Doc Holliday
&
Lords of the Land

Doc Holliday
&
Lords of the Land

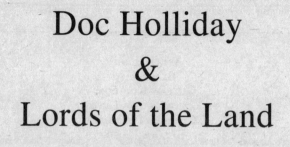

St. Martin's Paperbacks

These are works of fiction. All of the characters, organizations, and events portrayed in them are either products of the author's imagination or are used fictitiously.

Published in the United States by St. Martin's Paperbacks, an imprint of St. Martin's Publishing Group.

DOC HOLLIDAY / LORDS OF THE LAND

For information address St. Martin's Publishing Group, 120 Broadway, New York, NY 10271.

www.stmartins.com

ISBN: 978-1-250-23418-6

Our books may be purchased in bulk for promotional, educational, or business use. Please contact your local bookseller or the Macmillan Corporate and Premium Sales Department at 1-800-221-7945, ext. 5442, or by e-mail at MacmillanSpecialMarkets@macmillan.com.

Printed in the United States of America

Doc Holliday St. Martin's Paperbacks edition / August 1997
Lords of the Land St. Martin's Paperbacks edition / March 1996

10 9 8 7 6 5 4 3 2 1

Doc Holliday

TO

BETTIANE

WHO ALWAYS SHARED THE DREAM

Author's Note

DOC HOLLIDAY is the untold story.

All too many people believe the saga of Doc Holliday began with the Gunfight at the O.K. Corral. Historical chronicles offer abundant proof that nothing could be further from the truth. Doc Holliday was a legend long before he met Wyatt Earp.

A shootist and mankiller, Holliday was widely known across the Western frontier. Newspaper accounts of the day rank him with such heralded gunfighters as Wild Bill Hickok, John Wesley Hardin, and Clay Allison. He was a figure of mythical proportions, a gambler who lived by the gun.

Doc Holliday strode across the pages of the Old West. His name was respected and feared in boomtowns and mining camps from Dakota Territory to the wilds of Texas. He was formidable and deadly, and in his time, his reputation far overshadowed that of Wyatt Earp. He was a gunfighter who accepted any challenge, and never lost.

DOC HOLLIDAY is the story of those years before the Gunfight at the O.K. Corral. A span of time in which a dentist known as Dr. John H. Holliday was transformed into the Doc Holliday of legend. A tale of a gentleman who became a shootist without equal.

PART ONE

CHAPTER 1

"You can get dressed, John."

Holliday was bare-chested. He slipped into his shirt, which hung loosely on his thin frame. His trousers were too large, and when he tucked the shirttail into his waistband, he had to buckle the belt to the last notch. He began knotting his tie.

Tom Eckhart was a friend as well as a physician. He studied Holliday a moment. "How much weight have you lost?"

"Twenty pounds," Holliday said. "Perhaps a little more."

"Considerably more, I'd judge. I wish you had come to see me sooner."

Holliday was wracked by a sudden, harsh cough. He swabbed phlegm from his mouth with a handkerchief. "I thought it was pleurisy," he said. "These things sometimes linger on after a hard winter."

"You should have known better," Eckhart grumbled. "Dental college should have taught you the difference."

"The difference in what?"

"God, I wish it were someone besides me! Why didn't you go to another doctor?"

Holliday stared at him. "Just tell me."

Eckhart dropped his stethoscope on the desk. "You have

what's commonly called consumption. The correct term is 'pulmonary tuberculosis.' "

"You couldn't be mistaken?"

"No, John, I'm not mistaken. I've seen too much of it in the last few years."

A generation of Southerners had contracted the disease during the Civil War. Younger men, their condition weakened by general hardship and the shortage of proper foods, were particularly susceptible. Even now, eleven years following the end of the war, tuberculosis was still rampant throughout the South.

Holliday's features were stoic. "How bad is it?"

"Quite bad," Eckhart said gravely. "Your lungs are in an advanced stage of deterioration."

"You're trying to sugarcoat it, Tom. Give it to me straight."

"I'm afraid your condition is terminal. As you know, there is no cure."

"I see." Holliday nodded, silent a moment. He was tall, with ash-blond hair and a brushy mustache, and penetrating gray-blue eyes. Yet now his look was closed and inaccessible. "How long do I have?"

"A year," Eckhart told him. "Maybe longer if you relocate to a drier climate. Atlanta is no place for a man with consumption."

"What would you recommend?"

"Somewhere out West, perhaps Colorado or Texas. The sooner the better, John."

Eckhart thought Holliday, who was barely twenty-four, had taken the news with a maturity beyond his years. Some men, particularly one with a future in dentistry, would have accepted their fate with far less equanimity. He watched as Holliday shrugged into his suit jacket.

"What will you do with your dental practice?"

"Take down my shingle," Holliday said simply. "Let my patients know I'm moving west. There's no scarcity of dentists."

"I suppose not," Eckhart agreed. "When will you leave?"

"As soon as my affairs are in order. Nothing to hold me here now."

The matter-of-fact tone piqued Eckhart's curiosity. He knew Holliday was engaged to be married, and he told himself that it was none of his business. Yet, presuming on their friendship, he couldn't resist a personal question.

"Will you ask Mattie to go with you?"

"Would that make her a bride or a widow?"

Holliday departed on that cryptic note. He stepped through the door of the office, and turned south along Piedmont Street. Somewhere inside himself, he was struck by a bitter irony. One far too difficult to accept.

He had lost more than his life today.

The evening was lit by a primrose-yellow moon. Holliday sat beside Mattie on the porch swing, cloaked in the warmth of a gentle April breeze. Her arm tucked in his, she chatted on about plans for their wedding, set for June 6. He had yet to find a way to tell her.

The house was on Peachtree Road, north of the city proper, in one of Atlanta's finer residential enclaves. Like the phoenix of myth, Atlanta had risen from ashes after the Civil War. Mattie's father, the Honorable George W. Holliday, was a judge on the fifth superior court. He had survived the war, and the Reconstruction Era, to attain prominence in the new South.

Last year, upon graduating from the Baltimore Dental College in Maryland, Holliday had established his practice in Atlanta. The shingle outside his office read JOHN H. HOLLIDAY, D.D.S., and he was readily accepted into the professional community. But his welcome was lukewarm, and at times bordered on frosty, in the household of Judge Holliday. The situation was aggravated by the betrothal announcement of Mattie and Holliday, early in 1876. All of Atlanta, it seemed, loved a scandal.

Judge Holliday was the brother of Holliday's father. By

blood they were uncle and nephew, which meant that Mattie was Holliday's first cousin. The judge and his wife strongly opposed the engagement, for everyone knew that a union of first cousins resulted in offspring that were physically, and oftentimes mentally, impaired. But their daughter was willful and defiant, unconcerned that the man she loved was her cousin. Despite their protests, she accepted Holliday's proposal of marriage.

For his part, Holliday was willing to suffer the outrage and the gossip, even the stigma of cousins joined in wedlock. His deep feelings for Mattie stemmed from their childhood, when they were raised together in Lowndes County, in southern Georgia. After the war, when he'd gone off to college and her father had been appointed to the bench in Atlanta, nothing had changed to alter their lifelong bond. He chose Atlanta to establish his dental practice for no other reason than it reunited him with Mattie. She chose him to be her husband.

But now, beside her in the porch swing, Holliday searched for a way to begin, a way to tell her. She was vivacious and animated, a young woman of remarkable beauty, with auburn hair and a trim figure. In the face of her spirited manner, Holliday was at a loss as to how he might break the news. Finally, when she paused for breath, he decided the simplest way was the direct way. He steeled himself to the task.

"I went to see Tom Eckhart today."

"Oh, good," she said briskly. "I've been worried sick with all the weight you've lost. Did he prescribe something for your pleurisy?"

Holliday held her gaze. "Tom ruled out pleurisy. He diagnosed it as consumption . . . tuberculosis."

"What?" She suddenly looked stricken. "Oh, John, that's not possible. He must be wrong."

"No, I trust his judgment. He's seen too many cases over the years to make a mistake. He was quite certain about it."

"Well, what did he say? Surely there's something to be done."

Holliday had already decided that the whole truth would serve no purpose. To tell her that he'd been sentenced to death would destroy her, and he couldn't bear to see her hurt. Far better to let time and distance bring about a gradual loss of hope.

"I have to go away," he said gently. "A drier climate, somewhere out West. That's the only known treatment."

She squared her shoulders. "Then I'll go with you. We'll be married just as quickly as possible." She smiled bravely. "We'll go west together."

"Not so fast." Holliday took her hand. "There's no need to rush things. Give me time to get located out there, and try to recuperate. We'll get married when I'm better."

"How long will that take? Did Tom say?"

"Six months, maybe a year. Certainly no longer."

"A year!" She watched him, a dark edge of dread shading her eyes. "Are you telling me everything, John? You're not just putting me off . . . are you?"

Holliday smiled, reassured her with a bold lie. "Give me a little time and I'll be as good as new." He squeezed her hand. "You want a healthy husband, don't you?"

"I want you, John Holliday. Healthy or not, only you."

"You have me, Mattie, and that's the gospel truth. I've been yours since the day we met. Nothing will change that."

Her eyes welled with tears. "You promise?"

Holliday enfolded her in his arms. "Yes, I do, most solemnly. On my oath."

There was no lie in the promise, and he felt absolved in that. For he would love her until the day he died.

However long, or short, his time. All his life.

The following afternoon Holliday stepped off the train in Valdosta. The town was the county seat of Lowndes County, his hometown. The place of his boyhood and his rite of passage into manhood. He was there to see his father.

For the most part, his memories of Valdosta were pleasant ones. Walking toward the town square, he was reminded of a time, long ago, when he'd fallen for Mattie. His family,

and hers, were the landed aristocracy of Lowndes County
before the Civil War. Their lives were idyllic, filled with
the romanticism of youth, days of splendor. A time of in-
nocence.

Then, with the war's end, the society to which he'd been
born was destroyed. The Yankees came, and the carpetbag-
gers robbed his family of their lands, the genteel plantation
life. His father, who had fought with the Twenty-seventh
Georgia Infantry, became a lawyer, and Mattie's father,
through murky political connections, moved on to a judge-
ship in Atlanta. Shortly afterward, in the fall of 1866, his
mother died as much of lost dreams as failing health. A
grieving youngster, scarcely fourteen, he was appalled when
his father promptly took another wife. His time of innocence
ended with the wedding.

From that day onward, Henry Holliday's only son became
a rebellious troublemaker. He spent his time in the woods,
avoiding his stepmother and his father, content to hunt deer
and wildfowl. Lean and hard, gifted with quick hands and
exceptional coordination, he discovered an inborn talent
with firearms. Over the intervening years he won shooting
contests, defied the Yankee constabulary by carrying a re-
volver, and often ran away to Atlanta to see Mattie. Finally,
when he was twenty, and steadfastly refused to study for
the legal profession, his father shipped him off to dental
college in Baltimore. He had not returned to Valdosta since,
a matter of some four years.

The law offices of Henry Holliday were located on the
north side of the courthouse square. He looked up from a
sheaf of legal documents as his son came through the door
and halted before his desk. He managed a strained smile.

"Well, well," he said, somewhat taken aback. "The
prodigal son returns. To what do I owe the pleasure?"

"Good breeding," Holliday said dryly. "If nothing else,
you taught me duty, and manners. I've come to say good-
bye."

"Have you, indeed?" the elder Holliday replied. "And
where are you off to now?"

"Somewhere out West, perhaps Texas. I hear Dallas is more civilized than most."

"Why on earth would you move west?"

"A matter of health. I'm told my constitution requires a drier climate."

Henry Holliday appeared startled. He looked closer, saw that his son was pale and wasted, abnormally thin. "What is it, John? Are you ill?"

"In a manner of speaking," Holliday said. "I have tuberculosis. Otherwise known as consumption."

"My God, you can't be serious! How ill are you?"

"I'd thought to send you a telegram. But then, after some consideration, I thought it was better done in person. You might say this is our final parting."

"You're—" His father faltered, searching for words. "You came all this way to tell me you're dying?"

Holliday was struck by a sudden fit of coughing. He wiped his mouth with a handkerchief, noting that the sputum was tinged red. "I'm touched by your concern. You've made the trip worthwhile."

"You're my son, for God's sake! What did you expect?"

"Actually, I came here with a request. I could hardly tell all to Uncle George, particularly since he's not one to keep a secret. That being the case—would you look after Mattie for me?"

"You haven't told her the truth?"

"Let's say she believes it to be a temporary condition."

"So she still thinks you're to be married?"

"For now," Holliday amended. "Time will convince her otherwise."

"I see." The elder Holliday looked at him with a dimming stare, as though he wanted to say something but it was too late. "When the time comes, I'll do what I can for Mattie. You have my word on it."

"Good-bye, Father." Holliday extended his hand. "I'm catching the afternoon train back to Atlanta. I appreciate your help."

"Come now, John, why rush off?" His father held their

handshake a moment longer. "Won't you stay the night?"

"Thank you, no. I leave for Texas tomorrow."

"Well then, will you write me? Once you've settled?"

"We've never been much for letters, have we?"

"John . . . what do you want me to say—you're my son."

"I think that says it all, Father. I wish you well."

"Godspeed, John. You'll ever be in my prayers."

Holliday nodded, quickly turning away, and walked to the door. As he stepped outside, the clock on the courthouse tower tolled the hour. He paused, staring upward, oddly reminded of a poem he'd studied in college. He thought it was by John Donne.

> Never send to know for whom the bell tolls;
> It tolls for thee.

A slight, ironic smile touched the corner of Holliday's mouth. All of it seemed somehow fitting, appropriate to the moment.

He walked toward the train station.

CHAPTER 2

Dallas was located on the banks of the Trinity River. Late in April the noon train slowed as it entered the outskirts of town. A brassy midday sun stood high in a cloudless sky.

Holliday was seated in the lead passenger coach. He stared out the window, marking the date as April 27, as the train rolled through a residential section. His trip west had consumed six days, and the rigors of coach travel, combined with the constant jostling over rough roadbeds, had left him sapped of energy. He felt soiled and worn.

The engineer throttled down, further reducing speed as the train approached the depot. Holliday got a sudden scratchy sensation in his throat, and pulled a flask from his inside coat pocket. His coughing fits had grown progressively worse, and he'd discovered that a stiff shot of whiskey acted as a palliative. He uncorked the flask, tipped it to his mouth, and drank deeply. His urge to cough was quelled by the fiery bourbon.

A moment later the train chuffed to a halt outside the depot. Holliday gathered his carpetbag from an overhead luggage rack and moved to the end of the coach with the other passengers. Dallas was the terminus for the Texas & Pacific line, and everyone was eager to see the trip ended. Upon exiting the vestibule, he went down the steps and emerged onto the platform. He nodded to the conductor, who was standing nearby.

"I'm new to Dallas. Perhaps you could recommend a good hotel. Something comfortable."

The conductor was familiar with him from the trip westward. He knew that, apart from tippling a flask, which was a gentleman's personal business, Holliday wore tailored suits and was somewhat more cultivated than most who rode his train. He motioned uptown.

"The Regent," he said. "A fine establishment, the best in Dallas. Only a couple of blocks along Main Street."

"Thank you most kindly."

"Not at all, sir. Enjoy your stay."

Holliday moved into the shade of the stationhouse, waiting until the baggage car was unloaded. He signaled a porter, who claimed his steamer trunk and muscled it onto a handcart, along with his carpetbag. After being given the name of the hotel, the porter led the way around the corner of the depot. They walked toward the center of town.

Dallas was in the midst of boom times. The streets were jammed with wagons and carriages, the boardwalks lined with an array of shops and business establishments. Holliday was struck by the raw vitality of the place, strangely invigorated as they wound their way through the crowds. The porter, who had settled there with the advent of the railroad, proved to be something of a civic booster. A single question from Holliday elicited a spirited monologue on the town's growth.

Organized in 1841, Dallas began as a trading post on the Trinity River. During the Civil War, the town prospered and grew as the administrative center for Confederate army forces in the southwest. Following the war, it became the hub of banking and commerce for homesteaders and ranchers throughout the northern region of Texas. In 1872, with the arrival of the Houston & Texas Central Railroad, the town mushroomed. A year later, when the Texas & Pacific laid track to the Trinity, Dallas exploded in growth. By the summer of 1873, the population topped seven thousand people.

The great financial panic of 1873, spreading early that fall

from Wall Street across the nation, was the ruination of many Western communities. But Dallas, with two railroads and river navigation to the Gulf of Mexico, thrived as the center of trade for a sprawling frontier. The rail yards became a way station for the transshipment of goods to the reservations in Indian Territory. A string of military garrisons, stretching from Central Texas to New Mexico, were supplied out of Dallas by the government. All of this added to the normal trade of settlers and buffalo hunters scattered across the vast region. The population swelled to almost ten thousand by the close of 1875.

Even now, a frenzy of construction continued far beyond the banks of the Trinity. Carpenters and brick masons by the hundreds erected buildings as the boom went on unabated. The price of real estate skyrocketed, doubling and doubling again, fueled by enterprising speculators with an eye for profit. Southerners in particular, forsaking their war-ravaged homeland, flocked to Dallas seeking a fresh start, a new life. All in all, as Holliday listened to the porter's prideful boosterism, he thought he'd made an excellent choice. A man with no future might find a measure of cheer in a roaring boomtown.

The porter halted in front of the hotel. As he unloaded the steamer trunk, he ducked his chin farther upstreet. "A gentleman like yourself wants to be careful up thataways. Folks call it the sporting district, if you take my meaning."

"Do they?" Holiday said, amused by the warning. "Danger awaits the unwary, is that it?"

"Mister, it's three city blocks of unfettered hell. Grifters and whores the likes of which you ain't never seen. They'd rob you blind faster'n scat."

"I'll heed your advice." Holliday slipped him three dollars. "And I'm obliged for the commentary on your fair city."

"Helluva town! You're gonna like it here, mister. Ever'body does!"

Inside the hotel, Holliday crossed a carpeted lobby appointed with sofas and overstuffed chairs. As he approached

the desk, the room clerk snapped to attention. "Good afternoon, sir."

"Good afternoon," Holliday said. "I'd like one of your best rooms. I prefer a street view."

"Certainly, sir." The clerk swiveled the registration ledger around and handed him a pen. "How long will you be staying with us?"

Holliday smiled. "Indefinitely."

Upstairs, with a window overlooking the street, he waited while a bellman unlatched his trunk. He then ordered a tub and hot water brought to the room. After the bellman departed, he opened one of the trunk drawers and removed a quart of bourbon. He took a long slug straight from the bottle.

Walking to the window, he pulled a leather case from his pocket and extracted a cigarillo. He lit up in a haze of smoke, wryly aware that the tobacco would only kill him faster. Still, the whiskey held his cough in check, and he saw no reason not to indulge himself with a smoke. A man's vices, whatever the state of his lungs, were not easily discarded.

Yet his thoughts were not on mortality, or doom. He had decided that whatever time was allotted to him, he would live it to the fullest. His outlook was fatalistic: take the bitter with the sweet and make the best of it. The bitter, he'd told himself more than once, was in having lost Mattie. The sweet was to be found in the life he made for himself in the time remaining. He refused to enforce concessions on himself simply to prolong the inevitable.

Still staring out the window, he savored the pungent aroma of the cigarillo. His attention was drawn upstreet, and he idly wondered if the sporting district was all that dangerous. He recalled reading that everyone in the Wild West went armed, routinely settling their disputes with gunfire. Though amused at the time, he thought now the porter's warning was probably worth heeding. His lungs would kill him, but no man should be allowed that privilege. Irony had its limits.

The cigarillo wedged in the corner of his mouth, he moved back to the trunk. From the top compartment, he removed a Colt's New Line Pocket Revolver. The pistol was small and compact, perfect for concealment, and fired a .41-caliber slug. Before departing Atlanta he had purchased it on the premise that newspaper accounts, at the very least, bore an element of truth. Every man in the Wild West needed a gun.

He loaded five rounds into the chambers.

Early that afternoon, Holliday emerged from the hotel. After a soaking bath, which restored his vitality, he was ready to explore Dallas. He was attired in a dark serge suit, with a gold watch chain draped across his vest, and a narrow-brimmed hat. The pistol was tucked into his waistband.

The first order of business was to arrange a location for his dental practice. Finances were no great concern, for he'd cashed out his investments in Atlanta, and carried a bank draft for almost eight thousand dollars. But he was trained in dentistry, and he had no intention of falling into slothful habits merely because of illness. He was not yet infirm, and by no means lazy. He meant to practice his profession.

On a sidestreet, not far from the hotel, he found a vacant storefront suitable to his needs. He arranged with the owner to rent it by the month, and paid two months in advance. Through the owner, he was directed to a cabinetmaker, and ordered a reclining chair with a padded headrest. All of his dental instruments were packed in the steamer trunk, and it was a simple matter to purchase the necessary pans and other materials. He planned to open shop within the week.

An hour or so later, exploring the downtown area, Holliday wandered into the courthouse square. On the south side of the square, a small crowd was gathered before an oval-topped wagon. He heard the jaunty strains of a banjo, and strolled over to have a look. Emblazoned on the sides of the wagon were bright, gaily colored signs: HAMLIN'S WIZARD OIL & BLOOD PILLS. The back of the wagon dropped to the ground, supported by retractable legs, to form a stage.

The crowd was attracted to the medicine show by free entertainment. When the banjo player finished his tune, a large muscular man took center stage and proceeded to swallow a glistening sword fully half his body length. As he extracted the sword, bowing to cheers and applause, another man popped through the curtains at the rear of the wagon, brandishing a fiery torch. He drank from a bottle of clear liquid, then spat flames high in the air, and concluded by dousing the torch down his gullet. The crowd went wild.

The banjo player then strummed loudly, and brought out, with august pronouncement, Professor Omar Blackstone. The professor strode to the edge of the stage, attired in swallowtail coat and top hat, clutching bottles of patent medicine in either hand. His voice raised in sonorous cadence, he proclaimed the wonders of his wares, concocted from a secret formula discovered in the wilds of Borneo. Hamlin's Wizard Oil, he thundered grandly, would cure lumbago, rheumatism, heart trouble, and the loss of hair. The Blood Pills, he noted with a sly smile, were for those ailments peculiar to the female condition. "A dollar a bottle," he roared mightily, "and a cure in every bottle!"

The crowd surged forward. Holliday was tempted to ask if the professor's secret recipe would also cure consumption. But instead he turned away, certain in the knowledge that the Wizard Oil was at least fifty-percent alcohol, guaranteed to temporarily relieve any suffering known to man or beast. As he crossed the courthouse square, he blithely mused that the flask in his pocket was far more potent, and no less curative, than the professor's Wizard Oil. Unbidden, too sardonic to suppress, a more troubling thought flashed through his mind. The crowd, however fleetingly, took hope from Wizard Oil.

He wished the same could be said for bourbon.

That evening, after a light supper, Holliday went for a walk. His appetite was diminishing day by day, and no matter how tasty the dish, he had to force himself to eat. Whiskey and

cigars, though short on sustenance, were an acceptable solace. He lit a cigarillo.

Drawn by curiosity, he took an excursion through the sporting district. He was no stranger to whores, or games of chance, nor to the rougher element whose stock-in-trade was vice. In Baltimore, during his college years, he had frequented seamy gambling dives, and when the urge came over him, an occasional bordello. But he was nonetheless curious as to whether vice in the untamed West compared favorably with vice in the more sophisticated East. He quickly discovered that sin in Texas was the same, simply rowdier.

The sporting district occupied three city blocks. On both sides of the street there were saloons, gaming dens, dance halls, and a galaxy of whorehouses. Some of the dives were sleazier than others, and a few, clearly for select clientele, possessed a touch of class. The men crowding the streets were a democratic admixture of burly teamsters, rawboned cowhands, and well-dressed businessmen. They came there to satisfy lust, or drown their sorrows, or court Lady Luck. The sporting crowd catered to their every whim.

Holliday inspected several of the dives, pausing for an occasional drink. Finally, his curiosity dampened, he returned to the Acme Gaming Palace. The interior was pleasantly furnished, the atmosphere quiet if not genteel, and the patrons intent on the pursuit of fortune. The Acme was clearly the haunt of serious gamblers, wagering serious money on dice, roulette, poker, and faro. Holliday assumed many of them were professionals, and he drifted from table to table, casually watching the play. At length, determined to test the waters, he took a chair at a poker table where the players appeared to be evenly matched. No one commented as he placed a hundred dollars in greenbacks on the table.

The game was draw poker, jacks or better to open, check and raise permitted. The ante was five dollars, with a betting limit of ten dollars, and three raises allowed.

The first night in Dallas, he finished fifty dollars ahead.

CHAPTER 3

"Which tooth is it?"

"Last one on the bottom. Hurts like a bastard."

The burly teamster pointed to his lower left jaw. He was stretched out in the reclining dental chair, which was positioned in a spill of sunlight from the window. Holliday selected a steel probe from a tray on a nearby table, and peered into the man's mouth. He gently tapped the suspect tooth with the probe.

"Holy shit!" the teamster bellowed. "I felt that plumb down to my toes."

"Small wonder," Holliday said, placing the probe on the tray. "You have an abscessed molar, rather far along. The tooth has to come out."

"You're gonna pull it?"

"I see no alternative."

"How bad's it gonna hurt?"

Holliday silently remarked that large, rough men were often the most squeamish about such matters. There was something childlike about them when fear lanced the tough outer shell.

"No need to alarm yourself overly much. We'll have it out in no time."

"Hope to Christ you know your business."

"Would you prefer to consult another dentist?"

"Naw, hell, I'm already here. Just go easy on me."

Holliday took a pair of extractor pliers from the tray. He nodded with a reassuring smile. "Open wide, please."

The teamster stared at the extractor with a look of wide-eyed fright. Holliday clasped his lower jaw in one hand, and inserted the pliers into his yawning mouth. He gripped the tooth in the pincers, applying pressure, and gave it a forceful tug. When he met resistance, he strained harder, rocking the tooth back and forth. The teamster stiffened with a strangled moan.

"Awww. Awww!"

Holliday abruptly stepped back from the chair. His face flushed from the exertion, he was suddenly seized by a coughing spasm. He jerked a handkerchief from his pocket, wiping a wad of thick phlegm from his mouth. He wheezed harshly, took a slow, deep breath.

"Jesus," the teamster muttered. "Sounds like you need a sawbones yourself. You a lunger?"

"A slight cough, nothing more." Holliday got hold of himself. "You've no need for concern. Shall we proceed?"

"Yeah, if you're sure—"

Holliday grabbed his jaw in a viselock. He clamped onto the tooth, put one knee on the man's chest, and hauled upward with a mighty heave. The molar popped out in a mass of blood and rotted roots.

"Ohhh!" the teamster groaned, holding his jaw tightly. "You like to tore my head off!"

"I have no doubt you will recover."

Holliday dropped the tooth into a porcelain pan. As he returned the extractor to the tray, his features contorted and another coughing seizure shook his frame. He moved unsteadily to a cabinet, removed a quart of bourbon, and gulped a long dose. He corked the bottle, his color slowly returning to normal.

"Gawddamn." The teamster rose from the chair, watching him. "You're sure enough a lunger, ain't you? Feller in your shape oughtn't to be workin' on people."

"How very perceptive of you," Holliday commented. "I

suggest you rinse your mouth with salt water three or four times a day. You owe me two dollars."

The teamster dug silver cartwheels from his pocket. "I still say you got a helluva nerve. Last time you'll see me."

"A loss of incalculable proportions. Good day to you, sir."

The teamster hesitated, vaguely aware that he'd been insulted. But then, looking deeper into Holliday's eyes, he saw something that stifled any reply. He walked out the door.

Holliday scrubbed his hands in a pan of soapy water. As he toweled dry, he sourly reflected on this latest incident. A month had passed since he'd opened the office for practice. At first, with his framed diploma on the wall, and his well-bred Southern manner, he had attracted an enviable clientele, the gentry of Dallas. But word of his condition slowly made the rounds.

Talk spread, and the higher class of trade steadily dwindled off. Few people were willing to be treated by a dentist afflicted with what was commonly termed "galloping consumption." His cough had worsened over the last month, and he was often unable to hide the bloody refuse spat into his handkerchief. Though he was drinking more, sometimes a quart a day, the bourbon brought only temporary relief. His cough was constant, from the time he awoke until he drank himself to sleep.

Strangely enough, he felt energetic and otherwise healthy, which he attributed to the drier climate. He had discovered as well that he had an astonishing tolerance for alcohol. No matter how much he drank, he never became drunk, and the whiskey seemed to fuel his stamina. For all that, his dental practice had dropped off sharply, limited now to walk-in trade, teamsters and laborers, the rougher crowd. Some days he had only two or three patients, and some days none at all. His fees scarcely covered the rent.

In the quiet of the office, dwelling on it, he decided he'd had enough for one day. Even though it was still early afternoon, he quickly washed his instruments and laid them

out to dry. Then, gathering his hat, he moved through the door, locking it behind him.

He walked toward the hotel.

Seated at the desk in his room, Holliday stared at the blank sheet of paper. Her response to his first letter had arrived last week, and he'd put off answering day by day. But now, knocking back a shot of whiskey, he labored to find the right words, subtle yet not painful. He dipped a pen in the ink-well.

My Dearest Mattie,

Yours of May 20 arrived in good order, and most welcome it was, too. Not a day goes by but that I think of you, and wish myself back in Atlanta. Texas, for all one hears, lacks greatly in social amenities, hardly the place people of our background would choose.

I nonetheless concede that the dental trade here is brisk. One prospers at the expense of Texans who value many things above a full set of teeth. Only today I extracted a tooth from an affluent gentleman of modest age and exceptionally disturbing dental habits. Like many here, he will soon have a set of the false variety. A D.D.S. could scarcely fail to succeed in this frontier outpost.

Be that as it may, I cannot report that the climate here is as beneficial as Tom Eckhart suggested. My condition has improved to no noticeable extent, and I am still plagued by bouts of coughing. Not that I offer this as a complaint, but merely as an observation. The affliction I live with, as you know, recognizes no healer apart from time. Even so, there are no convenants that warrant cure. Still, one hopes.

I do most heartily regard the encouragement and kind wishes so lovingly expressed in your letter. Should ever a man seek salvation he would utter your name, and I do so with regularity. Yet I dread the

thought of you waiting there, too patient and too faith-
ful, with no life of your own.

I most sincerely urge you to avail yourself of the
social activities always present there, and not deny
yourself by my absence. To know that you heed my
wishes in this respect would bring me inordinate plea-
sure, and great happiness. For you surely know that
the certainty of happiness for me is to be found in
your joy, your fulfillment in life.

I remain, as ever, most fondly yours,
John

Holliday stared down at the words. He wondered if she
would read between the lines, see the message penned there.
To say it more openly was beyond him, for he could not
bear to inflict pain on her. He had to hope that she would
forgo hope, and forget.

In that moment, he realized that he had never felt more
lonesome, or alone. He was a stranger in a strange land, and
he damned the illness that had brought him there. He
damned life.

Quickly, before he could change his mind, he sealed the
envelope.

Early that evening Holliday emerged from the hotel. He
walked to the Bon Ton Cafe, where he now took most of
his meals. These days, as his appetite continued to wane, he
looked upon food as fodder, a source of energy. He had to
force himself to eat.

By now a regular, he usually sat at a table near the win-
dow. Tonight, he ordered beef stew, laced with vegetables,
and fluffy buttermilk biscuits. His waitress, a stout woman
named Bertha, had taken to fussing over him. When he fin-
ished, having eaten little of the stew and only half a biscuit,
she stopped by the table. She wagged her head as he lit a
cigarillo.

"Gracious sakes," she clucked. "You eat like a sparrow,
Dr. Holliday. How are we gonna fatten you up?"

"An unlikely prospect, Bertha. Fine cigars and good whiskey stoke my engine."

"One of these days you'll just dry up and blow away."

Holliday smiled. "I will endeavor to avoid high winds."

"All your funnin' doesn't change things. A solid meal would do you a world of good."

"Yes, I'm sure you're right. Perhaps tomorrow."

From the cafe, Holliday walked uptown to the sporting district. His evenings were devoted to poker, and the Acme Gaming Palace had become his usual haunt. Sometimes, when business was slow at the office, he even played during the day. His skill as a gambler had gradually improved, for he was analytical and quick to figure the percentages of good hands and bad. A month at the tables had proved to be an education.

One of the first lessons learned was that every game was assumed to be crooked. A boomtown served as a lure to cardsharps and grifters, ever on the lookout for an easy mark. Some worked alone, and others operated in league with one or more confederates. The game of choice was poker, and the wiles they employed were seemingly endless. Their craft, the ability to cheat, was more art than science.

A favorite dodge of tinhorns was to introduce marked cards into a game. The practice was so common that "readers," cards with secret marks on the backs of a deck, were widely advertised by manufacturers. Another trick was faint punctures on the surfaces, indiscernible except to a skilled hand, which revealed the high cards. Shaved cards, trimmed along the sides, and cards with slightly rounded corners, were employed by those with the dexterity to stack a deck, or deal from the bottom. Mastery of the various tricks required a deft touch, and constant practice. A cardsharp, no less than a magician, relied on sleight-of-hand.

Holliday, who considered himself an honorable man, had no interest in resorting to underhanded methods. Yet he played to win, and he was imbued with a fierce will to emerge the victor in any contest. So he became an avid student of cardsharps, and the varied dodges they used to

rig a game. He watched, alert to the unusual or unexplain-
able, anything that defied the mathematical odds. He slowly
came to understand the tricksters, and their trickery.

The regulars at the Acme Gaming Palace accepted him at
face value. He was a dentist, fairly adept at the game of
poker, and a man who minded his own business. He was
not considered one of the sporting crowd, but neither was
he considered a greenhorn, a sucker. Some thought him
aloof, too educated for their tastes, and others thought his
wry wit made for excellent company. He was welcome at
any table, and he seldom went away a loser. That alone
earned their respect.

The game tonight was five-card draw. In some Eastern
casinos the traditional rules of poker had been revised to
include straights, flushes, and the most elusive of all com-
binations, the straight flush. The highest hand back East was
now a royal flush, ten through ace in the same suit. By all
reports, the revised rules lent the game an almost mystical
element.

Poker in the West was still played by the original rules
observed in earlier times on riverboats. There were no
straights, no flushes, and no straight flushes, royal or oth-
erwise. There were two unbeatable hands west of the Mis-
sissippi. The first was four aces, drawn by most players only
once or twice in a lifetime.

The other cinch hand was four kings with an ace, which
precluded anyone holding four aces. Seasoned players
looked upon it as a minor miracle, or the work of a skilled
cardsharp. Four kings, in combination with one of the aces,
surmounted almost incalculable odds.

Shortly before midnight, at a nearby table, a tinhorn gam-
bler dealt himself the miracle hand. A cattleman, who held
four treys, loudly denounced the gambler as a card cheat.
Apart from conceding the pot, and being run out of town,
the tinhorn had only one option. He kicked his chair away,
pulling a bulldog revolver from his waistband as he backed
off from the table, and fired twice in the space of a heartbeat.

One shot plowed into the table and the other went wide of the mark.

The cattleman, by now on his feet, drew a holstered Colt Peacemaker. He extended his arm, sighting as lead whizzed past his shoulder, and coolly fired a single shot. The slug struck the gambler squarely in the chest the instant he triggered a third shot into the far wall. He lurched backward, his eyes rolling up into his head, and toppled to the floor. The cattleman holstered his Colt, then calmly raked in the pot. No one offered any objection.

The gambler was left where he'd fallen. Someone went to fetch the city marshal, and play quickly resumed at the other tables. Holliday, with a ringside seat to the shooting, was impressed by the cool nerve of the cattleman. Whether the tinhorn had actually cheated seemed to him a moot point. Of the two antagonists, only one was still standing.

The gunfight was the first he'd witnessed since arriving in Dallas. For a man who frequented gaming dives, he thought it was highly instructive. Arguments over cards were not uncommon, and any gambler, professional or otherwise, might be called upon to defend his honor. The only acceptable response was the one he'd seen tonight.

A man who gambled must be willing to risk it all with a gun.

CHAPTER 4

Holliday awoke with bright sunlight streaming through the window. He sat up on the edge of the bed and took his pocket watch from the nightstand. After an all-night poker game he'd got to sleep around five in the morning, and it was now going on noon. He yawned, arms curled in a wide stretch.

A sudden spasm erupted deep in his lungs. He reached for a bottle on the nightstand, popped the cork, and took a long pull. The whiskey was raw, molten fire searing him from gullet to stomach. But on the way down it stopped the coughing fit, and he tossed off a second dose for good measure. He was ready to face the day.

The room was stuffy with the forenoon heat of early July. He moved to the washstand, sloshing water from a pitcher into a wide oval basin. The image he saw in the mirror was a ghost of his former self, his features gaunt and pallid. Still, for a man whose closest companion was death, he wryly thought there were mornings he'd looked worse. He began stropping his razor.

For the most part, musing on it as he shaved, he thought the sporting life agreed with him. Toward the middle of June, when the coughing fits finally robbed him of patients, he had closed his dental practice. By then, he was spending more time in the gaming dives than fixing teeth, and it seemed logical to transform a pastime into a new vocation.

All the more so since he needed a steady source of income simply to cover routine living expenses. Virtually overnight, he became a professional gambler.

Oddly enough, he found that the regimen of a gambler agreed with him. Sometimes, as happened last night, he might play from late afternoon until the early morning. But these marathon sessions of ten or twelve hours rarely sapped his spirits. If anything, good cards mixed with liberal doses of whiskey seemed to restore his vigor. His lungs protested the strain, and some days he coughed with every other breath. Yet he not only survived, he thrived.

All in a short time he had earned a reputation among the sporting crowd. He won more often than he lost, particularly when the stakes were high, which was the mark of a professional. The larger contest was with rough, brawling men who thought his affliction made him an invalid, and therefore easily intimidated. He was quick to call their bluff, and let it be known that he subscribed to a deadlier credo. He operated on the premise that God made men, but Samuel Colt had made them equal. So far, no one had pushed it to the limit.

To underscore his point, Holliday went dressed for trouble. On his hip he now wore a Colt Peacemaker, chambered for .45 caliber, with a four-and-three-quarter-inch barrel. The finish was lustrous indigo-blue and the grips were custom-made of yellowed ivory. Beneath his suit jacket, in a spring-loaded shoulder holster, he carried a Colt Lightning, chambered for .41 caliber, with a three-and-a-half-inch barrel and a birdshead butt. The Lightning was officially scheduled for release by Colt in January, but his gunsmith had managed to obtain an early production model. The pistol was double-action, which eliminated having to cock the hammer for the first shot. A simple squeeze of the trigger got the job done.

Apart from hardware, Holliday had ordered a new wardrobe as well. Gamblers customarily wore dark suits, with white shirts and dark ties, which gave them the look of prosperous undertakers. To celebrate his new profession,

Holliday chose a more distinctive look, with tailored suits in a variety of colors. His wardrobe now included light gray, muted blue, and pale beige, and a selection of pastel shirts matched to complement the suits. The overall appearance was one of sartorial elegance, a spiffy dresser. He stood out from the rest of the sporting crowd.

Today, when he came downstairs, he was attired in a vested suit of gray, with a dove-colored shirt and a royal-blue tie. His one concession to local custom was a wide-brimmed Western hat with a domed crown. In the lobby, the desk clerk greeted him with a letter from the morning post. He glanced at the envelope, recognizing the perfectly ovaled script, and stuffed it into his pocket. Outside, the blast of summer heat brought an instant film of perspiration to his face. He crossed the busy intersection to the Bon Ton Cafe.

Bertha brought his usual breakfast of soft-boiled eggs, dry toast, and coffee. He laced the coffee with a shot from his flask, then read the letter while he ate. His appetite, never strong in the best of circumstances, was further spoiled by what he read. Mattie continued to ignore, or even acknowledge, his many hints that she should make a life for herself in Atlanta. She seemed determined in her belief that God, in some magical way, would cure his consumption and they would once more be together. The last paragraph stopped him cold.

> *The Lord in his infinite mercy will guide us through our moment of travail. We have only to trust in Him, and never allow our faith to waver. I know, just as you do, John, that the Lord meant us to be joined as one. You are utmost in my prayers, and though we are apart for now, I am with you in spirit and soul. We will come through this interlude for the better, and forever. Our love, all that we share, will endure.*

The words blurred. Holliday wanted to embrace her belief that all would come right in the end. He needed to hold her,

to smell the fresh scent of her hair, never to leave her again. Yet he was too much a pragmatist to trust in the Lord's mercy, or rely on the curative power of divine intervention. Her prayers would alter nothing, and one day, despite her faith, his lungs would kill him. Short of death, he wondered how she might be convinced to turn loose. To finally let go.

Still lost in thought, Holliday emerged from the cafe. Outside, waiting for him, was a young boy of thirteen, Joey Woodruff. A fortnight ago, upon casting his lot as a gambler, he'd hired the youngster to assist in a daily drill. Joey's assignment was to collect empty whiskey bottles from saloons, load them in a gunnysack, and meet him at the cafe. His wages were fifty cents a day.

"Good morning, Joey," Holliday said. "I see you've been busy."

"Yessir," the youngster said brightly, hefting his gunnysack. "I got a good load today."

"Well, then, let's be off."

Holliday led the way through the downtown area. A short while later they halted along a deserted stretch of the Trinity River. Without being told, Joey positioned himself upstream, dumping bottles from the gunnysack onto the ground. The empty bottles were corked and airtight, guaranteed to float. The purpose of the drill was to further hone Holliday's skill with a pistol. His new profession demanded that he be as proficient with firearms as he was with cards.

During his time in Dallas, Holliday had witnessed three gunfights. After some reflection, he had come to the conclusion that the victor was not necessarily the faster man. Speed was fine, but in his view, accuracy was final. The shot that killed an opponent, rather than the first shot, was what counted. More often than not, the man who hurried his opening shot was soon bound for the graveyard. So he practiced on a speedy draw, yet his focus was on placing every shot dead center. He was quick, but deliberate.

Joey tossed a bottle into the river. Then, one after another, he lobbed four more in rapid succession. The bottles bobbed to the surface, spaced several feet apart, and floated down-

stream. Holliday's hand snaked beneath his jacket and came
out with the Colt Peacemaker, the hammer cocked. His mind
closed down, his nerves went dead, and he reverted to a
state of reflex and instinct. Time fragmented into split sec-
onds, an instant of icy deliberation suspended within each
moment. There was an overwhelming sense of calm, and
the gun. He simply saw and reacted.

His arm leveled and the Colt bucked in his hand. The first
bottle erupted in a geyser of water and glass. He swung the
Colt in an arc and locked onto the second bottle. His eyes
sighted along the barrel—caught within an instant of delib-
eration—and he feathered the trigger. The second bottle in
line exploded. Then the next and the next, and finally the
last as the current swept it some yards below his position.
Less than five seconds had elapsed from the moment he
pulled the gun.

Timing himself, Holiday shucked the empty shells and
reloaded. He inserted a round into the first chamber, leaving
the next one empty, and loaded the last four chambers. On
a measured count of ten, he snapped the loading gate closed
and lowered the hammer on an empty chamber. After hol-
stering the Peacemaker, he looked upstream and nodded.
Joey began tossing bottles, until five more bobbed along the
surface. Holliday snapped the Colt Lightning out of the
shoulder holster and extended his arm. He fired double-
action, the hammer rising and falling with each squeeze of
the trigger. All five bottles exploded in shards of glass.

"Goldurn!" Joey whistled shrilly. "You don't never miss
no more."

Holliday began reloading. "I sincerely hope not, Joey. No
cigar for second best in this game."

The drill was repeated, alternating between the Peace-
maker and the Lightning. Finally, after twenty bottles and
no misses, Holliday was satisfied. The ravages of consump-
tion had not slowed his hand, and his reflexes were still
sharp. Later, at the hotel, he would clean and oil the guns,
cleansing the parts of black-powder residue. Before he went
to work, he would ensure that their action was butter-

smooth. For that, too, was part of the daily drill.

The pistols were tools of his trade.

" 'Evenin', Doc.''

Holliday nodded to the bartender. "Good evening, Harry."

"The usual?"

"Yes, I believe so."

The barkeep filled a shot glass, and left the bottle. Holliday knocked back the drink, waiting for the warmth to spread through his insides. He refilled the glass, turning with one elbow on the counter, and studied the room. Toward the rear, there was action at three of the poker tables.

George Palmer, owner of the Acme Palace, was observing play at one of the faro layouts. He saw Holliday and moved to the bar. "Looking for a game, Doc?"

"No pay unless a man plays, George. Another day, another dollar."

To those in the sporting district, he was no longer John Henry Holliday, the dentist. Once he adopted the mantle of a gambling man, someone had dubbed him "Doc," a play on his former profession. The nickname was a badge of acceptance, his induction into the fraternal order of gamblers. He was now known simply as Doc Holliday.

"Watch yourself," Palmer warned in a low voice. "Cole Younger's playing at the second table. He's a hothead when it comes to cards."

Holliday sipped his whiskey. "Cole and I are on mutually good terms. Neither of us would offend the other." His gaze drifted to a large man seated at the second table, and he chuckled. "All the world loves a rogue. Amusing, isn't it?"

Cole Younger and his brothers, Bob and Jim, had ridden into Dallas a week ago. They were members of the James Gang, and according to rumor, Jesse had ordered the band to scatter following a bank holdup in Missouri. Local peace officers, while aware of their presence, felt no great obligation to Missouri bankers. The Youngers were allowed the run of the town.

After finishing his drink, Holliday walked to the rear of the room. He exchanged greetings with Cole Younger, but took a seat at another table. A waiter brought him a fresh glass and a full bottle of bourbon. He lit a cigarillo, peeling a thousand dollars off his bankroll, and nodded pleasantly to the five men at the table. One of them, Clell Austin, had a reputation as a sore loser, and averted his eyes. He looked irked that Holliday had joined the game.

The rules were dealer's choice, restricted to five-card stud and five-card draw. Ante was twenty dollars, with a fifty-dollar limit and three raises. Check and raise was permitted, which made it a game perfectly suited to Holliday's style of play. He had developed his own technique for winning at cutthroat poker. The secret was to keep them guessing.

Over the next hour Holliday seemed unbeatable. He had an uncanny knack for reading the other players, and he won on what appeared to be weak hands. There was no pattern to his betting and raising; his erratic play made him unpredictable, and somewhat intimidating. He would bluff on a bad hand as often as he folded, and he seldom folded. More often than not his bluff went undetected.

On good hands, he would sometimes raise the limit, allowing the money to speak for itself. At other times, when he held good cards, he would lay back and sucker his opponents into heedless raises. On occasion, merely calling all bets and raises, he let the other players build the pot only to turn up the winning hand. No one was ever sure of what he held.

Into the second hour, the deal passed to Wally Bevins, a local businessman. He dealt five-card stud, the first card down and four exposed one at a time. On the opening round, Austin was high with an ace showing, and bet twenty. Holliday, with a ten up, raised fifty and the other players folded. Austin scowled, hesitating a moment, then called the raise. As the hand played out, Austin caught a jack on the fifth card, pairing one already on the board. He bet fifty, and Holliday, who had a pair of deuces showing, raised the limit.

Austin studied on it a while, then uttered a sour grunt. He folded his cards.

"What'd you have?" he demanded. "Three of a kind or two pair?"

"Why, Clell, you didn't call," Holliday said amiably. "Of course, as one sporting man to another, I've no objection." He turned his hole card, a queen. "It appears I have a pair—both deuces."

"You raised into my jacks with that! Who the hell you think you're kiddin', Holliday? There's something fishy here."

"Yes, I do believe you should have called. I plead guilty to a crass and unseemly bluff."

"Bluff, my ass!" Austin bristled. "Nobody raises with deuces. You rigged the game somehow!"

"Oh, Clell," Holliday said with a sardonic half-smile. "Are you accusing me of cheating?"

"You're goddamn right I am! You think I'm afraid of you?"

" 'A living dog is better than a dead lion.' Ecclesiastes, chapter nine, verse four. It's good advice, Clell."

"What's that supposed to mean?"

"Apologize"—Holliday's smile darkened—"or defend yourself."

Austin glowered at him with a furious expression. Then, like a jack-in-the-box, he sprang from his chair, clawing at a pistol holstered on his hip. Holliday remained seated, leaning back slightly as he popped the Colt Lightning from his shoulder holster. His arm extended across the table a beat before Austin's gun cleared leather. He pulled the trigger twice, one shot blending with the other.

Dark splotches appeared on Austin's shirtfront. The slugs were an inch apart, centered on his sternum. He stiffened, his gun pointed at the floor, a look of stark surprise on his face. His knees buckled and he collapsed, crashing backward over his chair. His right bootheel drummed a quick tattoo of death.

Holliday stood, holstering the Colt in a single motion. A

dense silence hung over the room as he circled the table, halting beside the body. He stared down a moment, then looked toward the bar, nodding to George Palmer. His voice was steady, curiously restrained.

"George, be so good as to send someone for the marshal. You might fetch the undertaker as well."

CHAPTER 5

Dallas sweltered under the brutal heat of August. Few men ventured into the sporting district until sundown, with the cool evening breezes. Vice suffered beneath the blaze of deep summer.

Holliday thrived on the heat. His general condition improved, though his cough remained constant, and he had energy to spare. With the poker tables slow during the afternoons, his attention turned to faro. He felt it important, as a professional, that he be versed in the frontier's most popular game. His education was trial by fire, for he was playing against the house. The game required quick insight into percentages, and a certain finesse.

Today, seated at one of the faro layouts, Holliday studied an abacuslike device, known as the casekeeper. Positioned to one side of the table, the casekeeper indicated the cards already dealt and allowed a player to figure percentages on cards remaining in the deck. Queens were still unplayed, and he decided to wager on the lady. He placed a five-dollar chip above the queen on the layout.

The dealer slipped two cards from a wooden box. The first was a queen and the second a four. "Four's a winner," he said smoothly, collecting the chip. "Tough luck, Doc."

"No apologies needed," Holliday said with a slow smile. "I like the game for its very perversity. Not all that different from life, wouldn't you agree?"

"Doc, that's too deep for me. I just deal 'em."

"Well, then, deal me a winner. I'm overdue."

Faro, even more than poker, was governed by the luck of the draw. An old and highly structured game, it had originated a century before in France. The name was derived from the king of hearts, which bore the image of an Egyptian pharaoh on the back of the card. All betting was against the house, known in Western parlance as "bucking the tiger."

A cloth layout on the table depicted every card from deuce through ace. After being shuffled, the cards were placed in the dealing box, and then drawn in pairs, displayed faceup. Before the turn of each pair, players placed bets on one or more cards of their choice. The first card out of the box was a losing bet, and the second was a winner. All bets were canceled if there were no wagers on either card.

By watching the casekeeper, players could bet win or lose on the layout. To wager on a losing card, they "coppered" their bet by placing a copper token on their chips. A daring player, or a confident high roller, would often bet win and lose on the same turn.

By late that afternoon Holliday had lost almost two hundred dollars. In his daily faro sessions, he'd learned a lot, but hardly enough to be a consistent winner. Though the education was costly, he looked upon it as an investment in the future. He thought a professional, as a practical matter, should be skilled at any game of chance. Then, too, the cost of his education was all relative. He financed it from his poker winnings.

The hour was early, and only one poker game was in progress. Cole Younger was seated at a table with three other men, one of them Amos Deckard, a railroad detective for the Texas & Pacific. Holliday was amused by the irony of a detective gambling with a notorious train robber, for the James Gang pillaged trains as well as banks. Still, that was one of the things he liked most about the gaming profession. At a card table, there were no class distinctions. There were only men with money.

Over the past month Holliday had grown friendly with Cole Younger. As a rule, he seldom gambled with friends, for cards and friendship were a poor mix. But he wanted to recoup his faro losses, and only one table was in play. He decided to lay off against Younger, and concentrate instead on the other men. When he approached the table, Deckard had just won a sizable pot. Holliday nodded pleasantly.

"Would you gentlemen like another player?"

"Grab a chair," Younger said, motioning at the detective. "Never saw a lawdog so lucky at cards. Maybe you can bust his streak."

"I'll certainly try," Holliday said, seating himself. "After all, losing is not my game."

Deckard gave him a dour look. "That why you quit at faro?"

"I often enjoy a change of pace, Mr. Deckard. Do you object?"

"Happy to take your money, Holliday. I'm on a roll."

Deckard's bravado proved to be misplaced. He was a cut above Younger and the others at a poker table. But he was scarcely able to hold his own against Holliday. The game seesawed back and forth into the early evening hours. Though Deckard won an occasional hand, his streak was clearly ended. Holliday bluffed, often controlling the play with heavy raises, and his stack of greenbacks grew ever taller. Cole Younger compounded the situation by laughing uproariously whenever Holliday pulled down a pot. Deckard slowly turned churlish, his mouth set in a tight line.

Toward mid-evening, the deck rotated to Holliday as dealer. The ante was ten dollars, and he called five-card draw, allowing the man on his right to cut after he'd shuffled. He dealt around the table, pouring himself a drink before looking at his cards. He had three fives.

Younger, who was on his left, checked. Deckard, seated directly across the table, bet twenty. The next two players folded, and Holliday, puffing his cigarillo, airily raised twenty. Younger reluctantly folded, and Deckard bumped it another twenty. Holliday took the last raise.

On the draw, Deckard held four and drew one. Holliday kept the three fives and dealt himself two. When Deckard squeezed his cards apart, the corners of his mouth lifted in a fleeting, telltale smile. He checked.

Holliday caught the smile. He figured Deckard had filled on two pair and was trying to sandbag him. He fanned his cards, only to discover that he'd drawn the case five. He hesitated a moment, as though weighing his options, and bet twenty. Deckard grinned broadly.

"Your twenty," he said with a smug look. "And twenty more."

Holliday feigned surprise, then called, pausing a moment, and raised. Deckard raised again, waiting for Holliday to call, and barked a short laugh. He spread his cards.

"Read 'em and weep. Full house! Kings over tens."

"How unfortunate," Holliday deadpanned, turning his cards. "I filled as well, Mr. Deckard. Four fives."

Deckard stared at the cards. "You dealt yourself the case five."

"I'm sorely embarrassed by my own luck."

"Luck don't cut it! More to it than that."

"Let's pretend you overstated yourself, and let it drop."

"Not by a damnsight!" Deckard roared. "I say you stacked that deck."

Holliday smiled. "And I say you are a liar, Mr. Deckard."

Deckard cursed, his features contorted with rage. He started to rise, his hand darting to a pistol in a crossdraw holster. The Colt Lightning appeared from beneath Holliday's jacket, and he fired across the table. The slug caught Deckard half standing, drilling him through the heart, and his hand dropped away from the holstered pistol. He sat down heavily, his head crooked at an angle, arms dangling over the sides of the chair. His bowels voided in death.

"Well, Doc," Younger said, batting the air at the stench. "I think you killed the son of a bitch."

Holliday holstered his pistol. "So it would appear."

"You're some sudden with a gun. Dumb bastard never cleared leather."

The other two players pushed away from the table. "Keep your seats," Holliday ordered. "You gentlemen are witness to the fact that Deckard made the first move. The marshal will want to hear your story."

Some while later City Marshal Owen Campbell and one of his deputies, Lon Donaldson, pushed through the crowd. They listened attentively, asking few questions, as Holliday related details of the shooting. Cole Younger and the other players corroborated his story, agreeing that Deckard had instigated the fight. At length, his expression puzzled, the marshal turned back to Holliday.

"Amos Deckard was no slouch with a gun. How'd you beat him to the draw?"

"All in the eyes," Holiday said with mock seriousness. "He blinked just before he made his play."

Campbell looked unconvinced. "There'll be a coroner's inquiry tomorrow. Make sure you show up."

"You may depend on it, Marshal."

Campbell instructed his deputy to attend to the body. As he walked toward the door, Younger and Holliday moved away from the table. "Lemme buy you a drink," Younger said. "You earned it tonight."

"Why, thank you, Cole. I accept your kind offer."

Several men at the bar, most of them gamblers, congratulated Holliday. But after a few drinks, he tired of their company, and talk of the shooting. The celebrity they accorded him, what smacked to him of notoriety, made him uncomfortable. He decided to call it a night, and begged off another round of drinks. Cole Younger finally let him go with a warm handshake.

He walked off toward the hotel.

Late that night Holliday stood at the window of his room. He had a drink in one hand and a cigarillo in the other, and his eyes were fixed on the starry sky. He was taking stock of himself.

In a matter of a month, he had killed two men. Honor permitted no other recourse, for in each instance he had been accused of cheating at cards. Yet he was struck by the fact that he felt no remorse, no sense of regret. All the more so since he'd never before killed a man.

The killing itself had been easy, perhaps too easy. There was no hesitation, no struggle with conscience, simply the act of drawing and pulling the trigger. The two men, Clell Austin and Amos Deckard, had forced the issue, pushing him to fight. Still, in retrospect, he thought he might have deflected the challenge with words, or humor, or simple indifference to their accusations. But then, taking it to the end conclusion, he saw that as impractical, fancy rather than solution. A gambler could not abide being branded a cheat.

All the same, with both killings, he was vaguely bothered by his lack of remorse. The truth, though the admission came hard, was that he felt nothing. The men had bought into trouble, and whatever they got was no more than they deserved. He wondered if his own shaky mortality, the consumption slowly devouring his lungs, might have affected the way he viewed life, and death. God had merrily robbed him of life, consigned him to a last boat ride over the river Styx and the land of the dead. Perhaps all that made it somehow acceptable, simpler.

A dying man might easily kill with godlike impunity.

The door rattled under a quick, insistent knock. His woolgathering abruptly ended, Holliday crossed the room. He opened the door to find Cole Younger in the hall.

"Well, Cole, what a surprise. I thought we'd said our good-nights."

"Gotta talk to you." Younger brushed past him. "Trouble's headed this way."

Younger was tall and sturdy, a man given to coarse language and rough behavior. He was an outlaw, no stranger to trouble, and his brusque warning was not to be taken lightly. Holliday closed the door.

"What's the nature of the trouble, Cole?"

"The law," Younger said gruffly. "You recollect that deputy at the Acme tonight? Donaldson?"

"Yes, of course. What about him?"

"After a fashion, Donaldson and me are friends. I make it worth his while to keep his ear to the ground. Tell me if the Texas Rangers or such are sniffin' at my heels."

Holliday nodded. "Are they after you?"

"Hell, Doc," Younger said, clearly agitated. "I'm trying to tell you the law's after you. You're gonna be arrested for killin' Deckard. Donaldson just slipped me the word."

"I hardly think so, Cole. Everyone agreed it was self-defense."

"Don't make no nevermind. You killed a railroad stooge, and the Texas and Pacific runs this town. The big muck-a-mucks ordered the marshal to bring you in."

"Even so," Holliday said without concern, "the charge would be thrown out of court. I have witnesses, you among them."

"Forget me," Younger told him. "I show up in court, they'll toss my ass in jail. Forget them other fellers, too. Don't matter what they say." He shook his head dolefully. "The skids are greased to put you on the gallows."

"Donaldson said that?"

"Just as sure as God made little green apples. The railroad believes in an eye for an eye, and Deckard was their boy. They aim to stretch your neck."

"But Deckard made the first move. Everyone saw it."

"So you say," Younger countered. "Think back, and you'll recollect he never cleared leather. His gun was still in the holster. How you think that'd look to a jury?"

Holliday frowned. "Not too favorable, I'm afraid."

"You gotta get out of town, Doc. I'm talkin' about right now and damn quick. Otherwise you're as good as hung."

"Under the circumstances, I think a train would be a poor choice. Any suggestions?"

Younger chuckled. "I stole you a horse off the street. He's tied out back of the hotel. Head for the Nations."

"The Nations?"

"Indian Territory," Younger explained. "Due north acrost the Red River. Find your way to Ardmore, in the Chickasaw Nation. Ask around for Ed Blanchard."

"Who's Ed Blanchard?"

"A friend of me and Jesse's. Robs a train now and then himself. Just mention my name. He'll treat you square."

Holliday looked around the room. "I assume there's no time to pack. Hate to leave all these fine clothes."

"Stole a horse, not a wagon," Younger said urgently. "Forget your fancy duds and save your neck. Let's get a move on."

Downstairs, Holliday clasped Younger's hand in a firm grip. "Thank you, Cole. You have my marker."

"You'd do the same for me. Go on now, Doc. Get outta here."

Holliday walked through the rear hallway and out the back door. Younger watched after him a moment, then turned to the desk clerk. He put a finger to his lips, warning silence, and the clerk quickly nodded. As he approached the entrance, Marshal Campbell and Deputy Donaldson hurried into the lobby. Campbell gave him a suspicious look.

"Where's Doc Holliday?"

"Whyn't you try his room, Marshal? Second floor on the front."

The marshal rushed to the stairs, and Younger glanced at the deputy with a sly wink. Then, cocking his hat, he went through the door.

He strolled off toward the sporting district.

CHAPTER 6

Holliday forded the Red River on August 15. The river lay some hundred miles north of Dallas, and his trip had taken the better part of five days. By traveling at night, and hiding out during the day, he had passed through the countryside without attracting attention. The eastern horizon paled as he gained the opposite shoreline.

On the north bank, Holliday paused and stared back at the river. From talk among the sporting crowd, he knew that the Red was a line of demarcation. Texas Rangers and county sheriffs, regardless of the crime involved, were forbidden to cross into Indian Territory. Their jurisdiction ended at the river.

To Holliday, all that seemed a mixed blessing. He had escaped certain prosecution and conviction, and the hangman's rope. But he was now a wanted man, a fugitive from the charge of murder. The river represented a point of no return, a departure for a former dentist turned gambler. He was now an outlaw.

The greater irony was that he was riding a stolen horse. So far as the law was concerned, that made him a horse thief as well as a murderer. He felt cheated in that respect, for Cole Younger, in the rush of the moment, had stolen a poor mount. The horse was a dun gelding, long of tooth and short of wind, on its last legs as they forded the Red. He felt lucky to have escaped at all.

From the river, he followed a rutted trail northward. A mile or so farther along he came upon a log house, surrounded by cleared fields, owned by a Chickasaw farmer. A full-blood, with braided hair and dressed in white men's clothes, he was the first Indian Holliday had met. His English was passable, and he informed Holliday that Ardmore lay some twenty miles to the north. For a dollar, his wife provided a breakfast of venison steak and boiled hominy.

The meal, though simple fare, restored Holiday's spirits. For the past five days, he'd eaten rabbits killed with his pistol. His cough, strangely enough, seemed improved from sleeping on the ground, exposed to fresh air, wrapped in a rain slicker he'd found on the horse. For another dollar, the Chickasaw replenished his flask with corn liquor, a home-made concoction with the taste of liquid fire. He rode out with renewed vigor.

Late that afternoon he sighted Ardmore. The town was a crossroads, with a trading post, a general store, and a livestock dealer. Throughout the day, much to his surprise, Holliday had passed one farm after another. Unlike anything he'd expected, the Chickasaw Nation was an agrarian society, farmers rather than warriors. The town was crowded with wagons, drawn by stocky workhorses, and everyone was dressed in store-bought clothes. Apart from the color of their skin, the tribesmen might have been Texas settlers.

Holliday dismounted outside the general store. He was dusty and bedraggled from five days on the trail, his face stubbled with whiskers. But it was his gray suit and pastel shirt, clearly a novelty in the backwoods, that drew attention. As he entered the store, he noticed two white men loading supplies into wooden crates. They glanced in his direction, inspecting him, then went back to work. A Chickasaw man behind the counter watched him with a stoic expression. He stopped, nodding pleasantly.

"Good afternoon," he said. "I would like to purchase a straight razor and a bar of soap. By any chance, do you stock cigarillos?"

"Got all the smokes you want."

"I'll have a dozen."

"Anything else?"

"Yes, there is," Holliday said. "Perhaps you could direct me to a man by the name of Ed Blanchard. I understand he lives somewhere around Ardmore."

The Chickasaw's eyes flickered past him. He turned to find the two white men staring in his direction. One of them, short and muscular with sandy hair, moved across the aisle. His gaze was cold, and guarded.

"Who's askin'?"

For a moment, Holliday almost gave his full name. Then, remembering who he was now, he kept it simple. "The name's Doc Holliday."

"What's your business with Blanchard?"

"That's my affair."

"Not anymore." The man jabbed himself in the chest with a thumb. "I'm Ed Blanchard."

"Are you?" Holliday said. "Then you know Cole Younger. He told me to look you up."

"Why would Cole do that?"

"I found it necessary to depart Dallas . . . in a hurry."

"Don't say?" Blanchard woofed a dry laugh. "What'd you do, kill somebody?"

Holliday cut a glance at the storekeeper. Blanchard caught the look and idly waved it off. "Nobody around here carries tales. Go ahead, what'd you do?"

"I was involved in a dispute over cards. The other man lost."

"So you did kill somebody. You a cardsharp?"

"A gambler," Holliday clarified. "I play a straight game."

"Take your word for it." Blanchard stuck out his hand. "Welcome to the Chickasaw Nation, Doc. The law won't bother you around here. Not unless you run across a federal marshal."

"Oh?" Holliday shook his hand. "What authority do the federals have here?"

"Let's get these supplies loaded. I wanna get back to camp before dark. We'll talk on the way."

Blanchard and the other man, one of his gang, loaded the crates into a wagon outside. Holliday paid for his cigarillos and the razor, then joined them in front of the store. He mounted, riding alongside the wagon, as they turned east out of town. Blanchard gave him a rundown on the oddities of an outlaw's life in Indian Territory.

The Five Civilized Tribes comprised what was known as the Nations. Apart from the Chickasaw, there were the Cherokee, Choctaw, Creek and Seminole tribes. By federal mandate, the tribes had been relocated from various southeastern states to Indian Territory in the late 1830s. All of the tribes had adopted the white man's ways, turning to farming as their principal means of livelihood. But their bitterness toward the federal government created a virtual haven for white outlaws.

Gangs made wild forays into Kansas and Missouri and Texas, and then retreated into the Nations. There they found immunity from the law, and perhaps the oddest sanctuary in the annals of crime. Though each of the Five Civilized Tribes was a sovereign nation, their authority extended only to Indian citizens. White men were untouchable, exempt from all prosecution except that of a federal court.

Yet there were no extradition laws governing the Nations. Federal marshals had to pursue and capture the wanted men, and return them to white jurisdiction. In time, the country became infested with hundreds of fugitives, and the problem was compounded by the Indians themselves. They had no use for white man's law, and the marshals were looked upon as intruders. The tribal Light Horse Police refused cooperation, and the tribesmen, more often than not, connived with the outlaws. A man on the run found asylum in the Nations.

"Don't that beat all!" Blanchard concluded with a laugh. "The lawdogs gotta come in here and dig us out, and that ain't no easy chore. Hell, we're pretty near heroes to the Injuns."

"Unusual, to say the least," Holliday observed. "Are the marshals aggressive in their pursuit?"

"Them that are got a fight on their hands. Me and my boys have killed our share."

Holliday made a mental note to proceed with care. Like most gamblers, he carried his bankroll in a moneybelt, usually in large denominations. Beneath his shirt, strapped around his waist, was something more than ten thousand dollars. Ed Blanchard and his gang would find such a sum tempting, perhaps too tempting. Killing one man was far easier than robbing a train.

For all that, he liked what he'd heard about the Nations. A lawless land, where anarchy reigned, was the perfect spot for a man unjustly charged with murder. A sanctuary where marshals ventured at their own peril.

Far better than being hanged in Dallas.

The hideout was a crude log cabin along the banks of Elk Creek. There were five men in the gang, all of them cutthroats of the first order. They robbed banks and trains, and retreated to the Nations to whore with Indian women and gamble among themselves. None of them expected to live to old age.

Holliday found them to be dangerous company, like a pack of wolves. Yet they accepted him as one of their own, a killer outside the law. His educated manner fascinated them, and they were amazed that he'd once been a dentist. Still, it was his mastery of cards that kindled their greatest respect. For hours at a time they sat watching him stack a deck and deal seconds, all quicker than the eye. They looked upon him as small boys behold a magician.

The cabin was sparse on comforts. Three double bunks stood end to end along one wall, and a rough-hewn table, flanked by a potbelly stove, occupied the central living area. Beyond the table, at the far end of the room, was a wood cooking stove and shelves packed with tinned goods. A jumble of saddlebags, filthy clothes, and weathered gear was strewn about the floor. The place smelled like a bear's den.

Holliday marked his first week among them on a Sunday night. A poker game was in progress, but he had them outclassed and they knew it, and he never gambled with them. As repayment for his card tricks, one of the men, Roy Smith, had taught him a skill learned from the Indians. Smith was a swift and deadly knife fighter, and he'd made a present to Holliday of a small, double-edged stiletto. The dagger was six inches long, with German toolmarks, and sharp as a scalpel.

Smith had crafted an ingenious scabbard which enabled Holliday to carry the knife in the breast pocket of his suit jacket. He'd then demonstrated quick, surgical strokes to various parts of the anatomy, all of which were meant to kill. A cut to the jugular, or a slash to the artery in the forearm, was certain, if not instant, death. A ripping stroke to the lower abdomen would disembowel a man, and spill his guts on the floor. Smith, who enjoyed his work, preferred a knife to a gun.

On a more practical note, Blanchard took it upon himself to find Holliday a reliable mount. He laughingly referred to Holliday's stolen horse as "crowbait," and yesterday he'd arranged a trade with the livestock dealer in Ardmore. The swap cost Holliday an extra sixty dollars, but he got a handsome new saddle and a spirited sorrel gelding. The horse was broad through the chest, fifteen hands high, and built for endurance. Blanchard joked that Holliday could now outrun the law from the Nations to Wyoming. Holliday wryly expressed the hope that the need would never arise.

Later that night, when the poker game ended, Blanchard's underlying motive became apparent. Good horses, he explained to Holliday, were a must for those who rode the owlhoot trail. After pulling a job, they required a mount with stamina for their escape, one capable of outdistancing a posse. A man on a slow horse wound up with his head in a noose.

"Reason I mention it," Blanchard went on, "me and the boys are fixin' to hit a bank up in Kansas. Oughta make a nice haul."

Holliday was aware of the other men watching him. He nodded, saying nothing, waiting for the gang leader to continue. "Well, anyway," Blanchard said expansively, "me and the boys took a vote. We'd like you to join us."

The compliment needed no elaboration. For a gang of robbers to invite a relative stranger into their ranks was a singular honor. Holliday knew a refusal would offend them, and the situation might turn sticky. He chose his words with care.

"You flatter me," he said, looking from man to man. "To ride with you would be a high honor, indeed. But I must decline your offer."

A mumbled protest arose, and he stilled it with an upraised hand. "Hear me out. You gentlemen pride yourselves on being professionals at your trade. Am I right?" Blanchard and the others bobbed their heads. "Well, then, imagine that you are as skilled with a deck of cards as I am. Would you willy-nilly toss it aside—quit your profession?"

"Hell, no!" Roy Smith blurted. "Way you play, it's legalized robbery. Shore beats the shit outta pullin' holdups with a gun."

The others murmured quick agreement. Blanchard nonetheless looked disappointed. "Sorry you're out, Doc. We'd have been proud to have you along."

"I sometimes think God cast me in the lot of a gambling man. I'm sorry, too, Ed."

"Well, what're you gonna do with yourself? You won't find no poker games worth a squat in the Nations."

"Good question," Holliday replied. "Perhaps I'll try California. I doubt the Texas Rangers would find me there."

Blanchard scoffed. "No need to travel that far. Christ, there's places in Texas ain't never seen a Texas Ranger." He chuckled scornfully. "Bastards'd likely get shot on the spot."

"What sort of places?"

"I reckon Jacksboro would head the list. Toughest gawd-damn hellhole there ever was."

"Jacksboro?" Holliday inquired. "I assume that's a town."

"After a fashion," Blanchard said. "Grew up around Fort Richardson. Nothin' but saloons, gamblin' dives, and whorehouses. Rough crowd."

Holliday looked quizzical. "Seldom much money around military posts. Are these gaming establishments of the penny-ante variety?"

"Godamighty, no! Hide hunters and cowmen are thick as fleas out there. All of 'em rollin' in money, too. They're what drew the sportin' crowd, not the soldiers."

"Out there?" Holliday repeated. "Where is Jacksboro, exactly?"

"Off in the middle of nowheres," Blanchard said. "I'd calculate it's mebbe a hundred miles west of Dallas."

"And you say they have no law out that way?"

"A man makes his own law in Jacksboro. Judge Colt and a jury of six hold court every night."

"You've been there, then?"

"Just once," Blanchard allowed. "When I was young and dumb, workin' for a cow outfit. Lucky I got out alive."

"You may have solved my problem, Ed. Jacksboro appears made to order for a gambling man."

"Well, one thing's for damn sure. You won't see no Texas Rangers out thataway."

Holliday thought it might work out very nicely. No law, no Texas Rangers, just the sporting crowd. Judge Colt and a jury of six.

He liked the sound of it.

CHAPTER 7

Holiday rode into Jacksboro early in September. The town was situated along Lost Creek, a tributary of the Trinity River. Fort Richardson was three miles west of town, on the south bank of the creek.

The garrison was one in a chain of army posts that guarded the western settlements of Texas. For generations, the Comanche and Kiowa had swept out of the north, crossing the Red River, to raid and pillage Texican settlers. The Red River war, a vast military campaign concluded only a year ago, had at last put an end to the bloodshed. The hostile tribes were now interned on reservations in western Indian Territory.

A stagecoach splashed across Lost Creek as Holliday entered town. Some thirty miles east lay the Chisholm Trail, the overland route for herds of longhorns into the Kansas cowtowns. The plains surrounding Jacksboro were now open rangeland, the terrain dotted with stunted pecans and scrub oak. Large ranchers, claiming thousands of square miles of graze, operated cattle spreads to distant points of the compass. Farther west, vast herds of buffalo still roamed the rolling plains.

Jacksboro was little more than a frontier outpost. There was no organized town government, and the military was barred by law from involvement in civilian affairs. Yet the small community was vital and prosperous, a center of com-

merce for buffalo hunters, ranchers, and homesteaders, and
the garrison at Fort Richardson. The principal connection
with the outside world was the stage line, crossing east to
Fort Worth and west to El Paso.

The town itself was a crude collection of buildings,
thrown together with ripsawed lumber and narrow board-
walks. The main street was rutted and dusty, baked hard by
the plains sun. Shortly before the noon hour, Holliday reined
to a halt outside a livery stable at the end of the street. He
was wearing rough range clothes, purchased during his stay
in Indian Territory, covered now with grime from five days
on the trail. For six dollars a week, he made arrangements
to stall his sorrel gelding at the livery. Warbag in hand, he
turned uptown.

The street was lined with saloons and dance halls, a mer-
cantile emporium, one hotel, and a trading post. There were
three cafes and several smaller establishments, but no sign
of a bank or a newspaper. The hotel was a ramshackle affair,
with plank floors and bare walls, and an outhouse out back.
At the desk, Holliday engaged a room for a dollar a day,
and inquired about laundry service. His one remaining outfit,
the gray suit and pastel shirt he'd worn upon fleeing Dallas,
was stuffed in his warbag. The desk clerk agreed to have it
sent out to a Chinese laundry which also pressed suits.

"By the way," Holliday asked. "Does Jacksboro have
such a thing as a tailor?"

"Matter of fact, we do," the clerk said. "Officers out at
the fort get uniforms tailored over at the mercantile."

"Your town is more civilized than it appears. I'm im-
pressed."

"Yessir, we're lots more citified than we look."

Holliday ordered hot water, a tub, and a quart of bourbon
brought to his room. His supply of corn liquor from Indian
Territory was almost exhausted, and he savored the thought
of a return to bourbon. His room was spartan as a monk's
cell, with a bed and washstand, a cracked mirror and one
chair, and a johnny-pot to avoid hurried trips to the out-
house. The sight of it brought on a mild coughing fit, and

he drained the last of the corn liquor from his flask. He thought the only saving grace was a window looking westward onto the plains.

The tub, brought by the hotel handyman, was a galvanized washtub. But with it were several buckets of hot water, and Holliday managed to bathe while jackknifed into the confined space. By the time he shaved, and stepped into his one fresh set of underdrawers, the handyman returned with his clothes and the bottle of bourbon. All in all, the suit was reasonably presentable, sponged of spots and sharply pressed.

With the Peacemaker on his hip, and the Colt Lightning in its shoulder-holster, he once more felt properly attired. The stiletto, with spring clips on the sheath to hold it secure, was secreted in his breast pocket. The flask, filled now with bourbon, went into the inside pocket of his jacket. After dusting his hat with a damp cloth, he inspected himself in the mirror. He was dressed for business.

Fortified by bourbon, Holliday left the hotel. His appetite was still at low ebb, but food was a necessary essential for energy. Upstreet, he stepped into a cafe and found the menu limited if somewhat exotic. He ordered antelope steak, a stack of buckwheat cakes covered with sorghum, and black coffee. The steak was tender, though gamey in taste, and he ate less than half of what was on his plate. He lingered over a second cup of coffee, spiked with bourbon. Lately, it seemed the best part of any meal.

Outside, surveying the street, he lit a cigarillo. Horses stood hip-shot at the hitch racks, and three wagons loaded with buffalo hides were parked in front of the trading post. There were few passersby on the boardwalks, and the town seemed somnolent in the warmth of a September afternoon. A post office sign, nailed beside the door of the trading post, reminded him of Mattie. Her letters were likely gathering dust in Dallas, and she was doubtless worried because he hadn't replied. He considered letting her believe he'd disappeared, or died; but deceit was more repugnant than the alternative. He made a mental note to write.

The thought was quickly put aside. A month had passed since his last time at the tables, and he was eager to try his hand. Directly across the street, with the name emblazoned on a plate-glass window, was the Lone Star Saloon. After scanning the other dives, he decided the Lone Star, based on outward appearances, looked to be the top spot in town. He crossed the street.

Holliday got a pleasant surprise. Upon pushing through the batwing doors, he found that the Lone Star catered to gamblers. Opposite a mahogany bar were faro layouts, dice and roulette, and chuck-a-luck. To the rear were four tables reserved for poker. The place was empty, except for a bartender, table men, and one faro dealer. Everyone stopped, silent a moment, inspecting his unusually debonair attire. To his amazement, the faro dealer was a woman. She gave him a dazzling smile.

"Care to try your luck?" she said. "No time like the present."

She was attractive, with high cheekbones, a pert nose, and upswept red hair. She wore a pale green gown which accentuated her slim waist and full breasts. Her eyes danced merrily, watching him as he approached the table. She laughed.

"I do love a man who dresses well. You are definitely a rarity in Jacksboro."

"No more rare than you," Holliday said, seating himself before the table. "I've never met a lady faro dealer."

"Lottie Deno," she said, introducing herself. "Are you a gambling man?"

"A pleasure, Miss Deno. And yes, I am a gambler of some small repute. My friends call me Doc Holliday."

She blinked. "*The* Doc Holliday? From Dallas?"

"The same," Holliday confessed, suddenly wary. "How do you know of me?"

"We receive the Dallas newspapers by stage mail. Your name made the headlines."

"An unfortunate incident all the way round."

"From what I read," she said in a cultured voice, "there

was more than one incident. The newspapers say you killed two men over cards.''

"Yes, that's true," Holliday admitted. "A matter of honor, and both were fair fights." He paused, assessing her. "Will I have trouble with the authorities here?"

Lottie Deno laughed. "There are no authorities in Jacksboro. Haven't you heard? No law west of Fort Worth, and no God in west Texas. You're perfectly safe."

"Well, I'm glad to hear that. I thought we might have to postpone our game."

"Spoken like a true sporting man, Doc. I take it you enjoy faro."

"Only if it's a square game. Do you deal straight, Lottie?"

"Try me and see."

Holliday's question, and Lottie Deno's reply, were sides of the same coin. Some dives hired faro dealers, and others leased the concession for a percentage. Either way, everyone took it for granted that all dealers were crooked. Holliday signaled the barkeep for a bottle of bourbon. He then bought five hundred dollars in chips.

"Suppose I catch you?" he said with a slow smile. "What's my reward?"

She batted her eyelashes. "We'll talk about it when it happens. But I must warn you—I'm good."

"I admire a woman with confidence. Deal, Lottie."

Holliday bet the nine to win and coppered the king to lose. He watched her hands closely, for cheating at faro required the skill to manipulate a deck of cards. The most common method was to use "strippers," a deck with certain cards trimmed slightly along the edges or on the ends. A dealer with sensitive fingers could then "read" the cards before slipping them from the box. By dealing "seconds"— holding back the top card and dealing the one below—a dealer could determine the outcome of bets on the layout. The house odds were vastly improved by an adept dealer.

Lottie Deno was unusually talented, smooth and quick. Alert to any irregularity, Holliday was still unable to spot

her sleight of hand. Yet he knew she was cheating, for he lost twice as often as he won. She was gracious, her hands flashing as she kept up an engaging patter, and she slowly ground him down. At the end of an hour, all his chips were on her side of the table. He shook his head with a rueful smile.

"I have to take my hat off. You are the best I've ever seen."

"Why, thank you, sir," she said lightly. "I consider that high praise."

A sudden spasm struck Holliday. He knocked back a shot of bourbon, then poured another and drained it off. When the coughing subsided, he wiped his mouth with a handkerchief. "Too much fresh air," he said with an offhand gesture. "One day it will be the death of me."

Lottie knew consumption when she saw it. She matched his casual manner. "A smoky gaming parlor should be the perfect cure. We always have a large crowd at night."

"Speaking of tonight—" Holliday gave her a bold smile. "After you close, perhaps we could have a late supper. I would count it an honor."

She detected in his courtly bearing, and his Southern accent, a man of breeding. A gentleman rogue, perhaps, but nonetheless a gentleman. The quality was uncommon in the wilds of Jacksboro, and she decided to overlook his cough. She nodded happily.

"Late supper for two sounds very nice. I accept."

Holliday quit her faro game. She had trimmed him quickly and expertly, and he thought it enough for one day. But the crowd, just as she'd promised, began building shortly after sundown. By early evening, the Lone Star was packed with buffalo hunters, cowhands, and soldiers. They were a rough and raucous bunch, there to swill whiskey and test their luck. Every table in the place was soon jammed with players.

At the rear of the room, Holliday found a poker game with a notions drummer, three ranchers, and a buffalo hunter. The ranchers considered themselves high rollers, and

the buffalo hunter, who had sold three wagonloads of hides that afternoon, was loaded with cash. The stakes were set for anything up to fifty dollars, with a ten-dollar ante.

Holliday was out of their league. The men were mediocre gamblers, several notches below the competition he'd faced in Dallas. They lacked insight into percentages and odds, often playing on the come, hoping to improve a poor hand. The buffalo hunter, a tough, thickset man who smelled of rancid hides, was the worst of the lot. A heavy drinker, loud and belligerent, he bluffed wildly trying to buy pots. He was a steady loser.

By late evening, Holliday was ahead by at least a thousand dollars. A good part of it had been won from the buffalo hunter, who was as easy to read as an open book. He became more pugnacious as his losses mounted, his anger fueled by whiskey. His resentment was directed more at Holliday than the others, for he saw his money neatly stacked on the opposite side of the table. Toward midnight he and Holliday were the only players left in a hand of five-card draw. Holliday bet fifty after the draw, and the hunter raised. Holliday returned the raise, and the man grunted coarsely. His features twisted in a scowl.

"Gawddammit, I'll just call. But you better have 'em!"

"I do," Holliday said, spreading his cards. "Three nines."

A shouted curse from the bar attracted their attention. They turned as two cowhands squared off in a windmilling slugfest. One of the men went down from a clubbing blow, and rolled away, trying to lever himself upright. The other one booted him in the ribs, then kicked him in the teeth, and he crumpled to the floor. The crowd cheered the victor, who called for a round of drinks. The men at the poker table turned back to the game.

Holliday reached for the pot. The hide hunter gave him a baleful once-over. "Bet you never had a fight in your life, did you?"

"I prefer poker to fisticuffs. Let's play cards."

"Listen to him, will you! Gawddamn runt all tricked out

in his fancy duds. Whyn't you find a game with girls?''

Holliday fixed him with a level stare. "I'm not looking for trouble.''

"Well, you done found it,'' the hide hunter growled. "Think I'll just whip your ass for the hell of it.''

" 'His looks do menace heaven and dare the Gods.' ''

"What's that again? You makin' fun of me?''

"Indeed not,'' Holliday said. "The line was written by Christopher Marlowe, an Englishman of letters. He might have written it for you.''

"That does it, you pansy sonovabitch! I'm gonna cripple you.''

Holliday stood as the man started out of his chair. He smiled. "I see you are heeled. Use it or turn tail.''

"You wanna try me with a gun?''

"Only if you insist.''

The hide hunter laughed out loud. His eyes crazed, he grabbed for the pistol at his side. Too quick to follow, Holliday's hand dipped beneath the skirt of his jacket and re-appeared with the Colt. He fired, and a puff of dust kicked off the buffalo man's shirt beneath the breastbone. Holliday fired again as the man struggled to bring his gun arm level. His eyes went dead, and his legs suddenly failed him. He toppled to the floor.

The crowd stood as though mesmerized, frozen in silence. No one moved as Holliday holstered his pistol in a smooth, fluid motion. Lottie Deno, watching from her faro table, was no less stunned than the crowd. Yet, somewhere deep inside, she felt a jubilant, tingling sensation. She thought the word would soon go out.

Doc Holliday had arrived in Jacksboro.

CHAPTER 8

Late morning sunlight streamed through the window. Holliday stood at the washstand, his face lathered with soap. His hand was steadied by bourbon, three heavy slugs since he'd awakened. The straight razor glided smoothly over his jawline.

After he finished shaving, he trimmed his mustache with a small pair of scissors. Then he splashed his cheeks with bay rum. Studying himself in the mirror, he noticed that his features were gaunt, his jawbone somewhat more pronounced, but his eyes were clear. He thought there were mornings he'd looked worse.

Almost two weeks had passed since his arrival in Jacksboro. His nights were devoted to poker, and though the crowd at the Lone Star was a rough, uncouth lot, the tables had treated him well. Today he felt chipper and reasonably healthy, his mood buoyed by memories of last night. Lottie was like an elixir, some magical potion that invigorated his life. He considered himself a lucky man.

A clothing rack had been installed along one wall of his room. On it were hung four new suits, and half a dozen shirts, fitted for him by the tailor at the mercantile store. He chose a light blue worsted, with a pale apricot shirt, and a patterned four-in-hand tie. His boots, new as well, were handmade of soft leather, with a low walking heel. He took his hat off a wall peg as he went out the door.

In the hall, he walked toward the end of the corridor. Three doors down from his room he stopped, rapping lightly with his knuckles. From inside, he heard footsteps on creaky floorboards, and the door opened. Lottie was still in her bed clothes, a filmy peignoir covering a low-cut nightgown. She inspected him with a sultry smile.

"My, my! Don't we look dapper today?"

Holliday grinned. "Tailoring makes the man."

"Or the other way round." She motioned him into the room. "As you can see, I'm not ready yet. Make yourself comfy on the bed. Your spot's still warm."

Holliday had left her room around four that morning. Their relationship had begun his second night in town, and he'd shared her bed every night since. She was a fiery lover, almost wanton in her needs, and he felt somehow rejuvenated by their affair. He never spent the entire night, for his cough kept her awake, and as she delicately phrased it, "robbed her of her beauty sleep." Though he suspected there was some lingering fear of his consumption, she never evidenced it by her actions. She smothered him with kisses when they made love.

"Why aren't you dressed?" he asked, seating himself on the bed. "I thought we were going for a drive."

"Of course we are! But I'm a working woman, remember? Just let me finish here."

Holliday enjoyed watching her. She was svelte, with shapely legs, and moved with the grace of a languid cat. She resumed her seat at the table where she'd been working when he interrupted. Before her was a small rectangular device known as a card trimmer, a tool of the trade essential to rigged faro games. The metal device was flat on top, with a gauge to position and measure cards, and what resembled a hinged cleaver on one side. She flashed him a smile, then bent to her task.

One card at a time was positioned in a recess on top of the device. By turning a knob on the left side, a thin plate moved the card a millimeter to the right, the edge held firmly in place. The razor-sharp cleaver, decorated with an

onyx handle, was then snapped downward in a slicing motion. The blade trimmed a millimeter off the side of the card, discernible only to an educated finger, and left the edge smooth. A deck of cards put through a trimmer allowed a skilled dealer to "read" individual cards simply by touch.

"There!" Lottie set the deck of cards aside. "That will hold me for tonight, anyway. I'll trim another deck tomorrow."

Holliday raised an eyebrow. "I wonder if your patrons suspect you're a cardsharp? Perhaps an attractive woman is all the excitement they require."

"Why do you think I wear peek-a-boo gowns? Those chumps would rather look at my cleavage than win at faro."

"Pity the rascal who sneaks too long a peek. Hmmm?"

"Honestly, Doc!" she said with a minxish smile. "A girl has to make a living."

Lottie was his confidante as well as his lover. In quiet moments they had revealed themselves, one to the other. Haltingly, though he'd said little of Mattie, he had told her of his pilgrimage westward. She in turn related the story of a Kansas City girl, born to a good family, who had fallen for an itinerant gambler. A year later, when he left her stranded in Abilene, she had put to use all he'd taught her about crooked cards. She became a faro dealer, traveling from town to town, pausing wherever money was loose and men were foolish. Jacksboro was the latest stop in her odyssey.

"Do you want an outing or not?" Holliday said now. "At this rate, I could have slept another hour."

"Give me a chance to get dressed, will you? I'll just be a moment."

A short time later they emerged from the hotel. She was wearing a respectable gown, her flaming hair covered by a fashionable bonnet, and carried a parasol. They had a quick breakfast in the nearest cafe, and then walked downstreet to the livery stable. The owner, a reedy man with scarecrow hair, met them as they came through the door. His head bobbed with a nervous grin.

"Mr. Holliday," he said in a squeaky voice. "I've got the buggy all hitched and set to go. Just like you ordered."

"Thank you kindly, Arnie. Expect us back before sunset."

"No rush, Mr. Holliday. No rush a'tall. Enjoy your ride."

The buggy was drawn by a coal-black mare with ginger in her step. Holliday had a good hand with horses, and he gently popped the reins, urging her along at a brisk clip. They drove west from town, on a wagon trace skirting the creek. Dappled sunlight spilled through tall cottonwoods bordering the road.

"Lord love us," Lottie said, unable to suppress a giggle. "I thought Arnie Fisher was going to bow down and kiss your boots. He was absolutely petrified to please you."

Holliday shrugged. "You make too much of it. He probably treats all of his customers with the same courtesy."

"Oh, of course he does! Especially if they kill a man a week."

"Well, as to that . . . I think you overstate the case."

"Don't go modest on me, Doc. You have a reputation to uphold."

There was no arguing the point. Holliday had been in Jacksboro scarcely two weeks, and he'd sent two men to the graveyard. The buffalo hunter, killed his first night in town, had set the sporting crowd buzzing. Then, three nights ago, he had called a tinhorn cardsharp for dealing from the bottom, and doing it poorly. The sharpie made the mistake of reaching for his gun, and found himself outclassed at more than cards. Holliday killed him with one shot.

The local undertaker sent Holliday a box of cigarillos. Some among the sporting crowd, though they never said it within his hearing, spoke of him as a shootist. The term was peculiar to the frontier, reserved for those considered to be a mankiller of some distinction. Everyone in town, aware of Holliday's previous disputes in Dallas, now placed the score at four men killed. His reputation, much as Lottie had observed, was spreading. Doc Holliday was not a man to cross.

"So how does it feel?" Lottie said at length. "To be the talk of the town?"

Holliday laughed shortly. "A dubious honor. Not one I would have sought."

"You know, I've often wondered about that. The way men fight and kill one another. Does it really matter who's cock-o'-the-walk?"

"I suppose it comes down to a matter of pride. Or perhaps male vanity. Every man likes to think he wears the badge of courage."

She smiled. "Spoken like a true Southerner."

"What does one have to do with the other?"

"Well, I've always heard that the Holy Grail for Southern men was the *code duello*. Death before dishonor."

"From all I've seen," Holliday said wryly, "the custom never traveled west. Out here things are a bit more practical."

"Oh?" She appeared puzzled. "In what way?"

Holliday briefly explained. The *code duello* of the Old South, he noted, was indeed based on honor. The parties to a dispute stood back to back, stepped off ten paces, then turned and fired. There was a protocol to such affairs, and a certain dignity, all conducted under a rigid and rather elaborate set of rules. A duel in the Old South was a ceremony steeped in tradition.

The code of the West, Holliday went on, was strictly a matter of survival. The practical approach to a gunfight was to shoot first, shoot straight, and answer to the law later. There were no rules, certainly no protocol, that governed conduct in a shootout, except the rule of fairness. A man could not fire on an unarmed opponent, or open fire without warning. Apart from that, every man looked for an edge, some slight advantage. The idea was to win, to walk away. To survive.

"Old fashioned pragmatism," Holliday concluded. "The loser gets buried, and the winner lives to fight another day. All very practical."

"What about honor?" she said mischievously. "You sort of skipped over that part."

"Like most things in life, it's haphazard. Some men are more honorable than others."

"And some have no honor at all."

"Hah! A good many of them to be found in Jacksboro."

She playfully squeezed his arm. "What code does the fearsome Doc Holliday follow?"

"Live and let live," Holliday said equably. "I won't be insulted and I won't be threatened. These are courtesies I extend to other men." He paused, underscoring the thought. "I require the same of them."

"No insults. No threats. That sounds simple enough. So what provokes men to try your temper?"

"The gods."

"Pardon me?"

" 'As flies to wanton boys, are we to the Gods. They kill us for their sport.' "

"Do they really?" She looked skeptical. "Where did you hear that?"

"Shakespeare," Holliday said with a faint smile. "*King Lear,* I believe."

"And I believe you're full of it! You don't actually think the gods provoke men to fight—do you?"

"Folly and fools are often traveling companions. Perhaps the gods winnow them out for lack of better sport."

She sniffed. "I would hardly call that sport."

"Well, after all," Holliday deadpanned, "the gods don't play poker. Or for that matter, faro. Of course, the way you deal it's far from a sporting proposition, either." He cast a sly, sidewise glance at her. "Wouldn't you agree?"

"Thank you, sir," she said with a delightful laugh. "I take that as a compliment."

"You should," Holliday told her. "I doubt there's a man alive who's your equal at dealing seconds. I speak from personal experience."

"Why, Doc, I only took you for five hundred."

"Lottie, I consider it money well spent. An education of sorts."

She uttered a low, gloating laugh. "I'll bet you still couldn't catch me."

"All too true," Holliday agreed. "But watching you these last couple of weeks has given me a decided edge. I think I could catch anyone else."

"Yes, I just imagine you could."

She was silent a moment. Her mind went to three nights ago, and the tinhorn Holliday had called out. She remembered the man's face as he went for his gun, and found himself staring into the muzzle of Holliday's pistol. She had witnessed many gunfights, in gambling dives from the Kansas cowtowns to the western reaches of the Texas frontier. But she had never seen a man so quick, or so deadly, as Holliday. Nor was she alone in that view. All of Jacksboro agreed.

Stranger still was the manner in which he killed. Twice now she had watched as he goaded other men into making the first move. He was cool and calculated, never raised his voice, relying instead on ridicule to force the other man's hand. His manner seemed somehow detached, oddly amused, as though he were an observer to some absurd, comic ritual. Which was perhaps the case, after all. He killed men with absurd ease.

The buggy rolled to a halt. Her reverie broken, she saw that Holliday had stopped on a low bluff overlooking the Western prairie. The sun shone brightly on verdant grasslands stretching endlessly to the horizon, cottony clouds scudding along on a southerly breeze. She was aware that he hadn't spoken in a long while, his gaze fixed on some distant point beyond sight. She wondered if his thoughts were on the future. Or perhaps the past.

"What do you see out there, Doc?"

Holliday stifled a cough. He pulled the flask from his pocket and took a long swig of bourbon. Then he capped it, balancing it on his knee, his eyes suddenly brighter. A curious, enigmatic smile tugged at the corner of his mouth.

"I see the plains, Lottie. I'm often touched by the harsh beauty of this land. Cruel and inviting, all at the same time. I think I like it."

She knew he was lying. Or at least being evasive. Whatever his inner thoughts, he chose not to share them. Yet she was struck by the timbre of his voice, and his gift for the language. Words that flowed, expressive words, a portrait of sound.

She thought him a paradox. A man who saw beauty in the cruelty of the plains. A man who quoted Shakespeare and obscure poets. A quiet, witty man who goaded other men to foolish anger.

And killed them while he smiled.

CHAPTER 9

The sun was high when Holliday emerged from the Lone Star. His features were sallow and a throbbing ache seemed rooted deep in his chest. He filled his lungs with crisp morning air.

The poker game had lasted two days and three nights. A cattleman, just returned from a trail drive to the Kansas railhead, had refused to quit, determined to recoup his losses. Holliday, as the big winner, had been obliged to stick with the game until the end. He figured he'd won close to three thousand.

The score was his largest since arriving in Jacksboro. He was exhausted, hollow-eyed and drained from almost sixty straight hours of poker. Apart from trips to the outhouse, the men had never left the game, their meals served while they played. Yet he was filled with a sense of triumph, and elation stoked his engine. However bad he looked, he was riding high from the big win.

A freight wagon rolled past as he crossed the street to the trading post. The place was a rainbow of odors, the smell of cured buffalo hides mixed with new saddle leather, foodstuffs, and tobacco. He was down to one cigarillo, and he ordered a fresh box from one of the clerks. As he dropped bills onto the counter, the clerk suddenly remembered that a letter had arrived with yesterday's post. It was addressed to Dr. John H. Holliday, and the clerk wisely refrained from

any humorous remarks. The handwriting was all too famil-
iar.

On his way out, Holliday noticed a calendar on the wall.
He marked the date as September 24, reflecting that he'd
been in town almost three weeks. Upon arriving, he had
written Mattie, advising her of his move to Jacksboro. He
explained his departure from Dallas by revealing that his
dental practice had failed, due to his cough. To earn a living,
he told her, he had turned to gambling, and was now fol-
lowing the western boomtowns. He casually remarked that
he had "fallen from grace," and plied his new trade as a
member of the sporting crowd. He thought perhaps the rev-
elation would persuade her to cut him loose.

In the privacy of his hotel room, he read her reply. She
was saddened by the failure of his dental practice, express-
ing sympathy for his loss. As for gambling, she was sur-
prised by his choice of a new enterprise, but in no way
critical. Her concern was not for the occupation itself, but
rather for his health. She begged him to keep regular hours,
to eat properly and get sufficient rest, and not to overtax
himself in pursuit of fortune. The important thing, she said,
was that he regain his health, and speed the day they would
again be reunited. She closed by reaffirming her love and
her commitment. She prayed their separation would soon
end.

Holliday dropped her letter on the nightstand. He
scrubbed his face with his hands, suddenly riddled with
guilt. How could he face a man with a gun, he brooded, and
yet lack the courage to tell her outright that there was no
hope for them? Granted, his intent was to avoid hurting her;
but perhaps he wronged her more with lies of omission. His
affair with Lottie Deno abruptly seemed to him a betrayal,
still another hard truth left untold. Or perhaps, because it
had been four months since they parted, the betrayal
stemmed more from his memory of Mattie. A memory of
the past, all the things gone from his life. A life that was
no part of his future.

Some time elapsed before he gathered himself. Seated on

the bed, he took pen and paper, and hunched over the night-stand. Even before he began writing, he knew he would hint and prompt, and once again skirt the truth. Her endearing words robbed him of resolve, the strength to break her heart. Time and distance were still his allies in that regard, dark forces that would bring her to accept what he was unable to write. There was no hope. No future.

> *Your letter was a touch of brightness in this forlorn outpost. The accommodations are starkly crude, and my "clientele" are, for the most part, an unsavory lot. Days and nights run together for a gambler, and I fear you would be appalled by the demands of the vocation. I can only say that it is more lucrative than dentistry.*
>
> *News of Atlanta, what seems now another lifetime, is ever most welcome. Still, reading between the lines, I detect that you have further isolated yourself from the gaiety of that city. You must not allow my absence to deprive you of an entertaining, and fulfilling, social life. I urge you to think less of me and more of your-self. To know that you have done so would please me greatly.*

Holliday finished the letter in a similar vein. His over-riding wish was that she would become disillusioned with the passage of time. With no encouragement, and no good news regarding his condition, she might succumb to the temptations of Atlanta's social swirl. A girl of her charm and family position never wanted for suitors, and there was an inevitability about such things. The right man would make her forget.

Exhaustion finally overtook him. His lungs rebelled, and a harsh, wracking cough bent him double. He fumbled for a bottle of bourbon beside the bed and knocked it over. As the bottle rolled away, eluding his grasp, there was an in-sistent rapping at the door. He lurched across the room, gripped by the spasm, and twisted the door key. Lottie stood in the hall.

"Are you all right?" she asked anxiously. "I was passing by and heard you coughing."

"I—"

Holliday pulled at his shirt collar, gasping for breath. His face purpled and a strangled cough tore at his insides. Lottie slammed the door, hurrying to the bottle, and pulled the cork. He took it greedily, gulping a long draught and then another, his eyes watering. His words came out in a low wheeze.

"I'll be all right now."

"Oh, sure you will," she said crossly. "You and your damn marathon poker games! Come on, I'm putting you to bed."

Holliday tried a burlesque leer. "Would you take advantage of a sick man?"

"You're a regular riot," she said, moving him to the bed. "Hush now, and let's get you out of those clothes. Save your jokes for later."

She got him seated on the bed, then pulled his boots off. Working quickly, she peeled away his clothes, dropping them on the floor. When he was down to his underdrawers, she handed him the bottle. He took a long, gurgling pull, his breathing easier. She reclaimed the bottle, swinging his legs into bed, and covered him. He gave her a drowsy smile.

"You are a gem of a woman."

"And you are a damn fool, Doc! Go to sleep."

Holliday obediently closed his eyes. Within moments, his breathing ragged but steady, he was fast asleep. She placed the bottle on the floor, pulling the room's one straight-back chair close to the bed. She sat down, heaving a sigh of relief, and watched him a moment. Her gaze strayed to the letters on the nightstand.

The struggle between conscience and curiosity was quickly lost. She first read the letter written in the oval script of a woman's hand. Startled, though she knew a little of Holliday's past, she was struck by the consummate love expressed in Mattie's letter. She then read his reply, and read it again, studying the words. She realized with a shock

that the letter, however subtly phrased, was meant to dissuade. He was trying to extinguish the desperate longing of a woman's love. A gentle smothering of the flame.

Lottie's eyes welled with tears. Though they had never spoken of it, she knew he was dying. The day-by-day death that ultimately claimed the life of any man with consumption. Yet his concern was not for himself, or how long he might live, as borne out by his letter. His concern was for a fragile young girl in Atlanta, and her life. A girl he clearly loved.

She thought Dr. John H. Holliday was one of a kind. She wished she'd met him first.

Holliday slept all day and through the night. Lottie checked on him periodically, and the next morning she had breakfast brought to his room. Her plan was to keep him confined to bed another day, force him to rest and recoup his strength. But she found him to be a poor patient.

A hearty breakfast, liberally chased with whiskey, seemed to restore his spirits. By early afternoon, feeling energetic and restless, he declared himself recuperated. When he tried to coax her into bed, she knew it was a losing battle. She reluctantly agreed, and discovered that nearly twenty hours of sleep had worked wonders. He made love to her like a frisky stallion.

Late that afternoon they strolled down to the Lone Star. Lottie opened her faro game, and Holliday spent the next hour or so chatting with Burt Elliott, the owner. The sporting crowd was still buzzing about Holliday's big score, and Elliott bought several rounds of drinks. By early evening the place was crowded, and Holliday, floating on a cloud of bourbon, began looking for a game. He was ready to play poker.

There were no high rollers around, and the best he could manage was a low-stakes game. Still, any game was better than no game, and he decided to amuse himself until something better developed. He took a seat at a table with the local barber, a couple of cowhands, and three soldiers. From

the conversation, he gathered that one of the soldiers, a sergeant named O'Meara, was new to Fort Richardson. A pugfaced Irishman, he had been transferred from a cavalry regiment stationed in Kansas.

Holliday played with his usual erratic style. He had found that men in a low-stakes game were little different from those in a table-stakes game. A cowhand placed as much value on a month's pay as a high roller did on several thousand dollars. One was as easy to bluff, or sandbag with a concealed hand, as the other. The secret was to confuse them, keep them guessing. Their uncertainty gave him the edge.

After an hour of play, Holliday was ahead almost a hundred dollars. The deal passed to him and he called five-card draw. The barber opened, the cowhands dropped out, and O'Meara raised. The other two soldiers folded, and Holliday bumped it with another raise. O'Meara and the barber merely called, each taking three cards on the draw. Holliday also took three, riffling his cards as the other two players checked. Holliday bet the limit, three dollars, and the barber folded. O'Meara gruffly called the bet.

"Two pair." Holliday spread his hand. "Sevens and treys."

O'Meara flung his cards on the table, revealing a pair of jacks. "You're good at that," he said sullenly. "Dealin' yourself winners."

Holliday smiled. "Luck of the draw."

"Too goddamn lucky! Man don't raise the first go-round on a little pair. Lessen he knows he's gonna catch another pair."

"What are you trying to say, Sergeant?"

"He ain't sayin' nothin'," one of the other soldiers interrupted, frowning at O'Meara. "This here's Doc Holliday, Sarge. Nobody you wanna mess with. Just leave it go."

"Hell I will!" O'Meara rumbled. "Goddamn tinhorn don't scare me off. The bastard cheated."

Holliday stared at him. "Sergeant, I am neither a cheat nor of illegitimate birth. I believe you owe me an apology."

"Apology, my ass! I wouldn't doubt you're a son of a bitch, too."

"And you, sir, are a whore's son liar."

O'Meara flushed beetroot red. He cursed, slamming out of his chair, knocking the table over. Cards and money rained through the air as he clawed at the flapped, crossdraw holster on his belt. Holliday shoved the upturned table aside, pulled the Colt Lightning from beneath his jacket, and fired. The slug struck O'Meara in the left eye, exploding the back of his skull in a bloody halo. He went down like a felled tree.

A leaden silence settled over the saloon. Everyone stared at the body as a wide puddle of blood spread across the floor. Then, as though galvanized, the other two soldiers bolted for the door. A moment later the drumming thud of hoofbeats sounded from the street.

Burt Elliott, assisted by one of his dealers, dragged the corpse outside. As they pushed through the door, play slowly resumed at the other tables. Holliday walked to the bar, ordered bourbon, and lit a cigarillo. Lottie closed down her faro game, hurrying forward. Her features were masked with concern.

"You have to get out of Jacksboro. And fast!"

Holliday calmly tossed off his drink. "Why would I run? Everyone saw it. He pulled first."

"You killed a soldier," she said hastily. "That's altogether different from killing a civilian. The army will come after you."

"Well, let them come and be damned. I will not be bullyragged by Yankee soldiers."

"Lottie's right," Elliott said, joining them at the bar. "Happened once before. A hide hunter killed a soldier and the army took him into custody. Threw him in the stockade and held him for the Texas Rangers. Only time I ever saw a Ranger set foot in Jacksboro."

"Doc, listen to him," Lottie pleaded. "You have an hour, two at the most. Then a whole cavalry detachment will come swarming in here."

"Lookin' for blood, too," Elliott added. "You put up a fight and they'll kill you. Figure you killed one of theirs."

Holliday deliberated a moment. "You make a strong case," he said with a bitter laugh. "Perhaps I've overstayed my welcome in Jacksboro."

Lottie took his arm. "Come on, I'll walk with you to the hotel. You have to get moving."

"Not so fast," Holliday said. "I'm not leaving without my clothes this time. I'll need a packhorse."

"God, I hope your vanity doesn't get you hung!"

"I have to stop by the livery, anyway. I'm sure Arnie Fisher will be delighted to sell me an extra horse."

"Well, let's go, then. Come on!"

Not quite two hours later they stood outside the hotel. Lottie had arranged for provisions from the trading post while Holliday emptied his room. The packhorse was loaded, his sorrel gelding saddled, and nothing to hold him longer. He kissed her softly on the mouth.

"I'll miss you, Lottie Deno."

"Me, too." Her voice was husky. "Take care of yourself, Doc."

"Who knows, maybe our paths will cross again."

"Look for the redhead dealing faro."

Holliday stepped into the saddle. He smiled, waving to her with an offhand salute, then reined north out of town. She watched from the hotel as he forded the creek and disappeared into the night. Now that he was safely away, she had no fear that he would be caught. A man on the run, given even a few hours' lead, could vanish forever into the mountains and plains across the West. But she nonetheless feared for him in ways that had nothing to do with lawmen and the law. For he rode with a companion far more certain than a hangman's rope.

She hoped they would meet again before his time ran out.

CHAPTER 10

The brassy dome of the sky shimmered under a midday sun. High overhead buzzards swooped and circled, quartering something on the land below. The rolling plains marched onward into endless distance.

Holliday paused to water the horses on a bend in the Canadian River. He was twelve days out of Jacksboro, by rough estimate some three hundred miles to the northwest. Yesterday he had skirted Palo Duro Canyon, once the impenetrable stronghold of the Comanche. He held steadily to a northwest course, occasionally sighting a ranch house and herds of longhorn cattle. His destination was Colorado.

Upon leaving Jacksboro he had traveled north, toward the Red River. His first thought was to once again take refuge in the outlaw sanctuary of Indian Territory. But then he remembered he'd quit the Nations to avoid involvement with renegades and train robbers. So instead, figuring the law would never track him to Colorado, he had turned west along the Red. He knew Colorado was somewhere off to the northwest.

Four days later he stumbled upon Doan's Crossing. The trading post was situated on the south bank, a way station for Texas cattlemen driving herds along the Western Trail to railhead at Dodge City. There he'd bought provisions for overland travel, as well as a Winchester carbine, and purchased a mackinaw to ward off the chill of autumn nights.

The owner of the trading post obligingly sketched a rough map, tracing a latticework of rivers that led westward across the plains. His route lay through the Texas Panhandle, once the domain of warlike tribes.

From the Prairie Dog Fork of the Red, Holliday had turned north, to the Canadian, where he now sat staring over the limitless plains. The terrain swept onward to the horizon, flat and featureless, evoking a sense of something lost forever. There were no trees, no ridges or distant hills, just endless space. Nothing moved as far as the eye could see, as though, in some ancient age, the land had been frozen for all time. A chill breeze, like the cold breath of a ghost, rippled over the curly mesquite grass, disturbing nothing.

Holliday had the feeling he was looking upon something no mortal was meant to see. For in an eerie sense, the vast trackless barren was like the solitude of God, somehow unreal and strangely ominous. Yet Texas cattlemen, following the defeat of the warlike tribes, had brought their herds to the fabled *Llano Estacado,* now called the Panhandle. The land was still sparsely populated, with a handful of ranches scattered along Palo Duro Canyon and the winding Canadian. There was a spooky sensation that man was an intruder here, forever an alien on the windswept plains.

For all that, a town had sprung to life along the upper reaches of the Canadian. At Doan's Crossing, Holliday had been told the place was called Tascosa, and its location was marked with an *X* on his crudely drawn map. From what he gathered, the town was a collection of saloons and whorehouses, thrown together to serve the randy tastes of cowhands throughout the Panhandle. Still, it was an oasis in the middle of nowhere, and he was weary from twelve days on the trail. He thought to replenish his supply of whiskey, and maybe, with luck, find a hotel. A bedroll on hard ground was not his idea of comfort, and his bones ached. One night in a real bed sounded good.

Late that afternoon he rode into Tascosa. The town's one street was located on the north bank of the Canadian, roughly parallel with the river. The buildings, hastily erected

from ripsawed lumber, were a squalid testament to the allure of vice. Along one side of the street were two saloons, a couple of whorehouses, and a blacksmith shop. On the other side was a third saloon, flanked by a cafe, a general store, a small hotel, and a livery stable. The whole thing looked to have been built in one day.

Holliday left his horses and trail gear at the livery stable. With the Winchester in one hand, and a warbag in the other, he walked upstreet to the hotel. He was wearing rough range clothes, bought a week ago at Doan's Crossing, and the clerk took him to be a cowhand. The room he rented was four walls, with a bed, a washstand, and no windows. After testing the bed, which sagged in the middle, he stripped and took a birdbath in the basin. A short while later, attired in the mackinaw and a fresh shirt from his warbag, he returned to the lobby. He nodded to the clerk.

"Which saloon would you recommend?"

"The Exchange," the clerk said without hesitation. "Don't water down their whiskey, like some I could mention. Owned by Mick McCormick and his wife, Frenchy."

"Unusual name for a woman."

"Well, she ain't no whore, if that's what you're thinkin'. Deals faro."

Holliday was surprised. "I've known only one lady dealer."

"Give the Exchange a try. You'll meet another."

Dusk was settling over the land as Holliday emerged from the hotel. The general store was closed for the evening, but lamplight spilled through the window of the cafe. He turned into the Exchange, a boxy room brightly lighted by coal-oil lamps. Three cowhands stood hunched over the bar, opposite a couple of poker tables, which were empty. At the far end of the room, an attractive woman with dark hair riffled cards at a faro layout. No one was playing at the moment.

The bartender was a large man, with a square jaw and a handlebar mustache. He finished serving one of the cowhands, placed a bottle on a back shelf, and turned as Hol-

liday stopped at the end of the bar. His mustache rolled upward in a smile as he moved forward.

" 'Evenin'," he said pleasantly. "What'll it be?"

"Good evening," Holliday replied. "I'll have four quarts of bourbon."

"Quarts, you say?"

"I'm traveling through, and a long ways yet to go. A man doesn't want to run dry on the road."

"Indeed not."

The bartender produced a shot glass and pulled a bottle off the back shelf. He poured to the brim. "Have one on the house. Not often I sell four quarts at a lick."

Holliday sampled the bourbon. He nodded appreciatively. "You must be Mick McCormick."

"In the flesh." McCormick extended his hand. "I'm pleased to make your acquaintance, Mr. . . . ?"

"Holliday." Holliday accepted his handshake. "John Holliday."

McCormick gave him a quizzical look. "Holliday? Holliday? The name has a familiar ring."

"Probably someone else. Not all that uncommon a name."

"Wait!" McCormick stared at him. "Now it comes to me! Would you be the one called—Doc Holliday?"

Holliday frowned. "Some people call me that. How do you know me?"

"By the Jeezus! An honor to meet you." McCormick grabbed his hand, again pumped his arm. "What with people coming and going, news travels out here, Mr. Holliday. You're more famous than you know."

"I'm sorry to hear it. Suppose we keep it to ourselves?"

"I will, indeed! You have my word on it."

Holliday changed the subject. "I understand your wife deals faro. Maybe I'll try a hand."

"Uh—" McCormick stammered, his eyes round. "A professional courtesy, one gambling man to another. I must caution you . . . she cheats."

Holliday smiled. "Well, I wouldn't want to compromise a lady. What about a poker game?"

"Oh, there's always a game at night. Most of the cowboys drift in around seven or so."

"I haven't had supper, anyway. I'll get something to eat and come back." Holliday fished a roll of bills from his pocket, dropped money on the counter. "Meantime, perhaps you could have that bourbon delivered to the hotel. Leave it with the clerk."

"I'll see to it personally," McCormick said. "No trouble at all, Mr. Holliday."

"You might as well call me Doc. I'm not one for formalities."

"An honor and a privilege, Doc. Enjoy your supper."

Holliday walked next door to the cafe. A lone cowhand was seated at a table, flirting with the waitress. She broke away as Holliday seated himself at a table by the window. He ordered the evening special, a tangy beef stew with sourdough biscuits and coffee. As he ate, picking at the food, he stared moodily out the window. His expression was dour.

In Jacksboro, he had grown accustomed to people treating him with wary deference. He was aware that the sporting crowd, among themselves, referred to him as a shootist, or a gunman. But it never occurred to him that his reputation would have traveled to the wilds of the Texas Panhandle, passed along by word of mouth. The notion left him perplexed, for it tagged him with an unwanted infamy. He had no wish to be placed in the same league with mankillers such as John Wesley Hardin or Wild Bill Hickok, who had been assassinated only last month in Dakota Territory. The idea that he was infamous was repugnant, and dangerous. Infamous men attracted trouble, not to mention the law. A double jeopardy of sorts.

He wondered if his reputation had spread to Colorado, or beyond. The thought gave him pause, and the irony of it soured his appetite. Life was sometimes more complicated than dying.

* * *

"Ace high bets."

The dealer nodded to Holliday. The game was five-card stud, and all the cards were on the board. Holliday pretended to hesitate, then shrugged. "Bet two dollars."

A jingle of spurs chimed musically as one of the men shifted in his chair. There were five cowhands seated at the table, three to Holliday's left and two on his right. The player beside him tossed his cards onto the table. "Too rich for my blood."

"Same here," the next man said. "I'm out."

The third cowhand was the heavy drinker of the bunch. A ruddy man, his face flushed with liquor, he studied Holliday through bloodshot eyes. "Think you're bluffin', but I'll just call."

The next man folded, and the last, with a queen high showing, called. Holliday turned his hole card, an ace. "Caught a pair, gentlemen. Beat the aces."

"Shit!" the drinker rasped. "Had tens wired the whole time."

"Quit your bitchin', Buford." The other man flipped his hole card. "I was holdin' queens."

Holliday was bored. The stakes were low and the cowhands provided little competition. When the deal passed to him, he decided to play one last hand and call it a night. The ante was a quarter, and he dealt five-card draw. The man on his left checked, and the next one, after studying his cards, bet fifty cents. Buford grinned, chortling drunkenly to himself, and raised two dollars. The last two men tossed in their cards.

Holliday fanned his cards, almost disappointed to see three fours. On the verge of raising, he broke into a coughing fit. Several times during the night his cough had interrupted the game. A bottle sat at his elbow, and he quaffed a shot of bourbon. He noted flecks of blood on his handkerchief when he wiped his mouth.

"Your two," he said, nodding to Buford. "And raise two."

The man beside him folded. Buford muttered something

unintelligible, and called. On the draw, Buford took three cards and Holliday took one. After squeezing his cards open, Buford cackled gleefully. He bet two dollars.

"Go ahead," he gloated. "Raise on your two pair now."

Holliday smiled indulgently. "I regret to say I have no choice. Your two . . . and two more."

Buford glowered at him, then called the raise. Holliday spread his hand. "Three fours."

"You suckered me!" Buford flung his cards down, revealing aces and jacks. "Drawed one to three of a kind. Never saw such!"

"All's fair in poker." Holliday raked in the pot, glancing around at the other cowhands. "I believe I'll call it a night. Thank you for a stimulating evening, gentlemen."

"Whoa, now!" Buford thundered. "You ain't walkin' away with our dinero that easy. Nobody quits big winner!"

Holliday ignored him, pushing back his chair. Buford suddenly stood, his features hostile and twisted. "You gawddamn fancy-talkin' lunger! You deaf, too? Sit your ass down!"

"No trouble there," McCormick called out from the bar. "Buford, hold your tongue and mind your manners. That's Doc Holliday you're talking to."

"Shut your trap, Mick! I don't care if his name's Jesus Christ. I'll plug him if he tries walkin' out of here."

Holliday spread his hands. "Don't even think about it, cowboy. You couldn't win."

"Cut your wolf loose, lunger!"

Buford grabbed at the pistol on his hip. Holliday pulled and fired before the cowhand's gun arm came level. A look of blank surprise came over Buford's face, and his eyes rolled back in his head. His knees buckled, the gun dangling from his hand. He slumped to the floor.

The cowhands started out of their chairs. McCormick stepped around the end of the bar with a sawed-off shotgun, thumbing the hammers. "You boys sit real still."

"No need for that, Mick," Holliday said. "I tried to warn him off. They know he started it."

"Won't wash," McCormick said dully. "Way they look at it, you're a pistolero and he was just a drunk cowboy. They'd hang you from the nearest tree."

Holliday glanced at their faces, and saw it was true. "What do you suggest?"

"I'll hold 'em here till you're clear of town. You'd best leave now."

"What happens to you after I'm gone?"

"Nothing much." McCormick grinned, wagged the snout of his shotgun. "The sporting crowd sticks together in Tascosa. These boys wouldn't try anything stupid." He smiled at them. "Would you, boys?"

The cowhands looked downcast, their eyes averted. Holliday moved away from the table, holstering his pistol. "I'm in your debt, Mick. The marker's good anytime."

"Doc, I consider it an honor. Be off with you now."

Holliday rode out within the half hour. He was leading the packhorse, with four quarts of bourbon tightly wrapped inside his bedroll. Outside town he took a fix on the North Star, and gigged his horse into a ground-eating trot. Distance, given the circumstances, seemed the prudent move.

The indigo sky sparkled with starlight. All around, the plains seemed to shimmer, bathed in a silvery glow. As he rode along, it occurred to him that he'd spent less than seven hours in Tascosa. His plans for a night in a comfortable bed had gone to hell in a hurry. Apart from buying whiskey, he had managed to win a few hands of poker and kill a cowboy. There was no pride in it, and an unsettling sense of regret gave him pause. But the vagary of it nonetheless made him laugh.

A gambler's life was never dull.

CHAPTER 11

Three days later Holliday crossed into No Man's Land. The Texas line, according to his crude map, was at a spot where the North Canadian made a sharp bend to the northwest. Once he forded the river, he felt an inner sense of relief. He was beyond the arm of the law.

During his time at Jacksboro, Holliday had heard talk of this remote strip of wilderness. Centuries ago Spanish explorers had called it *Cimarron,* which meant "wild and unruly." Through a hodgepodge of confused and poorly written treaties, it now belonged to none of the Western states or territories. So it was aptly dubbed No Man's Land.

Yet there was nothing confusing about its borders. Texas and Kansas were separated by its depth of some thirty-five miles, while its breadth extended nearly two hundred miles westward from Indian Territory to New Mexico Territory. Along its northwestern fringe, the isolated strip of grasslands formed a juncture with Colorado as well. To a large degree the raw expanse of wilderness had been forgotten by God and government alike. Texas Rangers never crossed the line.

Holliday marked the date at somewhere around October 6. After fording the river, he angled off toward the northwest, and Colorado. From the days of his youth, when he'd spent all his time off in the hinterlands of the family plantation, he was able to reckon direction by the angle of the sun. He felt comfortable in the wilderness, as though reliv-

ing his explorations as a boyhood hunter, and his Winchester carbine kept him supplied with game. Still, wrapped in his bedroll at night, he was anxious to have the journey ended. He missed the fast pace, and the rivalry, of the sporting crowd.

The following afternoon he rode into Wild Horse Lake. The spot was roughly located on his map, situated on the divide between the Beaver and Cimarron rivers. A prominent landmark, it was known to be the haunt of renegades and killers. Those who came there were predators, wanted men on the dodge, and the law of the gun prevailed. A man survived on cunning and nerve, and by minding his own business. Holliday thought he could manage it for one night.

The lake itself was centered in a large basin. Somewhat like a deep bowl, it served as a reservoir for thundershowers that whipped across the plains. Above the basin, sweeping away on all sides, was a limitless prairie where the grasses grew thick and tall. Wild things, the mustangs that gave the lake its name, no longer came there to feed and water. The basin was now the domain of man.

Every stripe of outlaw found refuge there. A sanctuary where those who rode the owlhoot could retreat with no fear of pursuit. Not even U.S. Marshals dared venture into the isolated stronghold, for lawmen were considered a form of prey anywhere in No Man's Land. Discretion being the better part of valor, peace officers stayed away, and a man on the dodge could find no safer place. There was absolute immunity from the law at Wild Horse Lake.

Several cabins dotted the perimeter of the lake. A trail from the south dropped off the plains and followed an incline into the basin. Holliday held his gelding to a walk, leading the packhorse, and rode toward the nearest cabin. He reminded himself that he was a stranger here, and in a land of outlaws, any stranger was suspect. Yet he was a fugitive himself, and given the rules of the game, that made him one of the brotherhood. Which nonetheless required that he establish his credentials as a desperado. He decided on the bold approach.

A corral with some thirty head of horses was positioned off to the side of the cabin. As he rode past, Holliday noted that many of the horses wore fresh brands, the hair and hide still singed. He was no expert on such matters, but it appeared that the brands had been recently altered. Four men stood outside the cabin, ranged along the front wall. They were a rough lot, unshaved and unkempt, armed with pistols and knives. A fifth man, sporting a brace of holstered Colts, stepped into the doorway.

Holliday reined to a halt. "Good afternoon," he said, nodding from one to the other. "Who's in charge here?"

The man in the doorway looked him over. "Who's askin'?"

"The name's Doc Holliday. Late of Jacksboro."

"We've heard the name. How do we know you're him?"

"I just told you," Holliday said flatly. "I'm not accustomed to having my word questioned. You can accept it or I'll ride on."

"Feisty as a rooster, aren't you?"

"No offense intended. A simple statement of fact."

The man held his gaze. "What brings you out here?"

"Necessity," Holliday replied. "The Texas Rangers took an interest in my personal affairs. I thought I'd try my luck in Colorado."

"Grapevine has it you've killed a few men."

"The grapevine has it correct."

"Anybody we'd know?"

"Ask around Tascosa," Holliday said. "Four nights ago a cowhand braced me over a card game. You might have known him."

"Tend to doubt it," the man said with a slight smile. "We don't have much truck with cowhands."

"Then you'll have to take my word for it."

"Guess I will at that. Climb down off your horse and stay a while."

Holliday stepped out of the saddle. His blunt manner, much as he'd expected, had paid off. Toughnuts abhorred weakness and respected strength, and boldness was the key.

The man in the doorway walked forward. "Glad to meet you, Doc," he said, his hand outthrust. "I'm Henry Borne."

The name was legend. All across Texas people spoke of Dutch Henry Borne with awe. He was considered the greatest horse thief on the frontier, a will-o'-the-wisp who had never been caught. His notoriety earned the wrath of peace officers and the grudging admiration of common men. He was all but a folk hero.

"A pleasure," Holliday said, shaking his hand. "You are a man of reputation, yourself."

Borne laughed. "I reckon there's no need to deny it. I've lasted longer than most."

"I've heard it said that lawmen stay clear of No Man's Land. Are you responsible for that, as well?"

"Took a spell, but we made 'em believers. Hate to tell you how many lawdogs we buried."

"Nor would I ask," Holliday said. "Do I call you Henry or Dutch Henry?"

"Friends call me Hank." Borne paused, openly inspecting him. "You as fast as they say you are?"

"Faster," Holliday said without expression. "I have the gift."

"Godalmighty!" Borne whooped. "I like a man that speaks plain. I think we're gonna get along, Doc."

"I never doubted it for a minute, Hank."

Borne motioned to his men. "You boys tend to Doc's horses. Treat 'em better'n your own."

The men led the horses toward the corral. Borne threw an arm over Holliday's shoulders. "C'mon, Doc, let's have ourselves a drink. Maybe you'll tell me how you got so fast."

Holliday smiled. "Perhaps we can trade secrets, Hank. I know nothing of stealing horses."

"Well, you sure as hell come to the right place!"

Borne roared at his own humor, leading the way into the cabin. Holliday hoped he wouldn't serve corn liquor.

* * *

Supper was antelope steak and beans. The cook of the outfit apparently believed taste was secondary to quantity, and the men clearly agreed. They ate like wolves gathered over a carcass, Dutch Henry Borne included, devouring every last scrap on the table. Their appreciative belches brought a smile to the cook's face.

Holliday ate lightly. He laced his coffee with liberal doses of rye whiskey. Earlier, drinking with Dutch Henry, he'd been pleasantly surprised to find that the gang stocked several cases of rye. The whiskey, like the beans and other essentials, was imported to Wild Horse Lake from a distant trading post. Though he preferred bourbon, the sharp bite of the rye kept his cough under control. He thought the men nonetheless suspected he was a consumptive.

Borne was amazed by his tolerance for alcohol. He quickly gave up trying to match Holliday drink for drink. Instead, under Holliday's casual questioning, he expounded on Wild Horse Lake. There were six gangs who made the basin their headquarters, only one as large as Borne's outfit. Some rustled cattle, others robbed banks and trains, but none dealt in stolen horses. Borne reserved that right to himself, and he enforced the mandate with an iron will. The other gangs went along, aware that Borne would fight to protect his interests. No one cared to tangle with him or his outfit.

After supper, with oncoming nightfall, coal-oil lamps were lighted. The men switched from coffee to rye, sloshing whiskey into their tin cups. Borne, who had clearly taken a liking to Holliday, ignored the other men. They watched, silently sipping their whiskey, as he rolled himself a cigarette. He popped a match on his thumbnail, then lit up and held it for Holliday's cigarillo. He snuffed the match, exhaling smoke.

"How's the whiskey?" he said. "Need a refill?"

"I'm fine for the moment, Hank. Thank you."

Borne nodded. "You talk like an educated man, Doc. Don't see many like you out here."

Holliday realized it was a subtle question. He was aware as well that the other men were watching him closely, await-

ing his reply. He puffed his cigarillo, wondering where the conversation was headed. His mouth quirked in a wry smile.

"Schooling has to be taken with a grain of salt. I've found experience to be the greatest teacher."

"No argument there," Borne agreed. "All the same, there's something to be said for book learnin'. Wish't to hell I'd got more."

"I'd say you've done quite well for yourself."

"Doc, you might be surprised. Lemme tell you how it works."

Borne warmed to his subject. He likened the operation to a game of checkers. Several livestock dealers, spread throughout surrounding states and territories, represented the squares on the board. Every week or so the gang would conduct a raid into Kansas, Colorado, New Mexico, or Texas. The stolen horses were then trailed back to No Man's Land, where the brands were altered with a running iron.

Once the new brands cured, Borne went on, the horses were never sold on home ground. Horses from Kansas were trailed to New Mexico, and those from Colorado to Texas. The herds were always moved in rotating order; horses stolen in Kansas were never sold twice in a row in Colorado. To muddy the waters further, the order of the raids was also rotated among the states and territories. As a result, local ranchers could never establish any pattern to the random nature of the raids. Yet it was all very methodical, nearly impossible to defend against.

Borne then explained how the checkers game was played out. The stolen horses were split into small herds, generally numbering ten head or less. After being trailed to a different location, never on home ground, the herds were sold to livestock dealers over a widespread area. Usually, there was a mix of altered brands, and to all appearances, the stock had been bought here and there by an itinerant horse trader. In the end, horses stolen in random order had been split into small bunches and sold across the breadth of four states. The checkerboard effect was complete.

"Damn near foolproof," Borne concluded. "Even if it

wasn't, livestock dealers are crooked as a barrel of snakes. We've never come close to gettin' caught.''

Holliday was impressed. By its very complexity, their operation virtually eliminated any chance of being detected. ''From the sound of it,'' he said, ''you should have been a general. You are a born tactician, Hank.''

''Suppose you're wonderin' why I told you all this?''

''The thought had crossed my mind.''

''Like to have you with me,'' Borne said simply. ''I admire a man with education, and two heads are better'n one. We could double the size of the operation in no time.''

Holliday wished he weren't so popular with gang leaders. Not two months ago, in Indian Territory, Ed Blanchard had tried to enlist him as a bank robber. Now, after an obvious attempt to impress him, Dutch Henry was trying to recruit him as a horse thief. He knew he should feel flattered, for Dutch Henry clearly meant it as a compliment. He warned himself to proceed with caution.

''I'm honored by your offer,'' he said. ''But I genuinely believe it would not serve your best interests. You see, I have a fever—''

''Fever?'' Borne interrupted. ''You talkin' about your consumption?''

''No, not that. A fever to gamble, Hank. I'm drawn to it like an addict to an opium den.''

''Well, hell, maybe you could break yourself of the habit. Lots of money to be made in horses.''

''For a gambling man,'' Holliday told him, ''money is merely a tool. The stuff that allows him to feed the fever. The *need* to wager it all on the turn of a card.''

''Damn shame,'' Borne said, clearly disappointed. ''You got the makin's of a first-class horse thief. Don't see that too often.''

''I consider that a high praise, Hank. High praise, indeed.''

''You're so full of shit it stinks!''

The outburst came from one of the men at the table. Holliday remembered him being called Dunbar, or maybe Dun-

ston. The man glared across the table, his hands knotted into
fists. Borne gave him a corrosive look.

"What got your bowels in an uproar?"

Dunbar snorted. "Christ, Hank, listen to the bastard! Too
damn good for us, him and his snotty ways. All the rest is
horseshit."

"I'll be the judge of that." Borne glowered at him. "I
want you to apologize to Doc—right now."

"Won't do it." Dunbar stubbornly shook his head. "I
stick by what I said."

Borne drew his pistol, sighting quickly. He fired across
the table and Dunbar's left earlobe vanished in a puff of red
mist. Dunbar squealed, grabbing at his ear, blood spurting
over his hand. Borne again thumbed the hammer on his
pistol.

"Next one's between the eyes. What'd you say, Floyd?"

Dunbar gritted his teeth. "Take it back," he muttered,
glancing at Holliday. "Spoke out of turn."

"That's better," Borne said sternly. "Won't have a man
in my outfit with no manners. You satisfied with his apol-
ogy, Doc?"

"I believe that will suffice, Hank. Consider the matter
closed."

Holliday reminded himself to avoid horse thieves in the
future. He thought the quicker he saw the last of Wild Horse
Lake, the better. Sunrise sounded none too soon.

He poured himself another cup of rye.

PART TWO

CHAPTER 12

Holliday adjusted his tie. After stepping back, he inspected himself in the full-length mirror of the armoire. He thought he would pass muster at the New Year's Eve celebration. Tonight they would usher in 1877.

A scratchy sensation spiraled upward in his throat. He walked from the bedroom to the sitting room, and moved quickly to a table opposite the sofa. A decanter and glasses were arranged on the table, and he poured a glass of bourbon. He downed it in a gulp, waiting for the bourbon to suppress the onset of a spasm. His breathing slowly returned to normal.

All in all he thought Colorado agreed with him. In late October, upon arriving in Pueblo, he had sold his horses and engaged a suite in the Manitou House Hotel. The rooms were handsomely appointed, and the hotel staff obligingly catered to the odd hours of a gambler. His health was neither worse nor better, despite the climate. He still relied on whiskey to control his cough.

From the vestibule closet, he removed a woolen greatcoat and his hat. Downstairs, the lobby was festooned with Christmas decorations and logs blazed in the fireplace. He exchanged greetings with the desk clerk, moving to the door, and stepped outside. A swirling snowfall, blown about by a north wind, was silhouetted against the pale, yellowish glow of streetlamps. He walked toward the sporting district.

Pueblo was situated in the southern foothills of the Rockies. The surrounding countryside was arid and rough, despite the proximity of the Arkansas River to the town. Eastward lay a vista of broken plains, and to the west towering summits were blanketed with snow. The mountains marched northward like an unbroken column of sentinels.

By the close of 1876, Pueblo had achieved prominence as the railway center of southern Colorado. The Denver & Rio Grande rails extended some ninety miles northward to Denver, and the Santa Fe line provided a link to points eastward. The downtown district was dominated by the county courthouse, and the streets were lined with all manner of stores, shops, and business establishments. A once-isolated outpost, Pueblo had been transformed by the arrival of two railroads in as many years. The town was now a bustling mecca of commerce.

Holliday noted a festive air in passersby on the street. Snowfall was an unusual experience for him, rarely ever seen in Georgia, and he thought it contributed to the lingering Yuletide spirit. Last week he had received a cheery Christmas letter from Mattie, and he reminded himself to comment on the snow when he replied. They had exchanged two letters since his arrival in Pueblo, and Christmas without her had left him despondent for a day or so. Yet her letters were still bright and bubbly, filled with hope, and what he considered a depressingly rosy outlook for their future. He oftentimes wondered if she would ever let him go.

West of the downtown area, he entered the sporting district. He told himself that Mattie would find it tawdry and vulgar, indecent beyond anything she might ever imagine. But the seamier side of Pueblo had proved a turning point for him, an unexpected revelation of a whole new world. He found immediate acceptance among the sporting crowd, for his name was known from an article in the *Police Gazette,* written by a journalist who regaled readers with overblown tales of Western gunmen. He was now a figure of no small notoriety.

The revelation came about in conversation with fellow

gamblers. He discovered that there was something known within the brotherhood as the "Gamblers' Circuit." From all he heard, the circuit extended from Dakota Territory southward to Texas, and westward from the Kansas cowtowns to Arizona. Within that vast land mass, there were dozens of boomtowns where money flowed freely and chumps were just waiting to be separated from their bankrolls. When the cards turned stale, or a man wore out his welcome, he simply took off for the next stop on the circuit. There was always another boomtown.

The idea held great appeal for Holliday. God and circumstance had already conspired to remake him into a vagabond gambler. He enjoyed the life of a drifter, without ties or roots, free to come and go as he pleased. The notion of a circuit, towns where gamblers congregated, seemed to him the best of all worlds. Listening to the tales of other gamblers, he had decided to travel the northern circuit, moving along as time and luck dictated. His first stop would be Denver, where some of the more fabled gaming dens on the circuit were located. He planned to leave tomorrow, on the noon train. A fresh start for the new year.

Not that Pueblo hadn't treated him well. As he walked through the flurrying snow, he calculated that he was over five thousand ahead for the two months. He was known as a square gambler, one who gave all comers an even break, and high rollers were drawn to his game. His name was respected, and while he was essentially a loner, he maintained cordial relations with the sporting crowd. His reputation with a gun was an asset of sorts, often forestalling trouble before it got started. He hadn't been forced to kill anyone since he'd arrived in town. All things considered, he thought Pueblo had been a wise choice.

The Tivoli Gaming Parlor was packed. A large barnlike structure, the Tivoli boasted the longest bar in town, assorted games of chance, and a stage theater. Holliday came through the door as a magician produced a rabbit from a top hat, and then immediately brought forth a pair of doves from a silk scarf. The crowd applauded the feat, some of them al-

ready drunk, clearly in a gala mood. They were there to
celebrate a year of thriving prosperity, largely due to the
railroads, and the recent admission of Colorado into the
Union as a state. New Year's Eve was an excuse to stomp
and shout.

Holliday checked his greatcoat and hat at a cloakroom
reserved for regular patrons. His suit was new for the oc-
casion, a subtle charcoal worsted, the drape of the jacket
tailored to conceal his pistols. As he walked to the end of
the bar, an act billed as the "Ethiopian Minstrels" pranced
onstage. The troupe of fifteen men, all in blackface, pro-
ceeded to rattle their tambourines while they sang and
danced and ribbed one another with colorful badinage. He
nodded to the bartender working the end of the counter.

"Good evening, Gus."

" 'Evenin', Doc. And a New Happy Year to you."

"Thank you most kindly, Gus. Many pleasant returns."

Gus placed a glass on the counter, poured from a bottle
of aged bourbon. "You playin' tonight, Doc?"

A table was reserved for Holliday every night of the
week. The management considered him a draw, and the
courtesy had been extended his first week in town. He rarely
missed a night.

"Yes, I'll play," he said now. "New Year's or not, I'm
sure to find a game."

"Reason I ask—" Gus ducked his head down the bar.
"The feller in the big hat and mackinaw was askin' about
you. Told me he'd heard you're the best in town."

"Do you know him?"

"His name's Gabe Miller. Just after Thanksgiving Day,
I read in the paper his wife had passed on. Guess he got
lonesome on New Year's."

Holliday took a sip of bourbon. Over the rim of his glass
he studied the man, who was watching the minstrel show.
Miller was broad and muscular, somewhere in his late for-
ties, dressed in range clothes. He never once laughed at the
Ethiopians' ribald wisecracks.

"Sober devil," Holliday commented. "Do you think he has money, Gus?"

"Sure oughta," Gus said with conviction. "Owns one of the biggest cattle spreads in these parts. I just expect he's loaded."

"How is it he's never inquired of my game until now?"

"Maybe his wife wouldn't give him a night off."

Holliday laughed. "Then we'll give him a New Year's to remember."

" 'Evening, Doc."

Frank Tyler, a gambler new to Pueblo, leaned into the bar. Gus drifted off to wait on other customers. Holliday nodded pleasantly. "How are you this evening, Frank?"

"Never better," Tyler said jovially. "All set for a big New Year's?"

"I am the soul of conviviality, Frank."

Holliday was on speaking terms with every gambler in town. He recalled hearing that Tyler had arrived in Pueblo three weeks ago, and specialized in low-stakes games. Some members of the profession ground out a living a few dollars at a time.

"Good crowd," Tyler said, looking around the room. "Are you open for business tonight, Doc?"

"How better to ring in the New Year? I suspect there's a game to be found."

"I'd lay odds you're right. Would you mind if I sit in at your table?"

"Why would I mind?" Holliday was nonetheless surprised. "I generally play fifty-dollar limit, Frank. Are you up for that?"

"Hell, I'm flush!" Tyler grinned confidently. "Have to warn you, I'm on a streak and feeling lucky. Won a bundle the last couple of nights."

"So you plan to press your luck. Hmmm?"

"When you're hot, you're hot. Figured I'd try my hand at a high-stakes game. Start the New Year off right."

Tyler was a genial man, easygoing and quick to smile. He seemed particularly exuberant tonight, anxious to play.

Holliday had trimmed many gamblers whose cocksure manner exceeded their skill. One more, on his last night in Pueblo, would be an amusing diversion. He downed his bourbon.

"Frank, a man on a roll shouldn't be kept waiting. Let's play poker."

Holliday led the way back to his table. His game attracted high rollers, and hardly before they were seated, other men rushed to claim a chair. A local merchant was first, followed by the superintendent of the Denver & Rio Grande, and then the rancher, Gabe Miller. The last man was a notions drummer, attired in a loud checkered suit and a bowler hat. He introduced himself as Horace Sprigg, from St. Louis.

The men agreed on a fifty-dollar limit, check and raise, with three raises. Every man at the table had at least a thousand dollars in front of him, and the merchant cut high card for the first deal. An hour or so into the game Frank Tyler appeared to be as good as his word. He had won several large pots, usually with cards that gave him only a slim margin. He seemed to have a sixth sense for when to fold and when to stay, and more importantly, when to raise. He won on modest hands, nothing higher than three of a kind.

Holliday slowly became suspicious. He noted that Tyler won more often when Horace Sprigg, the notions drummer, was dealing. Yet Sprigg was heavyset, with stubby fingers, and seemingly too awkward to manipulate the deck. Holliday noted as well that Sprigg stayed in whenever Tyler won, and was already a heavy loser. He inconspicuously tested the deck for shaved cards, or pinpricks, but found nothing out of order. The glaring tipoff was that Tyler won from the other men, but quickly folded anytime Holliday held a decent hand. To Holliday, it seemed clear that Tyler was at pains not to offend him. He knew then the game was somehow rigged.

Some while later the deal passed to Holliday. He called five-card draw, folding when he dealt himself a poor hand. After the draw, everyone folded except Tyler and the cattleman, Gabe Miller. Holliday thought it ironic that he'd

dealt Tyler a strong hand. All the more so since he couldn't spot how the game was rigged. He watched with mounting frustration as Miller, who was the heavy loser for the night, called a fifty-dollar raise. To his astonishment, Tyler turned over four deuces.

"What a night!" Tyler crowed. "Gents, I can't be beat."

Miller flung his cards on the table. He glared at Tyler, then nailed Holliday with a hard scowl. "You two are in cahoots," he said coldly. "I'm callin' you for what you are—cardsharps!"

"You're right and you're wrong," Holliday informed him. "The game is crooked, but I've no hand in it. Nor can I prove it."

"What the hell's that supposed to mean?"

"Our chubby friend"—Holliday gestured to the drummer—"somehow deals winners to Tyler. I haven't yet figured out exactly how."

"You take me for a dimwit?" Miller fumed. "You just dealt your partner *four* deuces!"

"I'm embarrassed by it myself. But think back . . . who's been dealing him winners all night?"

Miller turned his gaze first on Sprigg, and then Tyler. "You dirty sonsabitches are all in it together. See it in your faces."

Sprigg froze like a toad on a stump. Frank Tyler rose from his chair. "Watch who you're calling names, old man."

"I've got you pegged, sonny."

Miller shoved away from the table, fumbled for his gun. Tyler pulled a Remington derringer from his vest pocket, thumbed the hammer. All in a motion, Holliday jerked his Colt Lightning and fired. The slug caught Tyler in the throat and a fountain of blood splashed over his shirt collar. He reeled away, mouthing a strangled sound, and crashed to the floor. His eyes went blank, fixed on the ceiling.

Miller stood rooted in shock, gun in hand. Holliday motioned with his pistol. "Don't make me kill you," he said quietly. "Place your gun on the table."

After a moment of deliberation, Miller obeyed. His features knotted in a grimace. "You're not off yet, Holliday. You'll answer to the law."

"Excellent idea," Holliday agreed. "Someone send for the marshal."

An hour later Marshal Wilbur Stone stood talking with Miller at the table. Horace Sprigg had disappeared into the night, and Holliday was sipping bourbon at the end of the bar. Stone finally nodded, turning away from Miller, and crossed the room. He stopped beside Holliday.

"Two things," he said curtly. "One, you killed a man—"

"Who was trying to kill Miller."

"—and second, Miller says you killed him to keep his mouth shut."

"I run a straight game, Marshal. Tyler was not my confederate."

"Your word against Gabe Miller's. He's a God-fearing, tax-paying citizen, and you're a gambler. Get my drift, Holliday?"

"Are you charging me with something?"

"Nope." Stone stared at him. "I'm posting you out of town. Be on the noon train tomorrow. Savvy?"

"Nothing simpler," Holliday said with a sardonic smile. "Why not escort me to the station? Wish me bon voyage."

"What's so damn funny?"

"A private joke, Marshal. Not worth repeating."

Holliday collected his hat and coat, and went through the door. Outside the snow swirled on gusts of wind, the air crisp and sharp. He tugged his hat down and walked off toward the hotel. The idea that he had been posted out of town was amusing in itself. But doubly so when he'd already made plans to leave for Denver. Life was, after all, a droll jester.

He laughed and wished himself a Happy New Year.

CHAPTER 13

The engineer set the brakes with a racketing squeal. A moment later the train rocked to a halt before the Denver station house. Dusk was settling over the land and the snowy spires of the Rockies rose majestically against a backdrop of fading light. Passengers from Pueblo and points in between began deboarding the train.

Holliday stepped from the rear coach onto the platform. He pulled the collar of his greatcoat tighter against the evening chill, signaling one of the porters who waited outside the depot. When the baggage car was unloaded, the porter collected his new steamer trunk and wrestled it onto a handcart. As he followed the porter across the platform, he noticed a man watching him from the doorway of the station house. A badge was pinned to the man's overcoat, and he wondered if the law had been informed of his arrival in Denver. The idea of it amused him.

In front of the depot, he engaged a horse-drawn cab. He tipped the porter and told the cabbie to take him to the Brown Palace Hotel. From all he'd heard, it was the finest hotel in Denver, and he planned to establish residence in proper style. On the trip uptown he noted that the streets were cobbled and many of the buildings were constructed of brick masonry. Lamplighters were busy with approaching dark, and he was reminded that he hadn't seen gas street-

lights since dental college in Baltimore. He thought he was going to like Denver.

The Brown Palace was everything he'd heard from other gamblers. Thick carpets covered the marble floor of the lobby, and a central seating area was furnished with leather chairs and sofas. The whole of the lobby ceiling glittered with an ornate mural, and a wide, sweeping staircase led to the upper floors. The place had the look and smell of wealth, home away from home for the upper class. At the reception desk, he noted a calendar with the date January 1, and he thought it an excellent start to the New Year. He nodded to the clerk.

"Good evening," he said. "I would like one of your finer suites."

"Of course, sir. How long will you be staying with us?"

Holliday peeled a thousand dollars off his roll. "Let me know when that runs out."

"Yes, sir. I will have it credited to your account immediately. Welcome to the Brown Palace."

The clerk handed him a pen. With a flourish, he signed the register Dr. John H. Holliday. Upstairs, led by a bellman, he was shown into a lavish suite. A lush Persian carpet covered the sitting room floor and grouped before a marble fireplace were several chairs and a chesterfield divan. The bedroom was appointed in the Victorian style, connected to a bathroom with hot and cold running water. A series of handsomely draped windows overlooked the city.

Some while later, with his steamer trunk delivered and logs blazing in the fireplace, Holliday poured himself a tall glass of bourbon. He wandered through the suite, pleased with his accommodations, and halted before the sitting room windows. Flickering streetlamps marched into the distance, and windows in buildings across the town were lighted in a cider glow. Looking out, he recalled that Denver was now a center of finance and commerce for a large part of the West. A city grown from origins that were anything but humble.

Gold was discovered on Cherry Creek in 1859. Over the

next decade thousands of men in search of fortune crossed the Great Plains to Colorado Territory. Some perished, and some found gold, and the mining camp reproduced itself a hundredfold, until finally a glittering metropolis rose along the banks of Cherry Creek and the South Platte. Denver became a cosmopolitan beehive, with theater and opera, newspapers and a stock exchange, and three railroads. By 1876, with a population of twenty-five thousand and growing, the city was unrivaled on the Western plains.

Holliday's woolgathering was interrupted by a sharp knock at the door. He turned from the window, placing his glass on a table, and crossed the room. When he opened the door, a beefy man with stolid features stood in the hallway. The man wore a high-crowned hat, a badge pinned to his coat, and a pistol strapped at his side. Holliday smiled at him.

"The law in all its majesty."

"Are you Doc Holliday?"

"A *nom de guerre* of recent times."

"I'm Claude White. City marshal of Denver."

"Well, come in, Marshal." Holliday waved him through the door. "Won't you have a seat?"

"I'm not staying." White turned, thumbs hooked in his gunbelt. "I'll come straight to the point, Holliday. I'm here to put you on warning."

"Are you? And the nature of the warning?"

"We don't tolerate troublemakers in Denver. I've heard you could start a fight in an empty room."

"Let me guess," Holliday said lightly. "You received a wire from the marshal in Pueblo. Then you posted one of your men at the train station. And now you're here." He paused with a waggish look. "How am I doing so far?"

"Here's the message," White said with a dark frown. "You kill anybody in Denver and you'll answer to me. You got that clear?"

"I tremble at the thought."

"Don't say I didn't warn you."

White brushed past him. When the door closed, Holliday

reclaimed his drink and walked back to the window. For a moment, looking out into the night, his mustache curled with a crooked smile. He held the glass to the lights of the city in a satiric toast.

Welcome to Denver.

Later that evening, Holliday took a stroll through the sporting district. During his stay in Pueblo, talking with gamblers who traveled the circuit, he had heard wondrous tales of Denver's nightlife. He thought to acquaint himself with his new place of business.

For reasons lost to time, the sporting district was called the Tenderloin. There, within a few square blocks of Blake Street, every vice known to man was available for a price. Saloons and gaming dives catered to the sporting crowd, and variety theaters featured headline acts from the vaudeville circuit. Whiskey and gambling mixed with top-drawer entertainment was a unique combination. The racy blend attracted high rollers from all across the West.

One block over, on Holladay Street, was Denver's infamous red-light district. The similarity to his own name amused Holliday, and he wondered if some wayward kinsman had changed the spelling. Known locally as the Row, Holladay Street was a lusty fleshpot, with a veritable crush of dollar cribs. Girls posed in the windows, soliciting customers, available by the trick or by the hour. Hook shops dominated on the Row, but there was no scarcity of high-class whores.

The parlor houses offered younger girls and a greater variety, all at steeper prices. Something over a thousand soiled doves plied their trade on Holladay Street, and the expensive bordellos were the domain of the more exotic tarts. Yet, given Denver's down-to-earth municipal code, each in her own way was a civic benefactress. Their license fees kept the city treasury afloat.

Hop Alley satisfied the more bizarre tastes. A narrow passageway running between Larimer and Holladay, it was Denver's version of Lotus Land. Chinese fan-tan parlors

vied with the faint, sweet odor of opium dens, and those addicted to the Orient's heady delights beat a steady path to this backstreet world of pipe dreams. To a select clientele, China dolls were available day or night.

Holliday spent several hours roaming the Tenderloin. His inspection led to the conclusion that nothing he'd heard had done it justice. Finally, chilled from the night air and tired of walking, he stopped for a drink at Murphy's Exchange. Dubbed by its habitués as the Slaughterhouse, it was a hangout for the shady characters of Denver's underworld. Games of chance were a mere diversion for the grifters and bunco artists who frequented the dive.

Trade was brisk at the bar but slow at the tables. Holliday took a seat at an empty faro layout. The dealer was so inept that it entertained him to watch the man's clumsy attempts at dealing seconds. He bought fifty dollars in quarter chips, warming himself with bourbon, and tried to outguess where the crooked cards would fall. The dealer seemed lonesome, and loquacious, and Holliday gradually steered the conversation around to the Tenderloin. From what he'd seen, the Row and its girls, as well as Hop Alley, operated with the blessing of city hall. He was curious how it worked.

On a slow night, with Holliday the only chump in sight, the dealer happily gave him the lowdown. A man named Ed Chase owned the Progressive Club, a gaming den frequented by high rollers and the top professionals. Chase was considered the czar of the Tenderloin, as well as Denver's underworld element. He enforced his authority through a gang of hooligans who collected weekly payoffs from every saloon, gaming dive, and whorehouse in the sporting district. Their strong-arm tactics kept everyone in line.

Holliday occasionally asked a leading question. But the dealer was enjoying himself, revealing nothing that wasn't already public knowledge, and he needed little prompting. The rackets, he related with a sly smirk, operated under the protection of Denver's political machine. On the first of every month one of Chase's thugs, carrying a black bag, made the rounds at city hall. From the mayor on down,

every elected official in Denver shared in the spoils. The payoffs were the grease of politics.

Ed Chase's power, the dealer noted, was even more apparent at election time. The sporting crowd represented the swing vote in any election, and Chase controlled the Tenderloin. No politician got to city hall, or stayed there, without the swing vote, and that meant working hand-in-glove with Chase. His hooligans turned out the vote on Election Day, and everyone from bartenders to faro dealers voted the way they were told. Control of the ballot box, along with monthly payoffs, ensured a partnership between the politicians and the sporting crowd. The Tenderloin operated wide open, night and day, without interference of any sort. Everyone involved benefited by the arrangement.

Holliday made a mental note to check out the Progressive Club. From what the dealer said, it was where high rollers congregated, and that was the place to establish his headquarters. He thought it would be a wise move, as well, to cultivate an acquaintance with Ed Chase. A man with influence was a man worth knowing.

"This Ed Chase?" Holliday wagered a quarter on the queen. "How would I go about meeting him?"

The dealer clumsily slipped a queen from the box, followed by a nine, and collected Holliday's chip. "You got to understand, Chase only hobnobs with high rollers. No offense, but a quarter bet wouldn't get his attention."

"Does he play poker?"

"Uh-oh," the dealer grunted, staring past his shoulder. "Here comes trouble."

Holliday turned in his chair. He saw four men enter the door, one of them carrying a cane. They spread out on line, approaching three men who stood at the end of the bar. He twisted around, glancing at the dealer. "What's the problem?"

The dealer looked apprehensive. "Grifters on the warpath. One gang spoiled a swindle of the other one." He nervously licked his lips. "Gonna be hell to pay."

The man with the cane advanced closer to the bar. He

twisted the head of his cane and withdrew a wicked-looking sword. "Warned you, Jordan," he said, glaring at one of the men at the bar. "You should've got out of town."

"Don't mess with me, Cady. I'll kill you."

"Not tonight!"

Cady lunged with the sword. The blade struck Jordan in the left shoulder as he tried to dodge aside. He lurched backward, wrenching the blade free, and pulled a gun. Before he could fire, one of Cady's men raised a pistol and shot him in the chest. He went down as though poleaxed.

The men on both sides had by then drawn their guns. The distance separating them was less than five feet, and they opened fire in a withering volley. One man spun away with a wound in the side, another crumpled with a slug in his leg, and a third dropped dead, shot through the heart. Farther down the bar, the crowd scattered, running for cover. Two of them dropped in mid-stride, brought down by wayward slugs.

The gunfire became general, the front end of the room wreathed in smoke. On either side another man fell, and Cady was the only one left standing. Having dropped the sword cane, he extended a pistol, and shot a man struggling to rise from the floor. The bartender whipped a sawed-off shotgun from beneath the counter, triggering both barrels in a blinding roar of light. Jolted by a double load of buckshot, Cady hurtled backward into the wall. He slid to the floor in a bloody heap.

Holliday crawled from beneath the faro table. The room looked like a charnel house, with nine men down, four of them dead. The wounded lay splattered with blood, moaning piteously, their eyes wide with shock. All but deafened by the gunfire, Holliday stared at the carnage with a bemused expression. The faro dealer peeked out from behind the table.

"Holy God," he said in a shaky voice. "Would you look at that!"

An hour or so later, the dead and wounded had been carted away. Marshal Claude White stood talking with the

bartender, and a deputy was posted at the door. Outside, a crowd was gathered before the plate-glass window, gawking in numbed silence. A swamper slowly mopped blood from the floor.

Holliday sat alone at the faro table, sipping bourbon. Along with the other witnesses, he had been ordered to wait until the lawmen completed their investigation. He lit a cigarillo, watching as White turned away from the bartender and crossed the room. The lawman halted in front of him.

"Dangerous town," he said, exhaling smoke. "You should have warned me, Marshal."

White arched one eyebrow. "Trouble seems to dog your heels, Holliday."

"I was an innocent bystander. A spectator of sorts."

"So the barkeep tells me. Otherwise you'd be headed for jail."

"You are a hard man," Holliday said with mock solemnity. "I take it I'm free to go."

"Watch yourself, Holliday. I'll have my eye on you."

"Good night, Marshal."

Holliday walked toward the hotel. He was unconcerned with the hectoring manner of Marshal Claude White. Yet he was intrigued by the bloodbath he'd just witnessed. A cosmopolitan city, he told himself, was not necessarily a civilized place. Tonight proved the point.

Denver was no less dangerous than the wilds of Texas.

CHAPTER 14

Springtime was the best of times in the Rockies. By late April most of the snow was melted and green-leafed aspens fluttered on gentle breezes. The mountains surrounding the mining camp were ablaze with the riotous color of wild flowers.

Georgetown was located some forty miles west of Denver. The camp was the offspring of one of the richest silver strikes ever made in Colorado. At an elevation of eight thousand feet, the town itself was situated in a broad gorge shadowed by mountains. On the main street shops and stores were wedged together with saloons, gaming dives and dance halls. A rough form of free enterprise reigned in any mining camp.

Holliday stood at the window of his hotel room. He gazed out at the town, lost in a moment of contemplation. In late January, when he'd turned twenty-five, he had wondered if he would live to see spring. But today, thirteen months after he had departed Atlanta, his mood was surprisingly optimistic. The mountain air agreed with his lungs, and though his cough was ever constant, he was otherwise in good health. He had lived longer than anyone expected, himself included. He felt ahead of the game.

Sometimes he wondered if things might have been different with Mattie. Her attitude was still one of unshakable determination, and her letters dwelled on their future to-

gether. She wanted to come west and join him, all the more
so since his condition had not worsened to any marked de-
gree. He was often tempted, particularly during his stay in
Denver, for she would have enjoyed the relatively sophis-
ticated atmosphere. But he continued to dissuade her when-
ever he wrote, never losing sight of the hard reality, an
immutable truth. He was living on borrowed time.

There were other reasons as well. After three months in
Denver, he had found himself growing restless. He had
made friends there, and whether a matter of good fortune
or his reputation, he hadn't been forced to kill anyone. But
he slowly wearied of the town, and an urge to move on, to
see more of the Gamblers' Circuit, gradually came over him.
A month ago, having heard good things of Georgetown, he
had boarded a westbound stage. A mining camp lacked the
amenities of Denver, but the play was loose and fast, and
he liked the wild, no-holds-barred manner of a boomtown.
He decided to stay a while.

The sun was high when Holliday turned from the win-
dow. He left his room, moving through the hallway, and
went downstairs for his regular noontime breakfast. One of
the more pleasant surprises about Georgetown had been the
Hotel de Paris. The owner, Louis Dupuy, was French by
birth and an adventurer by choice, seeking fortune in the
mining camps. The hotel had been built shortly after the
silver strike, and Dupuy had created what seemed a holdover
from some opulent era of the past. His hostelry was now
considered a landmark in the remote mountain town.

Entering the dining room, Holliday was struck again by
the grace of the establishment. The ceiling was an inlaid
mosaic, offset by a floor of perfectly matched panels in dark
mahogany and light oak. Carved figurines encircled the
room at ceiling height, and a crystal chandelier swung in
delicate suspension. Old World etchings and fine engravings
decorated the walls, and spotted around the room were or-
nate, carved credenzas. The tables were covered with im-
maculate linen.

"Bon jour." Dupuy rushed forward to greet Holliday. He

was short and stout, with a waxed mustache and bright, eager eyes. "How are we today, monsieur?"

"I've felt worse, Louis."

The room was crowded with noonday diners. Dupuy led him to a corner table and bowed him to a chair. Some people thought the little Frenchman's accent, and his cultivated airs, were a showy masquerade for the patrons. Holliday considered it part of his charm.

"Now, let me see!" Dupuy briskly rubbed his hands together. "What may I offer you today, monsieur? Something substantial, eh?"

"The usual will be fine, Louis."

"Bon Dieu!"

Dupuy often accused him of eating like a sparrow. His breakfast, by now a standby, was eggs, toast, and coffee. He might have nothing during the day, and seldom more than a light supper when he finished for the night. Yet his weight held steady, though he was painfully thin, and he never lacked for stamina. Whiskey was his source of vigor.

After breakfast, Holliday strolled along the main street. Georgetown, like most mining camps, was open night and day. The miners were a hardy lot, with no thought for tomorrow, and spent their leisure time indulging in some form of vice. Halfway down the block, shouts and laughter spilled from the door of a hurdy-gurdy dance hall. Holliday paused a moment to watch.

The term "hurdy-gurdy" derived from a hand organ on which street musicians cranked out a tune. In Western mining camps, the name had been adapted to mean a dance hall. A battered upright piano, accompanied by a fiddler and a banjo player, provided the music. The girls, who worked for the house, were for hire at a dollar a dance. Few of them were pretty, but they were generally buxom and enthusiastic, willing partners. The booted miners, clumsy as draft horses, shoved them around the dance floor.

Whether it was the springtime weather, or the girls in their short skirts, Holliday realized he was feeling frisky. Since Jacksboro, and Lottie Deno, he had not formed a liaison

with any of the women he'd met. On those occasions when
he felt particularly randy, he sought out a parlor house. Still,
he was selective where women were concerned, and the girl
had to be personable as well as attractive. A quick encoun-
ter, merely to satisfy his rutting instincts, hardly seemed
worth the effort. He required more of a woman.

Farther down the street, he stepped into the bordello op-
erated by Belle London. His first week in town he had in-
spected Georgetown's three parlor houses and selected hers
over the others. She maintained a clean house, with five
handpicked girls who were all lookers. One in particular had
caught his eye.

Belle was short, with curly blond hair, and a sassy man-
ner. She greeted Holliday with a humorous smile. "Well,
hello there, Doc. Got the urge today?"

"I thought I might pay a call on Lorraine."

"I like your style, Doc. Always the gentleman caller."

Belle London, like everyone else in town, was aware of
Holliday's reputation. Word had it that he'd killed ten men,
though the count was thought to be inflated. Yet he was
easygoing, witty in a sardonic way, and someone she now
considered a friend. She welcomed his visits.

"Lorraine!" she called out. "Someone to see you."

A young girl moved from a rear hallway into the parlor.
She was voluptuous, wearing only a chemise, with dark hair
and sultry eyes. "Hello, Doc," she purred. "I'm so happy
to see you."

Holliday laughed. "The pleasure's all mine."

"Show him a good time," Belle said with a broad wink.
"Doc's one of our special customers."

Lorraine took his arm, squeezing it tightly into her breast.
As they moved into the hallway, a door opened at the end
of the corridor. Chalk Wheeler, a gambler who shared Belle
London's bed, walked toward them. He was handsome, with
sleek black hair, and some people thought him less a gam-
bler than a kept man. Holliday shared the opinion, for they
had met over a poker table several times in the past month.
Wheeler always went away broke.

"Well, Doc," he said with an oily grin. "Here to get your pole greased?"

"You have an unfortunate way with words, Chalk."

"Hey, no offense intended. How about I buy you a drink later? Maybe we can play some cards."

"I have no objection to taking your money."

Wheeler reddened. "Who says you're gonna win?"

Holliday smiled confidently. "I believe the record speaks for itself."

Lorraine tugged on his arm, leading him down the hallway and into her room. When the door closed, Wheeler turned on his heel and walked to the parlor. Belle looked up as he entered, but her smile quickly faded. His features were livid.

"What's the matter, honeybun?"

"Nothing," Wheeler snapped. "I need some money. A thousand ought to do it."

The other girls were still in their rooms. He never asked for money in their presence, and he'd never asked for such a large sum. She kept her voice calm. "That's a lot of green, sweetie. Why so much?"

"What the hell's it matter?" Wheeler said crossly. "I need it, that's all."

"You don't have to be so snippy."

"Just get the goddamn money."

Belle sighed heavily. She rose from her chair and walked to her room at the end of the hall. When she returned, she silently handed him a stack of bills. Wheeler stuffed the bills into his pocket, chucking her under the chin. On his way out the door he laughed.

"I'm liable to be late tonight. Look for me when you see me."

Belle sank down into her chair, her expression morose. She asked herself why she kept him around. Then, sadly, she answered her own question.

A woman needed a man, even if he was worthless.

* * *

The lamp cast an amber glow over the table. Holliday was seated across from Wheeler, with four men occupying the other chairs. The game was into its third hour, and Wheeler looked like he'd swallowed the canary. His mound of greenbacks kept growing.

Holliday's expression revealed nothing. Yet he was down almost seven hundred dollars and he thought it had nothing to do with luck. He was convinced that Wheeler was cheating. All the more so since Wheeler seemed to win whenever he dealt and there was a large pot. On small pots, he invariably dropped out.

For all that, Holliday was stumped. Throughout the evening, when he was dealing, he had checked the deck for shaved cards or pinpricks. So far, there was no indication that "readers" had been slipped into the game. Nor had he been able to detect that Wheeler was dealing seconds or dealing off the bottom. He was at a loss for an explanation.

Holliday nonetheless trusted his instincts. Wheeler was a sore loser, and he lacked the finesse needed to win at high-stakes poker. So it followed that he would hold a grudge, and try to recoup past losses by cheating. From previous games, simply observing Wheeler's dexterity with cards, Holliday knew that he possessed the skill for dealing crooked. But suspicion alone was no reason to brace a man.

A short time later the deal passed to Wheeler. He called five-card stud, adroitly dealing one card down and one up to the players. Holliday stayed in, tossing money into the pot, watching closely as the game progressed. On the fourth card, he suddenly felt like a blind man whose sight had been restored. All evening Wheeler's eyes had flicked down and up as he dealt the cards, almost a rapid blink. Holliday caught it on the last go-round, amazed by his own stupidity. The gaff was a shiner.

"Just noticed," he said idly. "You have a new ring. Quite handsome."

"Little present from Belle." Wheeler kept his fingers curled, displaying a square silver ring with an onyx stone. "You're high on the board, Doc. Care to bet?"

"Before I do, perhaps I might have a look at your ring. You wouldn't mind—would you?"

The other players exchanged startled glances, suddenly alert. "What's with the ring?" Wheeler said stiffly. "Nothing much to see."

"Maybe not." Holliday stared at him. "Unless you're wearing a shiner."

"You got a helluva nerve. I never dealt crooked cards in my life."

"Prove it," Holliday said. "Show us your ring."

A shiner was a ring with a flat bottom which had been polished to a mirror surface. Any man with a quick eye and nimble hands could catch the reflection of the cards as he dealt. The trick was to hold back the card he needed, dealing seconds until it came his turn. A cardsharp with a shiner was an unbeatable combination.

"Go ahead," Wheeler said in a flat, hostile voice. "See for yourself."

Slipping the ring off, he tossed it across the table. On the instant, thinking Holliday distracted by the ring, he went for his gun. Holliday ignored the ring, but he was still a beat behind. He popped the pistol from his shoulder rig as Wheeler touched off a hurried shot. The slug singed the sleeve of Holliday's coat.

Holliday fired so fast that three shots sounded like an unbroken roll of thunder. The lead slugs stitched a pattern of red dots straight up the front of Wheeler's shirt. He jerked upright in his chair, knocked backward in a nerveless dance. His mouth opened, spraying a gout of blood across the table, and he toppled to the floor. Holliday stood, checking to make certain Wheeler was dead, then holstered his pistol. He picked up the ring, held it to the light.

The bottom shone like a mirror.

Some time later, after the town marshal ruled it justifiable homicide, Holliday pushed through the crowd at the door of the gaming dive. He made his way downstreet and entered Belle London's parlor house. He found her seated in

a chair, a stunned, sick look etched on her features. Lorraine herded the other girls out of the room.

"Belle, I'm sorry," Holliday said earnestly. "He tried to gaff me with a shiner."

"I heard," she answered in a monotone. "He liked to brag when he used it on miners. I never thought he'd dare try it on you."

"Then you've heard that he pulled first. I had no choice."

She hugged herself, rocking back and forth. "Chalk was a prideful man. He couldn't bear it that you beat him so regular at cards." Her voice sounded brittle. "What earthly difference did it make? I gave him all the money he wanted."

Holliday shook his head. "Some men never know when to count their blessings. You were the best thing that ever happened to him."

"Yes, I was, Doc. Oh, I know he was shiftless and no-account. But I loved him something awful. Why couldn't he be satisfied?"

"I have no answer for that, Belle. Probably no one does."

"No, probably not." Her eyes were dulled with hurt. "I appreciate your coming here. God knows you didn't owe me any explanation."

"Let me know if I can do anything. All you have to do is ask."

Holliday left her huddled alone in her chair. He was filled with remorse at having brought her sorrow. But as he walked toward the hotel, he realized that his regret extended only to her. He felt nothing at having killed Chalk Wheeler.

The dumb bastard should never have pulled a gun.

CHAPTER 15

Holliday arrived in Cheyenne on June 4. As he stepped off the train, jagged streaks of lightning split the sky far in the distance. From the platform, he watched a moment while the storm clouds rolled across the empty plains. He wondered if all of Wyoming was so desolate.

A porter collected his steamer trunk and arranged a cab. On the way uptown, he was pleased to see that Cheyenne had all the earmarks of a thriving city. After a month in Georgetown, he had spent several weeks in Denver, and he'd grown accustomed to the luxuries of city life. He already missed the comforts of the Brown Palace.

Still, however much he enjoyed Denver, his sense of wanderlust proved stronger. A restlessness came over him, and on the spur of the moment he'd decided to have a look at the High Plains. He planned to travel the northern circuit with a stop in Cheyenne and then on to Deadwood, Dakota Territory. Time was not a consideration in his plans, assuming he found sufficient action at the poker tables to hold his interest. He would move on as the mood suited him.

The Stockman's Hotel was a three-story structure with a wide, shaded veranda. The porter saw to his steamer trunk and he entered a lobby filled with men dressed in range clothes. He had been told that Wyoming was cow country, and from all appearances, the cattle season was under way. His light gray suit and royal blue tie stopped conversation

and left a wake of silence as he crossed the lobby. He halted at the registration desk.

"Yessir," the clerk greeted him. "May I help you?"

"Good afternoon. The Brown Palace in Denver wired ahead for a suite in my name. Dr. John H. Holliday."

"Yessir, that's all arranged. We put you in a suite with a nice view of the capitol."

"Thank you most kindly."

The clerk glanced past him and nodded imperceptibly. A man of medium height, engaged in conversation with a group of cattlemen, caught the look. He was slender, with sharp eyes and a square jaw, and had a badge pinned to his vest. Excusing himself, he crossed the lobby, stopping beside Holliday. He nodded, extending his hand.

"I'm Amos Rodman. Town marshal."

"Are you my reception committee?" Holliday accepted his handshake. "I take it I've no need to introduce myself."

Rodman smiled. "Claude White wired me from Denver. Told me what train you were on and where you'd be stayin'."

"Marshal White is something of a gadfly. He takes uncommon interest in my affairs."

"Well, that's to be expected. You're a man of some reputation, Mr. Holliday."

Holliday was not misled by his genial manner. He saw in Rodman the cool confidence of an experienced lawman. "So tell me, Marshal. Am I welcome in Cheyenne?"

"Why don't we take a walk? I'll show you around."

"Good idea." Holliday glanced at the desk clerk. "Kindly have someone put my trunk in the suite. I'll return directly."

"Yessir, Dr. Holliday!"

Rodman led the way out of the hotel. On the street, Holliday fell in beside him. "May I inquire the purpose of our excursion?"

"Want to introduce you to someone. His name's Tom Kennedy. Owns the Cattleman's Saloon."

"Saloon?"

"The best place in town. You'll like it."

"Will I?" Holliday said. "Why is that?"

"You're a gambler," Rodman replied. "All the big ranchers and Eastern cattle buyers hang out there. They play high-stakes poker."

"You surprise me, Marshal. I'm unaccustomed to such courtesy."

"One hand washes the other, Holliday. I'll treat you right so long as you treat me right. Don't kill anybody and we'll get along just fine."

Holliday knuckled his mustache. "I sometimes feel hounded by this so-called 'reputation.' I've never yet killed a man who wasn't trying to kill me."

"So I've heard." Rodman was silent a moment. "Understand, I don't aim to tie your hands. I just like a peaceful town."

Holliday let it drop. "Tell me about your town, Marshal. I understand there's a good deal of money in Cheyenne."

"No two ways about it. We're right in the middle of cattle season. Everybody's flush these days."

Rodman went on to explain. The United Pacific had selected Cheyenne as its Western headquarters in 1867. In the ten years since, the town had grown from a single ribbon of steel to a bustling plains metropolis. As the capital of Wyoming Territory, it was growing rapidly and the population was approaching the twenty thousand mark. Cheyenne was now a center of commerce and the major Western railhead.

On the south side of town, bordering the railroad tracks, saloons and gambling dens, dance halls and bawdy houses, composed a thriving vice district. Farther uptown, the business district was packed with stores and hotels, restaurants and banks and two daily newspapers, and the territorial capitol building. A horse-drawn trolley car clanged through the center of town, and on a summer day, upwards of five hundred cowhands crowded the sporting district. For good reason, Cheyenne was known as the Magic City of the Plains.

Yet for all its growth, Cheyenne remained a curious ad-

mixture of cowtown and citified elegance. The Union Pacific
had transformed it into a hub of trade, an ever-expanding
business and financial center. As the territorial capital, fre-
quented by lawmakers and wealthy cattle barons, the city
had slowly assumed an aura of respectability and cultivation.
At the same time, it was the central railhead and shipment
point for Wyoming's vast cattle industry.

Every summer herds were trailed into Cheyenne from
ranches all across the High Plains. After being sold to cattle
brokers, the cows were shipped east for slaughter. A great
deal of money exchanged hands, and in the process the town
prospered. However progressive their outlook, everyone
from the governor to storekeepers catered to cattlemen for
the most basic of reasons. Cows were big business, the
mainstay of Cheyenne's economic growth.

The territorial capitol was located on the outskirts of the
business district. Rodman waved to it with some pride as
they waited for the trolley car to pass, then crossed a busy
intersection. Ahead, positioned between a bank and the
town's largest mercantile emporium, was the Cattleman's
Saloon. He noted that it was the only saloon north of the
sporting district, and by long-standing tradition, barred to
cowhands. The clientele was restricted to the uptown crowd
and visiting cattlemen. The power brokers of Wyoming Ter-
ritory.

"None of the rough crowd," Rodman said, as they
walked toward the saloon. "Haven't had so much as a fist-
fight in here in the last five years."

"I confess I'm curious." Holliday gave him a keen, side-
wise glance. "Why would you arrange for me to play in the
town's holier-than-holy establishment? Aren't you con-
cerned I'll . . . *injure* . . . one of your upstanding citizens?"

"Three reasons," Rodman informed him. "One, there's
no way I could keep you out of Cheyenne. No warrants or
charges on you in Wyoming."

"And second?"

"A house rule in the Cattleman's. Anybody caught cheat-
ing at cards is barred for life. Folks would sooner drink

arsenic than risk disgrace. So you won't have to brace any cardsharps in here.''

Holliday looked at him. "You mentioned three reasons.''

"Third one was I got waylaid," Rodman said with a lighthearted chuckle. "When the wire came in about you, half the folks in town got the news before I did. Our telegraph man spread the word like his pants was on fire.''

"I somehow missed your point.''

"Why, the point's real simple. Every high-roller cowman in Wyoming wants a chance to play against Doc Holliday. They'll be braggin' on it for months to come.''

"You don't say?" Holliday was genuinely astounded. "I hadn't realized that notoriety lends itself to celebrity.''

"Oh, hell, yes!" Rodman said quickly. "I got my marchin' orders damn near before your train left Denver. Told to personally deliver you to the Cattleman's.''

"I begin to feel like a trophy put on display.''

"Don't let it bother you. By your lights, there's not a decent poker player in the bunch. You'll probably wind up rich as Midas.''

Tom Kennedy hurried forward when they came through the door. He was a portly man with beaming features and a broad smile. He clasped Holliday's hand in a firm grip.

"Welcome to the Cattleman's, Mr. Holliday. Honored to have you as a guest in my establishment.''

Holliday reclaimed his hand. "The marshal tells me your customers like to play poker.''

"Do they ever!" Kennedy could hardly contain himself. "They'd stand in line for a seat at your table. And I've given you the best table in the house.''

"When does the game start?''

"Why, right now! Right this way.''

Kennedy led him to the center of the room. Seated around a baize table were six men in tall-crowned hats. Kennedy grinned, his eyes bright with cheer.

"Gentlemen, permit me to introduce Doc Holliday.''

Amos Rodman turned and walked to the door. His job was done.

* * *

Holliday was late for breakfast the next day. He entered the hotel dining room shortly after the noon-hour rush. His waitress tried to sell him on the blue-plate special, but he declined. She brought him eggs, toast, and coffee.

The game had ended around five that morning. The cattlemen went away happy losers, elated to have played at his table. Holliday figured he had won about a thousand, and another game was set for tonight. But he wasn't certain how long he could continue the charade, despite the easy money. There was no sport to shooting fish in a barrel.

A man appeared in the doorway. He was young, with a wild thatch of reddish hair, his face dusted with freckles. His suit was rumpled, almost baggish on his tall, gangly frame. He rushed forward, doffing his hat, and stopped beside the table. His expression was eager.

"Pardon me, sir." His voice seemed an octave too high. "Do I have the privilege of addressing Mr. Doc Holliday?"

Holliday looked him over. "Who are you?"

"Tad Watson," he said too loudly. "Reporter for the *Cheyenne Sentinel*."

"Does your father own the paper?"

"How the dickens did you know that?"

"Have a seat." Holliday poured bourbon from the flask into his coffee cup. He lit a cigarillo as the reporter whipped a pad and pencil from his coat pocket. "Was it your father's idea to send you here?"

"No, sir!" Watson blurted. "Not many chances to interview a . . . uh—a figure like yourself. I told Pa it was front-page news."

"Just a matter of curiosity, Mr. Watson. How old are you?"

"Well . . . I . . . I'm twenty-three. What makes you ask?"

"No reason." Holliday felt ancient, though he was only two years older. He sipped his laced coffee. "How may I help you?"

"For starters—" Watson hunched forward, his pencil poised. "Why are you called Doc?"

"Once upon a time, I was a dentist. I chose to become a gambler."

"The Deadly Dentist." Watson scribbled furiously. "People say you've killed twenty men, Mr. Holliday. Could you confirm that?"

Holliday no longer kept count. He thought it was more on the order of seven, maybe eight. "I never bothered to keep score, Mr. Watson."

"Say, that's rich! 'Never bothered to keep score.' You know, some people are comparing you to Wild Bill Hickok. Do you think you could have taken him?"

"You may quote me as saying Wild Bill was in a class all his own. I have no such aspirations."

Watson continued to pepper him with questions. Holliday was evasive on personal matters, revealing little of himself or his family background. On questions related to gambling and gunfights, he answered with a series of half-truths and wry fabrications. He was amused by the interview, and the gullible naïveté of young Watson. He thought fairy tales were concocted in just such a manner.

"By golly!" Watson finally said, closing his notepad. "This will make a whale of an article, Mr. Holliday. I don't mean just for our paper, either. I'll bet the *Police Gazette* will snap it up."

Holliday nodded wisely. "What more could a journalist ask?"

"You've been swell, Mr. Holliday. Just swell. I can't thank you enough."

"No thanks needed, Mr. Watson. Happy to oblige."

The young reporter hurried out, waving as he went through the door. Holliday stared after him, contemplative a moment. Though amused, something about the interview struck an odd chord. He rose and walked to the lobby. The desk clerk came to attention.

"Yessir? Help you with something?"

"Perhaps you could recommend a physician. The best in Cheyenne."

"That would be Dr. Cowen. Are you feeling poorly, Mr. Holliday?"

"On the contrary," Holliday said. "I believe I'm feeling too good."

An hour later he was shown into the office of Dr. Ambrose Cowen. The physician was a stout man, with shrewd eyes and a beneficent manner. He listened attentively as Holliday related his medical history in some detail. Consumption was a common problem, and he had attended many patients with the dread disease. To himself, he thought his patient today looked like death warmed over.

"I feel too good," Holliday concluded. "Hardly seems natural for a man given a year to live. Could the disease be in remission?"

"How bad is your cough?"

"No worse than six months ago. Fairly constant."

"Are you coughing up blood?"

"Generally more in the morning. Or when I'm unusually tired."

"I tend to doubt you're in remission. Let's have a look."

Holliday stripped down to his bare chest. The doctor listened to his lungs with a stethoscope, asking him to breathe deeply. For several minutes, with Holliday breathing in and out, he moved from chest to back, his expression alert. He then checked Holliday's throat and studiously inspected his eyes. He finally dropped the stethoscope on his desk.

"I smell liquor on your breath. Tobacco, too. How much do you drink?"

"A quart a day." Holliday shrugged. "Sometimes a little more."

"Good God," Cowen muttered. "Keep that up and you'll pickle your liver."

"I'm more concerned with my lungs. What's your prognosis?"

"You strike me as a man who prefers the truth."

"Speak plainly, Doctor."

"From the sound of your lungs, you should have been

dead months ago. I have no idea what's kept you alive. It's one for the medical books.''

Holliday began dressing. ''Ascribe it to the medicinal qualities of sourmash bourbon. Stranger things have happened.''

''Not in my years of practice. You are an anomaly, Mr. Holliday.''

''I believe that sums it up perfectly, Doctor.''

On the street, Holliday walked toward the hotel. He was neither surprised nor disturbed by the verdict. Nor was he any worse off than he was an hour ago. Some ancient sage had penned what was still an eternal truth.

Life was but a journey from the womb to the tomb.

CHAPTER 16

Holliday emerged from the hotel in the early afternoon. He paused a moment, lighting a cigarillo, and stared up at the mountains. The pine-forested slopes shimmered under a warm July sun.

The town of Deadwood was surrounded by the rough terrain of the Black Hills. Three weeks ago, after tiring of Cheyenne, he had boarded a stagecoach for the three-hundred-mile run to Dakota Territory. He sometimes missed the luxuries of a city, but he thought of it as a trade-off. The raw vitality of a mining camp was a welcome stimulant.

The town twisted through a narrow gulch. In all directions, wooden stairways intersected terraced sidestreets up and down the slopes. Wagons drawn by oxen clogged the main street, and bullwhackers scorched the air with the sharp pop of their whips. The boardwalks were thronged with men, and the bustling atmosphere of a gold camp pervaded the town. There was a sense of carnival madness to the hubbub and the milling crowds.

Some two years ago, the gold rush had transformed a wooded gulch into a boomtown. Deadwood's population swelled to almost twenty thousand, with more arriving every day, and no end in sight. The upper end of Main Street was packed with stores and cafes, three banks and some thirty hotels, and one public bathhouse. The lower end of town was reserved for the sporting district, saloons, gaming dives,

and cheap brothels. A local wit had dubbed it the Badlands.

Holliday turned downstreet. A few blocks along the way, he passed what was now considered a landmark. The No. 10 Saloon, located on the edge of the Badlands, was famed as Wild Bill Hickok's last watering hole. There, not quite a year ago, a deadbeat named Jack McCall had shot Hickok in the back of the head. The assassin was hanged, and Hickok was laid to rest in Deadwood's budding cemetery. The turnout for the funeral was the largest in the town's brief history.

Farther downtown, Holliday turned into the Bella Union. The best that the Badlands had to offer, the establishment was a combination saloon, gaming dive, and variety theater. He had made it his unofficial headquarters, and he was by now considered one of the regulars. Everyone in Deadwood knew his name, and his reputation, for his notoriety had spread through yet another article in the *Police Gazette*. The sporting crowd accepted him as one of their own.

Opposite a long mahogany bar were gaming layouts and several poker tables. Toward the rear, through an arched doorway, was a spacious variety theater. Holliday took a chair at one of the high-stakes tables, where a game was already in progress. Seated across from him was Turkey Creek Jack Johnson, a gambler of some skill, and a man he'd come to respect. The origins of Johnson's nickname were hazy, but rumor had it that he was originally from Texas. Like many men on the Gamblers' Circuit, he was vague about his past.

"'Afternoon, Doc," Johnson greeted him. "You're lookin' pretty spry today."

"Never better." Holliday signaled the waiter for bourbon. "In fact, I feel uncommonly lucky."

"What the hell, get a bunch, bet a bunch. Let's play poker."

The other four men at the table were outclassed. The game seesawed back and forth between Holliday and Johnson, with neither of them the clear winner. They enjoyed butting heads, bluffing on nothing and sandbagging on

strong hands. An hour or so later, after driving the other
players out with heavy raises, Holliday took a pot with a
pair of deuces. Johnson, who had stayed for the last raise,
laughed heartily.

"You got me good, Doc. Thought for sure I had you
high-carded."

Johnson's good humor abruptly faded. Two men, each
wearing crossed gunbelts, halted beside the table. Their
mouths were set in a tight line and their eyes were fixed on
Johnson. He returned their look with a steady gaze.

"Farnum. Rosser." His features were impassive. "What
can I do for you gents?"

Farnum was the taller of the two, lean and hard. "Time
to settle accounts, Johnson. We're here to call you out."

"I'd sooner talk than fight. Why don't I buy you boys a
drink?"

"Sorry bastard!" Rosser bridled. "We're all done talkin'.
You gonna fight or crawl?"

Holliday knew the men from around town. They were
suspected of stage robbery, and though the reasons were
unclear, their animosity toward Johnson was known
throughout the sporting crowd. Two against one seemed to
him a cowardly advantage, and on the spur of the moment
he decided to take a hand. He looked at Johnson.

"You have poor odds, Jack. Would you like me to even
it out?"

"Hold on now," Farnum said quickly. "We got no beef
with you, Holliday."

"You gentlemen interrupted my poker game. I'm of-
fended by your bad manners."

"Thanks all the same," Johnson broke in. "This here's
a personal matter, Doc. I'll tend to it."

"Are you sure?" Holliday asked. "You're playing
against a stacked deck."

"Maybe there's a way to lower the odds."

Johnson dictated his terms to Farnum and Rosser. From
what he described, it would be more of a duel than a bar-
room gunfight. Still, they had him outnumbered, and the

alternative was to deal with Doc Holliday. They agreed.

Half the crowd in the Bella Union tagged along to watch. A short while later they halted outside the graveyard on the edge of town. Holliday thought Johnson's intended irony, selecting the cemetery, gave him a slight edge. Farnum and Rosser, eyeing the grave markers, no longer looked so confident.

The cemetery bordered the road for some fifty yards. Johnson took a position at one end, facing toward town, and Farnum and Rosser positioned themselves at the opposite end. On signal, the men were to advance, two against one, and open fire at any point along the way. The duel seemed to Holliday as much about nerve as it did marksmanship. He held a handkerchief high overhead, then dropped it.

Farnum and Rosser opened fire the moment they started forward. The distance was too great, particularly when firing on the move, and their shots were wide of the mark. Johnson walked steadily down the road, pistol in hand, seemingly unrattled by the buzz of lead all about him. After advancing no more than ten yards, Farnum and Rosser had each exhausted the loads in one gun. They holstered the empty Colts, hastily drawing their second guns, and shifted the weapons to their right hands. Johnson had yet to fire a shot.

Then, as the distance closed, Farnum and Rosser lost their nerve. They began blasting away in a staccato roar, triggering shots so fast that it sounded like the *pop-pop-pop* of a Gatling gun. A slug plucked at the sleeve of Johnson's shirt and another sent his hat dancing in the air; but he never faltered, ignoring the near misses, moving forward at a measured pace. When the distance dropped to about twenty yards, he stopped, brought his pistol to shoulder level, and fired. Farnum windmilled backward, his shirtfront splotched with blood. He fell dead in the road.

Rosser got off a last, wild shot. Johnson thumbed the hammer, took an instant of deliberate aim, and feathered the trigger. His Colt spat a streak of flame and the slug drilled Rosser straight through the brisket. The impact spun him around, his legs tangled, and he went down, the gun still

clutched in his hand. One leg jerked, as though kicking at the doors of eternity; the crotch of his pants stained as his bladder voided. His eyes stared blankly into the sunlit sky.

Johnson stood in the middle of the road, looking at the bodies. A prolonged moment of silence slipped past, then the crowd rushed forward, shouting with excitement and pummeling him across the shoulders. Holliday watched with a thoughtful expression, impressed by Johnson's nerve. The gunfight seemed to him affirmation of what he'd determined long ago about a contest of arms. The outcome was seldom decided by speed alone.

By his count Farnum and Rosser had fired somewhere around fifteen or sixteen shots. Turkey Creek Jack Johnson had fired only twice. The result was indisputable.

Accuracy, in the end, was final.

"Twenty simoleons."

"Raise you fifty."

"I fold."

"Too rich for my blood."

"I'm right behind you."

"Call the raise!"

Holliday turned his hole card. "Three ladies."

"Judas Priest." The miner shook his head in mild wonder. "You're sure enough a hard man to beat."

"Luck favors those who are pure of heart."

Jack Johnson laughed. "That ought to make you an angel, Doc. You're plumb blessed tonight."

Holliday and Johnson were seated at a table with three miners. All evening the miners had been losing steadily, exchanging bags of gold dust for poker chips. As Holliday raked in the pot, the orchestra blared from the variety theater. He began stuffing chips into his coat pockets.

"Gentlemen, you will excuse me. The play is about to commence."

"The play!" Johnson groaned. "Goddamn actors don't hold a candle to poker. Stick around, Doc."

"Hold my seat until I return. I hear the call of the Bard."

"Who?"

"An old friend, Jack. I'll explain later."

Holliday hurried toward the arched doorway at the rear of the room.

The variety theater was large enough to accommodate two hundred people, and already filled to capacity. The audience was seated at tables arranged before a proscenium stage, brightly lighted by oil lamps arranged across the footboard. A table had been reserved for Holliday, and he took a seat as waiters scurried to serve the crowd. He signaled one of them for a bottle of bourbon.

Tonight's entertainment was a production of a traveling stock company. John Langrishe, the impresario and a thespian of some renown, wandered the West with his troupe of actors. Even in remote mining camps, there was an eager and appreciative audience for stage plays. The evening's main attraction was a wrenching melodrama with the evocative title of *A Husband's Vengeance*. To add a touch of culture, John Langrishe was to open the show with a selected reading from *Hamlet*. A sampling of Shakespeare was considered adequate in a rough boomtown.

The orchestra trumpeted a fanfare. A hush fell over the audience as the curtain rose and Langrishe walked to center stage. He was a handsome man, with a classic profile and an arresting manner, dressed in a period costume. His every move, particularly the gesturing of his hands, was effortlessly fluid, at once studied and wholly natural. His voice floated across the footlights in a sonorous baritone.

> To be, or not to be: that is the question:
> Whether 'tis nobler in the mind to suffer
> The slings and arrows of outrageous fortune,
> Or to take arms against a sea of troubles,
> And by opposing end them? To die: to sleep—

A miner pounded his table. "You're puttin' me to sleep, you gassy windbag." He stood, motioning around the

crowd. "What d'you say, boys? Let's have the gawddamn melo-drama!"

Holliday pulled his Colt Lightning. He fired and the miner's hat sailed into the air. "Sit down," he commanded. "I won't ask again."

The miner hastily obeyed. A stilled silence descended over the theater as Holliday holstered his pistol. He looked toward the footlights, nodding to the stunned actor. "All the world's a stage. Please continue."

Langrishe bowed gratefully, then struck a dramatic pose. He resumed the soliloquy and carried on as though never interrupted. Holliday listened attentively, nodding to himself, particularly taken with the passage. The rich language alluded to the "sleep of death," and he found a personal meaning in the words. Given the state of his lungs, he wondered when he might "shuffle off this mortal coil." Hamlet, he discovered all over again, spoke to the heart of the matter.

To his surprise, Holliday enjoyed the melodrama as well. An overdrawn tale, the story was wrought with angst and played to the hilt by the actors. The audience applauded wildly at the end, and the cast took an extra curtain call. Holliday remained in his seat, waiting for the stampede to subside as the crowd filed out. He poured himself another shot of bourbon.

John Langrishe came through a door leading backstage. He hurried forward, still dressed in costume. "Good evening," he said, halting at the table. "I'm told you are Doc Holliday."

"One among my many sobriquets, Mr. Langrishe."

"I wished to thank you personally for intervening tonight. Drunk or sober, that miner has no appreciation of Hamlet."

" 'When we are born, we cry that we are come to this great stage of fools.' "

"King Lear!" Langrishe exclaimed. "You are indeed a student of the Bard. I'm surprised that a—"

Holliday smiled. "A man of my profession?"

"Please take no offense, Mr. Holliday. But you are a man of some—"

"Notoriety."

"And of course, I've read of your exploits."

"To my great regret," Holliday said affably. "'Men's evil manners live in brass; their virtues we write in water.'"

"King Henry the Eighth!" Langrishe marveled. "A man of letters who lives by the sword. You must pardon my amazement."

Holliday waved it off. "'The prince of darkness is a gentleman.'"

"You pluck Shakespearean snippets out of the air like a magician. You are indeed a man of parts, Mr. Holliday."

"'One man in his time plays many parts.'"

"From *As You Like It*. You have an astounding gift, sir."

"I'm showing off," Holliday said with amiable good humor. "There's scant opportunity to quote the Bard these days. And few who would understand."

"Yes, well—" Langrishe fumbled for an appropriate response. "Once again, my most sincere thanks. You saved the show."

"Happy to be of service."

The actor bowed, moving toward the stage door. Holliday poured himself another shot, and held the amber liquid to the glow of the footlights. His mouth curled in a wry smile.

"'That which hath made them drunk hath made me bold. What hath quench'd them hath given me fire.'"

He thought there was some truth to be found in *Macbeth*.

CHAPTER 17

Holliday stood in front of a full-length mirror. The tailor fussed about, muttering through a mouthful of pins, adjusting the lines of his suit jacket. The material was an imported lightweight blend called tropical wool.

Through the streetfront window, Holliday stared at the distant Rockies. The peaks were still snow-capped, but the August heat had bared the slopes to a dull umber. Towering skyward, the spires touched the clouds, a majestic sight. He felt good to be back in Denver.

Toward the end of July he had grown bored with Deadwood. Once his interest flagged, the old wanderlust had come over him, and he'd decided to move on. From the mining camp, he had traveled by stage to Cheyenne, and then by train to Denver. He was again installed in a suite at the Brown Palace, and found himself exhilarated by the faster pace of city life. He thought he might stay a while.

"There!" The tailor stepped back, admiring his handiwork. "A perfect fit, Mr. Holliday."

Holliday studied himself in the mirror. The drape of the jacket concealed his shoulder holster, and the Colt Peacemaker on his hip presented only a slight bulge. Then, looking closer, he saw an oversight. He motioned to the tailor.

"I need something from my other jacket. Would you mind?"

The tailor took his old suit jacket from a hanger on a

nearby rack. Holliday unclipped the sheath knife and trans-
ferred it to the breast pocket of his new suit. He squared his
shoulders, looking in the mirror, and wagged his head. He
tapped his breast pocket.

"Far too obvious," he said. "You'll have to let out the
pocket. Allow more room."

The tailor gingerly worked around the knife. While he
chalked and pinned, he clucked to himself, his eyebrows
arched. He was appalled that anyone felt compelled to carry
two pistols *and* a sheathed dagger. But Holliday was a val-
ued customer, one who settled every bill in full, in cash. He
dutifully adjusted the pocket.

"All done," he said as he finished. "Let me help you out
of the jacket, Mr. Holliday. Careful of the pins."

"When will you have it ready?"

"Day after tomorrow. Would you like it delivered to your
hotel?"

"Thank you most kindly."

Holliday shrugged into his old jacket. He clipped the
knife into his breast pocket, nodding pleasantly to the tailor,
and went out the door. On the street, he caught a crosstown
trolley and some minutes later stepped off at the corner of
Seventeenth and Glenarm. He walked toward an imposing
stone building, four stories high and occupying nearly half
a block. A monolithic structure, it commanded the intersec-
tion.

The Denver Club was the sanctum sanctorum of the city's
power brokers. Membership was restricted to those of
wealth and position, the elite of the business world and pol-
itics. Their numbers included bankers and merchant princes,
railroad barons and financiers and lawyers. Their influence
was incalculable, and their connections extended to the
statehouse itself. They were, in a word, the aristocracy of
Denver.

The interior of the club was scarcely less imposing. Dark
paneling predominated, and a staircase facing the entrance
rose upward like an aerial corridor. An attendant escorted
Holliday into a room immediately off the central hallway.

The decor was opulent, with velvet drapes and damask-covered walls, all heightened by a black marble fireplace and luxuriant leather furniture. An immense oil painting of the Colorado Rockies hung resplendent over the fireplace.

Ed Chase turned from a sunlit window. He was slim and angular, with iron-gray hair, impeccably attired in a black broadcloth coat and an elegant silk cravat. He moved forward, extending his hand. "Glad you could make it, Doc. What would you like to drink?"

"Bourbon," Holliday replied, shaking his hand. "Thank you for the invitation."

"I thought we might talk a little business. Let's have a seat."

Holliday was intrigued. Chase was the undisputed boss of the Tenderloin, Denver's sporting district, and perhaps the most powerful political figure in town. Whenever he was in Denver, Holliday made his headquarters at Chase's Progressive Club, the finest gaming establishment in Colorado. Over time they had become passing friends, the respect of one gambler for another. But there had never been any overture about a business relationship.

Chase led the way to leather armchairs. After a waiter brought their drinks, he settled back with a disarming look. "You've become a man of no little fame, Doc. Even the newspapers take note when you visit Denver."

Holliday lit a cigarillo. "I find it a questionable distinction. Not one I would have sought."

"Even so, you're known to the public at large. Your name alone is a draw."

"A draw for what?"

"I'll be frank," Chase said earnestly. "I'd like to have you as a faro dealer at the Progressive Club. At a high-stakes layout, you would be a natural attraction, Doc."

"A natural attraction," Holliday repeated slowly. "Sounds more on the order of a sideshow freak. I think not, Ed."

"We could make a great deal of money. I'd even give you a piece of the action. A partnership arrangement."

"I've no wish to be a curiosity on public display. I believe I'll stick with poker."

"Take my advice," Chase said with a shrewd look. "Capitalize on your name and turn it to profit, Doc. Opportunity only knocks once."

A spasm erupted deep in Holliday's lungs. He hawked a wad of reddish phlegm and swabbed it into his handkerchief. Then, stubbing out the cigarillo, he took a long shot of bourbon. "Excuse the cough," he said, catching his breath. "I know you mean well, and I appreciate the offer. But it's not for me."

"The proposition is solid gold, Doc. At least think about it."

"Tomorrow or the next day, the answer would be the same. Thanks anyway, Ed."

Chase walked him to the door. They parted amiably, and outside Holliday turned toward the center of town. He thought he should feel complimented, particularly by an offer from a man the caliber of Ed Chase. Instead, he felt offended, somehow irked.

A circus fat lady might have as easily filled the bill.

The Alcazar Theater was hushed. All eyes were fixed on the stage, where Lola Montana stood bathed in the cider glow of a spotlight. Her exquisite features were tilted in a woeful expression, and her clear alto voice filled the hall. She sang a heartrending ballad of unrequited love, and her eyes were misty. Her voice somehow gave the lyrics a haunting quality.

Holliday was no less captivated than the rest of the audience. Upon returning to Denver, he'd heard that a bewitching creature with the voice of an angel had taken the town by storm. The owner of the Alcazar had arranged a front-row table for him, even though the house was sold out. Watching her now, he was taken by the way she acted out the song with poignant emotion, creating an overall effect of lost innocence. He found himself lost in her performance.

Yet the anguish in her voice somehow reminded him of Mattie. He thought perhaps it was guilt, evoked by the lyrics; but it was no less real. A week ago, when he'd arrived at the Brown Palace, several letters awaited him from Mattie. He had not informed her of his trip to Cheyenne, or Deadwood, and he hadn't written her in all that time. His hope was that she would become infuriated, or simply disgusted, and finally dismiss him from her life. He had misjudged her devotion.

Her last letter was frantic. With no word from him in almost two months, she was desperate with worry. He immediately penned a reply, assuring her that he was not yet at death's door, though his health continued to deteriorate. He offered no apology for failing to write, but rather provided a travelogue of his sojourn into Wyoming and Dakota. Once again, he urged her to rejoin the social swirl in Atlanta, noting that he'd been gone over a year. The Western climate, he gently informed her, was clearly no curative for his condition. He closed with a fond wish for her happiness.

Despite the tone of his letter, he had no great belief that it would change her mind. Nor was he yet able to sever the bond between them, brutally inform her that his death was certain, if not imminent. She was his only link with the past, a time when dreams still had a future, and he was unable to permanently cut the cord. However much he wished it otherwise, she was ever in his thoughts, and not a day passed that he didn't miss her. But late at night, when she was most in his thoughts, he nonetheless loathed himself for not being stronger. He lacked the moral courage to end it himself. He waited for her to do it.

Lola Montana's performance was flawless. Her voice was at once sultry and virginal, and she held the crowd captivated to the last note. A moment slipped past, then the theater vibrated to thunderous applause and wild cheers. She took a bow, then another and another, and still the house rocked with ovation. At last, throwing kisses to the audience, she signaled the maestro.

The orchestra segued into a rousing dance number. A line

of chorus girls exploded out of the wings and went high-stepping across the stage. Lola raised her skirts, revealing a shapely leg, and joined them in a prancing cakewalk. The girls squealed and Lola flashed her underdrawers and the tempo of the music quickened. The audience went mad.

Holliday found his toe tapping in time to the music. There was a wanton exuberance to the routine, with Lola and the girls cavorting around the stage. Then the orchestra thumped into the finale with a blare of trumpets and a clash of cymbals. The chorus line, in a swirl of upraised skirts and jiggling breasts, went romping into the wings. Lola waved and blew a last kiss as she strutted offstage. The crowd roared with delight.

When the curtain rang down, the applause dropped off to a hubbub of animated laughter. Holliday poured a glass of bourbon, his mood vitalized by the spirited dance number. He wondered that he took such pleasure in a tawdry display of short skirts and high-kicking legs. In another lifetime, a respected member of Atlanta's gentry, he would have been scandalized to patronize a bawdy variety house. But time and circumstance altered a man's outlook.

There were only memories of that past life. The future was here and now, and perhaps tomorrow. A thing to be lived to the fullest. One day at a time.

The Progressive Club was almost empty. The hour was late, and toward the rear of the room, one poker table was still in play. Holliday was the big winner for the night.

There were only three other men left in the game. One was a local businessman, and another was a land broker for the railroad. The third was Budd Ryan, owner of a parlor house on the Row. He was down by nearly a thousand dollars, and a sore loser. His manner became more offensive as the night wore on.

Ed Chase watched from the end of the bar. He was anxious for the game to end, and hopeful it would end without trouble. Ryan was a stout man, with mean eyes and a nasty disposition, and fancied himself a rough customer. When he

lost another hand, cursing roundly, Chase swapped a quick
glance with Holliday. He shook his head with concern. Hol-
liday merely shrugged.

The deal passed to Ryan. He called five-card draw, shuf-
fling with smooth dexterity, and allowed the land broker to
cut. His nose suddenly wrinkled, and he reared back in his
chair, his eyes pinched tight. The deck of cards still in hand,
he hunched forward, blasting a loud sneeze as he pulled a
handkerchief from his inside coat pocket. Then, placing the
deck on the table, he wiped his nose and stuffed the hand-
kerchief inside his coat. He prepared to deal.

Holliday was not fooled. The sleight-of-hand involved
switching a deck of cards wrapped in the handkerchief for
the original deck. The substituted deck, commonly called a
"cold deck," was already stacked, with a winning hand ar-
ranged for the dealer. Ryan clearly meant to recoup his
losses for the night by dealing good cards to everyone, and
better cards to himself. Which left Holliday in a quandary,
for exposure would provoke a fight, and he wanted to avoid
killing Ryan. He had no wish to be posted out of Denver.

"Hold on," he said, before Ryan could deal. "Either
you've switched a cold deck into the game, or I'm a liar.
Which is it?"

"You're a lying son of a bitch," Ryan said in a cold
voice. "I don't deal crooked cards."

"Prove it." Holliday stood, leaning across the table, sup-
porting himself on his left hand. "Sit very still while I take
that handkerchief out of your pocket. I'm betting we'll find
a deck in there."

"You touch me and I'll stop your goddamn clock!"

"I seriously doubt it, Budd. Let's have that handker-
chief."

Ryan dug at a bulldog pistol in his waistband. Holliday,
his left hand anchored to the table, pulled the sheath knife
from his breast pocket with his right hand. He lashed out as
the barrel of Ryan's pistol cleared the edge of the table. The
blade struck Ryan on the cheekbone and carved a gaping
slash to his jawline, exposing teeth. Ryan screamed, drop-

ping the gun, clutching at his face. A gout of blood spurted through his hands.

The other players scattered. Ed Chase hurried forward with a bar towel, clamping it over the wound. Holliday ignored Ryan's mewling cries, whipping aside the front of his coat. Cards fluttered across the floor when he jerked the handkerchief from the inside pocket. He tossed the handkerchief onto the table, nodding to the other players, satisfied that he'd proved his point. All neatly done and Ryan still alive, if somewhat worse for wear. The letter of the law had been obeyed, with no one killed. He told himself he was in the clear.

City Marshal Claude White disagreed. He granted the fact that Budd Ryan had been caught cheating at cards. He even accepted the word of Chase and other witnesses that Ryan had pulled a gun. But he was adamant that the incident could have been settled without resorting to violence. He blamed Holliday for provoking the fight.

Holliday argued forcefully, claiming the right to defend himself. All of it was to no avail, for Marshal White wore the badge, and there was no appeal to his ruling. Even Chase, despite his political connections, was unable to dissuade the lawman, who stubbornly refused to reverse himself.

Holliday was posted from Denver that night.

CHAPTER 18

The Clear Fork of the Brazos was bounded by rolling prairies and wooded hills. Holliday forded the river in late September, dressed for the trail and leading a packhorse. He rode into the town called the Flat.

Fort Griffin stood on a hill directly above the townsite. Established in 1867, the military outpost was almost a hundred fifty miles due west of Dallas. Some three hundred soldiers, cavalry as well as infantry, were quartered at the garrison. The windswept town sprawled around the base of Government Hill.

Holliday's odyssey had consumed the better part of a month. After departing Denver, he had entrained for Pueblo, where he was met by the town marshal. He was no longer welcome in Colorado's major cities, and he had tired of life in the mining camps. From fellow gamblers, he heard talk of a new and highly prized stop on the gambling circuit. The town was known simply as the Flat, an outgrowth of Fort Griffin.

In Pueblo, Holliday had bought horses and outfitted himself for the trail. He then drifted southward, through Raton Pass and into New Mexico, along the Pecos Valley. He eventually turned eastward across the plains, angling toward the Clear Fork of the Brazos. A year had passed since he'd killed the soldier at Fort Richardson, and fled Texas. Gamblers recently returned from the Flat at Fort Griffin informed

him that the killing was old news, and the army had lost interest. He was no longer being sought by the law.

The Flat was simply that, a stretch of flat prairie below Government Hill. Griffin Avenue, the main street, was lined with stores and saloons, several dance halls, and a single newspaper, *The Frontier Echo*. The town itself was an ant-hill of commerce, headquarters for a legion of buffalo hunters and the supply point for ranches scattered throughout west Texas. In season, trail herds bound for the Western Trail and Dodge City watered along the river. Outside town ricks of buffalo hides awaited transport to the distant rail-heads.

Closer to the river, where a grove of pecan trees towered overhead, there was a row of bawdy houses that rivaled anything yet seen on the Western plains. Among the towns-people it was known as Naucheville, a local metaphor for the world's oldest profession. Those operating the brothels were true advocates of the free enterprise system, offering whites and blacks, Indian breeds, and one pink-eyed albino dubbed White Lightning. Something to suit the demands of any man, whatever his tastes.

Hitch racks along the main street were jammed with sad-dle horses. From the saloons and dance halls came the stri-dent chords of rinky-dink pianos mixed with the sprightly wail of fiddles and an occasional banjo twanging in the background. Knots of men crowded every corner—hide hunters and mule-skinners, cowhands and soldiers—and along the boardwalks a rowdy throng made its way from one dive to the next. The Flat was a wilderness oasis for men whose appetites ran to fast women and popskull whis-key.

Holliday reined to a halt before the livery stable. As he stepped out of the saddle, the boom of a large-bore rifle reverberated through the town. Farther down Griffin Ave-nue, he saw a man seated in the middle of the street with a Sharps .50 and a cartridge belt. He loaded the buffalo gun, sighting on a building near the end of the thoroughfare, and blew out a window. A man appeared in the window with a

Winchester and let off three rounds, kicking up spurts of dust around the one seated in the street. Unperturbed, he in turn put another shot through the window.

"Them boys are a caution."

Holliday turned toward the livery. A sallow-faced man stood in the doorway, staring downstreet. He dolefully shook his head. "They're gonna kill somebody yet."

"What's the problem?"

"A woman," the liveryman said. "Hurricane Bill, the one in the street, he's a buffalo man. Every time he goes off on a hunt, the one in the saloon—barkeep named Mike O'Brien—steals his woman." He paused, spat a stream of tobacco juice. "Shootin' starts whenever Hurricane Bill gets back."

"How long has this been going on?"

"I'd judge nearabout a year. Neither one can shoot worth a darn, or they'd both be worm meat. Beats me how Hurricane Bill ever kills a buffalo."

"Where's the law?" Holliday said as the Sharps boomed again. "Why doesn't the town marshal stop it?"

"Got plumb fed up with 'em," the liveryman observed. "Figures one's bound to get plugged sooner or later. Let 'em solve it their own selves."

"Your marshal sounds like a practical man."

"Yeah, ain't no flies on Will Cruger. Not gonna get himself shot over a couple of hotheads and their tramp."

Holliday nodded. "I'd like to stable my horses. I'll pay by the week."

"Dollar a day's what I charge. How about your gear?"

"I'll have someone collect it. What's the best hotel in town?"

"The Bison House," the liveryman said. "Just down the street, on the corner. Careful O'Brien don't wing you with his popgun."

"I'll try to stay out of the line of fire."

Holliday strolled off down the street. At the corner, he paused a moment, watching Hurricane Bill trade shots with the bartender, Mike O'Brien. Horses tied to hitch racks

danced and snorted; but men crowding the boardwalks looked on with detached amusement. He thought nothing had changed in the wilds of Texas, and found himself pleased by the absence of lawmen. Anarchy was still the best of all worlds.

The Winchester cracked as he turned into the hotel. He doubted the accommodations would come close to those of the Brown Palace, in Denver. But he nonetheless had a good feeling about his return to Texas, a gambler's hunch. He nodded to the desk clerk.

"I would like a room, preferably on the street side. The best in the house."

"Yessir," the clerk said, swinging the registration ledger around. "Got just what you want."

Holliday signed his name. The clerk spun the ledger, scanning the signature. He looked up, his eyes round. "Dr. John J. Holliday. Any chance you'd be Doc Holliday?"

"I answer to the name. Have someone collect my gear at the livery stable. I'd like it right away."

"Why, sure thing, Mr. Holliday. We'll have it here pronto."

"I'll also need a bath. Would you arrange a tub and hot water brought to my room?"

"Yessir." The clerk handed him a room key. "Get right on it."

"You're most kind," Holliday said. "Which gaming establishment would you consider the best in town?"

"I'd have to say the Bee Hive. Owner's name is John Shanssey. He runs square games."

Holliday seriously doubted it. He started toward the staircase, then turned back as the Sharps .50 roared. "How long will the shooting contest continue?"

"Them goldurn fools," the clerk said sheepishly. "Generally don't stop till one or the other runs out of shells. Everybody in town wishes they was better shots."

"I endorse the sentiment."

Holliday mounted the stairs. His eardrums were ringing from gunfire, and he wondered if he would be allowed a

bath in peace. Yet he suddenly chuckled, struck by a way-
ward thought.

Anarchy sometimes came at a steep price.

Early that evening Holliday emerged from the Bison House.
He was shaved and bathed, and the spicy aroma of bay rum
hung in his wake. His charcoal-gray suit was freshly
pressed, and a gold watch chain stretched across his vest.
He turned downstreet at a leisurely pace.

The boardwalks were crowded with men. His fashionable
appearance was something new to the Flat, and drew atten-
tion. The men he passed stared at him as though a goldfish
in a bowl had appeared in their midst. A drunken cowhand
made a slurred wisecrack about his attire, but he ignored the
remark. A block downstreet he pushed through the door of
the Bee Hive.

The establishment was a combination saloon, dance hall,
and gaming dive. Opposite a long mahogany bar were faro
and roulette, and several poker tables. A dance floor at the
end of the room was surrounded by small tables, with a
piano player and fiddler providing the music. Saloon girls
in full warpaint mingled with a crowd of cowhands, soldiers,
and buffalo hunters. Men stood three deep at the bar.

Holliday paused in the doorway. All conversation ceased
toward the front of the bar as a group of buffalo hunters
gave his outfit a slow once-over. Then, through the crowd,
he saw Lottie Deno seated behind the nearest faro layout.
She glanced up, spotted him at the same time, and her fea-
tures brightened with a dazzling smile. He moved forward
with a wide grin.

"Doc!" She leaned across the table to kiss him on the
cheek. "So wonderful to see you again. I heard you were
in town."

"News travels," Holliday said. "That hotel clerk must
be a talkative fellow."

"Why should that surprise you? You're quite the famous
man these days."

A lone cowhand, seated before the layout, gathered his

chips and moved over to the next table. "No great loss," Lottie said, laughing. "I was about to bust him, anyway."

Holliday wagged his head. "Still dealing tricky cards, huh?"

"I should say so! A girl has to make a living."

"I've often thought of you since Fort Richardson. What brought you out here?"

"What else?" Her eyes twinkled. "All the buffalo hunters moved west, and I tagged along. This town's rolling in money."

"Just like old times," Holliday said with a roguish smile. "Perhaps we should celebrate with a late supper. A reunion of sorts."

Her features clouded. "Doc, I'm not at liberty this time out. I have a gentleman friend, and pretty special, too." She gestured around the room. "He owns the place."

"His good fortune is my misfortune. How did you get together?"

"Doc, I think it was fate."

Her expression was suddenly animated. She explained that John Shanssey was a former prize fighter. A contender for the Western heavyweight championship, he had lost the title fight not quite a year ago. Smarter than most pugilists, he had taken his purse winnings and set off in search of opportunity. Where buffalo hunters gathered, there was money to be made, and he'd opened the Bee Hive. They had met when she arrived in town some months past, looking for a faro concession. The attraction was mutual, and they'd been together since.

"I just know you'll like him," she went on. "He's a little rough around the edges, but a sharp cookie. And he's good to me."

Holliday shrugged. "Any time that changes, let me know. I'm always at your service."

"Uh-oh!" Her eyes went past him. "Here he comes now. Behave yourself, Doc."

"I am the soul of discretion. Diplomacy itself."

A large thick-shouldered man approached the table. He

was tall, with brutish good looks, his nose slightly off center. There was scar tissue over his left eye, and he gave the appearance of a prize fighter not far removed from the ring. Lottie held out her hand.

"Hi there, honey," she said gaily. "I want you to meet an old friend. John Shanssey. Doc Holliday."

"No joke!" Shanssey clasped his hand in an ore-crusher grip. "By God, it's an honor to have you in my place, Doc. Okay if I call you Doc?"

Holliday immediately warmed to the man. There was the congenial manner about him of a huge but amiable bear. "Any friend of Lottie's is a friend of mine. A pleasure to meet you, John."

"We heard you was in town. Hope you'll make the Bee Hive your headquarters. I'd be proud to have you at my tables."

"Well then, consider it done. Lottie tells me there's action to be found."

Shanssey chuffed a deep laugh. "No two ways about it. Least a quarter million buffalo hides will be shipped out of here this year. Hell, it's better'n a gold mine."

"Hide hunters," Holliday said wryly. "A crude lot, but congenital gamblers. What more could a man ask?"

"One thing's for sure, you'll never run out of chumps. You're liable to stay here forever, Doc."

A commotion erupted at one of the poker tables. Two men slammed out of their chairs, drawing their pistols, and fired in the same instant. Their faces were etched with astonishment, a study in disbelief. One slumped across the table and rolled onto the floor. The other folded at the knees, dead as he fell.

The musicians never missed a beat. Some of the crowd edged forward for a closer look at the bodies. But for the most part, the shooting was a matter of passing interest. "Dumb bastards," Shanssey said in a low rumble. "Couple of tinhorns always trying to outsmart the other. Guess they finally done it."

"So it would appear," Holliday remarked. "I'd wager

neither of them figured on a tie. But then, no man does.''

Marshal Will Cruger hurried through the door. A man of medium height, with muddy eyes and a bowlegged walk, he pushed through the crowd. After questioning the other players in the game, he ruled the shooting a double suicide. Holliday thought his inventive edict was probably typical of how he enforced the law. That and never being around when the shooting started.

Cruger sent someone to fetch the undertaker. Then, as though pressed for time, he strode toward the door. As he passed the faro layout, he noticed Holliday with Lottie and Shanssey. He stopped, one eye cocked in a quizzical look.

''You must be Doc Holliday. Heard you were in town.''

''Hasn't everyone?'' Holliday said casually. ''You have an unusually speedy grapevine, Marshal.''

''Hope you don't kill nobody while you're here. Got all the bother one man can handle.''

''I will endeavor to restrain myself, Marshal.''

Lottie stifled a giggle as the lawman walked away. Shanssey was unable to suppress a broad, jaw-cracking grin. He beamed at Holliday.

''Doc, I admire your style. Welcome to the Flat.''

CHAPTER 19

A brisk October wind rippled across the plains. Cottonwood trees along the river sparkled with leaves turning scarlet and gold. High overhead, a vee of ducks winged their way southward.

Holliday emerged from the hotel under a late afternoon sun. He took a deep breath, savoring the crisp air, and turned downstreet. By now, after a month in the Flat, he was known to everyone in town. Storekeepers and shop owners, as well as passersby on the street, greeted him by name. His fashionable attire no longer drew stares.

Today he was dressed in a sharp brown suit tailored from worsted wool. As he strolled along the boardwalk, it occurred to him that he felt at home in the Flat. The townspeople, as well as the sporting crowd, had accepted him with cordial respect. Unlike Denver, he was not considered an oddity, and there was no stigma attached to his reputation with a gun. Killings were common in the rough-and-tumble life along the Clear Fork of the Brazos.

For all that, he'd not had reason to resort to the gun. He was only too aware that his reputation gave other men pause. Yet he treated them with the respect and consideration that he himself demanded. So far, though he never missed a night at the tables, no one had attempted to sharp him in a game. Nor had anyone tried to bullyrag him because of his courteous manner, or his frail physical stature.

In that sense, his reputation worked to the benefit of all. He hadn't been forced to kill anyone.

Downtown, he turned into the Bee Hive. Shanssey and a gang of buffalo hunters were huddled at the end of the bar. Their voices were raised in argument, and he noted that Shanssey appeared to be the referee between opposing factions. The evening rush hadn't yet started, and Lottie Deno was alone at her faro layout. She waved him over.

"Hi, there, Doc," she said brightly. "You're looking spiffy, as usual."

"Why, thank you, Miss Deno. I bask in your appreciation of sartorial fashion."

She never ceased to be amused by his dry wit. Still, despite his tailored suits and Southern charm, she saw beneath the guise he presented to the world. His health was of particular concern, for the wracking cough deviled him day and night. More and more, though he was clever about it, she saw him spitting bloody phlegm into his handkerchief. She worried as well about his mental state, the letters he never spoke of to anyone. She knew he all but mourned the girl in Atlanta. He was a lonely man, bitter beneath the outer shell. He hid it with droll humor.

Holliday nodded toward the bar. "John seems to have his hands full. What's all the commotion about?"

"Another dogfight," she said with disgust. "I'll never understand why he involves himself in such a cruel business."

"Don't be so harsh. Men love their bloodsport, a throwback to our atavistic nature. John merely provides the forum."

"I still think it's too brutal for words."

"Whose dogs are to be pitted?"

"Two hide hunters," she said waspishly. "One has some sort of bulldog. The other has what he claims to be a wolf. They're arguing over the stakes."

"A wolf against a bulldog. Interesting match."

"Honestly, Doc! You're as bad as John."

"All men are base by nature. God made women to subdue the beast."

"Small chance of that."

One of the saloon girls wandered over to the table. She was a redhead, with green eyes and an impudent expression. Her figure was sumptuous, with long, shapely legs and a narrow waist. Holliday didn't recall seeing her before, and wondered why. He inspected her with open interest.

"Do I pass muster?" she said with a sassy smile. "Or do you ogle all the girls like that?"

"Doc Holliday," Lottie said quickly, "this is Kate Elder. She just started today."

"Miss Elder." Holliday bowed with his head. "To answer your question, I am a student of feminine pulchritude. You do indeed pass muster."

"Thanks . . . I think," she said in a flippant tone. "You always use two-dollar words?"

"Only when the two-bit variety won't suffice. Do you enjoy seeing dogs pitted, Miss Elder?"

"Forget the polite stuff. Everybody calls me Kate. And no, I've never seen a real pit fight."

Holliday glanced past her. Shanssey and the buffalo hunters were walking toward a door at the rear of the building. "Well, Kate," he said. "Today's your lucky day. Are you game?"

"I'll try anything once."

"Good for you." Holliday looked around. "Will you join us, Lottie?"

"God no!" Lottie said vehemently. "I wouldn't watch it blindfolded."

"Kate and I will apprise you of the outcome."

Holliday led the way. Kate followed him to the rear of the room, across the dance floor, and through the back door. When they stepped outside, they found nearly a hundred men gathered in a rough circle. Holliday eased through the crowd, with Kate close behind. He wedged out a spot in the front row of spectators.

Pitting dogs to the death was a popular sport in the West.

The men jostled for position around an open pit six feet square by four feet deep. The pit had been designed by Shanssey with considerable thought: large enough to allow fighting room and deep enough to discourage a cowardly dog from trying to escape. Apart from wagering bets of his own, Shanssey operated the pit to profit the Bee Hive. Bloodsport had a curious way of making men thirsty.

Kate caught her breath as one of the hide hunters moved to the edge of the pit. He restrained a full-grown male wolf on a short length of plaited rawhide. The wolf stood close to three feet at the shoulder and topped a hundred pounds. His chest was as broad as that of a young bull, and his yellow eyes glinted fiercely in the late afternoon sun. His mouth curled to reveal saber-sharp fangs, and he strained at the leash. Holliday overheard a spectator remark that the hide hunter had raised him from a pup.

A moment later the other buffalo man appeared on the opposite side of the arena. The bulldog he led was a brindle-colored brute, with short hair, clipped ears, and predatory eyes. Though somewhat shorter than the wolf, he was wider through the chest, with the massive, knotted jaws of a killer. Known more commonly as a pit bull, he'd been bred with no other purpose in life but to fight in the pits. The breed was vicious and strong, born without fear of man or beast.

Shanssey motioned the owners forward. The leads were let out enough to allow the animals to claw their way into opposite corners of the pit. The wagering quickened throughout the crowd as the slobbering brutes strained to get at one another. When Shanssey swept his arm downward, the hide hunters slipped their leads. The wolf and the bulldog sprang forward, clashing head-on in the center of the arena. The wolf nearly lost the fight in that first bloody exchange.

The bulldog was a scarred veteran of the pits. He dropped low under the wolf's opening lunge and came up with a hold on the throat. Only the thick, double-coated ruff around his neck saved the wolf. The bulldog's massive jaws, embedded in heavy fur, were unable to get a death grip. The

wolf reared back and slung the bulldog against the side of
the pit. The veteran kept his feet as he bounced off the wall,
and they began circling. The spectators watched spellbound
as the beasts gathered themselves with bared fangs.

The wolf launched himself in another attack. This time
he struck lower, jaws working in a maddened rage, and the
bulldog went down under his weight. They rolled, snapping
and biting, obscured within an explosion of dust. When they
separated, hunks of fur floating skyward, the onlookers
loosed a murderous roar. The wolf's muzzle was laid open
to the bone, blood spurting over his snout. Yet it was the
bulldog who had suffered most. One eyeball hung from its
socket on a silvery thread of tissue.

The monsters backed off and again resumed their shuf-
fling dance. The earth puddled red at their feet as they cir-
cled the pit with gnashing teeth. Then the bulldog snarled
with savage ferocity and leaped to the attack. He came in
low, lunging for the throat, and for an instant, his nape was
exposed. The wolf's jaws chomped down on the brindle
neck, and there was an audible crunch as the bulldog's spine
snapped. Head high, the wolf lifted the limp body and shook
it like a dead mouse. His yellow eyes glinting, he dropped
it disdainfully in the center of the pit.

The crowd went mad, cheering and shouting as they
surged around the arena. Kate clutched Holliday's arm in a
fierce grip, her eyes wide with a mix of excitement and
revulsion. The wolf calmly licked blood from his muzzle as
his owner jumped into the pit and hugged him around the
neck. On the opposite side of the hole the other hide hunter
stared down at the bulldog with an expression of shocked
disbelief. Then, suddenly, the strident voice of a man rack-
eted over the murmur of the spectators. Everyone turned to
look at two men squared off on the edge of the crowd.

"Don't gimme that shit!" one yelled. "We shook on it
and you lost. Pay up!"

"You're a lyin' asshole, Pritchard. You told me that wolf
hadn't never fought before. All bets are off."

"The hell you say! Fork it over."

"Kiss my rusty butt."

The man turned, about to walk away. Pritchard's eyes glazed with rage, his hand on the pistol holstered at his side. He drew and fired with a crazed oath, the distance less than three feet. The other man staggered, struck in the back, then stumbled forward and folded at the waist. He fell dead.

There was a moment of stunned silence. Then, led by Shanssey, several men jumped Pritchard and wrestled the gun from his hand. A muttered anger swept through the crowd, the dogfight abruptly forgotten. He had broken the code, the sacrosanct tenet that no man could be shot without fair warning. The ugly look of a mob came over them as they pressed forward.

"Hang him!" someone shouted. "Sonovabitch shot Wilson in the back."

"No!" Shanssey roared, holding them off. "There'll be no lynching here today. We'll try him fair and square."

"We ain't got no court here, Shanssey."

"Then we'll make our own. Better that than mob law."

"Let's get to it," a buffalo hunter rumbled. "Quicker we convict him, quicker he swings."

The crowd adjourned to the Bee Hive. By acclamation, Shanssey was appointed judge, to preside over the trial. Twelve men were selected at random as the jury, and took chairs positioned by the bar. Pritchard was seated in a chair in the center of the room, his hands bound behind his back. He looked like a man who had heard the death knell.

Holliday, standing with Lottie and Kate, watched from the faro table. As Shanssey brought the court to order, Marshal Will Cruger burst through the door. One look told the tale, and he argued strenuously against vigilante justice. The legal way, he declared, was to transport Pritchard to the county seat for a proper trial. The crowd hooted him down, threatening to hog-tie him unless he backed off. He stormed out of the saloon.

Shanssey asked for witnesses to the shooting. Several men stepped forward with their account of the argument, and the untimely death of Elijah Wilson. One of them, a

bearded hide hunter, pointed a thorny finger at Pritchard. "Seen it with my own eyes," he announced hotly. "Sorry polecat's a gawddamn backshooter. I say we string him up!"

The onlookers grumbled their agreement. Shanssey rapped the bar with his knuckles. "Joe Pritchard, you've heard the testimony. Have you got anything to say in your defense?"

"Lost my head," Pritchard said lamely. "Could've happened to any man here. Ain't no reason to hang me."

The churlish response from the spectators said otherwise. Shanssey motioned for quiet. "Gentlemen of the jury, all the evidence is in. What's your verdict?"

"Hang the bastard!" someone shouted over the roar of the crowd. The vote being unanimous, they hauled Pritchard from his chair and headed toward the door. Holliday followed along as they hustled the condemned man to a grove of trees bordering the riverbank. Shanssey, still acting as judge, selected a stout limb about ten feet off the ground. A rope whistled over the limb, and one of the men made it fast around Pritchard's neck. Others scrambled to grab the loose end.

Shanssey faced the prisoner. "We tried you fair and square, Joe. You got any last words?"

Pritchard's voice was weak. "Guess I'll see you boys in hell. Praise Jesus Christ. Amen."

Shanssey gave the signal. The rope snapped taut and Pritchard shot into the air. He twitched and kicked, his face slowly turning purple in the last rays of sunset. The men tied the rope around the base of the tree, and stood back to watch him strangle to death. When it was finally over, the body hanging limp, they trooped off toward the Bee Hive. Everyone agreed that it had been a memorable day, even for the Flat. A bulldog and two men dead. And the night yet to go.

Holliday had never seen a man hanged. Nor had he witnessed the crazed bloodlust that transformed ordinary men into a vengeful mob. There was an indelible impression in

his mind of the condemned man dancing on air, struggling against the stranglehold of the rope. He made a mental note to avoid mobs, and a personal promise that he would never allow himself to be hanged. There were better ways to die.

A celebratory mood followed the men to the Bee Hive. They toasted the dogfight, bragging on the wolf, and hoisted another round to Joe Pritchard's necktie party. Holliday took a seat at a poker table, and soon had a game with three hide hunters and a couple of ranchers. As the night went on, the laughter got louder and the men ganged around the bar began to wobble under the influence of popskull whiskey. Around midnight a drunken cowhand started pawing at Kate, trying to sneak a squeeze. Shanssey rounded the end of the bar with a bungstarter, but he was a step behind. Kate beat him to the punch.

Her green eyes flashing, she grabbed a bottle off the bar and broke it over the cowhand's head. The blow squashed his hat, and he went down as though struck dead with a broadaxe. The crowd roared with laughter, impressed by her spunk as well as the way she wielded a bottle. A couple of the men scooped her up and sat her on the bar, her legs dangling over the counter. Her gaze drifted across to the poker table, settling on Holliday, and a vixen smile touched her mouth. She lowered one eyelid in a saucy wink.

Holliday reminded himself to invite her out for a late supper.

PART THREE

CHAPTER 20

The curtains fluttered on a gentle April breeze. A noonday sun, streaming through the window, flooded the room with light. Outside, the curse of a muleskinner was followed by the sharp *pop* of a whip.

Holliday rolled to a sitting position at the edge of the bed. His lungs contracted and a spasm shook his thin frame. The rattling cough doubled him over, head between his knees, his sides heaving. He uncorked a bottle on the nightstand and gulped three long swallows. His labored breathing slowly eased off.

"Are you all right, sweetie?"

Kate scooted across the bed, one hand on his shoulder. Holliday took another slug of bourbon. "I'm fine," he said hoarsely. "The picture of health."

"You shouldn't sleep with the window open. I keep telling you, but you won't listen. The night air only makes it worse."

"Spare me another of your misguided lectures. Fresh air never killed anyone yet."

"C'mon, honey." She rubbed his shoulder. "I was only trying to help."

"Aside from bourbon, there is no help. You should know that by now."

Holliday instantly regretted the rebuke. For the past six months she had shared his bed, offering only comfort. She

was concerned for his welfare, evidencing no fear for herself, though consumption was known to be infectious. She had nursed him through a hard winter, warming him with her body when frigid winds whipped off the plains. Some days she was more attendant than lover.

Yet she never made demands. Unlike other girls, who expected lavish presents for their favors, she seemed content to be Doc Holliday's woman. In January, when he'd turned twenty-six, she had reversed their roles by presenting him with a fine silk shirt. Embarrassed by the gift, he'd had to ask her age, which was twenty-three, and her birthday, which fell in June. She revealed little about herself unless prompted to talk.

Over time Holliday learned that she was originally from St. Louis. A spirited girl, orphaned at sixteen, she had become the mistress of a riverboat captain. From there, the details were sketchy; but she had somehow made her way west. With no trade, living by her wits, she had drifted into the one profession always open to women. Before Fort Griffin and the Flat, she had worked saloons at other military garrisons across Texas. She was a dance hall girl whose charms were for sale. She whored on the side.

Holliday moved to the washstand. The water in the pitcher was warm, and he gave himself a birdbath. Then, his hand steadied by bourbon, he shaved and trimmed his mustache. In the mirror, he caught Kate's reflection as she selected a dress from the armoire. In the sunlight, her buxom figure was apparent beneath her gauzy nightgown, her shapely rump clearly defined. He smiled, watching her, thinking perhaps they might have a quick romp before breakfast. She was an eager lover, with no inhibitions whatever, and abandoned in her desires. But then, one thought intruding on another, his features darkened.

"Have fun last night?" he said caustically. "I saw you sneak off with that hide hunter."

"I didn't sneak," she said with cheerful insouciance. "He wanted a little and I didn't have the heart to say no. Besides, he gave me ten dollars."

"You have a convenient lapse of memory. How many times have I offered to match what you earn—if you'll quit?"

"How many times have I told you I don't want to quit? I like to spread happiness."

"You like to spread your legs," Holliday said gruffly. "I think you do it to annoy me."

"Nasty, nasty," she said with a mischievous grin. "You're a gambler and I'm a whore, and we've beat that horse to death. Why cover old ground?"

The argument was one of long standing. She was stubborn, with an independent streak, and refused to mend her ways. There were rooms upstairs at the Bee Hive, where the girls took customers and split the fee with John Shanssey. Her nocturnal jaunts upstairs were a constant source of aggravation to Holliday. All the more so since she'd moved into his room at the Bison House. But she blithely ignored his wishes in the matter.

Holliday rinsed his razor in the basin. "There's a bit of the alley cat in you, Kate. I think you enjoy your work."

"Don't be jealous," she scolded. "I mean, it's not like I'm bedding everybody who asks. I only turned one trick last night."

"Your logic escapes me. One or a dozen, what's the difference?"

"Well, I just won't be dependent on you. I told you that from the very beginning. A girl has to look out for herself."

There were times when Holliday seriously considered ending their liaison. But he always relented, for she was vivacious, loyal to him in her own way, and undeniably attractive. Of no small significance, she filled a void in his life, and if it wasn't love, it was an acceptable substitute. She took his mind off Mattie, whose letters continued to riddle him with guilt, and that in itself was a godsend. He thought it better to sleep with a whore than to sleep alone. Somehow, with her beside him, he dreamt less of Atlanta and days past. What might have been.

After they were dressed, they went out for breakfast. In

a cafe down the street, Holliday seated her beside the front window. She was a voracious eater, ordering ham and eggs, with fried potatoes, biscuits, and a bowl of gravy. He picked at his eggs and toast, topping off a mug of coffee with a slug from his flask. As she smothered a third biscuit with gravy, he pushed his plate away. He lit a cigarillo.

"Tell me something." He exhaled a thin stream of smoke. "You said a girl has to look out for herself. Were you talking about money?"

"Money makes the world go 'round," she replied, spearing a chunk of ham with her fork. "I always sock some away for a rainy day. Better safe than sorry."

"Well then, suppose I gave you an allowance? Let's say a hundred dollars a week."

"Why would you do that?"

"So you could save for a rainy day. You wouldn't have to . . . entertain . . . anymore."

"No, thank you," she said quickly, her tone offended. "I won't be a kept woman."

Holliday looked dumbfounded. "You sell yourself anyway. I fail to see the difference."

"A girl on the line is her own boss. She can stay or move on as she pleases. She's not beholden."

The term "on the line" was a frontier euphemism for "prostitution." Holliday considered it quaint but meaningless. "Kate, a rose by any other name smells the same. You are what you are."

"Of course I am." She munched gravy-sopped biscuit with relish. "But I'd rather be a whore than a kept woman. After all, Doc, I've got some pride."

Holliday conceded defeat. Her rationale was her own, and clearly immune to reason or logic. Perhaps, he thought, her time with the riverboat captain had soured her on the life of a mistress. Perhaps she was just a free spirit marching to the beat of her own drummer. Whatever she was, she wasn't about to change.

She was a whore and she thought like a whore. But the life he led hardly gave him a mandate to cast the first stone.

They were, in many ways, a mismatched pair. Yet at the same time birds of a feather.

He told himself that nothing was perfect. Half a measure would have to do.

Late that afternoon they walked down to the Bee Hive. The evening rush was still an hour away and Kate went upstairs to change into her peek-a-boo gown. Holliday ordered a bottle brought to one of the poker tables. He dealt himself a hand of solitaire.

Shanssey and Lottie Deno came down from their living quarters upstairs. Lottie paused at the poker table, chatting with Holliday for a few minutes. Then she moved on to her faro layout, and began arranging trays of chips for the night. At the bar, Shanssey stopped to check the inventory with the head bartender.

Shortly afterward, a man dressed in trail clothes came through the door. Holliday noticed that his eyes quickly scanned the room as he proceeded to the bar. Shanssey turned from the backbar, his features registering a mix of shock and surprise. Then he laughed, grinning broadly, and shook the man's hand with a firm grip. They talked for several moments, and Shanssey's expression slowly dissolved into a solemn frown. He walked the man to his cubbyhole office behind the bar.

A short while later Shanssey and the stranger emerged from the office. Shanssey left the man at the end of the bar and moved across the room. His features were uncharacteristically somber as he stopped beside the poker table, nodding to Holliday. He took a chair.

"Doc, I've got a favor to ask. See the fellow at the end of the bar?"

Holliday looked toward the bar. "What about him?"

"His name's Wyatt Earp," Shanssey said. "He's a lawman from Kansas. Deputy marshal of Dodge City."

Holliday knew the name. Texas cattlemen, who trailed their herds to railhead in Kansas, spoke of Earp in harsh terms. He reportedly ruled Dodge City with an iron fist and

a quick gun. "You appear to be friends," Holliday said. "How do you know Earp?"

"We go way back. When I was a pug, he refereed a couple of my fights up in Kansas. Damn good man."

"What brings him to Texas?"

"Train robbers," Shanssey said quietly. "Dave Ruda-baugh and his gang hit a payroll train outside of Dodge. The Santa Fe hired Earp to track him down."

Holliday was familiar with the gang. Outlaws frequently drifted through the Flat, which was on the fringe of the settlements, and seldom visited by peace officers. A week ago Dave Rudabaugh had played in his game.

"You mentioned a favor," he said. "I assume it has to do with Rudabaugh."

"Earp tracked him here," Shanssey acknowledged. "The trail's gone cold, and I thought you might lend a hand. You hear things, Doc."

Holliday smiled. "Some of my best friends are horse thieves and train robbers. Why would I help the law?"

"I'd count it a personal favor. For what it's worth, you'd have my marker. I'll owe you one, Doc."

"You feel that strongly about it?"

"Like I said, Earp and me go back a long way. Otherwise I wouldn't ask."

A moment of weighing and deliberation slipped past. Holliday felt no great compunction to get involved, for the law had branded him a killer and posted him out of several towns. On the other hand, John Shanssey was a friend, and his personal marker might one day prove valuable. A gambler sometimes had need of an ace in the hole.

"All right," he said at length. "Send Mr. Earp over. We'll talk."

"Thanks, Doc. You won't regret it."

Shanssey rejoined Earp at the bar. They spoke for a moment, then Earp nodded, walking toward the table. He was a solid six-footer, lithe and muscled, with light hair and a sweeping mustache. His eyes were the color of blue ice.

"Mr. Holliday." He extended his hand, surprised by the

strength of Holliday's grip. "John says you're willing to help."

"Have a chair." Holliday waited until he seated himself. "Anything I do will be done as a favor to John. For the most part, I find myself at odds with the law."

"So I've heard," Earp said in a level tone. "Your reputation is well-known, even in Kansas. I understand you are easily offended."

"Texans say much the same of you, Mr. Earp. I hear you crack heads at the slightest provocation."

"We don't brook troublemakers in Dodge City."

"Oddly enough, I play poker by the same rules."

"You got me there," Earp said with a slight smile. "I like an outspoken man, Mr. Holliday. What say we call a truce and start over?"

Holliday spread his hands. "You appeal to my better instincts, Mr. Earp. How may I help you?"

"Well, as John told you, I'm after Dave Rudabaugh. Any idea where he's headed?"

"Last week he lost a considerable sum of money at this very table. Where he went from here is anyone's guess."

"Are you personal friends with Rudabaugh?"

"We are more on the order of nodding acquaintances."

Earp studied him a moment. "Maybe you could ask around. Somebody in town likely knows where he headed."

"Yes, possibly so." Holliday was silent a moment. "I take it your own inquiries came to nothing."

"All I got was that he'd left town. Your marshal told me that."

"Will Cruger is a fount of information. You haven't inquired further?"

"Waste of time," Earp admitted. "A place like the Flat, there's not a helluva lot of respect for the law. Folks tend to get a sudden case of lockjaw."

"Whereas they might tell a man of my . . . credentials."

"The sporting crowd generally knows what's what and who's where. You're one of them, and I'm not. Guess it's just that simple."

Holliday's expression revealed nothing. Yet a vivid image abruptly flashed through his mind. A week ago, after the poker game, he recalled Dave Rudabaugh taking one of the saloon girls upstairs. Some men weathered heavy losses at the tables by asserting their manhood in a whore's bed. In a moment of passion, driven to brag, they often told a woman their innermost secrets. Whores were sympathetic listeners.

"I'll put out some feelers," Holliday said now. "You understand, I'm making no promises. All I can do is try."

"I'm obliged," Earp told him. "How long you think it might take?"

"Let's meet here tomorrow afternoon. I should know by then."

After they shook hands, Earp stopped at the bar for a word with John Shanssey. Then, as he started toward the door, Holliday saw Kate coming down the stairs. She was dressed for the evening, spangles and warpaint.

He waved her over to the table.

CHAPTER 21

Holliday finished shaving. His eyes were bloodshot from a poker game that had lasted until five that morning. He studied himself in the mirror a moment, then rinsed and dried his razor. He turned from the washstand.

Kate was preening in front of the armoire. She held a dress to her shoulders, inspecting herself with a critical eye in the full-length mirror. Holliday opened the other door on the armoire and selected a light gray suit from the clothes rack. He took a pale blue shirt from the bottom drawer.

"Let's not take all day," he said, as she continued to pose for the mirror. "I'd like to have breakfast."

"I don't know why." She held the dress over her breasts with a coquettish air. "You hardly eat enough to keep a bird alive."

"You eat enough for the both of us."

"Oh, honestly, Doc! I'm not that bad."

Holliday stepped into his trousers. He moved to the bed, sat down, and began pulling on his boots. He abruptly stopped, struck by a wayward thought. Last night Kate had left the Bee Hive while his game was still in progress. She was asleep when he'd finally crawled into bed, and they hadn't spoken since. He looked up at her.

"Were you able to find out which girl entertained Rudabaugh?"

"Oh, sure," she said, slipping into her dress. "Sally

showed him a good time. She remembered him right off.''

Holliday stamped his foot into a boot. ''Did she say where he was going from here?''

''I didn't ask.''

''Why not?''

''I changed my mind.'' She moved to the washstand mirror and began brushing her hair. ''I just didn't feel right about it.''

Holliday stopped, the other boot in his hand. ''Right about what?''

''About helping a lawman. I'd much rather help Dave Rudabaugh. He's more our kind.''

''I'm not interested in your philosophical beliefs. All I want is the information.''

''Well, I won't do it,'' she said petulantly. ''Who's this Wyatt Earp, anyway? What do we owe him?''

''We're not talking about Earp,'' Holliday informed her. ''We're talking about how I decide a matter will be handled. Is that clear?''

''For God's sake, sweetie! What's the law ever done for you? Why get yourself crosswise of your own kind?''

''Yours is not to reason why. You'll follow my wishes in this matter.''

She gave him a pouty look. ''And if I don't?''

''Listen to me, Kate.'' Holliday's eyes went cold. ''I'm not asking your opinion or your preference. I'm telling you what I want done. Do you understand?''

''Do what I'm told and don't bitch about it. Isn't that it?''

''In a word—yes.''

She avoided his gaze. ''You can be a real bastard sometimes. Do you know that?''

''So I've been told.'' Holliday stood, tucking his shirt into his pants. ''Have the information for me this afternoon.''

''What if she doesn't know where Rudabaugh went?''

''Sally strikes me as a girl who is versed in pillow talk. She'll know.''

A knock sounded at the door. Kate crossed the room,

opening it, and found the desk clerk in the hall. He held out an envelope.

"A letter for Mr. Holliday. Postmaster gave it to me when I went to pick up the mail."

"Thanks a bunch."

She closed the door, scanning the envelope. Her green eyes fired with jealousy and she flung it across the room. "There you go," she said tartly. "A love note from your Georgia peach."

"No need for spite." Holliday retrieved the envelope from the floor. "I explained to you the way things are."

"I'll bet you never gave your darling Mattie any orders?"

"Keep your voice down."

"Go ahead and read your damn letter. I'll see you when I see you."

"Just make sure you get the information on Rudabaugh. No more excuses."

"Yessir, Mr. Holliday!"

She flounced out of the room. When the door slammed shut, Holliday crossed to the nightstand. He uncorked a quart of bourbon and took a long pull. Then, seating himself on the bed, he tore open the envelope. The delicate script was all too familiar.

My Dearest John,

How I treasure your letters. Every day, when the post arrives, I run to the box with hope in my heart. Your latest arrived only this morning, and I read it over and over again. You cannot imagine the joy I find in your words, the simplest endearment. I am, truly, a different woman.

As always, I look for some sign of improvement in your health. You offer none, I know, but I have faith that your welfare is ever under the watchful eye of our Savior. Your quote from Shakespeare—"If I must die, I will encounter darkness as a bride, and hug it in mine arms"—sounds so unlike you, John. If you must embrace anything, or anyone, then tell me only that

*we are to be reunited. I will rush to your side, and
stay there forevermore . . .*

Holliday folded the letter over. There were two more
pages, but he knew the words as if by rote. Her unyielding
optimism, and her faith in God, were as immutable as a
rock. Even quoting Shakespeare on the finality of death had
failed to shake her sanguine belief in their future. She would
not let him go.

He wondered if death itself would alter her steadfast re-
solve.

After breakfast, Holliday returned to the hotel. Kate was
nowhere to be found, and he thought it best considering her
temper tantrum over the letter. He gathered two boxes of
cartridges from the room and turned back into the hall. It
seemed a good day to blast something to kingdom come.

In the lobby, he met Earp coming through the door. Their
hours were different, and he discovered now that the law-
man was also staying at the hotel. He briefly explained that
there was no news as yet, but he hoped to have word later
in the day. On the verge of leaving, Earp noticed the car-
tridge boxes in his hand. He caught the look.

"Pistol practice," he said by way of explanation. "In my
profession, a man doesn't want to lose the touch."

"Same here," Earp said. "Unless it'll bother you, maybe
I'll tag along. I could get some extra shells at the hardware
store."

"By all means, join me, Marshal. We'll have an outing."

Earp walked across to the hardware store. Holliday col-
lected a sack of empty airtight cans from the cafe, and met
him on the street. They cut across town, weaving through
alleyways, headed toward a deserted stretch along the riv-
erbank. By the time they reached the treeline, they were on
a first-name basis.

Holliday placed a row of cans on a fallen log. He stepped
off ten paces, and offered Earp the first round. The lawman
carried a Colt .45, with a five-and-a-half-inch barrel, hol-

stered high on his hip. He pulled, thumbing the hammer, and extended the pistol at shoulder level. When he fired, a can leaped into the air, and he continued until the chambers were empty. Four cans out of five were kicked off the log.

"You excel with a pistol," Holliday commented. "All dead-center hits."

"All but one," Earp said, frowning. "Good thing he wasn't shooting back."

"I suppose that's what makes the game interesting, Wyatt."

While Earp reloaded, Holliday set out a row of ten airtights. Last night, before the poker game started, he had questioned Shanssey about the Dodge City lawman. He learned that Earp was a former buffalo hunter who had made his mark as a peace officer. His first post was Wichita, during the town's heyday as a Kansas railhead, and from there he'd moved on to Dodge. He was considered the toughest of all the cowtown marshals.

Holliday took his position on the firing line. All in a motion, he brushed back the skirt of his suit jacket and drew the Colt Peacemaker. He thumbed and fired, not a heartbeat between shots, and five cans sailed off the log. Without a moment's hesitation, he holstered the Peacemaker and snapped the Colt Lightning from beneath his arm. His eyes steady, firing double-action, he sent five more cans flying toward the riverbank. From start to finish, not ten seconds had elapsed. He began shucking empty shells.

"Jee-zus," Earp said slowly. "That's pretty fancy shooting."

"And a measure of luck," Holliday said with offhand modesty. "I'm seldom so steady."

"Doc, from what I hear, you're steady all the time. Nobody's beat you yet."

"Not as of today," Holliday remarked. "I hear the same of you."

"Pure hogwash," Earp confessed. "Three years a peace officer, and I've never killed a man. Always managed to get the drop on them before it went too far."

"Well, that is certainly an enviable record, Wyatt. Perhaps you'll teach me the secret."

"Nothing in the world I could teach you, Doc. Not a thing."

Earp was an observant man. The nature of his work made him mindful of other men's traits, particularly those of dangerous men. By his manner, he recognized Holliday as a man of taste and breeding. From the constant cough, he knew that the gambler was a doomed man. A consumptive living on borrowed time.

Today, having seen it with his own eyes, he understood something more about Holliday. He knew now that all the stories circulating throughout the West were true. Holliday was unquestionably the deadliest man with a pistol he'd ever come across. The gambler was possessed of a fatalistic courage, virtually devoid of fear, born from the knowledge that he had only a short time to live. That fatalism, in tandem with his speed and uncanny accuracy, made Holliday a formidable mankiller. His contempt for death gave him the edge in any fight.

After their practice ended, Earp was impressed by another of Holliday's traits. The gambler insisted on returning to the hotel, where he carefully cleaned and oiled both of his pistols. To him, a gun was a tool, something to be treated with respect and kept in perfect operating order. Earp gathered from his offhand comments that he approached the matter from a practical, and somewhat pragmatic, standpoint. A tool designed to kill should be counted on to perform its intended function.

Later that afternoon they walked toward the Bee Hive. As they approached the intersection, a company of soldiers from Fort Griffin rounded the far corner. The men marched in columns of fours, led by a captain, Springfield rifles slung across their shoulders. The company wheeled column right onto Griffin Avenue, executing the turn in perfect cadence. The brass on their uniforms glittered under a westerly sun.

"Looks like a parade," Earp said. "What's the occasion?"

Holliday laughed. "The commander at Fort Griffin peri-
odically delivers a message to those who inhabit the Flat.
You're about to see an example."

"What's the message?"

"Some of the dives are notorious hangouts for card-
sharps. Now and then, they allow greed to cloud their com-
mon sense. Colonel Pratt takes personal offense when his
men are fleeced too flagrantly."

"So he parades troops through town?"

"The colonel subscribes to the theory that might makes
right. You'll enjoy this."

Farther downstreet, the captain brought his company to a
halt outside the Alamo Saloon. At his barked order, the men
performed a right face, with two rows kneeling and two
rows standing. Their rifles came up on the next command,
trained on the saloon's roofline. A shouted order to "Fire!"
rocketed along the street, and forty rifles simultaneously
belched smoke. The roof of the Alamo disintegrated under
the fusillade, blown to flinders, debris raining skyward. The
captain re-formed his men and marched off toward Fort
Griffin.

"I'll be dipped," Earp marveled, watching shattered tim-
ber settle to the street. "They shot it to hell and gone."

"Quite a spectacle," Holliday agreed. "The cost of a new
roof will put the Alamo on its good behavior. Are you im-
pressed?"

"Doc, that takes the cake. Never saw anything like it."

"I've always considered it one of Fort Griffin's more
amusing customs. The colonel has an eccentric sense of jus-
tice."

When they entered the Bee Hive, Holliday saw Kate com-
ing down the stairs. He excused himself, leaving Earp to
order a beer, and walked to the end of the bar. Kate stood
waiting, one hand on her hip, her expression sullen. He nod-
ded pleasantly.

"Your sulk tells me there's good news. What did Sally
have to say?"

"Fort Davis," she said, tight-lipped. "Wherever the hell that is."

"I knew you wouldn't let me down. Good girl."

"You're still a sanctimonious bastard."

"Yes, but I'm your bastard, Kate. Cheer up."

Holliday patted her affectionately on the cheek. He turned and walked back to the front of the bar. Earp looked up from his beer, his pale eyes quizzical. "All quiet on the domestic front?"

"We have our moments," Holliday said amiably. "Kate's bark is worse than her bite. In fact, she is the bearer of glad tidings."

"How so?"

"Dave Rudabaugh's destination was Fort Davis. I recall that's west of the Pecos River."

"And then some," Earp amended. "From here, it's likely a five-hundred-mile ride. Rudabaugh sure gets around."

"Will you go after him?"

"I've never seen that part of Texas. Maybe it's time I did."

Holliday signaled the barkeep for a bottle. He poured himself a shot of bourbon, placing the bottle on the counter. Then, lifting the glass in a toast, his mustache curled in a smile.

"I wish you good hunting, Wyatt."

"Doc, I owe you and your lady friend. Look me up if you're ever in Dodge."

"One day, perhaps. Who knows? Stranger things have happened."

They drank to the uncertainty of the future.

CHAPTER 22

The summer trail drives got under way in early May. Cattlemen fixed the distance from the Clear Fork of the Brazos to Dodge City at roughly four hundred miles. Barring stampedes and rustlers, they planned to reach the railhead by late June.

The Bee Hive was packed. Nine longhorn herds were bedded down along the river for the night. At sunrise, their trek would start northward on the Western Trail, which meandered through Indian Territory and on into Kansas. Once the drives began, there would be no break along the trail, and herd owners had allowed their crews one last night in town. There were nearly a hundred cowhands swarming through the Flat.

The usual mix of buffalo hunters and soldiers added to the crowd jammed into the Bee Hive. Holliday and six other men were seated around his regular poker table. The game was loose and fast, with three of the players, all from the same cattle outfit, determined to make the most of their night on the town. Their interest seemed equally divided between whiskey and poker. They were drunk, and losing.

Their outfit was the Circle T, the largest cattle spread in West Texas. One of them was the foreman, a beefy, hard-faced toughnut named Ed Bailey. He was loud and crude, clearly cock-o'-the-walk at the Circle T, with a rough, pugnacious manner. Losing heavily, his temper fueled by liquor,

he began cursing the cards and his run of bad luck. The other players eyed him warily.

Holliday ignored the outbursts. He was winning consistently, and an unruly drunk was one of the burdens all professional gamblers learned to endure. Some three hours into the game, the hide hunter seated next to him dealt a round of five-card draw. Bailey opened for five dollars, Holliday raised him five, and everyone except the dealer folded. On the draw Bailey took three cards, Holliday asked for two, and the hide hunter dealt himself three. They looked at their cards, waiting on Bailey, as the opener, to bet.

Bailey studied his hand a moment. Then, grunting to himself, he reached out and slyly picked up the deadwood of the dealer. In poker vernacular, the cards discarded by other players on the draw were called the deadwood. The practice was akin to cheating, for it gave a player an insight into his opponent's hand. The tactic was one used on a greenhorn, or by a hardcase trying to intimidate the other players. The standard penalty across the West was loss of the pot.

"Play poker," Holliday admonished him. "Leave the deadwood alone."

"Stuff it," Bailey said coarsely. "I ain't afraid of you, Holliday. I'll do whatever I damn well please."

"Don't press your luck. You've had too much to drink. Bet or get out."

"Hell, I'm gonna bet your ass off. Ten bucks!"

"Your ten—" Holliday tossed bills on the table. "And raise you ten."

The dealer folded. Bailey mumbled something under his breath, again inspecting his hand. He gave Holliday a venomous look and reached across the table. He casually flipped over Holliday's discards. His mouth split in a wet chuckle.

"Gonna call ten and raise—"

"You're out," Holliday interrupted. "Twice in the deadwood is once too often. The rule says you forfeit the pot."

"Don't gimme none of that shit! I'm still in the game."

"You're all through, cowboy."

Holliday leaned forward, started to scoop in the pot with

his left arm. Bailey muttered a sharp curse, lurching from his chair, and fumbled at the gun on his hip. Caught out of position, stretched over the table, Holliday was unable to reach either of his pistols. He pulled the sheath knife from his breast pocket with his right hand and slashed out across the table. The blade, honed to a razor's edge, opened Bailey like a gutted hog, from the sternum to his beltline. He howled a scream of bloodcurdling terror.

The crowd froze in a stilled tableau. Bailey stumbled backward, eviscerated, steamy intestines spilling down over his belt. Mesmerized by the sight, the crowd watched as he tried to hold his innards from leaching through the horrendous wound. One of the girls retched, gagging as she turned away, spewing vomit across the bar. Bailey dropped to his knees, still holding his guts in his hands, and his eyes rolled upward. He fell facedown on the floor.

There was an instant of doomsday silence. Suddenly, as though galvanized, one of the cowhands bolted from his chair. "Sonovabitch murdered him!" he shouted drunkenly, pointing at Holliday. "Ol' Bailey never had a chance!"

"Get hold of yourself." Holliday calmly wiped blood from the knife with his handkerchief. "Everyone here saw what happened. He went for his gun."

"Like hell!" the other cowhand yelled. "Looka there if you want proof. His gun's still in his holster."

The crowd strained for a better look. Bailey lay in a welter of blood and offal, the gun anchored in his holster. A guttural murmur swept through the room, and Holliday all but read their minds. What they saw was a man who had been killed without warning, with no chance to defend himself. A butchery that went against their sense of fair play, violated the code. Their faces abruptly took on the look of a mob.

"Hang him!" one of the cowhands cried. "Gawddamn murderer!"

Holliday slipped the knife into its sheath as the hide hunter beside him bellowed for silence. "You boys got it all wrong! Holliday never—"

The cattlemen in the crowd roared him down. They pressed forward, their faces cold with bloodlust, leading what was now a lynch mob. Holliday jerked the Peacemaker, switching it to his left hand as he backed to the wall. His right hand darted beneath his jacket and came out with the Colt Lightning. He leveled both pistols on the crowd.

"Stand fast!" he commanded. "I'll kill the first man who moves."

The men ganged before him stood as though rooted. Across the room he saw Kate, her features twisted in fear, and Shanssey watching from behind the bar. Out of the corner of his eye, he was aware of Lottie seated at the faro table. He knew they could offer no help, not in the face of a mob set on vengeance. His one out was to hold the crowd at bay, and somehow get clear of the saloon. The alternative was to go down fighting. He would not be hanged.

Marshal Will Cruger burst through the door. He took a tentative step into the room, then slammed to a halt. His eyes skittered from Holliday to the motionless crowd. His voice sounded parched. "What the devil's going on here?"

"Murder, that's what!" someone shouted. "Holliday killed a man in cold blood."

"Marshal Cruger," Holliday called out. "I am placing myself in your custody. Do your duty and cover my retreat."

"Hold on now, Holliday. You want me to put a gun on these men?"

"Unless you prefer that I open fire. I have ten shots, and I will take ten men with me. What's it to be?"

Cruger slowly drew his gun. "You men hold real still. Just be sensible and I'll get Holliday locked away in jail. Don't make me shoot nobody."

Holliday wagged his pistols, motioning men to clear a path. He kept his back to the wall, easing along the row of tables, never taking his eyes off the crowd. There were low rumbles of protest from the cattlemen, but no one dared risk being the first one shot. Finally, skirting Lottie's faro table, he moved to Cruger's side. They backed toward the door.

"Stay put!" Holliday ordered. "Anyone who tries to follow will be killed. Let's have no heroes."

Outside, waving his pistols, Holliday pushed through knots of men thronging the boardwalks. He turned upstreet at a fast clip, with Cruger rushing along at his side. The lawman kept darting looks over his shoulder.

"We better get you locked away damn quick. They'll hit the street any minute."

"I must decline the offer," Holliday said. "Your jail is far too easy to storm."

"You got something safer in mind?"

"I suggest we fort up in my hotel room. Given time, perhaps they'll cool off."

"And if they don't?"

"Then you will have to earn your pay, Marshal."

"Jesus."

The street was clogged with men. The mob had swelled to over three hundred in number, and they blocked the intersection outside the hotel. Their shouts carried through the town.

"We know you're in there, Cruger. You're not foolin' nobody!"

"Bring the gawddamn tinhorn out! Make it easy on yourself."

Cruger stood at the edge of the window, looking down at the street. His eyes were round with fear and his face was beaded with sweat. He saw a wedge of some thirty or forty cowhands in the front ranks of the mob. One of them was holding a knotted rope.

"Christ A'mighty," he said shakily, turning back into the room. "How'd they find us so fast?"

"You forget, we were seen coming into the hotel. Someone probably told them."

Holliday sat in a chair near the door. He avoided the windows, wary of someone in the crowd taking a shot at him. Instead, his ear cocked to the door, he listened for stealthy footsteps in the hall. A lynch mob, boiling with

fury, was short on patience. Before long, he expected them to rush the room.

"Them damn cowhands," Cruger said, peeking out the window. "They're the ones leading that pack."

"A tribe sticks together," Holliday commented dryly. "Bailey was one of their own. They want an eye for an eye."

"Why'd you have to gut him thataway?"

"Under the circumstances, a knife was more expedient."

Cruger sighed heavily. "They're not gonna wait much longer. Gotta figure some way to get you to the county jail."

Albany was the county seat, some fifteen miles to the south. Holliday knew they would never make it out of town, much less to the protection of the sheriff. On several occasions, he had seen Cruger back off in the face of a lynch mob, and he had no doubt about tonight. Cruger would surrender him rather than fight.

A stone shattered the window. Glass exploded across the room and the rock bounced off the far wall. Cruger jumped away as the howl of the mob took on a maddened pitch. A furious voice, louder than the others, ratcheted over the street. *"Send the bastard out. We want him now!"*

Cruger looked desperate. His features were contorted with alarm. "They're gonna be poundin' on the door pretty quick. You got any ideas?"

"Let them come," Holliday said impassively. "They'll pay a dear price before they break in here. I won't surrender."

"You expect me to get killed for you? Hell, that ain't part of my job."

A brilliant orange glow suddenly filled the room. They moved to the window as frenzied shouts erupted from the crowd outside. Downstreet, halfway along the next block, the rear of the hardware store was engulfed in flame. The blaze lit the night, burning brightly against an indigo sky speckled with stars. Smoke billowed as sparks leaped toward nearby buildings.

Fire was an ever-present dread in the Flat. The structures

along Griffin Avenue were dry as a tinderbox, slapped together with ripsawed lumber. Unless checked, the flames would leapfrog from building to building, and rapidly burn the entire town to the ground. The blazing hardware store was everyone's concern, saloonkeepers and hide hunters, gamblers and cowhands alike. The lynch mob scattered, Holliday abruptly forgotten, and rushed toward the fire. Men quickly formed bucket brigades from water pumps along the street.

There was a light rap at the door. Holliday pulled his Peacemaker, flattened himself against the wall. "Who's there?"

"Kate," a whispered voice replied. "Let me in."

Holliday unlocked the door. When he opened it, the pistol still in hand, Kate hurried into the room. She was dressed in men's clothes, with a baggy jacket and scuffed boots, her hair bunched inside a slouch hat. She ignored his astounded expression, brushed past Cruger, and grabbed a worn carpetbag from beneath the bed. She began stuffing clothes in the bag.

"C'mon, Doc," she demanded, glancing at Holliday. "Whatever you want, let's get it packed. We're short on time."

"I'll be switched." Holliday laughed with sudden understanding. "You started that fire, didn't you?"

"Well, of course I did, sugar. Somebody had to distract those fools away from here."

"Why are you wearing men's clothes?"

"I couldn't very well ride a horse in a dress. C'mon, Doc, let's get moving."

"You have horses?"

"Behind the hotel," she said. "I stole them off the street."

"Hold on now," Cruger interrupted, turning to Holliday. "You killed a man and she set the town on fire. I can't let you skedaddle out of here."

Holliday cocked his pistol. "Marshal, I place little faith in you or the law. Kindly hand your gun to Kate."

"For chrissakes, Doc! Them boys'll tar and feather—"

"Do it. Now."

Cruger obeyed, grumbling as he surrendered his gun. Holliday tore a bedsheet into strips and tied him hand and foot in a chair. After using a strip of cloth for a gag, he selected one suit from the armoire and crammed it into the carpetbag. He waved to Cruger on the way out the door.

"Invent some tall tale about how I got the drop on you. I doubt they would believe the truth."

Kate led the way down the back stairs. At the rear of the hotel, two horses stood hitched to a woodshed. Holliday got her mounted, then hooked the handles of the carpetbag over his saddlehorn. He stepped aboard, reining his horse about, and rode toward the edge of town. The sky was ablaze with firelight, the frantic shouts of men drifting on a southerly breeze. He chuckled out loud.

"Kate, I swear, you are a wonder. How did you manage it?"

"Simple as pie," she said from beneath her slouch hat. "The fire was John Shanssey's idea, and he loaned me the clothes. I stole the horses all by myself."

"A pair of tacticians," Holliday remarked with wry humor. "We'll be far away before anyone knows we're gone."

"That raises a good question, sweetie. Where are we going?"

"Our first stop will be Doan's Crossing."

"Where is that?"

"On the Red River," Holliday said. "A trading post of sorts on the Western Trail."

"You're kidding!" She looked at him, surprised. "We're going to Dodge City?"

Holliday smiled. "I have a standing invitation."

They rode north from Fort Griffin and the Flat.

CHAPTER 23

Holliday and Kate rode into Dodge City late in May. She was still dressed in men's clothes, and they drew stares as they crossed the bridge over the Arkansas River. The Santa Fe railroad tracks, which bisected the town east to west, were directly north of the bridge. The business district was spread along a broad plaza opposite the tracks.

Their journey had consumed almost three weeks. At Doan's Crossing on the Red River, Holliday had outfitted them with food supplies and camp gear. Generally following the Western Trail, their trip northward through the Indian Nations had proved uneventful. Yet they were weary from the long ride on horseback, and their clothes were covered with trail dust.

Holliday's spirits were nonetheless improved by their return to civilization. He felt he'd made a friend in Wyatt Earp, and he thought they would be welcome in Dodge City. The cowtown was also far removed from Texas, which made it unlikely that he would be sought for the killing at Fort Griffin. From a professional standpoint, Dodge was considered a major stop on the Gamblers' Circuit, ranked alongside mining camps in the Rockies. A railhead, and cattlemen fresh off a trail drive, offered easy prospects for a gambler. So far he liked what he'd seen.

Dodge City billed itself as ''Queen of the Cowtowns.'' On his way into town, Holliday's brief glimpse of the sport-

ing district indicated that it was larger and far livelier than
he had expected. He was surprised as well by the number
of longhorn herds on the holding grounds along the plains
bordering the Arkansas. From the looks of things, many
Texas ranchers got an early start on the drive to railhead.
The herds were money on the hoof, and hard cash in the
pockets of cattlemen. All of which boded well for a gambler.

Fort Dodge, the nearest army post, was situated five miles
east along the Arkansas. Until 1872, with the arrival of the
railroad, Dodge City had been a windswept collection of log
structures devoted to the buffalo trade. But now, hammered
together with bustling industry, it had sprung, virtually over-
night, into the rawest boomtown on the Western Plains. A
sprawling hodgepodge of buildings, the town was neatly di-
vided by the railroad tracks.

The dusty plaza along Front Street was clearly the center
of trade and commerce. Down at the end, flanked by several
smaller establishments, were the Dodge House Hotel, Zim-
merman's Mercantile, and the Dodge Opera House. Up the
other way were a couple of banks and the newspaper, bor-
dered by cafes and shops and varied business places, in-
cluding the Long Branch Saloon. Farther north, beyond the
plaza, was the residential district of town.

Holliday reined to a halt outside the Dodge House Hotel.
With Kate at his side, he entered the lobby, where a group
of Texas cattlemen stood talking among themselves. All
conversation ceased as the Texans stopped to gawk at a
woman, dusted in trail grime, dressed in men's clothes. She
ignored the strange looks, watching as Holliday signed the
register "Dr. and Mrs. John H. Holliday." He then ordered
a bathtub and hot water brought to their room, and arranged
to have his extra suit pressed. The clerk agreed to have their
horses stalled at a livery stable.

Their room overlooked the plaza. Holliday dumped their
tattered carpetbag on the bed and moved to the window.
Kate removed her slouch hat, fluffing her hair, and joined
him. She gave him a curious sidewise glance. "What was

that nonsense about Dr. and Mrs. Holliday? Are we getting married?''

"Not today,'' Holliday said evasively. "I just thought it would look better. A matter of propriety.''

"Who do you think you're kidding, sugar? You're trying to impress your lawdog friend, Wyatt Earp.''

"Here.'' Holliday peeled a hundred dollars off his roll. "Go buy yourself some clothes while I have a bath. Get dresses that are nice-looking, respectable. Nothing flashy.''

She took the money. Her gaze went across the railroad tracks, to the sporting district. "We're on the wrong side of town for my line of work.''

"As of today, you are retired. You have become a lady of leisure.''

"What if I don't want to retire?''

"You have a choice,'' Holliday said firmly. "Either you're my woman, or you are a bride of the multitude. I won't have it both ways.''

"Are you serious?'' she said, with a wounded look. "You'd kick me out it I went back on the line?''

"Kate, try to understand. All the time we were on the trail, I had you to myself. I want it to stay that way.''

"A lady of leisure.'' She examined the notion. "I suppose we could give it a shot. See how it goes.''

"Indulge me this one time. You won't regret it.''

"You are some sweet man, Doc. Why not?''

She returned an hour later. The dresses she'd bought were demure by her standards, colorful but high-necked and fashionably proper. Holliday was bathed and shaved, attired in a freshly pressed gray suit and apricot shirt. He dusted off his hat, placed it squarely on his head. She dropped her bundles on the bed.

"Are you going out?''

"I thought I might have a look at the town.''

"What about me?''

Holliday motioned to the tub. "I had it filled with fresh water. Have a bath and surprise me with one of your new dresses.''

Her eyes narrowed. "When will you be back?"

"Expect me in time for supper."

When he went out the door, she stared after him a moment. Then, stripping off her grimy clothes, she stepped into the tub. She sighed, luxuriating in the hot water, her eyes closed. A smile tugged at the corner of her mouth.

She thought being a lady of leisure might not be so bad.

The train depot was at the east end of the plaza. Directly across the track was the city jail, which housed a combined office for the town marshal and the county sheriff. The building resembled a fort, constructed of thick railroad timbers.

Holliday entered by the only door, which faced the sporting district. To the rear was a large holding cage, fronted by steel bars and a heavy metal door. In the outer office were four battered desks, with carbines and double-barrel shotguns chained in a wall rack. Wyatt Earp rose from behind one of the desks.

"I'll be damned," he said, slightly amazed. "Where'd you drop from, Doc?"

"Points south," Holliday replied, shaking his hand. "I tired of Texas."

"Well, that's easy to do. What brings you to Dodge?"

"I've heard it called the Babylon of the Plains. Anything so iniquitous has a certain intrigue."

Earp laughed. "We've got our share of sinners. No doubt about that."

"Speaking of wayward souls," Holliday said. "Were you able to capture Dave Rudabaugh?"

"Missed him by a week. Damn fool headed back to Kansas and got caught anyway. Like to introduce you to our sheriff."

A man stood at one of the other desks. "Bat Masterson," Earp said, "this is Doc Holliday. You'll recall he gave me an assist at Fort Griffin."

Masterson was of medium height, solidly framed, his brushy mustache neatly trimmed. The man seated at the next

desk bore a striking family resemblance. Earp introduced him as Ed Masterson, the town marshal.

"Heard a lot about you," Bat Masterson said. "Wyatt tells me you're an honest gambler."

Holliday shrugged. "I prefer the vagaries of chance. Why improve the odds?"

"How long you plan to stay in Dodge?"

"I haven't given it much thought. Why do you ask?"

"From your reputation," Masterson said, "you're a man with a short fuse. We frown on gunplay around here."

"An admirable policy," Holliday said in a neutral voice. "I am a staunch advocate of law and order."

Ed Masterson gave him a sharp look. "That why you've killed so many men?"

"Hold on," Earp interrupted. "We've got no shortage of toughnuts in town. No reason to single Doc out."

"We're not," Bat Masterson said gruffly. "Just call it a word to the wise. No gunplay allowed."

"I'll vouch for him," Earp said. "Doc won't be the one to start trouble. Am I right, Doc?"

Holliday spread his hands. "I will be on my best behavior. Decorum is the byword."

"Hope you mean that," Ed Masterson said. "Your name will just naturally draw attention. Try to avoid trouble."

"I always do, Marshal."

"Come on, Doc." Earp moved toward the door. "Let's you and me take a walk. I'll show you around town."

"Gentlemen." Holliday nodded to the Masterson brothers. "A pleasure to meet you."

Outside Earp led the way to Second Avenue, the main thoroughfare through the sporting district. Holliday wagged his head. "Your friends seem to have made the law a family business. Unusual, to say the least."

"Well, they're good men, sticklers for the law. Highly regarded by folks in Dodge."

"Do they disapprove of all gamblers . . . or just me?"

"Don't take it personally," Earp said. "Their job is to run a clean town. Gets rough sometimes."

"No doubt," Holliday observed. "How long have they been in office?"

"Bat was elected last November. Ed got appointed town marshal a few months ago. He was a deputy before that."

"I'm surprised you weren't considered for the job. You have an enviable record as a lawman."

"Never liked to be tied down," Earp told him. "I sign on only during the cattle season. 'Course, there's politics involved, too."

"I see," Holliday said. "Are the Mastersons skilled at the game?"

"Bat's the talker of the family. He could charm the birds out of the trees. Natural born politician."

"I tend to prefer your view of things. No permanent ties."

"That reminds me." Earp looked at him. "Your lady friend at Fort Griffin was a big help. Whatever happened to her?"

"We formed an alliance," Holliday said with a crooked smile. "In fact, she's over at the Dodge House right now. I brought her with me."

"She plan to catch on here as a saloon girl?"

"Kate has retired from the business. We have an . . . arrangement."

"Had a few myself, here and there. Nothing like a good woman."

Holliday laughed. "Or a bad one."

Before Earp could reply, they rounded the corner onto Second Avenue. The trailing season had only just begun, but the sporting district was jammed with Texans. A wild-and-woolly atmosphere permeated the street, with saloons, whorehouses, and gambling dives pandering to the rowdy nature of cowhands. A combination of fallen women and raw whiskey quickly separated most of them from their wages.

The district was known simply as the South Side. There, the trailhands were allowed to let off steam in a no-holds-barred pursuit of drunkenness and depravity, gunplay ex-

cepted. But at the railroad tracks, locally dubbed the Deadline, all rowdiness ceased. The lawmen of Dodge City, with a no-nonsense attitude toward troublemakers, rigidly enforced the ordinance. Anyone who attempted to hurrah the town north of the tracks was guaranteed a night in jail.

Holliday thought it a highly sensible arrangement. The wages of sin on one side of the tracks and the fruits of commerce on the other. The neutral ribbon of steel in between served as a visible, and clearly effective, dividing line. At first glance, containing the Texans to the sporting district seemed to work uncommonly well for all concerned. On the north side of the Deadline, the townspeople went about their business in relative peace.

Earp gave him a tour of the better gaming establishments. At the Lady Gay, one of the more popular watering holes, he was introduced to Ben Thompson. A Texan himself, and a veteran of Wichita and other cowtowns, Thompson was a high roller of some note. His attitude toward Earp was civil but distant, and Earp later explained the reason. Thompson was something of a hothead, and in gunfights from the Mexican border to the Kansas railheads, he'd reportedly killed ten men. He was on warning in Dodge City.

Uptown, across the Deadline, Earp stopped in at the Long Branch. He introduced Holliday to Chalk Beeson, the owner, who operated high-stakes games for wealthy Texas ranchers. The resident gambler was Luke Short, a fastidious dresser, small and wiry, with the quick hands of a professional. Holliday liked his natty attire, and found him to be a man of understated intelligence and jocular good humor. Afterward, on the street, Earp explained that Short was a former army scout turned gambler. He was reported to have killed six men in shootouts, but none in Dodge. His presence north of the tracks was tolerated because he behaved himself.

Holliday sensed a subtle message. "Perhaps you might yet have a place in politics. You are a man of some diplomacy, Wyatt."

"Diplomacy?" Earp feigned surprise. "How so?"

"Thompson is consigned to the South Side, and Short is accepted uptown. Unless I'm mistaken, you've cautioned me to keep my nose clean. Am I wrong?"

"Doc, when I left Fort Griffin, I said you'd be welcome in Dodge. I just wanted you to understand how things work."

"You need have no qualms," Holliday said earnestly. "I will do nothing to compromise your position as a lawman, Wyatt. You have my word on it."

"Never thought otherwise," Earp said. "Whatever anybody else thinks, I got your number down in Texas. You're a man of honor, Doc."

"Kindly keep it to yourself, will you? I wouldn't want my reputation spoiled."

They parted with a warm handshake. Earp turned toward the jail, and Holliday walked upstreet to the hotel. He realized now that Dodge City had been the right decision. Among the men he'd known, Wyatt Earp was unique, even singular. One of a kind.

A man worthy of friendship.

CHAPTER 24

The crowd began to drift off about three in the morning. Shortly afterward, with only a few cowhands still at the bar the gaming tables closed for the night. A swamper began gathering his mop and pail from the storage room.

On the dance floor, Kate swirled lazily in the arms of a young cowhand. By house rule, the band was not allowed to leave until the place emptied for the night. The Lady Gay was popular with Texans, and no customer ever went away thirsty. The doors were never locked.

Holliday was seated at a poker table with Ben Thompson and another gambler, Frank Loving. Over drinks, conversing in low tones, they discussed the night's action at the gaming tables. Loving, who dealt faro at the Long Branch, had walked down to the Lady Gay a short while ago. Saloons north of the Deadline usually closed an hour or so before the sporting district quieted for the night. By four in the morning the South Side dives were virtually empty.

A month had passed since Holliday's arrival in Dodge City. He was by now widely respected as a gambler of surpassing skill among those in the sporting crowd. For the most part, he played in high-stakes games at the Long Branch, routinely trimming Eastern cattle buyers and Texas ranchers fresh off the trail. But occasionally, when the action was slow uptown, he found a game at one of the dives below

the Deadline. Tonight, he'd taken a chair at Thompson's table in the Lady Gay.

Kate had insisted on coming along. She had kept her promise, referring to herself as a "reformed whore," and rarely ventured south of the tracks. But tonight was her birthday, and she felt entitled to celebrate among her own kind, the saloon girls of the South Side. Earlier, Holliday had given her an expensive mother-of-pearl brooch as a birthday present, and she was thrilled. She was nonetheless adamant about accompanying him to the Lady Gay. She wanted to party.

Holliday watched her now with mounting irritation. She was wobbly from too much liquor, and hanging on to the cowhand with a dreamy smile. Before taking a seat in the poker game, he had danced with her a couple of times. But afterward, left to her own devices, she had mingled with the saloon girls, informing anyone who would listen that it was her birthday. Texans bought her drinks, and she had spent the night whirling around the dance floor with a dozen or more trailhands. Short of a public quarrel, he saw no way to stop her.

"What do you think, Doc?"

Thompson's voice intruded on his woolgathering. He looked around. "I confess my mind was elsewhere, Ben. Did you say something?"

"Frank and me figured to grab a bite to eat. How about you?"

"Yes, of course. I'll just reclaim Kate. A meal would do her good."

Thompson and Loving exchanged a look. They were seasoned gamblers, and gunmen of some repute, and they felt a kinship with Holliday. Yet their respect for him was tempered by his relationship with Kate. In their opinion, he treated her with far more consideration than she deserved. Neither of them believed she was worth the effort.

Kate and the cowhand were the only couple on the dance floor. Holliday caught them in a slow turn and took her arm. "Time to go," he said. "The party's over."

"C'mon, Doc, not yet," she said in a woozy voice. "I'm just getting started."

"You heard me, Kate. Let's go."

"For chrissakes! You sure know how to spoil a girl's fun."

The cowhand released her, stepping back. Like every Texan in town, he was unwilling to provoke the anger of Doc Holliday. Stories around the campfire had it that the consumptive gambler, though frail and wasted, was sudden death with a gun. He watched as Holliday dragged her off the dance floor.

"Damn you anyway!" she screeched. "You're an ol' stick-in-the-mud, Doc. The night's still young."

"Behave yourself and act like a lady."

"I keep trying to tell you—I'm not a lady!"

Holliday led the way out of the saloon. On the street, with Thompson and Loving following along, he walked Kate to an all-night cafe on Second Avenue. She was still fussing and complaining as he got her seated at a table. A waiter came over, and the men ordered steak with fried potatoes and biscuits. Kate refused the thought of food, and Holliday told the waiter to bring her black coffee, lots of it. She lapsed into a pouty sulk.

A short while later Wyatt Earp came through the door. He started toward the counter, then saw them, and walked to the table. " 'Evening," he said, nodding to them in turn. "You folks calling it a night?"

"An end to the festivities," Holliday said with a trace of irony. "We are celebrating Kate's birthday."

"Congratulations," Earp said, smiling at Kate. "Many happy returns."

"Yeah, sure," she replied in a huffy manner. "All I need is a birthday cake. Fat chance of that."

There was a moment of strained silence. Holliday finally broke the tension. "Won't you join us, Wyatt? Always room for one more."

"Thanks all the same, Doc. I just stopped off for a cup of coffee. Still got to make my rounds."

"Another time, then."

"Sounds good."

Earp crossed to the counter, straddling a stool. The meal continued in silence, with Kate pointedly ignoring Holliday. A few minutes later, Earp dropped a coin on the counter and went out the door. Thompson shoveled potatoes into his mouth, chewing thoughtfully. He looked across at Holliday.

"You mind a personal question?"

"Not at all." Holliday shoved his plate away, the steak barely touched. "Ask me anything."

"Everybody's wondering how you and Earp got to be such chums. Whole town's talking about it."

"Do you find it unnatural, Ben?"

Thompson was stoutly built, with a walrus mustache and piercing eyes. He feared no man, and considered himself any man's equal with a gun. But he was nonetheless careful not to offend Holliday. He lifted his fork in a shrug.

"You'll have to admit it's not ordinary. I mean, you being who you are."

Holliday lit a cigarillo. "I suppose you have a point. Wyatt wears a badge and I wear a crown of infamy." He paused, exhaling smoke. "An unlikely pair, hmmm?"

"After a fashion," Thompson said, nodding. "Lawmen don't usually have much truck with our sort."

"True." Holliday's gaze went to Loving. "Are you curious as well, Frank?"

Loving shook his head. "Your business is your business, Doc. I tend to my own knittin'."

"An admirable trait." Holliday fixed Thompson with an enigmatic smile. "To answer your question, there is no answer. Wyatt and I choose to be friends." He tapped an ash off his cigarillo. "Who knows why?"

Thompson laughed. "You're a corker, Doc. Never saw your like."

"I sincerely hope not."

Later, walking toward the hotel, Kate gave Holliday a sullen look. "You ought to listen to your real friends. Ben Thompson was trying to give you a warning." She sniffed.

"Nobody in our crowd likes Earp worth a damn."

"Let me give you some worthwhile advice. Never question a man's choice of friends. Yours is not to reason why."

"You make that sound like a threat, or something."

"Kate, you are more sober than you appear."

Holliday was shaving when Kate awoke. A shaft of sunlight from the window blinded her and she put an arm across her eyes. Her head throbbed with a dull hangover.

"God," she moaned. "Close the curtains."

"Time to get up, lazybones. Let's go."

"I think I'm dying."

"Small wonder." Holliday held his jawline tight, stroked with the razor. "Fortunately, you have only one birthday a year."

She licked her lips. "I need a drink."

"What you need is a solid meal. Get out of bed and get dressed. I'll take you to breakfast."

"What time is it?"

"Going on two o'clock."

She groaned, levering herself upright, and sat on the edge of the bed. She shielded her eyes from the sun. "How come you never have a hangover? Not natural, the way you drink."

"I have a covenant with John Barleycorn."

Holliday dried his face, then moved to the bedstand. He poured a small dollop of bourbon into a glass and handed it to her. "A bracer to get you started. Don't ask for more."

She drank it down greedily. "I think you just saved my life."

"Yes, I am widely known for good deeds."

Holliday waited while she took a sponge bath. She brushed her hair, applied rouge to her cheeks, and got herself dressed. When they walked from the room, she looked presentable if not altogether steady on her feet. Her eyes were still slightly bloodshot.

Downstairs, the desk clerk handed Holliday a letter. The stationery as well as the delicate penmanship was familiar.

Kate recognized it even as Holliday stuffed the envelope into his pocket. Her eyes flared, but he quickly hustled her into the dining room and got her seated. A waitress took their breakfast orders.

"Don't mind me," Kate said testily, as the waitress turned away. "Go ahead and read your love note."

"No rush," Holliday said. "I'll wait till later."

"Oh, don't be bashful, Doc. See what your Georgia sweetheart has to say. I'm sure it's just too precious for words."

"Sarcasm does not become you. Let's hear no more of it."

"You've got a hell of a nerve! How do you think I'm supposed to feel?"

" 'The fault is not in our stars. But in ourselves.' "

"What?"

"Shakespeare," Holliday remarked. "A line from *Julius Caesar.*"

"So?" she demanded. "What's your point?"

"You allow yourself to get carried away with emotion. You have no reason to be jealous."

"Prove it! Quit with your fancy quotes and prove it. Ask me to marry you."

Holliday looked uncomfortable. "All in good time, Kate."

"To hell with time!" Her eyes darkened with anger. "Ask me now or I swear to God I'll go back on the line. I mean it."

"Extortion hardly makes for a sound marriage."

"Does that mean no?"

"Yes," Holliday said brusquely. "That's exactly what it means."

She slammed out of her chair. Before Holliday could stop her, she marched from the dining room and through the lobby to the street door. The other diners gave him a strange look, and in the next instant, the waitress appeared. Her eyes were questioning as she placed the plates on the table.

"Don't worry about it," he said casually. "I eat enough for two."

Holliday was unconcerned. Kate was temperamental, but in the end, she always came to her senses. He took out the letter, opening the envelope, and began reading as he salted his eggs. The contents were much as he expected, an expression of unwavering hope mixed with a belief in divine intervention. Time had done nothing to rob Mattie of her determination, or alter the depth of her feelings. She refused to take his hints, to read between the lines of his letters. She would never give up hope.

Brooding on it, he ordered another cup of coffee. He refolded the letter, shoving it into his pocket, and took out his flask. As he laced the coffee with bourbon, Luke Short suddenly burst through the door of the dining room. The gambler hurried forward, halting at the table. His features were grim.

"Doc, you'd better come quick. Kate's over at the Long Branch raising holy hell."

"Women," Holliday grunted with disgust, rising from his chair. "What's she doing?"

"Well, for one thing, she's guzzling liquor like there's no tomorrow. For another, she's offering to turn tricks for anybody with the right price. That's not allowed north of the Deadline."

"What she needs is a good switching. Lead the way, Luke."

A few minutes later they walked into the Long Branch. Kate was at the bar, arguing loudly with Chalk Beeson, the owner. When he saw Holliday, he stepped around her, rushing forward. His face was mottled with indignation.

"Get her out of here, Doc," he said, motioning wildly. "Otherwise I'll have her arrested."

"No need for that." Holliday brushed past him, taking hold of Kate's arm. "Don't say a word or you'll regret it. Come along."

Her eyes were glazed with drink. "Lemme go! Lemme go!"

Holliday abruptly stopped. Levi Richardson, a gambler of small repute, stood at the door with a pistol in his hand. A deathly silence settled over the saloon as customers at the bar, and those ranged along the gaming tables, scattered for cover. Richardson was known to have a running feud with Frank Loving.

"Time to settle accounts, Loving! Defend yourself."

Loving, who was dealing faro at the rear of the room, moved from behind his table. He halted beside a potbelly stove as Richardson raised his pistol, fanning the hammer with the heel of his left hand. The reports blended together, slugs thunking into the stove and crashing through the back wall. Richardson fanned off five shots before Loving was able to draw his gun. Untouched, Loving coolly sighted, and fired three spaced shots.

The slugs pocked red splotches along the front of Richardson's shirt. He reeled backward under the impact, dropping his empty pistol, and bounced off the wall beside the door. The light went out in his eyes and he slumped to a bloody heap on the floor. There was a moment of prolonged silence, and then the crowd broke out in cheers for Frank Loving. The faro dealer took a bow.

Holliday marched Kate toward the door. As he passed the body, he was reminded again that speed in a gunfight inevitably took second place to deliberation and accuracy. On the boardwalk, Kate began struggling, trying to free herself. Holliday gripped her arm in a viselock.

"I want you to stop acting like an alley cat. Get hold of yourself."

"Dammit, Doc, you're never going to change me. Why don't you give it up?"

"You are my hair shirt, Kate. I wear you for penance."

"Your Georgia peach sure put the guilt on you. What'd her letter say?"

Holliday managed a sphinxlike expression. Yet he thought her comment was a perceptive retort. One that struck much too close to home. He walked on toward the hotel.

CHAPTER 25

A dwarf on roller skates whizzed around the stage. Dressed in a clown costume, his face was painted white with crimson cheeks and a bulbous red nose. He leaped into the air and performed a flying, head-over-heels somersault, landing smoothly on his skates. Arms pumping, he rocketed upstage. The crowd roared approval. Texan trailhands, who packed the theater, had never seen anything like it. The Comique was combination saloon and gaming dive, with a spacious theater at the rear of the building. The variety acts were imported from around the country, some from as far away as New York. There was rarely an empty seat in the house.

Lloyd Franklin, owner of the Comique, personally escorted Holliday and Kate through the crowd. Their reserved table was down front, positioned directly before center stage. Franklin got them seated, snapping his fingers at a waiter, who quickly produced bourbon for Holliday and a bottle of iced champagne for Kate. Heads turned when the waiter popped the cork.

Onstage, the dwarf glided full speed in a circle, balanced on one leg, his arms outstretched. Then, sailing toward the footlights, he executed a dizzying pirouette, spinning round and round on the toe of one skate. He suddenly snapped to a stop in mid-spin, his tiny arms flung overhead, his clown's face gleeful in a peg-toothed grin. The audience applauded madly as he bowed and waved, skating backward offstage.

Kate clapped with merry abandon. Holliday watched, amused by her childlike antics, as a line of cancan dancers exploded out of the wings. For the past week, since her tantrum over Mattie's letter, he had devoted part of every evening to keeping her entertained. Sometimes he took her dancing, and other times they spent a few hours drinking and socializing with friends among the sporting crowd. By late evening, despite her grumbling protests, he escorted her back to the hotel room. He then went in search of a poker game.

Holliday understood that she was bored. She missed the excitement of saloons and dance halls, the carefree gaiety of the sporting life. Her only friends were below the Deadline, for the respectable women of Dodge City would have nothing to do with a former whore. Though he lavished her with fashionable clothes and fine jewelry, her manners, and her language, were still those of a saloon girl. She was simply out of her element with the uptown crowd. She longed for revelry and wild times.

Yet he was determined to transform her into a lady. He was fond of her, and though marriage was not a serious consideration, he nonetheless wanted a respectable woman to share his bed. On a deeper level he realized that he was trying to replace Mattie, to rid himself of demons. Still, as a practical matter, Kate was trustworthy, loyal in her own way, and a good companion. So long as he gave her attention, she said nothing more about going back on the line, and that seemed a step in the right direction. He was willing to make the effort to keep her straight.

The chorus line kicked and squealed, flashing their legs, and pranced offstage to thunderous applause from the crowd. The headline act was Eddie Foy, a song-and-dance man from the variety circuit back East, and the house was packed for his opening night. As the girls disappeared into the wings, the orchestra segued into a sprightly tune, with the horns muted and the strings more pronounced. Eddie Foy skipped onstage, tipping his derby to the audience, and went into a shuffling soft-shoe routine. The sound of his

light feet on the floor was like velvety sandpaper.

Foy was short and wiry, with ginger hair and an infectious smile. Halfway through the routine, he began singing a bawdy ballad that brought bursts of laughter from the trail-hands. He ended the soft-shoe number at center stage, and the orchestra fell silent with a last note of the strings. Framed in the footlights, he walked back and forth with herky-jerky movements, delivering a rapid comedic patter that was at once risqué and hilarious. The Texans honked and hooted with rolling waves of laughter.

On the heels of a last, riotous joke, the orchestra suddenly blared to life. Foy nimbly sprang into a high-stepping buck-and-wing dance routine that took him cavorting around the stage. Toward the end of the number, his voice raised in a madcap shout, he belted out the lyrics to a naughty tune involving a girl and her one-legged lover. His rubbery face stretched wide in a grin, he whirled, clicking his heels in midair, and skipped offstage with a final tip of his derby. The audience whistled and cheered, rocking the walls with ovation. Foy, bouncing merrily onto the stage, took three curtain calls.

"Holy Hannah!" Kate cried, her eyes bright with excitement. "Wasn't that the greatest thing you ever saw, Doc? He's wonderful!"

"A true jester," Holliday agreed. "He even made me laugh."

"Sugar, that makes him the funniest man alive. You're the original stoneface."

"Why, Kate, you strike to the quick. I've always thought myself a man of some humor."

"Oh sure," she mugged. "You keep me in stitches day and night."

Her face was suddenly arrested in shock. Lloyd Franklin halted at the table with Eddie Foy at his side. He waved a hand in introduction. "Eddie, I'd like you to meet a couple of friends. This here's Doc Holliday and Miss Kate Elder."

"A pleasure," Foy said genially. "Hope you enjoyed the show."

"We did, indeed," Holliday replied. "Won't you join us for a drink, Mr. Foy?"

"I'd be delighted. Dee-lighted. But only if you call me Eddie. Mr. Foy was my father."

To Kate's amazement, the entertainer dropped into a chair. Then, as Franklin walked away, she caught him nodding to Holliday with a sly wink. Even more astounded, she realized that there was nothing impromptu about the introduction. Holliday had arranged it.

A waiter materialized with another glass, and Holliday poured champagne for Kate and Foy. He lifted his own glass in a toast. "Welcome to Dodge City, Eddie. I think it safe to say you've taken the town by storm."

"Has he ever!" Kate bubbled. "You were just marvelous. I never saw anybody so light on their feet."

Foy smiled modestly. "A little of this and a little of that. A hoofer's stock-in-trade."

"Are you kidding? I used to be a dancer myself. I know a headliner when I see one."

"How about that, a fellow hoofer! Were you a solo act?"

"No, no." She shot Holliday a warning look. "I always performed with a partner, sort of a duo. That was before Doc retired me."

Holliday thought it a harmless lie. "Kate has a gift for ballroom dancing. I'm afraid I ended a promising career."

"Don't take it too hard." Foy patted her hand. "The variety circuit is a real grind, believe me. You're better off with a good man."

"Amen to that," she said with heavy irony. "Doc's made a regular little homemaker out of me."

"Domesticity becomes Kate," Holliday said lightly. He looked at Foy. "I understand you're from New York."

"Wonderful place, New York. You should visit it sometime, Doc. You're famous back there."

"So I've been told."

"Well—" Foy sensed he'd hit a nerve. "Hope I didn't

speak out of line. You know how newspapers are. Never get the facts straight.''

"Those rags!" Kate said with a grand air. "They don't know half the things Doc's done. Isn't that right, sugar?''

Holliday ignored her. "Is this your first trip west, Eddie?''

Foy brightened. "First trip to the Wild West. Quite an experience.''

"What is your impression of Dodge City?''

"Wild and woolly, just like I've always heard. They ought to rename it Baghdad on the Plains.''

"Certainly apropos," Holliday acknowledged. "We have our share of sin and sinners.''

"The more the merrier," Foy said. "I've never played to a better audience! These cowboys are just great.''

"You're pretty swell yourself," Kate marveled. "How long will you play Dodge?''

"I'm booked through July. Hope you'll catch my act again.''

"You bet your boots we will. Doc loves the theater, don't you, sweetie?''

Holliday spread his hands. "I am a patron of the arts, Eddie. You will see us here often.''

"Champagne's on me next time." Foy hitched back his chair. "Sorry to drink and run, but I have to get ready for the next show. It's been a pleasure. A real honor.''

Kate laughed. "The honor's all ours. Good luck, Eddie.''

Foy waved, moving off through the crowd. Holliday dropped money on the table, and Kate rose from her chair. She took his arm as they walked from the theater through the saloon. Dealers at the gaming tables nodded to Holliday, and cowhands along the bar cast admiring glances at Kate. She vamped them with a bright smile.

Outside, Holliday turned uptown. The boardwalks were jammed with Texans, and the sound of laughter and music mingled all along Second Avenue. As they moved through the teeming crowds, Kate kept peering into the doorways of

saloons and dance halls. Finally, her mouth downturned, she let out a deep sigh.

"Sugar, it's still early. Couldn't we stop for a drink somewhere? Maybe a couple of dances."

"I have a game awaiting me at the Long Branch. Perhaps tomorrow night."

She grimaced. "C'mon, have a heart, Doc. I'm tired of sitting in that room. A girl's got to live a little!"

"You've done quite well," Holliday remarked. "A show and champagne, not to mention meeting Eddie Foy. All in all, a pleasant evening."

"Yeah, I know, and that's fine as far as it goes. But what about the rest of the night? You expect me to sit around and twiddle my thumbs?"

"I expect you to be content with what you have, Kate. Don't try my patience."

"Your patience!" she screeched. "For chrissakes, you've all but got me in chains. I'm bored silly!"

Holliday looked at her. "Perhaps you should take up reading. Charles Dickens, or maybe Longfellow. It would improve your mind."

"What the hell's wrong with my mind?"

"Nothing a sampling of literature wouldn't cure."

"Next thing you'll want me to start attending sewing bees and church socials."

"Not a bad idea," Holliday said, chuckling. "God does love a sinner."

Gunfire sounded a short distance ahead. As they approached the Lady Gay saloon, they saw two trailhands standing in the middle of the street. The men were clearly tanked on rotgut whiskey, and out to tree the town. One raised his pistol overhead and fired.

"I'm a curly wolf from the Brazos. Lemme howl!"

"Whooeee!" the other one bellowed, firing his gun into the air. "We done cut the wolf loose!"

Ed Masterson, the town marshal, rushed out of a nearby gaming parlor. He crossed the street, slowing to a steady walk as he approached the cowhands. One was tall and

lanky, and the other was of medium height, stoutly built. He halted in front of them.

"You've had your fun, boys," he said in a firm voice. "Nobody's hurt and I aim to keep it that way. Let's have those guns."

"Like hell!" the tall one growled. "I ain't fixin' to spend the night in jail."

"No way around it. Town ordinance says there's no shootin' in the streets. Don't give me any trouble."

"Trouble's my middle name! Just lemme be, goddamn you."

Masterson grabbed his gun arm. The cowhand grappled with him and there was a muffled explosion. Shot in the stomach, his shirt on fire from the muzzle blast, Masterson staggered backward. He pulled his pistol, fire licking around his belt buckle, a ghastly expression etched on his face. The Texans were jarred out of their stupor as his pistol came level. An instant too late, they raised their guns. He triggered four shots in a blinding roar.

A slug caught the tall cowhand in the chest, and he went down with a strangled grunt. The shorter one was struck in the arm, the shoulder, and the chest, lurching backward under the impact. Yet he somehow kept his balance, wobbling across the street, and collapsed in the doorway of a saloon. Masterson stood there a moment, watching them, casually brushing out the flames on his shirt. His eyes suddenly went blank, and the pistol slipped from his hand. He slumped to the ground.

Upstreet, Bat Masterson bulled through the crowd and sprinted forward. A short distance behind, Wyatt Earp rounded the corner onto Second Avenue at a dead run. By the time he reached them, Masterson was on his knees beside his brother. The sharp odor of blood mixed with burnt cloth steamed off the body. Masterson stared down into his brother's sightless eyes.

"Sonsabitches!" He hammered the earth with a fist. "They killed him."

"Not any consolation," Earp said gently, "but he got

The page number 208 and "Matt Braun" is at the top - running header.

them, too. You wait here, Bat. I'll have a look.''

Earp checked the cowhand in the street, then walked to the door of Peacock's Saloon. As he turned away from the second body, he saw Holliday and Kate standing at the front of the crowd. He motioned them forward, nodding to Holliday. His voice was raspy.

"You see what happened here, Doc?"

"The marshal tried to disarm them. The tall one shot him and he still popped off four rounds. Do you know them?"

"Yeah, I know them," Earp grated. "Alf Walker and Jack Wagner. We've had them in jail three times since they hit town."

"Four times was too much," Holliday observed. "They were determined not to be jailed again."

"Bastards," Earp muttered. "Guess they got their wish."

"Yes, the hard way," Holliday said. "Offer Bat my sincere condolences. His brother was quite a man."

"I'll tell him, Doc."

Earp moved into the street and knelt beside Masterson. Holliday threaded a path through the crowd, and led Kate toward the Deadline. As they crossed the railroad track, she glanced up at him. Her expression was bemused.

"What's with the condolences? Bat Masterson doesn't have any love for you."

"Nor I for him," Holliday noted. "That's hardly the point."

"Then what is the point?"

"A friend of a friend, Kate. Nothing more, nothing less."

She thought it more than less, but held her silence. Wyatt Earp was one argument she would never win.

CHAPTER 26

Four men, sweltering in the July heat, sat around the poker table. The hour was late, and only a few of the gaming layouts were still in play. Apart from Holliday, who never removed his coat, the men were playing in their shirtsleeves. Their features were beaded with perspiration.

Earlier that night, at his usual table in the Long Branch, Holliday had organized a high-stakes game. By two in the morning, a Texas rancher and a cattle buyer, both heavy losers, had dropped out. Those remaining were Dog Kelly, the mayor of Dodge City, and a couple of wealthy cattlemen. The Texans were out of their league.

Jim Kelly owned the Alhambra Saloon, located in the next block along the plaza. Elected mayor last fall, he was universally known as Dog because he operated greyhound races outside town every Saturday afternoon. He made it a practice never to gamble in his own establishment, and usually played three or four nights a week at the Long Branch. He was considered one of the better poker players in Dodge.

Holliday was dealing five-card stud. He looked across at Kelly, who was high on the board. "Pair of nines bets. That's you, Dog."

"Not too proud of nines," Kelly said, thumbing a bill from his stack. "I'll just bet twenty."

The rancher beside him debated a moment. His high card was a ten, and everyone knew he had another one in the

hole. He tossed bills into the pot. "Raise you fifty."

Holliday folded, and the Texan seated next to him dropped out. Kelly deliberated on the raise a moment, and finally, with an air of some reluctance, he called. Holliday dealt the last card, a queen to Kelly and an eight to the rancher. After peeking at his hole card, Kelly mopped sweat from his face with a handkerchief. He checked the bet.

"The worm turns," said the rancher with a gloating laugh. "Cost you a hundred to stay in."

A hundred dollars was the table limit. Kelly stared at the Texan's hand a few seconds, then shrugged. "Just can't convince myself you've got tens. Have to raise you a hundred."

"Well, pardner, I say I got 'em. Your hundred and bump it a hundred."

"What the hell, I've gone this far. I'll take the last raise."

Holliday admired a craftsman who was able to sucker the other player. He watched as the rancher, certain of a winner, called the raise. Dog Kelly flipped his hole card, a trey, which matched one on the board and gave him two pair. His mouth quirked in a faint smile.

"Nines and treys."

"You sandbagged me!" the Texan hollered. "Flat talked me out of three hundred."

"It's only money," Kelly said smoothly, raking in the pot. "Where else could you have so much fun?"

"Who the hell's havin' fun? You just cost me ten cows."

"Yeah, but longhorns breed quick. Look on the bright side."

Kelly's comment was grounded in fact. On the holding grounds outside town, a sea of longhorns awaited shipment to Eastern slaughterhouses. More herds were arriving daily, and the Santa Fe estimated that three hundred thousand cows would be driven to railhead by the end of the trailing season. Texas cattlemen would collect something on the order of nine million dollars—and a good part of it would be

spent in Dodge City. All of which made it a banner year for the Queen of Cowtowns.

Yet there was a darker side to the boom times. The death of Ed Masterson, and the two trailhands he'd killed, had heightened antagonism between the Texans and town officials. In the month since the shootout, ugly rumors had surfaced of a loosely organized plot among the cattle outfits camped outside Dodge City. Word had it that the Texans meant to exact revenge for the deaths of the trailhands, even though their rowdy behavior had provoked the incident. Dog Kelly had fanned the flames by roughly ejecting a drunken cowhand from the Alhambra.

The Texans' general animosity was directed toward the town's lawmen. But Jim Kennedy, the cowboy manhandled by Kelly, added the mayor to the list of those targeted for reprisal. Not quite two weeks ago, late at night, Kennedy emptied his revolver through the bedroom wall of the mayor's house. The bedroom was occupied not by Kelly, but rather two saloon girls who worked at the Alhambra. One of them, Dora Hand, was killed in the blast of gunfire. Jim Kennedy, thinking he'd killed the mayor, lit out for Texas.

Before dawn, Bat Masterson and Wyatt Earp, along with two other deputies, rode south in pursuit. Late the next day they overtook Kennedy at a ford on the Cimarron River, in Indian Territory. The Texan elected to fight, and in the ensuing shootout, he was wounded and captured. Upon being returned to Dodge City, wealthy cattlemen provided Kennedy with a lawyer, who got him freed on the grounds that there were no witnesses to the murder of Dora Hand. Kennedy wisely departed for Texas the same day.

The upshot was even deeper antagonism. Dog Kelly, who by mere happenstance had escaped assassination, ordered harsh enforcement of town ordinances. Charlie Bassett, a political appointee who had replaced Ed Masterson as marshal, gave his deputies a free hand. Earp and the other lawmen were quick to respond to the slightest infraction, often with brute force. Below the Deadline disorderly Texans

were now routinely "buffaloed," a practice which involved cracking a man across the skull with a pistol barrel. The jailhouse was full every night.

Tonight, watching Dog Kelly rake in the pot, Holliday was amused by life's smaller ironies. He thought it somehow symbolic that the mayor of Dodge City was trimming Texas cattlemen at a poker table. In the larger scheme of things, he considered himself an impartial observer, almost a spectator. He had no fondness for the law, and apart from Wyatt Earp, he felt no great concern for the fate of the town's lawmen. Who won and who lost in the struggle between rebellious trailhands and peace officers was a matter of passing interest. A touch of anarchy merely added spice to the brew.

From a personal standpoint, he found life's little ironies even more amusing. A marshal and two cowhands had been killed, not to mention the aborted assassination attempt on the mayor. Yet, during his two months in town, he hadn't once drawn his gun, much less killed anyone. In part, his reputation discouraged trouble, and to avoid embarrassing Earp, he was not so quick to take offense. Still, after a hard night of gambling, he sometimes awoke wondering at his newfound flair for tact and diplomacy. He felt all but slated for sainthood.

The rancher seated beside him dealt a hand of five-card draw. Holliday spread his cards, his expression betraying nothing, and found himself holding three sixes. Kelly opened for fifty, and the other cattleman, clearly pleased with his hand, raised fifty. Holliday placed his cards on the table, sorting through bills.

"Get out while you can, gentlemen," he said in a genially confident tone. "I call the opener and the raise . . . and raise a hundred."

The other men stared at him like three owls contemplating a shared mystery. Over the course of the night he had bluffed relentlessly, and he'd been caught out twice, losing large pots. Whether he was bluffing now was a question the

other players pondered at length. His jovial confidence led them to fool themselves.

"I'll call," said the rancher to his left. "That's two hundred to me."

Kelly chuckled. "Doc, just to make it interesting, I'll take the last raise. Pony up another hundred."

"You're not runnin' me out," the other Texan said curtly. "I see the raises and wish't there was one left."

Holliday dropped a hundred on the table. "I do admire sporting blood. Your donations are most welcome, gentlemen."

The dealer called. On the draw, Kelly took three cards and the rancher to his left took one. Holliday kept four, holding the three sixes and a king, leading them to believe he had two pair. He suspected the cattleman on his right, who was a conservative player, actually held two pair. The dealer dealt himself three cards.

Wyatt Earp came through the door. He waved to Luke Short, who had one player at his faro layout, and walked back to the poker table. He halted, taking in the pot at a glance, and looked around at the players. " 'Evening, gents," he said, nodding to them in turn. "You've got yourselves a nice pot there."

"And Doc's trying to buy it," Kelly said with a grin. "Has some notion his two pair will hold up."

Holliday looked wounded. "Dog, where are your poker manners? Would I tell the table you have only a pair?"

"You just did!" Kelly took a quick peek at his cards. "Well, would you look at that. I think I've drawn the winning hand."

"Bet 'em, then," the dealer said. "You're the opener."

"Good idea," Kelly said with great bravado. "Run for the hills, boys. Opener bets a hundred."

"Your hundred"—the Texan next to him spread bills on the table—"and reckon I'll raise you a hundred. Who's runnin' now?"

Holliday squeezed his cards apart. He forced himself not to smile, or blink. On the draw, he'd caught a king, which

gave him a full house. ''In for a penny, in for a pound,''
he said with a trace of resignation. ''Call the two hundred
and . . . raise a hundred.''

The dealer chortled aloud. ''You gents damn sure better
have the goods. I'll just take the last raise.''

''Three hundred to me,'' Kelly said, flinging money into
the pot. ''Let's see what you're so proud of.''

The cattleman dealing spread his hand. ''Read 'em and
weep! Three jacks.''

''Christ on a crutch,'' Kelly cursed, turning over three
tens. ''Talk about being nosed out. Jesus!''

''Hell, don't bellyache.'' The other Texan tossed his cards
in the deadwood. ''Two pair was suckin' hind tit.''

Holliday started to reveal his hand. Before he could move,
Jim Masterson burst through the door and hurried toward
the table. The youngest of the Masterson clan, he had been
hired as a deputy when his brother was killed. He halted
beside Earp.

''Got trouble, Wyatt,'' he said, catching his breath.
''Some cowhands over at the Lady Gay are fixin' to cross
the Deadline. They're on the prod.''

''How'd you get wind of it?''

''Bartender snuck out and found me on the street. He says
somebody told 'em you're over here.''

''Hold on,'' Kelly interrupted. ''Are you saying they're
out to get Wyatt?''

''Sounds that way,'' Masterson affirmed. ''They likely
know Bat's off chasin' train robbers. Figured Wyatt was the
next best thing.''

''Where's Marshal Bassett?''

''Home in bed,'' Earp said with a tinge of sarcasm.
''You'll recall, Charlie doesn't work the night shift.''

''Well, roust him out,'' Kelly ordered. ''Get the day dep-
uties up, too. Let's have a show of force.''

''No need for that,'' Earp told him. ''These boys are
probably all wind and no whistle. Jim and me can handle
it.''

''What if they're serious, though? I ignored all the talk

about threats from Kennedy. Dirty bastard did his best to kill me.''

The two Texans at the table were listening with rapt attention. When Earp glanced at them, they hastily averted their eyes. He looked back at Kelly. "We'll scout around and see what's what. Might turn out to be nothing."

Earp nodded to Masterson, and they walked toward the door. After a moment, clearly flustered, Kelly motioned around the table. "Think I'll call it a night. Where'd we leave off?"

"With me," Holliday said, fanning his cards on the table. "I have a small full house. Sixes over kings."

"Looks pretty big to me," Kelly said. "You won yourself a nice pot, Doc."

The cattleman with the three jacks angrily brushed his cards aside. "Sat here and dealt myself second-best. Damn the luck, anyway!"

Holliday reached for the pot. From outside, the drumming thud of hoofbeats sounded across the stillness of the plaza. Across the room he saw Earp and Masterson move through the door. He kicked back his chair, registering the startled expressions of everyone in the saloon, and quickly circled the table. He was halfway to the entrance when the roar of gunshots split the night.

A window shattered and slugs drilled through the front wall of the saloon. Holliday was aware of men diving for cover as he drew his Peacemaker and stopped beside the door. Outside, their pistols at shoulder level, he saw Earp and Masterson returning fire on four horsemen some thirty yards away. The riders and their mounts were limned in faint starlight, the muzzle blasts from their guns flaming through the dark. Lead sizzled all around the lawmen.

Three of the riders suddenly whirled their horses and galloped off into the night. The fourth horseman triggered two rapid shots, then wheeled his mount and rammed hard with his spurs. Earp dropped to one knee, sighting along the barrel of his pistol, the rider silhouetted against the starlit sky. When he fired, the man straightened, arms flung outward,

and pitched sideways out of the saddle. The horse pounded across the plaza.

Earp walked forward, Masterson at his side. They cautiously approached the fallen horseman, stooping down to inspect the body. Satisfied that he was dead, they stood talking a moment, staring off into the night where the other riders had disappeared. Then Earp holstered his pistol and turned back toward the Long Branch. Holliday stepped through the door.

"Your lucky night," he said equably. "I wonder that you weren't hit."

"Goddamn cowhands," Earp said crossly. "Good thing they opened up at a distance. Otherwise I'd look like a sieve."

"Distance doesn't noticeably spoil your aim. You made quite a shot."

"Tell you the truth, I never figured to drop him. Surprised myself."

Dog Kelly rushed through the door of the saloon. "Jesus Christ, Wyatt! Sounded like a war out here. What happened?"

"Four cowhands looking for trouble. One dead and three got away."

"You think that'll stir up a hornet's nest?"

"I'd say the hornets are already loose."

"So what's to be done?"

"Whatever they try, give it back to them in spades. Right, Doc?"

Holliday smiled. "No question about it. Tit for tat."

Kelly groaned and walked back into the Long Branch.

CHAPTER 27

The bell over the door tinkled. Holliday was seated in a barber's chair, an apron pinned around his neck. He looked in the mirror and saw Dog Kelly enter the shop. The barber stopped snipping.

" 'Afternoon, Mr. Mayor," he said, motioning with his scissors. "Have a seat, won't be long. You're next."

There were no other customers in the shop. Kelly nodded to Holliday in the mirror. "Doc, how's tricks?"

"Win some, lose some, Dog. How is it with you?"

"No complaints." Kelly moved to a row of straight-backed chairs along the wall. "Fact is, maybe it's a little too quiet."

"Are you referring to the Texans?"

"Well, nobody else causes me to lose sleep. Just too damn quiet since that last dustup. Not natural."

Holliday smiled. "You sound superstitious."

The barber paused, interested in the answer. Kelly wagged one hand back and forth. "I'm no more superstitious than the next man. But I'm leery of too much good luck."

Some two weeks had passed since the shooting outside the Long Branch. The dead cowhand had been buried in Boot Hill, with over a hundred Texans attending the funeral. But there had been no retaliation against the town's lawmen,

or the mayor. All of Dodge City seemed to be waiting for the next move.

"Perhaps you overestimate them," Holliday said. "Even Texans are susceptible to common sense."

Kelly's brow wrinkled in a frown. "What's common sense got to do with anything?"

"Three cowhands have been killed this summer. Maybe they've decided it's a losing proposition."

"You think they've pulled in their horns?"

"I wouldn't be surprised," Holliday observed. "Their record against Dodge City lawmen isn't all that impressive."

"Hope to hell you're right, Doc."

The barber removed the apron. "All finished, Mr. Holliday. How does it look?"

Holliday rose from the chair. He dug a coin from his pocket, studying himself in the mirror. "You give a nice haircut," he said, turning toward Kelly. "Try not to worry so much, Dog. Things usually work out in the end."

Kelly snorted. "I'll just be glad when trailing season is over. I could use a good night's sleep."

Holliday suddenly coughed, phlegm rattling in his throat. He pulled out his flask, took a long slug, and returned it to his pocket. After a deep breath, he wiped his mouth with a handkerchief, moving toward the door. He waved to Kelly.

"Drop by the Long Branch tonight. We'll have a game."

"Maybe I will," Kelly said, as he climbed into the barber's chair. "See you around, Doc."

Holliday collected his hat from a wall peg. Outside, he turned upstreet and walked in the direction of the hotel. A blistering noonday sun hung over the town, heat waves radiating across the distant plains. At the corner, he met Earp crossing the intersection. The lawman nodded pleasantly.

"You're out early, Doc. What's the occasion?"

"Nothing more momentous than a haircut. Kelly came in as I was leaving. He seems fixated with Texans."

Earp shook his head. "Our mayor jumps at his own shadow. You'd think we were in a war."

"To hear him tell it," Holliday agreed. "What's your opinion?"

"I've got a hunch it's yesterday's news. Things are pretty much back to normal on the South Side."

"Exactly what I told Dog. Three dead cowhands send a convincing message."

" 'Course, there's always next year," Earp said in a jocular tone. "Texans tend to have short memories."

"Take it one day at a time, that's my motto. Who knows what the morrow brings?"

A startled expression suddenly came over Holliday's face. Earp saw the color leach from his features and followed the direction of his gaze. An attractive young woman, led by a depot porter carrying her bags, was crossing the opposite side of the intersection. He glanced back at Holliday.

"You look like you've seen a ghost, Doc. Something wrong?"

"I fear it's people who haunt our lives, not ghosts. You'll have to excuse me, Wyatt."

Holliday hurried off. His stride increased as he crossed the street and mounted the opposite boardwalk. He overtook the woman and the porter as they turned into the entrance of the Dodge House Hotel. He was breathing heavily when he entered the lobby.

"Mattie."

She turned at the sound of his voice. Her first impression was that of a man so thin he appeared emaciated. Some two years had passed since their parting, but she was unprepared for the change. His features were gaunt and haggard, with dark circles under his eyes. His clothes, unlike the somber attire he'd worn in Atlanta, were hardly less colorful than a peacock. She tried to hide her shock.

"John, it's you," she said, holding out her hand. "Oh, it's so good to see you."

"God, I couldn't believe my eyes." Holliday took her hand, suddenly awkward and fumbling for words. "Where did you come from? What are you doing here?"

"I had to come, John. I simply couldn't bear to wait any longer . . . no more letters."

"Why didn't you wire me, let me know?"

"I was afraid." She averted her gaze. "Afraid you would leave, if you knew I was coming here."

"I—" Holliday was at a loss for a reply. "Well, why don't we get you settled into the hotel?"

The porter was still waiting with her luggage. Holliday gave him five dollars, and then walked her to the registration desk. All the while his mind was riveted on the scene Kate would make if she happened into the lobby. At Holliday's insistence, the clerk gave her a ground-floor room, and wisely made no comment when she signed the register "Miss Mattie Holliday." He agreed to have her bags taken to the room.

Holliday escorted her into the dining room. The noontime crowd was clearing out, and they found a table in the far corner. She was too excited to eat, declining his offer of food, and he ordered coffee. While they waited, it occurred to him that she was untouched by the passage of time. Her features were exquisite, and she still possessed the verve and animation he remembered so well. The waitress shortly returned with their coffee.

"You haven't changed a bit," he said, when they were alone. "Still the girl I remember from Atlanta."

"Oh, John, it's so good to hear your voice again! You can't begin to imagine how happy I am."

A sudden spasm wracked Holliday's lungs. He poured a dollop from the flask into his coffee, and gulped it down. "Pardon my manners," he said, his features flushed. "These days I have little choice but to drink in public. Bourbon has a palliative effect on my cough."

"I didn't want to believe your letters." She smiled sadly. "I wanted to arrive here and find you in glowing health. I should have known you were telling the truth."

"So then, tell me your truth, Mattie. Why are you really here?"

"To be with you. I don't care how ill you are. We belong together!"

Holliday studied her. "Do your parents share your opinion?"

"No, they don't," she said softly. "But I'm a grown woman and I know my own mind. I belong with you. I always have."

Holliday was torn by mixed emotions. The eroding effect of their long separation melted away simply at the sight of her. Watching her now, he was reminded that she was the only woman who had truly touched his inner core, his soul. However much he might wish it otherwise, she was the one person in his life who engendered love and compassion, and some deeper sense of grace. He was flooded with memories of all they had shared, the bonds of the past.

Yet, though he was inwardly torn, he tried to put the memories aside. He was determined not to allow her presence to weaken his resolve, to overturn what he knew was right. His future was ordained by some higher power, and he still rode the pale horse of death. He told himself that she must somehow be dissuaded, forced to accept the hard truth of finality. To make her his bride, and quickly his widow, would be a corruption of all they had once shared, a stain on honor itself. He had to end it here, today.

"Listen to me," he said earnestly. "You still have some image of me as I was in another time, another life. I am no longer that man."

She held his gaze. "You are exactly as I remember you. Time doesn't change the man, John."

"No, you are very wrong. I am a professional gambler, one of the sporting crowd. Do you know what that means?"

"Not really."

"A fraternity of scoundrels," Holliday informed her. "I consort with cardsharps and thieves and ruffians of every stripe. Some people think I'm the worst of the lot."

"I'll never believe that," she said. "It simply isn't in your nature to cheat or steal, or even countenance such things. I know you too well."

"Do you?" Holliday said gravely. "Do you know that I am infamous, that men fear my name? Do you know I am called Doc Holliday?"

"No," she said in a small voice. "And it doesn't matter."

"Does it matter that I've killed nine or ten men since you saw me last? Not duels of honor, Mattie. Sleazy barroom gunfights, over cards and money. Am I the same man you remember?"

"Ohhh—" The sound died in her throat. "Why are you telling me all this?"

Holliday's stomach knotted. "I'm telling you the kind of life I lead. Sordid and low, oftentimes brutal." He paused, sighing heavily. "Not a life for you."

After a long silence, she looked at him. "Shouldn't that be for me to decide, John?"

"Would you martyr yourself?" Holliday's tone softened. "Think back to all those nights we read the classic poets. Do you recall the line Lord Byron wrote? 'The Angel of Death spread his wings.' "

"What does that have to do with being a martyr?"

"The wings of death are spread over me. You have only to look to see it in my face. I'm living on borrowed time, bankrupt of life. Why martyr yourself for a dead man?"

Her chin lifted, her eyes defiant. "Living or dead, you are the man I love, John. There will never be another." She smiled wanly. "So yes, I would happily accept whatever time remains."

A sinking feeling came over Holliday. He was so absorbed in his own thoughts that he failed to notice Kate crossing the dining room. She halted beside the table, one hand on her outthrust hip. Her eyes flashed with a wicked glint.

"Well, well," she said in a throaty huff. "Stepping out on me, lover?"

Mattie looked at her with a stunned expression. Holliday started from his chair, momentarily at a loss for an explanation. But then, struck by sudden inspiration, he wondered

that he'd never thought of it before. He saw a way to end it.

"Miss Mattie Holliday," he said with a formal gesture, "may I introduce Miss Kate Elder, my fiancée?"

"Your—" Mattie's face was a mask of pain. "You are betrothed?"

Holliday nodded. "I apologize most sincerely, Mattie. I should have told you before now."

Her eyes welled with tears. "Excuse me," she said in a choked voice, rising from her chair. "I have to see to my luggage."

She walked toward the dining room door, her head held high with dignity. Holliday watched, suddenly undone by his own cruelty, as she disappeared through the lobby. He felt as though he'd destroyed something rare and fragile with a blow of his fist. Kate gave him a venomous look.

"So that's your Georgia peach, huh, Doc? Who's being used here, her or me?"

"No more, Kate." Holliday fixed her with a cold stare. "Keep away from me until I have her safely out of town. Disobey me and you will regret it."

Her face went rigid. "Who the hell you think you're ordering around? Whatever you told Miss Priss, I'm not your fiancée."

"I won't warn you again. Stay out of this."

"Stuff it, buster," she announced sullenly. "You just lost yourself a personal whore. I'm going back on the line!"

"Go where you will," Holliday said wearily. "The farther the better."

Her laugh was wild, harsh and mirthless. "How's Cheyenne sound, Doc? One of the girls has been after me to go up there. That far enough?"

"Pack your things and get out of the room. I want you gone within the hour."

"You cheap bastard! What'd you ever buy me that's worth carting along? I'll be out in ten minutes."

She sniffed, her eyes filled with mockery, and flounced off toward the lobby. Holliday dropped back into his chair,

pulling the flask from his pocket. He took a long slug, then another, suddenly chilled and needing warmth. He felt cold to the marrow.

Shortly before dusk, Holliday escorted Mattie to the train station. She had decided that there was no reason to stay, and ample reason to leave. The evening eastbound would take her to Kansas City, and from there, she would travel on to Atlanta. She offered no protest when Holliday insisted on buying her ticket.

The train was on time. Holliday arranged for a porter to take her bags onto the lead passenger coach. He struggled for something to say as they crossed the depot platform in a cone of silence. Finally, on the verge of boarding, she turned back and lightly placed a hand on his arm. Her eyes searched his face.

"You do love me, don't you, John?"

Holliday swallowed. "I will love you on the day I die."

"Yes, I know it now." She touched his cheek, kissed him on the mouth. "God keep you safe from harm, my dearest."

The conductor assisted her onboard. Holliday walked along the platform, observing through the window as she took a seat in the coach. She stared out the opposite window, sitting perfectly straight, as the engine chuffed smoke and the train got under way. He watched until the lamps on the rear coach faded into the night.

Uptown, he met Earp crossing the plaza. The lawman gave him a strange look. "Get your friend off all right, Doc?"

"Yes, safely away," Holliday said dully. "Her stay was shorter than anticipated."

"Maybe she can stay longer next time."

"In another life, perhaps. Who knows?"

"Word's around you split with Kate."

"Wisdom prevails," Holliday said, forcing a smile. "In fact, I'm leaving in the morning myself. I think I'll try the mining camps."

"Sorry to hear it, Doc." Earp was silent a moment. "Any idea where you'll go?"

"Colorado," Holliday said with a dry chuckle. "I've heard Leadville is booming these days."

"One camp's pretty much like another. Why Leadville?"

"I thrive on anarchy, Wyatt. I thought you knew."

CHAPTER 28

Leadville was located some seventy-five miles southwest of Denver. Deep in the Colorado Rockies, near the headwaters of the Arkansas River, the town meandered through a gulch at an elevation topping ten thousand feet. There, scarcely a year ago, placer miners had discovered the richest silver strike in the history of the world.

Early on an August evening, Holliday stepped out of the St. Anne's Hotel. He paused, lighting a cigarillo, and then turned north along Harrison Avenue. Streetlamps flickered in the dusky light, and the boardwalks were crowded with miners, teamsters, and businessmen attired in fashionable suits. Heavy ore wagons, drawn by mules, lumbered toward the smeltering plants south of town.

Leadville operated day and night. Harrison Avenue was the economic center of the mining camp, and ranged along the three-block stretch were stores and restaurants, hotels and saloons, and several elegantly furnished gaming parlors. East and west of the main thoroughfare, wedged into narrow sidestreets, were the seedier lodging houses, clapboard dance halls, and the red-light district. On the northern edge of town was the Denver & Rio Grande railroad depot.

Holliday strolled along the avenue with a sense of anticipation for the night ahead. The high altitude sometimes played havoc with his lungs, but he was otherwise pleased with his stay in the mining camp. A month ago, after a

harrowing train ride through rocky gorges and along steep mountainsides, he had engaged a comfortable suite at the St. Anne's. In the time since, he had become a regular in the town's wide selection of plush gambling establishments. He was averaging better than a thousand dollars a week in winnings.

Unlike Deadwood and other mining camps, Holliday found that anarchy no longer reigned in Leadville. The magnitude of the silver strike had instead transformed the town into a wilderness mecca of prosperity and trade. The monthly payroll from the mines exceeded eight hundred thousand dollars and the population was at twenty thousand people and growing. There were five banks, three newspapers, over two hundred saloons and gaming dives, and close to fifty whorehouses. Three of the larger mines, capitalized at more than forty million dollars, were listed on the New York Stock Exchange.

If anything, Leadville resembled a small city, isolated in the fastness of the Rockies. Yet Holliday was willing to forgo anarchy, and tolerate the trappings of civilization, for the inexhaustible wealth exchanged nightly at the gaming tables. All in the brief span of a year, the town had become a lodestone for the sporting crowd, and a major stop on the Western gambling circuit. A legion of cardsharps, grifters, and con artists were drawn to the bonanza by the smell of easy money and gullible marks. The miners were routinely robbed of their wages, day and night.

Upon his arrival, Holliday had received a personal call from the town marshal. Edgar Spangler was a tough, ham-fisted lawman, who delivered a blunt, albeit courteous, message. Throughout the Colorado mining camps, Holliday's reputation was widely known, and peace officers considered him a lightning rod for trouble. He was told in a polite, businesslike manner that gamblers were welcome but gunmen were advised to behave themselves. The warning proved to be unnecessary, for everyone in Leadville was shortly aware that one of the foremost mankillers on the

frontier was now in residence. No one had yet been tempted
to provoke his anger.

. Tonight, under a sky flecked with stars, Holliday took
vigor from the bracing mountain air. A month without Kate,
and her constant temper tantrums, had done much to restore
his sense of freedom. He found that her absence lent an
added note of zest to life, and generally improved his mood.
These days, his only bothersome moments were when he
fell into a dark, brooding melancholy over Mattie. He knew
he'd done the right thing, though he often loathed himself
for breaking her heart. His one consolation was their final
moment of parting at the railway station in Dodge. A mo-
ment when he spoke what they both knew to be the truth.
She would go to his grave with him.

Near the Denver & Rio Grande rail yards, Holliday en-
tered a large warehouse. Bareknuckle fights were popular
sporting events throughout the mining camps, and a local
promoter had arranged a match for tonight. As he came
through the door, Holliday noted rows of benches aligned
around the center of the warehouse, forming a boxlike
square. Lighted by overhead lamps, the ring looked to be
about ten feet across, covered with a thick carpet of sawdust.
The benches were packed with spectators, and a dense haze
of cigar smoke hung in the air.

Holliday found a seat in the section reserved for the
town's high rollers. A few seats over, he saw Pete Richter,
who waved a lazy greeting. Richter was a professional gam-
bler, and in the past month, Holliday had clipped him for
something more than two thousand dollars. Holliday con-
sidered him a mediocre card player, hardly a match at the
tables, and they were scheduled for a session later at the
Board of Trade gaming parlor. Earlier in the day, over
drinks, they had wagered a thousand dollars on tonight's
prizefight.

The pugilistic exhibition was no run-of-the-mill fight.
Tom McKey, the Leadville champion, was so lethal in the
ring that challengers had become virtually nonexistent. On
his last outing he had all but crippled his opponent, and the

only way to arrange a match was to increase the odds. To-
night, instead of one opponent, he was pitted against two
bullyboys from the mines, fighting both at the same time.
Holliday was convinced the local champion would pull it
off, and he'd offered Richter an equal money wager. Richter
snapped it up, equally convinced that McKey was over-
matched.

A hush fell over the gallery. Tom McKey strode to the
far side of the ring, a towering brute of a man dressed in
fighting tights and a bright green sash. His arms were corded
with muscle, and under the flickering lights, his gnarled fists
looked like rock-crushers. On the opposite side of the ring
his opponents stood watching, stripped to the waist, their
chests covered with a sheen of sweat. One of the thugs was
flatnosed and heavily scarred, clearly the survivor of many
rough-and-tumble brawls. The other bullyboy was stumpier,
packed with muscle, not an ounce of suet on his burly frame.
The crowd waited expectantly as McKey flexed his massive
shoulders.

The referee moved to center ring. "Your attention,
pleeze!" he announced in a booming voice. "A night of
scientific fisticuffs for your edification and entertainment.
Joltin' Tom McKey, the undefeated cham-peen"—he mo-
tioned extravagantly to the far side of the ring—"against
two of Leadville's finest scrappers! Give the boys a hand
before the massacre starts."

The referee hurriedly stepped outside the ring as the spec-
tators applauded and cheered. From that point on, his only
function would be to raise the hand of the winner, for the
match was a fight to the finish, with no holds barred. As he
reached the outer edge of the sawdust a tense murmur swept
across the crowd, then stillness settled over the warehouse.
Holliday leaned forward to watch the action.

McKey advanced to the middle of the ring. He stopped,
eyeing his opponents, arms loose at his sides. The bullyboys
approached from either flank, ambling slowly forward, their
fists cocked. Studying them, McKey concluded that the pug-
nosed tough was the more dangerous of the two, and he

purposely maintained eye contact. Suddenly, shifting lightly on his feet, he feinted a blow at the man, who was circling on his right. The thug nimbly skipped backward across the ring.

The other man instantly attacked from the opposite side. McKey whirled, gauging the hooligan's movements perfectly, and kicked him in the kneecap. The man's leg buckled, and he retreated, hobbling toward the edge of the ring. McKey pivoted to the left, quickly closing the distance, and lashed out with a splintering left-right combination. The ruffian slumped at the waist, his legs collapsing beneath him, and McKey kicked him in the head as he went down. The first miner stepped in from the side, pummeling McKey with three rapid roundhouse punches. The champion's eyebrow split, slinging blood across the sawdust.

McKey spun around, swinging his elbow in a looping arc, and connected solidly with the miner's jaw. Knocked back on his heels, the man swayed unsteadily, his eyes cocked askew. Crouching, McKey flicked a punishing jab, followed by a searing left hook. The thug retreated, wobbly stepping out of the sawdust arena, and the crowd bodily threw him back into the ring. Bobbing and weaving, McKey feinted a left, then drove a paralyzing blow flush between the man's eyes. Spectators scattered as the miner smashed into the front row of benches and went down, out cold.

McKey stood alone in the ring, blood dripping from the gash on his brow. The mixture of sweat and blood coating his chest glistened in the reflection of the overhead lamps, and for a moment he stared curiously at the battered forms of the miners. Then pandemonium broke loose, and he slowly became aware of the crowd's roaring chant. The nearest spectators jumped into the ring, mobbing him, straining to get closer as they shouted themselves hoarse. Someone raised his arm in victory.

Pete Richter watched with a grim expression. Finally, collecting himself, he moved through the cheering crowd, halting beside Holliday. He fished a roll of bills from his pocket and peeled off a thousand dollars. ''You've got all the

luck,'' he said in a disgruntled voice. "Never saw anything
like it.''

Holliday folded the money into his own roll. "Don't de-
spair, Pete. You'll have a chance to recoup tonight. Perhaps
your luck will change.''

"You know—'' Richter hesitated, gave him an odd look.
"I wouldn't be surprised but what you're right. I'm long
overdue.''

"Of course you are.'' Holliday nodded toward the ring.
"I want to have a word of congratulations with the champ.
Suppose we meet at the club in an hour.''

"Yeah, that sounds good, Doc. I'll see you there.''

Holliday pushed through the mob surrounding Tom
McKey.

The Board of Trade was considered the finest gaming es-
tablishment in Leadville. A large diamond-dust mirror was
centered behind a mahogany bar that dominated the front of
the club. Opposite the bar were dice and roulette tables, faro
layouts, and other games of chance. The walls were adorned
with paintings of nude women and prancing horses, and
crystal chandeliers, blazing with light, were suspended over-
head. A section at the rear was reserved for a grouping of
six poker tables.

Holliday was losing. The game was into its fourth hour,
and he estimated he was down by at least two thousand
dollars. Richter sat opposite him, and ranged around the ta-
ble were three claims speculators and two mine owners. He
noted that Richter, who was the heavy winner for the night,
had an uncanny knack of dealing himself winning hands.
His own cards were serious betting hands, but he invariably
found himself holding second-best. Something about it
smelled fishy, and his suspicion centered on the man directly
opposite him. Richter won consistently whenever he dealt.

After a while, the deal again passed to Richter, who called
five-card draw. Holliday observed everyone closely, hardly
surprised to find himself holding two pair, queens and fours.
In the first round of betting he and Richter raised back and

forth, driving everyone out but one of the mine owners. On the draw he took one card, the mine owner drew three, and Richter dealt himself one. Upon spreading his cards, Holliday discovered he'd filled a full house, queens over fours. He no longer had any doubt that the game was rigged.

As the opener, Holliday had the first bet. Slowly, as though pondering on it, he riffled the five cards in his hand. He suddenly felt like a dunce, for in their many poker sessions, he had not pegged Richter as a cardsharp. With the tip of his finger, he detected that they were playing with a "stripper" deck, one in which the cards of high denomination had been trimmed a thirty-secondth of an inch on the edges. He had no idea how the deck had been introduced into the game, but it hardly mattered. Richter was dealing crooked cards.

Holliday smiled amiably. "You'll have to pay to play, gentlemen. Opener bets a hundred."

The mine owner folded. Richter feigned uncertainty, then laughingly shrugged. "What the hell," he said. "Get a hunch, bet a bunch. Raise you a hundred."

"And a hundred more on a sure winner."

"Got no choice but to bump you again."

"I call," Holliday said. "Full house, queens over fours."

"By golly, Doc." Richter chortled, wagged his head. "Guess it's my lucky night, after all. Filled mine, too. Aces over sevens."

"Hold it," Holliday said, as he reached for the pot. "Pass me your cards."

"What do you want my cards for?"

"Let's call it a moment of enlightenment."

Holliday gathered the deadwood. He adroitly shuffled, cut the deck, and then proceeded to deal seconds. His fingers were nimble and quick, and he dealt two sets of cards, facedown, three cards to a set. Then he placed the remainder of the deck on the table.

"Gentlemen, your attention," he said, looking around at the other players. "Here we have six cards, three aces and three queens. You may ask how I know."

Holliday turned the cards, one at a time. "I know because Mr. Richter is a card cheat. He has been dealing strippers."

The men stared at the cards, three aces and three queens. Richter's features went beet-red. "You're a goddamn liar, Holliday!" He slammed the table with the flat of his hand. "You pulled some kind of trick here."

"You, sir, are the trickster." Holliday fixed him with a level gaze. "The penalty is your bankroll, every red cent. Leave it on the table and walk away."

"Who you think you're trying to bullyrag? Nobody takes my bankroll!"

"That leaves but one alternative. Would you care to draw on me?"

Richter seemed to debate it a moment. Then, with his hands spread palms outward, he rose from his chair and walked toward the front of the club. As he neared the roulette table, he whirled around in mid-stride, drawing a gun from his waistband. His expression turned to stark amazement as he saw Holliday standing beside the poker table, a Colt Peacemaker extended at shoulder level. Holliday fired twice, the reports scarcely an instant apart.

Staggered by the impact of the slugs, Richter lurched backward and fell dead at the foot of the roulette table. A buzz of conversation swept through the club as Holliday calmly holstered his pistol. The men at the poker table watched openmouthed with astonishment as he resumed his seat. "Gentlemen," he said with unnerving detachment. "I estimate Mr. Richter clipped me for two thousand. You may divide the rest of his bankroll however you see fit."

Within minutes, Marshal Edgar Spangler hurried into the club. He paused briefly to inspect the body, then walked back to the table. "Nice shootin'," he said, glaring down at Holliday. "But I warned you I wouldn't tolerate gunplay."

Holliday looked at him with a droll smile. "Are you posting me out of town, Marshal?"

There was a prolonged moment of consideration. "A

man's got a right to defend himself," Spangler allowed. "We'll let it pass this time."

"In that event, I will relieve you of any future concern. Count on me to be gone within the week."

Holliday called for a new deck of cards. He shuffled expertly and permitted the speculator on his right to cut. Then, glancing around the table, he began dealing.

"Ante twenty dollars, gentlemen. The game is stud poker."

CHAPTER 29

Holliday came downstairs shortly after the noon hour. The lobby of the Dodge House was filled with cattlemen, and they fell silent, watching him with sidewise glances. He studiously ignored them.

" 'Afternoon, Mr. Holliday," the desk clerk said with unctuous pleasantry. "A letter came for you in the morning post."

"Thank you." Holliday accepted the envelope, looking at the oval script. "I see we have fair weather."

An early September sun stood at its zenith in a cloudless sky. "Yessir," the clerk agreed. "Guess we've seen the last of summer."

"A cool snap would be most welcome."

Holliday moved through the lobby into the dining room. He had returned to Dodge City three days ago, and immediately fell into his old routine. He took a table beside the window overlooking Front Street, and ordered his usual breakfast. The waitress brought coffee, which he laced with bourbon.

The envelope lay before him on the table. A month had passed since Mattie's unannounced visit, and he hadn't expected any further communication. He stared at the familiar script, and felt an inward sense of dread. When she departed Dodge City, he'd thought she had finally accepted the fu-

tility of their relationship. But now, opening the letter, he was no longer certain. He read it with growing unease.

> *Dearest John,*
> *I do hope this finds you well, and of good spirit. When we parted, I know you were more concerned with my welfare than your own. Your selflessness is but one of the qualities I have cherished throughout our lives.*
> *I write this final letter to allay your concern. God works His wonders in mysterious ways, and never more so than in my regard. As you read this, I will have taken vows as a nun in the Sister of Charity convent, here in Atlanta. You above all others will understand that I have found unimaginable peace as a bride of Christ.*

Holliday was stunned. He paused, grappling with the mental image of her in a nun's habit. No less staggering was the fact that she had converted to Catholicism. The thought of it boggled his mind, left him momentarily incredulous. He read on with deeper misgiving.

> *You must not feel that this was in any way precipitous, or hasty, on my part. I long ago decided that, apart from you, there was but one life for me. I am content to devote myself to God and His works, in the certainty that I will experience a divine state of grace. Few in this life, or the hereafter, are so blessed.*
> *A cloistered order permits no correspondence, so you have no need to reply. You will forever be in my thoughts and my prayers, and I ask our Lord to grant you happiness and good health. Know that the happiness we shared will be with me always in fondest memory.*
>
> > *Yours in faith,*
> > *Mattie*

* * *

Holliday dropped the letter on the table. He sloshed more bourbon from his flask into the coffee cup, and drank it down. The waitress returned with his eggs and toast, her eyes darting curiously from the letter to the stricken look on his face. When she moved away, he stared at the plate a moment, suddenly robbed of appetite. His gaze drifted off through the window, fixed on nothing.

The thought uppermost in his mind was one of sorrow for Mattie. He believed what she had written, that without him, she was content to be a bride of Christ. She was the most religious woman he'd ever known, and he was certain she did indeed feel blessed. Yet he wondered at the same time if she had chosen a convent as a sanctuary from life, cloistered from the world and all its disappointments. A place to escape the past.

A rap on the window broke his reverie. He glanced up and saw Earp looking at him from outside. Before he could react, Earp motioned along the boardwalk, then turned toward the hotel entrance. He quickly folded the letter, stuffing it into the envelope and slipping it in his pocket. He tried to collect himself as Earp appeared through the dining room door, moving to the table. He gestured to a chair.

"Join me," he said. "Have you had dinner?"

"I already ate." Earp seated himself. "Off your feed today, Doc? Your eggs are getting cold."

Holliday pushed the plate aside. "Today may be my day for a liquid diet."

"Never saw anybody get by on liquor the way you do."

"Well, it's the old adage, an apple a day. In my case, bourbon serves as nectar."

Earp studied him a moment. Something seemed oddly out of kilter, and he noted the hollow cast to Holliday's eyes. He wagged a hand back and forth.

"You look like a lost soul, Doc. What's up?"

"I've been more chipper, no question of that. Some days are better than others."

"Anything you want to talk about?"

Holliday was a private man. He neither sought nor welcomed the opinions of others. By his lights, it was a weakness of character to air personal matters in public. Yet he felt a kinship with Earp, and he knew it was mutual. Trust and respect were the bond between them, a bond of friendship. There was no need for artifice with Earp.

"You remember the lady who visited me here the first part of August?"

Earp nodded. "The one you put on the eastbound train. A fine-looking woman."

"We were engaged to be married. But I felt it an unlikely prospect, given the state of my health. I broke it off."

"She took it badly?"

"Judge for yourself."

Holliday handed him the letter. Earp read it through, surprise slowly registering on his features. He carefully refolded the letter and passed it across the table. His expression was sober.

"Quite a woman," he said. "She knows her own mind."

"Yes, that would be an apt description of Mattie."

"There's worse places than a convent, Doc. Sounds like she made the right decision for her."

"Strange," Holliday said in a low voice. "I feel like a man in mourning. It's almost as though she died."

A closed look came over Earp's face. "I was married once. Not many people know that."

"I've never heard you speak of it."

"She died in a typhus epidemic, seven years ago. I still mourn her, but what's past is past. You learn to put it behind you."

Holliday was momentarily at a loss. He realized that Earp had revealed a hidden part of himself, and all to a purpose. The message was couched in subtlety, one friend to another, but nonetheless straightforward. Leave the past behind, and get on with life.

"Wyatt, you give sound advice." Holliday raised his coffee cup in a toast. "Here's to the women in our lives. Gone but not forgotten."

Earp smiled. "I'll drink to that."

"So now, let's move on to cheerier things. Anything new around town?"

"Your old friend Dave Rudabaugh robbed another train. Masterson took off after him this morning."

"Bat has the knack for making headlines. I've no doubt he'll get his man. Nothing more noteworthy to report?"

"Depends on who's talking," Earp observed. "Word's around the Texans are on the prod again. Tobe Driskill's the ringleader."

"Driskill?" Holliday repeated. "I'm not familiar with the name."

"One of the biggest cattlemen in the business. He's got a high opinion of himself."

"An opinion you don't share, correct?"

"You might say we've had our differences."

Earp went on to explain. Driskill was a cattle baron, trailing upward of twenty thousand head to Dodge every season, and thought himself above the law. A year ago, with his herds sold and himself tanked on liquor, Driskill attempted to tree the town. Earp buffaloed him upside the head with a pistol barrel, and carted him off to jail. Driskill swore he would have revenge.

"Whiskey courage," Earp concluded. "Driskill talks a big fight."

Holliday lit a cigarillo. "How is it I haven't heard his name before?"

"Well, he only just got into town. Waited to come up the trail with his last herd of the season."

"From what you hear on the grapevine, there's to be trouble of some sort. Perhaps he's here to settle the score."

"Maybe so, maybe not," Earp said. "Hard to predict what Texans will do."

"Even so, keep your guard up," Holliday warned him. "As some sage once counseled, better to err on the side of caution."

"I never take anything for granted." Earp rose from his

chair. "I've got places to go and people to see. Let's have a drink later."

"I expect to be at the Long Branch all night."

Earp walked toward the door. Holliday took a drag on his cigarillo, exhaling a plume of smoke. His eyes fell on the letter, and he unfolded it, staring at one paragraph. The words seemed to leap off the page. A bride of Christ.

He poured himself another drink.

A full moon bathed the town in a spectral glow. The South Side was packed with trailhands, shafts of light spilling from dives along the street. Drunken laughter mixed with discordant music filled the night.

Tobe Driskill emerged from the Lady Gay saloon. A beefy man, broad and tall, he swayed unsteadily on his feet. Behind him, battling their way through the door, were some twenty cowhands, all of them ossified on rotgut whiskey. Driskill scowled up and down the street.

"Where's all the gawddamn lawdogs? You boys see anybody?"

The cowhands swiveled in unison, following his gaze. When no one replied, Driskill motioned toward the railroad tracks. "Yellow bastards are probably hidin' out uptown. Let's tree ourselves a coon!"

Someone loosed a Rebel yell as Driskill stepped off the boardwalk. He led the men in a ragged phalanx upstreet, their shouts and laughter rocketing off buildings as they moved through the sporting district. Trailhands lining the boardwalks paused to watch as they marched past.

"Here we come!" Driskill roared drunkenly. "You boys just remember, Earp's mine. Gonna cut the wolf loose!"

Earp stepped out of the jailhouse as they crossed the Deadline. All evening he'd been expecting trouble, warily alert as Driskill and his men caroused in the Lady Gay. But a saloon brawl had claimed his attention, and he had just finished locking away three of the combatants. Jim Masterson, the other night deputy, had been summoned to a melee in one of the whorehouses downtown. He was on his own.

Driskill and his trailhands began shooting as they crossed the tracks. Their first target was the Alhambra, owned by Dog Kelly, the mayor. They blew out the windows in a volley of gunfire, laughing uproariously, yipping wild Rebel yells. Then, turning west along the plaza, they paused to blast the storefront of Wright & Beverly's Mercantile Emporium. Shattered glass exploded in the silvery moonlight.

Earp sprinted behind a building east of their position. He turned west, running through the alleyway, headed for the Long Branch. There were at least twenty men with Driskill, and his one hope was to reach the sawed-off shotgun kept beneath the bar. His plan, concocted on the run, was to surprise them as they moved from store to store along Front Street. He thought they might back down in the face of a scattergun.

The plan went haywire when the Texans moved faster than he'd expected. As he emerged from a passageway alongside the saloon, he found the trailhands already gathered in front of the Long Branch. One of them spotted him, and they wheeled in his direction on the instant, their guns drawn. Driskill bulled his way to the head of the pack, his features twisted in an ugly leer. He wagged the snout of his pistol.

"Well, looky here!" he crowed. "Done caught Mr. Hardass his own self. Howdy do, Earp."

Earp kept perfectly still. "Driskill, you'd be smart to call it off. There'll be other deputies here any minute."

"Let 'em come, you sorry sonovabitch. We'll settle your hash long before then."

"Your fight's with me, Driskill. Let's settle it between ourselves—just you and me."

"Like hell!" Driskill countered. "You done killed two Texicans this summer. Time to pay the piper."

"You expect me to draw on your whole gang?"

"Don't make no nevermind. We're gonna kill you anyway, Earp. Start sayin' your prayers."

"Nobody move! I'll kill the first man who blinks."

Holliday stepped through the door of the Long Branch.

He was framed in a shaft of lamplight, directly behind the Texans. The Peacemaker in one hand, the Lightning in the other, he advanced into the street. His voice was cold.

"I am death itself, gentlemen. Do not try me."

None of the Texans moved. They stood locked in a rigid tableau, waiting for a signal from Driskill. Earp pulled his pistol.

"Drop your guns," he ordered. "Now!"

Driskill hesitated, staring hard at Earp. A trailhand in the middle of the pack suddenly raised his six-gun, thumbing the hammer. Holliday sighted, the Peacemaker extended at arm's length, and fired. The cowhand's skull blew apart in a mist of brains and bone matter, and he pitched to the ground. Earp moved before anyone could react, rapidly closing the distance, and thunked Driskill over the head with his pistol. The rancher went down as though chopped off at the knees.

"Hands up!" Earp thundered. "Ditch those guns!"

The trailhands jumped to obey. Their six-guns hit the ground, and they raised their hands overhead. Jim Masterson appeared out of the moonlight, his pistol cocked, and covered the Texans from the opposite flank. Driskill moaned, trying to lever himself erect, and one of the men helped him to his feet. Earp motioned toward the railroad tracks.

"Get moving," he commanded. "You boys are going to jail."

Holliday fell in beside him. The Texans trooped off across the plaza, with Masterson herding them from the front. After a moment, Holliday chortled softly. "You are a man to attract a crowd, Wyatt."

"Driskill will wish he'd come alone. He'll pay fines of a hundred dollars a man."

"Not to mention the cost of a funeral."

Earp looked around. "You saved my bacon, Doc. I'm obliged."

"Think nothing of it. After all, what are friends for?"

"Just the same, I owe you."

"Well, if you insist—"

"Yeah?"

"Buy me a drink and we'll count it even."

They marched the Texans toward the jailhouse.

Part Four

CHAPTER 30

"Kings bet fifty."

"I am forced to raise. Fifty more."

"Your fifty and another fifty."

"And one last time."

"Christ on a crutch, Doc. I'll just call."

"You are a gamecock, Josh." Holliday flipped his hole card. "It appears I have a pair of nines . . . with an ace kicker."

"Nines! Thought for sure you had two pair. Got you that time, Doc."

"I have only a modest talent for the game."

"Yeah, and bird dogs fly, too."

Joshua Webb raked in the pot. He was a gambler and sometimes peace officer, currently without a badge. The other players, seated at a table in the Long Branch, were Frank Loving, Dave Mather, and Ben Thompson. To while away the time, waiting for the 1879 cattle season to commence, they were forced to play among themselves. Their afternoons were generally spent at the Long Branch, and their evenings at the Lady Gay.

A warm May sun, dipping westward, slanted through the windows. Holliday poured himself a shot of bourbon, and tossed it off neat. He had wintered in Dodge City, and he welcomed the coming of spring. Cold weather played havoc with his lungs, but he'd decided that Kansas was marginally

better than the Colorado mining camps. The snow had melted, and the moderate springtime temperature was like a balm for his coughing fits. He longed for the heat of summer.

Loving dealt a hand of five-card stud. After a peek at his hole card, Holliday waited until the bet came around, then dropped out. He watched the play with no great interest, for he found himself bored with the same company day in and day out. For that matter, he was bored with Dodge City, having been there eight months, what seemed an eternity. The daily poker sessions with his fellow gamblers were now more ritual than sport. Win or lose, the tedium was ever present.

Yet, in what he considered the irony of ironies, Holliday had become an accepted member of the community. The citizens of Dodge City applauded his johnny-on-the-spot rescue of Wyatt Earp. Everyone agreed that his intervention had prevented another lawman being gunned down by the Texans. Even Bat Masterson, who viewed him with a jaundiced eye, was now cordial, if not friendly. His new respectability was further enhanced by the fact that his lone killing in Dodge—a trailhand—was thought deserving of a medal. He found it droll, but nonetheless a bore.

The deal passed to Thompson, who called five-card draw. Watching him shuffle, Holliday reflected that his long stay in Dodge had only one high point. In January, when snow lay heavy on the ground, he had marked his twenty-seventh birthday. Despite the odds, the Western climate generally agreed with his lungs, and he had survived another year. Some days were better than others, and any thought of Mattie, locked away in a convent, invariably depressed his mood. But he was alive, still mobile if not a strapping physical specimen, and he hadn't killed anyone lately. All in all, he could have done worse.

Dave Mather opened for twenty dollars, and Webb called. Holliday, who was holding a pair of queens, raised fifty. Loving folded, Thompson raised another fifty, Mather groaned but called both raises, and Webb got out. With an

idle gesture, as though tossing money to the winds, Holliday took the last raise. On the draw, Mather discarded three, Holliday held two, and Thompson dealt himself one card. Mather, who was the opener, checked to the raisers. Holliday spread his cards, looking at three queens. He checked.

Thompson grunted. "Price of poker just went up. Cost you fifty to stay."

A moment elapsed, then Mather folded. Holliday wet his thumb, counting bills. "As the spider said to the fly, step into my web. Raise you fifty, Ben."

"Your web, huh?" Thompson grinned with amusement. "I got an itty-bitty hunch you're bluffin'. Bump you fifty, Doc."

"One more time," Holliday said with a sardonic smile. "All contributions are greatly appreciated."

"Listen to the man talk, will you? Call the raise!"

Holliday fanned his cards. "Three ladies."

"Kiss my dusty butt," Thompson groaned. "Went in with two pair and come out with two pair. Damn the luck, anyway!"

"No luck to it, Ben. Poker, as we all know, is a science."

"Yeah, sure thing," Thompson mumbled. "Wish to hell trailing season was here. Them cowboys never learned the science."

"Won't be long," Loving said. "Another couple of weeks, three at the most. I can already smell the cowshit."

"Who cares?" Mather chimed in. "Their money don't stink, no sir. Sweet as lilacs."

Thompson chuffed. "Just thinkin' about it makes my mouth water."

Holliday glanced around as the door opened. He saw Joe Bascom, the desk clerk from the hotel, pause at the front of the bar. Bascom nodded to him, motioning with his head, a strange look on his face. Holliday pushed back his chair.

"Deal me out the next hand. I won't be long."

Bascom appeared jittery as Holliday walked along the bar. He bobbed his head with a weak smile. "Sorry to bust up

your game, Mr. Holliday. Figured I ought to come find you.''

"Something wrong, Joe?"

"Understand, it's not my fault, Mr. Holliday. Miss Kate showed up—"

"Kate Elder?"

"Yessir," Bascom said nervously. "She waltzed in and demanded a key to your room. Wouldn't take no for an answer."

Holliday frowned. "And you gave it to her?"

"Had to, Mr. Holliday. She was making a fuss they must've heard on the street. I was in a bind."

"She's in the room now?"

"Yessir, I'm afraid so. Sorry as the dickens about this."

"I'll attend to it, Joe. Don't concern yourself."

Holliday made his excuses to the players at the table. After pocketing his bankroll, he led Bascom on a quick walk to the hotel. Upstairs, as he approached his room, he heard the sound of a woman humming a dance hall tune. He stepped through the door.

Kate turned from unpacking her valise. "Hello there, lover," she said, batting her eyelashes. "Look who's come home."

Holliday closed the door. "I take it you tired of Cheyenne."

"Honest to God's truth, sugar? I got to missing you. So, here I am."

"You've been gone almost ten months. Why the sudden flowering of passion?"

She laughed a low, throaty laugh. "You're the only man for me, Doc. You always were."

"You are a poor liar, Kate." Holliday's eyes narrowed. "What happened, did the law run you out of Cheyenne? Or perhaps you tired of working for a living."

"C'mon now, sweetie. Don't be a sourpuss. Aren't you glad to see me?"

"Spare me the theatrics. What do you want?"

"Just you." She put her arms around his neck, her voice

husky. "Don't you want me, like it was before? I'll treat you good."

Holliday disengaged himself. "Let's understand one another," he said, moving away from her. "If you come back, there are conditions. Rules."

"Why sure, sugar. What sort of rules?"

"No drinking. No whoring. No scenes. You will comport yourself as a lady."

She vamped him with a look. "Nobody ever accused me of being a lady. You always liked me best when I was wicked."

"Times change," Holliday said impassively. "The foremost rule has to do with the South Side. You will not set foot across the tracks. Understood?"

"You don't mean that." Her smile slipped away. "Not even a dance now and then? A night out?"

"Those are the terms. The only terms."

"You'd expect me to stay cooped up in this hotel? Never visit the girls, or have a little fun?"

"I expect you to behave as a respectable woman."

Her temper flared. "I'm not your Georgia peach, Doc. I'm who I am."

"That is your misfortune," Holliday said coldly. "Either it's my way or no way at all."

"You watch out or I'll go back on the line! I'll fuck every Texan that comes up the trail. How'd you like that?"

"You give the word 'vulgar' new meaning, Kate."

Holliday closed her valise, cinched the straps. He carried it across the room and opened the door. "No need for a fond adieu. Good luck on the South Side."

"Goddamn you!" She grabbed the valise as she went past. "You're the lowest son of a bitch I ever ran across."

"Yes, I am one of a kind."

Holliday gently closed the door. He listened as she stomped along the hallway and down the stairs. A sense of relief, perhaps deliverance, suddenly came over him.

He felt as though an anvil had been lifted from his shoulders.

* * *

Holliday left the hotel shortly before dusk. He was sched-
uled to meet the other gamblers at the Lady Gay, for their
nightly poker session. The fact that Kate was working the
South Side seemed to him a minor annoyance. He would
not alter his routine to avoid her.

The South Side was fairly quiet. There was some local
trade, but the sporting crowd, in the main, awaited the ar-
rival of the first trail herds. As Holliday crossed the railroad
tracks, he saw Earp and Bat Masterson walking over from
the jailhouse. He waited for them at the corner of Second
Avenue.

" 'Evening, Doc,'' Earp greeted him. "You're regular as
clockwork.''

"Wyatt. Bat.'' Holliday nodded to them. "Why not join
our game? Fresh blood is always welcome.''

"Not for me,'' Masterson said agreeably. "But we'll
walk along with you. I've got an offer for you and your
friends.''

"What sort of offer?''

"The Santa Fe commissioned me to organize a militia.
Good pay for anyone handy with a gun.''

"Why would the Santa Fe need a militia?''

"Trouble with the Denver and Rio Grande, over in Col-
orado. I'll explain when we get everybody together.''

Holliday glanced around. "Are you involved in this, Wy-
att?''

"No such luck,'' Earp replied. "Some damnfool Texan
might bring in an early herd. The town council wouldn't
give me time off.''

Holliday thought it was business as usual. The Santa Fe
was a power in county politics, and Masterson danced to
the railroad's tune. Where Santa Fe interests were con-
cerned, he would forgo his duties as sheriff, and follow or-
ders. Even if it meant leaving county law enforcement to
his deputies.

"By the way, Doc,'' Earp said with a quizzical look. "I
hear Kate's back in town. Are congratulations in order?''

"Far from it," Holliday told him. "Kate and I have gone our separate ways. Permanently, I might add."

"Count your blessings," Earp commented. "She's always reminded me of a cat in heat. You don't need the grief."

"Wyatt, I couldn't agree more."

Downstreet, they turned into the Lady Gay. Holliday's poker cronies were already seated around a table at the rear of the room. Masterson took a chair, flanked by Earp and Holliday, and convened an impromptu meeting. He went straight to the point.

"The Santa Fe needs twenty fighting men. I'm authorized to offer you gents five thousand apiece. That's double what the others will get."

Thompson furrowed his brow. "What makes us so special?"

"I won't kid you, Ben. All of you boys have a reputation with a gun. If you sign on, the others will jump at the chance. It's just that simple."

"Hired guns," Webb remarked. "That's what it boils down to."

"For what?" Thompson demanded. "Who are we supposed to kill?"

Masterson launched into a quick explanation. The Santa Fe and the Denver & Rio Grande both claimed right of way through the Royal Gorge, a mountain canyon leading to several Colorado mining camps. The Denver & Rio Grande had taken the first trick by laying track and building station houses along the Arkansas River, which flowed through the gorge. But in a stunning reversal, the Santa Fe brought legal action and was awarded sole right of way by the Supreme Court. The court decision also awarded the Santa Fe all railroad construction previously built by the Denver & Rio Grande.

Defying the law, the Denver & Rio Grande retaliated with force. Gangs of armed men stormed the line of station houses, and put the Santa Fe workers to rout. Though illegal, might makes right, and the Royal Gorge was now in the

hands of the Denver & Rio Grande. Under the circumstances, the Santa Fe had no choice but to respond in kind, and fight force with force. The Dodge City militia was being organized to invade Royal Gorge and recapture the station houses. A special train would depart for Colorado tomorrow afternoon, with Masterson in command.

"That's it," Masterson concluded. "A couple of weeks at the most, and you're back in Dodge. We'll just overrun the bastards."

"Sounds good to me," Thompson said. "Easy money, and we'll be back in time for trailing season. What d' you think, Doc?"

Holliday was thinking of Kate Elder. She was a spiteful woman, and probably already devising ways to make his life miserable. Anything that put distance between them seemed to him a reasonable alternative. Then, too, summertime in the Rockies had a certain allure. The mining camps were El Dorado for a gambler.

"Well, why not?" he said with a waggish air. "Enroll me in your legion of mercenaries, Captain Masterson. Where do I sign?"

"Your word's good with me," Masterson said. "How about you other gents? You game?"

Holliday rose, followed by Earp, and walked to the end of the bar. The bartender brought him a bottle of bourbon, and a beer for Earp. He poured the shot glass to the rim, and downed it in a quick motion. His gaze went back to the table, where Masterson was conversing with the men. He shook his head.

"A jolly little war and a born leader of men. Who could ask for more?"

Earp sipped his beer. "What's bothering you?"

"Nothing at all, aside from boredom. That's why I signed on."

"Don't get bored when the shooting starts. Keep your head down."

"Why, Wyatt, you surprise me. Are you concerned for my safety?"

"Free advice," Earp said with a shrug. "You tend to be a daredevil."

"I wasn't meant to be killed by a bullet."

"What makes you so sure?"

Holliday laughed. "God has other plans."

Earp thought he had never known a better friend, or a lonelier man. He wondered if Holliday was bitter at God because of his disease, or because he'd lost the girl in Georgia. Or on second thought, maybe it was simply Kate Elder. A whore who could spoil any man's day.

All in all, he figured it was a toss-up.

Chapter 31

Trinidad lay in the shadow of Fishers Peak. A center of commerce for mining and cattle ranching, the town was situated along the banks of the Purgatoire River, in southern Colorado. Only a month past it had become the end-of-track depot for the Santa Fe.

By July, as the terminus for the railroad, Trinidad had been transformed into a boomtown. The population doubled and doubled again, with buildings sprouting across the landscape and the main street paved with masonry brick. Overnight the town became a new stop on the gambling circuit, attracting trainloads of grifters, whores, and con artists. Anything was for sale in Trinidad.

Holliday stepped out of the Baca House Hotel. He was freshly shaved, attired in a vested dove-gray suit, with a pale blue shirt and a royal-blue tie. An early afternoon sun slanted westward, toward the distant, snow-capped spires of the Sangre de Christo mountain range. He popped a match on his thumbnail and lit a cigarillo, strolling south along the main thoroughfare. The center of town was known locally as Corazon de Trinidad, the Heart of Trinidad, and a marble statue of Kit Carson commanded the central intersection. The sporting district was a few blocks farther south.

At the intersection, a crowd was gathered on the northeast corner. Holliday paused to watch one of the town's more artful grifters fleece the unwary with admirable sleight of

hand. From observing masters in the gambling fraternity, he was able to spot the gaff being used today. Yet the gullible nature of those who were so easily conned was always a source of fascination, and sardonic amusement. The grifter was a wiry man with nimble hands, dressed in a checkered suit and a bowler hat. There was a touch of the revivalist preacher in his melodious voice.

"Cleanliness is next to godliness! And I see men before me who are in need of both. Step right up, brothers!"

The crowd was hooked by his rapid-fire delivery. Their numbers had grown, spilling off the boardwalk into the street. The grifter dramatically held two bars of ivory-tinted soap aloft for all to see. The tempo of his evangelistic cadence quickened.

"Soap, brothers! Salvation for your skin and your soul alike. Concocted for miscreants and backsliders from an ancient formula evolved in the Holy Land. Who will be the first to step forward and give me twenty-five cents . . . a lowly two bits . . . for salvation—and a clean hide!"

No one stepped forward. He looked at them with bafflement, then sudden dawning. "Oh, yes, I know what you're thinking. Why would you pay two bits when you can buy common soap for a nickel at the mercantile? Well, here's the reason!" A hundred-dollar bill appeared in his hand, and he waved it around the circle of faces. "Lord God Jehovah ordained me to get people to use soap. And I'm willing to pay *you* to do it. Step up, my friends! Watch closely."

The onlookers jostled for a better look at the hundred-dollar bill. Before the pitchman stood a sample case on a tripod loaded with bars of unwrapped soap. His dexterous fingers swiftly twisted the bill around an ivory cube, then wrapped it in a square of blue paper, tossing it carelessly into the tray. Faster than the eye could follow, his hands wrapped one bar after another, enclosing ten- and twenty-dollar bills in each package. A hush fell over the crowd as he stopped including money and began wrapping plain bars of soap. His spiel picked up speed.

"Brothers, you're all sports! You wouldn't buy my soap

at twenty-five cents so I'll offer you another shot at salvation. There's over three hundred dollars tucked snugly here in my little pile. For the paltry sum of five bucks you get to select any bar in the tray. Cleanse your soul and win ten, or twenty, or a century note! Who's first? A fiver for a hundred!''

"Mister, you're pretty quick." A coatless man in a filthy shirt slapped five dollars into the grifter's hand. "But by grannies, you didn't catch me nappin'. Nosiree."

The man rummaged through the tray and selected a bar of soap. He eagerly unwrapped the package, and shouted, triumphantly, holding a crisp twenty-dollar bill. "I told you! You just wasn't fast enough. By golly, I'm gonna trade this twenty for four more chances. I'll get that hunnert yet!''

"Don't get greedy now." The grifter warded him off. "Only one bar to a customer. Let somebody else have a chance at that century note. All it takes is a keen eye and faith in the Almighty. Who's next? Take your pick!''

The crowd swarmed over him, thrusting gold pieces and greenbacks into his hand. Holliday turned away, crossing the intersection, as they fought to snatch the bars of soap. When the gaff started, he'd seen the grifter palm the hundred; the man in the tattered shirt was a shill, an instant winner to spark greed in the others. He estimated there were at least twice as many bars as there were men, and the odds were with the grifter. Some would win, but most would turn the blue wrappers inside out and find only a nickel bar of soap. The grifter would clear a tidy sum.

Holliday liked Trinidad. The anything-goes atmosphere acted as a stimulant, something he'd missed in Dodge City. He had arrived in town not quite a month ago, following the aborted railroad war. Led by Bat Masterson, the Dodge City militia had been outnumbered ten to one by Denver & Rio Grande workmen, and failed to take any of the station houses in the Royal Gorge. The Santa Fe had then sent them to Pueblo, again led by Masterson, to occupy a roundhouse that controlled the rail yards. There, besieged by a detachment from the U.S. Army, they were forced to withdraw in

short order. The campaign, from beginning to end, had proved a fiasco.

The one prize captured by the Santa Fe was Raton Pass. Located on the southern border of Colorado, the pass was a natural gateway through the mountains to New Mexico Territory. Some eight years ago, a cagey entrepreneur named Dick Wootton had finagled a charter authorizing him to operate a toll road through Raton Pass. Santa Fe officials, offering a princely sum, had purchased right of way from Wootton, and thereby closed the southern gateway to the Denver & Rio Grande. The Santa Fe was now laying track through the pass, some twenty miles south of Trinidad, and would soon establish a railhead in New Mexico. Neither Masterson nor the Dodge City militia had contributed anything to the skirmishing between rival lines.

Afterward, thoroughly disgusted by the whole affair, Holliday had decided to stay in Colorado. Through Masterson, he sent word to Wyatt Earp that he planned to follow the Santa Fe into New Mexico, moving along as new boomtowns were established. The hotel in Dodge City forwarded his belongings, shipped in a steamer trunk by railway, and with it a note from Earp. The lawman wished him good fortune, and expressed the cryptic thought that their paths might cross again before too long. Holliday had no idea where or when, but he felt he'd already played into good fortune. The Santa Fe had paid him five thousand, and in the bargain, he had escaped Kate. He was ahead of the game.

A block from the main intersection, on the fringe of the sporting district, he entered a cafe. The waitress took his breakfast order, and he laced his coffee with a liberal dose of bourbon. Every morning, upon arising, he still coughed up a wad of bloody sputum. But the mountain air generally agreed with him, and he'd found no dearth of high rollers in Trinidad. He felt no worse than usual, if he wasn't altogether the picture of health, and the cards were falling his way. All things considered, he thought the venture into Colorado had worked out for the best.

Dub Watson, a deputy town marshal, came in as he was finishing his eggs and toast. Heavyset, with meaty features and a stolid manner, Watson halted beside the table. He nodded with an empty expression. "The marshal sent me to fetch you. He wants you over at his office."

"Does he?" Holliday said genially. "To what do I owe the honor?"

"Don't know and didn't ask. Just told me to bring you."

"Well, then, let's not keep the marshal waiting. Lead the way, Dub."

Holliday followed him out the door.

"You ever hear of Kid Colton?"

"I don't believe so."

"Never got crosswise of him any whichaway? Cards? Women?"

"Not to my knowledge, Marshal. Why do you ask?"

"He means to kill you."

Frank Mott was seated at a battered rolltop desk. A spittoon was strategically located near his foot, and the walls of his office were decorated with wanted dodgers. His chair squeaked in protest as he leaned back, arms folded. Holliday looked at him with a bemused expression.

"Why would a total stranger want to kill me? Until now, I never heard his name."

Mott snorted. "You're no stranger to the Kid. Everybody in creation knows your reputation."

"Perhaps so," Holliday acceded. "But that doesn't explain the why of it."

"Hell, no mystery there. Damn fool wants to be known as the man who killed Doc Holliday. Figures that'll make his reputation bigger'n yours."

The concept was foreign to anything Holliday might have imagined. To kill another man simply to build a reputation seemed to him somehow farcical, even asinine. He spread his hands.

"This Colton?" he asked. "By any chance is he a simpleton?"

"Nothin' stupid about the Kid." Mott leaned forward, rang the spittoon with a squirt of tobacco juice. "He's just ornery, mean, no-account. A regular little sidewinder."

"You know him well, then?"

"Yeah, he rides for a cattle outfit over on the North Fork River. Fancies himself a badman pistolero. Only killed one man in his whole life—a Mexican."

"How old is he?"

"No more'n twenty, maybe younger. Name's Wilbur, but he calls himself the Kid. You know, after Billy the Kid."

Everyone knew of William Bonney, dubbed Billy the Kid, who had made national headlines during the Lincoln County War in New Mexico. Holliday nodded. "How did you hear of his . . . intentions?"

"Word gets around." Mott shifted his cud to the off cheek. "He's been braggin' on it ever since you hit town. Guess he finally got up the nerve. He aims to try it tonight."

"Will he call me out? A fair fight?"

"Oh, shore, no backshootin' for the Kid. He wants to be notorious, same as you."

Holliday considered a moment. "You pique my curiosity, Marshal. Why the friendly warning?"

"More a practical matter," Mott said equably. "I was hopin' you'd listen to reason. Maybe catch the next train out."

"I think not," Holliday said. "Perhaps you could reason with Mr. Colton."

"Hotheaded little squirt wouldn't listen. He already put his brag out. Just be a waste of time."

"You could disarm him, take him into custody."

Mott sighed heavily. "Dumb shit wouldn't come along peaceable. I'd have to kill him."

"I see." Holliday held his gaze. "From the sound of it, you prefer that I kill him. Or am I mistaken?"

"Don't care to say one way or the other. Whatever you do, just make sure it's on the up and up."

"In other words, kill him fair and square."

"Your words, Mr. Holliday, not mine."

"Well, in any event, I thank you for the warning. Good day, Marshal."

On the street Holliday wondered if he'd heard the truth. From all appearances, he had been designated to rid Trinidad of a troublesome misfit. But the personal irony of it struck him even more forcefully.

He was now a bullseye for aspiring gunmen. A target.

The Criterion was the finest gaming parlor in town. High rollers frequented the establishment, and those who followed the gambling circuit made it their headquarters. Hardly a night passed without fortunes being won and lost.

Holliday sat with his back to the wall. There were five other men at the table, and the game was into its third hour. By rough estimate, he calculated that he was almost a thousand dollars ahead. He thought it was more luck than concentration on the cards, or the players. His eyes were glued to the door.

Kid Colton swaggered in around nine o'clock. He was young, with a peach-fuzz mustache, short and slim, bright-eyed with liquor. He wore a brace of pistols in a double buscadero holster rig, the gun belt studded with silver conchas. The jinglebobs on his spurs chimed musically as he walked to the bar and ordered whiskey. The men standing nearby quietly moved away from him.

From the poker table, Holliday saw the Kid darting glances at him in the back bar mirror. He thought the Kid looked nervous, and suspected he was fortifying himself with whiskey courage. One eye on the bar, he collected his cards as a hand of five-card draw was dealt. He found himself holding a full house, jacks over fours, and raised the limit. Three players dropped out, and on the draw, he stood pat. The remaining two players each took one card.

The Kid downed a second shot of whiskey. He turned from the bar, skirting a roulette table, and crossed the room. His eyes were fixed on Holliday, and the jangle of his spurs resounded like church bells as the crowd fell silent. Every-

one knew who he was and why he was there, and they waited to see how it would play out. He halted a few paces from the poker table.

"Holliday," he said in a flat voice. "I'm Kid Colton."

"Yes, I know," Holliday said, nodding absently. "Be so kind as to wait a moment. I have the winning hand."

The Kid flushed. "You deaf or something? I'm callin' you out!"

Holliday rolled his eyes. " 'O death, where is thy sting?' "

"What's that you say?"

"Corinthians. Chapter fifteen, verse fifty-five. Shall I have it engraved on your tombstone?"

"You smart-mouth sonovabitch!"

The other players hurled themselves to the floor. All in a motion, the Kid pulled both pistols, thumbing the hammers as he cleared leather. Holliday, who was still seated, seemingly produced the Colt Lightning by some feat of legerdemain. He fired across the table, squeezing off two shots in the space of a heartbeat. The slugs punched through the Kid's breastbone.

Jolted by the impact, the Kid windmilled backward. The pistol dropped from his left hand, but his right arm swung upward, and he fired. A bullet plowed into the ceiling, and the lamp over the table swayed, casting shadowed waves of light. Holliday shot him again, a bright red rosette stitched in the center of his shirt pocket. He stiffened, erect as a wooden soldier, and toppled to the floor. His sphincter voided in death.

Holliday got to his feet. He peered over the table at the body, and it occurred to him that Wilbur Colton had died an ignominious death. Not for honor, or in answer to an insult, but rather in a foolhardy attempt to claim some measure of immortality. The saddest part was that fame of a sort would attend the death. Kid Colton, though not in the way he intended, would make the headlines. Briefly.

The game resumed as the body was carted away. Holliday bet the limit and the other players hastily folded. They had

no idea if he was bluffing, or actually held a full house. But they wisely refrained from calling a pat hand.

Though none of them remarked on it until later, they all agreed that Kid Colton had foolishly defied the odds. His wager was against death itself.

CHAPTER 32

Holliday finished shaving. He selected a beige suit from his wardrobe, and a tie the color of dark chocolate. The room was chilly from a late-September cold snap, and he hurriedly slipped into his pants and shirt. He took another shot of bourbon for good measure.

The window from his room afforded a view of the distant mountains. While he knotted his tie, he stared out over the adobe structures of Old Town. Once a sleepy village in northern New Mexico, Las Vegas was located a hundred miles south of Raton Pass and the Colorado border. The town was now end-of-track for the Santa Fe.

After strapping on his guns, Holliday shrugged into his suit jacket. He inspected himself in the mirror, making a final adjustment to his tie, and collected his hat off a wall peg. Downstairs he started across the lobby, which was furnished in the Spanish style and warmed by the blaze from a fireplace. The clerk greeted him with a diffident smile.

"Good afternoon, Mr. Holliday. I was just reading about you."

"Nothing too derogatory, I trust."

"No, sir, just the opposite. Not often we have a gentleman of your standing staying with us."

The clerk handed him a copy of the *Police Gazette*. Holliday scanned the front-page headline, and nodded. "Thank you most kindly. I'll read it over breakfast."

"The press sure follows your exploits, Mr. Holliday. You're right up there with Buffalo Bill."

"Yes, I travel in rarefied company."

Holliday entered the dining room. He took a table by the window, ordering his usual breakfast. After the waitress brought coffee, he dosed it with a shot from his flask. Then, unfolding the paper, he slowly shook his head, staring at the headline. DOC HOLLIDAY GUNFIGHT SENDS ANOTHER SOUL TO ETERNITY.

The article dealt with a shooting that had taken place almost a month ago. At the time, Holliday was headquartered in the town of Otero, the first end-of-track depot established by the Santa Fe in New Mexico Territory. A dispute with a cardsharp ended in gunfire, and Holliday was exonerated on the grounds of self-defense. After considerable hyperbole devoted to the shooting, the article went on to review Holliday's career as a Western gunman. The score, according to the reporter, now stood at twenty-four dead men.

Holliday pushed the paper aside. His opinion of Eastern journalists was further eroded by their flagrant exaggeration, often outright lies. The waitress brought his breakfast, and as he cracked open a soft-boiled egg, he tried to bring the number into sharper perspective. He never kept count, but he knew the score in the *Police Gazette* was nothing more than a bald-faced invention. A closer count, though he'd long ago lost track, would be on the order of eleven, perhaps twelve. He thought it irresponsible of the press to sensationalize, and inflate the numbers. But then, they lied about Bill Cody as well.

Thinking about it, Holliday wondered how the national press kept itself informed as to his whereabouts. Shortly after the shooting in Otero, the Santa Fe had laid track into Las Vegas, and he had moved on to the new terminus. The town was situated in the foothills of the southern Sangre de Cristo mountains, hardly more than an outpost for sheep herders and cattle ranchers in the district. The Spanish influence was apparent everywhere, in the architecture as well

as the customs of the people. Apart from Anglo merchants, the population was largely Mexican.

All that had changed with the arrival of the railroad. Old Town, the original settlement, was now bordered on the west by the Santa Fe depot and rail yards. On the opposite side of the tracks, what was quickly dubbed New Town sprang to life virtually overnight. The sporting crowd moved south, bag and baggage, and the natives watched with amazement as saloons, gaming dives, and whorehouses were erected in a frenzy of construction. Las Vegas, in short order, became a boomtown, flooded with people and trade brought by the railroad. The sporting district ran wild day and night.

A major part of the boom stemmed from future plans of the Santa Fe. The railroad was furiously extending track along a line that curved down the Rio Grande Valley and on into Albuquerque. Farther west, at the town of Rincon, the line would branch, with one fork to El Paso, in Texas, and the other to Deming, in southwest New Mexico. By 1881, scarcely two years away, the Santa Fe planned to forge a transcontinental link with the Southern Pacific, in California. The flurry of building brought thousands of people and millions of dollars into the territory.

Holliday prospered on the influx of trade. He spent his nights in the sporting district, trimming high rollers drawn by the boom. Yet he took lodging in Old Town, at a well-kept adobe hotel catering to New Mexicans. The old part of Las Vegas seemed to him a quaint frieze out of the past, somehow reminiscent of life in the South before the Civil War. The pace was slower, the people were unstintingly cordial, with a gracious air totally foreign to the hustle and bustle of New Town. He often thought he'd stepped backward in time, to a lost world. A place of manners, and genteel refinement.

The desk clerk entered the dining room as Holliday lingered over a second cup of coffee. He hurried across to the table, his features somewhat abashed, waving an envelope. He offered Holliday a lame smile.

"I started talking about that newspaper article and completely forgot, Mr. Holliday. A letter came for you in the morning post."

Holliday was momentarily nonplussed. He wondered how Mattie had managed to locate him in New Mexico, and why she would write. Then, accepting the envelope, he noted the handwriting and was even more astounded. The letter was from Kate.

"Thank you for remembering, George. I appreciate your courtesy."

"I won't forget next time, Mr. Holliday. You can depend on it."

When the clerk moved away, Holliday stared at the envelope for a long moment. He could think of no good news from Kate, or any reason for her to write. He took a sip of laced coffee, noting postmarks indicating the letter had been forwarded from Trinidad to Otero to Las Vegas. The postal service, as well as the *Police Gazette,* seemed to know of his whereabouts. He tore open the envelope.

September 10, 1879

Dear Doc,

Surprise! Bet you never expected to get a letter from yours truly (that's me). I sweet-talked Wyatt Earp into telling me you were in Trinidad. Believe me, it was like pulling teeth!

Anyway, here's why I decided to write. I got to thinking things over, and you were right and I was wrong. A man's got a right to expect that his woman won't fool around, or get drunk and make an ass out of herself in public. I ought to have listened and not let you run away mad. I could just cut my tongue out.

We always had lots of fun, Doc. Maybe we're not the best match under the sun, but we suit each other more than most. I'd like to make amends, and get back together, and pick up where we left off. You give the go-ahead and I promise to behave myself, just like you wanted. Write me and let me know what you think.

I miss you and want to come back. Hope you feel mutual.

Love & Kisses!
Kate

Holliday lit a cigarillo. Her words were conciliatory, but something about the letter rang false. He asked himself why she had waited almost five months to write. Then, glancing again at the date, it suddenly made sense. The summer trailing season was about to end, and she was facing a hard winter in Dodge City. A hard winter with no cowhands to pay for her services.

The thought occurred that she was looking for a meal ticket. He examined it, and found it a reasonable explanation for her abrupt change of heart. The tone of her letter had about it a forced sincerity, and between the lines, he discerned the wiles of a desperate woman. He had never known her to apologize, or willingly eat crow. But he had often known her to twist the truth to advantage.

Holliday wadded the letter into a ball. He placed it in an ashtray, struck a match, and set it afire. The paper flared, burning brightly, disintegrating into charred flakes. He thought it a wise decision.

Life without Kate was a new dawning every day.

Center Street was the main thoroughfare of New Town. Whenever he crossed into the sporting district, Holliday was struck by a sense of moving from the past into the future. Weathered adobe on one side of the tracks and ripsawed lumber, hastily splashed with whitewash, on the other. The contrast was somewhat like a lady rubbing shoulders with a whore.

Early that afternoon Holliday made his way to the Occidental Gaming Parlor. The place was owned by Jim O'Farrel, a toughnut Irishman who ran the classiest dive in town. All of the equipment was new, with the gaming tables opposite a gleaming mahogany bar. The saloon girls wore spangly outfits, short on the bottom and skimpy on the top.

A piano player enlivened the atmosphere with rinky-dink tunes.

Trade was unusually slow when Holliday came through the door. Dealers were idle at the gaming tables, and there were only two men at the bar. He caught their reflection in the back bar mirror, startled by familiar faces. One was Joshua Webb, who had served with him in the Dodge City militia during the aborted railroad war. The other was Dave Rudabaugh, the train robber with a talent for eluding the law. He thought them an unlikely pair.

"Look here!" Webb turned from the bar with a wide grin. "Doc Holliday in the pink."

"Good to see you, Josh," Holliday said, then nodded to Rudabaugh. "Long time since the last time, Dave. Where was it, Fort Griffin?"

"Think so," Rudabaugh mused. "I recollect I'd pulled a job and somebody was doggin' my tracks. More'n likely it was Bat Masterson."

"A fearless lawman," Holliday observed wryly. "Josh and I were under his command in the late, great railroad war. He led us merrily to defeat."

Webb laughed. "Bat wasn't cut out to be a general."

"Or a lawdog," Rudabaugh added. "I've outrun him six ways to Sunday. He's easy to slip past."

"Bat's a politician," Webb said. "For my money, Wyatt Earp's got him beat hands down as a lawman. Strictly no contest."

Rudabaugh grunted sourly. "Guess you haven't met Virgil yet, Wyatt's older brother. Town marshal over in Prescott, and nobody to mess with. Toughest sonovabitch in Arizona Territory."

"Have you met his younger brothers?" Holliday asked. "Wyatt once told me he has brothers who are marshals in Montana, or Wyoming. I gather the entire family wears a badge."

"Don't care to meet 'em," Rudabaugh replied. "I try to steer clear of lawdogs. Bastards got no sense of humor."

Holliday looked at Webb. "That leaves you in strange

company, Josh. I recall you've worn a badge on occasion.''

Webb and Rudabaugh exchanged a quick glance. "I gave up law work," Webb said after a moment. "Think I'll take a fling at the cattle business."

Holliday recalled hearing that Rudabaugh rustled cows in between train holdups. He wondered if Webb was a new partner in the venture. "So?" he said, changing the subject. "What brings you gentlemen to Las Vegas?"

"Just passing through," Rudabaugh said evasively. "Matter of fact, we oughta be on our way. Only stopped off for a drink."

"Why rush off?" Holliday said. "We could play a little poker."

"Maybe next time, Doc. We've got a ways to ride. You ready, Josh?"

Webb nodded. "I was born ready."

After a round of handshakes, the men walked toward the door. Holliday still thought them an unlikely pair, hardly birds of a feather. As he turned back, Jim O'Farrel came out of his office at the end of the bar. Holliday motioned around the empty room.

"Where's all the action, Jim? I came to play."

O'Farrel was a rawboned man, with square features and a sweeping mustache. "Got me, Doc," he said dourly. "Never saw it so slow."

"Well, for a diversion, I might try my hand at faro. Assuming, of course, I could get an honest deal."

"Hell, come on, I'll deal. I've got nothing better to do."

O'Farrel jerked his thumb at one of the faro dealers. He took a chair behind the layout and shuffled the deck, placing the cards in an ivory-faced dealing box. Holliday felt assured of an honest game, for the Irishman lacked the finesse to deal crooked. He bet the house limit, a hundred dollars.

The cards were favorable from the opening hand. A gambler sometimes hits a streak, and today Holliday could do no wrong. For every bet he lost, he won three, completely overturning the house odds. With luck at his side, he began coppering his bet, wagering the first card dealt to lose and

the second to win. The play was fast, and at two hundred dollars a hand, his stack of chips steadily mounted. By four o'clock that afternoon, he was twelve thousand dollars ahead.

"Jesus," O'Farrel said, his features tight as he paused to reshuffle. "You're breaking my back, Doc."

"Tell you what," Holliday said amiably. "I'll give you a chance to get even. Care to raise the limit to five hundred?"

"Done," O'Farrel announced. "Nobody stays lucky forever."

Holliday proved him wrong. By five o'clock, a small crowd was gathered around the layout, watching in awe. The chips stacked before Holliday resembled a mound. He was forty thousand dollars winner.

The crowd abruptly turned as a commotion broke out at the bar. One of the saloon girls shrieked, and a man's voice raised in anger stilled the room. Before anyone could react, the man backhanded her in the mouth. She bounced off the bar onto the floor.

O'Farrel crossed the room in three swift strides. He spun the man around, planting a fist in his belly, followed by a clubbing blow to the jaw. The man went down and out, and O'Farrel grabbed him by the collar. He dragged the unconscious man to the door and bodily tossed him into the street. Dusting his hands, he returned to the faro layout.

"Well done," Holliday said as he sat down. "Who's the ladies' man?"

"Goddamn thimblerigger named Mike Gordon. Him and his woman had a spat, and she came to work for me. He keeps after her, but she won't take him back."

"Smart woman." Holliday hesitated, studying his mound of chips. "Jim, I have a proposition for you. Suppose we play for double or nothing . . . all of it."

"The whole shebang?" O'Farrel stared at the stacks of chips. "Christ, Doc, there's better'n forty thousand there. That'd wipe me out."

"Or get you even," Holliday said lightly. "After all, it's only money, Jim. Easy come, easy go."

O'Farrel eyed the chips with open greed. On the turn of a card, he calculated Holliday's chances of winning at virtually nil. "You're on," he said in a rush. "What's your pleasure, Doc?"

Holliday looked at the casekeeper, the abacuslike device that kept track of the cards already dealt. He saw that none of the aces had been played, and a sudden, visceral instinct told him to take the odds. Leaning forward, he placed a chip in the center of the ace on the layout. Then, playing out his gut hunch, he coppered it. To lose.

A murmur swept through the crowd. O'Farrel appeared dumbfounded, his mouth open. "You coppered it, Doc. First card out of the box. Your bet's to lose?"

"A loser for a winner, Jim. Deal."

O'Farrel slipped a card from the box. He gingerly turned it over, and all the color drained from his face. He dropped the ace of diamonds on the table.

The onlookers stood hushed with wonder. O'Farrel recovered himself with the aplomb of a seasoned gambler. "You called a winner," he said evenly. "Looks like you just won the Occidental, Doc. Congratulations."

"Nothing so serious." Holliday was still staring at the ace. "I'll sell it back to you, Jim. What would I do with a gaming den?"

"Figure out a way to run it. I'm busted."

"You're broke?"

"Cleaned out," O'Farrel said. "You're the new proprietor."

Holliday slumped back in his chair. A lucky streak was one thing, but a gaming parlor was altogether different. His features knotted in consternation.

He wondered where to start.

CHAPTER 33

The word spread quickly throughout town. By dark, every-
one in Las Vegas knew that Doc Holliday had won the
Occidental in a faro game. The news was like an elixir to
workingmen who dreamt about beating the tables, and al-
ways fell short. They swarmed the Occidental to share in
the celebration.

Holliday was lost in an avalanche of detail. After signing
over the property, O'Farrel had given him a sketchy briefing
on the operation of a gaming parlor. But the Irishman was
disconsolate, embarrassed and embittered over the loss of
his grand enterprise. He departed with the hangdog look of
a man weighted down by defeat.

Left to his own devices, Holliday felt like he'd stepped
into quicksand. The crowd was three deep at the bar, and
men were wedged shoulder to shoulder around the gaming
tables. All of them wanted to shake the hand of the man
who had bucked the tiger and won the house. That the man
was Doc Holliday, notorious shootist and mankiller, merely
fanned their enthusiasm. He was swamped by admirers who
pumped his arm with unbridled glee.

Between accepting congratulations, Holliday tried to keep
a sharp eye on the tables. Operation of the tables was per-
haps the one thing he understood about running a gaming
establishment. Every professional gambler knew from ex-
perience that dealers were not to be trusted. Just as they

routinely cheated, boosting the house odds, they were equally capable of robbing the house. A crooked dealer, working with a confederate on the opposite side of the table, virtually had a license to steal. The trick was to catch them.

Holliday was all too aware that the first night was the most critical. Any dealer who meant to rob the house would capitalize on the excitement and distraction swirling around the new owner. He wandered from table to table, trying to avoid well-wishers, all the while watching the action. Whether faro or roulette, dice or chuck-a-luck, he knew any game could be rigged to reverse the house odds. The problem was, he couldn't be everywhere at once.

"Mr. Holliday!"

One of the saloon girls planted herself in front of him. She was a brassy woman with rouged cheeks and painted lips, her breasts spilling over the top of her gown. Her eyes popped with anger.

"Yes?" Holliday's attention was fixed on a dealer at one of the faro layouts. "What is it?"

"I need your help—right now!"

"Help with what?"

"See that man? The lard-assed bastard with the spiky beard. Down at the end of the bar."

Holliday followed the direction of her finger. He saw a man with a scruffy beard toss back a shot of liquor. The man was wobbly on his feet, clutching at the bar for support. He was obviously drunk.

"What about him?"

"He grabbed my tit!" she said, outraged. "Had to smack him to make him let go. I'll be bruised for a week."

"I see." Holliday tried to focus on the problem. "What is your name?"

"Dolly."

"Well now, Dolly, men get drunk and they try to sneak a feel. Isn't that part of the job?"

"Not on your tintype!" she huffed. "Nobody's allowed to get rough with the girls. That was Mr. O'Farrel's rule."

"And how did Mr. O'Farrel handle these matters?"

"He'd have tossed the bastard out on his ass!"

"I'll have one of the bartenders attend to it."

She arched an eyebrow. "Mr. O'Farrel always gave 'em the heave-ho himself."

"Yes, but I'm not a bouncer, Dolly. I'll hire one tomorrow."

Holliday stepped around her. As he approached the bar, he saw the girl whose jilted lover had backhanded her that afternoon. She was working a customer, all tease and smiles, plying him to buy drinks. He thought Dolly could learn from her example.

Out of the corner of his eye he spotted one of the bartenders downing a shot of whiskey. He edged through the crowd, signaling the barkeep. "Are you in the habit of drinking on the house?"

"Yeah, I guess," the bartender said hesitantly. "O'Farrel never minded if we took a nip now and then. Just so we stay sober."

Holliday made a quick mental calculation. Three bartenders with a nip now and then sapped considerable profit from bar sales. O'Farrel apparently ran a loose ship, and he wondered if the bartenders were pocketing money that should have gone in the till. He reminded himself to look into it tomorrow.

"The man at the end of the bar," he said. "The one with the beard."

"Yeah?"

"Throw him out."

The bartender frowned. "I don't do strong-arm work, Mr. Holliday. I keep bar."

Holliday stared at him. "Until I hire a bouncer, your duties have changed. Do I make myself clear?"

"Well, yeah, if you put it that way."

"I do, indeed."

Holliday turned away. Bartenders who nipped drinks forced him to consider whether O'Farrel had left him with a sieve, rather than a leaky boat. His attention was directed back to the tables, and he studied the play with new concern.

The realization suddenly struck him that he might never again have time to spend a night at a poker table. As the proprietor, he would have a full-time job contending with drunks and slippery bartenders, and dealers tempted to steal from the house. The Occidental, far from an unexpected godsend, abruptly seemed to him an albatross. He told himself he was gambler, not a tradesman.

The front window imploded in a shower of glass. The report of a gunshot sounded from outside, followed by another and another. A slug shattered the back bar mirror, and the third shot drilled through a row of whiskey bottles. Women screamed, and men hurled themselves to the floor, panic spreading across the room. Holliday hurried toward the door, drawing his Peacemaker as he went past the dice table. A voice from the street boomed out in a guttural roar.

"Lila! You hear me, Lila? I come to get you!"

Holliday stepped through the door. Framed in a spill of light from the shattered window, he saw Mike Gordon standing in the middle of the street. The thimblerigger was staggering drunk, and clearly intent on reclaiming the girl he'd belted that afternoon. He shook his pistol at Holliday.

"Send her out, goddammit! I want Lila!"

"Drop your gun, Gordon. Don't make me kill you."

Gordon brayed a drunken curse. Then, straightening his arm, he fired. The slug thunked into the door frame, and Holliday leveled the Peacemaker. He feathered the trigger, and fired again as Gordon tried to bring his gun to bear. The impact sent Gordon reeling, his legs tangled, like a puppet with its strings gone haywire. He pitched to the ground on his side and lay still. The gun dropped from his hand.

Holliday advanced into the street. Behind him, the crowd jammed the door of the Occidental, watching as he approached the body. He thought he'd never killed a man with less reason, and wondered that a thimblerigger, a common con artist, would challenge him with a gun. Liquor and love, he told himself, made for a deadly combination.

Owen Kimball, the town marshal, appeared around the corner. He moved forward, pausing to glance down at the

dead man, then halted beside Holliday. His eyes were guarded. "Mr. Holliday, I'll thank you to holster that gun. What happened here?"

Holliday holstered his pistol. "Gordon shot out the windows." He motioned to the empty window frame. "When he kept shooting, I tried to stop him. He fired on me."

"Gordon fired first?"

"Ask the people in the Occidental. They will verify my story."

"That's my job," Kimball remarked. "There'll have to be a formal hearing on this. Law requires it of any unnatural death."

Holliday looked at him. "Are you arresting me?"

"Have I got your word you'll show up for the hearing?"

"You have my word as a gentleman and a property owner. You may have heard, I now own the Occidental."

"I heard." Kimball nodded to the body at their feet. "This isn't the last time, you know. Even if you're cleared at the hearing, there's other gunmen will try you on for size." He pursed his mouth. "You owning a gambling joint is like a red flag to a bull."

"You may have a point, Marshal."

Holliday turned, staring back at the Occidental. The aggravation of the night suddenly came over him, and he realized operating a gaming parlor was not his lot in life. There was, moreover, the real possibility that he would serve as a magnet for men who wished to try their luck with a gun. His gaze settled on the body a moment, then snapped back to the Occidental.

He thought it was indeed an albatross.

The courtroom was in an adobe building on a sidestreet of Old Town. Holliday and the others involved in the hearing filed into the room early the next afternoon. Overnight he had arranged for O'Farrel and Lila Foster, and one of the bartenders, to testify on his behalf. The bailiff called the court to order at one o'clock.

Justice of the Peace Oren Hough took his place on the

bench. He was an imposing man, with a thatch of white hair and a walrus mustache. From a handwritten document, he read aloud the official purpose of the hearing. Then he glanced at a man seated at one of two tables directly before the bench.

"Are you ready to proceed, Mr. Sanchez?"

City Attorney Manuel Sanchez rose to his feet. Of Mexican descent, slim and dark-haired, he was an elected official, representing civil and criminal matters for Las Vegas. He nodded. "We are prepared, Your Honor."

Hough glanced toward the spectator benches. "Are you represented by an attorney, Mr. Holliday?"

"No, Your Honor." Holliday stood. "I will represent myself."

"That's highly unusual, Mr. Holliday. Particularly in a case involving a homicide."

"I have had some small experience in such matters, Judge. Given the circumstances, I have no need of counsel."

"As you prefer," Hough noted. "You may proceed, Mr. Sanchez."

The first witness was a local physician, who served as the county coroner. Under questioning from Sanchez, he testified that the deceased, one Mike Gordon, had sustained two gunshot wounds. He went on to state that a bullet to the heart had been the cause of death.

Town Marshal Owen Kimball was then called to the stand. He testified that upon arriving at the scene, he had found John H. Holliday, otherwise known as Doc Holliday, standing over the deceased with a gun in his hand. He further related that Holliday had admitted to the killing, but had not been detained. He felt Holliday would honor his word to appear in court.

"No further questions," Sanchez said. "That will be all, Marshal."

Judge Hough peered over his spectacles. "Mr. Holliday?"

"Thank you, Your Honor." Holliday approached the witness stand. "If you will, Marshal, tell the court what you

found upon inspecting the deceased's pistol.''

"Freshly fired,'' Kimball said. "Four rounds fired and one unfired cartridge still in the chamber.''

"Were you able to determine where the expended rounds struck?''

"Three rounds hit the window and the back bar of the Occidental. The fourth round lodged in the outside door frame. I pried it out.''

"For what purpose did the deceased fire at a door?''

"Witnesses to the shooting said you were standing in the door. Gordon fired at you and missed. Then you killed him.''

"In other words, Gordon fired first?''

"Yeah, all the witnesses agreed on that.''

"I've no more questions, Your Honor.''

Sanchez next called Holliday to the stand. His keen black eyes were alert, piercing. "You admit you killed the deceased, Mike Gordon?''

"I do,'' Holliday said firmly. "In defense of my life.''

"How many men have you killed, Mr. Holliday . . . in defense of your life?''

"No more than necessary, Mr. Sanchez. All forced upon me, I might add.''

Sanchez appeared skeptical. "Is it not true that you challenged Mike Gordon? Threatened to kill him?''

"No,'' Holliday countered. "I told him to drop his gun. I said something to the effect, 'Don't make me kill you.' ''

"Why did you take enforcement of the law upon yourself? Why did you not wait and permit a peace officer to arrest Mr. Gordon?''

"Gordon was endangering the lives of my customers. When I came outside, there were no peace officers in sight. His next shot might have killed an innocent bystander.''

"Of course,'' Sanchez said caustically. "So you shot him as a public service. Is that what we are to believe, Mr. Holliday?''

"I shot him,'' Holliday said without inflection, "because

he fired on me. To be more precise, he was trying to kill me.''

"Is it not true that Gordon was drunk? So intoxicated that he posed no real threat?''

"His first shot missed me by no more than six inches. I thought it imprudent to wait and see if his aim improved.''

"Are you not known as a shootist, Mr. Holliday? A professional gunman?''

"I am a professional gambler, Mr. Sanchez. Nothing more nor less.''

Sanchez sniffed. "I have no further questions of this . . . witness.''

"Very well,'' the judge said. "Anyone you want to call, Mr. Holliday?''

"Yes, there is, Your Honor. Thank you most kindly.''

Holliday briefly questioned two witnesses. Jim O'Farrel recounted that the deceased had manhandled one of his employees yesterday afternoon, and how he'd thrown him out. The bartender, Johnny McNamara, testified that he had witnessed the shooting through the shattered window. He substantiated Holliday's version of the incident. Mike Gordon had fired first.

Lila Foster was then called to the stand. After she was seated, Holliday positioned himself so that she was facing the judge. "You were formerly the companion of the deceased. For how long, Miss Foster?''

"Almost three years.''

"What was his vocation?''

She looked confused. "Vocation?''

"His occupation.''

"Oh.'' She sat erect. "Mike was a thimblerigger. Anything with a con to it, that was his game.''

Holliday nodded. "A swindler often finds himself in a tight fix. Was Gordon ever caught out?''

"Yes.''

"How did he respond?''

Her eyes dropped. "Mike was only caught twice. Once in Leadville and again in Denver. He murdered both men.''

"Were you a witness to these murders, Miss Foster?"

"Oh, no, I never got involved in Mike's schemes. But he liked to brag when he got drunk, and both men turned up dead. They were shot in the back."

"I see," Holliday said solemnly. "So it would be fair to characterize Mike Gordon as a man with a violent temper?"

"That's the reason I left him. I got tired of him beating on me."

"Were you ever in fear of your life?"

"All the time," she said, tears puddling her eyes. "He was a cold-blooded killer. He enjoyed it."

Holliday gave her his handkerchief. "You are a brave young lady, Lila. No more questions."

Judge Hough rendered his decision without deliberation. He declared the death of Mike Gordon, at the hands of John H. Holliday, a justifiable homicide. No charges were to be pressed, and he ordered the books closed on the case. He dismissed the court with a bang of his gavel.

Outside the courtroom, O'Farrel fell in beside Holliday. "Congratulations, Doc. You ought to have been a lawyer."

"Practice makes perfect." Holliday took a slug from his flask. "I regret to say that wasn't my first time before the bar of justice."

"Well, your luck's running strong. Won the Occidental and cleared yourself of a hanging offense. You're on a roll."

"Not one of my choosing. How would you like to have the Occidental back?"

"Like it fine," O'Farrel said. "But I'm just as broke to-day as I was yesterday."

"I have a solution," Holliday told him. "I'll take forty thousand of what I won, and you keep the rest to run the club. I retain a quarter interest until you've paid me another fifty thousand. Sound fair?"

"Hell, it's more than fair, Doc. But I'm confounded why you'd do it. The Occidental's a gold mine."

"I prefer a simpler life, no entanglements. Do we have a deal?"

"Damn right!" O'Farrel said boisterously. "I'll pay you off in no time."

"I'm sure you will, Jim."

Holliday felt he'd won and lost and won again. The burden of last night, operating a gaming parlor, was the euphoria of today. All at a tidy profit.

By its vagaries, he told himself, life was the clown prince of jesters. And all the rest a joke.

CHAPTER 34

The stagecoach rolled to a dust-smothered halt at the Wells Fargo station. The driver set the foot brake with a hard kick and looped the reins around the lever. He leaned over the side with a raspy shout.

"All out for Prescott!"

Holliday was the first passenger to alight from the coach. After stretching his legs, he dusted himself off and walked to the luggage boot. He fished out a match, waiting for his steamer trunk to be unloaded, and lit a cigarillo. Puffing smoke, he hooked his thumbs in his vest and scanned the street. All around him was a tableau of bedlam.

Prescott was located in central Arizona. The town twisted through a pine-forested valley along Granite Creek, at an elevation of a mile high. Looming northward were the Santa Maria Mountains, and to the south were the peaks of the Weaver Mountains. Wagons drawn by oxen clogged the street, and the shouted curses of bullwhackers intermingled with the pop of their whips. The boardwalks were thronged with men, and the uproarious commotion of a mining camp pervaded the town. There was a sense of maddened revelry about the milling crowds.

A week ago, having tired of following the end-of-track railheads, Holliday had decided to try another mining camp. He recalled that Wyatt Earp's brother, Virgil, was the marshal in Prescott, and he'd booked passage for Arizona Ter-

ritory. Once the decision was made, he was eager to be on his way, and he had settled his interest in the Las Vegas gaming dive for fifty cents on the dollar. The next day he had boarded a stage that took him from New Mexico on a winding route through the westward mountains. Folded in his money belt were cash and bank drafts for more than ninety thousand dollars, and he felt an itch to gamble. He thought Prescott had the look of a camp that would attract high rollers.

The weather was blustery, with low clouds framed against the distant mountains. Holliday marked the date at October 16 as a handyman from the stagecoach line loaded his trunk onto a cart. The finest hotel in town was the Mount Tritle, and he engaged a suite with a handsomely appointed sitting room. He arranged for a suit to be pressed while a galvanized tub and buckets of hot water were brought to his suite. The trip westward had been tiring, and he lazed around in the tub for the better part of an hour. A shave with a splash of bay rum made him feel like a new man.

Shortly before dusk Holliday emerged from the hotel. With directions from the desk clerk, he walked upstreet toward the town marshal's office. He was curious to meet Virgil, the eldest of the Earp brothers, and reportedly a lawman of Wyatt's stature. As he moved along the boardwalk, he noted several banks, and a newspaper, and the territorial capitol building at the far end of the street. The business district was closing for the night, but a steady stream of men on foot and on horseback were headed for the lower part of town. He suspected the sporting district was in that direction.

The marshal's office was in a wide frame building, with jail cells beyond a partition at the rear. As Holliday came through the door, a man looked up from behind a desk, his features bathed in the glow of a lamp. The family resemblance was striking, and there was no question that he was a member of the Earp clan. He was stoutly built, a solid six-footer, with hard eyes and a sweeping handlebar mustache. His expression was one of quiet resolve, and he looked to

be in his middle thirties. A Colt six-gun was holstered high on his hip.

"Help you with something?"

"Yes, I believe so," Holliday said with an amiable smile. "Unless I'm mistaken, you must be Virgil Earp."

"You have me at a disadvantage, Mr.—?"

"Holliday. John Holliday. Wyatt has told me a great deal about you."

Virgil's eyes narrowed. "Doc Holliday?"

"I answer to that name as well."

"Wyatt's told me about you, too. Leastways, what could be put in a letter."

"Nothing too unfavorable, I trust." Holliday extended his hand. "A pleasure to meet you at last."

Virgil rose from his chair. His handshake was firm, and dry. "What brings you to Prescott?"

"A gambler travels wherever there's action. I hear good things about your town."

"We have our share of high rollers."

Holliday sensed something less than a welcome in the other man's manner. He was accustomed to a cool, and sometimes hostile, reception from peace officers. But he had expected more from the brother of Wyatt Earp.

"Let me put your mind at rest," he said. "I am not here to presume on my friendship with your brother. I merely thought to introduce myself."

Virgil hesitated, then gestured aimlessly. "Wyatt wrote me how you'd saved his life with them Texans. So I'll give you more leeway than I would most gambling men." He paused, his jawline tight. "But you kill anybody, I won't bend the law to save your neck."

"Nor would I expect special treatment of any sort. I will endeavor not to be a bother."

"Just wanted to clear the air." Virgil motioned him to a chair. "Guess you haven't heard the latest about Wyatt. He's on his way here."

"Prescott?" Holliday was astounded. "Wyatt's coming to Prescott?"

"Yeah, I just got the wire day before yesterday. He ought to be here in a couple of weeks."

"Why would he leave Dodge City? He's very highly thought of there."

"Not for me to say." Virgil's look became closed. "Wyatt'll have to tell you that himself. You never met my other brothers, have you?"

"Morgan and Warren?" Holliday said. "No, I haven't, even though Wyatt told me a good deal about them. Why do you ask?"

"Well, they're headed this way, too. Everybody's supposed to get here toward the end of the month."

"I recall Wyatt saying they are lawmen, as well."

"Sort of runs in the family," Virgil remarked. "Morgan's the marshal up in Butte, Montana. Warren's assistant town marshal in Cheyenne."

Holliday considered why four brothers, all of them lawmen, would gather in one spot. He thought there was more to it than a simple family reunion. But Virgil was clearly reluctant to offer an explanation. He would have to wait for Wyatt's arrival.

"Quite an occasion," he said. "All of you together, again."

"Near as I recollect, it's been three years, maybe longer. Work kept us pretty much scattered."

"Has Wyatt resigned his position in Dodge?"

"Like I said, you'll have to ask him."

A searing spasm ripped through Holliday's lungs. He bent forward in a strangled cough, and hawked a clot of bloody waste into his handkerchief. After returning the handkerchief to his pocket, he unstoppered his flask and took a long slug. His features pallid, he managed an offhand smile.

"I do not recommend stage travel in Arizona Territory. God never meant man to breathe dust."

Virgil looked unconvinced. "Wyatt told me about your condition. You need to see a sawbones?"

"Thank you, no," Holliday said, returning the flask to his pocket. "I am an enigma to the whole of the medical

profession.'' His eyes became inquisitive. ''Wyatt seems to have given you my life history. I confess I'm surprised.''

''Well—'' Virgil faltered, choosing his words. ''Wyatt was gonna stop off and see you in Las Vegas. Anyway, that's what he said in his last letter.''

''How did he know I was in New Mexico?''

''Your name's a regular thing in the newspapers. Guess folks like to read about a shootist.''

Holliday let the comment pass. ''Why was Wyatt planning to stop in Las Vegas?''

''Wanted to talk with you,'' Virgil said. ''Got a proposition, but that's all I'll say. Let him tell you about it.''

''You make it sound . . . mysterious.''

''I've said too much already. It'll keep till he gets here.''

''Providence has a strange way of dealing the cards.''

''I don't follow you.''

''Wyatt would have missed me in Las Vegas. But here I am in Prescott. Perhaps it was fated.''

Virgil shrugged. ''I reckon anything's possible.''

Holliday's gaze went to the wall behind the desk. A wanted poster on William Bonney, otherwise known as Billy the Kid, caught his eye. Beside it, he saw one on Dave Rudabaugh, and the reward was dead or alive. He knew now where Rudabaugh had gone after their chance meeting in Las Vegas. He wondered if Josh Webb had also joined the Kid's gang.

''Interesting,'' he said, nodding at the poster. ''I see Dave Rudabaugh has joined forces with Billy the Kid. A poor choice of company.''

''Damn fool,'' Virgil said stolidly. ''He should've stuck to robbing trains. You know Rudabaugh?''

''Our paths have crossed here and there. I take it you believe cattle rustling to be more dangerous than train robbery?''

''Especially when you ride with the Kid. What he done in the Lincoln County War signed his death warrant. Anybody caught with him will likely get hung.''

''Too bad,'' Holliday commented. ''Rudabaugh isn't a

killer at heart. He just prefers the outlaw life."

Virgil searched his face. "Rudabaugh a friend of yours?"

"No, merely an acquaintance. A sporting man meets all kinds. Outlaws included."

Holliday detected skepticism. He suspected Virgil placed him in the same class as Rudabaugh, or the Kid. For a moment, he toyed with the idea of relating how he'd once put Wyatt on Rudabaugh's trail. But then, on second thought, he rejected the notion. He saw no reason to justify himself to anyone, or curry favor. He wasn't yet sure that he even liked Virgil.

"The Kid's as good as dead," Virgil said absently. "Lawmen from Arizona to Texas are lookin' to collect that reward. He'll more'n likely get shot before anybody has a chance to hang him."

"Do you know Joshua Webb? He once served as a deputy with Bat Masterson."

"I don't place the name. What makes you ask?"

"A matter of curiosity," Holliday replied. "The last time I saw Rudabaugh, they were partners. I wondered if Webb also enlisted in the Kid's gang."

"Well, if he did, that'd be a helluva note. A lawman turned outlaw deserves to have his neck stretched."

"There is a caprice to some men's lives. Circumstance often dictates their course."

"Not to my way of thinkin'," Virgil said shortly. "A man comes to a fork in the road and he's got a choice to make. No excuses for them that takes the wrong turn."

Holliday thought the statement revealing. Virgil had all the earmarks of a puritan, straightlaced and rigid in his views. Unlike Wyatt, he probably never saw both sides of the coin. He sounded intolerant and implacable. A stickler for the rules.

"Well, on to other things," Holliday said. "Perhaps you could recommend a gaming establishment in Prescott. I prefer high-stakes poker."

"The Gem's the best," Virgil told him. "Any high rollers in town, you'll find 'em there. Poker, faro, no nevermind."

"Sounds made to order."

"Why don't I walk you over? I'll introduce you to Harvey Fuller. He owns the place."

"That's most kind of you."

"Least I could do for a friend of Wyatt's."

Virgil led him downtown. A civic booster of sorts, he provided a monologue on points of interest along the way. Prescott was settled in the early 1860s, by prospectors who found gold along Granite Creek. In 1863, concerned that the Confederacy would attempt an occupation, President Lincoln granted Arizona territorial status. The town boomed in 1870 when modern technology reduced the cost of extracting ore from gold and silver. The population was now pushing the twenty thousand mark.

"Good town," Virgil went on. " 'Course, we have our troublemakers, like anybody else. But they get the message pretty quick."

"From the way you say that," Holliday observed, "I take it troublemakers are treated to a rough time. Do you follow Wyatt's practice—buffalo them with a pistol barrel?"

"Miners are a lot like cowhands. A few busted heads and everybody starts to toe the line. Got to keep 'em in their place."

"What works in Dodge City works in Prescott. Is that it?"

"Or vice versa. I showed Wyatt that buffalo trick a long time ago."

Holliday accepted the statement at face value. Virgil impressed him as an older, and somewhat tougher, version of Wyatt. He had no doubt that Prescott was run with a nononsense attitude, and an iron fist. A troublemaker was almost certainly assured of a busted head.

The sporting district was locally dubbed Whiskey Row. At the lower end of town, along a four-block section, saloons and gambling dens operated beside hurdy-gurdy dance halls and a surprisingly large selection of bordellos. The Gem Saloon & Gaming Parlor was much like a hundred such dives Holliday had seen across the West. The mirror

behind the bar was flanked by the ubiquitous nude paintings, with gaming layouts arrayed along the opposite wall. The poker tables were grouped at the rear of the room.

Harvey Fuller, the owner, beamed when Virgil made the introduction. "An honor, Mr. Holliday," he said grandly. "Your reputation precedes you as a high-stakes player. I'm proud to have you in my establishment."

"Thank you," Holliday said. "Marshal Earp tells me there are high rollers aplenty in Prescott."

"And they all come to the Gem," Fuller bragged. "Mine owners, ranchers, and of course, our resident politicos. We have a regular clientele from the territorial legislature."

"I have no objection to playing with politicians. As the saying goes, their money spends."

"Careful now," Virgil said, with his first glint of humor. "I got lots of friends up at the capitol. Don't trim them too hard."

"Virgil's quite popular in Prescott," Fuller said approvingly. "He made our town safe from cutthroats and ruffians. The powers-that-be think very highly of him."

Holliday smiled. "No public servant will leave my table a sore loser. I have the gift of flattery."

Virgil and Fuller stared at him a moment. Neither of them were certain whether he was serious, or merely indulging in a jest. Finally, after begging off on a drink, Virgil went on about the business of policing the town. Fuller got Holliday ensconced at a table reserved for high rollers, and quickly spread the word that he was looking for action. His notoriety drew a crowd within the hour.

The game lasted far into the night. Holliday won handily, bluffing and pressing his luck almost by rote. Yet he was distracted, his mind not fully on the cards. A thought kept buzzing through his head.

He wondered what sort of scheme the Earps were hatching.

Chapter 35

Holliday was attired in a dove-gray suit. A gold watch chain was looped across his vest, and a rich magenta tie was knotted at the throat of his shirt. He came downstairs shortly after the noon hour.

The lobby was filled with politicians. The legislature was in session, and lawmakers made the hotel home away from home when they were in Prescott. They were stuffed from the noon meal, and stood talking politics in small groups. A cone of silence followed Holliday as he moved through their ranks, his sartorial elegance a spark of color against their drab attire. Several of them smiled pleasantly, greeting him by name.

For the past two weeks many of the legislators had regularly taken a chair at his poker game. He was often amazed at the amount of money they lost, for few of them were personally wealthy. The other regular players, mine owners and local cattle barons, possessed the wherewithal to absorb heavy losses. But politicians were public servants, and he gathered that the annual salary for legislator was a mere pittance. He thought corruption was indeed a profitable enterprise.

The dining room was all but empty. At a table by the far wall, Holliday saw Morgan and Warren Earp, and they motioned to him. The younger brothers of the Earp clan had arrived in Prescott only yesterday, October 30, and he had

met them when Virgil brought them by the Gem for a drink. Walking toward the table, he was struck again by the family resemblance all of the Earps shared. Their size and rough-hewn features, and a preference for handlebar mustaches, were remarkably similar. He was reminded of four peas in a pod.

" 'Afternoon, Doc," Morgan said. "Grab a chair and take a load off your feet."

"Thank you most kindly. Good company always improves a meal."

Morgan and Warren were through eating, and the waitress came to collect their plates. She brought Holliday a cup of coffee, which he laced with a shot from his flask. As she moved away, Warren tapped a newspaper lying on the table. His expression was one of eager interest.

"We were just reading about you, Doc. You made the front page."

"Journalists make too much of too little. I weary of seeing my name in print."

Holliday glanced at the newspaper. The headline was below the fold, in bold print. DR. HOLLIDAY CONTINUES TO COURT LADY LUCK. The article dealt with his hot streak, lasting now for two weeks, and speculated that he had won in excess of thirty thousand dollars. There was the usual reference to the "notorious" Doc Holliday, shootist and gambler par excellence. He pushed the paper aside.

"There must be a dearth of news in Prescott. A poker game hardly merits such attention."

"Devil it don't!" Warren said earnestly. "Thirty thousand bucks in a couple of weeks. That's some haul!"

"Yes, I suppose so," Holliday agreed. "But then, you have to consider the caliber of men playing at my table. Their combined wealth makes my winnings look picayune."

"Yeah, but you've clipped them good, Doc. How'd you get 'em hooked on your game?"

"No secret there," Morgan said, rapping the newspaper. "Laid out in black and white, for everybody to read. They all want to play *the* Doc Holliday."

There was no arguing the point. Men of wealth and power were compelled to test themselves against a noteworthy professional. To keep himself interested, Holliday had turned it into a table-stakes game just within the last week. A man needed at least five thousand for a seat at the table, and there was no limit on the amount of a single wager. The pot on a hand was often ten thousand or more, and men dropped small fortunes every night. Yet there was a waiting list to get into the game.

"Still mystifies me," Warren said. "You've got 'em outclassed so bad they're losin' their butts. Why do they keep coming back for more?"

"A congenital condition peculiar to gamblers." Holliday paused, took a sip of laced coffee. "They believe my streak will end and the cards will turn in their favor. Quite simply, they believe in luck."

"You're saying luck's got nothin' to do with it?"

"Luck enters into any game of chance. But at the risk of braggadocio, skill separates the winners from the losers. Of course, I continue to foster the notion that luck comes to any man who waits."

"And while they wait," Warren whooped, "you clean their plow. Jesus H. Christmas! Flat takes the cake."

Warren's youthful enthusiasm was contagious. Holliday knew by now that Warren was twenty-four, and Morgan was twenty-eight. Though he'd met them only last night, he found himself somewhat partial to Warren. Morgan seemed to him a younger version of Virgil.

The waitress brought his eggs and toast. Weary of talking about himself, he moved to change the subject. As he cracked open an egg, he glanced from one to the other. "Have you heard anything further about Wyatt?"

"Not yet," Morgan said. " 'Course, we were set to meet here by the end of the month, and that's tomorrow. Knowin' Wyatt, he'll make it."

Warren laughed. "Wyatt was never late for anything in his life. He's liable to pop through the door any minute."

"I wish he would." Holliday spooned egg, took a bite of

toast. "I'm on tenterhooks waiting to hear of this grand scheme. Virgil treats it like a sealed dictum."

"Yeah, that's Virge," Warren said humorously. "Always was the tight-lipped one in the family. But don't worry yourself none, Doc. We're all gonna make a million—"

"Hold up right there," Morgan interrupted. "Virge said to wait on Wyatt, and that's that. No need to talk out of school."

"Hell, Morg, I didn't say nothin'. Don't get your bowels in an uproar."

"I'm just tellin' you, that's all. Virge knows best."

Watching them, Holliday was reminded that blood was thicker than water. The four brothers, until now, were scattered to the winds, and their parents owned a farm in California. Yet they were a westering family, having migrated from Iowa to all points of the compass, and their closeness was clearly untouched by time or distance. Together again after several years, it was as though they had never been separated. They were four, but oddly one. All of a mind.

"Doc, don't take it personal," Warren said jokingly. "Once Virge and Wyatt get their minds set, that's all she wrote. We're just along for the ride."

"That's a helluva thing to say," Morgan objected. "Nobody gave anybody else marchin' orders. We all agreed."

"Never said anything about marchin' orders. But we're here . . . aren't we?"

Holliday thought that Warren had got the last word. The youngest brother was a single man, and free to follow his fancy. But from conversation last night, it was apparent that Morgan had left his wife in Montana, and would send for her as circumstance dictated. Virgil, who was also married, had never once made reference to his wife, either directly or in passing. Whatever their plans, they were in it together, their wives excluded, and sworn to silence. All else awaited Wyatt's arrival.

Someone gave marching orders, and no one broke ranks. Holliday was left to ponder his role in what still remained a riddle.

* * *

Wyatt Earp arrived late the next afternoon on the westbound stage. After collecting his warbag, he walked over to the hotel and took a room. The desk clerk verified that Morgan and Warren, as well as Doc Holliday, were guests in the hotel. He was confident they could all be found at the Gem Saloon and Gaming Parlor.

A short while later Wyatt entered the Gem. Virgil, along with Morgan and Warren, were standing at the bar with Holliday. The table-stakes game was by now the main attraction in Prescott, and usually started around seven every evening. The Earps, like many of the townspeople, were there as spectators.

Wyatt greeted his brothers with a round of handshakes. The kinship was evident, and within moments it was as though they had never been apart. Then he turned to Holliday, extended his hand. He nodded with a slow smile.

"Long time, Doc," he said. "You don't look any the worse for wear."

"Welcome to Prescott," Holliday replied genially. "Your arrival has been much anticipated."

"I stopped off in Las Vegas and got a surprise. Found out you'd come on here."

"No doubt our paths were fated to cross."

"There's big things in the wind. Where can we go to talk? We need someplace private."

"You want to talk now? Won't it wait until tomorrow?"

"Some things won't keep, Doc. By tomorrow, we'll be on the trail."

The remark fired Holliday's curiosity. A few of the regular players were already waiting at his table, and a groan of protest went up when he excused himself from the game. After promising to return within an hour or so, he followed the Earps from the saloon. On the way uptown he suggested that they meet in his suite, which was large enough to accommodate everyone and still afford privacy. Some minutes later they trooped into the hotel.

Upstairs, Holliday got everyone seated. He removed

glasses from a cabinet and passed around a bottle of bourbon. After pouring himself a drink, he took a chair across from Wyatt. He arched an eyebrow.

"Virgil says you have a proposition. But so far, he's kept the cat in the bag. I am all ears."

"Don't blame Virge. I wanted to tell you myself. Have you heard of Tombstone?"

"The mining camp?" Holliday said. "Yes, I understand it's somewhere in southern Arizona. Quite a strike, from what I hear."

"Doc, it's the biggest silver strike since Leadville. Some say it's even richer."

A year ago a lone prospector struggled along the mountain slopes of southeastern Arizona. His name was Ed Schieffelin, and almost by accident, he stumbled upon the richest silver strike in history. With ore assaying at twenty thousand dollars a ton, the discovery sparked the greatest mining boom in the Southwest. Schieffelin named his strike Tombstone.

In a matter of months, the mile-high camp mushroomed into a boomtown. Men and machinery began pouring in, followed by merchants and speculators, and the largest contingent of the sporting crowd ever gathered in the Arizona barrens. From a few hundred tents and squalid shacks, Tombstone burst upon the map as a rip-roaring helldorado, with a population pushing ten thousand. A motherlode of silver still fueled the boom.

"The reason we're here—" Wyatt motioned around at his brothers. "We plan to take over Tombstone. Lock, stock, and barrel."

"Take it over?" Holliday repeated. "What does that mean?"

"It means the whole shebang. Tell him, Virge."

Virgil looked relieved to be released from his oath of silence. He explained that Tombstone was located in Pima County, with the county seat seventy miles away, in Tucson. The area was too large to effectively govern, particularly with the problems created by a boomtown, and the territorial

legislature planned to split it into two counties. Tombstone would shortly become a part of the new county, Cochise County.

"Law enforcement's at the top of the list," Virgil went on. "I've got friends in the legislature, and I managed to pull a few strings. We're gonna be all the law there is in Tombstone."

Holliday appeared bemused. "*All* the law?"

"All that counts. I wrangled myself a commission as a Deputy U.S. Marshal. I've resigned here as town marshal effective November first, tomorrow. I'll be the top lawman in Tombstone."

"And Wyatt?"

"That's the kicker," Virgil said, grinning. "I got Wyatt appointed a deputy sheriff, stationed in Tombstone. His campaign for sheriff of the new county—Cochise County— starts the minute we hit town. He's a cinch to get elected."

"I see." Holliday glanced around at their faces. "What about Morgan and Warren?"

"One way or another we'll get 'em a badge. That'll make it legal when we make our play."

"By your play, I assume you mean the political takeover of Tombstone."

"That's just part of it," Wyatt interjected. "Once we control the political machinery, the door's wide open. Every mine owner in town will jump at the chance to have us as partners." His mouth quirked in a crafty smile. "Same goes for the sporting crowd."

"For a man with an aversion to politics, you've certainly changed. Why the turnabout?"

"I finally saw the light. Politics makes the world go round, and politicians always ride the gravy train. Time to make my fortune."

Holliday thought it a grander scheme than he'd imagined. He reflected that it was Virgil, with the political connections in Arizona, who had put the pieces together. But he saw now that Wyatt, though a few years younger than Virgil,

was the driving force, the leader. He had no doubt they would take Tombstone by storm.

"I'm impressed," he said. "Granted, it is an audacious plan, but you have the audacity to pull it off. How does it involve me?"

"You're a full partner," Wyatt told him. "We stand to make a million, maybe more. You get an equal share."

"And how do I earn my share?"

"There's bound to be opposition. Nobody takes over a town as rich as Tombstone without a fight of some sort. We want you with us when it happens."

"Let me understand," Holliday said, watching him. "Am I to be a hired gun?"

"Doc, listen to me," Wyatt said solemnly. "There's five men in this room, and you're the only one not an Earp. We wouldn't invite anyone else into this deal. Am I right, Virge?"

Virgil spread his hands. "Wyatt says we need you, and I go along. We'd like you with us, Doc."

Morgan and Warren bobbed their heads in agreement. Holliday was touched by the sincerity of their invitation, almost as though he were being accepted into the family. From a personal standpoint, whether or not they made millions in Tombstone was of small import. But he found great appeal in the idea of a grand adventure with friends. Perhaps the one worthwhile venture left to him in the time remaining. A time to live.

"How could I refuse?" he said with an idle gesture. "Of course, if you're leaving tomorrow, I'll have to follow along. I will not quit a winning streak. No self-respecting gambler would."

"Then it's settled," Wyatt affirmed. "We'll get things rolling, and you come on when you're ready. Knew I could count on you, Doc."

"Yes, I am reliable to a fault. One of my few virtues."

Wyatt stood, and everyone got to their feet. He raised his glass in a toast, and all five glasses clinked together. His eyes were alight with the moment.

"To Tombstone!"

* * *

Holliday walked down to the livery stable late the next
morning. The men were saddling their mounts, purchased
by Virgil for the overland journey to Tombstone. The trip
would consume the better part of two weeks, and Morgan
and Warren were leading packhorses. Wyatt turned from
checking the latigo on a roan gelding.

"Well, Doc, we're off," he said. "Have to tell you, I'm
anxious to get the wheels in motion."

"I won't be far behind. A week, probably no longer. The
cards will tell the tale."

"Not wishing you bad luck, but I hope the worm turns.
I'd like you there sooner than later."

"I will see you in Tombstone, Wyatt. You may depend
on it."

They shook hands and Wyatt stepped into the saddle. The
others waved, then reined their horses four abreast as Wyatt
led the way south out of town. Holliday stood watching until
they were some distance down the street. He thought Tomb-
stone was in for a surprise. Sooner rather than later.

Uptown, Holliday moved along the boardwalk toward the
hotel. He checked his watch and noted that it was almost
twelve o'clock, time for breakfast. As he approached the
hotel entrance, the noon stage rolled to a halt at the Wells
Fargo station across the street. He stopped in his tracks,
momentarily stunned, as Kate waved to him from the coach
window. She called out in a laughing voice.

"Hi, there, Doc! Look who's come home!"

Holliday stared at her, unable to respond. For the first
time in his life, he was struck speechless. A mute rooted in
shock.

He wondered how the deuce she'd found him.

CHAPTER 36

Holliday snapped awake, his lungs on fire. He sat bolt upright, wracked by a harsh fit of coughing. The spasms shook his frame, and he turned, seated on the edge of the bed, his head between his knees. From the bedstand, he grabbed a handkerchief as the seizure tore at his innards. He spat a glob of bloody matter into the handkerchief.

Kate scrambled from beneath the covers, scooting across the bed. She uncorked the bourbon bottle on the nightstand and brought it to his mouth. He took a long, gulping swallow, then another, and pushed the bottle aside. The fiery liquid quelled his cough, but left his throat raw and scratchy. He gasped for air, a rattling sound deep in his chest.

Tenderly, as though ministering to a sick child, Kate cradled him in her arms. He slumped back against her, so wasted he felt almost weightless in her embrace. She rocked him back and forth, his labored breathing the only sound in the room. His color slowly returned, and he reached for the bottle, took another long pull of bourbon. He shrugged out of her arms, bracing himself with his hands on the edge of the bed. The sensation that he was suffocating gradually eased off.

"God, sugar," she said, gently rubbing his back. "You're worse than I've ever seen you. Haven't you been taking care of yourself?"

"I adhere to a regimen of whiskey and cards. Longevity is not my strong suit."

"You ought to try getting more rest, honeybunch. Those all-night card games will be the ruin of you."

" 'Doomsday is near,' " Holliday said in a hoarse voice. " 'Die all, die merrily.' "

She looked concerned. "What kind of crazy talk is that?"

"Shakespeare. *King Henry the Fourth*. A maxim for the ages."

"C'mon, Doc, you're not dying. You're just plain killing yourself."

"I pride myself on being incorrigible. Perhaps I will find redemption in the next life."

"Always got a snappy comeback, don't you? Honestly, sugar, you haven't changed an iota."

"I sincerely hope not."

Holliday stood, testing his balance. The morning dose of bourbon seemed to have restored his equilibrium, and he walked to the washstand. After sloshing water into the basin, he briskly scrubbed his face. Then, shaving mug in hand, he lathered up with a foamy brush. He began stropping his razor.

In the mirror, he saw Kate stretch like a languid cat. With the razor at his jawline, he idly pondered the question of why he'd taken her back. A week ago, alternately begging and cajoling, she had pleaded with him to let bygones be bygones. She swore she was a changed woman, reformed from her old ways and anxious to make a new start. All the whoring and drunkenness and fits of temper were behind her. She would be his alone, faithful and obedient. Just him.

Holliday placed little faith in reformed whores. He thought himself a brute for punishment to even consider rekindling their liaison. But he missed having a woman in his bed, and dreaded the dreams of Mattie that came so often in his darkest sleep. He told himself that Kate provided a distraction, and for however long it lasted, a pleasant companion. She was sincere today, concerned for his health,

anxious to make amends. Tomorrow would take care of itself.

After they finished dressing, they went downstairs for breakfast. Kate wore a simple gown, modest if not demure, all in keeping with her newfound air of respectability. Holliday, playing his role in their arrangement, held her chair as they seated themselves by a streetside window. She ordered a breakfast fit for a lumberjack, while he stuck with the usual eggs and toast. He spiked his coffee with an extra-strong dollop of bourbon.

"Feeling any better?" she asked, touching his hand. "You still look a little peaked."

"Have no fear." Holliday sipped coffee, gave her a wry look. "Like a phoenix risen from the ashes, I live to crow another day. I am indestructible, Kate."

"You're as full of gas as a pig's bladder. I never know when you're kidding or not."

"You see me at the top of my form. Fit as a fiddle, or perhaps the fiddler. Never better."

She laughed happily. "God, I'm glad we're back together, Doc. I missed the way you tickle my funny bone."

"And I admire a woman who enjoys a jest. Life's sour notes are not my style."

Holliday thought her remarkable in many ways. Not the least of which was her gift for deduction, the nose of a bloodhound. His long-running lucky streak was a matter of interest throughout the West, and his name alone was still news in Dodge City. She had tracked him to Prescott through widely circulated newspaper articles which were reprinted in the *Dodge City Globe*. Upon hearing that Wyatt Earp had departed for Arizona, she correctly deduced that Holliday was still in Prescott. She caught the first train west.

When he finished his eggs, Holliday lit a cigarillo. His lungs rebelled at the first puff and he coughed a spurt of smoke. Kate looked up from her plate as he hastily took a swig of laced coffee. She assessed him with a concerned frown.

"You really shouldn't play tonight. You're not up to snuff, even if you do say so."

"How could I disappoint my public?" Holliday said with a sly smile. "I have a certain reputation to uphold."

"Who do you think you're fooling?" She paused with a bite of flapjacks speared on her fork. "You'd play if you had to be carried there on a stretcher. Don't tell me I'm wrong, either."

"On the contrary, the very image of it has an unusual flair. Poker from the supine position. I like it."

Kate was genuinely worried. Some six months had passed since their parting in Dodge City, and in that time his condition had deteriorated markedly. His cough was worse than she remembered, and his bloody sputum looked as though it contained raw flecks of lung tissue. There was a jaundiced cast to his features that concerned her as well. She thought he was operating on grit, hardheaded nerve.

"Why not call it quits, sugar? I mean, you're ahead of the game and then some. What is it now, thirty thousand?"

"Forty thousand," Holliday corrected her. "I was in rare form last night."

"All the more reason to walk away before you keel over."

"A gambler never quits when the cards are running strong. Or when he's so far ahead. That would be considered bad form."

"Those chumps!" she said derisively. "You don't owe them anything."

"Perhaps not," Holliday allowed. "But I do owe it to myself. Who knows, I might press it to fifty thousand."

"You might press yourself into an early grave, too."

"Oh, I think not. I have a ways to go yet."

"What makes you so certain?"

"A sinner has an ear for the knell. I hear no tolls in the night."

Kate gave it up as a lost cause. To push him further would only incur his anger, and she was wary of pressing her own luck. Besides, she told herself, he lived to gamble, to defy

the odds. And so far, he was ahead in the one game that counted.

He was still alive.

The game started at seven. By nine o'clock Holliday was down almost eleven thousand dollars. When he held a decent hand, the other players held better cards. When he bluffed, someone always called with cards too good to fold. His hot streak abruptly turned cold.

Holliday was not a superstitious man. He subscribed to none of the hoary rituals practiced by many gamblers to reverse bad fortune. Walking around his chair three times, or changing seats, or any of the other mumbo-jumbo, was to him an exercise in the absurd. He had learned long ago that when the deck went cold a wise man went home. Under similar circumstances, he had seen even seasoned gamblers lose all they had won and dig into their pockets for more. To him, after a string of second-best hands, the sign was clear to read. Tonight was not his night.

Still, he found it difficult to quit when he was so far ahead. His forty thousand in winnings had dwindled to about thirty thousand, but it remained a sizable score. The high rollers seated at his table, politicians and mine owners and wealthy ranchers, expected fair treatment when the worm finally turned. For a gambler of his stature to walk away when the cards went sour would be considered bad form, poor sportsmanship. There was a certain etiquette to gambling, and a man's standing within the sporting crowd hinged upon such things. He would not sully his reputation.

Then, unexpectedly, the worm turned again. Holliday folded on a bad hand and was in the process of lighting a cigarillo. Over the flare of the match, he saw a man push through the door and walk to the bar. The man's name was Charley White, one of many gamblers who had drifted through Dodge City last spring. But he was a four-flusher, a seemingly respectable member of the sporting fraternity who placed little value on honor. He had left Holliday holding a marker for three thousand dollars.

Excusing himself, Holliday rose and walked to the bar. He halted beside White, who was about to down a shot of whiskey. White glanced around, then paused, his glass in midair. His face blanched.

"Well, Doc," he said weakly. "Long time no see. What're you doing here?"

"I was about to ask you the same thing."

"Just got in a couple of hours ago. Heard there was easy pickings in Prescott."

"Obviously, you failed to hear I was in town. Or you wouldn't be here, would you, Charley?"

White swallowed hard. "C'mon, Doc, that was a long time ago."

"Not long enough," Holliday informed him. "I could never abide a welcher. You stiffed me for three thousand."

"And I'll pay you, swear to Christ! You got my word on it."

"Your word has little currency, Charley. You'll pay me now."

"Wish I could," White mumbled dolefully. "But I've been down on my luck lately. Hard times are doggin' my heels."

"You are a poor liar," Holliday said coldly. "Hand over the money or I will put out the word. You won't find a game in all of Arizona Territory."

"Goddammit, I told you I haven't got it. Don't try puttin' the squeeze on me, Doc."

"I want you out of my sight, right now. Be careful we don't meet again until you can settle the debt."

"That sounds like a threat."

"Take it any way you please."

White was lithe and muscular, with ice-blue eyes. He was reported to have killed several men on the Gamblers' Circuit, quick to anger and quick with a gun. But now, his nerves deserting him, he was unable to hold Holliday's gaze. His drink untouched, his expression sullen, he pushed away from the bar. He walked out the door.

Holliday turned back toward the poker game. He thought

he would never see Charley White again, or the money, and he dismissed it from mind. As he approached the table, the door slammed open and he heard one of the bartenders shout a warning. A slug fried the air past his ear.

The gunshot sent men scurrying for cover. Holliday spun around, drawing the Colt Lightning, as another bullet plucked at the sleeve of his coat. He saw White framed in the doorway, and he quickly caught the sights, tripped the trigger. White staggered, a starburst of blood on his chest, his features frozen in a look of dull amazement. He tried to bring his pistol level.

Arm extended, Holliday took deliberate aim. The distance was some twenty paces, and he feathered the trigger, squeezing off a shot. When he fired, a puff of dust kicked off the breast pocket of White's suit jacket, directly over the heart. White took a step sideways, the gun clattering from his hand to the floor, then he buckled at the knees. He went down with his eyes fixed on infinity.

Holliday strode forward. The crowd got to their feet, watching in morbid silence, as he cautiously approached the body. He kicked the gun aside, then looked closer, and saw the fallen man's eyes locked in a death stare. A buzz of conversation swept through the room as he holstered the Lightning and walked to the bar. The bartender poured a shot glass to the brim, and he downed it neat. He told himself that Charley White was a damn fool. No man should die for the sake of bruised pride.

Ben Crowder, the new town marshal, hurried into the Gem moments later. He inspected the body, then questioned Holliday at some length. After several witnesses gave their account of the shooting, he rejoined Holliday at the bar. "Glad you're in the clear," he announced. "I wouldn't want to arrest you."

"No, Marshal," Holliday said stiffly. "You would never want to arrest me."

Crowder blinked, unnerved by the harsh tone. "Well, fair fight or not, there's got to be a hearing. I'll expect you to appear."

"You may depend on it, Marshal. I am nothing if not timely."

Holliday signaled the barkeep for another drink. All in a matter of hours his streak had gone cold and he'd killed a man. Some inner voice told him it was ended in Prescott.

Time to move on.

The hearing was held early the next morning. After all the evidence was heard, the judge ruled the shooting a justifiable homicide. A reporter tried to interview Holliday on his way out of the courtroom, but he kept walking. He had nothing to say to the press.

By late morning, Holliday had purchased a buckboard and a quick-stepping bay mare. When he arrived at the hotel, hopping down from the buckboard, he was in a chipper mood. The court hearing behind him, he'd decided that he had much to say grace over. His bankroll was fattened by some thirty thousand, and while the undertaker was busy today, he was still kicking. All in all, Prescott had treated him well.

Shortly after the noon hour, the hotel handyman loaded Holliday's steamer trunk and Kate's luggage in the back of the buckboard. Holliday assisted Kate into the front seat and climbed aboard on the driver's side. She unsnapped her parasol as he gathered the reins, clucked to the mare, and pulled away from the hotel. They were silent as they drove through the sporting district, each of them lost in their own thoughts. On the outskirts of town, they took the road leading south.

Holliday stared at the range of mountains ahead. Thunderclouds ringed the lofty spires, and he was somehow reminded that life was the ultimate jester. Every man got rained on, he thought, some more so than others. Consumption had robbed him of Mattie, and turned him into a rogue, and would one day claim his last breath. But in the course of things, he had prospered as a gambler and found a measure of peace in the mountains and plains of the West.

Perhaps the greatest joke was that he had survived. Not just his consumption, but a roll call of men who had tried

to kill him. A roll call of such distant memory that he had long ago lost count. So in the end, for all life's jests, he'd had the last laugh. The best laugh.

Kate finally broke the silence. "What are you thinking, sugar?"

"Nothing profound," Holliday said with an offhand gesture. "I was wondering if Wyatt thinks we've lost our way. He expected us before now."

"That Wyatt Earp!" she said in a huffy voice. "I still don't understand why you tag along after him. What's in Tombstone, anyway?"

"You have no sense of adventure, Kate. Wyatt wants the sun and the moon, and perhaps the stars, too. I suspect Tombstone will be one of our finer days."

"What if it's a bust? What if we travel to the end of nowhere and find out it's some harebrained scheme? What then?"

"Why then, we're no worse off than we were. We'll move on."

"Sometimes I think you're part gypsy."

Holliday chuckled. "That's the beauty of it, Kate. There's always another town."

"Honest to God, Doc, you're impossible!"

"Yes, I cannot deny it. I am a true-blue rascal."

Holliday drove on toward Tombstone.

EPILOGUE

Doc Holliday joined forces with the Earps in Tombstone. A staunch and loyal friend, he backed Wyatt's play to become sheriff of Cochise County. The campaign proved to be one of disappointment and frustration, for Wyatt twice failed to attain the office of sheriff. The Earps nonetheless became heavily entrenched in the political machinations of the county.

Virgil was appointed town marshal of Tombstone in October 1880. He retained his commission as Deputy U.S. Marshal, as well as his status as the top law-enforcement officer in Cochise County. Virgil's position as a lawman, and Wyatt's constant political maneuvering, led to friction with the Clanton and McLaury brothers, a gang of cattle rustlers and general troublemakers. The hostility between the factions slowly simmered into an open feud.

Holliday, who feared no man, willingly incurred the enmity of the gang. He provoked their anger, occasionally goading them to fight, but none of the gang members were so foolhardy as to accept the challenge. His reputation as a gambler was enhanced during his stay in Tombstone, while at the same time his relationship with Kate Elder gradually fell apart. In June 1881, after a bitter quarrel, Kate falsely accused him of attempted robbery and murder of a stage-coach guard. Holliday was quickly exonerated, and Kate

wisely departed Tombstone. They never saw each other again.

The feud between the Earps and the rustlers ultimately erupted into violence on a blustery day in October 1881. The Earps, with Holliday backing their play, went to arrest the gang at the rear of the O.K. Corral. The confrontation exploded into gunfire, and within thirty seconds, Virgil and Morgan were wounded and three gang members lay dead. Holliday made the difference at what became fabled in Western lore as the Gunfight at the O.K. Corral. His cool nerve and deadly accuracy were largely responsible for saving the lives of Virgil and Morgan Earp. Of the men involved, only Holliday and Wyatt were still standing when the gunfire ceased.

The aftermath of the O.K. Corral was a bloodbath. Virgil was ambushed at night, shotgunned by the remaining gang members, his left arm crippled for life. A short time later, Morgan was killed by assassins while playing pool in a local billiard parlor. Wyatt, now wearing the badge of a Deputy U.S. Marshal, rode out with Holliday and other supporters on a bloody vendetta. They killed three men in gunfights, and effectively put the rest of the gang to rout. But the political intrigue and rivalry of Cochise County resulted in their being charged with murder. With no hope of justice, or a fair trial, they fled Arizona Territory.

Holliday and Wyatt went their separate ways after crossing the border into Colorado. History records no reason, but they never again saw each other after March 1882. For the next five years, Holliday roamed the West, a celebrated gambler and shootist, adding to the list of those he killed. By 1887 his tuberculosis was in the final stages, his health ravaged to the point he was unable to continue on. He admitted himself to a sanatorium in Glenwood Springs, Colorado, and reportedly played poker each day with his attendant. No one from the old days came to visit, and he received only one letter during his confinement. The return address on the letter was the Sisters of Charity Convent, in Atlanta.

On a crisp winter day in November 1887, Holliday lay wasted and worn, too weak for the morning poker session with his attendant. He was still lucid, his mind clear, and his wry sense of humor was never sharper. He was quiet for a time, perhaps reflecting on his years as a vagabond gambler, and then his gaze went to the foot of the bed. He wiggled his toes beneath the covers, amused that a man who had survived so many gunfights would succumb at last to diseased lungs. He glanced at his attendant, again wiggling his toes, and remarked with droll good humor, "This is funny." A short time later he closed his eyes and died in peaceful sleep. He was thirty-five years old.

Wyatt Earp, in later years, was quoted by the *San Francisco Examiner* in words that serve as a lasting eulogy. "Doc Holliday was a dentist whom necessity had made a gambler; a gentleman whom disease had made a frontier vagabond; a philosopher whom life had made a caustic wit; a long, lean, ash-blond fellow nearly dead with consumption and at the same time the most skillful gambler and the nerviest, speediest, deadliest man with a six-gun I ever knew."

A legend was born the day Dr. John H. Holliday became Doc Holliday. Wasted by disease, a fatalist who never lost his sardonic wit, he was a figure of mythical proportions across the Western frontier. His exploits in life made him immortal in death.

Doc Holliday, the gentleman rogue, will live forever.

Lords of the Land

To
Nackey and Bill

A courageous lady
and a man of noble purpose

BOOK ONE

1865 -1867

Book Six

1863–1864

CHAPTER 1

A ghostly stillness hung over Brownsville. The streets were all but deserted, and every store in town had closed shortly after the troops rode out earlier that morning. Along the river a lazy forenoon breeze stirred, drifting cross current. Tiny ripples skimmed the surface of the water, and trees shimmered beneath the glare of the sun. With the breeze came an abrupt end to the silence, broken by three sharp blasts of a steamboat whistle.

Hank Laird walked from the warehouse several moments later. He paused, testing the wind out of habit, and gazed across the river at Matamoros. Nearly a dozen stern-wheelers lay docked and idle on the Mexican shore. But the *Mustang,* one of his own ships, had her boilers fired and was spewing columns of smoke from the twin stacks. Laird checked the cloudless spring sky and then moved off at a brisk pace toward the wharf.

A light skiff, with two oarsmen, waited at dockside. As Laird approached, his brother-in-law, Artemus Johnson, hurried forward to meet him. Johnson was a tall bony man, with shrunken skin and knobby joints, almost cadaverous in appearance. His features were set in a dour expression, and there was a troubled cast to his eyes. He shook his head, staring intently at Laird, and flung an arm in the general direction of the river.

"Hank, listen to me for once. This is madness! You haven't got a chance."

Laird never broke stride. "I've been listening to you all morning, and the answer's still the same. Now leave be! Let a man get on about his work."

"But the blockaders won't let you through. The war's over, Hank! They'll blow you out of the water."

"Not while I'm flying the turkey buzzard, they won't."

"You can't be sure of that." Johnson trailed alongside him down the wharf. "Maybe their orders have been changed. Now that the fighting's stopped, maybe they won't honor Mexican registry anymore."

"God's teeth, Arty! Why do you think our troops went downriver this morning? The fighting hasn't stopped. And the war's not over on the Rio Grande till the Yankees occupy Brownsville. That means I've got time for one last run, and I intend to take it. Blockaders be damned!"

"That's what I'm trying to tell you. So far as the Yankees are concerned, the war is over. Now you're just a freebooter or a privateer of some sort. All that Mexican flag will do is give them something to shoot at."

"Every cripple does his own dance, Arty."

"You and your Irish proverbs. It'll be the death of you yet."

"Aye, perhaps it will. But then it's my neck, isn't it?"

"Not altogether," Johnson countered. "What about Angela and Trudy? Shouldn't you be thinking about them?"

"I am, bucko. I am."

Laird halted at the end of the wharf and pointed across river, to the *Mustang*. The stern-wheeler was a shallow-draft riverboat, designed to navigate the sandbars and shifting channels of inland waterways. Yet today the craft rode perilously low in the water, for the main deck, from stem to stern, appeared to be a solid block of cotton bales.

"You're looking at two hundred thousand in gold, Arty. And believe me, gold speaks a language all its own. That'll spell the difference when the Yankees take over."

"And if you don't come back? Then what?"

"Quit being such a worrywart! Just do like I told you . . . go on out to the ranch. Ramon has his orders, and he'll see to it you're all safe while I'm gone."

Laird stepped off the dock into the skiff and motioned to the oarsmen. Then he seated himself and looked back over his shoulder, grinning at Johnson.

"Kiss the girls for me. Tell 'em it's in the bag."

The crew of the *Mustang* never questioned orders. Given a choice, they would have much preferred to remain at berth

in Matamoros. Lee had surrendered at Appomattox two days previously, and everyone on the river knew that the risks of blockade-running were now incalculable. Once they steamed into the Gulf, under the guns of Union warships, it could go either way. Yet today, despite that uncertainty, there was no grumbling as Hank Laird came aboard. The captains of his riverboats and their crews admired his cool judgment and nervy quickness in a tight situation. He commanded the loyalty of those around him, and by sheer force of character he had won the respect of every riverman on the Rio Grande.

Laird scrambled up a ladder to the Texas deck and entered the pilothouse. Waiting for him was Sam Blalock, captain of the *Mustang* and his oldest friend. After working together for nearly a decade, there was little formality between them. Blalock nodded and jerked his thumb at the chronometer.

"You're cuttin' it a wee mite close, Cap'n."

It was a title Laird had earned among rivermen, and he accepted it as his due. But now he detected mild reproof in Blalock's tone, and his eyebrows narrowed in a quick characteristic squint of mockery.

"The closer the better, Sam. Way I figure it, we'll squeak through and hit open water right about dusk."

"Squeak through!" Blalock grunted. "If it comes on dark, it'll be like a blind man tryin' to thread a needle."

"Aye, that it would. So you'd best get under way, hadn't you?"

Blalock muttered something to himself, then turned and crossed the pilothouse. He leaned out the window, hands cupped around his mouth. "Look alive down there! Make ready to cast off!"

On deck there was a flurry of activity. Lines were cast off fore and aft, and moments later the dull throb of steam engines sent a vibration throughout the entire ship. Blalock slowly maneuvered the *Mustang* clear of the dock and brought her into midstream. Then he ordered the engines all ahead full and settled down to outwitting the ever-changing hazards of the Rio Grande.

Once under way, Laird left the pilothouse and walked forward on the Texas deck. Outwardly bluff and hearty, he was nonetheless a shrewd, icy realist. He too had misgivings

about this last run; there was every likelihood, just as Arty
Johnson had said, that the Yankees would blow him out of
the water. But he made it a practice never to display inner
doubt to anyone. By nature he was a gambler, and he'd
learned early in life that confidence counted far more than
the odds. A man assured of himself bred that same convic-
tion in other men, and as a result, forever held the edge. It
was a belief that had served him well, and today, despite
certain qualms, he felt compelled to test it one last time
against Yankee cannons.

In truth, Hank Laird hated to see the war end. He enjoyed
the danger—thrived on it—and found himself eminently
suited to the life of a smuggler. Before the war, operating a
steamboat line had given him modest wealth and a certain
amount of personal satisfaction. It hadn't been easy; he'd
come to the Rio Grande as a deckhand and battled his way
up to the position of river pilot. Eventually he had earned his
captain's papers, and years later, with every penny he could
scrounge, he'd bought his first stern-wheeler. Then another
and still another, always undercutting the competition, until
finally he had only one rival left on the river. Yet, with all
he'd accomplished, he never felt any great sense of fulfill-
ment. Until the war.

By early 1862, the Union blockade had sealed all Atlantic
ports as well as the Gulf Coast. Virtually overnight the Rio
Grande became the back door of the Confederacy. King
Cotton was the South's one commodity, negotiable on the
world market for arms and munitions and the materials of
war. European ships anchored offshore and a lively trade
developed under the noses of Union blockaders. Flying the
neutral flag of Mexico, with ownership of their riverboats
hidden behind dummy registry, Hank Laird and his rival,
Joseph Starling, became a vital link in the Confederate war
effort. They handled cotton on commission, bought and sold
on their own, and always demanded payment in gold. Laird
even bought a ranch north of Brownsville, and established a
way station for the wagon trains of cotton being transported
overland to the Rio Grande.

Yet profits and patriotism were merely offshoots of a far
greater reward. Hank Laird was in his element, a legitimate
buccaneer blithely thumbing his nose at Yankee warships.

Never in his life had he enjoyed himself so immensely. Nor
was it likely that he would ever again find an enterprise so
fitted to his character. And with the Confederacy in a sham-
bles, the cause lost and the war ended, he felt a very personal
sense of loss. Standing there on the Texas deck, gazing
blankly at the shoreline, he was gripped by the vision of a
bleak and dreary future.

Things simply wouldn't be the same. Not after today.

A curious blend of commerce and war was centered around
the mouth of the Rio Grande. Union troops were encamped
on the north bank of the river, while across from them, occu-
pying the village of Bagdad, were the Imperialist forces of
Emperor Maximilian. Civil war also raged in Mexico, and
within the past week, the *guerrilleros* of Benito Juárez had
been driven inland by renegade generals who supported the
emperor. Yet the tides of commerce were unaffected by ei-
ther war; the world's merchants, loyal to no cause but their
own, traded with victor and vanquished alike. Offshore, up-
ward of a hundred vessels, ranging from creaky schooners to
iron-hulled steamships, lay at anchor awaiting a cargo of
smuggled cotton. Their counterparts, three Union warships,
patrolled the coastline like seagoing watchdogs. With the fall
of the Confederacy, and Imperialist victory on the border, it
was an explosive situation. Everyone waited, eyes fixed on
the mouth of the river. Throughout the merchant fleet, it was
even money that the next blockade-runner caught in open
water would be sunk.

Shortly after sundown the *Mustang* steamed past Bagdad.
Paddles churning furiously, the riverboat plowed into the
Gulf and set a bold course for the offshore fleet. Sam Bla-
lock manned the wheel, and beside him, Laird kept a sharp
watch northward along the coast. The *Mustang* had scarcely
cleared breakwater when Laird stiffened, peering intently
into the fading light. Off the port side, a Union man-of-war
loomed out of the dusk and quartered leeward to intercept.
Laird recognized the ship instantly, the U.S.S. *Portsmouth,* of
twenty-two guns, their chief adversary since the blockade be-
gan in earnest.

"God a'mighty!" Blalock yelled over the roar of the en-
gines. "Look at that scutter come!"

"Hold your course, Sam. Steady does it."

"You're awful goddamn calm for a dead man!"

Laird smiled. "Speak for yourself. I've got more lives than—"

The captain of the *Portsmouth* cut short his reply. One of the forward guns belched smoke and a cannonball sailed across the bow of the *Mustang*. An instant later a second gun boomed and a geyser of water erupted thirty yards off port. Salt spray splattered against the windows of the pilothouse, and Blalock involuntarily ducked.

"I told you, Hank! It's heave to or get the deep six. That bastard means business!"

"Faith, Samuel! Have faith. He's bluffing!"

"Like hell! He's got us bracketed. The next one'll take us midships!"

Laird walked to the port window, hands clasped behind his back. The *Portsmouth* was closing fast and the range had been reduced to a few hundred yards. Even at top speed, the *Mustang* was a ponderous target, sluggish and impossible to maneuver in choppy waters. Evasive action was out of the question, and he knew the Yankee gunners wouldn't miss if their captain swung broadside and ordered a salvo. Yet he wasn't convinced. Some visceral instinct told him it was a matter of whose nerves lasted the longest. Eyes fastened on the warship, he turned slightly and called out to Blalock.

"A hundred says it's a dodge. All bark and no bite."

"Done! But how the hell will I collect if we're—"

"By the Sweet Jesus!" Laird whooped wildly. "You won't collect, jocko! You'll pay. Look!"

Blalock glanced over his shoulder and saw the Union man-of-war fall off, then slowly come about on a westerly tack. With a great sigh of relief, he eased the *Mustang* two points to starboard and headed for the nearest merchant ship. At his side again, Laird uttered a low gloating laugh, and elbowed him in the ribs.

"Thank you, Sam. Easiest hundred I ever made."

CHAPTER 2

The girl finished dressing, then walked to the door and looked back. There was a question in her eyes, but Laird wasn't interested in a return engagement. While she was attractive enough for a *puta*, he hadn't been impressed by her talents in bed. He'd had better, and since there was no scarcity of whores in Matamoros, he saw no reason to encourage her. After a moment he rolled out of bed and padded barefoot to the washstand. He poured water from a pitcher into a cracked basin, and finally glanced up at her in the mirror.

"*Qué quieres, chiquita?*"

"*De nada, señor.*"

"*Bien! Hasta pronto.*"

She opened the door and closed it softly behind her. Laird waited until the latch clicked, then he cupped water in his hands and briskly scrubbed his face. The water was tepid but refreshing and he let it drain down over his body. After rinsing his mouth, he smoothed his hair back and caught his reflection in the mirror. He stood for a moment studying himself.

The vestiges of a violent youth marked his face. The bridge of his nose was slightly off center, and above the ruddy wind-seamed features an angry scar was visible over one eyebrow. It was by no means a handsome face, with a square jaw and wide brow, but it was ruggedly forceful under a thatch of chestnut hair and a bristling mustache. All that saved it from being hard were the eyes, smoky blue and inquisitive, the brash, spirited look of a born trickster.

He stepped back, watching himself in the mirror, and patted his belly. Still lean and tough as leather, not bad for a man approaching forty. Though he wasn't exceptionally tall, he was full-spanned through the shoulders, with wrists thick

as a singletree and arms knotted with muscle. Standing there, posing for the mirror like some barroom bullyboy, it suddenly struck him as a little absurd. Particularly for a man of his age and position. Yet despite himself, he felt a twinge of pride in the fact that there were few deckhands who would care to tangle with him in a rough-and-tumble slug-fest.

Abruptly the muscle-flexing gave way to a look of mockery, and he turned from the mirror, laughing at himself. He'd been cooped up in this fleabag hotel too long. A whore a day, swilling tequila till his head felt juiced, bored to tears and frustrated by the endless waiting. It was no life at all, and damned inconsiderate of the Yankees. An imposition of the worst sort.

Hank Laird was temporarily a fugitive. The federal Amnesty Proclamation required all former Rebels to take an oath of allegiance to the United States. Yet tens of thousands of Confederates, both military and civilian, were denied amnesty under the broad restrictions laid down by the government. Among those ineligible, the most notable were men who had held high office in the Confederacy, and anyone who owned property valued in excess of $20,000. While Laird's steamboats were still docked at Matamoros, his holdings in Brownsville and the ranch north of town automatically consigned him to this latter group.

The path to absolution was studded with pitfalls. The first step was a special application for amnesty, to be reviewed by the local commander of the Union occupation forces. Afterward, with proper endorsement by the military, the miscreant could then be pardoned directly by the president. But approval or disapproval rested solely in the hands of conquerors, and once the judgment was rendered there was no appeal. With absolute power, few military commanders were immune to corruption, and bartering for amnesty became one of the more profitable spoils of war.

Always the pragmatist, Hank Laird simply retired to Matamoros and, through his lawyer, conducted negotiations from the opposite side of the Rio Grande. It was a seller's market, however, and the Union commander, General John Stark, drove a hard bargain. Almost daily, offer and counter-

offer crossed the river, and after nearly a month, Laird was still trying for an acceptable compromise.

Today, while he shaved and dressed, it occurred to him that the situation had now reached a point of diminishing return. His steamboats were idle and he was fast losing the economic influence he'd once enjoyed in Brownsville. Worse, he was being played off against his only competitor, Joe Starling, who was also negotiating with the Yankees. If Starling weakened and suddenly made a deal, that would undermine his own position, perhaps force him out of business. On the personal side, he hadn't seen Angela and his daughter for nearly six weeks, and while he knew they were safe, he missed them. All in all, he was simply fed up with the life of an exile. He wanted to go home and be with his family and once again see his riverboats plying the Rio Grande.

On impulse, he abruptly decided to end it. The time for stubborn pride was past, and the consequences of further delay might very well prove disastrous. He would strike the best bargain he could, and then worry about outfoxing the Yankees. It was just that elemental, and given the alternative, another night in Matamoros, it was no choice at all.

Hardly was the decision made, when a knock sounded at the door. Laird called out, quickly stuffing his shirt into his pants, and the door opened. His lawyer, Warren Pryor, stepped into the room.

"Good morning, Hank." Pryor was a gnome of a man, with a perpetually constipated expression. His eyes flicked about the room, then shifted back to Laird with a look of mild reproach. "Another night of debauchery, hmmm? It's really quite remarkable, Hank. Your stamina, I mean. Even the Yankees are talking about it."

Laird nodded. "Aye, that's the way of it. Them with a wee set of balls always does the talking." Suddenly he laughed, watching Pryor redden, then went on. "But enough of that. What's the news? Has our greedy friend come around?"

"Yes and no," Pryor remarked stiffly. "General Stark has agreed to endorse your amnesty request. But the price has gone up. He now wants twenty-five thousand dollars."

"God's teeth!"

"And he insists it be paid in gold."

"Of course. The man's a bloody pirate!"

"I agree. But we've little bargaining power left at this point. His troops are running short of supplies, and it's down to a matter of whether you or Starling receive the quartermaster contract. Naturally, the general still demands a percentage off the top."

"How much?"

"Five percent. He was very firm about that."

"Yes, but it's lower than his original demand. Which means Starling must have offered him a bit less."

"I got the same impression."

Laird deliberated a moment, knuckling his mustache back as he considered the alternatives. At last he slammed a meaty fist into his palm, and turned on the lawyer with a cryptic smile.

"Tell him it's a deal. But I want it wrapped up today. All of it, his endorsement and the quartermaster contract."

"Just like that?" Pryor hesitated, clearly surprised. "No counterproposal?"

"Just like that. Get it in writing and he gets the gold."

"Hank, you're a sly and devious man. I can see it in your face. You've got something up your sleeve, don't you?"

"Hide and watch, bucko. Just hide and watch."

Laird rode into the ranch headquarters shortly after nightfall the next evening. Built like a fortress, the *casa grande* stood on a small knoll overlooking Santa Guerra Creek. Clustered around the main house were the adobe huts of vaqueros and their families; corrals for livestock and a blacksmith shed; storerooms, workshops, and a chapel where a lookout kept watch in the tower night and day. A thick adobe wall enclosed the entire *casco,* and in the event of raids by *bandidos* or Indians, it quickly became a fortified village.

The main gate swung open with a massive groan as Laird approached. A figure, armed with a double-barrel shotgun, emerged from the shadows and stepped into a patch of moonlight. His features were obscured by a wide sombrero, and a serape hung draped over his shoulders, but there was no mistaking the *segundo* of Santa Guerra Hacienda.

"Hola, Ramon!"

"Hola, Patrón! Welcome home."

"Qué pasa?" Laird reined his horse to a halt. "Have the Yankee soldiers returned?"

"Cabrónes!"

Ramon Morado spat the curse, mouth set in a tight grimace. His face looked as though it had been hewn from rough walnut, with an angular nose and high cheekbones and the brooding eyes of an eagle. A jagged knife scar, relic of some ancient duel, marked one jaw from his earlobe to the corner of his mouth.

"Twice they came, *Patrón.* Each time they herded *Los Lerdeños* into the courtyard like cattle. Then the barbarians searched every building with the thoroughness of starved dogs. But I did as you ordered. I held my tongue and made the vaqueros appear before them unarmed. There was no violence, and the *gringo pinches* found nothing. Your gold is safe, *Patrón.*"

Laird understood perfectly. His *segundo* was a man normally given to few words; the outburst had been a tactful display of rage and shame. The vaqueros called themselves *Los Lerdeños*—Laird's People—a name they bore with pride and great dignity. To humble themselves before anyone, particularly *yanqui soldados,* was an unspeakable humiliation. They had done it to protect his gold, nearly $300,000 put back during the war, buried beneath the earthen floor of the blacksmith's forge. Ramon Morado had politely reminded him of the vaqueros' loyalty and their willingness to suffer any indignity for the *patrón.* Unstated but tacitly understood was his own obligation to *Los Lerdeños.*

"Bueno! You have done well, Ramon. Our men too, eh?"

Gracias, Patrón. I will tell the people of your pride in them."

"And Doña Angela? What of her and my daughter?"

"They are well, *Patrón. La Madama* faced the soldiers with great bravery. She has the courage of a true *guerrero,* and none dared offend her."

"Bien! God smiles on us, Ramon. But now . . . enough of this talk! I have business at home. *Hasta luego, compadre!"*

Ramon grinned, his teeth flashing like rows of dice in the moonlight, and stepped aside. Laird feathered the horse with his spurs and burst through the gate at a dead lope. Moments later he slid to a halt in front of the house and

dismounted. He left the horse ground reined, certain Ramon would have it fetched, and hurried up the porch stairs. The door opened and suddenly Angela was there, framed in the cider glow of lamplight.

A long stride took him across the porch, and he pulled her into a rough embrace. Neither of them spoke, but her cheeks were flushed and a faint smile haunted the corners of her mouth. Then her lips parted and her arms went around his neck with a gentle urgency. He kissed her, aware of her scent, fresh and clean yet musklike, somehow sensual. Her body pressed against him and he drew her closer, felt her tremble. After a long while she pulled away, buried her face into his chest, clutching him to her with fierce possession.

"You're home." Her voice was a whisper, almost inaudible. "Praise God, home and safe. That's all I prayed for, Henry."

Only Angela called him by his given name, and the sound of it brought a surge of anticipation he hadn't known in weeks. For all his whoring and drunken brawls, his passion for her had never diminished. She was his wife, the mother of his child, and the one woman in all his life to whom he'd never been unfaithful in spirit.

He laughed and nuzzled the curve of her neck. "Aye, lass. Home from the war and hungry as a bear in rut."

"Henry, your language. Have you no shame in your own house?"

"None a'tall! And you wouldn't have me any other way."

"That's not true. You know it's not."

Without a word, he lifted her in his arms and walked into the house. She struggled briefly, but as he kicked the door shut behind them, her arms circled his neck and she lowered her head to his shoulder. On the way down the hall, she suddenly laughed and began nibbling his earlobe.

CHAPTER 3

Angela lay motionless, burrowed deep in the hollow of his arm. Moonlight flooded the bedroom, and she watched her breath eddy through the matted curls on his chest. She felt languid and sated, limp with an exquisite kind of exhaustion. Yet there was the other thing, the part that always crept over her afterward. Emotionally she felt wretched, loathing herself and the weakness of her own body.

Nothing changed. In all their years together, it was the same whenever he returned home after a long absence. Her need was no less urgent than his own, consuming mind and body in a haze of agony the instant he touched her. All else forgotten, they took one another in a frenzied burst of craving, lost in an incandescent thrash of arms and legs. It was only afterward, locked beneath him in a world cloyed with the musk of warm flesh, that the disgust set in.

There was no tenderness to the act, nothing of a spiritual union between them. It was merely animal hunger, together yet apart, satisfying brute lust without words or emotion. Then, panting and disheveled, drifting on a quenched flame, she was always overcome by a sense of uncleanliness. She condemned herself for yielding to the witless demands of the flesh. But even worse, she despised him for how easily he aroused that wanton need.

He made her feel like a whore.

A tear scalded her cheek, and suddenly she felt revolted by her own nakedness. Fearful of waking him, she slipped from his arm and slowly eased out of bed. She stopped, searching the floor for her nightgown, then found it and quickly pulled it on over her head. But the gown fitted snugly across full breasts and tightly rounded buttocks, and did little to hide her figure. She was a small, compact woman, neither

delicate nor plump. Childbirth hadn't spoiled her figure, though she was perhaps a bit wider through the hips, and the natural symmetry of her face seemed untouched by time. Her oval features were framed by hair dark as obsidian, and her eyes, large and expressive, forever betrayed her innermost thoughts. Incapable of guile or deceit, she was nonetheless haunted by guilt. She kept her eyes averted as she passed the bureau mirror, unwilling to look upon even a reflected image of herself.

"You've a damn poor sense of timing."

Startled, she turned to find him watching her. "I'm sorry, Henry. I thought you were asleep."

"Asleep or awake, where's the difference? You're still quitting my bed, aren't you?"

"That's not true! I was simply going . . . to the . . ."

"On your way to the privy?" Laird grunted, shook his head. "No, if it's the necessities you're after, there's a johnnypot under the bed."

"You needn't be coarse, Henry."

"And you've no need to rush off and have yourself a good cry. It's a queer sort of a welcome—damned if it's not!—right after a man's made love to his wife."

"I wasn't"—She faltered, fought back the tears. "I'm not crying."

"Ah, lass, it's no good, don't you see that? The time for mourning is past, and you've not yet buried the dead. You must put it from your mind or you'll drive yourself crazy."

"Is it really that easy, Henry?" Her mouth went tight, scornful. "Perhaps it wouldn't be . . . if you'd been there . . . when it happened."

"He was my son too! Or have you allowed yourself to forget that part?"

"Yes, but you weren't there . . . were you?"

"By the Sweet Jesus, you'll not talk to me that way!" Laird sat up in bed, glaring at her. "It's not the boy—and never was! It's your father. Him and his saintly ways—you've never got over it, have you?"

"Oh god, Henry." Her voice was a mere whisper. "How can you be so cruel? That's a terrible thing to say . . . terrible."

"Aye, but all the same true. Any time I ever touched you I

knew it for a fact, and it's not gotten better since he died; it's gotten worse."

"He didn't die—neither of them did—they were killed!"

"A distinction, I'll grant you, but one I hardly need thrown in my face."

"I'm not so sure, Henry . . . perhaps you do."

"And what the bloody hell is that supposed to mean?"

A look of agony twisted her features, and she appeared on the verge of speaking. Then her mouth clamped in a straight line and she lowered her head, staring dully at the floor. Laird watched her for a moment, thoroughly confounded, and finally let out his breath with a deep sigh.

"I've no wish to be cross, but it's gone on too long now. You're still living with ghosts and there'll be no peace between us till you've laid them to rest."

He smiled, held out his hand. "Come on, get back in bed and we'll chase away the miseries."

"I can't, Henry." She edged toward the door. "Please, not again . . . not tonight."

"Suit yourself." Laird fell back against the pillow and rolled onto his side. "But don't say you weren't invited."

Angela turned and fled. Still barefoot, she walked quickly along the hall, went through the kitchen, then out the door and onto the back porch. She took a deep breath, slowly released it, tried to distract herself by watching low clouds that scudded across the moon. But the thought persisted, and under the pale light, tears glistened in her eyes.

There was so much to forgive. So little she could forget. Sometimes she wished he would stay away forever. Then, when he left her alone and went to Brownsville on business, she bitterly resented the emptiness of being without him. Yet whenever he returned, like tonight, it was always a time of joy. A sudden deliverance, filled with laughter and happiness and his devilish, teasing ways. Until he took her to bed. Ruined everything by making her feel dirty and ashamed of herself and . . . guilty.

It was her father, of course. Even in death he stood between them. The Reverend Hiram Johnson, self-appointed messenger of Jehovah. Since childhood, particularly after her mother's death, he had drummed it into her head that lust was sinful, that those who fornicated for pleasure rather

than procreation were doomed to the fires of Hell. Try as she might, she couldn't drive his warped vision of the Scripture from her mind. Not even twelve years of marriage had erased the sound of his voice, those nightly sermons on the evils of man and the pitfalls of temptation. Nor could she absolve her husband of blame—the horrors of that final night—her father's unswerving belief even in the face of death.

The memory always jolted her, arriving unbidden from some dark corner of her mind. She blinked back tears, trying to push the nightmare aside, not to remember. Never to see it again . . .

Brownsville was in flames. The Confederate commander, upon hearing that the Union army had landed on the coast, put the torch to Fort Brown and retreated in panic. The fire touched off a powder magazine, and the force of the explosion showered fire-brands all across town. Buildings kindled and burst into flame, and along the levee, thousands of bales of cotton burned with an eerie brilliance under a pall of smoke. Darkness brought the drunken border scum from both sides of the river, looting and rioting unchecked through the streets. Stores were plundered, homes sacked, men who resisted were killed outright and their women ravaged.

And Angela waited, listening to the mob, her husband downriver with another load of cotton. Then the howling came closer, rose to a murderous pitch, and men began pounding on the door. Her children, Trudy and little Hank, were hidden in the bedroom. But her father stood before the door, disdaining weapons, certain that not even border ruffians would harm a man of the cloth. At the last instant, when the door splintered and tore loose from its hinges, she armed herself with a shotgun. Her father raised both arms, like a holy man warding off evil spirits, and gunfire erupted from the doorway. He slumped to his knees, still imploring mercy, then pitched forward on his face. And Angela pulled both triggers on the shotgun. The blast ripped into the mob, shredding bone and flesh with a double load of buckshot. Several men fell dead, others screamed, and those at the

rear of the pack turned and fled. The door emptied and a sudden stillness settled over the room.

Angela gagged—sickened by the carnage—slowly dropped the shotgun, and turned away. Then she froze. Little Hank lay in the doorway of the bedroom, the top of his skull blown off, brains and gore puddled around his head. A scream shattered the stillness, and she threw herself down beside him, only dimly aware that the cries she heard were her own.

Even now, after nearly two years, she couldn't forget or forgive. The screams still echoed through her mind, and she saw there, fixed forever in a grisly vignette, a little boy with his head destroyed by a stray bullet. Yet it was all so confused. A common thread somehow linked the loss of her son and the death of her father to that older guilt she felt in the bedroom. In her heart, she told herself that Henry wasn't at fault. His grief had been no less than her own. Perhaps deeper, since she would never give him another son. Still, if he hadn't been downriver that night it wouldn't have happened. If he were a gentler man, tender and understanding, perhaps she wouldn't feel like a common whore with her own husband. So if not Henry, then who was to blame?

Angela swayed, clutching at the banister for support. A wave of dizziness swept over her, and for a moment, the moon tilted crazily in the sky. Then her vision blurred and a splitting pain drew a sharp intake of breath. She put both hands to her head, pressing with all her strength, as though her skull would burst apart unless she held it together. Her knees buckled and she slowly collapsed on the porch, her body wedged up against the banister. Softly, like some wounded creature of the night, she began to cry.

Trudy speared another flapjack onto her plate and drenched it with molasses. Then she stuffed a large bite into her mouth, chewing thoughtfully for a moment, and glanced up at her father. "Pa, couldn't you change your mind? Please! Just this once."

"I've already told you, sprout. Business comes first. Steamboats don't run themselves, you know. Takes a firm hand at the wheel."

"Oh fiddlesticks! Uncle Art could look after those silly old

boats. Besides, it's the captains that run 'em anyway, isn't it?"

"Don't talk with your mouth full. And watch that saucy tongue or I'll box your ears." Laird faked a swat across the table, and Trudy ducked, giggling playfully behind her hand. He grinned, gave her a broad wink, then settled back in his chair. "Now, just to set you straight, it's the company I'm talking about, not the boats. There's where the firm hand is needed and, sad to say, your uncle Art isn't the man for the job."

Angela turned from the stove, on the verge of speaking. But she merely shot him a dark look, then took the coffeepot off a back burner and walked to the table. As she seated herself, Trudy gobbled down the last of the flapjack, licked her lips with a loud smack, and smiled at her father.

"I'll betcha Ramon could do it, Pa. He can do anything! Why don't you let him go take care of your boats?"

"Think that'd solve it, do you?"

"*Porqué no?*" she replied with a charming little shrug. "That way you wouldn't have to worry, and you could stay home all the time, couldn't you?"

Laird never ceased to be amazed by her wiles. For an eleven year old, she seemed uncommonly knowledgeable about men, and how to play on their weaknesses. He often wondered if she practiced on the vaqueros; these days she spent every spare moment astride a horse, apparently fascinated with the rough life of cows and men. The combination of elfin flirt and tomboy was at times disconcerting, yet he found it thoroughly enjoyable. He saw much of himself in the girl, both in her looks and her irreverent humor. Though her eyes were the color of wild honey, she favored him rather than her mother, and her hair had about it the golden umber of his family. Nature had cheated her in a sense, for she hadn't the promise of Angela's beauty, but he was not at all displeased with the result. Having lost a son, it gladdened his heart to have a daughter with the very traits he prized the most.

"I'm on to your tricks, you know." Laird halted her protest with an upraised palm. "No matter. You'll still get your wish. Quite soon now I'll be home every night." He paused, let her dangle a moment on his words. "I've ordered the old house

to be put shipshape, and when it's ready we'll move back to town."

"No!" Angela cried. "We won't! This is our home, not Brownsville."

Trudy was so astounded by her mother's outburst that her eyes went wide with fright. Angela tilted her chin defiantly, and Laird held himself in check, trying to divine her mood. After a prolonged silence, he glanced across at Trudy and smiled.

"Be a good girl and do your old dad a favor. Run tell Ramon to have my horse saddled. I'll be along directly."

Trudy merely nodded, darting a quick look at her mother, then scampered out the back door. Laird removed a cigarillo from his jacket pocket, carefully clipped the ends, and lit it. He studied the fiery tip a moment, his expression abstracted, and finally turned to Angela.

"I'll not comment on your manner in front of the girl, but I would like an explanation."

"Henry, I won't move back to Brownsville. You can do as you please, but Trudy and I stay here. That's all there is to it."

"No, lass, not all. Even after last night, you haven't rid yourself of it, have you? The bad memories?"

Angela stiffened, averted her eyes. "That has nothing to do with it. I simply won't live among Yankee trash and watch you humiliate yourself and this family. I understand about the oath of allegiance, and I know it was necessary. But this army contract is beneath you, Henry. It's corrupt and dirty and . . . well, it's just contemptible."

"Mother of Christ! It was part of the deal. Would you have had me rot in Matamoros rather than do business with Yankees?"

"I'm sorry, Henry. I can't help how I feel."

"Yankees be damned! Fool yourself if you want, but don't lay it off on me. It's that house that's got you spooked, and we both know it."

"That's not true. But regardless, it doesn't change anything. I won't leave this ranch, Henry. So let's not argue . . . that's my final word on it."

"Then by the Holy God, you'll be seeing little of me,

woman! And *that's* bloody well final! You can mark it down as gospel."

Laird slammed out of his chair and walked from the kitchen without a backward glance. Several moments later Angela heard voices and shouts of good-bye, then the sound of hoofbeats growing fainter and fainter, slowly fading away. She blinked, staring into a prism of tears, suddenly numb but no longer afraid. The threat had come and gone, and she was still safe. Safer than ever before.

Never again would she return to Brownsville. Or that house.

CHAPTER 4

Laird arrived in Brownsville early that afternoon. He left his horse at the livery stable, took the ferry to Matamoros, and walked along the wharf to a large warehouse. Shortly before two o'clock he was admitted to the office of Joseph Starling.

Fierce competitors, the two men had battled one another for the river trade with a sort of atavistic pragmatism. Their unsavory tactics were mutually acceptable, however, and several lesser rivals, caught in the middle of a larger struggle, had been eliminated piecemeal. Yet the two men were like amiable duelists. Similar in many ways, they both shared the same dream, and each had developed a grudging admiration for the other over nearly a decade of river warfare.

Starling rose from behind his desk as Laird entered, and extended his hand. He was a beefy man, with the bulbous nose of a heavy drinker and the girth of one who indulged himself in all the good life had to offer. But his eyes were small and bright, and for all his bulk, he was a nimble infighter in matters of business. Laird never underestimated him, and as they shook hands, he wasn't in the least deceived by the cordial smile.

"Have a seat, Hank." Starling waved him to a chair. "Can I offer you a drink? Got some mighty fine bourbon."

"No, thanks. I've not come on a social call."

Starling gave him a cool look of appraisal. "It's business, then?"

"Aye, Joe. Business, it is. I've come to make you a proposition."

"I wondered about that, when I heard you'd crawled in bed with the Yankees. Thought to myself, 'Yessir, old Hank probably figures he's got me by the short hairs.'"

"I do." Laird regarded him with a great calmness. "Took a

war to pull it off, but I've finally got the edge. You're up
against it, Joe. Hard times 'round every bend."

"So it's sell out or you'll bust me, hmmm?"

"That's about the size of it. With the army contract in my
pocket, I can afford to undercut you and take a loss on the
rest of the trade. You'd last six months—maybe a year—but
in the end I'd scuttle you just the same. Today, I'm offering
to buy you out. A year from now, maybe you'd have nothing
left to sell."

"Possibly." Starling nodded and was silent, thoughtful.
"'Course, there's always the Imperialists. I'm in pretty thick
with the emperor, and he'd likely stick with me since you'll
be haulin' for the Yankees. Could be I'd weather through,
what with him payin' so regular in gold."

"All the more reason to get out now. Juárez will whip him
sooner or later, and we both know it. You stick with Maxi-
milian and the *guerrilleros* will put you up against the wall.
Tell you the truth, Joe . . . I'd hate to see you end up dog
meat."

"You're all heart, Hank. All heart! Regular Good Samari-
tan."

"I can afford to be charitable. It's you that's got the prob-
lem."

"Yeah, and cleverly rigged, I'll give you that. Very neat and
tidy . . . for an ax job."

"Nothing personal, Joe. You would've done the same to
me."

Though it had never been proved, both men were aware
that Starling had in fact done worse. Shortly before the war,
with competition for the river trade at its peak, one of
Laird's boats had exploded and sunk under mysterious cir-
cumstances. At the time, several rivals were still working the
Rio Grande, and it was impossible to single one out from the
others. Yet Joe Starling was the least scrupulous of the lot,
and it was a tactic uniquely typical of his methods. Laird had
confronted him with a blunt warning: Unless it stopped
there, every boat Starling owned would go to the bottom.
Aside from the normal hazards, which all rivermen accepted
as part of the trade, there were no further incidents. It ap-
peared Laird had talked to the right man.

Now, confronted by yet another ultimatum, Starling knew

his operation was in imminent peril. After a long silence—his gaze fixed on Laird—he shrugged and spread his hands in a bland gesture.

"Awright, for the sake of argument, let's say you've got me euchred. What's your best offer?"

"Hundred thousand. Lock, stock, and barrel."

"The hell you say!" Starling slammed his fist into the desk, face mottled with anger. "That's not an offer. It's a goddamn insult! The boats alone are worth double that, maybe more."

"Take it or leave it," Laird said flatly. "It's my only offer, and I'll not haggle. But remember, Joe . . . either I'll buy you out or I'll scuttle you. No two ways about it."

A moment elapsed while the two men stared at one another. Then Laird's mouth twisted in a gallows grin. "How much have you got stashed away from the war, Joe? Half million? Easy that, I'll wager, and likely more. So be a smart fellow—take it and get out—live to spend it. You fight me on this and I'll feed you to the wolves."

"You're a number one bastard, Hank. Do you know that?"

"Coming from an old river pirate like yourself, I take that as a compliment. Now, quit grinding your molars and just give me a straight answer. What's it to be, Joe?"

An instant of weighing and calculation slipped past, but Starling found the younger man's logic unassailable. His choice was simple: win a little or lose a lot. Perhaps all! He inclined his head in a faint nod. "You've got a deal."

"Wise decision, Joe." Laird stood, his expression curiously bemused. "I'll miss you, though, and that's the God's own truth. Wouldn't have been any fun without you."

Starling merely grunted. But his eyes were cold and hooded, and inwardly he promised himself it wasn't over. Not by a damnsight! The river hadn't seen the last of Joe Starling. Not yet.

Nor had Hank Laird.

"A hundred thousand! Come now, Hank, you must be joking. That's ridiculous!"

"Starling was of the same opinion."

"Precisely my point. For that price, you must've put a gun to his head. He'll back out on it, you mark my words."

"He'll not back out. We shook hands on it."

"Shook hands! Why, the man's a scoundrel—a cutthroat! He's welshed on half the deals he ever made. He's notorious for it, you know that."

"I've not asked your advice on his character. All I want are the proper documents. And I want them by nightfall! Signed, sealed, and delivered. Now, is that clear enough for you, or must I write the bloody contracts myself?"

Warren Pryor flushed and bobbed his head in agreement. Laird towered over his desk, and the diminutive lawyer suddenly felt like a sparrow trying to outstare a hawk. His lips peeled back in a weak smile.

"Whatever you say, Hank. I'll draw up the papers and bring them to your office for signature before I see Starling. Assuming there's no difficulty in obtaining his signature, we should conclude the deal by late this afternoon."

"There'll be no difficulty. He's expecting you, and he'll sign."

Laird turned away from the desk and walked to a large topographic map mounted on the wall. Stretching roughly fifty miles northward from the lower Rio Grande, it was crisscrossed with boundary lines and a few meandering streams. Laird studied the map a moment, then rapped his knuckles on a spot some thirty miles upstream from the mouth of the river. It was a wide land mass separating the Rio Grande from a sheltered cove labeled LAGUNA MADRE.

"Buy me a slice of that." His thumbnail scratched parallel lines on the map. "All the way across. Doesn't have to be much, but it has to stretch from the river to the bay."

"The San Martin grant?" Pryor gave him a bewildered look. "It's worthless! Why the devil do you want that?"

Laird grinned, as if sharing a private joke with himself. "You'll see, when the time's right. For now, just do like I say."

"Certainly, Hank. I'll begin tracking down the *derechos* tomorrow."

"Start early. I want it done *muy pronto*. Savvy?"

Before the lawyer could reply, Laird again stabbed at the map. His fingertip rested on an inked block representing Santa Guerra Hacienda. Slowly he circumscribed a broad circle around the ranch holdings. He pondered it at length, eyes narrowed in concentration, then nodded.

"Buy it! Every last league." His finger touched the coast and skipped westward into the interior. "I want to own everything between the Gulf and the headwaters of Santa Guerra Creek."

Pryor bounced out of his chair, utterly astounded. "Have you lost your senses? My God, Hank, that's"—his eyes darted to the map, measuring distance with a look of disbelief—"that's nearly five hundred thousand acres. Maybe more! At least ten times your present holdings."

"Aye, that it is. And I want a deed to every square inch."

"But you don't understand. That includes the Espíritu Santo grant and the Santa Isabel grant, and even part of De Carricitos. The number of *derechos* are . . . Good Lord, they're incalculable! Not to mention who knows how many Texas grants. Don't you see, it would take a lifetime to bring that under legal title."

The lawyer's point was well taken. All of the land within a hundred miles of the Rio Grande was a convoluted maze of ancient, and often conflicting, land grants. The original grants, awarded by the Spanish Crown, as well as later Mexican grants, were recognized under Texas law. Descendants of the original grant holders had multiplied generation by generation, and while few of them actually lived on the land, each held an undivided *derecho,* or inheritance right. To acquire title to a land grant, it was necessary to buy up all the *derechos* from countless heirs scattered across the border. The problem of multiple ownership was further complicated by land certificates, usually for 640 acres, issued by the Republic of Texas to the veterans of past wars with Mexico. The task of securing incontestable title was not only monumental and costly, but highly improbable. There were simply too many families, too many heirs, and a whole new generation of *derecho* holders being born every day.

Yet Hank Laird had little patience with either his lawyer or the legal complexities. He waved his hand across the map, as though dusting away the problem. "Don't bugger me with details. Just get it done! Spend what you must, but *bring me the titles.*"

Pryor regarded him thoughtfully for a moment, then shook his head. "Hank, I hate to be the one to say it, but you've got visions of grandeur. It simply won't work. No mat-

ter how many *derechos* we acquire, there'll always be a hundred more who lay claim to the land. And some of them will hold out until you're forced to pay an astronomical price in order to validate title."

"By the great crippled Christ! Are you deaf? Do like I told you, and let me worry about the holdouts. I'll tend to 'em in my own time and my own way. Now, that's my last word on it, so leave it lay."

"Very well, Hank." Pryor spread his hands in a bland gesture. "But don't say I didn't warn you. I have, and most emphatically."

"Duly noted, Counselor. Duly noted. Now get to work."

Laird swatted him across the shoulders, and walked out the door chuckling to himself. Warren Pryor stood there for a long while, wondering if the insanity of Irishmen was congenital or merely a defect of the race. Finally he turned back to the map, peering at it with owlish scrutiny, and realized he hadn't the least idea where to start.

Late that afternoon Artemus Johnson ushered the riverboat captains into Laird's office. None too sober, Laird was in a dazzling good humor, and he greeted each of the three men with a warm handshake. A half-empty bottle was on the desk, and he poured drinks around while the captains seated themselves.

Behind the desk again, Laird raised his glass and laughed. "A toast! To the King of the Rio Grande, and the finest goddamn captains that ever manned a wheel."

The three men exchanged puzzled glances. Sam Blalock held seniority, but Lee Hall and Oscar Gilchrist had been with Laird since before the war. By now they were accustomed to his extravagant moods, and each of them knew better than to ask questions. Blalock silently knocked back his drink, and the other two quickly followed his lead.

Laird took a swipe at his mustache, beaming down on them. "Aw, look at you! Three wise men scratching their heads. Well, boys, it's simple." He flung an arm at the wharfside window. "Come dark, I'll own that whole bloody river. Every drop of it!"

Thumbs hooked in his vest, grinning broadly, he told them the story with all the gusto of a drunken lord. Skipping de-

tails, he related the highlights of his meeting with Joe Starling, and proudly informed them that he now owned every riverboat on the Rio Grande. Starling was out, and the Laird Steamboat Company at last had a monopoly on the river trade. The captains were held spellbound by his performance, and as he concluded they sat watching him with the expression normally reserved for sword-swallowers and trapeze artists.

Finally, the three men shifted uneasily, looking everywhere but at Laird, and Sam Blalock cleared his throat. "Cap'n, it's a neat piece of work, and damn me, if you're not the only man alive who could've pulled it off. But there's them that won't like it. They'll say you sold your soul to the Yankees just so you could keelhaul Joe Starling."

"They'll like it even less come morning," Laird announced. "Tomorrow I'm posting new freight rates. Ten percent hike across the board."

There was a moment of stunned silence, then Gilchrist rose from his chair. "I'm as hard as the next man, Cap'n. But I don't hold with skinnin' people. Not when you got 'em down. It just ain't my way, and I don't like it."

"Nobody asked you to like it. And it's me they'll blame, so don't let your conscience bother you. Just stick to business and keep your lip buttoned."

"I'd sooner not, Cap'n. It goes against the grain."

Laird kept his gaze level, and cool. "Oscar, you're a good captain. You've got a feel for the water, and you know how to work a crew." He paused, jawline set in a scowl. "But either you follow orders or I'll put you ashore and there you'll stay. Now, that's that, and if you care to argue the matter, we'll step outside and I'll gladly oblige you."

Blalock jumped to his feet and moved between them. "C'mon, Cap'n! You know Oscar'd never refuse an order. Hell, he's a riverman!" He turned back to Gilchrist, deadly earnest. "Tell him, Oscar. That's the straight of it, isn't it?"

Gilchrist studied the floor a moment, then shrugged and looked up. "Aye, Cap'n. Forget I said it. Whichever way you want it, that's how it'll be."

Laird's mood changed instantly. The scowl dissolved into a huge grin, and he hurried around the desk, arms outstretched. He herded the men toward the door, pounding

them across the shoulders and rumpling their hair with a genuine display of affection.

"Boys, it's a night to celebrate! And I know just the place. Good liquor and *señoritas* hot as chili peppers. Warm your innards and boil your blood. Guaranteed, by god! Guaranteed!"

CHAPTER 5

Summer lay across the land with fiery brilliance. At midday the earth shimmered under glaring shafts of light, and the sun at its zenith seemed fixed forever in a cloudless sky. Far in the distance waves of heat pulsed and vibrated, distilled small mirages from crystal air, and left the plains bathed in a glow of illusion.

Under the brassy haze, a buckboard and team clattered westward toward the headwaters of Santa Guerra Creek. Art Johnson held the reins, and beside him Angela sat perched beneath the shade of a parasol. At Trudy's insistence, she had agreed to accompany him, but not at the risk of her complexion. The plains sun aged women before their time, turned their skin leathery and coarse, eventually left them brown as a Mexican. Unlike her daughter, who became more of a tomboy every day, Angela was quite determined to remain a lady. The parasol was her constant companion.

The buckboard was trailed by a group of vaqueros, all armed to the teeth. Over her mother's protests, Trudy rode with them, mounted astride a roan gelding. She enjoyed their jabbering, carefree banter, and delighted in the fact that they accepted her as one of their own. Beside her were the sons of Ramon Morado, who acted as her companions on all such outings. Roberto was two years her senior, solemn and darkly handsome, with the grave manner of his father. The younger brother, Luis, was Trudy's age, with laughing eyes and a clownish smile, something of a prankster. Since Trudy refused to behave like a girl, the boys were with her almost constantly; their father had assigned them to accompany her whenever she rode with the vaqueros. Trudy considered the Morado brothers her *compañeros*—her clos-

est friends on Santa Guerra—and they treated each other with the off-handed familiarity of equals.

Yet despite the easy camaraderie, there was always a tinge of deference in the manner of both the boys and the vaqueros. She was, after all, the daughter of *El Patrón,* and their lives would be in serious jeopardy if she were allowed to fall into the hands of *bandidos* or marauding Indians. Under standing orders from Ramon Morado, the girl was never permitted outside the compound without an armed escort. Since *La Madama* was along today, the guard was heavier than normal, and Trudy was immensely pleased with herself.

She had arranged it all quite neatly, badgering her mother into joining Uncle Art on his errand, and the result was double the number of vaqueros who usually escorted her. Nearly twenty armed men! She felt like a *generalissimo* leading her own private army.

Angela simply felt bored. She rarely ventured outside the compound, and was of the firm opinion that anything pertaining to the ranch was best left in the hands of Ramon Morado. Certainly her husband knew nothing about cattle, and exhibited little interest aside from his monthly inspection of the account ledgers. His preoccupation was with riverboats and . . . other things . . . and this sudden urgency to acquire more land left her mildly puzzled. It was perhaps the only reason she had agreed to take part in today's excursion. Her brother was a perfect dunce, and she invariably learned more from him than she did her husband.

She sighed, and patted her forehead with a hanky. "Honestly, this heat isn't to be endured. Won't we ever get there?"

"It's not much farther. Couple of miles, maybe a little less."

"You're sure that's all Henry said? Check the boundary mark . . . nothing more?"

"That's it. For some reason or another, it's important to him that he own the headwaters of the creek."

"I thought that's why he retained that dreadful little man —Pryor, the lawyer—to look after such things."

"Shoot! He's had me doggin' Pryor's tracks for the last six months. You know Hank! If he can't do it himself, then it has to be checked and double-checked."

"No, I'm not sure I do know him. Not anymore. All this

flurry of land buying, and that unconscionable raise in freight rates." Her breast rose and fell, and she dabbed again with the hanky. "He's not the man I married, Arty. The war changed him, made him harder."

Johnson gave her a quizzical side-glance. "Aren't you being a mite hard yourself? You know, running a steamboat line's not like holdin' a church supper. The whole idea is to make all the profit the traffic will bear."

"Now you sound like Henry." Angela was unable to resist the temptation to display virtue, particularly when it served her purpose. "I shudder to think what Father would have thought if he'd heard you make such an uncharitable statement."

"Hold off a goldarn—" Johnson hesitated, unsure exactly how to defend himself. "You got no call to say that, Sis. I've never done a dishonest thing in my life. Not for Hank or anyone else."

"Really?" Angela lifted an eyebrow in question. "Are you telling me you're not a party to Henry's scheme?"

"Scheme! What scheme?"

"Oh, don't be a fool, Arty Johnson. Can't you see that he has a design in all this . . . a conspiracy of some sort?"

"You mean this land-buyin' deal?"

"Yes, the land, that's part of it. And then gaining control of the river. And trying to buy the railroad charter to connect Brownsville with the coast. My goodness, it seems to me any ninny would see that it's all somehow connected."

"Yeah, I suppose," Johnson agreed somewhat reluctantly. "Except for one thing. Hank could've bribed the Yankees if he'd wanted to, but he didn't. He bid fair and square on that railroad charter. Otherwise Joe Starling would've never beat him out."

"Of course he did! That's what I'm talking about. A railroad could destroy Henry's steamboat business. But he submitted a ridiculous bid, and now that Starling has the charter, he doesn't appear to be in the least concerned. So just stop and ask yourself the question, does that sound like the Henry Laird we know? Or does it sound like someone who's hatched a grand scheme of some sort?"

"Yeah, I guess so. But what? What kind of scheme?"

"Heaven save us! I don't know, Arty. That's what I'm asking you."

"Beat's me. All Hank said was to check the boundary mark."

Angela turned away in disgust. At that moment she detested her brother—who was an even greater fool than she'd suspected—and she was bitterly frustrated by her husband's secrecy. Not that his sharp business practices really bothered her. Nor for that matter his underhanded scheme, whatever it was! But she was positively livid that he'd excluded her from every aspect of his life in Brownsville. It was petty spite, she told herself, simply another way he'd found to punish and humiliate her. And all because she had a mind of her own, refused to consort with Yankees or return again to that dreary little house in town.

Suddenly her wrath turned inward. She despised herself and the shrew she'd become. For an instant she even hated her father, whose missionary zeal had uprooted them from their home and brought them to the border. Except for that, she might have remained in New Orleans forever, become a fine lady with broods of children and a prosperous, God-fearing husband. Instead, like some dizzy schoolgirl, she'd been swept off her feet by a laughing, wild-eyed Irishman. Sometimes she even wondered about that; was it love that caused her to marry or had she merely used it as a pretext to escape her father? The thought revolted her, dredged up emotions about her father she'd buried long ago, and she quickly cast it from her mind.

Her gaze wandered out across the plains. A brooding loneliness, like the hazed blue of the sky, hung over the land. The vaqueros called it *El Desierto de los Muertos*—the Desert of the Dead—for scores of Mexican families who originally attempted to settle the interior had been slaughtered by Comanche war parties and savage gangs of *bandidos* who roamed the border. Even now, there were only a few haciendas in this vast wilderness, strongholds established by men like her husband. Yet for all its cruelty and danger, it was a land of raw, untamed beauty. A great sea of grass, broken by mottes of laurel and scattered bosques of mesquite, stretched endlessly to the horizon. Along the creek stately groves of live oak wavered in the breeze, and around marshy

resacas there were occasional thickets of palmetto and chaparral. Not a hospitable land, for its rugged vistas were better suited to horses and cows than to men, but a land of immense tranquility, soothing in its stillness and sometimes ghostly silence.

Lately Angela had tried to convince herself that it was enough. The land and the ranch and the almost mystical adoration of *Los Lerdeños.* And of course Trudy. It was a good life, a peaceful life, without complication or worry or unwanted intrusion. A life to which she might devote herself and her energies, and someday, with the Lord's help, cleanse herself of those distasteful memories. Forget what her life might have been, had her father not heard the call and gone forth in search of sinners. Set aside faded dreams and lost hopes, the way one presses dead flowers between the pages of a book. Dwell no longer in the shadow of bitterness, haunted by thoughts of a little boy, and the ache in her womb when she saw again his childlike innocence and laughing face.

The word "cloistered" sprang into her mind, and with it an overwhelming sense of serenity. Abruptly it occurred to her that the answer might very well be within her grasp. Perhaps the inner peace she sought would one day . . .

Her reverie was broken. She became aware of her brother's voice, and realized he was watching her with an odd expression. She tilted the parasol, turning sideways, and gave him a disarming smile.

"I'm sorry, Arty. The sun's enough to paralyze the mind. Did you say something?"

"Well, yeah. You being so mad and all, I just got to thinking that maybe it didn't have nothin' to do with business. Thought maybe it was personal. You know, between you and Hank. So I was tryin' to explain that he doesn't mean any harm. He's just ornery and full of the dickens, and that's his way of blowin' off steam."

"I'm sure I don't know what you mean."

"C'mon, Sis." Johnson squirmed uncomfortably in his seat. "Don't make me spell it out. It's the whiskey and his . . . you know . . . the company he keeps."

Angela's smile seemed frozen. "Henry has always been

free to choose his own company. I've never interfered, even though I do find those riverboat captains a despicable lot."

"I'm not talkin' about—" Johnson sounded baffled. "Look here, now, are you funnin' me or what?"

"Arty, don't raise your voice. I gave you a civil answer, and I assure you it wasn't meant in jest."

"Well, I sure as the devil wasn't talkin' about riverboat captains!"

"Then suppose we let it rest there, shall we? I know you mean well, but there's nothing between Henry and myself that needs discussing."

Johnson looked at her with some surprise. "I get the feelin' you just told me to shut my mouth."

"Gracious, this sun's a caution, isn't it? I hope it's not much farther, Arty. I'm just dying for a drink of that cool spring water."

Angela sat stock-still, staring straight ahead across the prairie. She appeared serene and collected, but in the depths of hidden feelings a new anxiety burned bright. On those infrequent occasions when Henry came to the ranch, they kept their conversation on a surface level. And these days they never touched, especially in bed. It was as though there was some silent agreement, mutually acceptable, to avoid anything that might cause distress. She had Trudy and the ranch, and he had his steamboat business. Very tidy, everything in its own little niche, a civilized arrangement between two civilized people. Or at least she had hoped, even believed, that they had finally come to terms with one another.

Now she knew better, understood what lay behind his thoughtful manner and that polite veneer of concern. Unwittingly, her brother had spoken out of turn, and now she knew the truth.

It wasn't riverboats or riverboat captains. It was whores.

CHAPTER 6

Blalock reversed engines and slowly maneuvered the *Mustang* into shallow water. Deckhands waded ashore with hawsers, securing the boat to several stout trees, and a gangplank was lowered off the bow. Nearly thirty crewmen, all of them armed, stood bunched together on the forward deck. Laird approached them, a double-barrel shotgun cradled in his arm, and began issuing orders. He ticked off a dozen men, who each hoisted ten pound kegs of gunpowder onto their shoulders, then he walked forward and led the way down the gangplank.

On shore, Laird headed inland at a brisk pace. He set a winding course through the trees and undergrowth, but held generally to a north-by-northeast bearing. The crewmen strung out behind him single file, loaded down with an assortment of gear. There was no talking, none of the jesting and tomfoolery of a normal morning, and their faces were somber, almost subdued. Some three hundred yards inland, Laird broke clear of the scrub and halted, waiting for the men to gather round. Before them was a wide clearing, and stretching eastward toward the coast was a ribbon of steel. The rails were narrow gauge, newly laid, and glistened brightly as false dawn gave way to the glare of sunrise.

When the last of the stragglers stepped into the clearing, Laird turned back to the assembled group. His look was sober, and he studied them for several seconds, his gaze moving slowly from face to face. Not a man among them had been ordered to accompany him on today's mission. But they were rivermen, and loved a good scrap, and were of the common opinion that Hank Laird had hung the moon. He possessed that rare and undefinable thing called the common touch, and had he led the way, most of them would

have followed him across a bed of live coals. It was a loyalty he sometimes took for granted, yet this morning he was acutely aware of it, and never prouder that they counted him one of their own. After a while he grinned and patted the shotgun underneath his arm.

"Boys, this here's your signal. So remember what I said. There'll be no fireworks unless I start it. Just keep your eyes on me, and for the love of Christ, don't get itchy. I'll not have blood spilled unless there's no other way. Any questions?"

There were no questions. "All right, then, let's get to work." Laird jerked his thumb at the railroad tracks. "Dig your holes deep and plant that powder the way I told you. And make sure you get it right the first time! We've got a half hour, maybe a little more, before our company arrives."

The men broke into small work parties and walked toward the rails. Those with shovels began digging holes between alternate crossties, while others trimmed fuses for the powder kegs. From his position by the trees, Laird kept a lookout down the tracks, ready to signal the men the instant he saw smoke. But his eyes shifted constantly, moving around the clearing as he reviewed his plan one last time.

The rails ended midway through the clearing, where track crews had halted work yesterday evening and returned to the base camp on the coast. A railbed, extending across the rest of the clearing, had been freshly graded and tamped in preparation for today's track-laying. A stone cairn, partially hidden by brush, marked the eastern boundary of Laird's property. It bisected the rails some fifty yards below end-of-track, and unquestionably placed the Gulf & Rio Grande Railroad on private land.

Laird studied the terrain a moment longer, then nodded and chuckled softly to himself. His scouts had accurately reported the situation, and he was satisfied that this morning's welcoming party was perfectly legal. It had taken a year of waiting—and an endless summer while the rails inched toward his property—but he had every confidence that 1866 would prove the turning point in his grand design. He was congratulating himself on the virtue of patience when Sam Blalock crashed out of the brush and entered the clearing.

"We're all squared away, Cap'n. Boat's ready to shove off whenever you say."

"Thank you, Sam. It's them that'll be doing the running, but it never hurts to have an escape hatch . . . just in case."

"Then you still figure they won't fight?"

"Not unless Joe loses his head." Laird smiled. "The man's a great tub of lard, but he does have a temper."

"You really think he'll show?"

"Aye. Him and his partner both. They've no choice."

"I suppose not." Blalock rubbed his chin, watching the work crews. "Say it does get stickery, though. What happens then?"

Laird swept the clearing with his arm. "We'll split the boys along both sides of the track. You with one bunch, me with the other. Of course it's surprise we're after, so make damn sure they stay hidden in the trees. That way, we'll have Starling and his crowd caught between us."

"Yeah, and then what? After he gets here, I mean."

"Then I'll go down and have a little talk with Joe. Explain to him how I've got his balls in a nutcracker."

"Down there! Are you sayin' out in the open, by the tracks?"

"Naturally. Would you have me duck behind a tree and shout at him?"

"Cap'n, I don't like that idea. None a'tall! Least little thing goes wrong, and you wouldn't stand a Chinaman's chance. Not out there in the open."

"Calm yourself, Sam." Laird tapped the shotgun. "With this trained on his belly, Joe won't make any foolish moves. Take my word on it."

Blalock frowned, shook his head. "You're awful sure of yourself, Cap'n. What if he loses his temper, like you said. Then what?"

"Then you and the boys open up with your rifles, and I'll treat you to a display of fancy footwork. It's fast I am when I'm running for my life, jocko. Mortal fast."

"I hope so," Blalock muttered. "You're liable to need all the speed you've got before we're done here."

"Aye, that I will. But not for the reasons you mean." Laird gave him a cryptic smile. "Now, be a good fellow and hurry

the boys along. I've an idea our visitors got an early start this morning."

Blalock began a question, then appeared to change his mind. He shrugged and turned away, mumbling something under his breath. Laird fished a cigar out of his jacket pocket, juggling the shotgun while he lit it, and went back to watching the skyline. He had a hunch it wouldn't be long.

Less than a quarter-hour later, a locomotive, pulling several flatcars, rolled into the clearing. Loaded aboard the flatcars were stacks of rails and crossties and a track gang of perhaps a hundred men, nearly half of them armed. A groaning squeal racketed across the clearing as the engineer throttled down and set the brakes. The train ground to a halt, belching steam and smoke, scarcely ten yards from the end-of-track.

Hank Laird stood in its path, puffing on a cigar, shotgun cradled in his arms.

The steam drifted away on a light breeze as Joe Starling stepped down from the engine. Behind him was his partner, Earl Roebuck, and the two men presented a sharp study in contrasts. Roebuck was lean and swarthy, with splayed cheekbones and muddy eyes and sleek, glistening hair. He wore rough work clothes, with mule-eared boots and a slouch hat, and strapped around his hip was a Colt Dragoon. His eyes remained fixed on Laird, but he whispered something out of the corner of his mouth to Starling as they walked forward. Starling merely nodded.

Laird waited until they were near the end-of-track, then he lowered the shotgun and centered it on Starling. The two men halted, and he smiled. "Morning, Joe. See you got my message."

"Your man just said to meet you here. He didn't say nothin' about being greeted with a shotgun."

"A mere precaution, Joe. Nothing personal."

"C'mon, Laird! Save your malarkey and just spit it out. What the hell do you want?"

"Why, that's simple, Joe. I've come to warn you that you're trespassing. I want you off my land."

"Your land!" Starling shook his head like a man who had walked into cobwebs. "Since when is it your land?"

"Since I bought it and duly recorded it in Corpus Christi."

Laird paused and gave him a sad smile. "It's a pity, Joe. But you should've checked the title. Now you've gone and laid your rails on private property."

"In a pig's ass! I bought the charter off the Union army. The commanding general himself signed it! And you know goddamn well his orders supersede civil authority."

"Aye, that it does. But only where the charter is concerned. You see, the war's over, Joe, and we're back to the old rules. You must obtain right-of-way before you build a railroad. That's the law."

"Like hell it is! That charter's all I need."

"Nooo, there's still the matter of right-of-way. Your Yankee friends really should've told you about that, Joe. Of course, everyone knows they're sharp traders, so it's to be expected."

Starling's face went ocherous. "Get out of my way, Laird. I won't be stopped . . . not again."

"Careful now." Laird cocked both hammers on the shotgun. "You're already on my land, and I've the legal right to deal with trespassers."

Earl Roebuck stiffened, edging sideways, and Laird wagged the shotgun in his direction. "Easy with that pistol, Mr. Roebuck. Don't make me stunt your growth."

"You're not scaring anybody," Roebuck blustered. "Take a look back at those flatcars. Lots of armed men there, Laird. Think you can stop all of 'em with a lousy scatter-gun?"

"It's you that'd best take a look, Mr. Roebuck. Try the trees on either side of the tracks."

Starling and Roebuck swiveled in opposite directions, then back again. The tree line on both sides of the train bristled with rifle muzzles. They exchanged a baffled look, and Starling suddenly turned on Laird, his face pinched in an oxlike expression.

"You're just a sackful of surprises, aren't you?"

"Joe, those bullyboys of yours wouldn't have changed things one way or another. You're all wind and no whistle, and we both know it."

"Dirty sonovabitch!" Starling rasped. "You'll live to regret it, Laird. I promise you that."

"Temper! Temper!" Laird laughed without humor. "Don't lose your head, Joe. You've still got big problems."

"Oh yeah?" Starling eyed him warily. "And what the hell's that supposed to mean?"

Laird puffed on the stub of his cigar, took it out of his mouth, and blew ashes off the coal. Without a word, he walked along the tracks, knelt beside the front of the engine, and touched his cigar to a tip of cord protruding from the earth. There was a wisp of smoke followed instantly by a hissing sound and the flare of sparks. Starling and Roebuck stood slack-jawed, watching with stunned disbelief as he moved from fuse to fuse, lighting them in rapid succession. After the third fuse had caught, he glanced back over his shoulder and grinned.

"Joe, these are two-minute fuses. Now, if I was you, I'd get my fat ass on that engine and get it the hell out of here. Otherwise it'll get blown to Kingdom Come."

Starling and Roebuck took off running as he lit the fourth fuse. The engineer was hanging out of the cab, urging them onward with a sort of pop-eyed terror, and the moment they scrambled aboard he hooked into reverse. The great driving wheels spun and screeched, clutching at the rails, and there was a jolting groan as the locomotive slammed into the flat-cars. The train slowly picked up speed, chuffing smoke like a maimed dragon, and went hurtling backward out of the clearing.

Laird stepped across the tracks and quickly ran the line of fuses on the opposite side. Then he jumped clear and burst into a headlong sprint toward the wooded undergrowth. The crewmen were shouting and whistling, waving him on, and after what seemed an eternity, he flung himself to the ground behind the trunk of a live oak. Sam Blalock dove in beside him, mouth clamped tight, and gave him a dirty look as they ducked their heads. An instant later a dull *whump* sent tremors rippling through the earth.

The railbed suddenly buckled, split apart, and erupted skyward with a volcanic roar of fire and smoke. Timbers and steel and chunks of sod climbed higher and higher, blotting out the sun, and slowly blossomed into a gigantic black rosebud. The force of the explosion hurled shards of wood and twisted rails across the clearing, showering debris far beyond the tree line. Then it was gone, the thunderous blast and fiery wind replaced by an eerie silence. Smoke hung over the

clearing in a silty cloud, and where the tracks had ended only moments before, there was now a scorched crater almost the exact dimensions of a locomotive. It had the look and smell of a freshly ravaged battlefield.

Laird and Blalock climbed to their feet, peering around the tree, and after a long while the riverboat captain grunted with disgust. "You're fast awright, Cap'n. I'll give you that. But you're awful goddamn lucky too."

"It's me Irish blood, Sam. Tells every time."

CHAPTER 7

Laird managed to dismount without losing his balance. He gave the horse an affectionate swat on the neck and stood there a moment, breathing deeply of the crisp autumn night. He was none too steady on his feet, bracing himself like a man walking into a strong wind. But his vision was clear, and though his lips tingled with a numb sensation, his mind functioned perfectly. He'd never felt better in his life.

Since leaving Austin, his mood had grown more expansive, and every mile, his spirits had soared steadily higher. Three days on the road, with little sleep and even less food, had affected him none at all. His trail south was marked by a string of empty bottles, and he'd found whiskey to be a stimulating companion. He stank of horse sweat, bearded stubble covered his jaws, and he'd brought with him the grandest prize imaginable. The big casino.

Listing slightly, he mounted the steps and crossed the porch with a determined stride. At the door he paused, squaring his shoulders, then threw it open and entered the parlor with an air of Caesar triumphant. Angela sat in a rocking chair beside the fireplace, crocheting a finely worked doily. The firelight and a table lamp cast her face in an amber glow, and her dark hair glinted with flecks of russet and gold. She brought the rocker to a halt, the crochet needle gone still, and looked around.

"Good evening, Henry. I trust your trip went well."

Laird closed the door and took in the parlor with a baroque sweep of his arm. "Aye, well indeed! In fact, you may henceforth address me as King Henry the First."

"How nice," Angela murmured. "Of course, Henry VIII might dispute the claim, mightn't he? If he were alive, I mean."

"Never fear, lass. It's not England I'm claiming, but a kingdom of my own. Laird's Kingdom! The Rio Grande and every twist and turn along a hundred miles of border. By the Sweet Jesus, it's all mine! To rule as I bloody well please."

"And your subjects, are they now governed by royal edict?"

"In a manner of speaking, they are. Him that rules the tides of commerce rules the people. And sure as there's a God in Heaven, that's me!"

Angela sniffed and looked away. "You're drunk, Henry."

"Aye, drunk as a fiddler's bitch!" Laird whirled across the parlor, dancing a wobbly jig, and lurched to a halt behind the rocker. He leaned forward, cupping her cheeks in his hands, and laughed in her ear. "Hate whiskey worse'n the devil hates holy water, don't you?"

"You know very well I do."

"But still you've got the urge, don't you? Sitting there with your mouth tight as a peach pit, but all the time you're thinking how you'd love to get me in bed. Do all them dirty, filthy things that sets you to clawing and screaming like a wildcat." His hands slid down over her breasts and his voice dropped to a whisper. "Tell me it's not so. I dare you! On the head of your dear, departed father, let me hear you say it's all a pack of lies."

"You're disgusting!" Angela wrenched away, pushing his hands aside. "You come home drunk and blasphemous, and if that's not bad enough, then you have to paw me like one of those . . . one of your whores!"

"Now it's whores, is it?" Laird moved around the rocker, chortling in mock wonder, and turned with his back to the fireplace. "Could it be that you're jealous, lass? Not of me, you understand. Of them . . . the whores! Tell the truth, now. Wouldn't you trade your key to the Pearly Gates if you could let your hair down . . . not roast yourself to perdition for all those wicked thoughts whirling round in your head?" He cocked one eyebrow, watching her intently. "You would, wouldn't you? Even for a single night! Kiss the cross and tell me it's not true."

There was no answer. The silence grew, stretched, broken only by the crackling of logs in the fireplace. Angela set the

rocker in motion, eyes fastened on her hands and the furious blur of the crochet needle. It took her a long while to regain some measure of composure. When at last she spoke, her tone was one of distant civility. A tone she had cultivated over the past year, impersonal and reserved, brought into play with the deftness of a stiletto.

"Henry, until tonight you've faithfully honored our agreement, and I deeply appreciate that. What you do in Brownsville is your own affair. The drinking—the other things—it's no part of our marriage. I rarely even give it a thought, and if you hadn't goaded me, I wouldn't have spoken of . . . those things."

The crochet needle stopped, and she looked up. "I apologize for snapping at you. And although you're drunk, I hope you'll have the decency to behave as you normally do in our home. Now, why don't you sit down, and tell me about your trip to Austin? I never quite understood the purpose of your going, but from your manner it's evident you met with success."

Laird appeared bemused. His gaze was inquisitive, oddly perplexed, as though she were something he'd bought on impulse and now, upon reflection, he couldn't quite decide what he'd got for his money. She was absolutely the damnedest woman he'd ever known—a regular grab bag of contradictions—and he seriously wondered that he would ever fully understand what went on inside her head. Finally, with a great shrug of resignation, he flopped down in a leather wing chair, legs outstretched toward the fire.

"I'm not sure I'd call the journey a success. It was more on the order of a conquest."

"Conquest? My goodness, Henry, that does sound imperial."

"Well, as I told you, it's a kingdom I've returned with."

"Yes, but I thought you were just carrying on . . . exaggerating."

"Drunken bragging? No, far from it." He paused, staring into the flames, and his dampened spirits slowly rekindled. "I went to the capital with my saddlebags stuffed full of gold, and I returned with the charter for a railroad. The one and only charter that will ever be granted for a railroad to Brownsville."

"You're not serious!"

"Oh, I'm in earnest. It's hardly a matter to jest about."

"But how on earth—well, you know—the Yankees and all their trash."

"How'd I pull it off?" Laird's mouth curled in an ironic smile. "Simplest way possible. Austin's thick with thieves, so I bribed every carpetbagger and scalawag I could lay my hands on."

With mounting enthusiasm, Laird went on to relate the highlights of his visit to what was now the Yankee capital of Texas. Angela merely listened, coldly silent, eyeing him with a mixture of dismay and surprise. She knew that Texas, and all the South, was at the mercy of the Yankees. She knew as well that her husband was utterly pragmatic concerning business, whether he was dealing with competitors or corrupt Northern officials. But the ranch was a refuge of sorts, isolated from the terrors of Reconstruction, and until now she had never fully appreciated the extent to which Texas had been subjugated. Nor had she gauged the true ruthlessness of Hank Laird.

By the autumn of 1866, Union occupation forces were coordinating a program of reprisal and vengeance against a conquered land. The military possessed godlike powers, along with a taste for the spoils of war, and across the South the jackals gathered to share in the kill. The carpetbaggers, Northern-born loyalists, came by the thousands and, for the right price, were appointed to civil posts vacated at the despotic whim of military commanders. Next came the scalawags, Southerners without conscience or scruples, swearing allegiance to the Union in return for a license to rob their neighbors and kin. Many became governor, state senator, attorney general and, in league with the carpetbaggers and corrupt military commanders, set about performing civil and economic rape on a defeated land.

With the law in the hands of the conquerors and their henchmen, former secessionists were faced with a stiff choice. Either they learned to suffer in silence, or else they came to terms with vandals who literally held the power of life and death. Which was precisely what Hank Laird had done. To control the Rio Grande, and insure his monopoly

of the border trade, he needed an absolute license on all forms of transportation. It had cost him dearly, better than $50,000 in gold, but he now possessed a charter for all future railroad construction into the lower Rio Grande. The document effectively anointed him lord of commerce and trade for southern Texas, and in a very real sense, it had transformed the border into his own personal kingdom.

"So there you have it," Laird concluded. "The rascals would sell their mother if she'd fetch the right price, and once they sniffed gold, I practically dictated the terms of the charter word for word."

"But that doesn't make sense," Angela countered. "Last year you let Joe Starling outbid you on a charter, and then you purposely ruined him. Now you spend a fortune on a new charter . . . but why?"

"Lots of reasons. Starling's deal was nothing more than a link between Brownsville and the coast. The charter I've got covers *any* overland construction to the lower Rio Grande. Besides, last year I'd not yet sewed up title to all the ranchland. Now I own a strip that sits like a wedge between Brownsville and Corpus Christi. Any way you spell it, that means I'm the one who's got the leverage. And I've got it all."

"I still don't understand. I thought all along that you wanted to protect your steamboats. If Starling was a threat, then won't your own charter amount to the same thing?"

Laird slapped his knee and laughed. "Aye, but there's a difference, lass! You see, Joe meant to build his railroad. I've no such intention."

"You went to all this trouble, and you're not—"

Angela's face went pale, and suddenly she couldn't keep her hands still. Her mouth narrowed and her eyes took on the dull gleam of an icon. She drew a deep, unsteady breath and her voice rose quickly.

"Henry, you can't do it! Not again. It's unfair, don't you see that?"

"Fair! What the hell's fair got to do with anything? It's business. I set the rates and them that don't like it can take their trade elsewhere. There's no law that says they must use my boats."

"Now there is—your law—Laird's Law! You've all but put

them in bondage. The merchants have no choice. The towns-people and all those poor Mexicans have no choice. Either they pay your price or they'll go hungry, lose everything they own."

"Oh, they'll pay well enough, but I'll not crowd them too close. After all, lively trade makes for full boats, and that's the whole idea. I'll merely charge them what the traffic will bear . . . and perhaps a bit more."

"But that's monstrous!" Angela cried. "It's what I would expect from some Yankee trash. Don't you see that, Henry? It makes you no better than those carpetbaggers and scala-wags you've been talking about. If anything, it makes you worse. You'll be nothing but a spoiler . . . a common robber."

"God's blood!" Laird shouted, biting off the words. *"I'll—not—hear—more!"*

Standing, he walked stiffly to the door, then suddenly turned, his face ashen. "You're a miserable excuse for a woman, and what's worse—you've the tongue of a viper! Until I've had your apology, you'll not see me again. And there's the last of it!"

The door slammed behind him, and Angela felt an almost uncontrollable urge to run after him. To apologize then and there. To tell him she'd spoken in the heat of the moment, too quickly, without regard for his feelings. But she gripped the arms of the rocker and suppressed the urge. Forced herself to sit there and let him ride off, knowing full well that he might never return. Not after tonight.

Yet there was nothing to be done, he was wrong! And she'd spoken the truth! It was a monstrous thing he intended. Evil and mean, almost diabolic in the way he'd planned it. And however intolerant, she couldn't judge him by any code except the one she'd followed all her life. The code of right and wrong, and do unto thy neighbor. Nor could she make allowances for his own code, the riverman's belief in dog-eat-dog and devil take the hindmost. He was wrong, and it was just that simple.

Angela jumped, startled by a faint noise. She turned and saw Trudy peering at her from the corner of the hallway. She stood, took a step around the rocker, words forming in her throat, then she froze. The girl's face was rigid and hard,

blazing with fury. An instant of tomblike silence slipped past while they stared at one another. Then Angela collected herself, spoke the girl's name, started toward her.

Trudy whirled and fled, lost in the darkness.

CHAPTER 8

The cork floated lazily on the surface of the water. Trudy lifted her fishing pole, jiggling the hook, and settled back with a small sigh. On the creek bank beside her were the Morado boys. The fish weren't biting and none of them had spoken for a long while. Luis was stretched out, hands locked behind his head, gazing at the sky and whistling softly through his teeth. Roberto sat motionless, seemingly lost in thought. His fishing pole was jammed into the grassy bank and he watched the bobbing corks with a fixed expression.

The weather was unseasonably warm, a listless Indian summer day in late autumn. After the noon meal all activity in the village had ceased. Beneath a cloudless sky, with the sun at its zenith, the people had retired to their adobes for a brief siesta. But Trudy seldom observed the midday interlude, and she was in no mood to return to the house or chance another strained afternoon with her mother. The past few weeks had been an uncomfortable time, the worst of her life, and the thought of being trapped in her mother's presence any longer than necessary was simply unbearable. She had taken the noonday meal with the Morados and then talked the boys into a fishing excursion. Walking upstream to the swimming hole, a deep pool on the outskirts of the village, they had baited their hooks and entered into a contest of patience with the fish. So far it had been a draw, without so much as a nibble.

As the minutes wore on, the frown lines around Trudy's mouth deepened. She was in a bleak mood, thoroughly dispirited by events over which she had no control. She felt helpless and alone—somehow forsaken—like an abandoned puppy wandering aimlessly through dense woods. Even worse, she had difficulty separating emotions, balancing one

conflict against another. She waffled between anger toward her mother and an aching hurt for her father, uncertain from one moment to the next which bothered her the most. It was all very confusing, a heavy burden for a twelve year old, and one she was ill prepared to handle.

Nearly three weeks had elapsed since her father walked out of the house. In that time he had written her a couple of cheery little notes, brought to the ranch by courier, but there had been no mention of when he would return or if she would be allowed to visit him in Brownsville. Nor had he corresponded at all with her mother. Apparently he was as good as his word, and had no intention of setting foot on the ranch until he'd had an apology.

The thought hit Trudy with a new jolt each time it went through her mind. *He might never come back!*

Yet she wouldn't permit herself to believe it. The idea terrified her, left her queasy and light-headed, almost feverish. She couldn't imagine not seeing him, never hearing his voice again or feeling the strength of his arms when he hugged her. It just wasn't possible that such a thing could happen, that he would walk out of the house and out of her life and never again return. Still, however much she told herself it wasn't possible—and she repeated it to herself constantly these days—her every waking moment was filled with a sense of dread. Anything was possible with her father. To her, he was unlike all other men, an almost mystical figure given to acts of loving tenderness interspersed with godlike fits of rage. She wouldn't let herself believe it, but she knew it was true: Angered enough, it was entirely possible he'd never return.

Her mother, of course, was to blame for the whole thing. Thinking back to that night, Trudy recalled little except his look of fury. Yet one thing stuck out in her mind, an accusation he'd shouted at the very last. *You've the tongue of a viper!* So it was something her mother had said that had touched off his anger. Trudy had heard most of the argument, standing paralyzed in the doorway, but she understood virtually nothing of its substance. In her mind, grown-ups were a mystery wholly as incomprehensible as the Scripture, and it simply made no sense. One point was clear, however, and the

more she thought of it, the more vivid her impression became. Her mother was a fool!

Only someone without a lick of common sense would purposely anger her father. And it was clear now, just as it was clear then, that her mother knew what she was doing. Her mother always knew exactly what she was doing! So it wasn't her father who had caused the argument, and he couldn't be faulted for slamming out of the house. Or staying in Brownsville all this time. Instead, it was her mother who drove him away, and it was her mother who caused him to stay away. Until she apologized he wouldn't come home—those were his very words—and in Trudy's view that simply made her mother all the more a fool. Anyone who could keep a man like him at home with an apology was an absolute ninny to do otherwise. Of course, being a fool in no way excused her mother. She and her viper's tongue were to blame, and—*Válgame Dios!*—why didn't she just apologize, and say whatever needed saying, so he'd come on home?

Suddenly Trudy was more confused than ever. She couldn't understand her mother, and on those occasions when her mother attempted to raise the subject, it was all she could do not to scream and burst out in tears. As a result, they spoke less and less to each other, and the gap separating them widened daily. Yet Trudy desperately needed to talk to someone. She was lost and groping blindly in a thicket of questions that seemed to have no answers. Which made her feel something of a fool herself.

She darted a glance at Roberto. Though a boy himself, a mere fourteen, he had always seemed much older, and infinitely wiser about all manner of things. Besides, he was her best friend—a true *compadre*—and she knew she could trust him with her innermost secrets. As for Luis, he faithfully followed Roberto's lead, so there was little fear of him talking out of turn. Then, too, if it became necessary, she was reasonably certain she could whip Luis in a fair fight. So she had nothing to lose, and maybe, with Roberto's help . . .

"Roberto?"

"*Sí?*"

"Can I ask you a question?"

"*Sí.*"

His expression was one of amiable tolerance. By next

spring he would take his place among the vaqueros, and Trudy already considered him a man. She constantly badgered him with questions, for her curiosity about horses and cows was seemingly unbounded. While she was a bother at times, her admiration enhanced their friendship and in no way displeased him. She was, after all, the daughter of *El Patrón.*

"Well, I was wondering—" Trudy faltered, groping for words, then blurted it out. "Do your folks ever fight . . . get *furioso* at each other?"

Roberto twisted around, studying her a moment. He was startled, but alert to something unspoken in the question. "Why do you ask?"

"Oh, just because," Trudy replied vaguely. "C'mon, you can tell me . . . do they?"

"Sí." Roberto shrugged, watching her eyes. "Sometimes."

"Sometimes!" Luis hooted, quickly levering himself into a sitting position. *"Madre mío!* They fight like *gato montés* . . . all the time!"

Roberto silenced him with a frown. "Enough, little brother! You have a loose tongue and the laugh of a *burra.*"

"But they do fight," Trudy persisted. "Maybe not like wildcats, but they do fight . . . *verdad?*"

"Of course," Roberto conceded. "All married people fight. It is to be expected."

"Why?"

"Who knows? Perhaps they enjoy it."

Trudy nodded, gave him a conspiratorial look. "When they fight . . . your folks . . . who wins?"

"Mi padre!" Roberto told her. "He's a tough one—*puro hombre!*—no one gets past him."

"Ah, chihuahua!" Luis laughed, winking at Trudy. "Don't be fooled by such talk. Our *mamacita,* she always wins! Not at first, but in the end she leads the old man around like a *manso* with a ring in his nose."

"Ramon!" Trudy's mouth popped open. "She gets the best of Ramon?"

"Sí, always," Luis grinned. "She has magic—like a *bruja*—all women have it."

"Silencio, imbécil!" Roberto ordered. "You speak of things that . . . have no place here."

Roberto was alarmed now, wary of the conversation, and disturbed by his brother's careless remarks. It was no secret that the *patrón* had left Santa Guerra in a rage. Nor was the reason for his continued absence any great mystery. Among *Los Lerdeños,* there was considerable worry and open speculation that *La Madama* might never regain his favor. Roberto had suddenly sensed the purpose of Trudy's questions, and he warned himself to proceed cautiously. Not even his father would dare meddle in the affairs of the *casa grande.*

A prolonged silence followed, with Roberto glaring at his brother and Luis looking properly abashed. At last, thoroughly bewildered by his outburst, Trudy turned on him. "You ought to be ashamed of yourself, talking to Luis that way. It's not fair and . . . I want to know what he meant—!"

"It was loose talk, nothing."

"He said all women have it. Now, damn you, Roberto, tell me—have what?"

"Por favor, little one. Let it pass. There are certain things . . . things such as this . . . that you should hear from women. It is not right that we speak of it here."

"Are we *amigos?"* Trudy demanded. *"Compadres?* Are we, Roberto?"

"Sí, you know we are. But it has nothing—"

"Yes, it does too! There are no women I could ask, and I sure couldn't ask my mother. So that leaves you, and if you won't tell me, then how will I ever find out?"

Roberto was quiet so long she began to think he wouldn't answer. But he finally sighed and spread his hands wide with resignation. "Luis meant that women work their magic at night . . . when they are in bed."

"In bed?"

"Sí." Roberto looked acutely uncomfortable. "In bed with their men."

"Oh!" Trudy suddenly flushed.

"Comprendes?"

"Mi sabe. You mean like the cows . . . the way they tease the bulls . . . and finally . . . well, you know . . . like that."

"Sí, it is the same."

"And that's how they win?"

"So I am told." Roberto gazed out across the creek, thoughtful for a time. "It is said that no man can resist, not if the woman . . . encourages him properly."

"Encourages . . . oh, you mean like the cows . . . teases him?"

"*Aiiii caramba,* must I draw pictures?"

Trudy glanced away, then fell silent and stared for a long while at the water. "*Gracias,* Roberto."

Roberto merely nodded, eyes fixed in the distance. The silence stretched, each of them lost in their own thoughts, oddly solemn now and yet somehow closer than before. After several minutes, Luis began fidgeting and finally jumped to his feet. A slow smile spread over his face, then he shook his head, mocking them, and laughed.

"What a pair you are! All this talk about *compañeros* and look at yourselves. *Cuacha!* You act like one broke wind and the other fears to hold his nose."

Trudy giggled and exchanged a glance with Roberto. She saw a slight tremor at the corner of his mouth, and realized he was trying very hard not to smile. A rush of understanding, unlike anything she'd ever experienced before, swept over her. Roberto wasn't aggravated with her, he was embarrassed! Suddenly she laughed and gave him a rough shove that sent him sprawling sideways. Then she leaped to her feet, jerked her fishing line from the stream, and threw the pole to the ground.

"*Sangre de Cristo!*" She cursed, kicking the pole. "Luis is right! All this talk bores me, and I'm tired of sitting here. Even the fish have taken a siesta. *Valga, compañeros,* let's do something!"

"Yes! Yes!" Luis agreed. "Let's do something. Anything!" He stopped, suddenly at a loss, and looked at her. "But what, Trudy? What shall we do?"

"Well, let's see." Trudy frowned, biting her lower lip. She gazed past them, caught up in a moment of indecision, and her eyes drifted to a patch of sunlight on the water. Then her face brightened and she clapped her hands. "A swim, that's it! We'll go swimming."

"No!" Roberto said sharply. "Not today."

"What's wrong with you?"

"Nothing. I just don't feel like a swim, that's all."

"Oh, bull! You've always felt like it before."

"Today is different."

"Different? *Qué pasa,* Roberto? How's it different?"

"Things have changed." Roberto averted his eyes, slowly reddened. "It would no longer be proper . . . for you to swim . . . that way."

"Porqué no?" Trudy asked with a charming little shrug. "We're still *compañeros,* aren't we?"

Trudy began undressing and Roberto kept his head turned away. Luis looked from one to the other, his expression puzzled, then began tearing off his own clothes. "Roberto, are you loco? Nothing's changed! It's just a swim."

"He's right, Roberto!" Trudy stepped out of her drawers and ran naked into the water. *"Anda! Anda!* Last one in is a tar baby!"

Her challenge, along with a smug look from Luis, was too much for Roberto. As his brother cannonballed into the stream, he hurriedly stripped, all the while telling himself it was wrong and foolish and a huge mistake. But he couldn't back down, even though he knew she'd taunted him, purposely dared him. Perhaps another time, but not today. Finished undressing, he turned and dove off the creek bank, a bronzed streak in the sunlight, slicing cleanly through the water.

When he surfaced, Trudy and Luis were in a dead heat, racing across the swimming hole. Trudy won by a stroke, neatly reversed course, her bare bottom flashing in the sun, and left Luis panting at the shoreline. She swam toward Roberto, and as she drew closer, he caught a devilish glint in her eye. He backpeddled furiously, but she quickened her stroke and overtook him with a whooping laugh. She lunged, grabbing his hair in her hands, and tried to duck him beneath the surface. He thrashed and shoved, unable to break her hold, then locked his arms around her waist, dragging her underwater as he went down. Her firm young body was pressed against him, thighs splayed around his hips and budding breasts rubbing softly on his chest. Too late, he sensed it, knew it was happening, and even as they floated upward he lost control. His manhood stiffened, engorged with blood, rose thick and swollen between her legs.

Trudy gasped, wide-eyed and breathless, as their heads

broke clear of the surface. She felt a strange hardness thrust
into the warm crevice of her thighs. The shock rippled
through her, mixed with a curious tingling in her loins, and
for a fleeting instant she almost panicked. Then she realized
it was Roberto, that part of him she'd seen so often, hanging
limp and pudgy, like a small brown pickle, whenever they
went skinny-dipping. Only now it was long and astonishingly
hard, very much like . . . like a bull!

With a wild look in his eyes, Roberto pushed away, es-
caped her arms, and quickly swam toward the opposite bank.
She floated on her back, watching him, but even after he'd
reached Luis, he kept his head turned away. She saw Luis
cast an odd look in her direction, an amazed look not of
bafflement but of understanding. She ignored him, turning
her face to the sun, floating in lazy circles near the shore.
Her body still tingled, and in her mind there was the feel of
Roberto's hardness. She was astounded, really quite proud
of herself, and now, more than ever, filled with doubt.

She wondered if that was what her mother had failed to
do, the thing she'd done to Roberto. She thought it was
perhaps the reason her father hadn't come home, for now it
seemed the simplest explanation of all.

There was no magic in her mother's bed.

CHAPTER 9

A raw, blustery wind whipped in off the river. Hank Laird and Sam Blalock left the warehouse shortly before dusk and walked toward the ferry. They kept glancing at the sky, which was dingy and overcast, threatening another storm. For the past week hard rains had gusted inland from the coast, and like all rivermen, they harbored certain superstitions about the weather. Winters were seldom harsh along the Rio Grande, particularly in late January, and the signs indicated an uncommonly foul spring. That bothered them.

"Never seen it fail," Blalock observed, squinting querulously at the sky. "You no sooner get things headed your way, and sure as hell, up jumps the Devil."

"Aye, but let's not be borrowing trouble, Sam. Likely it'll take a turn for the better."

"Humph! Sounds to me like wishful thinkin', Cap'n."

"Even so, we've always weathered 'em before, haven't we?"

"Damned if that's not a fact! Reminds me of the time we was making the run 'tween Biloxi and Mobile. Judas Priest, what a night!"

Laird merely nodded, listening with one ear. He'd heard Blalock tell the story countless times—days of long ago, when they were young deckhands riding out their first storm —but today his mind was very much in the future. And despite himself, he'd been dwelling on the exact thought Blalock had voiced only moments before.

Everything was definitely headed his way, almost as though he had the magic touch. Since last fall, when he'd acquired the railroad charter, he had moved swiftly to tighten his hold on the lower Rio Grande. Not unlike a sleight-of-hand artist, he had used misdirection to beguile

merchants on both sides of the river. The first step was to hire a survey crew and start them north, plotting a track line to Corpus Christi. But it was mere eyewash, and while everyone was congratulating him on his progressive views, he had quietly increased freight rates on his riverboats by another five percent. Then, with the utmost secrecy, he had ordered construction of two new steamboats, to be delivered in New Orleans late that spring. Before their arrival on the Rio Grande, he would announce that the railroad venture was more than he'd bargained for; to complete it would require time and massive investment. By stalling, forever crying the need of greater funds, he had the perfect excuse to raise freight rates from time to time. And the longer he stalled, the stronger became his dominance of the river trade. Which was precisely as he'd planned it.

But lately he'd begun to wonder how long his luck would last. Everything was too smooth, too simple. All his life he'd had to fight for what he wanted, and it wasn't in the nature of things to win without a struggle. It made him leery, increasingly watchful, for if a man's plan went too well that was invariably when it happened. *Up jumps the Devil!* And anyone caught flat-footed generally took a real shellacking. So he had to be on his toes, ready for a fight, careful not to lower his guard. Sooner or later it was bound to happen, he told himself. Always had and always would. Merely a matter of time.

Then, too, there was the matter of Angela. Only yesterday, after four months of silence, he'd received her note of apology. It was a terse note, lacking even a pretense of humbleness, but indicated quite clearly her desire for reconciliation. With subtle understatement, she had admitted defeat, requesting his pardon, and asked him to return home. Yet, upon reading the note, Laird had experienced little of the satisfaction he'd anticipated, and no feeling of triumph at all. Indeed, he was struck by a curious sense of guilt.

Though Angela made only casual reference to Trudy in the note, it was easy enough to read between the lines. Apparently her relationship with their daughter had suffered greatly because of his absence; Angela had finally submitted not out of regret toward him but out of fear she would lose Trudy. For Laird, it was a Pyrrhic victory. His purpose was

never to humiliate Angela, and he'd had no intention of using Trudy as a pawn in their struggle. Yet, however inadvertently on his part, that was the upshot of the whole affair. Even worse, it was the girl who had suffered most, victimized by his thoughtlessness and stubborn pride. All in all, a sorry performance.

Perhaps a less superstitious man would have dismissed the matter as unfortunate, one of life's minor tragedies, and gone on about his business. But Laird was of the firm belief that personal wrongs, especially those visited on a loved one, inevitably returned to haunt a man. So he was on edge, doubly vigilant. The accommodation with his wife, won at Trudy's expense, merely reinforced his uneasiness about business ventures. He waited for the Devil to jump him around every corner.

Later, looking back on the evening, Laird would always ponder the curious blend of instinct and coincidence. Trouble intercepted them as they approached the ferry. It came in the guise of two Brownsville merchants, Fred Tate and Oscar Whitehead, who were among Laird's most outspoken critics. The men hurried forward, halting Blalock in the midst of his story, and Laird felt a prickly sensation on the back of his neck. He knew, even before they spoke, that this was no chance meeting.

"Laird! Hank Laird!" Whitehead called. "Hold on a minute."

The men stopped in front of Laird, ignoring Blalock, and Fred Tate jerked his chin toward the warehouse. "We were just on our way to see you."

"Were you now?" Laird gave them an amiable smile. "Well, I suppose I can spare a moment. What's on your mind?"

Neither of them seemed quite sure how to start, but Whitehead finally took the lead. "The fact of the matter is, we've just come from a meeting of the Merchants Association. They've elected us their spokesmen."

"Oh, the Merchants Association, is it? Sounds quite grand, Oscar. Tell you the truth, though, I've not heard of it."

"Well, it's new," Whitehead admitted. "We formed it this afternoon."

"Uh-huh! And you say you've been elected spokesmen?"

"That's right. Fred and me, unanimous vote."

"Then I take it I'm your first order of business."

Whitehead fidgeted, glancing quickly at Tate, then shrugged. "Hell, no need to pussyfoot around, I guess. The plain fact is, we've got it from a pretty reliable source that you never intended to build a railroad."

"And the same little bird," Tate interjected, "tells us it was nothing more than a dodge to protect your steamboat business."

"So the merchants sent us here," Whitehead added, "to ask you straight out whether or not it's true."

"This source of yours," Laird mused, "would you mind telling me his name?"

"Sorry, that'll have to remain privileged, leastways for now. But you can take my word for it, everybody thinks he's pretty damn reliable. Otherwise we wouldn't have gone to all this trouble."

"Aye, trouble's the word for it. You see, boys, you've already tried and convicted me—without letting me face my accuser—and that puts a bad taste in my mouth. I've no liking for kangaroo courts, nor the men who sit on them."

"It's not a kangaroo court!" Whitehead declared hotly. "It's a merchants association, same as they've got in almost every town."

"Every town except Brownsville," Laird countered. "You've never felt the need for one before. So evidently your *reliable* source must've put the bee in your ear."

"What if he did?" Tate edged forward with a feisty scowl. "Now look here, Laird, quit beatin' around the bush and give us a straight answer. Is it true or not?"

"Tell you what, Fred. You give me the name of your source, and I'll give you a straight answer. That's fair enough."

"Like hell!" Whitehead grunted sharply. "You're still hedging, and we mean to get to the bottom of this or—"

"Or what?" Laird regarded him with a brash impudence. "You'll take your business elsewhere, is that it, Oscar?"

"By God, we'll go to Austin, that's what we'll do. We've got somebody that can talk for us now, and he'll convince 'em you put one over on everybody, Yankees included."

"You should never threaten me, Oscar. It's not in your best interest." Laird paused, regarding the men with a dour look. "To show you I mean what I say, you can report back to your merchants association and tell 'em their freight rates go up another five percent tomorrow morning."

"Don't kid yourself, Laird. That's extortion, and I'm warning you, we'll never pay it. We'll fight you!"

"Now it's ten percent," Laird informed him. "Keep talking and you'll ruin yourself, Oscar. Along with Fred and the rest of your crowd."

Whitehead sputtered to a halt, glowering at him with a look of blunted anger. Fred Tate appeared on the verge of saying something, but evidently thought it over and changed his mind. Laird waited, watching them with a look of amused contempt, then turned brusquely on his heel and walked off. Blalock fell in beside him, and after they'd stepped aboard the ferry, Laird glanced back at the two storekeepers.

"You're a grand pair, but spokesmen you're not. Tell the boys I sent my regards. Ten percent, effective tomorrow."

Twenty minutes later Laird and Blalock crossed the plaza in Matamoros. Their plans for the evening were unaltered, and they proceeded directly to *El Borrachito*, the gambling dive frequented by rivermen. Laird was still chuckling to himself as they entered the door and walked to the bar. One aspect of the conversation continued to puzzle him, but all in all he was vastly amused, and he ordered tequila to celebrate the new freight rates.

The bartender poured, producing a salt shaker and a bowl of freshly sliced limes from beneath the counter. Laird spilled salt onto the web of his thumb, licked it, and then downed the tequila in a single gulp. He bit into a slice of lime, slammed the glass on the bar, and pursed his lips as though his teeth hurt.

"Awful stuff, bucko. Awful! But it does warm the innards."

Blalock grimaced, waiting for the tequila to hit bottom, and nodded. "Yeah, if it don't rot your pipes. I've heard tell it'd peel rust off a boiler."

Laird laughed and turned, leaning back against the bar. His eyes wandered across to the gaming tables on the oppo-

site side of the room. It was still early but *El Borrachito* was doing a brisk business. Rivermen mingled with Mexicans and a scattering of tradesmen from Brownsville, all crowded around the tables with the murmured hush common to gambling parlors. Except for dealers calling the cards, and the musical clink of gold coins exchanging hands, the spell was broken only by the occasional curse of a loser. Laird's gaze drifted past a faro table, then suddenly halted and snapped back to the players. He stiffened and pushed away from the bar.

Joe Starling was seated at the table, directly opposite the dealer. A mound of coins was heaped in front of him, and his hands flashed across the layout before each turn of the cards. He was betting heavily and winning, laughing the expansive laugh of a fat man every time he raked in another pile of coins. Earl Roebuck stood at his shoulder, on the left, watching the dealer work the card box. True to form, Starling trusted no one, and he had his partner acting as a spotter.

Laird nudged Sam Blalock with his elbow, and nodded toward the table. Though neither of them spoke, their thoughts followed along the same line. Joe Starling hadn't been seen on the border for nearly a year, and it was no accident that he'd returned on this particular day. Nor was Roebuck's presence to be discounted. The partnership had obviously endured, and such men rarely stayed together without the prospect of an unusually large payoff. It was clear now that they planned to collect at Hank Laird's expense.

Blalock and Laird exchanged a look, and this time it was the riverboat captain who nodded. Laird crossed the room, quartering off to the right, and paused for a moment at a monte layout. Then he walked toward the faro table, screened by the crush of gamblers, slowly weaving his way from table to table. Blalock held his position at the bar, shifting to a slightly better angle, and eased his hand inside his coat.

Starling laughed, pulling in another stack of coins, as Laird moved past a player at the end of the table and halted. There was a momentary lull as the dealer called for new bets, and Laird tossed a Mexican gold piece on the felt layout.

"Twenty says the fat man loses."

The gold piece bounced once, then came to rest in front of Starling, and he swiveled around in his chair. Roebuck took a step away from the table, eyes alert and wary, hand poised over the Colt Dragoon on his hip. Several onlookers quickly moved aside, leaving the three men in a pocket of silence across from the dealer. After a prolonged hush, Starling finally chuckled and shook his head.

"Hank, you should never buck a man on a winning streak. It'll put you in the poorhouse."

"Did you hear that now?" Laird grinned, glancing at the dealer with a look of amiable wonder. "I ask you, in all your born days, have you ever heard a worse bet?" The dealer gave him a weak smile, and his gaze swung back to Starling. "Oh, Joe, you have a fine way with words, indeed you do. But you've a short memory, and I'm thinkin' tonight's not your night." He paused, still grinning, and cocked one eyebrow. "In fact, if I was you, Joe, I'd pull down my winnings and call it quits. Your luck just ran out."

Roebuck tensed. "You're the one that's pushin' his luck, mister. Odds are all different, not like last time."

Starling quieted him with an upraised palm. "Hold your horses, Earl. Let's hear what he has to say . . . might be good for a laugh."

"Aye, a real bellywhopper," Laird agreed. "But the laugh's on you."

"Now, is that a fact? Why don't you tell me about it?"

"I'll not bandy words with you, Joe. I just took care of your friends across the river—"

"How's that . . . my friends?"

"Whitehead and his crowd. You stirred 'em up proper— I'll grant you that—but you forgot they're a bunch of ribbon clerks. No backbone. So you can scratch the Merchants Association."

"Not yet, Hank. No siree! They'll rally 'round when the time's right."

"There won't be anything for 'em to rally 'round. You and your pal are headed downriver on the next boat."

"That's one bet you'd best copper. I'm headed nowhere."

Laird's brow seamed and his jawline hardened. "Twice now I've warned you to clear out and quit meddling in my

business. It was good advice, and you should've taken it.
Now I've no choice but to convince you the hard way."

"You're loco! I'm here and I'm staying here . . . and
there's not a goddamned thing you can do about it."

"On your feet, Joe." Laird spat on his large-knuckled
hands and rubbed them together. "It's time somebody
hauled your ashes."

Starling's face blanched, and for an instant he seemed par-
alyzed with fear. Then his hand darted inside his coat and
came out with a .41 Derringer. Laird struck, his fist lashing
out in a shadowy blur, and the blow caught Starling flush on
the jaw. His chair seemed to collapse beneath him, and he
toppled over backward, the Derringer skidding across the
floor. But even as he fell, Earl Roebuck's arm moved and the
Colt Dragoon appeared in his hand.

A gunshot blasted across the room, and Roebuck reeled
sideways in a strange, nerveless dance. He stumbled into the
faro table, a bright red dot staining his shirtfront, then some-
how straightened himself and slowly brought the pistol to
bear. Almost as though he had winked, his left eye disap-
peared in another roar of gunfire, and the slug blew out the
back of his skull. The impact buckled his legs, bowels voided
in death, and he slumped to the floor without a sound.

Laird glanced over his shoulder and saw Sam Blalock,
ashen-faced, a navy Colt extended at arm's length. A wisp of
smoke curled out of the gun barrel, and as Blalock lowered
his arm, Laird turned back to the table. He dropped to one
knee, scooping the Derringer off the floor, and backhanded
Starling across the mouth. The blow jolted Starling out of his
daze and he jerked half-erect, then suddenly went very still.
The cold snout of the Derringer was pressed firmly between
his eyes, and he heard a metallic click as Laird thumbed the
hammer to full cock.

"Your choice, Joe. The deep six or down the river."

Starling blinked, swallowed hard. Then he very gingerly
nodded his head. "Down the river."

"Wise decision."

Laird lowered the hammer on the Derringer and stuck it
in his pocket. Then he hauled Starling to his feet, dusted him
off, and clapped a thorny paw around his shoulder. Starling
glanced at the bloody mess wedged in between the gaming

tables, but quickly looked away. Laird chuckled, and an ironic smile tinged the corner of his mouth.

"C'mon, Joe, we'll have a bon voyage drink. To you . . . and Mr. Roebuck."

CHAPTER 10

"*Hasta la vista, niños míos.* And mind you, now, be prompt!"

Angela stood in the doorway of the school as the children filed past her. The girls went first, according to the rules of courtesy she insisted upon, each of them glancing at her with looks of shy adoration. Crowding close behind, the boys were all bashful smiles and restrained exuberance, their eyes lowered with respect. Once outside, however, any sense of decorum fast disappeared. The boys took off in a howling pack toward the creek, scattering the girls in their rush to be the first to reach the swimming hole. For a moment the girls stared after them longingly, then separated and trudged home to help prepare the evening meal.

Inwardly sympathetic, Angela watched the girls fan out across the ranch compound. It was a man's world—even for young boys yet to become vaqueros—and she sometimes felt disheartened that her little girls accepted a life of drudgery with the stoicism common to all Mexican women. Last fall, filled with a need to enrich her own life, she had organized a three-day-a-week school for the children of *Los Lerdeños*. The classes were split into morning and afternoon sessions, and separated by age groups. Even then, it was necessary to exclude those youngsters old enough to work, for the ranch now employed nearly three hundred vaqueros and there were upwards of a thousand children in the compound. Her hope had been to instruct the children in the basics of their own language, simple reading and writing to combat what she considered an appalling rate of illiteracy. But now, in early April, even that modest goal was still to be realized. The children were slow learners, and she'd discovered that centuries of ignorance weren't to be overcome in a matter of

months. With spring roundup already under way, and the compound a beehive of activity, she was looking forward to closing school for the summer. It would give her time to think, and ponder the wisdom of creating elusive dreams in the minds of the young.

"Ready, Mama?"

Trudy paused before the doorway, her face expressionless. She resented being pulled away from roundup on school days, and never let her mother forget that she attended only under protest. Yet she rarely neglected her own studies, and had proved an indispensable help in teaching the younger children. Angela loved having her near, felt they had grown closer working together, and for that reason was reluctant to close the door on the old storehouse she'd commandeered as a schoolroom. Once the classes ended, she would see little of her daughter until after fall roundup.

"Yes, honey, I'm ready. Let's go home."

Trudy followed her outside and they walked in silence for a few steps. Then the girl glanced around. "I thought maybe I'd take a ride . . . see how the branding's going."

"Isn't it a little late? They'll be quitting before long."

"I know, but there's a couple of hours of sunlight left and that's plenty of time."

"Time you could just as easily devote to your French lessons. *N'est-ce pas?*"

"I'll do it tonight. Cross my heart!"

"Gracious, sometimes I think you're truly envious of those boys."

"Who?"

"Who indeed! Roberto and Luis, of course."

"Oh, them." Trudy feigned indifference. "Who cares?"

Angela laughed. "I suspect you know the answer to that. Or is it just a coincidence how your spirits improve after you've spent the day with them at roundup?"

"Holy cow! They're not even vaqueros yet, Mama. It's their first roundup, and Ramon still has them working the horse herd."

"Yes, but that's the first step, isn't it, to winning their spurs?"

"Sure, everybody starts out the same way."

"And you're not even the least bit jealous . . . that they have a head start on you?"

"The only thing I'm jealous about is that they got their saddle sores honestly."

"I don't understand, dear. Honestly how?"

"On horses," Trudy said wistfully. "I got mine riding a school seat."

"Perhaps that's true. But you can also speak two languages —three, if you took your French lessons seriously—and those boys, I'm sorry to say, can barely write their own names."

"C'mon, Mama, please! I promised I'd do it tonight, and I will. *De bonne grace.* Honest!"

Angela pretended to think it over, knowing very well she wouldn't refuse in the end. Still, a few minutes one way or the other wouldn't matter, and she enjoyed having the girl beside her on these walks through the compound. Not all lessons were learned from books, and she was aware that Trudy's attitude toward her had undergone a slow change since the school began. Angela credited that in great part to the example set by *Los Lerdeños.*

The compound had become a sprawling village, extending westward along the creek. Adobe houses were packed in tight clusters, one indistinguishable from the other, with scarlet *ristras* of peppers hung on the walls baked yellow by the sun. Wherever there was a patch of shade, old men sat and talked, smoking cornhusk cigarettes, while small children, clad only in cotton shirts, rolled and played in the dirt. For the women, the center of activity was the nearest well. Before supper each evening they gathered there to exchange gossip and draw the night's water. With the approach of sundown and the return of their men, they hurried home, carrying the water in clay ollas suspended from a yoke that hung over the shoulders. Then the compound quickly became saturated with the pungent aroma of *frijoles.* On school days, however, the evening meal revolved solely around Angela's walk through the compound. Not even a tortilla was cooked until the people had greeted her on her way back to the main house.

Yet it was their manner of greeting rather than their words that mattered. Commonplace pleasantries were spoken with

a warmth that bordered on veneration, and *Los Lerdeños* humbled themselves as though a queen were passing through their midst.

Children paused in their play and drew back, watching silently. A woman with water ollas hung over her shoulders bobbed her head and murmured softly, *"Buenas tardes, La Madama."* Several old men, withered vaqueros of another day, doffed their sombreros and rose from the shade of an abode. The eldest took a step forward, flashing a toothless smile, and addressed her with a personal reverence befitting his age and her station. *"Cóma está, Doña Angela?"*

"Bueno, ancianito," Angela replied. "And you?"

"Vivo, La Madama. Graciadios! I think I will live another day."

"Qué tal, Tomaso? You will live forever."

The men chuckled, captivated by her wit, and bowed in unison as she passed by. It was the same throughout the compound. Everything came to a halt the moment she appeared, and people edged forward, their cares forgotten, to exchange a word of greeting with *La Madama.* For Trudy, these walks were an endless revelation. By now, she understood that the feelings of *Los Lerdeños* involved something more than mere respect. There was genuine affection for her mother, almost a sense of love, and to a young, impressionable girl it was a persuasive force. Since the school began she had come to see her mother in a different light, vaguely aware that her own feelings of resentment and hostility were being tempered. She was no longer sure that her mother was wrong. Nor was she quite so confident that her father was right. Instead, there was now a blend of emotions, tugging her in opposite directions, and she found it all very confusing.

At the stables, Angela kissed her on the cheek and cautioned her to be home before dark. A few minutes later, accompanied by her usual escort, Trudy rode out the front gate. But her mood had changed, and her thoughts were no longer on the roundup. She was thinking of Roberto, and something that had been on her mind since their last visit to the swimming hole. The day she'd learned about the magic of women and the weakness of men. Only now, it was no longer an idle daydream. On the walk with her mother that

afternoon, it had become something altogether new and far more exciting. A bright hope fanned alive . . . by her mother . . . by some indefinable change in the woman. And perhaps in the woman's magic as well.

Late that evening, after supper, the customary battle began. Trudy had returned from her ride caked with dust, reeking of horse sweat, and Angela insisted she have a bath. Their nightly squabbles on the subject were by now something of a ritual: Angela alternately coaxed and threatened, and Trudy surrendered by slow stages. But tonight Trudy's protests seemed curiously halfhearted, almost a formality. She complied, with only token resistance, and although surprised, Angela didn't pause to question the ease of her victory. The servants were quickly ordered to fill *La Madama's* porcelain bathtub.

Trudy hated the tub. It had a virginal aura about it, with chubby little cherubs dancing through garlands of roses that ringed the sides and spilled out over the rim. The mere sight of it was a threat to her inner image of herself. She knew that no self-respecting vaquero would be caught dead in the thing, and she always approached it with the manner of a condemned man mounting the gallows.

For Angela, the tub represented all the hopes and dreams she had for her daughter. It was feminine and graceful, a thing of delicate beauty, and possessed elegance enough for even the finest of ladies. Yet these were the very traits lacking in her daughter, who had lately taken to swearing in the ornate idiom favored by vaqueros.

Sitting on a stool, watching the girl bathe, Angela was painfully aware of time and its fleeting quickness. Trudy would be thirteen in less than a month, still a little girl but fast losing her girlish ways. Already there was a budding of youthful breasts, and any day now she might become afflicted with the curse. Then she would have crossed the line, become a girl-woman, and each day afterward would be a day lost in the race against time. The girl was infatuated by horses and vaqueros, blinded by the excitement of ranch life, but she mustn't be allowed to make the same mistake Angela had made. Trudy must be sent to New Orleans, enrolled in a fashionable school for young ladies. There she would

acquire culture and breeding, the gentility and polish so necessary to a suitable marriage. And it must be done soon, Angela told herself, within the next year or so. Otherwise the girl would be trapped forever. Bewitched by her father, failed by her mother, doomed to a life fit only for a penitent, or Mexicans. No, that mustn't be allowed to happen. Never, under any circumstances—!

"Mama, I was wondering."

Startled, Angela realized she had drifted off, star-gazing about the girl's future. Trudy was immersed in water up to her chin, but there was an odd questing quality to her eyes, and Angela felt a sudden dread. Her daughter was going to ask her some horrid question about making babies. Or perhaps the curse. Maybe it had already happened, right there in the bathtub! She leaned closer, inspecting the water.

"Yes, honey, wondering what?"

"Well, mostly about Daddy, I guess." A small frown puckered the girl's brow, and her voice trailed off slightly. "Do you miss him?"

Angela blinked, sat erect on the stool. "Why of course I do, sweetheart. I always miss your daddy when he's away. You know that."

"Yeah, but do you miss him a lot? A whole bunch?"

"Yes, honey, I do. Very, very much."

"Then if you miss him so much, how come he stays in town all the time? Why doesn't he come home more'n he does?"

It was a deceptive question, and Angela wasn't at all sure that the phrasing was unintentional. Some months past she had written a note to her husband, apologizing for her behavior the night he'd walked out. Hardly an act of contrition, it was a calculated effort to bring him home and thereby restore herself in Trudy's eyes. The note had the desired effect, and now, once or twice a month, he made the trip out from town. But he went out of his way to avoid her, devoting most of his time to Trudy, and it was clear to everyone that he considered Brownsville his home. Angela had gained little ground in the skirmish for Trudy's affections, although lately, within the last few weeks, she'd noticed a lessening of tension. Now, confronted with it openly, she realized that

tonight's questions were a test of a different sort. The girl
wasn't nearly so innocent as she appeared, nor was she ask-
ing out of idle curiosity.

"Your daddy's a very busy man, honey. I know he'd like to
be with us more often, but you've heard him say it yourself
. . . business comes first."

Trudy pursed her lips and nodded solemnly. "Maybe he
just says that, though. Maybe it's not what he really means.
I'll bet he'd come home more if you asked him to."

"But I have," Angela assured her earnestly. "Honestly,
sweetheart, I have."

"Not the way I mean, Mama. I can tell, just by the way he
acts."

"Oh, really now—" Angela stopped, warned herself to go
slowly. "All right, honey, why don't you tell me exactly what
you mean."

Trudy's frown deepened. Her eyes wandered to the roses
along the edge of the tub, and she began tracing a petal with
her finger. "Well . . . maybe if you asked him to make up
. . . then he wouldn't be so grouchy . . . and things could
go back to being the way they used to be." She paused,
studied the rose with great concentration. "Don't you
think?"

"I'm not really sure about the makeup part. In what way?"

"Awww, you know. Kissin' and huggin' and . . . all that
stuff."

Angela knew exactly what her daughter meant. And she
had the very strong suspicion that the vaqueros had taught
Trudy as much about bulls as they had cows. Yet she saw
opportunity here, the chance to heal old wounds. Not so
much between herself and Henry—though that was within
the realm of possibility—but between herself and Trudy. It
was worth any price, even cozying up to Henry, if she could
reclaim her daughter in the process. Before the opportunity
could slip away, she seized it.

"Honey, you know something? I've felt that same way my-
self for the longest time now. And it was foolish of me not to
do something about it. So I've just decided. I'll write your
daddy tonight, and tell him about our little talk, and ask him
to come home and make up. That's exactly what I'll do."

"Ooo, you will!" Trudy bounced out of the tub, sloshing water across the floor, and threw her arms around her mother's neck. "Honest, Mama, will you?"

"Yes, I will, sweetheart. I certainly will. This very night."

CHAPTER 11

On a sunny June afternoon Laird steamed into Brownsville. He manned the helm of the *Border Queen* himself, and fifty yards astern he was trailed by the *Sam Houston.* It was the maiden voyage for both boats, and Laird came into port with banners streaming and steam whistles blasting the traditional river greeting.

A crowd of townspeople quickly gathered on the wharf, and more came running with every blast of the whistles. There was a buzz of excitement mingled with dark mutterings, for there had been no prior announcement concerning the new boats. Everyone knew that Hank Laird had disappeared nearly a month past; his activities, both business and personal, were the principal source of gossip in Brownsville. But only a handful of associates knew he'd gone to New Orleans, and the purpose of his trip was a closely guarded secret. Now it was a secret no longer, and like wildfire, word spread through town within a matter of minutes.

While the crowd watched, marveling at the size of the *Border Queen,* Laird deftly maneuvered her to dockside. Close behind, Captain Lee Hall brought the *Sam Houston* to berth. Both boats were side-wheelers, the smaller one of conventional cargo design, with twin stacks and the pilot-house perched on top of the Texas deck. But the *Border Queen* was a floating showpiece, with triple decks, wide promenades outside the passenger staterooms, and a grand lounge large enough to accommodate a full boarding. Clearly a luxury craft, designed for comfort rather than cargo, nothing like it had ever been seen on the Rio Grande. It created an instant sensation among the onlookers, and considerable puzzlement. Everyone knew Hank Laird was no fool, but such a riverboat on the border certainly seemed

a folly, and they began speculating as to what he had up his sleeve this time.

Sam Blalock and Art Johnson were no less astonished than the crowd. The *Border Queen* was one secret Laird hadn't shared with them, and the sight of her came as a complete shock. They went aboard to greet him with round-eyed wonderment, thoroughly confounded.

Laird hurried along the lower promenade, hand out-stretched, and pumped their arms vigorously. Then, before they could catch their breath, he hustled them forward and spun them around, facing the superstructure. He threw up his arms, grinning broadly, and swept the *Border Queen* with an elegant gesture.

"Sam. Arty. Let me introduce you to a grand lady. Queen of the Rio Grande! And a lovely piece of work she is . . . just lovely!"

"She's all that," Blalock agreed cautiously. "But if you don't mind tellin' me, Cap'n, what the hell are you gonna do with her?"

"Do with her?" Laird roared. "Great thundering cannon-balls! I'm going to run her back and forth with settlers and tradesmen and land speculators. We'll haul 'em in by the thousands!"

"Thousands—where from—god a'mighty, Cap'n—what settlers?"

"The settlers coming west, you great dunce. We'll lure them right here, to Brownsville. Garden of Eden on the Rio Grande! By this time next year, we'll have ourselves a land boom and a high tide of commerce all rolled into one. It'll be a circus, bucko. A circus!"

"I dunno," Blalock grumbled. "Sounds a little bit like pie in the sky to me."

"Aye, but if you're a dreamer, Sam, then you must dream big. And by the Living Jesus, this is it! Everything I've been planning since the war ended. The land's here. The settlers are headed west. And if you haven't already guessed, we're the only ones with a way to get 'em up the Rio Grande."

Laird laughed and smote him across the shoulder. "Go on now! Bite down on that and see if it don't taste sweet."

"Uh, Hank." Johnson tugged at his sleeve, slowly got his

attention. "Hank, I think you'd better have a talk with War-ren Pryor."

"Later, Arty. Later! I've no time for him today."

"Maybe you'd better make time. He's been awful nervous the last couple of days. Told me to get you over there the minute you pulled in."

"Nervous, you say? Nervous about what?"

"Beats me. He acted like his jaws was wired shut. But he said it was important . . . no, wait a minute. What he said was, it's urgent. Something about the railroad charter."

"The charter!"

Johnson nodded, suddenly nervous himself. "Yeah, that's all he said. The charter."

Laird turned and walked off, hurrying toward town.

There were several minutes of silence as Laird stared out the window at the river. The lawyer waited, watching him closely, expecting another outburst at any moment.

"Last week?" repeated Laird at length. "Why in the name of Christ did they wait till then? Why not last month or even six months ago? Why last week?"

Pryor leaned back in his chair, hands steepled, tapped his forefingers together. "Well, it's nothing more than supposi-tion, you understand—guesswork, actually—but I believe you took delivery on the boats last week, didn't you?"

"Aye, ten days ago, on a Thursday it was."

"Then I suspect that's the answer. Less than a week after you take possession of the boats, the legislature revokes your charter."

Laird turned from the window, his jaw set in a bulldog scowl. "You're saying someone used the boats to stir up the legislature?"

"Actually, it was the attorney general who brought things to a head, but that's neither here nor there. The point is—someone used the boats as proof that you had no intention of building a railroad, and then laid out some heavy bribes in all the right places."

"That was part of the deal! The bastards knew all along I never meant to lay track. They even laughed about it, told me it was a nifty piece of work."

"Politics change, Hank. Last year you dropped a bundle in

their laps, and this year someone upped the ante. On the face of it, I'd say it's someone who's been watching your activities closely."

"Watched!" Laird fixed him with a baleful look. "Are you saying someone had me followed . . . spied on?"

Pryor studied his nails, thoughtful. "Either that or else you have a traitor in your own camp. You'll have to admit, the timing sort of strains the laws of coincidence. Offhand, I'd venture a guess that they had one of their own men bird-dogging your trail. Then the moment you took possession of those boats, the telegraph wires started humming between New Orleans and Austin. It all ties together quite neatly."

"They! You keep saying that, but who the hell are *they?*"

"Hank, you know your enemies better than I do. Of course, the merchants here in town aren't exactly your big-gest supporters, so that might be a place to start."

"Aye, except there's not a thimbleful of guts amongst them."

"Well, perhaps it's a new group, someone we don't know. Austin's crawling with scavengers these days, and they're all looking for an easy kill."

"I wonder. A new group or a ghost of the old?"

"Sorry, I don't take your meaning, Hank."

Laird grew silent, staring at a spot of sunlight on the floor. His expression was abstracted, a long pause of inner deliber-ation. Finally he glanced up, dismissed the thought with a brusque sweep of his hand.

"No matter. New or old, it's clear the legislature means to award them the charter."

"Yes, I think we can safely surmise that. Of course, ac-cording to my informants, the official order revoking your charter doesn't take effect for thirty days. So it'll be a while before we learn who's at the bottom of all this."

"As I've just said"—Laird rocked his hand, fingers splayed—"it's six of one and half-dozen of another. We know we're in for a fight, and it doesn't much matter who we'll be fight-ing. What counts is that the fools have given us a little lee-way in terms of time . . . and we must use it to be prepared."

"Prepared! Now, hold off a minute, Hank. What kind of a fight are you talking about?"

"The only kind bastards like that understand. A keg of gunpowder and a damn short fuse."

Pryor shook his head in exasperation. "It'll never do, Hank. Not this time. Whoever pulled this off evidently has support in high places. That means he can call on the military, and there's every likelihood they'll back his play."

"Let them. By the Jesus, I'll not roll over and play dead for anybody!" Laird flung his arm at the wharfs. "In case you've forgot, I just spent a fortune on a couple of boats, and I'm of no mind to sit idly by while someone cuts my throat."

"Come now, Hank. It's hardly a matter of being wiped out. They'll need a year, perhaps longer, to build a line from Corpus Christi. That gives you plenty of time to recoup your investment."

"It's not the investment, you bloody fool! I'm talking about profits. In the next five years I stand to clear a million, maybe double that. Would you have me crawl off and suck my thumb instead of fighting?"

"If you resort to violence," Pryor said grimly, "they'll ruin you. Take my word for it, Hank. These are evil times, and there are men in Austin who wouldn't hesitate to use Yankee troops if it suits their purpose."

Laird brushed away the warning with a quick, impatient gesture. "I've fought Yankees before, counselor. And besides, I'm not all that sure they're willing to risk another shooting war. Not even a little one. There's lots of Texans that might like the idea."

Pryor gave him a bleak smile. "You may have a point. But then, a prudent man wouldn't provoke violence until he'd exhausted all the alternatives."

"What alternatives?"

"The courts."

"Carpetbagger courts? Don't make me laugh."

"Oh, there's no chance we would win. Not with the situation as it stands. But we could stall. An injunction here and an appeal there, it all take time. With a bit of luck, we might stretch it out to two years, maybe even three, before they lay the first foot of track."

Laird was suddenly very quiet, eyes boring into the lawyer. "Are you just trying to hold me in check, or do you really think it would work?"

"I think it would work very well. As a stalling device, of course."

"Then do it. And if it falls through, I've a few tricks of my own to spring on the bastards."

"We're back to gunpowder and short fuses."

"Counselor, the first rule of survival is that you never let the other man pick the spot for a fight. The idea is to sucker him along and take him unawares."

"I'm afraid that's a bit too cryptic for me, Hank."

"Hell, it's simple. You fight him on your own home ground."

CHAPTER 12

The barometer level read 29.89 inches.

Laird studied it a moment, knuckling back his mustache with a thoughtful frown. The mercury held constant, and after a brief deliberation he moved through the door onto the front porch. He walked to a cane-bottomed rocker and sat down, chin cupped in one hand as he watched the distant skyline.

To the west, the sun went down over the creek in a great splash of orange and gold. But there was an ominous darkening to the south-southeast. He knew it had been raining on the coast for four straight days, and now the clouds appeared to be moving inland with uncommon speed. Clearly a storm was brewing, yet all the signs were at variance with the barometer. The mercury level hadn't moved since he'd returned from Corpus Christi earlier that afternoon. It was a paradox, unlike any he'd encountered before, and it left him in a growing quandary.

The door opened and Angela stepped outside. She crossed the porch and seated herself in a rocker beside him. All afternoon he'd been brooding around the house, withdrawn and curiously silent, even though she knew he was smoldering about the court decision. She felt it would do him good to talk about it, and she was concerned that he'd kept his rage bottled up within himself. It wasn't characteristic of him, not at all his normal reaction to a setback; but she wasn't quite sure how to broach the subject, or his silence. She glanced at him hesitantly, exploring his face for any telltale change. At the supper table he'd hardly spoken, and now he had a faraway look in his eyes, as if he were staring toward something dimly visible in the distance. After a while

she set the rocker in motion, determined to draw him out, hopeful he might respond if she took the oblique approach.

"Trudy's worried about you. When we were clearing the dishes, she told me you looked like a volcano."

"That so?" Laird roused himself, took a swipe at his mustache. "Where'd she get off to?"

"Well, just between us"—Angela smiled—"she didn't want to be around for the eruption. She's doing her French lessons."

"Infernal nonsense. She's got to where she mixes it in with Mexican, and I can't understand half the jabber she throws at me."

"Oh really, Henry. Why do you insist on calling it Mexican? It's Spanish! And so far as the French goes, all educated people consider it *the* universal language. One day you'll be proud of Trudy. After all, it's not everyone who has a daughter that can speak three or four languages."

"Aye, that's a mortal comfort, no doubt about it."

His ironic tone carried little of the old sting. Over a dry and dusty summer, he and Angela had slowly worked out a truce. He no longer felt like a stranger in his own home, and though their lovemaking was sporadic, Angela had made a genuine attempt to discard her passive manner. It had been touch and go for a while, neither of them really confident that past grievances could be swept aside. But with time, and Angela's curious appeal for compromise, there was a gradual discovery of unexpired emotions. Then, too, adversity had drawn them closer together; Angela exhibited complete sympathy with his legal problems, and supported him in a manner wholly unexpected. She was always there, willing to salve his pride, and within the last couple of weeks, the urge to be with her had become somewhat like the temptation to bite on a sore tooth. He found it difficult to resist, for the time spent with her and Trudy, who lately seemed to bubble with happiness, was a time that revitalized him for the fight ahead.

Even now, despite his gloomy mood, he took pleasure in having Angela seated beside him. She was wearing a gingham dress, and its bright pattern, along with her smile, was a small cheerfulness in a gray day. He shifted in the rocker,

part of his mind still focused on the skyline, and turned to her.

"Pay no attention to my foul temper. I couldn't be prouder of the girl if you'd taught her Gaelic. And that's a fact. You've done a grand job."

"Well, thank you, Henry. It's very sweet of you to say so."

"Simply giving credit where credit's due. I should've mentioned it before, but the last couple of months I've started to feel like a one-legged man in a kicking contest."

Angela regarded him evenly. "Tell me about it, Henry. You've said very little, except that you lost the suit. Exactly how bad is it?"

"Who knows?" Laird shrugged and glanced away. "When you're dealing with carpetbaggers, you're never sure of anything from one day to the next."

"Yes, but Warren Pryor must have some idea. Hasn't he at least given you an estimate of your chances?"

"That little runt! Damn me if he's not as shifty as the Yankees. Just keeps telling me to be patient, and let him see what he can arrange."

"Well, perhaps that's very good advice. I mean, he has filed an appeal, hasn't he? That's what you said."

"Aye, an appeal." Laird's voice was suddenly edged. "But in the same breath he tells me it depends on whether or not he can buy the judges. So he scoots off to Austin and leaves me to wonder what the hell comes next."

"You mean he's trying to bribe them . . . buy a reversal?"

"Of course. How else does a man deal with carpetbaggers? We've been trying to buy a decision since this thing started, but the other side's outbid us every time. It's not a matter of law, never has been. It's a matter of money—a bloody auction!"

Angela was silent for a time. It occurred to her that corruption manifested itself in many forms. Seemingly there was a guise suitable to every situation, not to mention the individual man. The carpetbaggers and scalawags, venal men in a political marketplace, were corrupted by greed. Yet their corruption was a thing apart from that of bolder men, the visionaries and builders. With her husband, it was nothing so mean and petty as simple greed. Hank Laird had been cor-

rupted by ambition and a thirst for power, some inner need to leave his mark on the land and its people. His corruption was on a grander scale, almost sovereign in dimension, and perhaps, upon reflection, altogether necessary in a world where integrity was forced to compromise merely to survive. Still, however much she excused his behavior, she could never fully share his compulsion, nor the vastness of his dreams. She would have gladly settled for a simpler life and the brash young Irishman she'd married so long ago.

At length, she straightened her shoulders, took a grip on herself. "I suppose you've been right all along. Not that I approve, but it seems there's no choice with Yankees." She paused, thoughtful. "You mentioned the other side. Have you been able to find out who's behind it?"

A vein pulsed in Laird's forehead. "I've no proof, but I'd wager my soul it's Joe Starling. Everything we've learned—and that's precious little—convinces me it's somebody with a grudge. You see, it's not the railroad he's after—it was set up too crafty just for that—he's out to ruin me."

Laird had reason to suspect a vendetta. Throughout the summer, he and his lawyer had fought a delaying action in the courts. But their every effort had been stymied with maddening regularity. At the outset, an injunction was denied and appealed, only to have the lower court's ruling upheld. Then suit was brought charging that the legislature, because there was no time limitation or nonperformance clause in the original document, had revoked Laird's charter without sufficient grounds or a proper hearing. Only yesterday, after a protracted legal tussle, that too had been dismissed in district court. It was now clear, based on Warren Pryor's negotiations with the judge, that the decision had gone to the highest bidder. Someone was spending vast amounts of money, all the while hiding behind a battery of lawyers, to ensure that a new railroad charter would be granted. With some justification, Laird had little faith that he would prevail in carpetbagger courts. Though an appeal was to be entered, he'd already written it off as a lost cause.

By late fall the mystery man would have his charter. That seemed a foregone conclusion, and while it grated, Laird was slowly shifting the focus of his attention to the months

ahead. The real fight, much as he'd predicted in the begin-
ning, would be fought on home ground.

"Hindsight's a grand thing," Laird added without humor.
"I should've killed the devil when I had the chance."

"Killed! Are you talking about Joe Starling?"

"Aye, none other. I took mercy at the last minute and let
him slip through my fingers. But it'll not happen again. This
time I'll settle his hash for good."

"This time? I don't understand, Henry. That sounds as if
you *expect* to meet him again."

"Of course I do! Don't you see, that's been my ace in the
hole all along. Unless he wants to lay an extra fifty miles of
track around the ranch, then he has to cross my property to
get to Brownsville. Naturally, he'll try, and when he does, I'll
be there waiting on him."

"But you couldn't win. If he has enough influence to con-
trol the courts—not to mention the legislature—then he
could get some sort of legal order forcing you to let him
build across the ranch."

"Even so, it changes nothing. I'm betting the Yankees will
back down before a show of force. And the minute Starling
sets foot on my property, I'll send him straight to Hell. No
warning, either. Not this time."

"What show of force?"

"Why, a couple of hundred armed vaqueros. That ought
to convince anybody, even Yankees."

Angela stared at him reproachfully. "Isn't that a little
cold-blooded, Henry? You'd risk the lives of our people . . .
and kill a man . . . just to stop a railroad."

"Aye, that I would. Although it's not so much a matter of
stopping the railroad as it is saving my riverboats."

"Oh yes, how could I have forgotten? You and your pre-
cious riverboats. It wouldn't be the first time you sacrificed a
life to save them, would it?"

Laird could see anger, resentment, and a trace of fear in
her eyes. He shook his head. "Now it's me that's confused. I
went through the whole war without losing so much as a
deckhand, and proud of it."

"My god, Henry, are you that inhuman?" Something odd
happened to her face. She paled, her mouth tightened, and

there was a harried sharpness in her voice. "I'm not talking about deckhands. I'm talking about my son. Our son!"

"You're daft! I had no hand in that."

"Didn't you? Think back, Henry . . . where were you when it happened?"

"Downriver, running the blockade. But what's that got to do with anything?"

"It has everything to do with it. If you'd been home—where you belonged—it wouldn't have happened."

"By the Sweet Jesus! Are you saying the boy's death was my fault?"

"You knew there would be trouble that night. Admit it—you knew, didn't you? But you still left us alone, took your boats, and just sailed off without a care in the world."

"We were at war, or have you forgotten? I had a duty to perform—responsibility! A man can't turn his back on that—not in wartime—and you know it very well."

"Why not?" Angela demanded. "You turned your back on us."

"Where's your reason, woman? I was no different than a soldier, don't you understand that? I had to go, it was my duty."

"Oh for god's sake, Henry! Quit hiding behind lies, face the truth for once. You were running cotton, not fighting battles. You could have gone the next day or the day after—anytime!"

"You've a short memory, and a damn fine way of twisting the facts. We thought the Yankees were marching on Brownsville, everything pointed to it. I had to go that day or . . ."

"Or what?"

"Or risk losing the cotton—everything I'd worked for—maybe even the boats."

"Of course! I couldn't have said it better myself—*always the boats.* Forget your wife and children—leave them to the mob or the Yankees—but never, never risk your precious boats."

Laird flinched at the words, but he met her look. "That's it, then, isn't it . . . the boy? All these years and you've never forgiven me."

"Have you forgiven yourself, Henry? With God as your witness, have you?"

There was no answer. Laird's eyes dulled and appeared to turn inward on something too terrible for speech. A sickness swept over him, and there was a sensation of devastating loneliness, all the agony of grief and despair he'd buried with his son so long ago. Beads of sweat glistened on his forehead, and the ache became violently physical. He heaved himself out of the chair, walked to the edge of the porch, and took a deep breath.

Suddenly he stiffened, even in the midst of his sorrow, reverting to instinct. The night had become unnaturally warm and muggy. His head felt queer, almost as though his eardrums were blocked, and on a listless breeze he caught the crisp scent of the seashore. He whirled away and rushed inside the house, halted before the barometer.

The mercury level had fallen to 28.95 inches.

Laird stared at it for several moments, immobile with disbelief, then tore himself away and hurried out the door. As he crossed the porch Angela came to meet him, her face stricken with a look of dread and uncertainty.

"Henry! My god, Henry, what is it?"

"Hurricane! On the coast. You and Trudy stay inside!"

Angela ran for the door, calling Trudy's name. A few minutes later, huddled beside a window, they saw him spur his horse into a lope and disappear into the darkness. He rode toward Brownsville.

CHAPTER 13

His horse faltered within sight of town.

Laird swung down out of the saddle an instant before the gelding collapsed. He'd ridden through the night, never once pausing for a breather, and he counted himself lucky to have made it this far. Too late, he wished he'd brought a pistol, but he hadn't and there was nothing to be done for the animal. He dismissed it from his mind and took off running toward town.

Out of the corner of his eye, he saw the sun slowly crest the earth's rim. But it was the smoke that claimed his attention. A dead calm, without a whisper of sound, had settled across the land. Ahead, tendrils of smoke drifted skyward, then hung there, suspended over Brownsville like a dark shroud. Nearer the edge of town, he caught a faint smell, harsher than woodsmoke but mingled with a sweetish odor. He recognized it as the stench of burnt flesh, and picked up the pace, sprinting the last fifty yards in a burst of apprehension.

It was worse than anything he'd imagined. The hurricane had swept inland from the south, raging along the border with gale force, and tore a swath through the heart of Brownsville. The town's main street had simply disintegrated, transformed by titanic winds into a tangled mass of bricks and glass and timber. Flames still licked through the ruins, every store in the downtown area reduced to a smoldering ash heap, and it was apparent the entire business district had been enveloped in a roaring holocaust.

On the outskirts of town, the devastation was only slightly less complete. All through the residential area, the hurricane had blown off rooftops and then battered the houses to flinders. It seemed another world, eerie and spectral, somehow

demonic, the streets dotted with crackling flames and twisted
rubble. Corpses littered nearly every yard, charred and man-
gled beyond recognition, and survivors clawed through the
wreckage with a look of numbed horror. The stench of death
grew stronger as the sun rose high, and in full light it was as
though some diabolic force had struck the earth, leaving be-
hind a blotch of scorched destruction.

Laird stood for a long while, regarding the havoc of the
storm in a kind of witless stupor. Once before, when he was
a young deckhand, he'd weathered a hurricane at the port of
Mobile. But it was nothing like the carnage before him now.
A lifetime of violence and death hadn't prepared him for the
virtual annihilation of a town. He could only marvel that
anyone had survived, and in the back of his mind, he won-
dered how many had perished beneath the fury of the squall.
Finally, with the sense of entering a nightmare, he collected
himself and walked toward the river.

Along a side street, the steeple of the Methodist church
had toppled over, blocking the road. He veered around it,
cutting through the yard of a house that had been leveled to
the ground. As he passed the spire, a figure emerged from
the ruins of the house, one arm dangling loosely, blackened
from head to toe with soot. The man limped toward him,
calling his name, and only then did he realize it was Fred
Tate, the hardware dealer.

"Laird! Help me, Laird. I can't find her."

He stopped and Tate hobbled closer, clutching at his arm.
"Have you seen Martha? Or the kids? Have you, Laird?"

"Sorry, Fred, I haven't. I just got to town."

"Oh Jesus. They've got to be somewhere! Somebody
must've seen them."

"Weren't they with you?"

"No, I was at the store. When it hit." Tate blinked, licked
his parched lips. "Her and the kids were in the house—they
must've been—but goddamn, Laird—it's gone. The house is
gone!"

"Take it easy, Fred. You'll find them. Maybe they're over
in the church."

"I looked there, first thing. Right after the wind stopped."

"Why didn't you come home before then, before the
storm hit?"

"No time. No warning. Jesus Christ a'mighty, it was rain-ing one minute and then the whole world just blew apart! You never saw anything like it, Laird. It was . . . it was just . . ."

Tate's voice trailed off, and a pinpoint of terror surfaced in his eyes. Whatever he'd gone through, it was too horrible to articulate, and his mouth froze in a silent oval. Laird watched him a moment, almost certain now that Martha Tate and her children were buried in the house. He sensed that Fred Tate knew it as well, and simply couldn't bring himself to accept the truth. Yet there was nothing he could do, and by the looks of the town, he had problems of his own waiting at the docks.

"Fred, listen to me. You keep looking and I'll send some of my men up to help. That's a promise, just as quick as I can."

Tate gave him a glassy-eyed stare, then turned and wan-dered back toward the pile of rubble. Laird hurried down the street, avoiding everyone he encountered, paused only long enough to chase a couple of dogs off the body of a woman lying black and bloated in the sun. Then he broke into a run, goaded by his own fears and a sudden urgency to reach the riverfront.

The wharf had vanished. Laird trotted past a mound of brick and embers—what had once been the Mercantile Na-tional Bank—and abruptly slowed to a walk. For an instant, he couldn't comprehend the enormity of the destruction, and he had the fleeting impression of a world turned topsy-turvy. Then it registered, jolted him into a state of acute awareness. It wasn't that at all. It was the end of the world. His world.

The hurricane had snuffed out the warehouse, and like so many matchsticks, simply uprooted the docks. Then it shred-ded beams and stanchions and pilings into kindling wood, and scattered the remnants of the debris across a wide path below the business district. To the west, along the shoreline, the trees had been stripped clean of bark and leaves, stand-ing ghostly white against the brown earth. A haze of smoke drifted listlessly in the still air, and throughout the wreckage, tongues of flame blinked and flickered with the erratic bril-liance of fireflies darting through the gloom of night. Yet, terrible as the destruction was, Laird saw it through a prism

centered on his own personal hell. He was staring at the boats.

The *Mustang* was aground, heeled over on her starboard side, the bow wedged within a tangle of refuse. Another boat had been beached and gutted on the rocks, then slammed back into the shallows with its stern underwater. Several older craft had simply ruptured and sank, either blown apart or cleaved into splinters by the force of the wind. Three of the newer boats had been hurled into the wharf, upended and overturned, then twisted together in an unrecognizable mass of timber and steel. But the onshore wreckage was mere prelude to a still greater disaster.

Berthed upstream of the warehouse, the *Border Queen* had snapped her hawsers and careened away from the docks. Adrift and floating downstream, it was apparent the crew had fired her boilers in a valiant effort to gain power and ride out the storm. With only modest luck they might have pulled it off, but one of the older boats, docked below the warehouse, had also slipped her moorings. Swung hard astern by the wind, the boat had hurtled into midstream and rammed the *Border Queen* amidships. The collision breached the larger boat below waterline, and almost upon impact, her boilers exploded with a molten roar. Now little more than ravaged hulks, it was evident the boats had been consumed by fire and quickly settled to the river bottom. The superstructure of the *Border Queen* had collapsed, buckling inward, but the stern rose defiantly from the water and her flag still flew.

On shore, Laird stood for several minutes, his face a mask, eyes fixed on the smoldering wreck. It had been his grandest dream, and in the death of the *Border Queen* he sensed the end of many things. The kingdom he'd won was a kingdom no longer. With the loss of his riverboats, and the threat of the railroad, his rule of the Rio Grande was a thing of the past. Yet it all fit together like a template—too precisely— events dovetailed one to the other with uncanny timing. And he wondered if the God of retribution—the one Angela worshiped so devoutly—hadn't exacted the cruelest punishment of all. Her words still echoed through his mind, and it occurred to him that if a man couldn't forgive himself, then even a merciful God might find it difficult to grant absolu-

tion. Perhaps that was the answer. Perhaps God lurked in the shadows, waiting for a man to erect his kingdom on earth, then destroyed it in the blink of an eye. Let the winds blow and summoned a hurricane to act as the instrument of punishment.

It was one answer. Perhaps the only answer that accounted for such uncommon coincidence, and luck turned sour. Certainly no Irishman's luck deserted him without reason, and if ever he needed convincing, he had to look no farther than the middle of the river.

Laird had no idea how long he'd been standing there. He vaguely sensed crewmen picking through the rubble, was aware that several of them had spoken to him, but he hadn't replied. His thoughts were hardened around an indrawn bleakness, and he couldn't seem to take his eyes off the *Border Queen*. At last, someone placed a hand on his shoulder, and he turned. Sam Blalock nodded, clearly groping for words, then lowered his gaze to the ground.

"Sorry, Cap'n. We did the best we could, but it wasn't no use."

"Aye, from the looks of things, nothing would've helped. I'm obliged to you all the same, Sam. Nobody could've done more."

Blalock's features were worn and haggard. His clothes hung in tatters, and the whites of his eyes seemed to pop out from a face blackened by woodsmoke. He still appeared dazed, and after a moment he shook his head.

"Goddamnedest thing I ever saw, Cap'n. The mercury dropped close to two inches in less'n an hour. We was still trying to secure the boats when the sonovabitch come howlin' in and just chewed us up and spit us out. Never had a chance."

"Forget it, Sam. It was a freak and nothing to be done. Just be glad you pulled through in one piece."

"Only by the skin of my teeth. And that's the God's truth."

"Well, it's over now." Laird glanced past him, searching the ruins. "That reminds me, though. Where's Arty? I don't see him around."

"He's dead, Cap'n." Blalock gave him a hangdog look, then gestured toward the demolished warehouse. "Caught it right off, when the roof went. Never knew what hit him."

Laird scanned the debris, spotted it quickly, felt his stomach knot and tasted bile. A falling timber had impaled Artemus Johnson, spiked him to the floor, arms and legs splayed outward by the impact. Oddly enough, the sight somehow brought the Crucifixion to mind, and it occurred to Laird that Angela might take solace in the thought. Then he noticed the charred skin and burst blood vessels, all clothing consumed by flames, and made a mental note. That part he wouldn't tell her.

"Sorry we haven't got to him yet, Cap'n. We're still diggin' to see if there's any survivors."

"Of course." Laird swallowed, eyes grim. "What about the skippers?"

"Don't know about Gilchrist. He was downriver on the *Sam Houston.*"

Blalock paused, and the timbre of his voice changed. "Lee Hall went under with the *Queen*. I was on the dock when her hawsers broke and she drifted past. Lee waved at me—grinnin' big as life—then the wind sucked her away. 'Course, he had her boilers fired and he was makin' a game fight of it till the *Lone Star* took him broadside." His Adam's apple bobbed and he cleared his throat. "That's the last I seen of him."

"How about Gilchrist, think there's any chance?"

"None a'tall, Cap'n. It must've been ten times worse closer to the coast. God knows, I hope he pulled through . . . but I wouldn't count on it."

"The crewmen—the ones here—how many made it?"

"Half, maybe a few more. Like I said, we're still sortin' through the wreckage and—awww goddamnit to hell! I'm just kiddin' you and myself and everybody else. There's some of 'em we'll never find!"

"Easy does it, Sam. You've no cause to fault yourself."

"Yeah." Blalock's eyes misted over and his voice cracked. "Brave lads, Hank. Uncommon brave. None of 'em run, not the first man. Stuck it out and tried to save their boats. You would've been proud of 'em. Real proud."

"Aye, that I would. They're of a breed, these rivermen."

Laird's jawline tightened, and his gaze drifted cross river. Matamoros looked as though it had been bombarded by thunderbolts. Buildings and houses had simply crumbled be-

fore the wind, and the town was pocked with smoldering heaps of adobe. The shrieks of women mourning their dead were audible even on the north shore, and Laird was reminded of an ancient Mexican proverb.

Suerte y mortaja del cielo bajan.

It was true. Fortune and death come from above. Yet he was struck by the irony of it, for the thought stemmed from an older and even more stoic maxim of a people who had learned to endure. *Con el favor de Dios.* If God wills it. And perhaps, within the bittersweet irony, there was a message for all men, most especially an Irishman whose luck had turned sour.

For a long while no one spoke. Blalock stared wretchedly at the ground, and Laird studied Matamoros with the look of a man who had stumbled upon an unexpected revelation. The sunken hulk of the *Border Queen* merely reinforced his vision of all that lay ahead. It unfolded before him with blinding clarity, and fearful he might change his mind, he suddenly turned to Blalock.

"Will we be able to salvage any of the boats?"

"Only one, Cap'n. The *Mustang.* She's stove in pretty bad, but nothing that can't be put right."

"Would you like to buy her?"

"Buy her? I don't follow your meaning."

"God's teeth! It's simple. I'm asking if you'd like to go into the steamboat business?"

"I dunno. Hell, I never . . . well, yeah . . . I suppose so."

"Done!" Laird motioned grandly toward the boat. "We've a bargain and she's all yours—for a dollar!"

"Cap'n, if it's not too much trouble, what the hell are you talkin' about?"

"Exactly what it sounds like, jocko. I've quit the river."

BOOK TWO

1873 -1875

CHAPTER 14

On New Year's morning Laird and Trudy rode west from the Santa Guerra compound. A full day lay ahead of them, and despite a thundering hangover, Laird himself had suggested the ride. He felt it was important that the people see *El Patrón* mark the beginning of a new year in the saddle. It would serve as an example, and set the pace for what he already envisioned as a banner year in the fortunes of the *Ele Flecha* brand.

A squad of vaqueros fell in behind them as they rode through the front gate. These days not even Laird ventured outside the compound without an armed escort, but he quickly motioned the riders to trail them at a distance. This morning his head felt the size of a melon, and the drumming thud of hoofbeats merely aggravated his condition. Yet Trudy was in customary high spirits, completely undaunted by his gruff mood. She began peppering him with questions the instant their little column wheeled west along the creek.

"Pa, have you decided about roundup yet?"

"Aye, I've decided."

"Well . . . c'mon, tell me . . . when?"

"The end of the month."

"Honest? *Válgame Dios!* Why so soon?"

"Because I intend to get an earlier start this year."

"Earlier start . . . are you talking about the trail drives?"

"Naturally. Is there a better reason to hold roundup?"

"How many drives?" Trudy demanded impatiently. "More than last year?"

"*Claro que, sí.* Ten, maybe more, depending on the gather."

"But that's . . . that's twenty thousand cows!"

"Aye, it was the figure I had in mind."

"Madre mío! Why so many?"

"Porqué no?" Laird shrugged. "Why not?"

Indeed it was the very thing Laird had been working toward since he'd quit the river. In a brief stretch of six years he had extended his landholdings to 600,000 acres, and the Santa Guerra herds now exceeded 100,000 longhorns. His lodestar was the image of himself as a cattle baron, and he went at it with all the determination he'd once devoted to riverboats. In his mind, ranching was merely an enterprise, not all that different from the steamboat business; it was susceptible to organization and efficiency, and could be operated to yield maximum profit. His goals were long range and far-reaching, predicated on an ever-growing market for beef, and he approached it with the systematic calculation of a man whose dreams were the offspring of reality.

The ⌐→ brand—commonly called *Ele Flecha*—was now known from the Rio Grande to the Kansas cowtowns. Hank Laird himself was older and wealthier, though hardly mellowed, and still a man to be reckoned with along the border. He had forced Joe Starling to lay track to Rio Grande City, instead of Brownsville, which made him a pariah among the townspeople. And aside from *Los Lerdeños,* he was considered a scourge by the Mexicans. Any *derecho* holder laying claim to Santa Guerra land was offered payment; those who refused were dealt with harshly, and Laird was only too willing to demonstrate that possession was nine points of the law. Having lost a river kingdom, he had built himself a cattle empire, and no one doubted his ability to hold it.

Still, for all his boldness, trail-driving twenty thousand cows in a single season was no small undertaking. Few would have believed it possible, even for the owner of *Ele Flecha,* and the look on Trudy's face reflected her own sense of wonder.

"C'mon, Pa." She arched one eyebrow in question. "What's the real reason? Why so many this year?"

"We've got the cows. And I figure the market's ripe. So we'll send 'em up the trail to Wichita."

"Wichita! What happened to Abilene?"

"Abilene's dead. The rails moved south and now Wichita's the new cowtown. It's as simple as that."

Trudy was thoughtful a moment, then gave him a disarm-

ing smile. "Pa, you know, I've never seen Kansas, and I was thinking—"

"No."

"Wait a minute, I haven't even asked yet!"

"The answer's still no. A cowtown is no place for a girl."

"Why not? I work in the roundup, don't I? Even Ramon says I'm as good as some of the vaqueros."

"One has nothing to do with the other. You'll not go, and that's final."

"Caramba!"

"Watch your tongue. I've warned you before about cursing."

"Well, you cuss. And you say lots worse things than I do."

"Aye, but you're a girl, and there's the difference. It's not proper."

"And you're an old stick-in-the-mud. I stopped being a girl a long time ago, even Mama admits that."

Laird could scarcely dispute the point. His daughter was a blonde tawny cat of a girl, with bold, inquisitive eyes. Today, she was dressed in charro clothes—broad hat, short vest with tight pants, black boots and roweled spurs—and for a girl of eighteen, she looked very mature indeed. She had a sumptuous figure, which the charro outfit greatly accentuated, but while attractive, she hadn't her mother's orthodox beauty. Instead, she favored her father, with freckles and full lips and a short, impudent nose. Yet she was bright and personable, with an infectious laugh, and generously endowed with all the things that captivated men. Laird worried about that, even among his own vaqueros, and he took her swearing to be a bad sign.

"We'll not argue the matter. I said no more cursing, and that's the end of it."

"Oh, you're just grumpy today. Otherwise you wouldn't even notice. And besides, that's not important anyway. What we really have to talk about is me going along to Wichita."

"Mother of God! Will you never quit? You're like a bloody gnat."

"Poco y poco, Papa." She mimicked his dour look, then suddenly laughed. "All right, I'll stop for now. But you think about it . . . agreed?"

"Aye, but that's all. No promises. You'll not slip around me the way you do your mother."

Trudy knew better. If anything, her wiles usually worked wonders on her father. But she left it there for the moment. She smiled, satisfied to let him think he'd had the last word. In truth, she had no intention of going to Wichita or anywhere else. She planned to spend the entire summer on Santa Guerra. It merely suited her purpose to allow her father to believe otherwise . . . for a while longer.

Shortly before noon, some miles upstream, Laird reined to a halt beside a fenced pasture. The enclosure covered nearly a thousand acres, and was one of three such holding pens on the ranch. Unusually sturdy, the fence was constructed of mesquite posts, sunk four feet into the ground, with galvanized wire stretched taut and fastened to the posts by wrought-iron spikes. The wire alone, freighted in by wagon, had cost Laird a fortune, but once the project was begun, he'd spared no expense.

Always a visionary, Laird foresaw a need to upgrade the quality of his livestock. Longhorns were lean and hardy, perfectly suited to the arid climate, but produced almost as much bone and gristle as edible beef. Accordingly, Laird had imported ten Durham bulls and a hundred brood cows, then embarked upon a program of crossbreeding. The Durhams were built wide and hefty, packing nearly twice the beef of a longhorn, and he hoped to create a strain with the best traits of both breeds. Thus far, the project had been a dismal failure.

Durham cows, along with calves sired by longhorn bulls, grazed across the pastureland. But the cows were slowly losing weight, and their offspring, very close to yearlings now, fared only slightly better. In another pasture, farther upstream, the results were much the same with longhorn cows topped by Durham bulls. The crossbreed, by whatever combination, produced a chunkier animal, yet one that lacked the hardiness of native longhorns. It was obvious, after nearly two years of effort, that the strengths of both breeds had been diluted in the new strain.

Laird regularly visited the breeding pens each week, always hopeful for some sign of improvement. Today was no different from other days, however, and he stared at the herd

for a long while in silence. Finally, he hawked and spat, eyes rimmed with disgust.

"Damn me, but they're a sorry sight! Spoils my appetite every time I ride out here."

Trudy chewed her lower lip in concentration. "You know, Pa, I've been thinking . . . maybe it's the Durhams. Maybe a cross with Hereford or Angus would turn the trick."

"I've wrestled a bit with that myself. But then, they're no stouter a breed than the Durham, so what's to be gained?"

"Well, they sure couldn't do any worse. *Verdad?*"

"Aye, but there's no guarantee they'd do better. And I've no need to tell you, lass, as a business venture it's been a bloody loss."

Laird spotted a group of vaqueros riding along the far fence line, and the sight merely reinforced his statement. For the past two years, he'd had no choice but to station permanent guards, armed with Henry repeating rifles, to patrol the breeding pastures. With the death of Benito Juárez, and the rise to power of Profirio Díaz, Mexico had once again fallen into anarchy. Bands of outlaws crossed the border at will, raiding and plundering gringo haciendas with virtual impunity. The situation had been compounded by the election of a scalawag politician, E.J. Davis, as governor of Texas. Once in office, Davis formed the Texas State Police, to replace Union occupations troops and enforce his own edicts. But he left border settlements to fend for themselves, and outlying ranchers were hard pressed to stave off the attacks of Mexican *bandidos.* Laird had lost thousands of longhorns to the raiders, and except for his vaquero patrols, the Durham herd would have been rustled long ago. In round numbers, he calculated the breeding program had cost him in excess of $100,000. And still, he had nothing to show for either his money or his effort.

"There's always next year, Pa."

Trudy's voice broke the train of his thought, and he glanced around. "How's that?"

"Well, maybe if you cross a Durham-longhorn cow with a Durham bull . . . or a longhorn bull—" She paused, suddenly baffled by the intermix. "Well, anyway, you see what I mean. One way or the other, maybe crossing the next generation will get what you want."

"Perhaps, though I've little faith in it. Here lately, I've come to suspect it's the land instead of the Durhams."

"The land?"

"Aye, the weather and the graze. Too hot, too coarse, not what they're accustomed to. Could be I'm simply playing a fool's game all the way round . . . wishful thinking."

"What about the horses, though? That worked."

"You've a point there, lass. As a matter of fact . . . to hell with cows!"

Laird spun his horse around and signaled to their escort. *"Vamonos, muchachos!"* Trudy laughed, and roweled her own mount across the flanks. Trailed by the vaqueros, father and daughter took off upstream, running neck and neck, quirting their horses into a dead lope.

Several minutes later they slid to a halt before another pasture. On the opposite side of the fence a magnificent stallion charged toward them, suddenly pulled up short, and whinnied a shrill blast of greeting. He was a barrel-chested animal, all sinew and muscle, standing fifteen hands high and well over a thousand pounds in weight. A blood bay, with black mane and tail, his hide glistened in the sun like dark blood on polished redwood. He held his ground, watching them, and pawed the earth as though he spurned it and longed to fly.

Laird's mood always improved whenever he came to inspect the mares and Copperdust. He had imported the stallion from Kentucky, three years ago, and begun a selective breeding program. A *manada* of mustang brood mares was chosen from the ranch stock, picked for their conformation and speed. They had the spirit of their noble ancestors, the Barbs, and from generations of battling both the elements and predators, possessed an almost supernatural endurance. Yet, unlike Copperdust, the mares were essentially creatures of the wild, and no amount of breaking ever fully tamed a mustang. From this fusion, Laird hoped to breed the ultimate range horse, with all the qualities necessary for working cattle.

And the results had been spectacular.

By culling the mares, continually breeding up, nearly half of Copperdust's offspring now met the test. They had stamina and catlike agility, intelligence and an even disposition,

and a near sixth sense for the quirky ways of longhorns. Those who fell short of the requirements were nonetheless superb stock, and easily sold to the army for saddle mounts and pack animals. Not only had Laird developed a strain of horse suitable to his own needs, but in the process he had organized a highly profitable business. Before the year was out he figured to clear upwards of $50,000 from army contracts and the sale of young studs to other ranchers.

As Laird and Trudy watched, Copperdust came on at a prancing walk, moving with the pride of power and lordship. Always protective of his mares, who had retreated to the center of the pasture, he halted a few yards short of the fence. Then he stood, nostrils flared, testing the wind, like an ebony statue bronzed by the sun.

"God's teeth!" Laird chuckled. "Look at the devil strut. Thinks he owns Heaven and Hell, and everything in between."

Trudy nodded, her gaze abstracted, mouth set in a faint smile. The stallion fascinated her, and whenever he came this close, she always felt a curious sensation in her loins. His blood-red hide rippled, and she squirmed, pressing herself against the saddle horn. Oddly enough, every time the feeling came over her, Trudy experienced a fleeting image of her father. It was all very confusing, for the two of them, the stallion and her father, were somehow intertwined in her thoughts. On occasion, when she looked at her father, a sudden glimpse of Copperdust flashed through her mind. And the feeling never varied. It was warm and made her skin tingle, and brought a quick rush of dizziness that left a sweet aftertaste in her mouth. Almost as though she'd bitten into a moist peach.

"Something wrong, lass?"

"No, Pa." Trudy blinked, licked her lips. "Nothing . . . why?"

"Well, you've a damned queer look on your face, that's why."

"Oh, I was just thinking about Copperdust . . . what you said."

"And?"

"And you're right. Even without the fence, it wouldn't make any difference. He'd still own it all, wouldn't he?"

"I've no doubt he would. You see, in there or out here, it's all one kingdom. And fences mean nothing to a king."

"Or a Laird."

The words were spoken softly, but with a curious inflection, and immense tenderness. Trudy kept her eyes fixed on the stallion, unable to look at her father, and there was a prolonged silence. At last, convinced he'd read something into her words, Laird laughed and turned his gaze on Copperdust.

"Aye, it's the God's own truth. We'll not be fenced, him or me . . . except at our pleasure!"

At the supper table that evening, Trudy wolfed down her food, then excused herself and hurried off to the compound. One of her girlhood friends had recently become betrothed, and an informal *baile* was being held to honor the couple. Angela cautioned her to be home early, and Laird, who had little interest in such affairs, retired to the parlor for a cigar and whiskey.

After the servants had cleared the table, Angela joined him in the parlor, eyeing the decanter with distaste. Over the years, she had resigned herself to his drinking, for the alternative was incessant bickering which in the end accomplished nothing. But she endured with the quiet despair of a martyr being spiked to the cross; while never openly critical, she seemed forever in the act of biting her tongue. Tonight, she watched him drain his glass, waited in silence while he refilled it, and finally cleared her throat.

"Henry, I want to discuss something with you."

Laird took a sip of whiskey, glanced at her over the rim of his glass. "From the look on your face, I've an idea I won't like it."

"Perhaps not, but we still need to talk."

"All right, what's on your mind?"

"Trudy."

"What about her?"

Angela folded her hands in her lap and took a deep breath. "I'm worried about her, Henry. I have been for a long time, and tonight . . . well, I suppose tonight just brought it to a head."

"Are you talking about the dance?"

"I most certainly am. That and . . . all the rest."

"Jesus, must you forever talk in riddles? All the rest what?"

"Her friends, Henry! Her *only* friends."

Angela had faded delicately with the years. She was weary of life, often depressed by the gray in her hair and the cobwebs of time lining her face. Yet, for all the futility and frustration of her own world, she still clung to a brighter dream for her daughter. In that, she had received scant encouragement from Trudy, and none at all from her husband, but her hope was undiminished. She believed that patience was a great abrasive and could wear away even the obstinacy of Henry Laird. She had waited, ever watchful, confident the right moment would present itself, and tonight she meant to force the issue.

"I'm concerned, Henry. Deeply concerned. I only pray we haven't closed our eyes too long and allowed a very unhealthy situation to develop."

"God's blood! Would you get to the point?"

"Well, that is the point. Trudy simply doesn't have the proper companions. No girls her own age, and certainly no young men."

"Other than Mexicans, is that what you're saying?"

"Yes, that's exactly what I'm saying. And I find that very unhealthy, perhaps even dangerous."

"Now, hold it right there! Are you trying to tell me she's got her eye on someone . . . one of the vaqueros?"

"No, I'm not. But she's your daughter, Henry. She's impetuous and headstrong and if the notion struck her . . ."

"You think she might, huh?"

"To be perfectly honest about it, I'm not sure. But I do know that all the girls her age are married and having babies, and she might very well pick up some foolish ideas. Frankly, it's not a risk I care to take."

"And how do you propose to stop it?"

Angela squared her shoulders, looking him straight in the eye. "Henry, she's nearly grown, and it's long past time that we started thinking about her future. I want to send her to New Orleans, to a school for young ladies."

"Oh, for the love of Christ!"

"Henry, listen to me, please."

"I had a hunch that's what you were up to!"

"Please don't shout. I only want what's best for Trudy."

"Aye, and there's no need to go into your little song and dance. I've heard it so often I know it by heart."

"That's not fair!" Angela's tone was hotly defensive. "You make it sound like some silly game, and it isn't. I'm only thinking of Trudy . . . and if you weren't so afraid of losing her, you wouldn't act like such a fool."

"Oh, it's a fool, is it?" Laird puffed on his cigar, glowering at her. "Well now, maybe that makes two of us. All this high-and-mighty talk about New Orleans, would you like to know what the girl wants?"

"Why, of course, Henry. I'm sure you've filled her head with nonsense, but go ahead, tell me anyway. What does she want?"

"She wants to go to Wichita—with me!—and it was her own idea."

Angela paled. "Wichita?"

"Aye, and I've half a mind to take her. By the Sweet Jesus, she'd learn more there than she would in New Orleans."

"You really would, wouldn't you? You'd take her there and ruin her chances forever, just to spite me."

"I'll tell you one thing! You mention New Orleans once more and I'll take her to Kansas so fast it'll make your head spin."

"I see."

Angela fell silent, considering the threat. These days she never quite knew how to approach her husband. Their relationship had undergone a pronounced change in the last six years, and curiously enough, it was Hank Laird who had changed the most. Since the night of the hurricane, when she'd confronted him with the death of their son, his attitude toward her had become one of mixed emotions. At times he was considerate and gentle, almost courtly. On other occasions, especially those times she defied him regarding Trudy, he turned sullen and churlish. Slowly, despite his bluff air of assurance, she came to understand that he harbored some inner dread of losing Trudy. She traced it directly to the hurricane and the loss of his riverboats, and an intuitive belief, later confirmed, that he was saddled with guilt about their son. Quite by accident, she had discovered he was se-

cretly visiting the chapel, generally late at night, with some regularity.

Whether or not Hank Laird had got religion was a moot question. But Angela suspected he had developed a deep and abiding fear of a vengeful God. Clearly, his prayers were a way of appeasing that God, prompted by some dismal horror that Trudy would also be taken from him. For a man who had always treated God with a sort of hairy-chested bravado —not unlike a wrestling match between equals—it indicated a new awareness, even acceptance, of his own mortality. Yet Angela thought it typically Irish—almost barbaric—like some primitive cave dweller offering burnt sacrifice to pagan idols. In her eyes, it had less to do with atonement for past wrongs than an attempt to avert any further personal tragedy. Still, under whatever circumstances, she was pleased by his trips to the chapel, and gratified that it had tempered, to a modest degree, his attitude toward her. Of course, in certain matters, it simply made her life all the more difficult. Once having acknowledged the fearsome nature of his God, the thought of losing Trudy constantly preyed on Laird's mind. He would resort to any measure, however harsh, to hold on to the girl. Today's threat was in earnest, and upon reflection Angela realized she had placed herself in an untenable position. Unless she reversed herself, and accomplished it with a certain finesse, she would jeopardize any future efforts on Trudy's behalf. Her husband was entirely capable of making her the scapegoat where their daughter was concerned.

At length she sighed, her features rigid, and met his look. "Henry, you're wrong and selfish, and we both know it. But if I were to let the matter drop . . . what then?"

"Then we'll call it a standoff. She stays here with you and that's the end of it."

"Oh, you'd like that, wouldn't you? Trudy will blame me for spoiling her trip to Wichita, and you get everything just the way you want it."

"No, I'd not do that." Laird took a thoughtful sip on his whiskey, then shrugged. "What the hell, I'll take the blame myself. Tell her it's simply no place for a young girl."

"How very charitable of you."

"Don't mention it. After all, I'm not the sort to come between mother and daughter."

Angela studied him a moment, her face masked by anger. Then her eyes went dark and vengeful. "Henry, I never thought I'd tell you this—and I'm ashamed you could make me say it—but you really are a bastard."

"Aye, that I am. And proud of it."

Laird raised his glass and saluted her. "You're right about something else too. She's her father's daughter, and that's a bloody fact. Damned if it's not."

CHAPTER 15

The dancers ringed a huge bonfire. Flames leaped skyward, distorting their shadows, as the music increased in tempo and the beat of their steps grew faster and faster on the hard-packed earth. The crowd edged closer, gathered around them in a loose circle, laughing and shouting, urging them onward with cries of *"Olé! Olé!"* The betrothed couple responded to the chant, certain it was for their benefit. Yet the center of attention, watched closely by the crowd, was another couple on the opposite side of the fire. All eyes were fixed on the *patrón's* daughter and her partner.

Trudy advanced to meet Roberto, smiling and coquettish, gracefully performing the stylistic moves of the *jota*. Her eyes flashed, brilliant in the firelight, and she turned her head, taunting him with the traditional look of innocence as they retreated from one another. Then they skipped sideways, moving in opposite directions, suddenly reversed themselves and came together an instant before repeating the steps. Her skirts were lifted high, displaying a delicate ankle, and Roberto laughed, softly clapping his hands in time to the music. He was lithe and muscular, incredibly nimble in motion, matching her grace with an almost fluid counterpoint that was at once sensual and boldly inviting. The *músicos* launched into rapid verse, again increasing the tempo, and the dancers began a series of intricate steps keyed to the words of the song. The onlookers burst into applause, enthralled by the wild gaiety, the excitement of raised skirts and bare legs. A moment later, with a flourish of guitars and a piercing note from the lone cornet, the *jota* ended to thunderous ovation.

The dancers froze, poised an instant on the last note. Then the girls dipped low, eyes downcast and skirts spread

wide, and the men bowed, their arms outstretched, heads inclined in admiration. Roberto hovered over Trudy, bent at the waist, and his whisper was so faint his lips scarcely moved.

"I'll go first . . . take care."

Her look betrayed nothing. When they rose and stepped back, Roberto nodded, his mouth set in a formal smile. *"Gracias, señorita.* I hope you will permit me another dance before the night ends."

"Of course, Roberto. Perhaps a *jarabe,* eh? I always feel I do it better with such an accomplished partner."

"You are too kind, *señorita,* and too modest."

Trudy favored him with a smile, then turned and strolled away. The band struck up a *zorita* and Roberto immediately claimed one of the village girls as his partner. Several other girls followed him with their eyes, envious but ever hopeful he might choose them next time. A man of inordinate good looks, with the hawklike intensity of his father, he was by far the most popular young vaquero on Santa Guerra. Among the men, it was a standing joke that he had deflowered *virgens* beyond counting. Yet mothers wept and their daughters sulked whenever a *baile* passed without some acknowledgment, however slight, of his interest. As the eldest son of Ramon Morado, *segundo* to the *patrón,* he was considered most eligible indeed, and a prize catch for any girl. To families with marriageable daughters it was thought a great pity that he gave no indication of settling down. He seemed content instead to remain unattached, available to all.

Strolling through the crowd, Trudy kept one eye on the dancers, and Roberto. She paused here and there to chat, attentive to everyone, exchanging greetings with the warmth and affection *Los Lerdeños* had come to expect of her. Though the *baile* was in honor of the betrothed couple, her presence marked it as an event of special significance. Yet she was natural and unassuming, merely one of the people rather than the *patrón's* daughter. She wore a peasant's blouse with a low-cut bodice, and a simple skirt, the dress common to women throughout the village. It endeared her to them all the more, and by its very simplicity was a token of tribute to her hosts and the betrothed couple.

The *baile* itself was a lavish affair by village standards.

Only family and close friends had been invited, but there were upward of a hundred guests. They were gathered in a small clearing beside the creek, which was reserved for parties and festive occasions. A steer, donated by the *patrón*, simmered over a pit of live coals, and on a long table, the women had arranged steaming platters of frijoles and *carne asado* and other native dishes. For the men, there were jugs of *aguardiente* and tequila, and for the young people there was dancing. The musicians, seemingly inexhaustible, were kept fueled with liquor, and strains of all the traditional tunes filled the night. Around the bonfire, one dance swifly followed another, and the crowd cheered the young couples on with lusty approval.

A fandango ended, and Trudy, who was talking with the women at the serving table, saw Roberto detach himself from the dancers. Pleading thirst and promising to return, he joined a group of men at the edge of the crowd. There he took a pull on a jug of tequila, then casually drifted off, moving from one group to another. Aimlessly, in no apparent rush, he wandered ever farther from the bonfire, and finally disappeared into the trees upstream. If anyone noticed, it drew no comment. Men frequently stepped off into the darkness to relieve themselves.

Trudy waited several minutes, then excused herself and turned away from the serving table. The moment she turned she had the odd sensation of being watched. Her gaze swept the crowd, moved past the dancers to the opposite side of the fire, and suddenly halted. Luis Morado was staring straight at her, and as their eyes locked, his mouth curved in a sardonic smile. It was a look of disapproval mixed with sadness, and she knew he'd seen Roberto leave the party. For an instant, returning his stare, she was struck by the paradox of two brothers so dissimilar in all things.

Within the last few years, it was as though Roberto and Luis had exchanged skins. Once the boy jester, Luis had matured into a responsible and very industrious man. At eighteen he was married, shortly to become a father, and so knowledgeable of horses and cows that it was only a matter of time until he was promoted to *caporal*. Yet Roberto, always the solemn one when they were children, apparently had no taste for responsibility. He was wild and reckless,

willing to take risks that awed even the older vaqueros, and quite content to be considered the *macho hombre* of Santa Guerra. Trudy often wished it were the other way round, for if Roberto were more like Luis it would have eased her plans for the future. Then, too, she sometimes worried that Roberto was acting a role—for her sake—to avoid entanglements that would limit his freedom to come and go. On the other hand, it was a guise perfectly suited to their arrangement. Of all the people on the ranch, only Luis suspected, and she knew their secret was safe with him. While he disapproved and feared for the consequences, he would never betray his brother—or her.

Trudy laughed and tossed her head. The gesture made Luis wince, and he looked away, unable to mask his concern. A moment later the crowd began calling for a special *jarabe* by the betrothed couple. People hurried forward, jabbering excitedly, shoving and jostling for a better position around the fire. Amidst the commotion, no one noticed that the *patrón's* daughter held her ground, allowing them to push past her. After the music started, she waited awhile longer, until someone shouted "Bravo!" and the crowd quickly took up the cry.

Then she turned and melted unseen into the trees.

She came to him in the dark, the sky like a dim opal flecked through with stars. He held out his arms and she ran the last few steps, throwing herself into his embrace. Her hands went behind his neck, pulling his mouth down, and she kissed him with a fierce, passionate urgency. His arms tightened, strong and demanding, and when at last they separated, her voice was breathless, warm and husky.

"Oh, Roberto *mío,* how I've missed you."

His mustache gently brushed her cheek, and he kissed her. "It is the same for me, *querida.* I ache to hold you, and when we are apart there is no sleep."

"I know." She leaned against him, head buried in his chest. "It's torture . . . the waiting . . . never really sure when I'll see you again. Sometimes I think I'll go crazy . . . it hurts too much, Roberto . . . not knowing."

"*Sí,* but we are together now. Let us be thankful that Maria and Tomaso had their *baile* tonight."

"It's not enough! I want to be with you every night."

"Be happy with what we have, *cara mía.*"

"I won't . . . I can't . . . it grows more difficult . . . impossible."

"No sabe, little one. How more difficult?"

"I'm watched, questioned all the time. Everywhere I turn, there's my mother—like a hawk!—always watching, watching."

"Do you think she suspects?"

"I don't know . . . yes . . . yes, she probably does. But I don't care anymore, Roberto. I'm sick to death of her prying and her questions . . . and always being watched."

Her voice trailed off and he held her close, lightly stroking her hair. Each time they met she grew more wretched, and within the last few months a bittersweet quality had entered their relationship. The things he'd resigned himself to—the secrecy and stealth—were the very things she had never really accepted. A year ago, almost as though they were fated to become lovers, she had arranged a chance meeting and surrendered her maidenhead with joyful abandon. But even then, in that first flush of discovery, he'd known it couldn't last. She was still a girl in many ways, spoiled and hopelessly romantic; yet he had seen her develop into a proud and spirited woman. For her, there were no halfway measures. It offended her dignity, somehow marred her sense of worth, to skulk and deceive. However much she loved him, the intrigue made her uncomfortable and increasingly unhappy. He thought it her only flaw, common to all Anglos, and often wished she were truly one of *Los Lerdeños.* It would have simplified life greatly had he not fallen in love with a *gringa aristócrata.*

"Qué quieres?" He lifted her chin, kissed the top of her nose. "What is it you want . . . tell me?"

She sighed, pressed her face to his hand. "I want to stop sneaking around and lying to everyone, especially to myself. *Dios mío,* Roberto, we have nothing to be ashamed of—nothing at all!"

"Others would most surely disagree. There are times, little one, when the truth cannot be told."

"Cómo no?" she demanded. "Why not?"

"Be honest, now, would your mother approve?"

"No, of course not. But she certainly couldn't stop us, so she could just learn to live with it."

"Ah, and if that were so, would she then share our secret?"

"Keep quiet, you mean . . . not tell my father?"

"Sí, that is exactly what I mean."

She eyed him in silence for a moment. "I think it would be better if I told him myself."

"Mil Cristos! You're not serious?"

"You forget"—she smiled, tweaked his mustache—"I have a way with men."

"Aiiii caramba! We're not talking of men, we're talking of *El Patrón."*

"Oh, don't worry about that, I can handle him."

Roberto looked at her in astonishment, shook his head. "Can you also teach eagles to scratch the earth like chickens?"

"I don't understand."

"Then ask yourself a question, *querida.* What would your father do if he knew you were here . . . tonight . . . with a greaser?"

"Por Dios!" she protested. "He doesn't think of you that way. He doesn't!"

"Perhaps," Roberto said grimly. "But then again, perhaps I know your father better than you do."

"You actually believe he would—?"

"Sí, little one. I believe he would. You are his daughter—*hija inocente del Patrón!*—and for him, that alone would be reason enough."

"Oh god, Roberto, I couldn't stand the thought of that."

"It has little appeal to me either."

"But if you're right—"

"Accept it as a truth, *cara mía."*

"—then that means we must go on the way we have been. There's no other way, is there?"

"De seguro," he assured her. "No way whatever."

"Well, in that case, to hell with the whole damned world!"

Trudy laughed an indolent deep-throated laugh. She pressed her body against him, arms clutched about his neck, and hushed his reply with a soft kiss.

"Don't say anything," she whispered. "Not another word
. . . just make love to me . . . make me forget."

Roberto lowered her gently to the ground, and in a few
moments they were naked. She snuggled close in his arms,
felt an almost unbearable excitement as his hand caressed
her breasts, teased her nipples erect. Her mouth found his,
eagerly sought his tongue, then her hand grasped that hard
questing part of him, fondled it lovingly until he was aroused
and aching for her. His hand slid down her stomach, went
lower still, tantalizing and elusive, until she arched to meet it
and a tingling shock rippled through the core of dampness
between her legs. She was ready for him, moist and yeilding,
the moment he touched her. He moaned, trembling with
need, and she pulled him onto her, accepted him slowly, felt
him penetrate and probe tenderly. His arms went beneath
her and she was lifted, pressed closer still, felt him growing
inside her. Time lost measure and meaning, and within that
single instant, she crossed a threshold far beyond the limits
of her most vivid fantasies. Her legs tightened around him
and his stroke quickened, thrusting faster and faster, ever
deeper. She peaked, clamping him vise-like, and explosive
little shudders wracked her body. Her nails clawed his back,
drawing blood, and when he burst inside her, hot jolting
eruptions one after the other, her mouth opened in a gasp-
ing cry of agony.

"Ohhh Roberto! Tu amor, Roberto. Tu amor!"

CHAPTER 16

By late March the roundup was completed. Nearly 22,000 head had been gathered and driven to holding grounds around the ranch. Altogether there were ten herds, each comprised of something over two thousand cows, and their current market value exceeded $500,000.

The immediate problem was getting them to market. Between Santa Guerra Creek and the railhead in Kansas lay almost eight hundred miles of hard trail-driving. The herds would be started out a day apart, moving northward toward the Red River and Indian Territory. There they would connect with the Chisholm Trail, which followed a meandering course through the wilderness and eventually ended in Wichita. As yet, the major railroads had not laid track into Texas; since there were no branch lines with a connecting link, the ranchers had no choice but to trail their herds to Kansas. The drive took upward of three months, and along the way the drovers would encounter flooded rivers, hostile Indians, and the everpresent danger of stampede. It was unknown for a herd to arrive intact at the railhead. But the hazards were accepted as part of the trade, and any cattleman who lost less than ten percent on a drive considered himself fortunate indeed.

Hank Laird had never personally gone up the Chisholm Trail. Instead, he went by steamboat from New Orleans to St. Louis, then proceeded by train to Kansas, and met his herds at the railhead. He thought of himself as a businessman—cattle were merely the commodity in which he dealt—and he left trail-driving to those who were experienced at the game. Every spring he contracted with veteran trail bosses, offering them a generous share of the profits, and thereby insured their utmost concern for each cow bearing the ⌐→

brand. Unlike other cattlemen, who preferred to drive their own herds, he had narrowed the odds drastically. In the last five years, with nearly sixty thousand cows trailed to Kansas, he had averaged less than six percent loss every season. This year, given a firm market and nothing catastrophic along the way, he stood to clear better than $250,000.

Today, under the brassy dome of the sky, a crew of vaqueros was working to ready the first herd for the trail. Laird and Ramon Morado sat their horses on a slight rise, watching the operation. Outriders were stationed at the cardinal points, containing the cows on the holding ground and hazing bunch quitters back into the fold. The rest of the crew was busy doctoring blowfly sores with the standard range remedy. Bawling cows were lassoed and thrown, then the sore was cleaned and the proud flesh cut away. A vaquero carrying a rag dauber and a wooden bucket quickly stepped in and coated the raw spot with axle grease. The cow was released, certain to heal before the trail drive ended, and the next patient was hauled forward to have its sores doped.

The vaqueros wasted little effort, working together as a team, and Laird regarded the operation with an approving look. He was in an expansive mood today, one leg hooked over the saddle horn, puffing on a cigar, thoroughly pleased with himself and his world. He grinned, glancing at Ramon, and gestured with the cigar.

"You've done a grand job, *amigo*. And the men too! There's not a slacker in the bunch."

"*Gracias, Patrón.* But we merely followed your orders. Nothing more."

"Well, it's been a tough couple of months, and without everyone pulling together, we'd have never stuck to the schedule. I appreciate that. You tell 'em I said so."

Ramon's smile puckered the scar along his jawbone. "The vaqueros will take pride in your words, Patrón. Great pride."

"Aye, but I'm thinking they deserve more than a pat on the back. You tell 'em the day the last herd takes the trail, we'll have ourselves one *muy grande fiesta.* With presents for their women and all the *niños* too."

Laird often indulged himself in feats of impulsive generosity, but this was something more than a token of appreciation. There were easily five hundred vaqueros on the Santa

Guerra spread, and along with their families *Los Lerdeños*
now numbered over two thousand people. It would indeed
be a grand occasion, worthy of *El Patrón* and one the people
would not soon forget. Ramon was about to express that very
thought when the rumble of hoofbeats cut him short.

Laird twisted around and saw Trudy galloping toward
them, trailed by her usual escort. The vaqueros reined up
some distance away, and a moment later, enveloping her
father and Ramon in a cloud of dust, Trudy slid her mount to
a halt in a flashy display of horsemanship.

"Hola, Papa! Ramon! Qué pasa?"

"Nothing out of the ordinary"—Laird squinted at her
through the dust—"till you got here."

"Oooo." Trudy's voice was light and mocking. "Don't
scold me again, Papa. Please."

"Very funny. But that was a fool stunt, young lady, and no
way to handle a horse. Mark my word, you'll break your neck
one of these days."

"Don't be an old spoilsport. You know very well I can ride
rings around you any day of the week."

"Bullfeathers! There's not a word of truth to it."

"And besides, I need a *little* fun out of life. I mean, after
all, you're running off to Wichita and I'm stuck here on this
dull old ranch. So what's a girl to do?"

"Here now, no more of that. The subject's closed, and I'll
not have you browbeat me about it further."

"Why, Papa, no one's browbeating you. That's just your
guilty conscience speaking."

"Mother of God! Would you listen to that? My own
daughter, and she has the tongue of an adder."

"Well it's true, Papa. And you know it very well too!"

"I know nothing of the sort. You've had my reasons, and
all your harping won't change a thing. So let's have an end to
it, right now."

Trudy put on her best pout. "Well, I can see I'm not appre-
ciated here, and that's all right by me. I think I'll just find
myself some better company."

"Hold on a minute. You were supposed to inspect the
second herd. Have you no word for me?"

"Claro que sí, Papa. Two days, three at the most, and
they'll be ready to go. And when you meet them in Wichita,

don't let it bother your conscience that I'm not there. Not much!"

With that, Trudy heeled her mount sharply about and rode off toward the holding groud. Laird watched her go with an indulgent smile. Hardly a day passed without some barbed exchange about Wichita. But all in all she'd taken it rather well, and he was proud of her spunky manner. Still, once he'd gone, she might very well start feeling sorry for herself, and that bothered him. He turned to Ramon.

"You can do me a favor, *compadre.*"

"*Sí, Patrón.* Anything you wish."

"The girl takes after her father. She has a wild streak, and sometimes that's a bad thing."

Ramon made a small nod of acknowledgment, and Laird went on. "When I leave for Kansas, she may allow her anger to overrule her common sense. She is a woman who still thinks with the mind of a girl, and she might harm herself in a way which she believes would hurt me."

The shadow of a question clouded Ramon's eyes, then quickly moved on. The *segundo* had never lacked wisdom, but with age came a deeper insight that made him a truly wise man. For all the *Patrón's* affection and generosity toward *Los Lerdeños,* he knew that at bottom it was the affection of a lord for those who served faithfully and without question. Henry Laird ruled the people of Santa Guerra through example, and through a bond of loyalty unbroken into the third generation. Yet beneath it all, there was a quiet force that would never brook disobedience. Nor would it allow familiarity. Watching him now, Ramon sensed that they were discussing a very delicate matter. The *Patrón* would kill any vaquero who touched his daughter, and he was trying to convey the message without actually stating it.

"I understand, *Patrón.* It will be as you wish."

"*Bueno.* After I am gone, I will sleep easy knowing that you stand in my place."

"*Hecho!* I will watch over her as though she were of my own flesh."

"*Gracias, amigo.* I am in your debt."

"*De nada, Patrón.* You honor me."

Laird nodded and there was a moment of deliberation. He gazed off into space, staring past the holding ground, and

seemed to fall asleep with his eyes open. Presently he blinked, took a couple of quick puffs on his cigar, and swung back to Ramon.

"There is another matter we must anticipate. Our friends from below the river, *Los Renegados.*"

"*Sangre de Cristo!*" Ramon's nut-brown features colored with rage. "They grow bolder each day, *Patrón.* Always they strike where we least expect it."

"Too much land, that's the problem. And too many cows."

"*Sí, Patrón.* And too few men. Our vaqueros try, but they cannot be everywhere at once. The thieves know this, and they raid our herds with little fear of being caught."

"Once I'm gone, they'll grow bolder still."

"I do not understand, *Patrón.*"

"Think on it. What would you do if you were Cordoba?"

"*Hijo de puta!*" Ramon exploded. "Son of a whore!"

"He's that and worse. But he's also sly as a coyote. He'll know the exact day I leave for Kansas, and in his mind, my absence will appear to weaken our defenses. I have no doubt he will encourage more raids than ever, and we must be prepared to counter that threat."

"You are right, of course, *Patrón.* But how?"

"A good question, and one I ask myself a great deal these days."

Laird fell silent, thoughtful. It was a burden that weighed heavily, for he planned to spend most of the summer in Wichita, and he knew the people of Santa Guerra would be put to the test. Juan Cordoba wasn't a man to overlook opportunity.

With the Díaz regime firmly entrenched in Mexico City, General Juan Cordoba had been appointed commander of the lower Rio Grande. His selection particularly galled the Texans, for he had fought them under one flag or another for the past twenty years. Time had done nothing to dim his hatred, and once he'd occupied Matamoros, the plunder of ranches north of the border quickly assumed the guise of a holy crusade. Cordoba openly sanctioned the raids, stating that everything between the Nueces and the Rio Grande had been taken from Mexico by force, and therefore belonged to the Mexican people. The cattle rustling intensified, and the marauders were soon bragging, "The gringos raise our cows

for us." In return for official protection, Cordoba himself profited handsomely. He had stocked a ranch in the interior with stolen cattle, and regularly filled beef contracts for the Cuban and Mexican governments with cows bearing Texas brands. It was a lucrative and highly organized enterprise, and within the last year alone, Texans had lost more than 200,000 head to the raiders.

Laird had devoted considerable thought to the summer ahead. His presence in Wichita was essential, yet his absence on the Santa Guerra would leave the ranch more vulnerable than ever. He saw only one recourse, and while it was extreme, there seemed no alternative. At last, determined to thwart Cordoba at all costs, he made the decision he'd been toying with for several days.

"There is no easy way, *compadre*. But there is a way. Once the herds are on the trail, you will assign half the vaqueros to patrol duty for the balance of the summer."

"Blessed Virgin!" Ramon muttered. "Surely you're not serious, *Patrón*. That would cripple us. How can the work of all be done by only half?"

"Hire more men," Laird informed him. "Do whatever you must, but I want our boundary lines patrolled night and day. Those are my orders."

"*Sin falta, Patrón*. It will be done."

"One other thing. Tell the men who ride patrol that it is my express wish that they take no prisoners. *Quién sabe?*"

"*De los enemigos los menos.*" Ramon shrugged and smiled. "The fewer enemies the better."

"Aye, my thought exactly."

"Of course, there are some who have no stomach for such business. So I will assign my own sons to lead the most dangerous patrols. *Los Lerdeños* will then understand that your orders are in earnest. *Verdad?*"

"*Sí, compadre.* It would be an unmistakable gesture. But the thought worries me . . . Roberto and Luis are quite young . . . and the risk is great."

"Have no fear, *Patrón*. These *hijos* of mine are men—*duro hombres!*—they will instruct Cordoba and his bravos in the proper manner."

"*Hecho!* I leave it to your judgment, old friend."

Laird's gaze drifted out across the holding ground, and a

slow smile tugged at the corner of his mouth. Trudy was standing tall in her stirrups, hurling mock insults at the vaqueros, berating one and all for their laziness and lack of skill with the lariat. He shook his head, watching her antics with a sense of wonder, and finally stuffed the cigar in his mouth.

"I think you're in for a long summer, *amigo*."

Ramon followed his gaze, and nodded soberly. *"Sí, Patrón.* Already it appears endless."

"Buena suerte. I've an idea you'll need it."

CHAPTER 17

The lobby was deserted when Laird came down the stairs. From the bar he heard the drone of voices, mixed with laughter and the clink of whiskey glasses. The cattle buyers had already begun the evening ritual, spreading good cheer and hard liquor while they dickered on a herd of cows. It was a tricky game, one in which fortunes were made or lost on a handshake, and some cattlemen seemed to spend their lives trailing longhorns north only to be bamboozled by Yankee sharpers.

Laird debated having a drink, then decided against it. The buyers had been after his herds for a week now, but he was still holding out for top price. Tactics were everything, and he'd learned long ago that a man who appeared anxious to sell seldom got a fair offer. Crossing the lobby, he stepped onto the hotel porch and took a seat in a rocker. He trimmed and lit a cigar, snuffed out the match, and propped his boots up on the porch railing. The day had been a scorcher, typical of the Kansas plains in June, and he could feel rivulets of sweat running down his backbone. Exhaling, he watched the smoke hang in the still air, then let his gaze wander over the dusty street.

Wichita had become the reigning cowtown earlier that spring. The major railheads until then—Abilene, Ellsworth, and Newton—promptly lost the cattle trade once the Santa Fe tracks hit town. Wichita was farther south, saving the Texans a week on the trail, and it was a natural holding ground for longhorns. A vast sea of graze stretched in every direction, and the town itself was settled on the banks of the Arkansas, which was shallow and easily forded. Almost overnight the railroad had transformed a sleepy village into a boomtown.

Yet, like most cowtowns, Wichita wasn't much to look at. It was simply bigger and brassier, with the carnival atmosphere imported by the sporting crowd. Main Street and Douglas Avenue, the town's only real streets, were lined with saloons and gaming parlors, several dance halls, and a few mercantile emporiums. The lone hotel was a three-story brick structure that looked curiously out of place amidst the sleazy, falsefront establishments surrounding it. On the opposite side of the river was Delano, the red-light district. With remarkable foresight, the city council had banned the kingdom of whores to the west bank of the Arkansas. Trailhands were forced to cross the river in search for women, and for those who disliked wading water, the town had conveniently erected a toll bridge.

Still, despite its shabby appearance, Wichita was no town for pikers. The prairie was already dotted with longhorn herds, and it was estimated that upward of a half million head of cattle would be funneled through the railhead during the five-month trailing season. The stakes were big, the play was fast, and, before the end of September, somewhere around $15 million would have exchanged hands.

Which was the very thing that concerned Laird. Within the past week six of his herds had reached Wichita, and the others were arriving daily. Normally, he held off selling, waiting for the market to peak, and until now he'd stalled any serious negotiations with buyers. But there were ominous tremors in the financial world back East, and cattle prices had fluctuated wildly over the last few days.

On Wall Street the robber barons were slugging it out with brass knuckles. Vanderbilt and Gould, Morgan and Cooke, along with several lesser luminaries, were fighting for control of railroads, banks, and hundreds of millions in stock. While Laird knew little of high finance, he'd already grasped a truth which as yet eluded most cattlemen. The West was forever susceptible to the slightest disruption in the structure of a distant money market. As he saw it, a gathering storm loomed just over the horizon. When it broke, a wave of economic chaos would be set in motion, gaining momentum as it swept westward across the plains. And unless he misread the signs, hard times were about to overtake anyone who failed to hedge his bet.

Puffing on his cigar, oblivious to the throngs of trailhands crowding the street, he considered the knotty question of when to sell. If the market held firm and he sold too early, then he would lose tens of thousands of dollars in profit. On the other hand, if the market softened and he sold too late, then he might very well suffer a loss for the entire season. It occurred to him that greed had proved the downfall of more than one high roller. A smart gambler knew when to cut his losses and—of still greater consequence—he knew when to fold his hand and walk away winner. A sudden impulse told him to play his hunch, and after a moment's thought, he set a dollar figure in his mind. That would be his limit, and once it was offered, he made a mental promise not to succumb to greed.

Laird became aware that someone had taken the rocker next to him. Looking around, he found Josh Campbell, one of the Eastern cattle buyers, watching him with an amiable grin.

"Josh, how goes the battle?" He flipped the cigar stub into the street. "Thought I heard you in the bar trying to sucker some cowman."

Campbell laughed. "Why, Hank, you know me better than that. I'm the soul of charity, just trying to make a living."

"Aye, aren't we all?"

Though Campbell's convivial manner was never to be trusted, Laird wasn't offended by the mercenary nature of their friendship. He liked the dour little Scotsman, even enjoyed his caustic humor, and together they had sampled the delights of every cowtown in Kansas. But that in no way obligated him when it came time to talk money. The vagaries of the beef market were merely compounded by Campbell's slippery methods, and he warned himself to go slowly.

"Wee man that you are, Josh Campbell, you're still a first-rate robber. And I'm on to your tricks, so you've no need to spread the blarney thicker than usual."

"Always the cynic." Campbell stared back at him with round, guileless eyes. "I came out here to make you an honest offer, and all you do is subject me to personal abuse."

"Don't make me laugh. I told you I'll not sell till I've got my price. And you know me well enough to know I'll wait till Hell freezes over."

"It's Kansas that'll freeze over, not Hell. You hold out for thirty dollars a head and you'll end up wintering those cows on the Arkansas."

Laird chuckled. "Aye, and the way you dicker I'd likely come out ahead doing just that."

"Now there you go again, letting personal feelings stand in the way of business."

"Nothing personal about it. My price is the same for you as anyone else."

"Tell you what I'll do, Hank. Twenty-two, for the whole works."

"By Judas! You'd steal the gold out of a man's teeth. Twenty-eight and not a cent less."

"Hank, you're a hard man to do business with. Twenty-three, and that's my last offer."

"Twenty-seven and you've got yourself a deal."

The Scotsman did a quick calculation. "Call it four hundred eighty thousand dollars even."

Laird was no slouch with figures himself. "Josh, you just bought yourself some cows."

The men grinned and shook hands, then stepped back inside to seal the bargain with a drink. Campbell thought he'd saved himself three dollars a cow, and Hank Laird had turned an extra $20,000 profit. His rock bottom had been twenty-three from the outset.

Late that night Laird and Josh Campbell crossed the toll bridge to Delano. Their celebration, begun in the hotel bar, had progressed through a string of dance halls and saloons in Wichita proper. Between them, the men had consumed copious amounts of liquor, and after a brief stop at the Keno House, Laird was feeling especially festive. He'd won nearly $3000 at the faro tables, and he suggested they top off the evening with a visit to Mattie Silks's parlor house. Since he considered himself the big winner all the way round, he insisted that it was to be his treat.

Campbell thought it a grand gesture. Secretly, each man still figured he'd skinned the other, but tonight they were warmed by drunken camaraderie and effusive goodwill. An interlude among ladies of negotiable virtue seemed a fitting tribute to their friendship.

Upon entering the red-light district they had to pass a warren of cheap cathouses. These establishments were operated by the likes of Rowdy Joe Lowe and the Earp Brothers, Wyatt and James, and catered to cowhands who couldn't afford better. Down the street, Mattie Silks and Dixie Lee were in fiece competition for the parlor house trade. They had imported redheads and blondes, sloe-eyed Chinese and high yellow octoroons, and the girls were trained to pamper their customers in ways considered daringly exotic by Texans. Yet the charge for their services was purposely steep, and the parlor houses were usually frequented by men of substance, drummers and cattle buyers and ranchers flush from the sale of a herd.

Laird stormed into the brothel and let out a roar that shook the house. Followed by the austere little Scotsman, he entered the parlor to find Mattie Silks and her girls on their feet staring wide-eyed in alarm. The bouncer, Handsome Jack Ready, rushed from one of the back rooms with a lead-loaded bung starter in his hand.

"Mattie, my love!" Laird greeted her with a tottering bow! "You're looking lovely as ever."

"And you look like you're pickled."

"Aye, that I am. But with reason, lass, with reason. Me and my wee friend here are celebrating, so bolt the doors and lock the windows. I'm buying your house for the rest of the night. Every girl you've got."

The girls squealed with delight and started forward, but Mattie Silks halted them with an upraised palm. She was a plump woman, heavily corseted, with hair the color of corn silk and a pert oval face that lacked the hardness of most cowtown madams. Still, she knew how to handle Texans—drunk or sober—and she wasn't about to have the decorum of her parlor house unsettled. She drew herself up, hands on her hips, and fixed Laird with a stern look.

"That isn't the way I operate, Hank. And you've been here often enough to know it."

"Awww, Mattie, don't spoil my fun. It's a rare occasion! Haven't I just told you we're celebrating?"

"Yes, and you're welcome to the hospitality of the house, but I won't have my regular customers inconvenienced. Not for you or anyone else."

"Regular customers!" Laird howled. "And what in the name of Christ would you call me? In all the years we've known each other, have I ever patronized any house but yours? Have I?"

"Hank, as much as I'd like to oblige you, I can't. It's just not good business. Now that's final, so mind your manners and stop being unreasonable."

"Oh, it's final, is it?"

Laird scooped her up by the waist and swung her high over head in a billowing shower of petticoats. The madam screamed and thrashed, her tiny fists pounding at him in a fit of indignation.

"Let me go! Goddamnit, Hank Laird, you put me down!"

"Not till you've agreed. C'mon now, be a good girl and say it. Say the house is mine for the night."

"No, I won't! And if you don't put me down, I'll have Jack beat your brains out."

Handsome Jack Ready dwarfed everyone in the room. He circled them, slapping the bung starter in his open palm, looking for an opening. Laird pivoted, roughly jiggling her around, and presented her bottom to the bouncer. She screeched and kicked and he laughed uproariously.

"Call your gorilla off, Mattie. Do it or I'll rattle your teeth!"

"All right! All right! But put me down, you dirty—!"

Laird tossed her high in the air, laughing at her shriek, and effortlessly caught her with his arms outstretched. But as he lowered her to the floor, all the color suddenly drained from his face. He gasped, unable to get his breath, and clutched at his chest. The pain blurred his vision and a film of sweat popped out on his forehead. Then he seemed to lose his balance, staggering sideways, and crumpled to the floor.

For a moment no one moved. His face turned a peculiar shade of blue and spittle leaked down over his chin. Then Mattie dropped to her knees, rolled him onto his back, and tore his shirt collar loose. Handsome Jack Ready brought a tumbler of brandy and, assisted by Campbell, managed to get some of the liquid down his throat. He coughed, sputtering hoarsely, and his stomach heaved as he sucked in several quick breaths. Slowly his vision cleared, and as the pain

in his chest diminished, his breathing became less labored. After a few seconds the color returned to his face and he became aware of their worried expressions.

"Quit frowning. Lost my wind, that's all."

"Like hell!" Mattie snapped. "You damn near croaked."

"No, I told you, I'm all right. Nothing wrong except I overdid it a little too much."

"I think we ought to send for a doctor."

"Don't you dare," Laird grumbled. "Wouldn't trust one of the bastards with a hangnail. Just give me time to catch my breath and I'll be good as new."

His eyes closed, and Mattie watched him silently for a few moments. Then she stood, motioning the girls away, and nodded to Campbell. She drew him aside, lowering her voice. "Hank's not kidding anyone but himself. He's a sick man, and if you're any sort of friend, you'll get him to see a sawbones."

Campbell shook his head. "That's easier said than done."

"Well, he can rest here tonight, but you'd better read him the riot act tomorrow. Another one of those and it's all over."

"Yes, of course, you're right. I'll talk to him first thing in the morning."

Laird was asleep, snoring softly. Handsome Jack Ready lifted him off the floor and carried him toward the rear of the house. No one spoke for a long while, then Mattie shrugged and looked around at the girls.

"All right, let's see some smiles. Off your butts and look sexy! The evening's still young."

CHAPTER 18

The compound lay still and dark under a midnight sky. Trudy paused at the window of her bedroom, eyes watchful, alert to any sign of movement. Fireflies darted through the night, brief flickers swiftly dimmed, but everything appeared normal. She eased onto the windowsill, sat listening a moment longer, then dropped silently to the ground.

Walking to the corner of the house, Trudy again hesitated, once more scanning the darkness. Her heart was thumping, a steady drumbeat in her ears, and her pulse quickened. By now, after all the times she'd sneaked out of the house, she would have thought to control her fears. Yet it was always the same, her palms damp and a fluttering sensation in the pit of her stomach. She drew a deep breath, calming her nerves, and gathered her skirt in a wadded bunch above her knees. Then she ran, hurrying across the open ground toward the stables. There, without pausing to catch her breath, she circled the building and disappeared into the trees along the creek.

Behind her, a figure emerged from the shadows of the blacksmith shed. Her direction was obvious, and there was no need for haste. She was easily followed.

Once in the trees, Trudy turned upstream, walking now but still clutching her skirt for speed. The scary part was crossing the compound, and her fears always diminished after she'd gained the safety of darkened woods. Her excitement mounted and her skin began tingling with anticipation. Her thoughts leaped ahead, to the swimming hole . . . and Roberto.

She felt giddy and slightly flushed, knowing he was already there, waiting for her. A warm dampness spread between her legs, and her loins began to ache. She tried to slow her pace,

mocked herself for rushing to meet him. All her urgency and need was shamelessly apparent. She should tease and tantalize, force him to wait long past the appointed hour. Instead of throwing herself at him, she should madden him with elusiveness, play indifferent to his charms. But she had no pride where he was concerned, nor was she cut out to play silly games, act the coquette. She wanted him, needed to feel him inside her, and to pretend otherwise might somehow spoil it.

Besides, she could never fool Roberto anyway. Even as children he could divine her moods, understand what she was thinking before she thought it. In that sense he was very much like her father. He could see through her in an instant! Her secrets laid bare at a glance.

Hurrying along in the dark, it occurred to her that lately she'd thought of little else. For some reason, since her father had left for Kansas, the similarities between them had become more pronounced in her mind. It had nothing to do with looks or build, for in that way they were almost exact opposites. Of course, she had to admit they were uncommonly handsome—very attractive men—but it was still something aside from physical attributes. Though it was difficult to pinpoint, it seemed to her the similarities were of an inner nature. On the surface, one was brash and outspoken while the other was solemn and reserved, so that pretty much eliminated character traits. Or at least the kind that were obvious. Instead, it had to do with . . . strength . . . assurance . . . some certainty of self that emanated from within . . . felt rather than seen. Perhaps nothing they displayed, but rather a quieter force that somehow affected those around them. A sense of being sheltered . . . perfectly secure . . . less vulnerable with them than alone. Still, she could take care of herself, and she wasn't given to the vapors in times of stress. The very idea of a . . . protector . . . seemed to her a sign of personal weakness, and yet she somehow felt snug, curiously safe, in their presence. It was all very confusing.

Then she broke clear of the trees, stepped into the glade, and saw him. Roberto was standing beside the swimming hole, smoking a cigarette; as he took a drag, the fiery tip glowed, outlining his profile in a flare of light. Trudy was mesmerized, the aura of his features captured forever in her

mind's eye, and a moment slipped past before she found her voice. When she spoke his name, Roberto turned, tossing his cigarette into the water, and moved toward her. She ran the last few steps and he laughed, caught her in his arms and swung her around, brought her down in a tight embrace. His mouth covered hers, and she thrust herself against him, clutching him in fierce possession. The kiss was warm and long, their tongues entwined, and at last he groaned, pulled his head back, and looked into her face.

"Madre mío! You make a man wait all night and then you drive him loco."

"You!" Trudy kissed the tip of his nose. "No, *caro mío,* I'm the one who's crazy. Just look at me! I ran all the way, and now I'm hot and sweaty and smell of goats."

"You smell of love, *querida.* The scent of it fills my head and makes me dizzy."

"And you lie; but don't stop, you do it beautifully."

"Hmmm." Roberto pursed his lips, studied her with mock gravity. "Perhaps you're right. I do detect a faint aroma. Shall we have a swim . . . before we make love . . . just to refresh ourselves, eh?"

"Válgame Dios! Have I run all this way for a swim?"

"Well, one never knows when a woman talks of sweat and goats. *Verdad?"*

"You fool!" Trudy laughed, and took his head in her hands. "Would you waste our night on talk when I beg to be loved?"

"Sí, no more talk. We will love and swim and love again, and who knows what the night—"

A branch snapped in the woods. Roberto stiffened, head raised, and quickly pushed her aside. His hand went to the pistol on his belt, and he advanced a few steps, peering into the darkness.

"Quién es? Show yourself, pronto!"

There was a moment of silence, then a figure emerged from the trees. Trudy gasped as he stepped into the clearing, and Roberto seemed turned to stone, the pistol forgotten. Ramon Morado advanced a few steps further and halted, his features set in a grim scowl. He ignored his son, eyes fixed instead on Trudy. Even in the dark she could feel the inten-

sity of his gaze, and when he spoke, there was an undercurrent of rage, barely restrained, in his voice.

"We will say nothing of this night, *señorita.*Not for your sake, or the sake of this *traidor*"—he dismissed Roberto with a gesture—"but for the sake of your father. Agreed?"

"Ramon, listen to me." Trudy moved to Roberto's side, took his arm. "I love Roberto! We want to be married and—"

"*Silencio!* You will go home . . . now!"

"Ramon, *por favor,* you must—"

"Now, señorita! Do not test my patience further."

Trudy wilted before his fury. She cast a terrorstricken glance at Roberto, and he nodded. For an instant no one moved, then she turned, tears streaming down her cheeks, and ran toward the trees. At the edge of the clearing, she paused and looked back—father and son were immobile, staring at each other—and her hand went out to them like a wounded bird. She seemed on the verge of saying something, but suddenly she whirled away and vanished into the darkness.

An eerie stillness settled over the clearing. For a long while neither of the men moved, and between them there was a sense of suppressed violence. Ramon's eyes were hard and cold, unforgiving, and Roberto regarded him with a look of wary hostility. At last, his mouth twisted in a grimace, Ramon broke the silence.

"Were the *patrón* standing here, you would be a dead man."

"Perhaps." Roberto nodded. "But I would not die easily."

"*Mil Cristos!* Are you so stupid? I stand in the *patrón's* place, sworn to protect his daughter."

"*Sí,* Papa, your footsteps were always those of the *patrón's* shadow. So what will you do now, kill your own son?"

"Do not mock me! You are a curse upon my name . . . *bicho* . . . vermin!"

"Why, because I laid with a *gringa* lady? You heard her yourself, she loves me. And if it eases your conscience, I feel the same."

"You truly are an *imbécil.* You think with your *cojones* and talk nonsense."

"Careful, old man." Roberto's voice was edged. "There is no shame in what we've done."

"No shame!" Ramon thundered. *"Sangre de Cristo!* You have betrayed the *patrón*. You have violated his daughter . . . his only daughter!"

"Don't talk to me of shame! In the same breath you condemn me, you say a Morado is not good enough for a *gringa* lady. Yet I am good enough to risk my life killing the *patrón's* enemies. *Verdad?"*

Roberto paused, his eyes filled with disgust. "The shame is yours, Papa! You place the interests of *El Patrón* before those of your own family—"

"Enough!"

"You even talk like a gringo . . . *El Patrón's loro!"*

Ramon hit him. The blow caught Roberto flush on the jaw, staggered him backward, and he dropped to one knee. His expression was a mixture of shock and outrage, and he fixed his father with a look of feral savagery. As he climbed to his feet, Ramon struck again, smashing his nose, then buried a gnarled fist in his stomach. Roberto folded at the waist, gasping for breath, his lungs on fire. Wordlessly, with a sort of methodical stoicism, Ramon beat him into the ground. The blows were measured and brutal, delivered without mercy, driving him sideways, then to his knees, and finally flat on his face in the dirt. Ramon stood over him, hardly winded, waiting to see if he would rise. After a time, when there was no sign of movement, he hooked a toe under the youngster's shoulder and rolled him onto his back.

Roberto groaned, slowly regained his senses, then began retching and levered himself up on one elbow. His face was a bloody mask, lips swollen, and his nose crooked at an odd angle, no longer a handsome sight. He gagged, spit out a broken tooth, and shook his head. At last, eyes still glazed, he pushed himself to his hands and knees, looked up at his father. His mouth moved, frothing crimson bubbles, the words fragmented.

"Well done, Papa . . . he will be proud of you . . . your *patrón."*

"He will never know my shame," Ramon said coldly. "And as for you, listen to me well, *bicho.* Leave Santa Guerra

tonight, and never look back. You are no longer *mi hijo!* I wipe you from memory . . . *sabe?*"

Without waiting for a reply, Ramon turned and walked away. Roberto heaved to his feet, wobbled backward and almost fell, then caught himself, stood erect. His eyes were wild, homicidal.

"I'll be back, Papa. We have a debt—the *patrón* and I—a blood debt. . . . I swear it on your head!"

Ramon halted, hand resting on the butt of his pistol, tempted to end it there. He felt Roberto's gaze boring into his shoulder blades, and he knew it was no idle threat. Yet too much had passed between them tonight, and he decided to wait, hopeful there would never be another time. His hand slowly relaxed and he continued on into the woods. Out of the dark, without a trace of emotion, his voice drifted back across the clearing.

"If you return, Roberto, I will kill you myself."

CHAPTER 19

"Go ahead and get dressed. Then we'll have a talk."

Tom Parker left Laird in the examination room and returned to his office. He walked to the desk, sat down, and methodically filled his pipe from a humidor. After tamping down the tobacco he struck a match and sucked the pipe to life. Then he leaned back in the swivel chair, which creaked ominously under his weight, and studied the ceiling with a look of deliberation.

The physician was an old man, with a face like ancient ivory and hands webbed by blue ropy veins. He'd practiced medicine in San Antonio for nearly forty years, and in that time he thought he'd become hardened to misery and death. But today was different. He suddenly felt the weight of responsibility and resented having to play the role of God. He admired Hank Laird, considered him a friend, and the prospects of the next few minutes were particularly bitter. There was no way to approach it tactfully, not with a man like Laird; he found himself wishing the conversation could somehow be postponed. It wouldn't be pleasant.

After a few minutes Laird entered the office, shrugging into his coat. He crossed the room and took a seat beside the desk. The two men stared at one another a moment, almost like duelists sizing up an opponent, then Laird smiled.

"What's the verdict, Doc? Think I'll live?"

"A poor choice of words, Hank."

"Hell, it's no worse than your bedside manner. You look like you've just come from a wake."

"Hank, you can joke all you want"—Parker hesitated, slowly removed the pipe from his mouth—"but it's not making it any easier on either of us."

"That bad, huh?"

"Yes, I'm afraid it is."

Laird regarded him with a level gaze. "Let's have it, then. And none of your fancy lingo. Give it to me in plain English."

"You've got a bum ticker," Parker informed him. "To be precise, angina pectoris."

"You're sure . . . no doubts?"

"Very sure. It's hardly a diagnosis I'd make lightly. All the symptoms are there, and the seizure you had in Kansas was . . . merely a warning."

"God's teeth!" Laird growled. "It just doesn't make sense. I'm strong as a horse. Never felt better in my life!"

Parker nodded, took a couple of puffs on his pipe. "Hank, your heart's like a piece of machinery. It was made to handle a certain load, and when you overwork it then you run the risk that one day it'll just quit."

"Aye, and you're a sneaky old bird, aren't you? I've the feeling you're trying to tell me something."

"I'm saying you've pushed yourself too hard for too many years, and it's got to stop. Otherwise your heart's liable to stop."

"Liable to or will?"

"Depends." Parker knocked the dottle from his pipe and placed it in an ashtray. "If you give up cigars and whiskey—"

"Christ!"

"—get plenty of rest and take it easy with women, then you could live to a ripe old age."

"And if I don't?" Laird's eyes bored into him, demanding frankness. "How long have I got?"

"A year at the outside, maybe less. Right now, you're like a fine timepiece that's been overwound. A few more turns on the stem, and one day the mainspring will just pop. I couldn't explain it any better than that."

Laird's expression revealed nothing. He uncoiled from the chair and rose to his feet. "Thanks, Doc. I'll let you know how it comes out."

"Hank, a word of advice." Parker leaned forward, very earnest now. "I believe Angela's with you?"

"Her and the girl both, over at the hotel."

"Then I suggest you have a talk with her. You're not a

man to shed his vices easily, and I suspect you'll need all the help you can get."

"Aye, it's a thought."

Laird nodded and jammed his hat on his head. He walked to the door, then paused, looking back. He seemed on the verge of saying something but apparently changed his mind. His mouth ticked in a smile, then the door opened and closed and he was gone.

On the street, Laird walked toward the center of town in a mild daze. For all his outer calm, he'd been shaken by Doc Parker's report, but he found it difficult to accept the truth. In Wichita, the morning after his attack, he'd felt fine except for a monstrous hangover. All the way back to Texas he had experienced only minor discomfort, like a band being tightened around his chest. And upon arriving in San Antonio, where Angela and Trudy met him for their annual shopping spree, he'd convinced himself there was no reason for concern. Still, he hadn't forgotten the knife-edged pain, those moments of choking for air, and Josh Campbell's stiff lecture the next morning. Merely as a precaution, certain it was some passing ailment, he'd gone to see Doc Parker.

Now, with an almost grudging sense of realization, he knew he'd been wrong. The ailment wouldn't pass, and only by turning himself into a monk could he hope to prolong his life. Yet he couldn't reconcile himself to such an existence. Perhaps he could cut down on his work load at the ranch, delegate greater responsibility to Ramon and some of the older vaqueros. That was something he could accept, for it in no way diluted his authority, and he would still have the final word. But a life without women or whiskey—purged of his favorite vices—that was no life at all. The very thought sickened him, for he would no longer be a man but rather a *manso*, a tame bull. And that wasn't his idea of living! Better to be dead and buried than gelded by his own hand.

Crossing the plaza, his eye was drawn to the Alamo, and the sight of it somehow strengthened his resolve. There were ways of dying and there were ways of living, and if a man was to retain his self-respect, then he had to make the choice for himself. Of course, he had to consider Angela and Trudy, and that would involve a certain amount of compromise. But he was confident it could be done, and without resorting to

lies. A little evasion, spiced with a few half-truths, would serve very nicely. His stride suddenly brisk, chin jutting out defiantly, he crossed the plaza and hurried toward the hotel.

Upstairs, he entered the suite in the midst of a family squabble. Trudy had a new hand-tooled saddle thrown over the back of an easy chair, and was sitting astraddle it, her dress hiked up past her knees, beaming with pride. Angela stood off to one side, her expression cloudy, delivering a sharp rebuke on the girl's unladylike behavior. As he came through the door, they both turned, and Angela greeted him with a look of immense relief.

"Oh, I'm so glad you've returned, Henry. Honestly, your daughter has just driven me to distraction. She's simply impossible!"

"Is she now? And what seems to be the problem?"

"Look, Pa! Look here!" Trudy flung her legs wide, rearing back in the saddle. "Got a new rig. Center fire and tapaderas, the whole works. And look at this!" She kicked free of one stirrup and thrust an ornate, hand-stitched boot high into the air. "Aren't they beauties? Soft as calfskin and fits like a glove!"

"See! See what I mean!" Angela declared. "I took her shopping and she insisted on buying all this . . . this equipment!" Laird sensed there was something more involved than the saddle. A curious discord between mother and daughter—nothing he could put his finger on—but an element of conflict that hadn't existed before his trip to Wichita. It puzzled him, for Trudy was attempting to mask her defiance with a sort of sportive impudence. That wasn't at all like his daughter, and vaguely disturbing; she normally went out of her way to flaunt her defiance. Still, he could handle only one problem at a time, and at the moment Angela was on a tear. Her voice rose in pitch.

"On top of everything else, I practically had to drag her into a dress shop! And after I went to all the trouble of choosing new gowns, she won't even try them on. She's been perched—literally perched!—on that saddle ever since we got back."

"Awww, that's not fair, Mama! I told you I'd try 'em on.

But they haven't brought the water up, and there's no sense spoiling a new dress when I'm all hot and sticky."

"That's another thing, Henry," Angela gestured imperiously at the washstand. "I ordered fresh water so we could have a sponge bath, and that was over an hour ago. I must say, after all the years we've stayed in the Menger you'd think they could at least give us decent service."

Laird went to the washstand, collected the pitcher, and left the room without a word. Outside, he walked to the edge of a balcony which looked down upon the marble-floored lobby. He leaned over the balustrade, sighting carefully, and dropped the pitcher. An instant later crockery exploded across the lobby, and the desk clerk ducked for cover.

"If we can't get water," Laird thundered, "then by the Sweet Jesus, we've no need of pitchers!"

He turned, marched back into the suite, and slammed the door. "You'll have water in a jiffy. Now, why don't you run along and slip into one of your new gowns. It's not often I get to see you all gussied up, and I'm sure it would please your mother."

"Whatever you say, Pa." Trudy dismounted from the chair and moved to the door of a connecting bedroom. Over her shoulder she laughed and looked around. "I'm not taking my boots off, though. Not for anybody!"

The door closed and Angela collapsed into a chair with a deep sigh. "Honestly, she grows more like you every day, Henry. And that little episode with the pitcher hardly set a good example. It was crude of you, Henry. Very crude."

"Aye, but it'll damn sure fetch the water."

Angela couldn't argue the point. Within minutes every pitcher in the suite had been filled, and the hotel manager dropped by with a personal apology. Laird finally shooed them all out, chuckling to himself, and went to stand by the window. Gazing across the plaza at the Alamo, his expression slowly changed, became somber and somehow pensive. Angela sat watching him for a long while. Her temper was improved by the appearance of the water, but she was puzzled by the look on his face. He appeared cocky and assured, which was all quite normal, but there was something in his eyes that troubled her. Something she'd never seen before.

"Is anything wrong, Henry?"

"No, nothing's wrong. Just thoughtful, that's all."

"Are you sure? You seem rather . . . far away."

"Oh, I was just thinking of the financial panic back East. It's fortunate I sold when I did. There's many a cattleman that'll be wintering his herd in Kansas this year. And more than a few of them will go broke."

The room was pleasantly dark and cool, but his face was framed in a spill of sunlight. She studied him a moment in silence, unsettled by some feeling she couldn't define. "You're not being honest with me, Henry."

"Honest?" Laird caught her eye for an instant, looked quickly away. "I don't take your meaning."

"I think you do. You're worried about something, but it's not those other ranchers. I know you too well to be fooled by that, so there's no need trying to hide it from me."

"Aye, I suppose you're right." Laird pursed his lips, seeming to deliberate. "I went to see Doc Parker this afternoon."

Angela stiffened, sat erect. "Then something *is* wrong."

"Well, there is and there isn't. I was off my feed a bit up in Kansas, so I thought it was worth having him look me over."

"And?"

"Oh, he says I have a spot of heart trouble—"

"Your heart!" Angela rose, her face chalky. "Not a stroke?"

"No, no." Laird waved the thought aside. "Nothing like that. The doc said it's common for men my age, especially them that've overworked themselves. Told me I'd have to take it easier, not push myself so hard. That's all."

"Don't you lie to me, Henry Laird. Is that all he said?"

"God's blood! Would I lie about my health?"

"You haven't answered me. Did Dr. Parker say anything else?"

"Nothing much. Only that I'd be wise to shift some of the duties at the ranch. Let someone else take on a bit of the worry for a while."

"Well, I should think so! And that's exactly what we'll do when we get home."

"We?"

"Don't argue with me, Henry. I know as much about that ranch as you do, and I'm perfectly capable of assuming some of the responsibility."

"Aye, I've no doubt you are. But that wasn't exactly what I had in mind."

"Perhaps not. But the vaqueros certainly won't take orders from an outsider, so I'm the logical choice. Until you're recuperated I'm afraid that's how it will have to be."

Laird gave her a quizzical look. "I never thought you cared that much for the ranch."

"Honestly, there's no fool like an old fool."

Angela crossed the room, halted in front of him. "I don't care two hoots about that ranch, Henry." She ran her arms around his waist, watching his eyes, and smiled. "But I still care about you, even if you are a heathen."

"I'll be damned."

"Oh, you were damned long ago, Henry Laird. But perhaps there's time to save you yet."

"Aye, lass, perhaps there is."

Laird bent to kiss her when suddenly the connecting door swung open. Trudy swirled into the room, hobbled somewhat by her boots, and pirouetted across the floor in a yellow organdy gown. Angela disengaged herself from his arms, blushing like a schoolgirl, and Laird glanced from his wife to his daughter with a lopsided smile. Trudy laughed, whirling faster and faster, and spun back through the door into her bedroom.

"Encore! Encore! Just call me in time for supper."

The door closed. A moment later they heard the latch click into place, then Laird took her in his arms and they were alone.

A week later Laird left the house and walked toward the stables. With Angela and Trudy, he had returned to Santa Guerra the day before, and almost immediately his suspicions were confirmed. All around him, particularly among *Los Lerdeños,* he sensed a conspiracy of silence. Angela and the girl continued their pretense—went out of their way to act normally—yet the false note he'd detected in San Antonio was still there. The servants, on the other hand, lacked the guile for deception. Everyone fell quiet when he approached, unable to meet his eyes, and their natural gaiety seemed to have vanished. Even the vaqueros were acting strangely; but he was troubled most by his old friend Ramon

Morado. The *segundo* wasn't himself, and since the family had returned he'd scarcely spoken to Trudy. Once they were thick as thieves, and now they treated each other like . . . lepers.

It was damned odd, and he wouldn't tolerate being played the fool. He meant to have some answers.

Laird found Ramon at the corral. The *patrón's* grulla stallion was being curried and groomed by a stablehand, and *segundo* was leaning against the fence, supervising the morning ritual. He straightened as Laird approached, his expression guarded and tense, almost as though he dreaded the meeting.

"*Buenos días, Patrón. Cómo está usted?*"

"*Bueno, Ramon. Y tu?*"

"*Muy bueno, gracias.*"

Their exchange was formal, curiously strained. Laird was accustomed to being greeted with the warmth of times past, and the change irritated him, made him uncomfortable. He decided to force the issue.

"You seem troubled, *compadre*. What bothers you?"

"Why, nothing, *Patrón* . . . nothing at all."

"*Sí*, there's something. Be frank with me, is it our new arrangement? Do you object to taking orders from Señora Laird?"

"*La Madama?* No, *Patrón*, I swear to you. Never!"

"Then perhaps it's Cordoba . . . the *renegados*. Have you told me everything?"

"Everything, *Patrón*. We cannot catch all, but those we catch, we hang. And that leaves fewer *ladróns* to steal our cows."

Laird eyed him, thoughtful. "Your sons, then? I know we've lost men. Were either of them wounded . . . killed . . . fighting Cordoba's bravos?"

"*Gracias, Patrón*, but neither of them have come to harm."

"Then they're still leading the patrols . . . *sí?*"

Ramon glanced aside. "Only Luis, *Patrón.*"

"And your eldest, Roberto? What of him?"

"Roberto . . . he left Santa Guerra, *Patrón* . . . a month ago, perhaps longer, I forget."

"You forget!" Laird's eyebrows drew together in a frown.

"You're a poor liar, old friend. Roberto's whole life was here —*Los Lerdeños* and his family—why would he leave?"

"A personal matter, *Patrón*." Ramon shrugged, and his voice trailed off. "A thing between father and son, nothing more."

Laird studied his downcast face, considering. Somehow it all tied together—the funeral atmosphere around the ranch, Angela and Trudy, and now—suddenly he made the connection! He felt a stab of fear, some inner dread that warned him to walk away and leave it alone. Yet he had to know. His mouth hardened, and when he spoke the words were clipped, brittle.

"There is great sadness among our people these days. It has to do with Roberto, doesn't it?"

Ramon winced, unable to meet his gaze. *"Sí, Patrón."*

"And you say Roberto left a month ago?"

"A month, perhaps a little longer."

"Perhaps a great deal longer," Laird observed. "Perhaps shortly after I departed for Kansas . . . isn't that true?"

Ramon stared hard at the grulla, watching the stablehand brush and stroke the stallion's sleek hide. His expression was like that of a trapped animal, grievously hurt and afraid, jaws locked tight against the pain. When he remained silent, Laird took his arm, slowly turned him around.

"Let there be no lies between us, old friend. Roberto would never leave Santa Guerra, not of his own will. You sent him away, didn't you?"

"I had no choice, *Patrón*. He was my son."

Laird nodded. "You couldn't kill him, so you ordered him to leave. Isn't that it?"

A bleak stare was his only answer, and Laird went on. "But it happened right after I left, didn't it, Ramon? I asked a personal favor of you—and you gave me your word—and you kept your word, didn't you? What was it you said—you'd watch over her like she was your own flesh and blood—and that's what you did, wasn't it, Ramon? You watched over her too well. You caught her! You caught her and Roberto, wasn't that how it happened? The two of them, Ramon . . . *together* . . . you caught them together!"

There was a prolonged silence. Laird glowered at him, breathing heavily, barely able to control himself. A sharp

pain knifed through his chest, but he ignored it, and then, infuriated by the silence, his temper snapped. For the first time in all the years they'd known each other, he cursed Ramon Morado.

"Goddamn you, say something! Answer me!"

Ramon closed his eyes, slowly shook his head. "I would cut off my arm for you—"

"I don't want your bloody arm! I want an answer!"

"Perdónenme, Patrón. Forgive me. I cannot."

Laird turned from him and strode toward the house.

Laird was seated behind his desk, eyes fixed on the ceiling. For the past hour, he'd sat perfectly still, trying to collect himself. The pain in his chest had gradually diminished, but his anger was merely smothered, like banked coals. He wasn't at all certain he could control it, even though he knew the effort was necessary. The girl had his temper, and a shouting match between father and daughter would accomplish nothing. With no real conviction, he kept repeating the thought to himself while he waited.

When the front door opened, he sat forward and busied himself with a stack of correspondence. There were footsteps in the hall and a moment later Trudy entered the study. She was dressed in a charro outfit and appeared to be out of breath. The jingle bobs on her spurs chimed melodically as she hurried across the room.

"You sent for me, Pa?"

"Aye, that I did." Laird tossed the papers aside, motioned with a brusque gesture. "Sit down."

Trudy gave him a quick, intent look. Outwardly he appeared calm and impassive, but she wasn't deceived. He was seething inside, and she knew it the instant he'd spoken. She removed her hat, brushing back a damp curl, and took a chair in front of the desk.

"Hope it's important, Pa. I just about ruined a horse getting here." She glanced airily around the room. "Where's Mama?"

"Your mother's taking inventory in the commissary." Laird hesitated, considering. "In fact, that's one reason I sent for you. We've something to discuss, and it's best done while she's not around."

"Oh? What's the big secret?"

"Secret indeed! You and your mother evidently thought to keep it just that—or did you even talk about it?"

"Talk about what?"

"No, probably not. Her being so delicate about such things, she couldn't even mention it to me."

Laird pondered it a moment, and then, almost as though he was thinking out loud, he went on. "I suppose the pair of you figured it would go away if you ignored it long enough. Or at least I wouldn't find out—which pretty much amounts to the same thing—doesn't it?"

"I don't follow you, Pa."

"I think you do," Laird said flatly. "I had a talk with Ramon this morning."

Trudy's gaze was bland, revealing nothing. "I still don't see your point."

"Well now, it's quite simple, though it seems I was the last to learn of it. He told me Roberto has left the ranch."

"What's that got to do with me? I knew he was gone, but I just assumed—"

Laird's fist crashed into the desk top. "None of your lies! I'll have the truth, and by the Living God, I'll have it from you . . . not somebody else."

"Now, wait right there!" Trudy flared. "Are you trying to say there was some sort of funny business going on . . . between Roberto and me?"

Laird squinted at her. "Are you telling me you're still a virgin? Are you, lass? Look me in the eye and say it's a fact. Can you do that?"

"All right, it's true!" Trudy looked at him with utter directness. "But it's not like you think, Pa. Roberto and I intended—"

"Damn your intentions!"

Laird rose, flushed with anger, and moved around the desk. Trudy stood, quickly backed away a few steps, then stopped and faced him defiantly. He halted, glaring at her, and his words were hard, contemptuous.

"Are you blind, or have you simply lost your wits? Everyone on Santa Guerra knows what you've done, and they care nothing for your intentions. You've cost Ramon a son and you've made me look the fool . . . and the vaqueros—

Sweet Mother of God!—can you imagine what they're saying about the *patrón*'s daughter? Can you just imagine?"

"To hell with them! Let 'em think what they want!"

"Then you've no shame, none a'tall?"

"C'mon, Pa, don't talk to me about shame. You're not worried because I lost . . . my virginity . . . you're only worried because you lost face. That's it, and you damn well know it!"

"You little fool, it's not you or me that lost. It's Ramon!"

"What a crock of—"

Laird slapped her. The blow left a vivid welt on her cheek and brought tears to her eyes. Her mouth fell open, and she stood, blinking with childish astonishment, as her father walked to the door. There he paused, motionless, for several seconds and finally looked around. His eyes were moist, rimmed with sadness, and his words were a distorted whisper.

"Someday you'll understand how much I love you. When you do, you'll know what it cost Ramon to lose his son."

Laird stepped into the hall, and there was a moment of leaden silence. Then Trudy gasped, suddenly covered her mouth with her hand. A rush of tears blinded her and she slumped into the chair, softly began a low, keening cry.

She understood.

CHAPTER 20

The trial was a circus. Newspapers ballyhooed it as a milestone, and called it the biggest event to take place since Texas's scalawag governor departed office earlier in the year. By late April the sensationalism had crested, and people converged on Corpus Christi from all directions to see the spectacle. Their mood was carnival and a holiday atmosphere settled over the city. They had come to gawk at Hank Laird and watch him brought to earth.

Unlike his previous legal battles, Laird wasn't defending himself against railroad cartels or carpetbagger politicians. The plaintiff was John Kelton, a veteran of the war against Mexico. He claimed that Laird had appropriated his land grant, 640 acres on the eastern boundary of Santa Guerra, awarded to him by the state for two year's service in the army. The newspapers billed it as a David and Goliath extravaganza, the common man challenging the ruthless land baron. It fired the public's imagination, but those who flocked to Corpus Christi were only marginally concerned with justice. Their chief interest was in witnessing one of their own perform the role of giant killer.

John Kelton became an instant celebrity. He was the first man, Mexican or white, ever to sue Henry Laird over land rights. Although eighty-two years old, and an admitted drifter without family, he was lionized by press and public alike. His lawyer, a young firebrand from a prominent Corpus Christi family, made equally good copy. He promptly established the validity of Kelton's land grant, then paraded to the stand a long line of witnesses who testified to Laird's outrageous methods. Several Mexicans, all of them *derecho* holders, told of relatives who had mysteriously disappeared after making demands on the *patrón* of Santa Guerra. Like a

phoenix, Joe Starling even made a brief appearance, describing the violent tactics Laird had used against him in past railroad ventures. The key witnesses, however, were three men who had observed the plaintiff—repeatedly described as a doddering old man—physically ejected from Santa Guerra land by Laird's vaqueros. It was damning testimony, and resulted in explosive newspaper headlines.

Warren Pryor objected often and strenuously, filed several motions for mistrial, and ultimately drew a contempt citation when he charged the court with prejudicial conduct. But his histrionics did little for Laird's defense, and it was clear even to the spectators that he had alienated the judge. Throughout it all Hank Laird merely listened and watched, wisely refusing to take the stand. His only display of emotion came with the appearance of Joe Starling, whom he hadn't seen in nearly six years. Then the atmosphere grew charged with violence, and afterward an armed deputy was assigned to escort Starling to the train station. During the remainder of the trial, Laird stared off into space, utterly contemptuous of the entire proceeding.

On the final day an overflow crowd filled the courtroom. Down front, Laird and Warren Pryor were seated at the defense table. Across from them were John Kelton and his counsel, Ernest Kruger, and on the bench sat Judge Marcus Grisham. Earlier that morning Pryor had presented closing arguments for the defense, and now it was time for the plaintiff's lawyer to deliver his summation. With the stage set, and the spectators hanging on his every word, Kruger rose and approached the bench.

A tall man, lean and muscular, he had a deep baritone voice and a commanding presence. His gestures were restrained; his manner brisk and businesslike. And he wasted no time on formalities.

"Your Honor, we have before us a classic example of one man holding himself above the law. In the past three days we have heard testimony from eight witnesses regarding the piratical acts and the villainous methods of Henry Laird. That testimony has withstood cross-examination, and in no way has it been refuted by the defense. In fact, the reluctance of the defendant to take the witness stand—and subject himself

to sworn testimony—in large measure corroborates everything we've heard in this courtroom."

Kruger paused for effect, slowly turned from the bench. Then he leveled his finger at Laird. "There sits a modern-day feudal lord! A throwback to the Dark Ages, and all that was vile and base in the human spirit. We know that he rules his vaqueros as if they were vassals. We know that he rules his land as if it were a medieval kingdom. We know that on Santa Guerra his word is law, and there are none who dare oppose him. Those who have tried have simply vanished, never again seen by their families. But then, we are not here investigating murder—nor is Henry Laird charged with killing poor, defenseless Mexicans."

A low murmur swept the courtroom, and the crowd watched in awe as the young attorney attempted to stare down Laird. Neither man wavered, and after a moment Kruger shook his head in disgust, then turned back to the bench. The onlookers waited, hushed and expectant.

"Henry Laird is charged with robbing an old man of his legal land rights. There is evidence that he took the land by force, and there is evidence that he held it by force. Further, there is proof that he used his vaqueros as an instrument of intimidation to bully and threaten a man who honorably served his country in time of war. I ask the court to award the plaintiff his rightful land. I ask the court to award the plaintiff one hundred thousand dollars in punitive damages. I ask justice for John Kelton, and through it, the swift and certain censure of Henry Laird."

The crowd broke out in applause, and several men rose to their feet, cheering the young lawyer. Presently, after the spectators were quieted and order restored, Kruger rested the case for the plaintiff. Judge Grisham immediately called noon recess, informing them he would hand down his decision that afternoon. His announcement caught everyone by surprise, for in a case of such magnitude the decision was normally delayed several days. Before counsel for either side could respond, the judge stepped from the bench and hurried into his chambers.

Warren Pryor conferred briefly with his client, expressing guarded optimism. It appeared they had lost, he admitted, but the judgment could be delayed almost indefinitely

through appeals. Laird gave him a dark look, suddenly reminded that the tactic had been of limited value in past cases. He was about to raise the issue when Ernest Kruger approached and halted in front of them.

"Warren." Kruger nodded. "Mr. Laird."

Laird bristled, his features livid, and Pryor quickly took the lead. "Very nice presentation, Kruger. What can we do for you?"

"Nothing. But I thought I might do something for you."

"Oh? And what's that?"

"It occurred to me that both parties could benefit by an out-of-court settlement."

"That's a bit presumptuous, isn't it?"

"Not at all," Kruger countered. "You've obviously lost the case, and while I assume you'll appeal, that would only delay things for my client. From the look on Judge Grisham's face, I suspect it would also result in a harsher judgment against Mr. Laird."

Pryor shrugged. "I don't necessarily agree, but we're willing to listen. What sort of settlement did you have in mind?"

"A quitclaim deed in exchange for thirty dollars an acre."

"Go to hell!" Laird grated. "And take your goddamn client with you!"

"Not so fast, Hank." Pryor took his arm and pulled him aside. Lowering his voice, he motioned for Kruger to wait. "Now, let's be reasonable, Hank. Everything he said is true, and under the circumstances it's not all that bad an offer."

"In a pig's ass! It's triple what the land's worth, and I'll not be sandbagged by some young squirt with a fancy education."

"Hank, listen to me and try to control your temper. We've lost the case—that's a foregone conclusion—and Kruger's right. Thirty dollars an acre is less than a quarter of what the judge might award in damages. And you'd still lose the land in the bargain, so it's a compromise very much to your advantage."

"I pay you to win cases, not compromise."

"I know, but that's not what we're discussing. And before you get too huffy, there's something else you should consider. If the old man wins a big judgment, then a thousand more like him will crawl out of the woodwork. On the other

hand, if we settle out of court, then it won't look so tempting, and it just might discourage a lot of people from bringing suit."

"If you'd done your job," Laird informed him, "then we wouldn't be in this fix. You were supposed to find people like Kelton and buy 'em out, or have you forgot?"

Pryor flushed, gave him a hangdog look. "I've done the best I could, Hank. Unfortunately, we have a more immediate problem, and all the recriminations in the world won't solve that."

"Aye, it's a sorry kettle of fish, and there's no denying it."

Laird pondered it a moment, then turned and gestured to Kruger. The young lawyer joined them, and before Pryor realized what was happening, he found himself excluded from the conversation.

"I'll give you twenty dollars an acre," Laird announced. "Take it or leave it."

Kruger smiled. "I won't haggle with you, Mr. Laird. And if you'll allow me to say so, you're in no position to horse-trade."

"Think you're pretty goddamn smart, don't you?"

"Smart enough to know when I have the upper hand. It's thirty dollars an acre, Mr. Laird." Kruger paused, met his gaze with an amused expression. "Take it or leave it."

"Mother of Christ! You'd kick a man when he's down, wouldn't you?"

"Every time, Mr. Laird. Wouldn't you?"

"Aye, I suppose I would." Laird studied him for several seconds, found no sign of weakness. Finally he threw up his hands in defeat. "You're a bloody thief, but it seems I've got no choice. Tell the old man he's got himself a deal."

"A commendable decision, Mr. Laird. I'll draw up the papers and have them ready for signature in the morning."

Kruger nodded and walked away. Laird watched him rejoin John Kelton, boiling inwardly as the old man listened a moment, then let out a gleeful cackle of victory. A bit crestfallen, Pryor edged forward, his smile tentative.

"Well done, Hank. Couldn't have handled it better myself."

"Aye, and it cost me a pretty penny to find that out. You're fired, Warren. Crate up my files and send me a bill."

Pryor's jaw dropped open, then he began muttering, trying to summon back his voice. But the momentary lapse cost him any chance to reply. Laird jammed his hat on his head and stalked from the courtroom.

Early that evening Laird left the hotel and walked along the streets of Corpus Christi. His mood was somber, and he scarcely noticed passersby as he reflected on the problem at hand. He was absorbed with thoughts of mortality, and the fact that no man, not even one as rich and powerful as himself, could exert his will from the grave. If the course of events was to be altered, then it must be done while he still lived.

Laird still felt the compulsion to wager against time and the vicissitudes of age. Given a choice, he would have followed his original impulse, and ended life as he had lived it. But these days he controlled the urge with an iron discipline. He drank sparingly and harbored his energy, for it had become apparent within the past several months that the timing was all wrong. He couldn't indulge himself with one last fling at the sporting life, nor could his family afford the luxury of his death. All he had built must be consolidated and strengthened, left impregnable so that his legacy would endure whatever threat the future held. Then and only then would he feel free to end it the way he'd planned.

Some aspects of the problem were at least partially resolved. Angela had proved herself to be a capable manager, assuming the administrative duties and day-by-day details of running a large ranch. Ramon Morado, with a beefed-up force of vaqueros, had made rustling a hazardous occupation, and the outlaws now paid dearly everytime they raided Santa Guerra. And this year, for the first time, Laird would forego the pleasures of a summer hiatus in the Kansas cowtowns. He had contracted with a cattle agent to handle the sale of his herds, and while he begrudged the commission, it guaranteed that the agent would be satisfied with nothing less than top dollar.

Still, there was the problem of the ranch itself. Santa Guerra was vulnerable to lawsuit, and today's court action made it clear that possession was no longer nine points of the law. Times had changed, and the tactics he'd used in the

past wouldn't work in the future. Until he had secured title to the land, there was no assurance his family wouldn't lose it all once he was gone. He saw that now, and it had become a matter of utmost priority, one he must resolve without delay.

And then there was Trudy. Every night he lay awake thinking about his daughter, but thus far there were no answers, only tough questions. Her involvement with Roberto—and the boy's hasty departure—was a constant reminder that he hadn't a moment to spare. Though he was certain Angela suspected—or knew—the thought of discussing it with her made him acutely uncomfortable. As a result, they both pretended it hadn't happened, and never once had the incident been mentioned. But he was aware it could happen again, perhaps with disastrous consequences; he realized now his daughter had the appetites of a woman, and no more regard for convention or temperance than he himself possessed. Before it was too late, he had to take whatever steps necessary to preclude another . . . escapade . . . which meant removing the temptation once and for all.

What he had in mind would have to be performed with discretion and craft, and no one, especially Trudy, must ever have a clue. Yet he hadn't the faintest notion of where to start, or at least he hadn't until this morning. Now, though he wasn't fully committed to the idea, he was determined to explore the possibility of killing two birds with one stone.

Laird paused before a building, studying the neatly lettered sign on the ground-floor window. He'd thought to broach the idea tomorrow, but he saw the glow of a lamp inside, and it occurred to him that tonight might be better all the way round. It would be private, with no distractions, and he'd have an opportunity to test the man's character before making a firm decision. He walked to the door and knocked.

Several moments later the latch clicked and Ernest Kruger opened the door. A fleeting look of puzzlement crossed his face, then his expression became flat and guarded. "Good evening, Mr. Laird."

"Evening. I was out for a walk and happened to see your sign. Thought we might have a talk."

"Actually, I think tomorrow would still be best, Mr. Laird.

As a matter of fact, I'm working late tonight trying to finish the Kelton documents."

"It's not Kelton I want to discuss. We've already agreed to terms, so that's water under the bridge."

"I see." Kruger considered briefly, then nodded and stepped aside. "Come in."

Laird moved through the doorway and followed him to an office in the rear of the building. Kruger offered him a chair, crossed behind a desk littered with papers, and took a seat. Though he was barely thirty, there was something impenetrable about the young lawyer. His composure was monumental, and he possessed a sort of personal insensitivity regarding other people's opinion of him, either as a lawyer or a man. Only his eyes moved, alert and penetrating, and he studied Laird with a look of clinical appraisal. Finally, he folded his hands across his vest and settled back in his chair.

"Very well, Mr. Laird, how can I be of service?"

"First off," Laird said shortly, "you can answer a question. Why'd you say all those things about me in court this morning?"

"I had a case to win"—Kruger shrugged, eyebrows raised —"besides which, they were true."

"True! Have you ever set foot on Santa Guerra? Have you talked to any of my people and asked them whether I've set myself up as some sort of tin god?"

"No, I haven't. But before we brought suit, I made it my business to investigate you and your ranch quite thoroughly."

"Now, is that a fact? Suppose you tell me where you got your information . . . Joe Starling . . . that crowd of backbiters in Brownsville? Is that how you collect your dirt?"

"Mr. Laird, my sources are confidential." Kruger opened a drawer, removed a sheaf of foolscap, and tossed it on the desk. "If you care to examine it, there's a list of nearly all the vaqueros employed on your ranch. By a curious coincidence, the same family names appear over and over again. And unless I'm mistaken, those families are now into their third generation of service on Santa Guerra."

"Aye, that they are, and I'm damn proud of it."

"No doubt, but it nonetheless constitutes peonage. Oh, granted, you give them houses and every family a little plot

to garden, but you pay them practically nothing, and we both know it. That's precisely the way the feudal system operated during medieval times, Mr. Laird. So I wasn't exaggerating this morning. You're lord and master, and you operate Santa Guerra like it was a sovereign kingdom beyond any law but your own."

"Who has a better right?" Laird demanded. "I took land nobody wanted and turned it into the biggest ranch in the state of Texas. Of course, now that the herds are built up and all my people sleep with their bellies full, every spoiler this side of Kingdom Come wants a piece of the pie. If they were so bloody set on becoming ranchers, where were they when I was fighting off Comanches and pouring a fortune into improvements? You're a bright young fellow, so answer me that."

"The difference," Kruger observed neutrally, "is that you *took* part of the land. That's no fine distinction, Mr. Laird. You took it rather than bought it. And anyone with valid claim is entitled to legal redress. Years ago, might made right, but that's outdated now. Today, no man is above the law, not even Henry Laird."

"Aye, and I've that little runt of a lawyer to thank for one grand headache."

"Come now, Mr. Laird. Warren Pryor was as much a serf as any of your vaqueros. Unless I miss my guess, he simply did as he was told and tried not to get trampled in the process."

"Judas Priest! You believe in drawing blood, don't you?"

"No offense intended, merely a statement of fact."

Laird pulled in his neck and stared across the desk with a bulldog scowl. "How'd you like to work for me?"

"I beg your pardon?"

"You're not deaf. I said, how'd you like to be my lawyer?"

Kruger pondered the question, then slowly shook his head. "Nothing personal, Mr. Laird, but I don't believe it would work. You see, I don't take orders from my clients, and I suspect that would put us at loggerheads from the very outset."

"Suppose I gave you a free hand, no strings attached?"

"You know, of course, that I would insist on searching out

every derecho holder and land claimant, and paying fair market value for their rights."

"Aye, and you'd have a blank check to do your buying. I can afford it now, so we'd not squabble over money."

"I wonder." Kruger gave him a blank stare, finally dismissed it with a gesture. "No, really, I don't think it would work. If nothing else, I'm opposed to your system of . . . operation . . . and that would always intrude on our business relationship."

"Maybe, maybe not. Suppose you came out to Santa Guerra for a visit? Suppose you talked to my people and found out you're not so almighty right as you think? Would that change your mind?"

There was a moment of calculation while Kruger studied him. The silence grew, stretched. Laird stared him straight in the eye, challenging him, and at last the lawyer nodded.

"Yes, I'll agree to that. But only on the conditions you've just stated."

"God's teeth! Then it's a deal. And let me tell you something, young fellow—you're in for a helluva surprise!"

"I hope so, Mr. Laird. I genuinely hope so."

CHAPTER 21

A swollen ball of orange dipped westward toward the horizon. Laird and Kruger reined to a halt some distance from the holding ground, and their escort fanned out to the rear. Without a word, Trudy rode ahead into the dusty, bawling melee of men and cows. She was lost from sight for a moment, then appeared at the branding fire where she was greeted by the vaqueros with good-natured shouts and a rapid exchange of insults. Kruger understood the gibes, and knew by now that it was her customary way of greeting everyone on the ranch. But he felt a sudden twinge of resentment at her easy, carefree manner with the vaqueros. She had studiously ignored him since his arrival at Santa Guerra.

Their day had begun with an inspection of the compound. Kruger was impressed by the rows of clean, substantially built adobe houses, and even a bit startled by the rigidly enforced sanitation system. Laird explained that cholera had been eliminated on Santa Guerra, and bragged at some length on the low infant-mortality rate among his people. Yet it was *Los Lerdeños* themselves who dispelled any lingering doubt. Laird allowed him to wander freely throughout the compound, and Kruger was pleasantly surprised by his conversations with the people. He found them fiercely loyal to *El Patrón,* and voluble in their praise of all that had been done to provide the good life for them and their families. Despite himself, he had to admit that their condition was better than that of other Mexicans. It went against all his preconceived notions, especially those regarding peonage, but there was no denying that Laird's people lived very well indeed.

Operation of the ranch itself was equally revealing. The vaqueros worked from dawn till dusk, with an enthusiasm

and spirit that belied all Kruger's suspicions. Like spurred centaurs, they herded Laird's cows as though Santa Guerra were their own hacienda, and it was obvious even to an outsider that they took immense pride in their work. By late afternoon, when he'd seen several herds gathered for spring branding, Kruger was slowly forced to the conclusion that he had misjudged both the man and the vitality of his people. It was a kingdom and Laird ruled it according to his own standards, but there was no hint of peonage or servitude. *Los Lerdeños* looked upon themselves as part of Laird's family, and while the word of *El Patrón* was law, no one was under obligation of any sort. The people remained on Santa Guerra because they considered it their home.

Kruger's greatest surprise by far, however, was Trudy Laird. She was unlike any girl he'd ever seen, and not at all what he had expected. People in Brownsville and Corpus Christi spoke of Angela Laird as a grand lady, and he'd thought to find a daughter of the same mold. Instead he found a young hellion with tawny hair and smokey eyes who looked through him as though he weren't there. She was polite but distant, utterly immune to even the slightest compliment, and he was fascinated.

Several times during the day Laird had caught him sneaking peeks at the girl, and now he tried to concentrate his attention on the branding. It was difficult, for Trudy seemed to be everywhere he looked, but he kept his expression bland and directed his remarks to Santa Guerra.

"Very impressive, Mr. Laird. Of course I know little or nothing about the cow business, but if you'll overlook the pun, you run a tight ship."

Laird smiled, pleased by the choice of words. "Aye, it's taken a while, but we've got ourselves a profitable operation. Matter of fact, I sent close to thirty thousand head up the trail this year."

"Evidently you have faith that the economy has recovered."

"Not a matter of faith. My banker in New Orleans keeps me advised, and I'm satisfied the financial panic's run its course. People back East want beef, and if I'm any judge, the market will be higher than ever this season."

"That's curious—about New Orleans, I mean. I'm surprised you haven't opened your own bank."

"Bank! By the Saints, why would I do a thing like that?"

"Well, for one thing, it appears you have a heavy influx of cash every fall. And I suspect the return on your money would be greater by extending loans in Brownsville than it is by merely drawing interest in New Orleans."

"I've no wish to be a moneylender. Besides, as you've just pointed out, the logical place would be Brownsville, and I'll not lift a finger to help those ingrates."

"Yes, of course."

Kruger nodded, smiling to himself, and Laird gave him a narrow look. "What's so funny?"

"Oh, nothing really. I was just thinking of something I heard in Brownsville."

"Don't be bashful, I've a thick skin."

"Well, people there apparently feel you drive a hard bargain when it comes to business. They're fond of saying that beggars throw down their crutches and flee at the sight of Hank Laird."

"Bloody fools!" Laird chewed at his lower lip, thoughtful. "Maybe I'm hard but there's none that'll say I'm unfair. You've seen that here today, or if you haven't, then you're blind as a bat."

Kruger understood he'd been asked a question. "It's tempting, but I can't truthfully say I've made up my mind as yet."

"What's holding you back?"

"I'm the type of person who looks before he leaps, Mr. Laird. Let's just say that certain situations require a longer look than others."

"I've nothing to hide, so look all you please. But I'll expect your answer before you leave in the morning."

Kruger's reply was cut short. A commotion erupted near the branding fire, and Trudy's voice rose to a pitched yell. *"Sangre de Cristo!* Gently, you butchers. Gently!"

Several vaqueros were struggling with a yearling bull that had somehow escaped last fall's roundup. Although the bull was thrown and tied, four men fought to hold him still while a fifth tried to castrate him with a small knife. Trudy was hopping about, shouting instructions, urging the knife-

wielder to take care with his blade. At last, with dope smeared on his scrotum, the new steer was released and Trudy clapped her hands as the vaquero displayed a bloody pair of testicles.

All eyes, Kruger sat motionless, his jaw popped open. Laird watched him a moment, wondering if perhaps he hadn't seen too much, and quickly signaled Trudy with his hat. She swung aboard her horse, hurling a final insult at the vaqueros, and rode toward them.

"If you'll allow me to say so—" Kruger paused, cleared his throat, "—your daughter seems a most remarkable girl, Mr. Laird."

"Aye, there's not another like her. Got more grit than most men could handle, and that's a fact."

Kruger merely nodded, his gaze fastened on the girl. Her face was radiant, glistening with sweat and excitement, and as she joined them Laird turned his horse into the falling dusk. Their escort fell in behind and they rode toward the compound.

Angela laid out an elegant table that evening. Her husband seldom invited guests to Santa Guerra, and Kruger's presence at dinner was a festive occasion. Her family silver and the crystal were arranged on a lace tablecloth, and Cook had been ordered to prepare roasted squab with honeyed wild rice. Oddly, Laird made no comment on the arrangements. Any other time he would have scoffed, remarking on his wife's grand airs, but tonight he was uncharacteristically quiet, almost an observer.

Under soft candlelight Angela appeared somehow younger. She was vivacious and animated, utterly charming in her role of hostess. And she was very inquisitive. Sipping wine, her eyes warm and guileless, she directed her conversation almost exclusively to Kruger.

"Oh yes, Ernest," she said in wistful remembrance, "I knew your mother and father quite well. Of course, I was much younger then and, sad to say, we lost track of one another over the years."

"You do yourself an injustice, Mrs. Laird. My parents spoke of you often, and their recollections were always with great fondness."

"Imagine that! Of course in a way it was quite natural. You see, when my father brought us to Texas there were so few people of breeding and culture. I suppose we were attracted by mutual interests, exiles in a foreign land, you might say."

Kruger smiled. "I recall Mother expressing those exact sentiments. She never quite resigned herself to Texas—or Texans, for that matter. Even at the end, when she lay dying, she hadn't forgiven my father for dying first and leaving her behind."

"How sad. But then, she must have been very proud of everything your father accomplished. And I'm sure her last days were brightened knowing you would follow in his footsteps."

"Not really. I'm afraid I saw too much of politics when I was a youngster, and it's never interested me. You see, even a county judge has to strike a balance between compromise and principle. I prefer to be my own man."

"Mercy sakes!" Angela laughed, quite spontaneously, and wagged her head. "Now you sound like Henry. He's forever grumbling about the state of affairs in Austin."

"And with reason," Laird informed her. "They're a pack of rascals! The only reason one of 'em would die a saint is if he hadn't been offered the right price."

"Times do change," Kruger noted. "Perhaps with the scalawags gone and a new governor in office, we'll see less corruption in government."

"Aye, and perhaps we won't. Coke's a good man, but it's still too early to tell."

Kruger glanced across the table at Trudy. "What about you, Miss Laird? Do you think we can expect reforms now that there's been a housecleaning in Austin?"

Trudy had merely listened throughout the meal, picking at her food. Now her face remained expressionless, her eyes impersonal. "I try not to think about it, but I agree with my father. Politicians aren't worth the powder it'd take to blow them to . . . Hades."

"God's blood!" Laird rumbled. "Mind your tongue, young lady. We'll not have a guest leave our house thinking we've no manners."

"No, it's quite all right, Mr. Laird. I not only share the thought, but I endorse the verdict as well."

"Well now, we're of a mind." Laird made an expansive gesture, grinning. "You'll oblige me, though, and pardon her manner. She's blessed with her mother's looks, but the Good Lord slipped up somewhere. As you can see, she's got my temper."

Angela fixed her husband with a curious look. Never before had she heard him excuse Trudy's behavior, not even to her. He felt her gaze and their eyes met for an instant. Something unspoken passed between them, almost as though he were reading her mind, then his chin moved in an imperceptible nod. She quickly collected herself and turned to Kruger.

"Not to change the subject, but these days politics and business are so intertwined it's almost the same thing. I just want you to know how happy I am that you'll be representing my husband and Santa Guerra."

Kruger suddenly looked uncomfortable, and Laird laughed. "You've put him between a rock and a hard spot. He wasn't to give me his decision until tomorrow, but I suppose now's as good a time as any." Laird settled back in his chair and stared down the table. "So what's it to be . . . are you or aren't you?"

There was a moment of silence. Kruger unwittingly glanced across at Trudy, and she met him with a defiant look. The organdy gown seemed to accent her tanned features, and golden flecks of candlelight were mirrored in her eyes. It crossed his mind that she was a creature of the wild, not at all the kind of woman he'd known in the past, and he felt drawn to her in some strange way he couldn't define. At last he blinked, broke the hold, and swung his gaze back to Laird.

"Yes, I believe I will accept your offer."

"Aye, I thought you would, and I'm proud to have you on board."

Laird raised his wineglass in toast. He tipped it first to his wife, then to Trudy, and finally to the young lawyer. "*Salud,* and welcome to Santa Guerra."

CHAPTER 22

Angela's days and nights seemed to blend together. Before she quite realized it, summer and fall had passed, and the year spun into early November. Her time was devoted almost exclusively to management of the ranch, and she had found it the most rewarding experience of her life. With Henry to advise her and the guidance of Ramon Morado on day-by-day matters, she had completely overhauled the operation. And it had been the most profitable year in the history of Santa Guerra.

Her confidence in herself, along with the degree of authority she exerted, had developed gradually. Upon assuming many of her husband's duties, she had allowed several months to broaden her knowledge of the overall operation. She asked endless questions, all the while inspecting the herds and delving ever deeper into the books, and with a sort of methodical determination slowly came to understand the complexities of a cattle ranch. Almost from the outset she had won the respect of the vaqueros. She was, after all, *La Madama,* and with Ramon to relay her orders there was never any question that she had in fact become the mistress of Santa Guerra. But as her preoccupation grew and she took on added responsibility, she encountered several unforeseen problems. Not the least of which was Henry Laird himself.

Their first clash came when Angela cut back drastically on his breeding program. Though the horses continued to be a profitable venture, his crossbreeding of Durham-longhorn cattle was a constant financial drain. Over his strong protests, for he was never a man to admit defeat, she simply withheld funds and phased out the program in piecemeal fashion. Shortly afterward, she clamped down on all expendi-

tures, revamping his rather loosely organized administrative procedures, and their arguments intensified. The underlying problem, which became apparent only with time, was that Hank Laird simply couldn't let go. It was his ranch, the creation of his own boldness and vision, and despite all his good intentions, he found it nearly impossible to relinquish even token authority.

Angela eventually stumbled upon the idea of diverting his attention. For a while she kept him busy organizing patrols to intercept and pursue cattle rustlers. Then, before spring roundup, she inveigled him into making a complete assessment of the demand for beef and the Eastern cattle market. Later, as the trail-driving season got under way, he was occupied negotiating with drovers and various cattle agents in Wichita. Yet she was freed of his interference only sporadically, and the interludes ended altogether when the last herd took the trail north. With the bickering about to resume full tilt, she viewed it as something of a godsend when he was hit with a land suit and forced to settle out of court.

The change in her husband, after being humiliated in court, was remarkable. Seemingly overnight, he awoke to the fact that Santa Guerra was vulnerable to a form of legal extortion. He became obsessed with validating claim to every acre of the ranch and, all the better from Angela's standpoint, he was actively involved in mapping out strategy to acquire the rights of every *derecho* holder. It came at the very moment she was groping for a new diversion, and at last it got him out of her hair.

Of no less consequence, at least in Angela's mind, was his attitude toward Ernest Kruger. She found it a curious alliance, for the young lawyer possessed all the traits of character she felt her husband lacked. He was scrupulous to a fault, the product of an old, respectable family, and a man of deep religious convictions. In a matter of months he had altered Laird's cutthroat philosophy to one of benign generosity and, even more astounding, her husband deferred to his judgment with only an occasional outburst of temper. To Angela, it was all but incomprehensible, for Henry Laird was actually accepting direction from a man half his age.

Several times when she attempted to broach the subject, Laird had dismissed it as a matter of smart business. She

thought that a rather lame excuse, if not an outright evasion, but after a while she'd let it rest. There were currents to her husband she had never understood, most especially his sly pragmatism, and she knew things were not always as they appeared in his business dealings. In good time, when it suited his purpose, he would reveal his hand. Until then it was a waste of breath to belabor the point, and she pursued it no further.

Yet she was nonetheless elated by the prospect of Ernest Kruger. His sudden appearance in their lives seemed almost providential. For years now she had worried herself sick about Trudy; though no one suspected, she'd nearly taken to bed after that dreadful episode with the Morado boy. Not that she condemned Roberto—all men were brutish and disgusting in matters of the flesh—nor did she blame Trudy for yielding to temptation. The root of the problem was Henry, and until recently there was slim hope the situation would ever change.

All her life Angela had heard old wives' tales about daughters idolizing their fathers to the point of love, even physical yearning. It was scarcely an emotion she would have experienced herself—the memory of Hiram Johnson provoked fear, not love—but she was under no illusions concerning Trudy. The girl worshiped her father, with an almost godlike reverence, and in her eyes no man would ever measure up to Hank Laird. Angela knew her husband encouraged the feeling, though she never for a moment believed his motives were anything more than that of a selfish father fearful of losing his little girl. Still, it was an unwholesome situation, one that might already have stunted the girl emotionally. Certainly it had driven Trudy to seek a substitute—the Morado boy—and the mere thought of it left Angela wretched.

Within the past few months, however, she had found reason for hope. Ernest Kruger was clearly bewitched by the girl. It was apparent to everyone but Trudy, not so much by word or action, for he was a man of great reserve, but rather in the hidden looks he gave her, and the mere fact of his presence. Kruger visited the ranch at least once a week, always with some flimsy pretext regarding business, and yet he constantly went out of his way to be near Trudy. It was done

with the artlessness of a man who knew little about women or courting, and Angela often wondered why her husband allowed it to continue. But she didn't dwell on the seeming contradiction, nor did she ever once open it to discussion. She simply thanked her God for the reprieve, and prayed for time to nurture things along.

Today, with fall roundup completed and winter approaching, she could at last afford a moment from her hectic schedule just to sit and think. Thanksgiving was only a couple of weeks off, and she thought that the perfect excuse to invite Ernest Kruger for a long holiday. He had no family of his own, and he was now her husband's closest business associate, so it was not only proper but highly appropriate. A week's stay as their houseguest might prove very beneficial all the way round. Seeing them together that long, Trudy could easily awaken to the fact that there was at least one man who dared stand up to her father. And afterward, assuming all went well, the possibilities were unlimited. She might even persuade Trudy to visit Corpus!

On impulse Angela left the study, which had now become her office, and hurried across the parlor. The hall clock struck four and she took that to be a good omen. It would never work if Trudy thought she'd planned all the details in advance; the girl was as bullheaded as her father, often impervious to any view but her own, and quite blunt about expressing her opinion. Better to use the oblique approach, very casual and offhand, simply a spur-of-the-moment thing. And—God forbid!—not the slightest hint of a mother playing matchmaker.

Angela stepped through the door, quickly crossed the porch, and took a seat in her rocker. She closed her eyes, willing herself to relax, and set the rocker in motion. At times like this she often wished she had Henry's gift for subterfuge and guile. But it was unnatural to her, hardly the type of thing one learned by rote, and she felt thankful he'd gone to Corpus on business. One look at her face and he would have seen through her little scheme in an instant.

Several minutes later she heard footsteps and recognized the quick, purposeful stride. Trudy always rushed back to the house, threw on her range clothes, and went for a ride before supper. So like her father in so many ways! A creature of

habit, yet horribly unpredictable, and never to be taken for granted. She slowly opened her eyes, blinked several times as Trudy mounted the steps, and stifled a small yawn.

"Oh hello dear. Back from school already?"

"Not soon enough," Trudy replied, halting by the banister. "Another day like today and I'll be ready to tear my hair out."

"Gracious sakes, don't be too harsh on them, honey. All children are rambunctious, you know that."

"*Válgame Dios!* I wish those brats were unruly, but they're not. They're just stupid!"

"Now you're being intolerant," Angela admonished. "And always remember, they haven't had your advantages. They're simple people, and education takes time, not to mention patience."

"Damn patience! I love *Los Lerdeños* as much as you do, Mama. But they're a lot easier to take when they're full grown, and if that sounds intolerant . . . well, I'm just sorry. It's the truth."

Trudy lacked the even disposition necessary to instructing small children. Her mother had coaxed her into supervising the school, and even trained several Mexican girls who displayed an aptitude for teaching to assist with the classes. But the school was a constant source of aggravation to Trudy; early each spring she dismissed the children for the summer, and only grudgingly did she resume classes in late fall. Except for her mother, who shamed her into accepting the burden, she would have left the school in disarray and gone on about her own business. Unlike Angela, she had little regard for education and almost no sympathy at all for the uneducated.

"Come sit down." Angela patted the rocker next to her, and smiled. "You're upset, and I know the children can be a chore at times . . . but perhaps the day won't be a total loss. Come on, just for a minute."

Trudy crossed the porch and flung herself down in the rocker. "All right, but make it quick, will you, Mama? I asked the men to saddle my horse, and I don't like to keep them waiting."

"Of course, dear. It's just an idea I had that might put you in a better frame of mind."

"Oh, what's that?"

"Well, I've been sitting here sunning, and my mind got to wandering . . . and it occurred to me that it's gotten very dull around here since we finished roundup."

"Boy, you can say that again—in spades!"

"Yes, exactly. And that's why I've decided we need something to break the tedium. Something we haven't done in a long time . . . a party!"

"Party?" Trudy repeated blankly. "I don't follow you, what kind of a party?"

"A Thanksgiving party. One of the old-fashioned kind, with lots of guests and a big turkey and all the trimmings. Like we used to have when you were a little girl . . . before the war . . . in Brownsville."

"Doesn't sound like much of a party. Who would we invite, some of those one-cow ranchers from the Cattlemen's Association?"

"Well, I haven't given it much thought, but let's see." Angela frowned, thoughtful a moment, then suddenly brightened and clapped her hands. "Of course! We'll invite Captain Blalock. After all, he's your father's oldest and dearest friend, and I recall Henry saying he'd finally married, so naturally we'll ask him to bring his wife."

"That makes two," Trudy noted. "Better tell Ramon to shoot a small turkey."

"On the contrary, I just thought of another one. We'll invite Mr. Kruger to be our guest for the holidays. Poor man, you know he hasn't any family left, and he probably hasn't had a decent Thanksgiving since his mother passed on."

Trudy gave her a quick, guarded glance. "Why him? He sure won't add much to the holiday spirit."

"Why, Trudy Laird! What an uncharitable thing to say. I mean, really, he is your father's closest business associate . . . and besides, I thought you liked Mr. Kruger."

"Mama, you'd better get yourself some spectacles. Ernest Kruger is the stuffiest man I've ever met in my whole life. And on top of that, he can bore you to tears in nothing flat."

"Oh, fiddlesticks! He's a very cultured gentleman. Even your father is impressed by his manners and . . . well, I don't know . . . his charm, I suppose."

"He's charming all right. Especially when he sits around

and stares at me like I was some sort of freak. *Ugh!* Talk about the fish-eye."

"I think you're being cruel. Mr. Kruger probably admires you, that's all. Goodness gracious, you're nineteen and all grown up, and it's certainly no secret you're a very pretty young lady."

"Oh c'mon, Mama!"

"No, it's a fact, men do notice things like that. Perhaps it's been a few years, but I'm not so old I don't remember the looks they give attractive women."

"Suit yourself." Trudy uncoiled from the rocker and stood. "I'll tell you something, though. If he starts tagging around after me while he's here, I'll blister his ear with some words he'll never forget."

"Honestly, Trudy, you might at least give him the benefit of the doubt. First impressions are often very misleading, and I suspect you'll find there's more to Ernest Kruger than meets the eye."

"I can't help it, Mama. The man gives me the willies. But like I said, you suit yourself. I'm late, and I've got to run. See you at supper."

Trudy shrugged, then turned away and walked into the house. Angela closed her eyes, gently rocking back and forth, and began humming a church hymn. A tiny smile appeared at the corner of her mouth, and it occurred to her that she had handled a delicate situation with admirable tact. The seed was planted, whether Trudy knew it or not, and after Thanksgiving they could very well expect an invitation to Corpus Christi. Perhaps a long invitation.

CHAPTER 23

Laird heard the rumor in early April. All along the Rio Grande the border grapevine was alive with talk of Juan Cordoba's latest countermove. An audacious man, with the pride and vanity of a martinet, the Mexican general had at last reached the limits of restraint. He placed a bounty of $10,000 on the head of Hank Laird.

On the north side of the river gringo ranchers were shocked but hardly surprised. Over the past two years Laird had led the fight against *bandidos* who preyed on Texan herds. He'd organized the Cattleman's Association, convincing outlying ranchers to form a coalition for mutual defense. An alert system was established between haciendas; at the first sign of a raid, mounted couriers spread the alarm; within hours, pursuit columns converged on the border in an attempt to trap the marauders in a pincer movement. Though the *bandidos* always had the advantage of surprise, the plan produced modest results and had added a new element of risk to cattle-rustling.

Yet it was Laird and *Los Lerdeños* who formed the vanguard of defense. Santa Guerra now employed upward of seven hundred vaqueros; night and day ten patrols, each comprised of seasoned fighting men, rode the far-flung boundaries of the ranch. The raiders became increasingly cautious, resorting to hit-and-run tactics, and learned to strike only after a patrol had passed through a given area. For all their cunning, however, it was nonetheless a deadly contest: Los Lerdeños had accounted for nearly forty rustlers killed or hung in the last year alone. Without Laird and his vaqueros, the war would have been lost long ago, and it was their steady attrition of *bandidos* that prompted the bounty.

General Juan Cordoba, who served in the dual role of
military commander and bandit chieftain, slowly became
aware that his rustling operation was in serious jeopardy.
And he knew that the Texas ranchers without a strong leader
to unite behind would lose their determination to fight. He
concluded the simplest solution all the way round was to kill
Hank Laird.

Forewarned, Laird took immediate measures to tighten
security. He increased the size of his personal escort, and
instructed Ramon Morado to add another fifty vaqueros to
the patrol force. Angela and Trudy, who had made several
trips to Corpus Christi during the winter, were restricted to
the compound until such time as the danger passed. At Ra-
mon's suggestion, Copperdust and several prize brood mares
were also moved from the breeding pasture to the com-
pound stables. And within the month, Juan Cordoba retali-
ated by burning out four ranchers whose property abutted
the southern boundary of Santa Guerra.

Early in May, with murder and pillage increasing at an
alarming rate, Laird dispatched a request for assistance to
Governor Richard Coke. Elected the year before, Coke was
a native Texan and had no ties with the Reconstruction poli-
tics of carpetbaggers and scalawags. One of his first acts was
to disband the state police and reorganize the Texas Rang-
ers, who had themselves been disbanded by occupation au-
thorities at the close of the Civil War. The Ranger force was
limited in numbers, however, and by now Texas was infested
with outlaws. Their orders were to clean out the state county
by county—only recently they had put John Wesley Hardin
to flight—and they were slowly working their way south.
Governor Coke responded to Laird's request, promising
help within a few weeks, and advised him to hang on until
the Rangers arrived.

Laird knew the delay might very well prove disastrous to
his neighbors. They lacked the manpower to protect their
herds—even their homes, in many instances—and the
bandidos had stepped up the tempo of attack. But he was
only marginally concerned about Santa Guerra itself. Secu-
rity was tighter than ever, and his vaqueros were spoiling for
a fight. Watchful if not overly alarmed, he felt confident the
raiders wouldn't dare stick their heads into a hornet's nest.

In that, Laird dreadfully underestimated his opponent. Juan Cordoba borrowed a trick from the Indians, and sent three columns of raiders fording the Rio Grande at full moon. Texans called it a Comanche moon, for in times past the warriors favored brilliant moonlit nights when raiding *tejano* horse herds. It served the *bandidos* no less admirably as they rode north and split into dozens of small parties, each comprised of four or five men. The plan was simple, yet coordinated with elaborate attention to detail. For Juan Cordoba enjoyed an advantage never dreamt of by Comanche horse thieves. Into the ranks of his bravos he had recruited a man who was once esteemed by all of *Los Lerdeños.* A man of bitterness and hate, and one who was intimately familiar with the clockwork precisor of Henry Liard's vaquero patrols.

By midnight the raiders had infiltrated Santa Guerra, slipping past the patrols, and regrouped once again into columns as they closed on the headquarters compound. They came like dusky shadows along the treelined creek, and while greatly outnumbered, their tactical advantage—the element of surprise—promised to make it a costly night for *Los Lerdeños.*

Shortly after one o'clock, three men slithered over the compound wall and set fire to the horse stable. Within moments the building was engulfed in flames, and squeals from the terror-stricken horses could be heard a mile away. Vaqueros poured from their homes in their nightclothes, forgetting all else in their rush to save *El Patrón's* prized breeding stock. Among the first to reach the blazing stable was Ramon Morado, and an instant later Laird hurried from the main house tugging on his pants. Shouting commands above the raging inferno, they formed the vaqueros into two lines and quickly organized a bucket brigade.

Waiting patiently, the raiders bided their time as the crowd thickened around the stable. Soon the vaqueros were frantically engaged in dousing the fire, and the flames silhouetted their every movement within the confines of the *cuadrilla.* Suddenly the night came alive with the yellowish flash of gunfire, and lead hissed across the compound. Vaqueros fell right and left, clutching their wounds, and those left unscathed ran for cover. One glance was enough to con-

firm Laird's worst suspicions. Their attackers had them scissored in a crossfire, and unless something was done fast, every man in the *cuadrilla* would be killed.

"*Dispersad, hombres!*" Laird shouted over the roar of flames and rifle fires. "Scatter! Get your guns and form along the walls. *Andale! Andale!*"

The vaqueros leaped to their feet and ran at his command. Scuttling crablike across the open compound, they dodged and weaved in headlong flight toward the adobe structures. The gunfire increased in tempo as they ran, upending several men before they reached the sanctuary of the buildings. Moments later, they boiled from their homes, clutching rifles and bandoliers as they darted toward the walls. Laird emerged from the main house with a shotgun and shell belt. But even as he crossed the porch, the *bandidos* suddenly switched tactics.

One band of raiders along the south wall, and another positioned at the east wall, poured a devastating barrage into the vaqueros, forcing them to seek cover. Simultaneously the third group, who were still mounted, stormed the front gate and burst into the compound. With the defenders pinned down, there was only scattered opposition to their assault, and they rode in a direct line toward the main house.

To Ramon, who had ducked into the blacksmith shop with several vaqueros, their purpose was immediately apparent. The riders formed an execution squad, and their mission was to kill the *patrón*. Heedless of the crossfire, Ramon gathered the vaqueros in the smithy and led them in a rush across the open *cuadrilla*.

Taken unawares, Laird was caught on the porch steps, with no place to run. He stood his ground, bullets thudding all around him as the horsemen charged forward, then leveled the shotgun and triggered both barrels. A double load of buckshot, fanning out in a hail of lead, swept the lead riders from their saddles and dumped three horses at the head of the column. The charge broke apart, splintered by the tangle of men and horses, and the raiders skidded to a halt before the house. Laird retreated up the steps, ejecting spent shells and hurriedly reloading the shotgun. But as he gained the porch, a rifle slug smacked into his shoulder and sent him reeling backward. His knees buckled, then another bullet

struck him in the side, and he sprawled motionless on the porch. Trudy appeared in the doorway with a carbine, levering round after round into the riders. Her fire was murderous at point-blank range; three men were killed and another horse went down under the steady blast of her carbine. The sight of a *gringa*—cooly hammering shot after shot into their ranks—momentarily stunned the other raiders. There was an instant of hesitation, the attack blunted, then they recovered and turned their fire on Trudy.

Suddenly the *bandido* leader emerged from the melee of men and horses. Even as the first slugs splintered the doorway around Trudy, he spurred his mount to the forefront of the fight. Caught in the crossfire, his move seemed suicidal, but he ignored the maelstrom of lead, waving his sombrero overhead and shouting frantically.

"Alto! Alto! Vamos, hombres! Vamonos!"

Trudy froze, oblivious to the gunfire, slowly lowered her carbine. She watched with a look of tragic bewilderment as Roberto rode back and forth, cursing the bandidos, ordering them to withdraw. Her mouth opened, fixed in a silent scream, and the sudden horror of comprehension jolted her into rude awakening. It was no nightmare. It was truly him. Roberto!

Her Roberto!

While Trudy stood petrified, there was a moment of confusion. Roberto's shouts were punctuated by scattered gunshots and squealing horses, all blended together in a fury of noise. Several raiders had already wheeled their mounts, but those nearest the house raked the porch with one last volley. Even as they fired, Angela slipped through the doorway and ran toward her husband. Bullets pocked the front of the house, shattering windows on both sides of the door, and a slug meant for Trudy caught Angela in midstride. A surprised look came over her face, then a crimson dot blossomed wider across her nightgown and she slumped gently to the porch. Trudy screamed, dropping the carbine, and rushed outside as her mother fell.

Suddenly Ramon and his vaqueros appeared on the raiders' flank. Their rifles barked, spitting streaks of flame, drawing ever closer in a staccato roar of gunfire. Before the *bandidos* could get themselves sorted out, another half-

dozen were blown from their saddles. Their leader was curs-
ing and screaming, urging them to retreat; his horse reared
and he fought the reins, outlined an instant against the blaze
of light from the fire. Ramon halted, eyes wide and gaping,
thunderstruck by the sight of his son. The color drained from
his face, and a sense of rage swept over him. All thought
suspended, acting on reflex alone, he threw the rifle to his
shoulder, blindly triggered a shot. The slug went wild, cutting
a furrow across the flank of Roberto's horse. The animal
bolted, and before Ramon could get off another shot, the
raiders were gone, pounding toward the gate at a gallop.
Then, as abruptly as it began, the battle ceased. There were
scattered shots as bandidos along the walls withdrew and,
moments later, the fading sound of hoofbeats.

An eerie silence settled over the compound. The stables
burned out of control, and vaqueros stood silhouetted
against the flames, too dazed to move. Somewhere in the
night a wounded man groaned, crying out for help, then the
roof of the stables buckled inward and the building collapsed
in a shower of sparks and fiery timber.

Ramon slowly collected his senses, lowered the hammer
on his rifle, and turned toward the house. He saw Trudy bent
over her father, the servants peeking out the door, and he
took off running. As he mounted the steps he spotted An-
gela, lying small and crumpled, the front of her nightgown
soaked with blood. He halted, one foot on the porch,
glanced at Trudy with a look of stark disbelief.

"La Madama?"

"Muerto."

"El Patrón?"

"Alive, but he's hurt bad. I can't stop the bleeding."

Ramon dropped to his knees beside Laird, who was bare-
chested and still unconscious. The shoulder wound appeared
clean, drilled through below the collarbone. But the wound
in his side, slightly above the belt line, was inflamed and
puckered, seeping blood.

"Graciadios!" Ramon whirled on the servants. "A knife!
Boiling water! *Pronto, imbéciles. Pronto!"* The women
jumped, hurrying inside, and he turned to Trudy. "I must
take the bullet, and quickly. It is the only way."

Trudy's features were grim, eyes dulled. "Will he live?"

"Sí, niña mía. Con el favor de Dios."

Laird moaned and his eyelids fluttered open. He attempted to rise, clutched at the pain in his side; then allowed Trudy to ease his head down on the porch. He was groggy, but his vision slowly cleared and his gaze shifted to Ramon.

"How bad is it?"

"The bite of a flea, *Patrón*. You will live forever."

"And the others . . . everybody all right?"

Ramon flicked a warning glance at Trudy. "Nothing of consequence, *Patrón*. We drove the *bandidos* off with only minor losses."

"Bueno. Bloody bastards! That'll teach 'em not . . ."

Laird's voice trailed off and his eyes glazed. His lips moved but there was no sound, and after a moment, his eyelids drooped closed. Then he slept.

CHAPTER 24

The funeral services were simple. Though there was no priest on Santa Guerra, it was necessary, because of the heat, that a mass burial be quickly arranged. Carpenters spent most of the morning hammering together rough coffins, and by early afternoon, the dead had been laid out in their finest garments. An hour later Angela and thirty-four vaqueros were lowered into the ground in the graveyard north of the compound. Ramon Morado delivered a halting prayer, and Laird, despite his wounds, read a few passages from the Bible. Then it was over, and the gravediggers were left to complete their work.

The wailing of widows and mothers grew even louder as dirt was shoveled onto the caskets. But there were no tears from either the *patrón* or his daughter. With Ramon in the lead and Trudy at his side, Laird was carried away on a stretcher. The little procession slowly made its way back to the house, and though Trudy held his hand the entire time, neither of them spoke. Her eyes were sunken with fatigue, and her features were heavy and smudged, drawn with grief. Until this morning, when she'd bathed and dressed her mother's body, she had known nothing of death. Now it was a mystery no longer, and her tears had been replaced by a hollow ache, some deeper and very final sense of loss.

Laird had a tight grip on himself, teeth clenched against the pain, and he kept his sorrow hidden. But his expression was murderous, eyes garnet with rage. As they crossed the *cuadrilla,* he turned his head and stared at the charred ruins of the stable. Copperdust and five brood mares had perished in the fire. The thought sickened him, and yet, however senseless the act, it was not an irreversible loss. The stallion had sired many fine sons, some of them already at stud, and

the bloodline would continue. For *Los Lerdeños* it was an altogether different matter. There was no way to bring back the dead vaqueros—or Angela—and he felt stricken with guilt. By mere chance, he had survived while the attempt on his life had brought about the wanton slaughter of innocent men . . . and his wife, who in those last moments had braved gunfire to come to his aid. Even now, though Trudy had told him about it shortly before dawn, the thought of Angela on that porch shriveled his stomach into a hard knot of rage. He promised himself that retribution would be swift, and paid in kind.

One thing Trudy hadn't mentioned was Roberto Morado. She simply couldn't bring herself to tell either her father or Ramon that she had identified the *bandido* leader. Though Roberto had saved her life, he was nonetheless responsible for the death of her mother. She felt the circumstances were extenuating, but in no way forgivable. Roberto had also tried to kill her father. Yet, while she deplored his part in the raid, she couldn't wholly condemn him. She loved him still—even now she was convinced he'd been unjustly banished from Santa Guerra—and after last night she understood an emotion she'd never before experienced. She understood what it was to hate, and how it could drive men to kill. She too wanted Juan Cordoba dead, and given the chance she would gladly have pulled the trigger herself.

Unknown to Trudy, however, her father was painfully aware that Roberto had participated in the raid. Shortly before the funeral, Ramon had dutifully reported the details to Laird. He felt obligated to inform the *patrón* that it was Roberto who had led the execution squad. Purposely or not, the death of *La Madama* was brought about by his son, and for that he could never forgive himself. Nor could he excuse his miserable shooting in those last moments. It was his son, and therefore his responsibility, and he felt personally cheated in not having killed the *traidor*. After discussing it at length, both Laird and Ramon had decided it was best to keep the matter to themselves. There was nothing to be gained in telling Trudy and upsetting her further. Yet the men were in agreement about Roberto. He had cast his lot with Juan Cordoba, and like the bandit chieftain his life would be forfeited.

Nearing the house, Ramon suddenly stiffened and barked out a warning. A column of riders had been passed through the front gate, and the guards were signaling all clear. But Ramon was wary after last night's raid; he hurried the stretcher-bearers up the steps, intent on getting Trudy and the *patrón* out of sight. Laird twisted around, watching the riders over his shoulder, and caught a glint of metal in the sunlight. One arm was in a sling, but he raised the other hand, halting the vaqueros, and spoke to Ramon.

"Alto! Get me off this thing and on my feet."

"That would be unwise, *Patrón.* Better to have you inside until we question these men."

Trudy nodded agreement. "He's right, Pa. You're in no condition—"

"Don't argue! Just do as you're told. *Pronto!"*

Ramon glanced at Trudy, then shrugged and motioned to the vaqueros. They lowered the stretcher, gently lifted Laird to his feet, and assisted him to the edge of the porch. His legs were wobbly, but he slumped against the banister, supporting himself with his good arm, and waved them away. The vaqueros spread out along the porch, with Ramon in the center, their pistols drawn. Trudy stepped inside, hurried back with her carbine, and positioned herself in the doorway.

Several moments later the riders reined up before the house. Their leader swung down out of the saddle and walked toward the porch. He was a wiry man, of medium height, with pallid features and the quiet manner of a bookkeeper. But his eyes were a peculiar shade of gray, cold and hard, and he assessed the situation at a glance. Halting at the bottom of the steps, he waited, allowing the vaqueros to inspect the badge pinned on his shirt, then nodded at Laird.

"You must be Hank Laird."

"Aye, that I am."

"My name's McNelly. Captain L.H. McNelly, First Ranger Battalion."

"You'd be the Texas Rangers, then?"

"That's correct. We were ordered down here by the governor after you sent a request for help."

"Well, you're a little late, Captain McNelly. And I've no need of your help any longer."

"Sorry, Mr. Laird, I don't follow you."

"Why, it's simple enough. In case you hadn't noticed, we were raided last night."

"Yes, I saw . . ."

"You saw nothing! We've just finished burying thirty-four men and my wife. Shall I repeat that, Captain McNelly—my wife! So climb on your horse and ride on back to Austin. You're of no use to us now."

"I can't do that, Mr. Laird. You have my deepest condolences—"

"Damn your condolences!"

"—but I've been ordered to clear the border of outlaws, and that's exactly what I intend to do."

Laird scowled, glancing past him at the Rangers. There were some forty men in the column, all of them lean and tough, cold-eyed as their leader, obviously seasoned fighting men. After a moment, Laird grunted and shook his head with contempt.

"Do yourself a favor, McNelly. Go back to chasing bank robbers. You haven't enough men for the job."

"We're accustomed to long odds, Mr. Laird."

"Then I'll put it another way. I'm going after Cordoba and his gang of butchers myself, and I'll not having you spoiling the game. Now, is that plain enough, or do I have to spell it out?"

McNelly looked down and studied the ground, then his pale eyes came level. "I can't let you do that, Mr. Laird. I'm the law here now, and if there's any fighting to be done my boys will do it."

"Oh, it's the law, is it? Don't make me laugh, McNelly. I do as I please—always have and always will—and you'll not stop me."

"No, Mr. Laird. You won't budge off this ranch. We're going to handle Cordoba my way, and if you don't like it then I'm afraid you'll just have to sit on it."

"By Judas!" Laird exploded. "I'll not take orders from any man."

"On the contrary." McNelly's voice was barely audible, but there was an undercurrent of authority to the words. "Either you stay put, or I'll haul you down to Brownsville and throw you in jail. You see, it's my game now, Mr. Laird,

and I feel the same way you do. I won't allow anyone to spoil it for me."

There was a long pause of weighing and appraisal as the two men examined one another. McNelly saw urgency and homicidal fury in Laird's eyes, and knew he was dealing with a man whose sole reason for existence had now become vengeance. Still, he had a job to do, and it was essential that the Rangers establish their reputation from the very outset. Everyone along the border, on both sides of the Rio Grande, had to be convinced that law and order had been restored. And the place to start was with Hank Laird.

At last, with a faint smile, McNelly broke the tension. "Look at it this way, Mr. Laird. You're wounded, and it's plain to see you're in no shape to go off hunting bandits. So there's nothing to lose by letting us handle it, and you've got my word, we'll settle the score with Cordoba."

Laird considered a moment, then gave him a slow nod. "One week, McNelly. By then, I'll be mended and well enough to ride. Either show me some results or you've got my word on it—I'll take matters into my own hands."

"I wouldn't advise it, Mr. Laird, but we'll leave it there and see how things work out. Been nice talking with you."

McNelly glanced at Trudy, touched the brim of his hat, then turned and walked back to his horse. He stepped into the saddle, signaled his men, and wheeled the column out of the yard. A few moments later, the Rangers rode through the front gate and disappeared across the prairie.

After a prolonged silence, Laird pushed away from the banister and hobbled to his rocker. He sat down heavily, face drained of color, one hand clutching the wound in his side. Trudy crossed the porch, eyes filled with concern, and placed an arm around his shoulders.

"Don't worry, Pa. He's all talk and no show."

"Aye, but then again, he puts me in mind of a banty rooster. And they're damn good fighters. Might be he'll turn the trick."

"Maybe so, but I wouldn't bet on it."

"Funny thing, now that I think about it . . . I would."

The public square was all but deserted. Business came to a standstill at noon, and Brownsville, like all border towns,

wisely observed the custom of siesta during the midday heat. Yet today there was an ominous quality to the stillness, and while Brownsville appeared somnolent, the townspeople waited indoors with a sense of expectancy.

On the hotel veranda, Laird and Sam Blalock were seated in cane-bottomed rockers, talking quietly. Their attention was fixed on the north end of the plaza, where Ramon Morado and fifty vaqueros squatted in the shade of a huge live oak. Time seemed protracted, creeping past with interminable slowness, and their conversation ceased as a clock inside the hotel struck the half-hour. Blalock pulled out a pocket watch and clicked open the cover. He consulted it a moment, mouth pursed in a frown, then looked up.

"Twelve-thirty. Think he'll still show?"

"Aye, I've no doubt he'll be here."

"Well, he sure as hell's not the punctual type, is he?"

"You underestimate the man, Sam. He said noon, but he wouldn't have spread the word unless he meant to draw a crowd. It figures he'd be late."

"Crowd?" Blalock arched one eyebrow, slowly inspected the square. "Hope he's bringin' a brass band. He'll need it to wake up this burg."

"I've an idea McNelly has something better in mind."

"Yeah, maybe so." Blalock snapped the watch closed and returned it to his vest pocket. "Well, anyway, like I was saying . . . walked into the saloon and there was Joe Starling big as life. Had the mayor and half the town council with him. The way I got the story, he's promoting a bond issue and telling everybody he means to lay track between here and Rio Grande City."

"Joe should've been a pitchman. He's got the knack for it."

"That's pretty tame, comin' from you. There was a time you'd've run him out of town just for the hell of it."

"And I might again. But right now I've got other problems."

"McNelly?"

"Aye, him and Cordoba. One way or another, I intend to have it settled."

Laird clamped a cigar in his mouth, puffing on it with a cold expression. Almost two weeks had passed since his ex-

change with McNelly at Santa Guerra; despite his promise to take the field against Cordoba, he wasn't fully recuperated from his wounds, and none too graciously he'd conceded to Trudy that he wasn't yet in fighting trim. But he could manage to sit a horse, and before dawn he'd left the ranch, trailed by a heavily armed escort. The trip to town, though it had sapped his energy, was prompted by a summons from McNelly. One he could hardly refuse.

Late yesterday evening a courier had ridden into Santa Guerra. He brought word of a battle between McNelly's Rangers and a large band of cattle rustlers. Apparently the fight had taken place on Palo Alto prairie, some miles northeast of Brownsville, but the details were sketchy, and other than McNelly's cryptic message, the courier had little to relate. McNelly requested that Laird meet him in town, no later than noon the following day, and indicated that a message had been dispatched to the authorities in Brownsville. No reason was given, nor was McNelly's purpose entirely clear. It was simply a hook, baited with scraps of information, and Laird took it.

Now, puffing on his cigar, he waited, staring off across the plaza, wondering what it was McNelly had up his sleeve. All the way into town he had thought about it, examining various possibilities, yet he'd arrived at only one conclusion. Angela's death was still to be avenged, and whatever happened today, McNelly wouldn't stop him from going after Cordoba. The debt was owed and he meant to collect.

Sam Blalock suddenly grunted an oath, and Laird started, glancing quickly toward the north end of the square. For an instant his attention was drawn to the horsemen, then he saw the wagon. He stood, slowly removed the cigar from his mouth, and walked to the edge of the veranda.

Led by McNelly, the Rangers were split into two columns, with an old farm wagon in the center. Several Rangers bore the signs of battle, their wounds wrapped in crude bandages, and a Mexican, whose features appeared swollen and bruised, drove the wagon. Laid out in the wagon bed, arms and legs akimbo, were the bodies of nearly a dozen *bandidos*.

Staring straight ahead, McNelly led the column to a tree in the middle of the plaza. There, the Rangers dismounted and four of them clambered aboard the wagon. Quickly, like men

unloading cordwood, they began grabbing arms and legs, and dumped the bodies on the ground. The *bandidos* were blood-spattered, putrid in the noonday heat, and a breeze carried the stench of death across the plaza. By the time the Rangers were finished, doors began opening around the square and along side streets. The people of Brownsville, Anglo and Mexican alike, gathered near the buildings, hesitant to come closer, staring at the grisly scene.

McNelly, who was still mounted, waited a long while, eyeing the crowd. At last, when the square filled with onlookers, he barked a command. A rope was thrown over a low branch on the tree, and two Rangers hustled the *bandido* driver to the rear of the wagon bed. His hands were tied behind his back and a noose quickly cinched around his neck. The tailgate was lowered, and at McNelly's signal, another Ranger led the team forward. The *bandido* swung off the wagon, thrashing and kicking, his walnut features slowly turning purple and then black as the noose cut deeper into his throat. Several minutes passed, with the crowd watching in awed silence, before the *bandido* choked to death. Then his body went slack, on plumb with the rope, twisting gently in the wind.

An oppressive quiet settled over the square, and a moment later McNelly reined his horse around. He rode across the plaza, halted before the hotel, and stepped down from the saddle. His expression was stoic, revealing nothing, and he walked directly to the veranda, eyes fixed on Laird.

"I'm a few days late, Mr. Laird, but as you can see, I've kept my part of the bargain."

"Says who?" Laird demanded. "What've you got there, twelve, maybe fourteen dead ones? That's not enough. Not near enough."

"Perhaps, but it's a good start. You see, I deal in examples, Mr. Laird. By tonight, the families of those men will have their bodies back across the river, and it'll make a nice object lesson for anyone with ideas about turning cow thief."

"Come off it, McNelly. You haven't even made a dent in Cordoba's bravos, and you're standing here talking about object lessons. I'll thank you not to play me for a fool."

McNelly jerked a thumb over his shoulder. "See the one on the rope?"

"Aye, I'm not blind."

"Last night some of my boys persuaded him to talk. Told us a real interesting story about a place called *Las Cuevas.* Ever heard of it?"

"Of course I have. It's the biggest ranch in Tamaulipas. Belongs to some retired Mexican general."

"Not altogether," McNelly observed. "Seems like Cordoba and his *bandidos* have taken it over. Last year or so, they've been using it as a way station for rustled cows."

Laird regarded him with a quizzical look. "I'll be damned. You mean to cross the border, don't you?"

McNelly nodded. "That's the only way to end it. Strike south of the river and catch the whole bunch. Otherwise, we'll have to chase around after small raiding parties till Hell freezes over." He paused, thoughtful. "My orders are to get it done fast, so I reckon we'll take the fight to 'em for a change."

"And high time," Laird added. "Of course, you know you won't get any help from the army. The brass will start yelling about international boundaries and that'll put an end to it."

"I suppose, but it won't matter one way or the other. I'm still crossing the river."

Laird chuckled, glancing at Sam Blalock. "Told you he was a fighter, didn't I? Always could spot 'em, and still can too." He turned back to McNelly. "All right, Captain, lay it out for me. We'll join forces and settle Juan Cordoba's hash once and for all."

"No, not this time, Mr. Laird. Like I told you before, it's Ranger business, and we can't have civilians mixin' in. Specially when we're headed across the border."

"Now you're talking nonsense. You'll need all the help you can get once you hit *Las Cuevas.*" Laird gestured across the plaza. "There's fifty vaqueros sittin' under that tree, every one of 'em spoiling for a scrap. And I guarantee you, they'll fight rings around your Ranger boys."

"Maybe so, but the answer's the same. You stay and we go, and I won't argue about it."

"Oh, it's orders you're giving, is it?"

"Call it anything you want, but there's only one way . . . and that's my way."

"In a pig's ass! You're not the only man that knows his way

across the river. Hell, if it's a race you want, I'll have my men in *Las Cuevas* before you even get your toes wet."

"Don't push it." McNelly's pale eyes bored into him. "You try crossing the river and I'll guarantee you something, Mr. Laird. You'll lose more vaqueros than you already have."

"By the Holy Christ! It's you that'll have a fight on your hands. I've a thirst for vengeance, McNelly, and I won't be denied."

"I don't take kindly to threats, Mr. Laird."

"Well, you're damn sure free about handing them out. Indeed you are . . . and I find that very strange . . . particularly from a lawman. Seems to me you're letting pride get the better of your judgment, McNelly. Or haven't you the stomach to admit it?"

"I'm warning you—"

"Damn your warning!" Laird's eyes took on a peculiar glitter. "I've told you what I intend, and if you mean to stop me then there's no need waiting till I've crossed the river." He leveled a finger across the plaza. "There's my vaqueros! If it's a fight you want, we can get it settled right now."

Blalock suddenly came to his senses, and stepped between them. "Hank, listen to me! You're in no shape for a fight, not with him or Cordoba or anyone else."

"Stay out of it, Sam."

"For god's sake, use your—"

"Leave be!" Laird roughly swept him aside, glaring down at the lawman. "Your choice, McNelly. Either we fight together or we fight each other. What's your pleasure?"

"Your friend's right," McNelly told him. "You'd just be a hindrance to us, Laird."

"God's teeth! I'll outlast the bunch of you, and there's a fact. Now, quit trying to muddy the water and be kind enough to give me your answer. Who's it to be . . . Cordoba or me?"

McNelly walked to his horse, stood for a moment with his hand on the pommel, then stepped into the saddle. His gaze settled on Laird, and their eyes locked in a silent clash of strength. At last, with a look of resignation, McNelly slowly nodded his head.

"Cordoba."

"Wise decision," Laird chuckled. "You'll not regret it."

"Maybe, maybe not. But let's get one thing straight, Laird. I'm in command of this outfit, and that goes for everybody, including you. I'll deputize you . . . just to make it official . . . but when it comes to giving orders, you're just another Ranger. Understood?"

"Why, it's honored I am, Captain McNelly. Honored indeed!"

"Yeah. I can see it written all over you."

Laird turned his head and winked at Sam Blalock. McNelly muttered something under his breath, then reined his horse away from the veranda.

"We ride in an hour, Mr. Laird. Be ready!"

CHAPTER 25

A dingy haze lighted the sky at false dawn. With McNelly in the lead, they forded the river some hundred miles upstream from Brownsville. On the opposite shore, the men were dismounted and told to check their weapons. *Las Cuevas* lay a few miles south of the border, and their attack was to be timed with the moment of brightening at full dawn.

Laird was bone-tired, sore and weary after fourteen straight hours in the saddle. He hadn't slept since leaving Santa Guerra—yesterday before dawn—and he envied the men around him, begrudged them their youth and endurance. When he dismounted, his legs went rubbery, and he hung on to the saddle horn, stamping his feet to restore the circulation. But he saw McNelly watching him and quickly summoned some inner reserve of energy. He was determined the banty-assed little bastard wouldn't catch him weakening, not now, with the fight less than an hour away.

All around him there was the creak of saddle leather and the metallic clank of shells being levered into Winchesters. He broke open his shotgun, dropped fresh buckshot loads in both tubes, then snapped it closed and thrust it into the saddle scabbard. Though he had little use for pistols—preferring the advantage of a scattergun—he pulled his Colt and checked the loads, lowering the hammer on an empty chamber. He'd always thought it ironic that it was called a six-shooter, when for safety's sake everyone carried it with five chambers loaded. After holstering the pistol, he turned, almost certain McNelly was still watching him, and grinned broadly, thumbs hooked in his gun belt. McNelly shook his head and looked away.

Laird watched him move among the Rangers, nodding and offering last-minute words of encouragement. Somewhat

ruefully, he had to admit there was much about the man to
be admired. Even with the vaqueros, which effectively dou-
bled the strength of the Ranger battalion, they would still be
seriously outnumbered. Yet to hear McNelly talk, it was all
in a day's work.

At McNelly's invitation, Laird had joined him at the head
of the column shortly before dark last night. The Ranger
commander wasted little time on amenities, launching im-
mediately into a discourse on tactics. His manner was gruff
and straightforward, and the purpose of his lecture was
never in doubt. Laird and the vaqueros, in his view, were not
professional fighting men. Their previous skirmishes with
outlaws, while commendable, hardly qualified them for what
lay ahead. A blunt reference to the raid on Santa Guerra
stilled Laird's objections, and afterward, much as McNelly
had intended, the matter of rank was no longer in question.
It was a novel experience for Laird. He was accustomed to
giving orders; whether deckhand or vaquero, he expected to
be obeyed instantly. For the next hour he kept his mouth
shut, and listened.

According to McNelly, the *bandido* he'd hung in Browns-
ville had been a veritable encyclopedia of information. It
seemed Juan Cordoba was a man who thought on a grand
scale; his cattle-rustling operation far exceeded anything the
Texans had imagined. The raiders operated as far west as
Nuevo Laredo, covering some five hundred miles along the
Rio Grande border; upward of a quarter million cattle were
stolen every year, funneled through *Las Cuevas* to the inte-
rior of Mexico and several Latin countries. The magnitude
of such an operation required a small army, and Cordoba,
with his military background, had organized the raiders into
squadrons seldom containing less than fifty men. Although
the squadrons were constantly on the move—either raiding
Texan ranches or herding cattle deeper into the interior—
Las Cuevas was heavily defended at all times. On any given
day, no less than four or five squadrons were camped in a
perimeter around the main *casa,* the headquarters. By sim-
ple calculation, that meant *Las Cuevas* could muster at least
two hundred *bandidos,* all of the veteran fighters, in the
event of attack. Which placed the odds at roughly two to one
. . . perhaps worse.

McNelly had paused there, underscoring the point with a grim look. Laird was duly impressed, and despite himself he couldn't resist the temptation. He'd asked the obvious question.

"You're a queer one, McNelly. Without my vaqueros, you would've been outnumbered four to one! Why in the name of Christ did you make me force them on you?"

"For the best of reasons, Mr. Laird. I can depend on my men to follow orders, and I've seen them tested under fire. Your vaqueros are an unknown quantity."

"You're saying they might spoil your plans somehow . . . zig when you've told them to zag . . . is that it?"

"Our single advantage—in fact, our one hope to come out of this alive!—is the element of surprise. You and your vaqueros jeopardize that advantage, Mr. Laird. Why? Because you're accustomed to fighting as individuals, not as a unit. In any military engagement that's a dangerous flaw . . . perhaps fatal."

"You're worried, then, that we'll not follow orders?"

"Precisely."

"You seem to forget that we want Cordoba more than you do. It's personal with us—we've got the graves to prove it—for you, it's simply another job."

"You just made my point, Mr. Laird. Emotion has no place on a battlefield. It gets the wrong men killed."

"Well, you can belay your fears, Captain McNelly. I'll follow your orders down to the letter—and by the Sweet Jesus! —the same goes for my vaqueros. Maybe their blood's a little hot, but they'll not be losing their heads. You've my word on it."

"I pray you're right, Mr. Laird. You see, we're not likely to have such an opportunity again."

"Oh, how so?"

"Because Juan Cordoba's no fool. Once he knows we're willing to cross the border, he'll run all the way to Mexico City. So unless we kill him this time out, we probably never will."

"Aye, you're right. We've only the one chance, and damn little room for error." Laird hesitated, gave him a quizzical look. "That's why you've been lecturing me the past hour, isn't it?"

"I don't lecture, Mr. Laird. I'm a lawman, not a teacher. All I've done is explain how we might kill a man . . . in the most expedient manner."

Watching him now, Laird was reminded that a simple statement of fact had revealed much about the Ranger commander. However cold and impersonal, he was the right man for the job. Not that they would ever be friends, but under the circumstances it was possible to overlook his abrasive manner. McNelly was as deadly as the outlaws he hunted—a mankiller—the very attribute needed if ever law was to be brought to the border. Laird found it a tantalizing thought: peace on the Rio Grande. Almost enough, he told himself, almost but not quite. Juan Cordoba's head would give him true peace.

A flicker of movement caught Laird's eye. Alerted, he saw a Ranger ghosting through the trees, and suddenly realized McNelly had sent a man ahead to scout *Las Cuevas.* Clearly he was more exhausted than he'd thought. He hadn't seen the man leave the column! In fact, it hadn't even occurred to him to scout the enemy camp. He cursed himself for a smug fool, and wondered that he'd ever considered taking the field against Cordoba. Left to his own devices, he would have botched it! Probably got himself and a bunch of vaqueros killed, and in the end, accomplished nothing. Which was essentially the message McNelly had delivered last night.

Still mumbling to himself, Laird walked forward to where McNelly and the scout were squatted down on the riverbank. In the soft earth, the scout had sketched a diagram of *Las Cuevas,* and McNelly was studying it intently. As Laird halted, he nodded, apparently having arrived at a decision, and glanced up.

"Laird, have a look." McNelly poked at the diagram with a stick. "Here we are. There's the road a couple of hundred yards upstream. Then you follow the road about two miles and there's *Las Cuevas."* The stick jabbed at symbols scratched in the dirt. "Now, this square is the main house, and these X's are outbuildings, probably used to quarter Cordoba's regular hands. This wavy line, over to the west, is a creek, and these circles are *bandido* camps." He smiled, tapped a pair of circles along the wavy line. "That's where we got lucky. There's only two squadrons camped on the

creek. Allowing for the men in these outbuildings, I figure their forces at about a hundred and fifty, maybe a few more. Couldn't ask for better odds than that, could you?"

"Aye," Laird agreed, "it's certainly better than we expected. As you've said, though, they're fighters. What happens when we stir up the hornet's nest?"

"All depends," McNelly observed. "If they hold their ground, then we hit and run. Kill as many as we can and ride like hell. On the other hand, if me and my boys scatter this bunch along the creek, then we'll stick around and do the job proper."

"Well, that's splendid, except for one thing. You haven't yet mentioned my vaqueros."

"I thought you told me you wanted Cordoba?"

"Aye, we do indeed. But I don't take your meaning."

"Cordoba will be in the main house."

"I've no doubt he will. So—"

"So," McNelly informed him, "while me and my boys handle the creek, you and your vaqueros can have General Cordoba all to yourselves."

"Ah, McNelly!" Laird beamed. "You're a lovely man, that you are. By the Jesus, I could almost kiss you!"

"Spare me the pleasure, Mr. Laird. It's not sentiment, it's just good tactics. Now, suppose you pay attention, and I'll explain what I have in mind."

Laird clapped him across the shoulder and knelt down in the dirt. McNelly suppressed a smile, exchanging a look with his scout, and then directed their attention to the diagram.

CHAPTER 26

A faint blush of dawn lighted the sky. With the Rangers in the lead, their horses held to a walk, the column advanced quietly along the road. The men were grim-eyed, staring straight ahead, their features cold and hard in the sallow overcast. Abruptly, perhaps a hundred yards in the distance, the *Las Cuevas* compound came into view. The road opened onto the main *casa,* and beyond that several outbuildings were scattered in random order. At the front of the column, McNelly stood up in his stirrups, looked back down the road, and waved.

Trailing the Rangers by several yards, Laird acknowledged the signal and halted his vaqueros with an upraised palm. At his side, Ramon Morado motioned the vaqueros off the road, and within moments they were screened from sight by scrub undergrowth. Then, as prearranged, Laird removed his hat and waved.

McNelly instantly spurred his horse. Behind him, the Rangers gigged their own mounts, and the column thundered toward *Las Cuevas.* As they neared the compound, each man pulled his pistol; their rifles were held in reserve, to be used in the event of dismounted fighting. If all went according to plan, however, there would be no need for rifles. McNelly was gambling that surprise, combined with a lightning-quick mounted assault, would put a speedy end to the morning's work.

A man stepped from one of the outbuildings, water bucket in hand, as the Rangers swept past the main house. His mouth popped open and he stood transfixed, too astonished to raise a cry of warning. Since he was unarmed, the Rangers ignored him, and he watched as they skirted east of the compound. The steady drumbeat of hooves split the dawn still-

ness, and many of the *bandidos* camped on the creek were
awakened. But they were momentarily confused, unable to
identify the source of the sound, for the riders were con-
cealed behind the outbuildings. It was their uncertainty that
gave McNelly and his Rangers the element of surprise.

Upon clearing the compound, McNelly wheeled westward,
signaling a change in formation. Still at a gallop, the Rangers
maneuvered from column of twos, splitting left and right
until they came on line. With McNelly in the center—twenty
Rangers abreast of him on either side—they pounded
toward the creek. The distance was less than fifty yards, cov-
ered in a matter of seconds, and the *bandidos* were caught in
their bedrolls. McNelly fired the first shot, killing a man who
stumbled from his blanket, barefooted and wild-eyed, des-
perately working the lever on an old Winchester. Then the
Rangers cut loose, firing at point-blank range as their charge
carried them through the camps of both squadrons. For a
moment, with nearly thirty men killed and not a shot fired in
return, it almost became a rout. But the *bandidos* were fight-
ers, and while some ran, the majority held their ground.
Frantically, shouting and cursing, they threw aside their bed-
rolls and armed themselves.

Yet despite their determination, there was no time for
an organized defense. At the edge of the creek, McNelly
wheeled his Rangers and charged back into the camp. The
bandidos rose to meet them, and almost instantly, the gunfire
became general. It was every man for himself.

Within moments of the attack, McNelly's tactical genius be-
came apparent to Laird. Hidden in the chaparral beside the
road, he had a clear view of the compound. As the volume of
gunfire intensified on the creek, men began streaming out
of the main house and the outbuildings. Though hastily
dressed, they were all armed, and not one so much as
glanced in Laird's direction. Their attention centered on the
creek, and, to a man, they hurried to the aid of their *com-
pañeros.*

Laird waited, curbing his impatience. The urge to join
the fight was almost more than he could withstand. Yet
McNelly's orders had been explicit, based on the sequence of
events that were now unfolding. Laird was to delay until the

outbuildings had emptied and the *Las Curevas* regulars were
exposed on the open ground between the creek and the com-
pound. Then he was to attack from the rear, closing the trap.
With the Rangers on the front and the vaqueros to the rear,
the forces of *Las Cuevas* could be driven together in the
open and annihilated.

Yet, ironically enough, it was General Juan Cordoba him-
self who triggered Laird's attack. His gaze fixed on the com-
pound, Laird saw a man, dressed in the gaudy uniform of a
Mexican officer, emerge from the main *casa*. Brandishing a
silver-plated pistol in either hand, the man was joined by
a small contingent who had gathered outside the house. To-
gether, they hurried toward the rear of the compound.

To Laird, watching spellbound, there could be no doubt. It
was Juan Cordoba and his personal bodyguards! Clearly the
men would have delayed for no one except the *generalissimo*
himself. Laird twisted around in his saddle, grinning wolf-
ishly at Ramon Morado. Then he motioned the vaqueros
onward, spurring his horse, voice raised in a jubilant cry.

"Anda, hombres! Muerto a Cordoba! Anda!"

The vaqueros responded with a savage chorus, yipping and
shouting as they crashed their horses out of the brush. With
Laird in the lead, and Ramon trailing him, they took off
down the road at a full gallop. Moments later, surging
around the main *casa,* they broke ranks and streamed past
the outbuildings. Laird cleared the compound first, followed
closely by Ramon and several vaqueros. Ahead, on the open
ground, he saw a large body of men running toward the
creek. Vaguely, he sensed a lessening in the tempo of gunfire
from the creek; for a fleeting instant, he wondered if the
Rangers were holding their own. Then he spotted the gaudy
uniform—Cordoba and his bodyguards—rushing to catch up
but still separated from the main body by a good thirty yards.
All thought of McNelly and the Rangers vanished. Laird
waved the vaqueros onward to the creek, then turned his
horse on a direct line for Cordoba. He wrapped the reins
around the saddlehorn and cocked both hammers on his
shotgun. Leaning into the wind, he brought the shotgun to
his shoulder and charged.

Within the same split second, Cordoba and his men
turned, alerted by the drumbeat of hooves. At the general's

side was Roberto Morado; thunderstruck, his jaw agape, he stared as Laird bore down on them. Then he stiffened, stared harder, saw his father directly behind Laird, closing fast. Before he could react, Cordoba raised both pistols and fired. Laird's horse broke stride, slowed by the impact of a heavy slug, then suddenly went down beneath him. But as he tumbled headlong from the saddle, Laird instinctively triggered the shotgun. A load of buckshot fanned through the little cluster of men, killing two of them instantly. Roberto took a ball in the shoulder and spun sideways, struggling to keep his feet. Juan Cordoba dropped one of his pistols, clutching at his groin, and staggered forward in a drunken dance. The last man, miraculously unwounded, drew a bead on Laird, who lay sprawled on the ground not ten feet away.

In that final instant, Roberto Morado acted unwittingly. A dim spark of loyalty flared, and without thought, he trained his pistol on the man who was about to kill the *patrón*. Stunned, rolling awkwardly to one knee, Laird saw it all in a glimpse. A *bandido,* staring down the sights of a carbine, and to the rear, Roberto extending his pistol at arm's length. To the boy's father, however, the deadly tableau had an altogether different meaning. Skidding to a halt behind Laird's fallen mount, Ramon saw two men—one of them his son—aiming in the direction of the *patrón.* His choice was simple. Father and son fired simultaneously, and Ramon's pistol was centered on the boy's chest.

The *bandido* slumped forward, blood staining the back of his shirt, and discharged his carbine into the ground. Behind him, Roberto stood perfectly still, a great splotch of red covering his breastbone. Slowly, like a felled tree, his legs collapsed and he toppled facedown in the dirt.

The gunfire seemed to jolt Juan Cordoba out of his daze. Bent double at the waist, still clutching his groin, he raised his head and fastened a murderous glare on Laird. In his resplendent jacket, hastily thrown on over his nightshirt, the general made a grotesque figure. But there was nothing comic about the look in his eyes, nor was his courage in question. He was dying, yet he fully intended to take Laird with him. The two men scowled at each other, Laird on his knees, Cordoba folded in a low bow, so close they could have

touched. Then, with an expression of profound concentration, Cordoba slowly lifted his pistol.

Laird jammed the shotgun upward into his chest and pulled the trigger. The blast shredded Cordoba with a fist-sized pattern of lead, and he hurtled backward from the impact. His bare feet flapped the air, and, like some garishly costumed scarecrow, he settled to the earth in a puddle of blood. A moment passed while Laird stared down on the body, his nostrils assailed by the stench of burnt flesh and bowels voided in death. He gagged, choking back the taste of vomit, then strong hands went under his arms, lifted him to his feet. He turned, found himself mirrored in the sorrowful gaze of Ramon Morado.

"Cómo está, Patrón? Are you hurt?"

A sudden barrage of gunfire cut short Laird's reply. Startled, he and Ramon whirled toward the creek, prepared to join the larger fight. But they were too late, mere spectators to the final onslaught. As they watched, their vaqueros struck the *Las Cuevas* regulars from the rear. Through a pall of dust and gunsmoke, there were screams of men caught under trampling hooves and the murderous crack of pistols at close range. From the opposite direction, McNelly and his Rangers drove the *bandidos* away from the creek, forcing them to retreat into the path of their fleeing comrades. When the two groups came together, trapped in a last-ditch stand, the open ground became a charnel house. The vaqueros, joined in slaughter with the Rangers, took no mercy. *Bandidos* who attempted to surrender were simply gunned down on the spot.

McNelly, who was in the very thick of the fight, seemed indestructible, heedless of personal risk. He urged the attackers onward, and though their own losses were heavy, they pressed the *bandidos* relentlessly. The gunfire swelled in pitch, sustained for several seconds at a deafening level, then abruptly ended. As the smoke drifted away, it became apparent that the defenders of *Las Cuevas* were finished. The ground was littered with bodies, not a man left standing, the dead and the dying sprawled together in a welter of blood. For a moment there was absolute silence, vaqueros and Rangers alike staring dull-eyed at the carnage. Then a *bandido* groaned and McNelly rapped out a sharp command.

Several Rangers dismounted and walked through the tangle of bodies, dispatching the wounded with deliberate shots to the head. The reports sounded flat, somehow muffled, but final. Afterward, there were no moans, the stillness was complete.

From a distance, his features grim, Laird watched, waiting for it to end. With the last shot he felt somehow freed, all debts settled. Yet there was no personal joy, no sense of triumph, in his vindication. All the killing had left him drained, curiously saddened, and for a moment he pondered the reason. Then it flooded over him, the vivid image of a boy who had saved his life . . . lying dead now . . . struck down by . . .

"Ramon." Laird turned to his old friend. "About your *hijo* . . . Roberto."

"Put it from your mind, *Patrón.* I killed the *traidor* with my own hand, and for that I have no regrets. He deserved to die."

"No, you don't understand—"

"*Sí Patrón,* I do understand. He was about to kill you! I saw it all, and I thank the Virgin I was in time."

Laird realized then it was hopeless. To blurt out the truth would destroy whatever peace of mind remained for Ramon Morado. Bad enough that he must live with the knowledge that he had killed his own son. Were he to be told it was a mistake . . . that he'd killed the boy in error . . . there would be no redemption for him as long as he lived. He would crucify himself, go early to his grave with the guilt of what he'd done. Better to leave it alone . . . bury the dead . . . and the deed.

"If it is your wish, *compadre,* we will bury him on Santa Guerra. Whatever else he was, he was a Morado . . . your son."

"*Gracias, Patrón,* but he long ago ceased to be my *hijo.* We will bury him here, with the *bandidos* and his general. It is where he belongs."

Laird nodded, reluctant to press the matter further. There was an awkward silence, with Ramon staring at his son's body, dispassionate and cold-eyed yet unable to hide his grief. Laird touched his shoulder, about to speak, when the moment was interrupted by hoofbeats. He turned as

McNelly reined to a halt and stepped down out of the saddle.

"Well done, Mr. Laird! We wiped the bastards out to a man."

"Aye, we were detained but we saw it."

McNelly smiled, indicated the uniformed corpse. "Cordoba?" Laird merely nodded, and he went on. "I sort of figured you'd find him, one way or another. Guess your thirst for vengeance got a dipperful and then some, hmm?"

Ramon lowered his head, suddenly tight-lipped, and Laird glanced at him with a grave expression. McNelly saw the look, caught an undercurrent of something unspoken, and studied them a moment. Then his gaze settled on Laird.

"Something wrong?" His eyes narrowed. "Let's keep it straight, Mr. Laird. That is Cordoba . . . isn't it?"

"Aye, it's Cordoba."

"I don't know . . . the way you two look . . . you're damn sure about that, now?"

"God's blood! Are you calling me—"

A sudden rush of color flooded Laird's features and he gasped for breath. He staggered, clutching his chest, and slumped at the knees. Ramon caught him under the arms, holding him upright, and McNelly hurried forward. The attack ran its course quickly, however, and within moments Laird's breathing was even, if labored. Though his features were pallid and his speech thick, he brushed McNelly aside with a weak shove.

"Leave me be. I don't need your help."

"Maybe not, but you need somebody's help. I'd suggest you sit a spell, Mr. Laird, take it easy. We can handle it from here."

Laird straightened, filled his lungs with air, and his eyes took on a strange cast. "We're not done yet. I want *Las Cuevas* burned to the ground! Do you hear me, McNelly . . . leveled!"

"Don't worry about it. I was of the same thought myself."

"And one other thing."

"Yeah, what's that?"

"I want these . . . Cordoba and his men . . . I want them buried."

"We don't bury outlaws, Mr. Laird. The buzzards do it for us."

"By the Holy Jesus, you'll bury these, McNelly. You'll bury them—and you'll do it proper!"

McNelly eyed him for a long while, then shrugged and walked back to his horse. As he rode away, Laird seemed to collapse, slumping heavily against Ramon. Their eyes met, and Laird smiled. His old friend swallowed hard, slowly nodded.

"Gracias, Patrón. Gracias."

CHAPTER 27

Laird sat brooding into a cheerful blaze. The weather was unseasonably brisk for September, and despite the warmth of the fireplace, his bones felt cold. His chin was sunk on his chest, and a cigar jutted from his mouth like a burnt tusk. The flames held his gaze, mirrored in a hollow stare, almost as though he were mesmerized. Yet he was alert, inwardly on edge, absorbed in thought.

All his problems—save one—were now resolved. The summer had been a time of immense progress and high triumph. Exactly as he'd predicted, the beef market recovered by late July, and after deducting all expenses, his cattle operation had cleared better than $300,000 for the year. Though he had anticipated an excellent return, this was more in the nature of windfall profits, and to no small degree he credited the result to Angela's management of Santa Guerra. It left him bitter, often depressed, that she hadn't lived to see her efforts rewarded.

On the other side of the ledger, however, all accounts had been squared. Captain L.H. McNelly, true to his word, had virtually halted rustling along the lower Rio Grande. The attack on *Las Cuevas* had set the tone of his campaign; no quarter was asked and none given, and throughout the summer his Rangers all but annihilated a generation of cow thieves. By late August, with Juan Cordoba dead and his squadrons decimated, the *bandidos* who survived rarely ventured north of the border. Only last week, McNelly had called a halt to the campaign and, with his Rangers, ridden off to another assignment. Their work was done.

Laird was satisfied with the outcome, if not wholly content. His one regret concerned Roberto. Upon returning from *Las Cuevas,* he'd called Trudy into the study. There, as

gently as possible, he told her how Roberto had died saving his life. She began crying even before he'd finished, confessing that Roberto had saved her as well on the night Santa Guerra was raided. Only then did he realize how very much the youngsters had meant to each other; in retrospect, he saw that his own intolerance had triggered an unfortunate chain of events, with tragic consequences. Still, though he hadn't admitted it to Trudy, he knew the affair would have ended badly however it was handled. *He would never allow her to marry a Mexican!* Even as he consoled her, he'd told himself that *Las Cuevas* was the better ending after all. Under different circumstances, he would have killed Roberto himself.

Yet he was genuinely touched by her grief, and he'd held her until she cried herself out. Then he swore her to secrecy, and explained all the reasons why he'd chosen to keep the truth from Ramon. A good man, practically her second father, had killed his own son by mistake. It was important that she understand—and accept the fact—that Ramon had acted in the belief he was protecting his *patrón.* She mustn't blame Ramon for the boy's death, for that would be a terrible injustice. Nor was she ever to reveal the truth of the matter, for that would destroy a decent and honorable man. Indeed, she must make her peace with Ramon, for now that her mother was gone, she would assume the administrative duties of Santa Guerra. She would be working more closely than ever with Ramon, and it was essential that there be harmony between them. Trudy had agreed, her sympathy toward Ramon almost as great as her grief for Roberto. She promised to put aside the past . . . to forgive . . . and forget.

In subsequent days, it became apparent that Trudy, however well intentioned, was no administrator. She simply had no gift for organization, and temperamentally she was unsuited to the drudgery of musty ledgers and ink-stained fingers. Nor was she capable of handling liaison with Ramon and the *caporals.* She acted as a buffer of sorts, insulating Laird from worrisome details, but her disorganized manner was a continuing source of aggravation. Even Ramon, who had taken her underwing, found himself hard-pressed to excuse her lapses.

Several times, as the situation worsened, Laird had toyed with the idea of relieving her and once again assuming the burden himself. But on reflection, particularly after his last visit to San Antonio, he had discarded the notion. Doc Parker bluntly warned him that his heart condition had deteriorated; any strenuous activity, even excitement or unusual stress, might very well result in a stroke. It was a dim prognosis, and the physician cautioned him not to be a fool. The alternative was a risk that needed little elaboration.

So Laird heeded the advice and, with uncharacteristic restraint, put aside any thought of resuming his old work load. But he was by no means idle, for he was quick to grasp, after Doc Parker's warning, that time dictated the urgency of a far greater problem. Santa Guerra needed a master and the Laird bloodline needed a sire. And if he was to accomplish all that, Trudy needed a husband.

As to the proper man, Laird's view had merely been strengthened over the past year. Ernest Kruger was the logical choice on all counts. A man of iron discipline, who could contend with Trudy's unruly spirit, and a man who had exhibited growing fascination with the world of Santa Guerra. Of course, Kruger had proved somewhat awkward in his courtship, and Trudy suffered his advances with imperial disdain. But Laird could no longer afford to wait; their curious mating dance offered little hope of resolution. Nor could he rely on added proximity, however artfully contrived, to bring them together. Time was precious, slipping past like sand in an hourglass, and he sensed the need to act. Cleverly staged, perhaps, but nonetheless a direct approach.

Ever punctual, Ernest Kruger arrived late that afternoon. One of the servants ushered him into the study, and Laird greeted him with a warm handshake. Ostensibly, the young lawyer had been summoned to discuss business. Within the last year, he had worked tirelessly to validate claim on nearly 100,000 acres of ranchland; his dedication, along with a burgeoning loyalty to Santa Guerra itself, had earned Hank Laird's complete trust. If not friends, the two men were easy in one another's company, and their mutual respect was enormous. But today, unlike past meetings, Laird reverted to his old self. He became demanding, and devious.

"I've been wondering about the boys in Austin . . . that's one reason I sent for you. Have they seen the light?"

"Yes and no." Kruger stood for a moment at the fireplace, then took a chair. "I suppose they're like most politicians; they would prefer it under the table rather than out in the open. But we're making headway."

"Aye, but slowly. That's my point."

"We agreed in the beginning that we wouldn't resort to bribes. . . ."

"And a damn fool promise it was!"

". . . so it's campaign contributions or nothing."

"You've still not answered my question."

"Yes, some of them have seen the light. And no, others haven't. Keep in mind, though, elections are next year, and once our men are in office, we can legitimately demand favors. In the long run, contributions will be far more binding than bribes."

"It's the short run I'm worried about, especially if we get hit with another land suit. I want some judges in your pocket, and I want it done by the end of the year."

"Oh?" Kruger crossed his legs, brought his hands together, fingers steepled. "Why the rush?"

Laird brushed the question aside. "Tell me about your land dealings . . . any problems?"

"As a matter of fact, we're progressing quite smoothly. Of the original five hundred seventy thousand acres, we now have nearly four hundred thousand under valid title."

"Airtight?"

"Absolutely. And by this time next year, we'll have it all . . . one block of land."

"Not fast enough. Offer the holdouts more money—do whatever you have to do!—but speed it up."

"I detect a note of urgency. May I ask why?"

"Simple. I don't expect to be around this time next year." Laird paused, watchful. "I'm dying."

"Hank—" Kruger started from his chair. "My God, Hank, are you . . ."

"Aye, I'm sure. And let's have no sentiment about it." Laird waved him down, waited until he'd composed himself. "One other thing. It's strictly confidential, between you and me. Trudy mustn't be told."

"Yes, of course, if you feel . . ."

"It would serve no purpose, and that's the way I want it. Agreed?"

"Agreed."

"Fine. Now, let's get down to brass tacks."

Laird's eyes narrowed, and a smile appeared at the corner of his mouth. "It's my wish that you marry Trudy."

Kruger blinked. "I beg your pardon."

"You heard me. She needs a husband and Santa Guerra needs someone with a firm hand. To my way of thinking, you're the man that fits the ticket."

"You make it sound like a business proposition."

"It is, in a manner of speaking. You'd get Santa Guerra— as part of the bargain—and absolute control to do as you please. Of course I'd expect a promise that you'll carry on what I started, keep building." His fist struck the arm of the chair. "The land, Ernie, that's what counts. Nothing else! And it's the very reason I've chosen you. When I go, I want to make damned certain the dream doesn't go with me. I know you wouldn't let me down on that score."

"And Trudy?"

"You let me handle Trudy."

"I begin to see," Kruger said quietly. "It's an arranged marriage, with a rather generous dowry. Isn't that about the gist of it?"

"I'll tempt you, but I'll not try to buy you."

"Very commendable. What about Trudy, though? Don't her wishes enter into it?"

"Aye, to a degree. But I'm more concerned with her welfare than her wishes." Laird smiled, and the craftiness gleamed behind his eyes. "You love her, don't you?"

Kruger nodded. "You knew the answer to that before you asked."

"Then we've no argument, have we?"

"No, I suppose not . . . except for Trudy. She's not exactly smitten with me. Or hadn't you noticed?"

"Trudy's no obstacle, if we've a deal."

There was a moment of silence. "Very well, Hank, it's a deal."

"You'll look after her and carry on with Santa Guerra . . . the same as I would?"

"You have my word on it."

"Aye, and I'll have your hand on it too."

Laird heaved himself to his feet, standing tall and commanding in front of the fireplace. Still a bit dazed, Kruger rose and stepped forward. Then, quite solemnly, they shook hands.

Trudy left the commissary shortly before sundown. In her father's stead, she had taken on the administrative duties of the ranch, and quickly found it to be a loathsome task. She had no head for figures, and her mother's accounting ledgers, which detailed every transaction on the whole of Santa Guerra, left her in a constant state of bafflement. She detested the work and despised herself for allowing it to make her life so miserable. And she was plagued by the thought that the wild, carefree days were gone forever.

A group of vaqueros rode into the compound as she neared the house. She waved, calling out to them, but the men merely nodded, smiling soberly, and tipped their sombreros. The catcalls and vulgar insults, all the good-natured ribbing she'd once treasured, were now a thing of the past. She had become *La Madama Poco*—little mistress of Santa Guerra—and the old ways were no longer proper. These days, *Los Lerdeños* accorded her respect and great deference, for in their minds, considering her new station, it was unthinkable to do otherwise. She missed their ribald humor and bitterly resented the change. Sometimes, in the dark of night, she lay awake and yearned for those simpler days. The laughter and gaiety, fandangos and music and midnight trysts at the swimming hole. The freedom she'd known and lost . . . and the man . . . Roberto.

Upon entering the house, she was met by a servant and informed that *El Patrón* desired her presence in the study. She found her father and Ernest Kruger standing before the fireplace, and her already frayed temper took a sudden turn for the worse. She considered Kruger a pest and a bore and an intruder on her privacy. His unwanted attentions were a constant source of annoyance, and it galled her that yet another evening would be wasted fending off his clumsy overtures. On top of a dreadful day, it was simply too much. *Hijo de puta!*

With a thin smile, she greeted Kruger, noting his strange expression, and started across the room. Then she glanced at her father, saw the cocksure grin, and some intuitive sense warned her to beware. She stopped, studying them a moment, finally came a step closer, and regarded her father with a bemused smile.

"You two look like you got caught with your hand in the cookie jar. Anything wrong?"

"On the contrary," Laird chortled, "it's been a red-letter day."

"Oh, something special?"

"Aye, lass, very special indeed." Laird hooked his thumbs in his vest pockets. "I'm delighted to inform you that not ten minutes ago this young fellow asked for your hand in marriage." He turned his head just far enough to rivet Kruger with a look. "Isn't that so, Ernie?"

Kruger nodded, abjectly uncomfortable under the older man's stare, then glanced at Trudy. "I would be honored—truly honored—if you will consent to be my wife."

"There, didn't I tell you, lass? A proper proposal if ever I heard one."

Trudy gave her father a lightning frown. Something cold and visceral flashed inside her, a blinding thing that made her go rigid. She eyed him in silence a moment, utterly dumbfounded and speechless with rage. Then she threw her head back and laughed.

"You're loco! Both of you! Especially you, Pa."

"Watch your tongue, girl. It's no jesting matter."

"*Válgame Dios!* You're the joker, not me. But I'll tell you one thing, Pa . . . and you can damn well mark it down as fact. I'm not marrying anybody, and most especially"—she stabbed at Kruger with her finger—"I'm not marrying him!"

Kruger flushed, gave her a wounded look, and turned to leave. Laird halted him with an upraised palm. "You've no chance if you take to your heels now. Do you want to marry her, or don't you?"

"Of course I do," Kruger replied angrily. "But I won't beg anyone, not even your daughter."

"You'll not have to beg. Not in this house."

Laird swung around, fixed the girl with a dark scowl. His

tone was curt and inquisitorial. "Have you no respect for your father's wishes?"

"I won't be bullied, Pa. So don't you try . . . don't you dare!"

"Well then, if not me, what about the ranch? Have you no thought for the good of Santa Guerra?"

"Santa Guerra?"

"Aye, I'll not be around forever, you know. Santa Guerra needs a man with a firm hand and a head on his shoulders. I say Ernie's the man for the job, and on top of that, he'll make you a good husband."

"Like hell he will!" Trudy said fiercely. "I don't need him and Santa Guerra doesn't need him. *Sangre de Cristo!* He's not even a cattleman."

"No, he's not. But he's a quick learner and he's got backbone. And he's got a way with *Los Lerdeños*. Have you thought about that? What happens to them when I'm gone? You can't hold it together by yourself and don't tell me different. Judas Priest! You can't even keep the books straight on your own."

"So what? I can always hire some flunkey to keep books. They're a dime a dozen."

Laird dismissed the idea with brittle indifference. "You're talking nonsense. You need a man . . . a husband . . . there's no way you can run Santa Guerra by yourself. Hold your temper and think about it a minute. You'll see I'm right."

Trudy said nothing, offered no encouragement.

A moment passed, then Laird shrugged, his voice softer. "It's not just the ranch, lass. I want what's best for you, and funny as it sounds . . . I'd like to live long enough to see some of my grandchildren. Would you deny me that?"

"Oh Pa, don't—" Trudy stopped, head cocked to one side. "What's all this talk about 'when you're gone' and 'while you're still around'? Has your heart been acting up again? And none of your bull, Pa . . . has it?"

"I'm stout as an ox!" Laird assured her. "Never felt better in my life."

"Then why the sudden rush to marry me off?"

"God's teeth! Are you deaf? I've just explained my rea-

sons. I want things settled, and I want it done proper. Now, that's it, plain and simple, nothing more."

"Nothing's that simple, Pa. Not with you."

"Well, whether you credit it or not, when a man gets up in years, he starts thinking about things like that. He wants to know that his family and everything he's built will be looked after proper. And I'm damn glad Ernie proposed when he did. Seems to me he's the right man all the way round."

Trudy glanced at Kruger, and he held her gaze for a moment. Then he averted his eyes, staring down at the floor. But his expression betrayed his thoughts, and in that instant, she knew her father was lying. Some sensory perception told her that she'd heard only one truth here today. Her father wanted assurance about the future. Not for himself, but for her and Santa Guerra and their people. Before it was too late.

Suddenly she knew she couldn't deny him. Nor could she expose the charade he'd so cleverly arranged. It was his life, and however much she would have preferred it otherwise, only he could determine how it was to be played out. She was obligated to accept her role, to give a little in return for all he'd given her. To be Hank Laird's daughter.

She took a firm hold on herself before she turned back to her father. Then she brightened and smiled, threw up her hands with a look of resignation.

"All right, Pa, you win. I'll consider it."

"I knew you would! Knew it all along."

"But no more meddling. Ernest and I will talk it out and decide for ourselves. Fair enough?"

"Aye, fair enough and more. But make it soon, lass. Soon."

Laird held out his arms and she came to him. He enfolded her in a great hug, beaming with pride, and kissed her gently on the cheek. Then he grinned looking over her shoulder, and winked at Ernest Kruger.

Kruger nodded and smiled, and looked away.

CHAPTER 28

The wedding was an elaborate affair. Trudy would have preferred something simpler, even private, and quite reasonably she had argued in favor of the chapel at Santa Guerra. But her father was unyielding, determined to stage an event worthy of Hank Laird's daughter. By virtue of a large donation, the ceremony was held in the Brownsville Presbyterian church.

Unknown to Trudy, her father's decision had little to do with sentiment. Nor was it a matter of personal pride. Laird approached the affair with his usual pragmatism, one eye on the future and the other on Ernest Kruger. It was important that his son-in-law—the new master of Santa Guerra—be presented to all the people who counted. The ranch was simply too remote, far too inaccessible, which made it altogether unsuitable for Laird's purposes. Instead, he selected Brownsville for the wedding, and along with every rancher in the Cattlemen's Association, invited a gaggle of politicians from Austin. They all came, and much as Laird had planned, it was an event that catapulted Ernest Kruger from obscure lawyer to a man of prominence and wealth.

For her part, Trudy endured without complaint, and allowed her father to arrange everything to suit himself. She was packed off to Corpus Christi, where she was fitted for a bridal gown and trousseau, and even submitted to a week-long session with the dressmaker before she escaped back to the ranch. In the month since her engagement she had acceded to her father's every wish, holding her temper in check, and never once had she let slip her apprehension regarding the hasty preparations. The one exception had been the night Kruger proposed. After dinner that evening

she suggested a talk, and on the porch she had faced him with the blunt truth of their situation.

"If we're to marry, then I think we should have a couple of things understood from the beginning."

"Trudy, I hope you'll believe me . . . I *want* to marry you. I have for a long time. Your father just brought things to a head, that's all."

"Oh, I believe you, all right. But that doesn't change anything between us. I want you to know that I don't love you, and sometimes I don't even like you."

Kruger bobbed his head. "I know."

"I also refuse to become a pot-walloper with a bunch of kids hanging on my skirt-tail. I intend to have a hand in running the ranch, and if you want children, then you'll just have to catch me in a damned good mood."

"Are you saying that we wouldn't—"

"What I'm saying," Trudy cut him short, "is that you don't exactly stir my blood. So there won't be a lot of monkey business, not unless you show me good reason."

"I understand."

"And you still want to marry me?"

"Yes, I do, very much."

"Then I've only got one last question."

Trudy paused, looked him straight in the eye. "How long does my father have to live?"

"I can't—" Kruger faltered, shook his head. "You're asking me to betray a confidence, and I won't do that."

"You missed the point, Ernest. I already know, so it's not a matter of breaking your word. All I'm asking is, how long?"

Kruger wrestled with himself a moment, then shrugged. "From what he said, I gather he has a year, perhaps less."

"A year." Trudy's voice trailed off, and she was thoughtful for a time. Then her eyes snapped around, hard and demanding. "All right, Ernest, that'll be our secret. But between us, we're going to make it the best damn year of his life. Do I have your promise on that?"

"Yes, of course, I'll do anything you ask."

"Good. Now why don't you kiss me, and we'll go tell Pa it's all settled."

In the course of all the activity and planning, Laird never suspected that Trudy knew the truth. He seemed revitalized

by the impending marriage, personally supervising every detail as the whirlwind preparations went forward. On the night before the wedding, Sam Blalock brought a boatload of politicians upriver, and Laird threw a lavish bachelor's dinner for his prospective son-in-law. Brownsville's one hotel was the scene of laughter and drunken revelry until the early hours of the morning; but at the appointed time, Laird appeared at the church, freshly shaven and immaculately groomed, positively jubilant. When he gave the bride away, he had the look of a man watching a dream brought to life. All through the ceremony he listened raptly, nodding to himself, as though the words were spoken in benediction, spiritual sustenance.

And now, outside the church, oblivious to the well-wishers tossing rice, he watched his daughter descend the steps with her husband. For an instant his thoughts were a kaleidoscope of the past; instead of the vision drifting toward him, gowned in white silk with a lace veil, he saw the freckle-nosed tomboy of so long ago. Then she was there, standing before him, her eyes misty, blue as larkspur, touched with a vulnerable look. He took her in his arms, brushed her cheek with a soft kiss, and his voice went husky.

"You've made me proud, lass. Proud as a man can be."

"Oh Pa . . . I love you."

She hugged him around the neck, tears streaming down her face, and he forced himself to laugh. "Here now, let's have none of that. It's a day for dancing and clicking your heels."

"I know"—her voice cracked—"but I hate to leave you, Pa."

"You'll not be gone for long." He pried her loose, gently tipped her chin. "And I'll be right here waiting when you get back. Just the way we planned."

She gave him a bright little nod. "Yes, Pa . . . just the way we planned."

"Off you go then." He helped her into a waiting carriage, squeezed her arm, suddenly grinned. "And God's teeth, girl! Dry your eyes before you get to the hotel. It's your wedding party, and I want to see a smile . . . *muy risa!*"

He turned quickly away, and stuck out his hand to Kruger, who was standing to one side. The younger man pumped his

arm, smiling nervously, and Laird clapped him across the shoulder.

"She's yours now, Ernie. Treat her right and she'll make you a good wife."

"I will, Hank. And thanks . . . thanks for everything."

Kruger stepped into the carriage, and as they drove off, Sam Blalock walked forward. He stopped beside Laird, who was waving to Trudy, and watched in silence for a moment. Then he caught the look on his old friend's face and glanced away.

"Grand day, Cap'n."

Laird cleared his throat. "Aye, grand indeed."

"Want to join your guests? I think they're waitin' on you, Cap'n."

"How long till boarding, Sam?"

"Eight bells, thereabouts. We've plenty of leeway."

"Then let 'em wait! I need a drink."

Laird stepped into the street, hands jammed in his pockets, and went striding off toward the riverfront. Sam Blalock cast a perplexed look at the crowd in front of the church, then shrugged and hurried along behind him.

"Salud!"

Laird hoisted his glass and downed the drink. He waited, savoring the crisp bite of the liquor, then set his glass on the bar. His eyes drifted to the mirror, fronted by a gaudy clutch of bottles, and he squinted at his own reflection. The image he saw was annoying but not unexpected; the man staring back at him appeared sullen, somehow morose. There was a certain irony to it, and he found it grimly amusing that today of all days had suddenly turned sour. After a long while he rapped his glass on the counter and motioned to the bartender.

When their glasses were filled, Laird told the barkeep to leave the bottle. Blalock gave him a curious look, but said nothing as he quickly knocked back the drink. He poured himself another shot and glanced at Blalock, whose glass remained untouched.

"Drink up, Sam. You're falling behind."

Blalock turned, one elbow hooked over the bar. "You plan on gettin' drunk, Cap'n?"

"Who's got a better reason?"

"Depends. Are you celebrating or tryin' to drown your sorrows?"

"What's that supposed to mean?"

"Well, for a man whose daughter just got married, you don't seem none too chipper."

Laird had to concede the point. After a reception at the hotel, Trudy and Ernest were to depart on the afternoon steamboat to Corpus Christi. From there, they would proceed by train to New Orleans for a month's honeymoon. Even now, they would be in the ballroom, greeting their guests, and all too quickly they would be gone. Before, he'd thought it a splendid idea, but outside the church his mood had changed to one of dread. He had the sinking feeling he would never see Trudy again. A brief good-bye at dockside and then—

"Damnedest thing, Sam. Back there at the church something came over me. I wanted her married and settled—hell, I practically pushed her into it!—but I don't want to let her go. Hardly makes any sense, does it?"

"Guess you wouldn't be the first daddy that's had second thoughts. 'Course, like they say, you're not losing a daughter, you're gainin' a son. Got to look on the bright side, Cap'n."

"That wasn't exactly what I meant."

"Maybe not, but whatever's bothering you, it won't solve anything by gettin' drunk. Fact is, I seem to recall the doc told you to lay off liquor."

Laird's smile was cryptic. "Aye, that he did. But there's no need for worry, Sam. I'm all set now. All set and ready to go."

"Go where?"

The question went unanswered. Laird glanced past him as the door opened, and suddenly stiffened. Blalock looked around and saw Joe Starling, accompanied by another man, halt at the end of the bar. The saloon was almost empty, and Starling became aware of them the moment he leaned into the counter. A guarded look touched his eyes, swiftly there and swiftly gone. Then he laughed, pounding the bar, and ordered drinks in an assured tone of voice.

Laird studied him with a thoughtful frown. Though they hadn't seen each other in years, Starling had changed little

with time. He was heavier, with huge jowls and a great paunch of a stomach, but otherwise he appeared in jovial good health. All of which fitted with the stories of his immense success in both business and politics. As the railroad baron of southern Texas, he lived in high style, and it was obvious he indulged himself to the limit. It was apparent as well that he still clung to old habits. The man beside him was a bruiser, heavily muscled, with a thick neck and powerful shoulders, clearly a railroad tough elevated to the post of bodyguard. And that, too, fitted the pattern. Joe Starling had always had a wealth of enemies, even in the old days, and his companion merely confirmed that the years had changed nothing.

On their second round of drinks, Starling nudged the bruiser, muttering something under his breath, and chuckled softly to himself. Then his voice became louder—purposely stressing Laird's name—and his companion's mouth split in a vulgar grin. Starling threw back his head, face flushed with laughter, and whacked the bar with the flat of his hand. After a moment the laughter subsided, but he kept chortling and shaking his head, vastly amused with himself.

Laird took a sip of whiskey and carefully knuckled back his mustache. Slowly his face congealed into a scowl, and without warning he pushed away from the bar. Sam Blalock swung around, grabbing his arm, pulled him up short.

"Don't get your nose out of joint, Cap'n. He's just a loudmouth, always was and always will be. It's not worth the aggravation."

"Leave go, Sam. I've some unfinished business to tend to."

"Cap'n, it's your daughter's—"

"God's blood, man, leave me be!"

The command jolted Blalock. He nodded, dropping his hand, and stepped aside. Laird held his position, staring toward the end of the bar, waiting until the two men fell silent and Starling glanced his way.

"Joe, I believe you were speaking to me."

"To you?" Starling wagged his head. "No, Laird, I wasn't speaking to you. I was speaking to my friend here. And it was a private conversation."

"Then you were speaking about me."

"Only in passing. As a matter of fact . . . we were talking about your daughter."

"Were you now? And what was it you had to say about her, Joe?"

"Never change, do you, Laird? Always butting in where you're not invited."

"When you discuss me or mine," Laird said evenly, "it's no longer a private conversation. Or haven't you the nerve to repeat it out loud?"

Starling laughed, spread his hands. "What the hell, she's your daughter." He paused, gesturing toward three men seated at a rear table. "You're sure you want me to repeat it? Right out in front of God and everybody?"

"Aye, Joe, I insist."

"Well then . . . I was telling my friend how this young fellow—Kruger—he's in for a big surprise. Thinks he married himself a real lady, and the fact is, everybody's been talking about her for years."

"Talking about what?"

"Why, what else? How she's been playing stink finger and hide the wienie with every vaquero on Santa Guerra. Hell, it's common knowledge."

Laird smiled without warmth. "You've always had a foul mouth, Joe, but I never took you for a fool."

"You . . . you're calling me a fool?"

"Aye, I am indeed. You see, you've just gone and committed suicide."

"Spare me your cheap threats. I'm not impressed."

"You will be," Laird informed him. "I warned you once before to stay out of Brownsville, and you should've listened. Time to pay the piper, Joe . . . in full."

"A privilege and a pleasure!" Starling blustered. "But you'll have to get past my friend here before you get to me." He paused, then his jowls spread in a grin. "Allow me to introduce you to my vice-president in charge of discord and altercation, Mr. Pigiron Johnson."

The bruiser roused himself, shifting away from the bar, and Sam Blalock immediately ran his hand inside his coat. Laird caught the movement out of the corner of his eye and waved Blalock off.

"Stay out of it, Sam."

"Cap'n, for Christ's sake, don't be a fool! You're in no shape to tangle with him. And besides, he's probably heeled and you're not. Call it quits!"

Johnson snaked a hand inside his coat, withdrew a bulldog revolver, and carefully laid it on the bar. Then he smiled, motioning Laird forward. "Come on, old man. I don't need no help, not with you."

Laird barked a sharp, short laugh. Before the other man could get set, he feinted and punched him in the nose, felt it squash under his fist. Johnson didn't even blink. His arm lashed out in a searing left hook and Laird went down as though he'd been poleaxed. The whole right side of his head turned numb, and a brassy taste spread through his mouth as blood leaked down over his chin.

Johnson moved toward him with uncommon agility, striking swiftly with his foot, and the kick grazed Laird's forehead. Laird rolled away, slinging blood from a split eyebrow, scattering tables in every direction as he slithered across the floor. The tactic worked, carrying him well past the reach of Johnson's boots; even as he spun in the last roll, he came to his feet. But the respite was short lived. Johnson advanced on him, fists cocked, snarling an oath as he ambled forward.

Winded, blood seeping down into his eye, Laird waited, coldly inviting the bruiser to make his move. Johnson took the bait. His shoulder dipped, faking another left hook, then he launched a murderous haymaker. Laird ducked under the blow and buried his fist in the younger man's crotch. Johnson's mouth popped open in a roaring whoosh of breath. He doubled over, clutching his groin in agony, and Laird exploded two splintering punches on his chin. Dazed, Johnson shook his head, sucking great gasps of wind, and Laird kicked him squarely in the kneecap.

There was a loud crack and Johnson screamed in pain, grabbing at his knee. Laird shifted quickly, clouted him flush between the eyes, then broke his jaw with a hard clubbing blow. Johnson reeled backward, his crippled knee collapsing beneath him, and slammed into the bar. His head struck the brass rail and the impact sent whiskey bottles and glasses crashing to the floor. When the debris settled, Pigiron Johnson was flat on his back, his nose ballooned like a rotten apple, out cold.

Laird stumbled forward, chest heaving, his breathing labored. Blood oozed down over his cheekbone and an ugly cut split his upper lip. He lurched to a halt, pinwheels of light flashing in his head, stood for a moment gazing at the fallen man. Abruptly the glaze disappeared from his eyes and a surprised look came over his face. He hawked and rolled his tongue around, then spat out a bloody molar in the palm of his hand. He held the tooth at arm's length, inspected it with clinical interest, and slowly the expression dissolved into a broad grin. He turned, thumb cocked behind the tooth, and fired it like a marble at Joe Starling.

"Aye, you great tub of guts, you're next."

Starling backed away from the bar, eyes wide with terror, beads of sweat glistening on his forehead. Laird shuffled toward him, laughing silently, his features twisted in a gloating look of triumph. Halfway along the bar he stopped, as though he'd walked into a wall, and his face went chalky. He gasped, clutching at the bar for support, then an icy shudder swept over him. His heart seemed to burst, exploding deep within his chest, and suddenly the light went out in his eyes.

Hank Laird fell dead.

CHAPTER 29

The casket was borne up the hill by six vaqueros. Leading them was Ramon Morado, and a few steps behind the pall-bearers, Trudy Laird Kruger followed slowly with her husband. The procession entered the family cemetery and halted. The casket was lowered onto planks laid across the grave, then the vaqueros stepped back, removing their sombreros. Trudy walked to the head of the grave, supporting herself on Kruger's arm, and Ramon came to stand beside her.

Los Lerdeños were packed row upon row around the small cemetery. Altogether there were nearly two thousand people gathered on the hill; except for Sam Blalock and a few ranchers, the mourners were comprised totally of vaqueros and their families. Standing shoulder-to-shoulder in the front row were the *ancianitos,* elders of the village, now bent and withered, who had begun riding for Santa Guerra in their youth. Behind them, stunned and grief-stricken, were four generations of Laird's people, all come to pay homage to *El Patrón.*

For Ernest Kruger, there was a sense of the unreal about the burial. Several hundred women in the crowd were sobbing and moaning, and he saw hardened vaqueros, proud yet unashamed, tears streaming down their faces. But it was the contrast in his wife that struck him most forcibly. Only two days ago, vibrant with youth, she had been gowned in blazing white when Sam Blalock entered the ballroom and approached them on the dance floor. Today she wore black, the same dress she'd worn to her mother's funeral, and she looked older, somehow aged in a way Kruger couldn't quite define. The suddenness of it all, compounded by Trudy's odd behavior, left him vaguely uneasy; for reasons he hadn't yet

examined, he still felt very much the outsider, almost an interloper, and he wanted Hank Laird laid to rest without further delay. He opened his Bible and began to read.

"The Lord is my shepherd; I shall not want. He maketh me to lie down in green pastures; He leadeth me beside the still waters. He restoreth my . . ."

Trudy scarcely heard the words. Her eyes were like glazed alabaster, flat and unseeing in the bright sunlight. She stared at the coffin and saw nothing, yet revealed in her mind's eye was the image of all that had once been and would never be again. Since returning to Santa Guerra, she had shut herself off from everyone, searching for answers that proved elusive and spectral. Her mind was suspended in the emptiness of dead years and unexpired emotions, and within the darkness of her torment she groped blindly for the truth of a time now gone.

Alone and thoughtful, virtually cloistered the last couple of days, she had awakened to the realization that nothing remains constant. She grieved for her father's senseless death, and was haunted by the thought that his life had been extinguished to no purpose. Deep inside, she herself felt cheated; they were to have had another year together, the best of all years, and now there was nothing. It was as though she had closed her eyes for only a tiny moment and upon opening them found that the order of all about her had changed.

Yet there was constancy even in the midst of change. Santa Guerra lent a permanence all its own, and *Los Lerdeños* were as immutable as the earth itself. And while her father was gone, he would never really cease to exist. A part of him would forever be . . .

"—with the certainty that we shall all meet again at the Resurrection, through Jesus Christ our Lord. Amen."

There was a moment of leaden silence. Then the sound of ropes sawing on wood jarred Trudy back to the present. She blinked and saw the vaqueros gently lowering her father's casket into the ground. All around the cemetery *Los Lerdeños* were crossing themselves, and as the top of the casket disappeared, the wailing grew louder. Trudy took hold of herself, fought the sudden rush of tears, slowly gained a measure of composure. Her thoughts hardened to indrawn

bleakness, focusing on the task ahead, and she forced herself to look away from the grave.

A hand touched her arm and Kruger drew her aside, lowering his voice. "I thought we'd ask the guests back to the house, serve a little something. It won't take long and . . ."

"You mean the ranchers?" He nodded and Trudy shook her head. "Maybe another time. I'm not entertaining today."

"Yes, of course, but they've come a long way . . ."

"Then they're probably in a hurry to get home. Suppose you say my good-byes for me."

She turned to Ramon. "Will you see me back to the house, *compadre?*"

"*Sí, La Madama, a sus órdenes. . .*"

Trudy glanced at her husband, then walked from the graveyard on Ramon's arm. *Los Lerdeños* opened a path before them, murmuring her name, and as she moved through the crowd, Trudy paused here and there to touch an old friend or exchange a word of sorrow. Then the throng slowly closed in behind her and she was lost to sight.

Alone in the study, Trudy sat curled in an ancient wing chair, legs tucked beneath her on the leather cushion. She held a faded tintype in her lap, her gaze fixed on Hank Laird and his crew grouped before the first steamboat he'd captained on the Rio Grande. Her father was in the center, young and cocky, staring back at her across the years. He stood with his thumbs hooked in his belt, lean but broad through the shoulders, his mouth crooked in a brash, defiant smile.

The tintype evoked vivid memories. Her mother had been simply a warm presence during the years of her childhood. Someone she took for granted, smothering her with affection, forever lecturing on grace and manners and gentility. But her father was the one who had touched her life with some indelible part of himself. By sheer force of character, always laughing and pugnacious, he had taught her to challenge life; to ignore circumstances and convention and, despite the hidebound ways of those around her, to take what she wanted with eagerness rather than guilt. Until the day of his death he had retained that wild, unrepentant lust for living, and it was the reason she had idolized him with an almost godlike adoration. She cherished the memory of him

in life, and loved him perhaps even more in death. His legacy was one of pride and determination, and an utter certainty of self.

Staring at the tintype, a slow smile warmed her face. A part of her had been buried with him, but by far, a greater part of Hank Laird lived on in her. She sensed it, felt him all around her, and knew she would never be alone in the days ahead. She would endure.

There was a light knock and Ernest Kruger opened the door. She laid the tintype on a side table, then waited silently while he crossed the room. She saw concern in his eyes, a flicker of doubt, and she motioned him to a chair. He sat down warily, like a hawk perched on a branch, his look guarded.

"Have they gone?"

"Everyone except Captain Blalock. I asked him to spend the night."

"That was very considerate of you, Ernest."

"Well, it's been a difficult time . . . for all of us."

"And I haven't helped things, have I?"

"You were upset." His tone was moderate, but he glanced down, studying the carpet. "Only natural, under the circumstances."

"But you still think I should have held a wake for all your cronies?"

Trudy had refused to hold funeral services in Brownsville. She insisted that her father be buried on Santa Guerra, beside her mother, and she adamantly rejected any thought of delay. The wedding guests from Austin were left in a quandary, for a journey to the ranch and back entailed several days' travel. Over Kruger's protests, the casket was loaded into a wagon early next morning, and he had no choice but to accompany his wife. The politicians boarded a steamboat that afternoon, thoroughly mystified by the whole affair, and headed downriver.

Kruger was hardly less bewildered himself. Even now, watching her, he sensed there was more to it. Like her father, she could be devious when it suited her purpose, and he felt very much on the defensive.

"Trudy, whether you believe it or not, those men aren't my cronies. As a matter of fact, it was your father who invited

them to the wedding. He always had his eye on the future, and he saw it as a device to strengthen our political ties."

"I know."

"You know?"

"Of course," she replied flatly. "Pa wanted everyone to see that he'd personally tapped you as his son-in-law."

"Do you know why?"

"I can make a pretty good guess. He figured after he was gone—and you'd taken over running Santa Guerra—that would make it easier for you to pull all the right strings in Austin. He always said money talks; evidently he thought you could spread it around where it would do the most good."

"That's incredible." Kruger leaned back in his chair, eyed her keenly. "If you knew what he had in mind, then why did you go out of your way to offend those people?"

"Because the rules have changed."

"Rules . . . what rules?"

"You were picked by Pa," she pointed out, "and he's dead now. That sort of changes everything."

"I don't see how. We're still married."

"Are we? I seem to recall that our marriage hasn't been . . . what's the word for it . . . you know, the one all the nice people use?"

Kruger flushed. "Consummated."

"That's it . . . consummated . . . and you might say we're still unconsummated, aren't we?"

"Good god, Trudy, we just finished burying your father! There hasn't been time for anything like that. A proper wedding night, I mean."

"You missed the point, Ernest. Technically we're not married."

"Well, I can assure you we are legally."

"You're the lawyer, but would you really want to test that in court?"

"I beg your pardon?"

"Suppose I went to court and asked to have the marriage annulled. Let's even suppose the court ruled in your favor. You'd still be the laughingstock of Texas. And you damn sure wouldn't carry much weight around Santa Guerra, would you?"

Kruger met her gaze, but the words came hard. "What is it you want, Trudy?"

"I want a new deal," she told him. "Not the one you and Pa had . . . whatever that was . . . but something just between us. An arrangement."

"Very well, I'm listening. What sort of arrangement?"

"Let's take first things first. Did Pa change his will?"

"No, although he intended to after we were married. As it stands now, you are the sole heir."

"In other words, he promised you part of Santa Guerra."

"That's correct. With the proviso that I would look after you and carry on the work he'd begun."

They lapsed into silence. Trudy's look became abstracted, and a long while passed as she sat perfectly still, staring at him. Finally she shifted around, pulling her legs from underneath her, and motioned toward the window.

"Santa Guerra needs someone like you, Ernest. Not that I couldn't run it properly, but if it's to become everything Pa envisioned, then we have to expand our landholdings, and at the same time we have to establish ourselves as a political force. I've given it a lot of thought, and I see now that Pa was absolutely right . . . you're the man for the job."

Kruger looked annoyed. "Your flattery overwhelms me. But to be quite frank about it, I have no intention of acting as your front man. Perhaps it's a sound business arrangement, but as a marriage it stinks."

"Oh, don't worry," Trudy replied with a vague wave of her hand. "I'll honor Pa's bargain. So far as the world knows, you'll be the new *patrón* of Santa Guerra."

"We're to be partners, is that it?"

She hesitated, then shrugged. "Since you're my husband, I suppose that's only fair. But I want your word that you'll consult with me straight down the line. If it involves Santa Guerra, I get the last vote . . . understood?"

"I understand perfectly," he said in a resigned voice. "What I don't understand is our personal relationship. Are we to be man and wife . . . or business associates?"

"Like I told you before," she reminded him, "you'll have to catch me in a good mood. But just to show you my heart's in the right spot . . . suppose we consummate it tonight?"

"The final seal," he noted dryly. "Very appropriate."

"Well, it's almost final, but not quite. There's one last condition."

"And that is?"

"I want you to destroy Joe Starling."

"Starling?"

"You heard me. I want him ruined financially and I want him driven out of politics. And I want him to know who did it."

"If you're after vengeance, why not pull out all the stops? Hire yourself an assassin and finish him off completely."

"No. I want Joe Starling to live a long time. Every night before he goes to bed, I want him to remember that Hank Laird reached out of the grave and crushed his *huevos.*"

"And if I refuse to . . . geld him . . . then what?"

"Then you're not the man Pa thought you were, and all bets are off. You wouldn't be welcome on Santa Guerra."

Kruger rubbed the stubble along his jawline, lips pursed, reflective a moment. He had the sensation of a man sinking ever deeper into quicksand, and he wasn't at all sure that he was a match for the woman he'd married. It occurred to him that life with her would never be free of conflict; the best he could hope for was an occasional standoff, or perhaps a truce; and even then she would merely be resting, gathering her strength, forever intent on gaining the upper hand. But of course he loved her and wanted her desperately, and however irrational, it was her wild streak that had attracted him in the first place. On balance, he'd got everything he bargained for and, with a bit of luck, perhaps more.

At length, he drew a deep breath and nodded. "Hank would have approved of your plan. In a way it's a little uncanny, but then I suppose it was to be expected. You're really very much your father's daughter, aren't you?"

"The Mexicans have a proverb. *Un cabello haze sombra.* Even a hair casts a shadow." Trudy laughed, mocking him with her eyes. "I can't promise you a tranquil marriage, but it won't be dull."

Ernest Kruger never doubted it for an instant.

Book Three

1906 - 1909

CHAPTER 30

High in a leaden sky the buzzards wheeled and circled on an updraft. There were at least a dozen of them, sluggish black specks etched against the clouds, quartering a sector of land with unhurried interest.

On the ground, its muzzle dripping blood, the coyote went on feeding. A strayed calf had been brought down several minutes before, quickly killed, then its paunch ripped open in a spill of viscera. The coyote was lean and ravenous, gulping huge chunks of intestine, methodically gorging itself. Ever the wary hunter, it wouldn't return to the carcass for a second feeding; all that could be eaten would be eaten now. The remains would be left to the scavengers overhead.

Nearly sated, the coyote paused, licking warm blood off its snout. Then its ears pricked, suddenly alert to danger, and the coyote lifted its head to the wind. Across the prairie came the distant thud of hoofbeats, and an instant later the scent of something far worse. A blend of human odors mixed with horse sweat, and strongest of all, the dreaded scent of the killer beasts. The coyote turned from the calf and fled.

The sound of hoofbeats grew louder, but even before the horsemen appeared, a pack of five wolfhounds topped a low rise and coursed out ahead on the grassland. Their leader was a monstrous brute, almost three feet tall at the shoulders, outweighing all but the largest of men and heavily padded with muscle. He sighted the coyote immediately—a dun-colored streak of fur on the prairie—and burst into a lope that covered ground at a deceptively swift pace. Close behind, three bitches and a younger male lumbered after him, and the chase began in earnest. Since early spring, when cows commenced dropping calves, the wolfhounds had

hunted constantly; in slightly more than a month the pack
had become known to every predator on Santa Guerra, and
their quarry today sensed he wasn't merely running for his
life. The coyote was fleeing instead from death.

As the wolfhounds strung out in pursuit of the coyote,
Hank Kruger and several vaqueros rode into view. The
young *patrón* was a rock of a man, with rugged features and a
square jaw and intent blue eyes that took in the situation at a
glance. He wore rough range clothes, topped off by batwing
chaps and a grimy high-crowned Stetson. Brought up
amongst *Los Lerdeños,* he understood the ways of the earth
and all its creatures; he knew the coyote could never outrun
his wolfhounds, that it would resort to trickery rather than
speed; and he divined at once the general direction of the
chase. Without breaking stride, he quartered southwest from
the line of pursuit and roweled his horse into a gallop.
Hunched low over the saddle, his voice buffeted by the wind,
he urged the vaqueros onward.

"Andale, muchachos! Ándale!"

The chase was quickly run. The coyote followed a twisted,
convoluted path, winding through palmetto thickets and
snaggy chaparral, gradually bearing toward a boggy resaca
southwest of Santa Guerra Creek. But the wolfhounds stead-
ily closed the gap, and as the coyote skirted a bosque of
mesquite, one of the bitches sprinted ahead in a sudden
burst of speed. Losing ground, the coyote cleared the mes-
quite only to find its way blocked by the horsemen, who were
fanned out in a rough crescent. There was a split second of
delay while the coyote, skidding furiously, attempted to alter
course. Then the bitch struck from the rear, and in the next
instant the pack joined the fight.

Obscured by an explosion of dust, the coyote went down in
a tangled thrash of fur and snarling wolfhounds. A moment
later the pack leader emerged in a shower of grit and blood,
holding the coyote aloft, his massive jaws clamped around its
neck. There was a brutish growl, followed by an audible
crunch, and the coyote's spine snapped in half. The wolf-
hound lifted the limp body and shook it like a furry pelt,
then tossed it disdainfully to the rest of the pack. The young
male and the bitches savaged the body. Fangs bared, pulling

and tugging, they quickly ripped it apart in a frenzied blood-
lust.

The vaqueros whooped and shouted, laughing wildly as
the hated killer of calves was torn to pieces. Hank Kruger sat
quietly, allowing the pack its reward, but after several mo-
ments he put his fingers to his lips and blasted a shrill whis-
tle. Though not yet twenty-four, there was a certain
magnetism about the young *patrón,* an air of confidence and
enormous strength of character that somehow set him apart
from other men. Among themselves, the vaqueros called him
El Onza, a mythical beast of great ferocity, thought to be
sired by a jaguar and whelped by a wolf. It was a fitting
name, one he had earned.

At his whistle, the wolfhounds instantly separated, drop-
ping the mangled coyote, and formed around the pack
leader. The vaqueros fell silent, looking on with awe as the
brutes assembled, standing quiet and watchful, alert to their
master's command. Several moments passed while he stared
at the wolfhounds and the vaqueros stared at him. Then he
laughed and wheeled his horse.

"Vamonos, amigos! Our supper grows cold and our women
grow warm. Let's go! Let's go!"

Hank rode into the compound shortly after dusk. The house
had undergone several renovations during his childhood,
and it bore only scant resemblance to the modest dwelling
his grandfather had built. A wing had been added, as well as
a second story, and the front of the house was now orna-
mented with cornices and green shutters and tall pillars that
had transformed the old porch into a sweeping veranda.
Stretching south for almost a mile, flanked on either side by
trees, was a white clamshell driveway. It glowed even on the
darkest of nights.

In Hank's mind it was all a bit pretentious, the worst part
of Santa Guerra. Each of the renovations had been at his
father's insistence, always strenuously opposed by his
mother, and there were no good memories associated with
the house itself. As a child, he could never understand why
his parents fought so much, and later, when he was grown
and realized they both thrived on an adversary relationship,
it simply didn't matter anymore. There were too many good

things in life to let it be spoiled by the quarrels and their incessant bickering.

Tonight they were at it again. Even as he entered the house he could hear their voices from behind the closed study door. His mother, as usual, sounded slightly undone, and his father rumbled on in that sardonic monotone, dispassionate as a block of ice. He paused, wondering if they would take a break for supper, then decided to skip it altogether. He had an engagement tonight with a little *chica* in the village, and saw no reason to risk that by getting involved in the latest squabble. As he eased the door shut and quietly made his way toward the kitchen, it occurred to him that his parents were both slightly daft. Good folks, but queer as a three-dollar bill.

There was a sudden outburst in the study, and as Hank disappeared down the hall the discussion became even more heated. Trudy was pacing around the room, her expression cloudy, darting quick defiant glances at her husband. Ernest Kruger watched her with a look that belied his own sense of anger and frustration. He was seated in a chair, legs crossed, solemn as an undertaker. In the face of her intemperate manner, he'd learned long ago to suppress his own emotions; the tactic never failed to unnerve her, and invariably it allowed him to win. After several seconds, his voice moderate and calm, Kruger broke the silence.

"Perhaps if you explained your objection I might understand. Doesn't that make sense?"

"I don't have to explain," Trudy snapped. "There'll be no railroad, and that's that!"

"Yes, but why? Surely you have a reason."

"Just because, Ernest. Because I say so and because I won't hear of it."

"Come now, my dear," Kruger admonished her. "Because is an excuse, not a reason."

"The reason," Trudy said with an unflappable lack of logic, "is because my father swore that tracks would never cross Santa Guerra. They haven't and they won't and that's final."

"Good lord, Trudy! It's the twentieth century, and your father's been dead thirty years."

"Thirty-one years, come October. And you don't need to remind me."

"Well, someone certainly should. Times change, and what made sense yesterday only makes perfect nonsense today."

"Whatever his reasons were, they're still plenty good enough for me."

"He only had one reason—Joe Starling—and even that was simple spite. Stop and think about it a minute—the reason no longer exists. Starling's dead himself, or had you forgotten?"

"That's a closed subject, Ernest. I don't want to talk about it."

Kruger shook his head, staring at her in mild astonishment. "If it weren't so absurd it would be ironic. Every spring we trail our cattle fifty miles to the nearest railhead. And who owns it, who's making a fortune off a two-bit feeder line by shipping *our* cattle back East? Joe Starling's heirs, that's who owns it!"

"I don't give a damn who owns it. We've gotten along without a railroad so far, haven't we?"

"No, we haven't, and that's precisely my point. We pay through the nose every summer simply because we have no choice but to use their line. How do you think your father would feel about that, knowing we've made Starling's heirs richer than Midas?"

Trudy halted, glaring at him. "That's dirty pool, and I don't appreciate it one bit."

"Sorry, but it's the truth." Kruger sensed a weakening, and on impulse decided to play his trump. "Have you considered the fact that if we build a railroad, we'll have to have a terminal, and around that terminal we'll almost certainly build a town?"

"What's that got to do with anything?"

"Suppose I told you I intend to name the town after your father."

"The town . . . after my father?"

"That's right. Lairdsville, Texas. Has rather a good ring to it, don't you think?"

Trudy cocked her head and examined him with a kind of bemused objectivity. She hadn't fully comprehended his motives, but she knew her husband had the influence to build a railroad and a town, and if he took a notion to call it Lairdsville, then Lairdsville it would be. Ernest Kruger was the

most powerful man in southern Texas. His political connections extended to the statehouse, and beyond. By virtue of his wealth and prominence, he controlled legislators from several surrounding counties, and his wishes were rarely ignored in the state legislature. Through political clout, legal maneuvering, and shrewd timing, he had increased the Santa Guerra landholdings to more than one million acres . . . and yet . . . he still wasn't satisfied. She wondered what it was that drove him, and where it would end. Sometimes she found herself likening him to her father, and then at other times, like tonight . . .

"Where would you get the money?" she inquired skeptically. "A railroad from Corpus to Brownsville would cost a fortune, maybe a couple of fortunes."

"In round figures, three million dollars. Of course that's merely an estimate, but the money's no problem. I've already lined up an investor's syndicate, and I'm confident we could raise additional capital in Brownsville. All pending your approval, naturally."

"Why are you so concerned with my approval? Other than to keep peace in the family, what difference does it make?"

"The deeds," Kruger informed her. "We're equal partners in Santa Guerra, and that requires your signature to deed over the right-of-way and certain land grants to the railroad."

"Land grants . . . what sort of land grants?"

"Oh, nothing much, merely a cushion to satisfy the investors. Probably fifty thousand acres, maybe less, all of it along the coast."

"That's a pretty stiff price for a railroad, isn't it?"

Kruger shrugged. "It's land we seldom use anyway. Besides, every rancher between Corpus and Brownsville will have to do likewise, so it's only fair that we set the example."

"What would the land be used for?"

"Collateral, perhaps security notes for the investors. That's really up to the syndicate. Of course, I would insist that a large chunk be set aside for the town . . . Lairdsville."

"Lairdsville."

Trudy took a chair across from him, suddenly thoughtful.

Her lips moved, silently forming the word, and she repeated it to herself several times. Finally, a smile appeared at the corner of her mouth and she nodded.

"Yes, you're right. I think Pa would have liked that."

CHAPTER 31

On a brilliant summer day Trudy rode out from the compound. Once a month she visited every division on the ranch, and in an otherwise humdrum existence, these were marked as the best of times. Though largely ceremonial, her inspection tours had become something of a tradition on Santa Guerra; to the vaqueros she was still *La Madama,* and wherever she rode they greeted her with genuine affection. Her spirits always soared once she gained the open plains and lost sight of the house.

Yet there were constant reminders, even on the vast grasslands of Santa Guerra, that time altered all things. The ranch was no longer the majestic wilderness of her youth, nor was there anything but a dim memory of emerald prairies stretching endlessly to the horizon. Progress had settled slowly across the land, and her husband, like some demon god of change, had used it to remold Santa Guerra in his own image. At bottom, Trudy admired his innovative approach to ranching, and for the most part she could only agree that Santa Guerra had prospered under his management. But she'd never quite forgiven him for the barbed wire.

Unlike her father, Ernest Kruger was no visionary. He was a methodical man, with a speculative mind and a passion for careful observation. For months after Hank Laird's death, he had ridden Santa Guerra from daylight to dusk, probing and asking questions, recording everything he learned in a leather-bound journal. Gradually he became aware that Santa Guerra embraced three very distinct types of land, each of which complemented the other in terms no one had ever before imagined. The prairie lands toward the coast, with temperate climate and flat topography, were eminently

suitable for breeding ranges. The blackland plains to the northwest contained rich, loamy soil and produced graze on which livestock could be fattened prior to shipping season. To the south grew a hardier vegetation, perhaps not as nourishing but capable of sustaining cattle even during a drought. It was apparent to Kruger that Santa Guerra had to be separated into three divisions—and fenced—before the ranch could be managed in an orderly fashion.

Trudy resisted the idea at first, appalled by the thought of barbed wire. But in the end, when the older vaqueros endorsed the wisdom of her husband's plan, she had finally relented. Afterward Kruger was often heard to remark that management of Santa Guerra was somewhat like a sophisticated game of checkers. It was played with cattle and land; the primary goal was to convert grass into marketable beef; and he had proved himself to be a master of the game. Santa Guerra annually shipped upward of thirty thousand head to the slaughterhouses in Chicago.

The cattle themselves, however, had proved to be one of Kruger's less notable experiments. Instead of Durhams, which Laird had crossbred with range stock, he imported Herefords and began a systematic breeding program. The results were marginal at best, and after thirty years Trudy still took perverse delight in the fact that he'd been no more successful than her father. But Kruger was a determined man, not easily discouraged, and while the problem continued to plague him, there was never any question of suspending the program. He kept on experimenting, confident that he would one day find the key to a superior breed of cattle.

Curiously, though he was confounded by cows, Kruger experienced no difficulty whatever with horses and mules. Standardbred stallions were brought in to service range mares, producing animals that were highly sought after for both saddle horses and the carriage trade. Next he bred Kentucky jacks to Clydesdale mares, and the result was an outstanding mule much in demand by farmers and cotton planters all across the South. Within a decade, the operation became the largest of its kind in the entire nation, and by shrewd management Kruger enabled the ranch to net a

greater profit on horses and mules than it realized on the beef market.

Still, none of it would have been possible without the land, and Trudy was the first to admit that Ernest Kruger had fulfilled the promise to her father. She often thought he'd even exceeded Hank Laird's dream, and on occasion pondered the similarities between the two men. Certainly he had become obsessed by the same dream, and at the opportune moment he had displayed all the pragmatism once attributed to her father. In light of his scrupulous manner, it had come as one of the greatest surprises of her life.

The long drought of the early 1890s, combined with the widespread financial panic of 1893, had brought many cattlemen to the edge of ruin. With water holes baked dry, the graze scorched, and livestock slowly starving, several small ranchers were forced to sell out. Land could be bought for fifty cents an acre, and Ernest Kruger, always paying in cash, quickly capitalized on the misfortune of his neighbors. If honest, it was nonetheless hard business practice, scarcely to be expected from a man whose code of ethics was considered unimpeachable. Those ranchers with land bordering Santa Guerra were offered rock-bottom prices—cattle included— and Kruger's proposal was on a take-it-or-leave-it basis. When the money market finally recovered, Santa Guerra had become the largest single landholding in Texas, encompassing 1,104,912 acres.

But if money was again plentiful, water was still scarce. Without adequate rainfall, ranching remained a precarious business, and Kruger began the search for an alternative to natural creeks and dammed earthen tanks. Intrigued by the thought of deep artesian wells, he embarked on a program to tap the subterranean waterways. Heavy drilling rigs were imported, and during the summer of 1895, on a stretch of land some miles west of the compound, a column of pure artesian water burbled out of the earth. By the turn of the century, windmills became a commonplace sight; when the drilling program was completed there were nearly eighty wells scattered around the ranch. Kruger's innovative concept, along with his methodical approach, had solved yet another hoary problem, and drought would never again touch Santa Guerra.

All things considered, Trudy felt her husband had kept his end of the bargain. With the exception of Joe Starling, he had delivered on every promise made, and in that instance he'd simply had no chance to resolve the matter. A few weeks after her father's funeral, Captain Sam Blalock had marched into Starling's office and shot him dead. Afterward the old riverman turned the pistol on himself, which seemed to confirm later rumors that Hank Laird's death had affected his sanity. Trudy would have preferred to see Joe Starling ruined financially, and Blalock's suicide somehow weighed on her conscience, but none of that was the fault of her husband. He'd faithfully kept his word, transforming her father's dream into a reality, and their marriage, if not exactly a love match, had evolved into a mutually acceptable arrangement.

Not that it had been easy. Their relationship was rocky from the very start, with a constant battle for dominance regarding Santa Guerra. While Ramon was alive it had been a fairly uneven contest. Through him, she ran the ranch pretty much to suit herself, and in the process suffered two miscarriages because she refused to stay off horseback. But with Ramon's death, and her third pregnancy, the situation reversed itself. The doctor warned that another miscarriage might kill her, and even if she came to term, it would have to be her last baby. Suddenly, with only one chance to extend the Laird bloodline, Trudy wanted the child very much. She enforced upon herself a strict regimen of rest and proper diet, and in the latter months of her term, rarely left her bed. Henry Thomas Kruger, named after his grandfather, was born the fall of 1883.

The proud father, meanwhile, had been busy consolidating his position as *patrón* of Santa Guerra. During the months of her confinement, he had selected his own men from among the vaqueros and appointed them as *caporals* of the three ranch divisions. When Trudy finally emerged from the main house, it became apparent that she had lost control of Santa Guerra. The people revered her as much as ever, perhaps even more now that she had produced a son. But the *caporals* reported directly to her husband, and she quickly discovered he had instilled in them a fear of Ernest Kruger matched only by their fear of God.

Afterward Trudy learned that her husband could be hard as a Prussian drillmaster once he assumed full authority. To his face, he was addressed as *Patrón,* but among themselves the vaqueros called him *El Alacrán*—The Scorpion—and apparently with good reason. He was demanding but fair in his dealings with *Los Lerdeños* . . . until aroused. Then his sting was swift, without warning, and vaqueros who had suffered his wrath quickly spread the word that *El Alacrán* was not a man to be crossed. It was no mean compliment among men who prided themselves on courage and gritty toughness.

Always redoubtable, Trudy attempted to regain lost ground, but her position was hopeless. The vaqueros answered only to her husband, and their attitude toward her had changed; they looked upon her now as a mother and wife, the mistress of the house, truly *La Madama*. She remained as contentious as ever, fiery-tempered and outspoken, spiteful to the point that she kept her bedroom door locked for several months after young Hank was born. But by her own choosing, the battles with her husband became private affairs, for she invariably lost. Ernest Kruger had at last become *patrón* of Santa Guerra.

At the time, Trudy was particularly hurt by what she considered the betrayal of Luis Morado. Appointed *caporal* of the Coastal Division, Luis had evidenced complete loyalty to her husband, politely refusing to take her part in the dispute. In the beginning she thought Luis might still harbor a grudge over the death of his brother. But upon reflection she had to admit he'd never blamed her for Roberto's tragic misadventure. If anything, Luis was even more understanding than his father; though the matter was never discussed, Ramon and the entire Morado family knew her grief was no less than their own. They also approved of her marriage to Ernest Kruger—a proper match for the daughter of *El Patrón*—and understood that her grief, as a result, must be borne silently. As the mistress of Santa Guerra, it was best for all concerned that her affair with Roberto be forgotten. So in the end, once she'd thought it through, she knew there was nothing personal in Luis's decision. He had supported her husband—accepted Ernest Kruger as his *patrón*—simply because he believed it the wisest course for Santa Guerra.

With the years, Trudy had resigned herself to the situation,

though she was by no means content with the secondary role
of wife and mistress of the *casa grande.* In time, she even
forgave Luis, and he once again became her closest friend,
almost a confidant. Through him, she was able to influence,
to some small degree, the daily management of Santa
Guerra. Yet there were certain matters, notably her mar-
riage, on which they seldom agreed. Luis was of the old
school, very much the son of Ramon Morado, and believed
men's work should be left to men, especially where it in-
volved her husband, the *patrón.* Trudy tolerated his views,
but she never fully reconciled herself to defeat. One day,
when the time was right, she still thought it would be possi-
ble to wrest control away from Ernest Kruger.

Today, with Luis Morado at her side, Trudy sat her horse
on a rise overlooking the breeding pastures. Apart from her
status on Santa Guerra, she had few regrets. Nor was she any
longer bedeviled by illusions about herself. Time had treated
her harshly in many ways, and thirty years had added gray to
her hair, worry lines to her face. Yet she was strong and
healthy, still a match for her husband whenever she allowed
him into her bed. Of greater consequence, and perhaps the
chief source of her fortitude, was the fact that she had ac-
cepted a truth spoken by her father so many years ago. Santa
Guerra needed a man! For the moment, that man was her
husband, and though she'd never told him so outright, he
had accomplished far more than she had ever dreamed pos-
sible. Over the years she had come to respect and admire
him, and while he'd never once stirred her blood, there were
times when she genuinely liked him. Yet age and experience
had taught her that the only constant in life was the inevita-
bility of change.

What was true today might prove patently false tomorrow.
Santa Guerra needed a man, but there was no man for all
seasons. And where she had failed, another might succeed.
Not easily or quickly but, with the proper guidance, inevita-
bly.

She sat for a long while watching a mare and its foal graze
in the pasture below. And her thoughts turned to young
Hank.

CHAPTER 32

"Three to one, señor. No more!"

"*Válgame Dios!* I asked for odds, *hombre*. Don't insult me!"

"Ahhh, it is you who insult me, señor. The *negro* is a killer —*El Diablo's asesino!*—he's never been beaten. Twenty times he's been pitted, maybe more, and still he lives!"

"*Sí*, but always against one bird. Tonight he faces seven— count them, *hombre!*—seven blooded *gallos*. Each of them a *guerrero* . . . a warrior!"

"*Pollitos*, señor . . . chickens not cocks! . . . no match for the *negro*. It will be a slaughter!"

"But think, *hombre!* You have seven chances—all fighters who have survived the pit before!—and I have only the *negro*. The odds are seven to one, clearly in your favor. *Verdad?*"

"Seven to one! No, señor, impossible! Perhaps four to one . . . for a modest wager . . . but no more. That's all!"

"A thousand pesos, *hombre*. For a sporting man such as yourself, that should be modest indeed."

"*Sí*, I would venture a thousand."

"Then it's done?"

"Agreed, señor."

"*Hecho!*"

Hank Kruger grinned, exchanging a firm handshake with the Mexican. Then he turned to the girl on his arm and winked. She smiled, quite impressed by the way he'd boosted the odds. Yet there was something tentative in her eyes, a question. As they edged through the crowd, moving closer to the pit, she gave him a searching look.

"It is a great deal of money."

"A modest wager," Hank replied, mimicking the Mexi-

can's voice. "Any more and I would have frightened him off."

"Then you are certain of the *gallo negro* . . . certain you will win?"

"Of course, *chica!* With you at my side, how could I lose?"

The girl giggled. "Do I really bring you luck, señor . . . *buena fortuna?*"

"Ask the Virgin to make it so, little one. If the *negro* wins, I will give you a share."

"A share . . . for me, señor . . . truly?"

"*Sí, quinientos pesos,* all for yourself."

The girl squealed and hugged his arm to her breasts. She was one of hundreds of *putas* who practiced their trade in Matamoros. Younger than most, her attractiveness not yet dulled, she could hardly envision five hundred pesos. A night's work normally brought less than a tenth that amount, and always the *policía,* with their hands out, greedily demanding half of all she earned. She thanked the Virgin that this fair-haired gringo had wandered into the cantina tonight. She mentally crossed herself that he had selected her over the other girls, that he hadn't taken her straight-away to bed but had instead brought her to the cock-fights. She blessed him for his generosity, and promised herself— whether the *negro* cock won or lost—that the gringo would experience a night in bed such as he'd never known before. A man with so little regard for money must be encouraged to return another night . . . and another . . . always to *her* bed.

The girl was new to her trade, lacking the cynicism of a veteran *puta,* and still a poor judge of character. Hank Kruger regularly visited Matamoros, often for days at a time. Among the sporting element, his was a familiar face. There was hardly a gambling dive or cantina or whorehouse in the whole of Matamoros where he wasn't known. Tales of his grandfather—the hard-fisted riverman—were part of local folklore, and it was commonly agreed that the grandson had been formed in the same mold. Sober, he was the soul of courtesy, generous to a fault. Drunk, he was sullen and abusive, with a hair-trigger temper, ready to administer a brutal beating at the slightest affront. It was in Matamoros that he had earned his nickname—*El Onza*—and few questioned

that, within him, something of the mythical beast was unleashed by liquor. Yet his trips to Matamoros were begun in a spirit of revelry and escape. He came there to gamble and carouse and spend himself on whores. And to forget Santa Guerra.

With the girl hanging on his arm, Hank cleared a path through the crowd. There were few Anglos among the spectators, and though he rudely jostled several Mexicans, none of them took offense. A cock-fight was often more dangerous for those attending than for the spurred *gallos* in the pit. The combative aura, enhanced by liquor and feverish betting, transformed even the mildest of men into a *macho hombre*. Knives flashed at any provocation, real or imagined, and the action outside the pit was frequently the highlight of the evening. Yet few men, unless pushed to the limit, cared to tangle with the young gringo from Santa Guerra. His work was known and respected, and his eagerness to fight was considered unnatural. Like the *gallos,* he seemed to enjoy it.

Tonight, Hank was still in an amiable mood, not yet drunk. After making a place for himself and the girl in the front row, he pulled a pint of tequila from his coat pocket. He offered it to the girl, but she shook her head and he tipped the bottle, downing a quick shot. He corked it, wiping his lips, and returned the bottle to his pocket. Then he leaned forward, elbows on a wooden railing which encircled the pit. His eyes were drawn to the *negro* and a slow smile touched the corner of his mouth.

The pit was roughly twenty feet in diameter, a hard-packed dirt arena perhaps three feet below floor level. Crude bleachers, already jammed with spectators, surrounded the pit, which was located in an old warehouse near the waterfront. Overhead, suspended from beams, kerosene lanterns lighted the room through a haze of smoke. A smell of sweat and tobacco, blended with the musty odor of rotting timber, permeated the warehouse. Nearer the pit there was a different smell. The earthen floor, stained chocolate brown with old blood, now reeked of fresh blood and recent death.

Already that evening there had been ten mains, traditional fights in which two gamecocks were pitted to the death. But the event of the night, about to be conducted, was a *batalla real.* Brought to Mexico from ancient Spain, the battle royal

pitted eight cocks at the same time, and was allowed to continue until all but one, the victor, were either killed or crippled. The rivalry among cockmasters was intense, and the betting heavy; the victor of a *batalla real* was considered to be a supreme *gallo,* bestowing honor and great prestige on his owner. The cocks were subjected to a rigid training program in the week prior to the event; daily sparring sessions were held, in which the natural spurs were covered with leather to avoid injury; wing feathers were trimmed, the hackle shortened, and a special diet slowly brought the bird to fighting trim. On the day of the event, the *gallos* were allowed no food, only water, and an hour before the actual pitting, they were dosed with stimulants to increase their ferocity. Then, at pitside, each cock had fastened to his natural spurs specially crafted steel spurs two inches in length or longer. A tiny feathered warrior, shanked with steel, the *gallo* was at last ready for the *batalla real.*

The eight cockmasters were spaced evenly around the pit, awaiting the signal to release their *gallos.* Most of the cocks were bronze red in color, with a couple of duns and a lone black. Held in his owner's hands, the black was immobile, staring calmly at nothing. His eyes were fierce bright buttons of malevolence, yet he seemed utterly oblivious of the other cocks. It was almost as though he couldn't be bothered, not while he was still pinioned. His look was one of hauteur, withdrawn and solitary.

Watching him, Hank felt a curious kinship with the *negro.* Though he wasn't drunk, he had the sense of gazing into a mirror, staring at an oddly fashioned image of himself. The look in the *gallo*'s eye was one he recognized, for it was his own. A detached look, very private and somehow disinterested. Not so much cold as simply uncaring, remote and uninvolved. A look of one who holds himself aloof from the crowd, not out of contempt but rather out of preference. The look of a loner, alone yet never lonely.

Hank pondered it a moment, found an unexpected revelation in the *gallo negro*'s manner. With the girl at his side, standing in a warehouse jammed with men, he was still alone. There, one of the crowd, yet apart; with them but not of them. Nor was it simply Matamoros, time and circumstance, attributable to strange men and a strange girl. He

was the stranger! Even on home ground—on Santa Guerra!
—he was the oddball. The outsider.

The one who somehow never belonged.

The thought jolted him. Yet it explained the sense of . . .
indifference . . . he'd lately experienced toward so many
things. And people. His mother and father, the ranch, even
his oldest friends among *Los Lerdeños*. A man who didn't
belong gradually drifted away, cut himself off. Eventually, all
sense of obligation diminished, he chose to stand alone. It
was just that simple.

Or was it? Hank considered it a moment longer, and real-
ized there was a nagging uncertainty in the back of his mind.
Not about his folks necessarily. He knew his whoring and
rowdy behavior worried his mother, and for her sake he felt
a stab of regret. At bottom, though, he'd always known that
she secretly delighted in his deviltry. She was concerned he'd
catch the clap or get a knife planted in his ribs, but she'd
never once raised the subject of the family name. She just
didn't give a good goddamn about the opinion of anyone
outside the boundaries of Santa Guerra. His father, on the
other hand, was practically cross-eyed with disgust. To him,
public opinion meant everything, and he was deeply humili-
ated by Hank's unsavory reputation. None of which con-
cerned Hank one way or another. His father was fussy as an
old maid—a regular pain in the ass!—and he'd told him so
the last time they clashed. Since his father couldn't whip him
in a fight, that pretty well settled the matter. By mutual
agreement, they avoided each other whenever possible.

So it wasn't his folks that troubled Hank. The thorn of
doubt had to do with Santa Guerra and *Los Lerdeños*.
Though he'd tried to convince himself otherwise, the feeling
persisted, and he'd never been able to make a clean break.
His every instinct told him to cut loose and make a life for
himself—on his own terms—yet something held him on
Santa Guerra. For reasons he'd never quite unraveled, he
felt an intense core of loyalty toward the ranch and *Los
Lerdeños,* who were as much a part of Santa Guerra as the
earth itself. Somehow he felt responsible for their welfare,
and in a way that baffled him completely, he sensed some
inner commitment to the land. Not the dirt and rocks and
grass, but something intangible, embodied in the vision of

Santa Guerra. It was all very confusing, and the sort of obligation he'd long ago hoped to outdistance. In that, much as he hated to admit it, he'd failed miserably.

Then there was Becky. Still another quandary, and perhaps all the worse because it was an emotion he understood and deeply feared. If anything, a personal commitment was even more burdensome than what he felt toward Santa Guerra. A man could always walk away from a ranch, maybe not without regret, but it could be done. A wife was an altogether different matter, one that fettered a man with chains heavy enough to root him forever. Yet he'd thus far been unable to exercise any control over himself or the situation. Everytime they were together he got himself in a little deeper, and sooner or later he knew she would raise the specter of marriage. To his great annoyance, he realized he hadn't the faintest notion of how to handle it. He wanted the honey without the sting, and as any damn fool knew, one went with the other. It was a sorry mess, and getting sorrier all the time.

Suddenly it occurred to him that these were the very things he'd come to Matamoros to forget. Time enough to worry about them later, when he had no choice. For now, he had a pocketful of money and a regular little chili pepper hanging on his every word. With only modest effort, he could down enough pop-skull to wash away his troubles, and get himself screwed blue in the process. A man could hardly ask more out of life. Happy times, a *chiquita* willing to perform all sorts of bizarre and raunchy acts to astound him, and a thousand pesos at four-to-one on the meanest little sonovabitch of a cock ever to set foot in a pit. He pulled the bottle of tequila and knocked back a liberal dose in salute to the *gallo negro*.

As he corked his bottle, the signal was given and the cocks were pitted. Several of the birds spread their wings, strutting about in a menacing stance, while the others glared around the pit with looks of ferocious indecision. But there was nothing hesitant or indecisive about the *gallo negro*. He'd come to fight, and when his handler released him, the little cock's toes barely touched the ground. With a lightning-swift movement, he leaped high in the air, twisting sideways, and drove a steel spur through the head of a dun *gallo* on his

immediate right. The dun was killed instantly, thrashing about in a welter of blood, and the *negro* whirled without pause, attacking a red *gallo* to his rear. Amidst squawks and beating wings, spurs flashed under the glow of lanterns, and the red was dispatched in a flurry of blood-soaked feathers. The savagery of the *negro*'s assault seemed to break the spell, and suddenly the *batalla real* began in earnest. Of the remaining cocks, two reds squared off and the dun quickly engaged another red. That left only one red, alone in the center of the pit, confronted by black death itself. The *negro* ruffled his wings, standing a moment tall and stiff-legged, then he stalked eagerly to resume the kill. Even as he struck the red, the other *gallos* jabbed and slashed, weakening themselves in a furious battering of one on one. The crowd roared, on their feet now, shouting and screaming, caught up in a frenzied contagion of bloodlust. Under the lanterns, the pit filled with dust and explosions of feathers, and the flailing spurs of a swift black streak.

Hank leaned across the railing, unaware that the girl was hopping up and down, wildly pounding his shoulders. His eyes were fixed on the *gallo negro* and there was a fierce look of affection in his gaze. His lips moved, mouthing silent words, fists clenched.

"Kill! *Asesinato, negro!* Kill them!"

CHAPTER 33

A lone building marked the townsite of Lairdsville. It was little more than an elaborate shack, constructed of raw lumber, with one window and a door. The exterior had been whitewashed, and it stood like a mote of ivory on a broad plain some four miles inland from the coast. Over the door, firmly anchored to the roof beams, was a bold hand-lettered sign.

THE KRUGER LAND COMPANY
ERNEST KRUGER—PRESIDENT
LAIRDSVILLE, TEXAS

Wooden stakes delineated Main Street, which was wide and grassy, bordered on either side by rectangular building sites. To the north, working under a dog-day September sun, surveyors laid out adjacent streets and residential lots. At the west end of Main Street, where the railroad tracks would pass, there was a designated spot for the train depot, and a half-mile to the northwest another series of stakes for the cattle yard and shipping pens. The townsite encompassed a square mile of prairie, with bright red flags fluttering on corner pins, and at the very center stood the land company headquarters.

Inside, seated behind a litter-strewn desk, Ernest Kruger gazed out the window. His eyes followed the surveyors, but his expression was pensive, lost in thought. What he saw through the window was not a web of stakes pegged together with string; in his mind's eye he saw buildings and people, merchants and trade, a bustling community with stores and homes and the pulsebeat of commerce. Yet, in the same instant, he knew it was a trick of the imagination, wishful

thinking. There were merely stakes pounded into the ground, surrounded by miles and miles of prairie, waiting for all the rest to happen. He was impatient, a thirsty man rushing toward a mirage. He wanted it to happen now.

The past five months had been a time of immense progress. Kruger's days were at first filled with whirlwind negotiations and planning sessions that lasted long into the night. After forming a syndicate and raising capital, he had personally steamrollered a railroad charter through the state legislature. Then, within a matter of weeks, he had convinced ranchers all along the coast to grant right-of-way for the nominal sum of one dollar. It was to their advantage, providing a nearby terminus during shipping season, and even the diehards admitted it would raise property values throughout southern Texas. But in the aftermath, with the planning done and contracts let for the actual construction, his marriage had come perilously near collapse.

Trudy, upon learning that the other ranchers had not been asked for land grants, demanded an explanation. It was then she discovered—in her words—that she had been duped by her own husband. The syndicate had decided that seeking land grants would prolong negotiations and delay the project; the single land grant made to the Southern Texas Railroad was the fifty thousand acres deeded over by Santa Guerra. All the more incriminating, the railroad had promptly transferred the entire parcel to Ernest Kruger, terming it a commission for his services in obtaining right-of-way from Corpus to Brownsville. Trudy had turned the air blue with curses.

"Goddamnit, Ernest, I won't stand still for it. You lied to me! You never had any intention of getting land grants from the other ranchers."

"Come now, aren't you being a little unreasonable? If we had held out for those grants, the project would have taken another year, maybe longer. The important thing is the railroad . . . to get it built . . . in operation."

"Oh, now you're telling me the land grants weren't important, is that it?"

"Let's say they weren't imperative. Certainly not at the risk of delaying construction, perhaps even killing the project."

"Then why was the Santa Guerra land deeded over?"

"You have a short memory, my dear. Not only was it an article of good faith, but the land was needed to build a town . . . Lairdsville."

"A town! You needed fifty thousand acres to build a town?"

"Of course not. But there were other considerations that entered into our planning."

"Were there now? Well, suppose you tell me about it, Ernest . . . what other considerations?"

Kruger stared at her a moment, then shrugged. "The syndicate felt we needed something more than cattle shipments to insure a profit. Some economic base to provide the railroad with a steady source of revenue."

"Would you please stop beating around the bush and just tell me what the hell you're talking about?"

"I'm attempting to explain that the cattle business is seasonal, and since a railroad operates year round, we decided to open the land to settlement."

"Settlement? What sort of settlement?"

"To be specific"—Kruger paused, cleared his throat—"what we had in mind was farmers."

"Farmers!" Trudy exploded. "You lousy—rotten—lying bastard!"

"Now wait . . . hear me out before you get carried away."

"More lies?"

"No, merely a question. Would you have agreed to the railroad if I'd told you about the farmers beforehand?"

"You know damn well I wouldn't have . . . never!"

"Then there's your answer. Everything I've done is for the good of Santa Guerra." Kruger stilled her with an upraised palm. "No, don't interrupt, give me a chance to explain. You see, there are other factors involved, the railroad is merely the first step. As an example, for business reasons, as well as political appearances, it was necessary to separate the town and the farmland from the ranch."

"Why? What difference does it make?"

"Because all revenues from land sales and property taxes will be allocated toward the growth of the town. By bringing in farmers, we create the necessary trade to support the rail-

road and an adequate tax base to support Lairdsville. The ranch gets a railroad, which is what we wanted all along, and it hasn't cost us a dime."

"Like hell! It cost us fifty thousand acres."

"Yes, that's true. On the other hand, you would have resisted the idea of farmers, and I couldn't jeopardize the entire venture on the strength of your prejudices. We simply had too much to lose."

"That's a crock of applesauce!"

"On the contrary, it's very sound business."

"You must really take me for a fool, Ernest. It's not the ranch that stood to lose. It was you! You're the one that would've lost . . . you and nobody else!"

"I'm afraid I don't follow you."

"Follow me! Hell, you're miles ahead of me. You planned all the time to get your hands on that fifty thousand acres, didn't you? The day you had me deed it over to the syndicate, you knew damn well they were going to turn right around and hand it back to you. Not the investors . . . or the railroad . . . or anyone else . . . *you!*"

"Be reasonable, Trudy. I told you it was necessary to separate the town from the ranch. Politically, it was the only expedient way to handle it."

"Politics be damned! You wanted it for yourself. You wanted me out of it, Ernest! You purposely rigged the whole goddamn thing . . . so you could build yourself a little empire that had nothing to do with me . . . something totally independent of Santa Guerra. . . . It's true, damn you, isn't it? It's true!"

"That's ridiculous!" Kruger protested. "I was thinking of you and Santa Guerra. I wanted to create a railroad and a town—Lairdsville!—a tribute to your father."

"You leave my father out of this! You're what he used to call a wee little man, Ernest. Anything you build won't be a tribute to Henry Laird. It'll be a mockery. You're building it for yourself—because you're a greedy scheming sonofabitch! —and that's the plain truth of it."

"Oh, and I suppose your father was a paragon of virtue? The benevolent *patrón* who clothed the poor and fed the hungry masses."

"Up beside you he was Jesus Christ and the Three Wise

Men all rolled into one. You're a piker, Ernest! A penny-ante hustler that had to trick his own wife. Yessir . . . *poco hombre* . . . a wee little man in the flesh."

Kruger reddened, suddenly lost his composure. "You've always compared me to your father, haven't you? That's been the problem since the day we were married. In your mind, he's a tin god. . . . There's not a man on earth that could take his place! . . . Is there?"

"I'm warning you, Ernest—"

"Well don't! I've lost patience with your threats and your patronizing me with your body and the way . . . how you act when we're in bed. . . . God, it makes me sick!"

"What do you mean, how I act?"

"Oh, for the love of God, Trudy, do you think I'm naïve? Don't you think I know what's going through your mind when you . . . let me . . . when you condescend to have me in your bed?"

"Damn you, quit talking riddles! Say it straight out."

"I'm talking about your father. And please, don't insult my intelligence by pretending you're surprised. I've known for years, almost from the first night. It's me you're . . . holding . . . but it's not me you're thinking of. . . . It's your father. It was always your father!"

"That's a lie! A filthy lie!"

Trudy appeared outraged, but beneath her anger she was unnerved by the accusation. It struck very close to the truth. Whenever they made love, her thoughts were actually of Roberto. Her memories were vivid, and with little effort she could transport herself backward in time . . . to the swimming hole and a moonlit night and the boy who had taught her the meaning of love. For thirty years, though it was her husband who performed the act, she had fantasized that it was Roberto inside her. But now, confronted with it openly, she was shaken by an older memory, an uglier memory. On those moonlit nights, at the swimming hole, when Roberto made love to her, her fantasies were always of someone else . . . an older man . . . her father.

Kruger was silent a moment, watching her intently. Then his features darkened, eyes venomous and spiteful. "No, I can see it in your face. . . . It's no lie, Trudy . . . it's the truth. It always was."

"You've got a dirty mind, Ernest. A dirty, vicious—"

"Me!" Kruger shouted. "You have the nerve to call me dirty when you've spent your life—your whole life!—wanting to sleep with your *own father.*"

Trudy stared at him with a look of speechless horror. Her expression was one of sudden realization turned inward on some festering corruption of her inner self. A tear rolled down her cheek, then her eyes filled and she seemed unable to catch her breath. She turned away, stricken by a truth so loathsome it revolted her, and buried her face in her hands. Kruger walked from the room. He closed the door and paused a moment in the hall, listening as she broke down in choking sobs. His mouth was set in a grim line, and he took no comfort from the fact that he'd at last found her weakness. She was vulnerable now, and he could use it decisively in the months ahead, but the advantage had been purchased at a grievous cost. He still loved her . . . needed her and wanted her . . . even though her father shared their bed.

Afterward, avoiding any mention of their argument, Kruger went through the charade of justifying his plans for the future. It took several days to convince her there was nothing ulterior in his scheme, and even then she was never fully persuaded that he hadn't manipulated her to his own ends. Their relationship slowly returned to normal, but it required great tact on his part . . . for she hadn't guessed the whole truth. Always a secretive man, he now became a liar by omission.

On the whole Kruger felt he'd handled the situation rather shrewdly. Trudy would have found out anyway, and from a tactical standpoint it was better sooner than later. With her objections neutralized, he could proceed openly, and much faster than he'd originally intended. He immediately organized the land company and brought in surveyors to begin plotting quarter-section farm tracts. Next, he had several scattered parcels cleared and tilled; then he planted cotton and other varieties of dry crops. At the right time, these parcels would serve as his showpiece, living proof that the land could be cultivated and farmed.

The critical factor, of course, was the railroad. All his plans revolved around the end-of-track reaching Lairdsville. Only then could he lure farmers into the lower Rio Grande

Valley; already he had formulated a campaign, based on methods employed by railroad barons of a generation earlier, to attract immigrants and settlers westward. When they arrived, he planned to have Main Street completed, with an established business community to serve their needs. And once all that was accomplished, he could then implement what he considered the masterstroke of the entire project. It would place Lairdsville on the map, and at the same time, it would bestow an even greater honor on the Kruger name. A tribute to himself, but more important, a legacy for all the generations to come.

His preoccupation was broken as a buggy halted in front of the building. He glanced out the window and saw Hank assisting Rebecca Hazlett to the ground. The visit was unexpected, and from a father's viewpoint, something of a pleasant surprise. Hank normally played the field, hopping about from girl to girl like a bee pollinating flowers. But since he began keeping company with Becky, there had been no other girls. Or at least no other Anglo girls. Hank's outrageous behavior in Matamoros—not to mention his quieter forays on Santa Guerra itself—were a source of unremitting embarrassment to Kruger. It was a subject they no longer discussed, simply because Hank's response to exhortation and threat was some new and even more scandalous episode. He took orders from no one, least of all his father.

Becky's presence, then, was all the more welcome here today. To Kruger, it was a sign of maturity, a trait seldom displayed by his son to any degree. It also fitted nicely with his own plans for the future. Becky's father, John Hazlett, was the largest rancher south of Santa Guerra. As such, he would play a key role, albeit unwittingly, in the latter stages of the land program.

Kruger walked to the door to greet them. When he stepped outside he was struck again by Becky Hazlett's remarkable poise and attractiveness. Today she wore a high-necked taffeta gown, with a fetching little bonnet, and carried a gaily colored parasol. She was small but compactly built, and she had a way of speaking as though she were almost out of breath, somehow very intimate. Her smile was smoky and warm, eyes the color of damp violets, and there was a sensuality about her as palpable as musk. Hank, who

seemed oxlike and clumsy in her presence, was aware of her in the way of a man seated beside a bonfire. Which was precisely the effect she intended.

Watching them, Kruger thought it a curious match. She was dark and vivacious, with hair the color of a raven's wing, utterly in command of herself and her emotions. By contrast, Hank had pale eyes of the most vivid blue, and a broad, ironic smile. The look of a man who found life one immense joke and, ever the rogue, took his sport with no more self-restraint than a bull in rut. Still, they evidently saw something in each other, and Kruger was reminded of the old adage that opposites attract. It seemed the only explanation.

Becky approached, smiling, and extended her hand. "Mr. Kruger, how nice to see you again."

"The pleasure's all mine." He squeezed her fingers, nodding over the parasol at his son. "Special occasion, or are you just playing hooky?"

"Little of both," Hank said affably. "Figured things wouldn't fall apart if I took the day off, and besides, I've been promising Becky I'd show her your town."

Kruger ignored the barb. His son seldom referred to Lairdsville by name; in fact he seldom referred to it at all. There was a conspiracy of sorts between mother and son, and their attitude seemed to be one of wait and see where the town was concerned. On the subject of farmers, however, there was no pretense of diplomacy. Hank, even more than his mother, resented the oncoming encroachment of what he termed "sodbusters."

The girl took Kruger's arm. "Actually, I had to badger him into bringing me here." She gave Hank a look of mock wonder. "Whether you know it or not, Mr. Kruger, your son is still a bit of a ruffian. He thinks progress reached its zenith with the invention of the wheel."

"He's a problem, all right." Kruger chuckled, patting her hand. "Perhaps you can smooth off the rough edges, civilize him a little, hmmm?"

"I'm not sure he's worth it."

"Probably not, but it would be a real challenge, wouldn't it?"

"Challenge!" Becky's eyes gleamed with mischief. "Just

between us, I think it would be more on the order of a miracle."

"C'mon, now!" Hank groaned. "You two are ganging up on me."

"No more than you deserve." Becky twirled her parasol, gazing past him at the townsite. "Let's just ignore him, Mr. Kruger. Now that I'm here I want to see Lairdsville and hear all about your plans."

"Well, there's not a lot to see, not yet. But I've got the plans and the survey maps in the office. Maybe you'd like to see what it'll look like when we're all finished?"

"Oh yes, I would! I really would."

Kruger held open the door and she stepped into the office. Hank threw up his hands, exchanging a glance with his father, and trudged along after them. Inside, Becky walked to a large map tacked on the far wall and Kruger came to stand beside her. She frowned, studying the map intently for several moments, then suddenly clapped her hands.

"That's where we are, isn't it? And these are stores . . . homes?"

Kruger nodded. "All the business places will be on Main Street, and we'll build the houses back off on these side streets. Ought to be a fair-sized town when we get it done."

"And these are the farms"—her finger traced a jumble of blocks between the railroad tracks and the coast—"all through here?"

"That's right. Almost three hundred quarter-sections, hundred-sixty acres each. By rough count, including women and children, I figure we'll end up with close to two thousand settlers."

"How exciting! You must be very proud, Mr. Kruger."

"Yes," Kruger said with exaggerated gravity, "it's a big responsibility."

"I would think so. Not many men have that kind of vision . . . to create a town out of a wilderness and open the land to—"

"Pig farmers," Hank interjected, "and plow pushers."

They turned to look at him, and his mouth curled in a sardonic smile. After a moment Kruger grunted, shook his head. "You're awfully intolerant, son. There's room enough here for all kinds, farmers included."

"Not for my money. You clutter up the country with that many people and pretty soon there won't be any room for cows."

"Unfortunately, cows won't support a railroad or build a stable economy. Besides, we have more people than that on Santa Guerra, and it's never created any problems."

"*Los Lerdeños* belong here! You're talking about outsiders."

"We were all outsiders at one time."

Hank shrugged. "Thanks all the same, but I'll stick to cows. They're lots less headaches than most people, especially farmers."

"Well, it's a moot point anyhow, isn't it? The farmers will settle east of the railroad and that pretty effectively separates them from Santa Guerra. So there'll be no conflict either way."

Hank began a reply, but Becky made a face and cut him off short. "That reminds me, Mr. Kruger. When will the railroad get here—do you have any idea?"

"Oh yes," Kruger said, relieved by the interruption. "We expect to be in operation by the end of the year, perhaps a bit sooner. They're already twelve miles south of Corpus and laying track at the rate of a mile a day."

"That fast?" Becky asked, fascinated. "How on earth do they do it, Mr. Kruger? I mean, I've ridden on railroads, but it never occurred to me that one could be built so quickly."

Later, after explaining the dynamics of railroad-building, Kruger stood at the door watching them drive off. He had mixed feelings about the visit. Becky was a delight, intelligent and lighthearted, altogether captivating. But Hank had embarrassed him; the boy was irresponsible, perhaps incorrigible, always taking it upon himself to play the spoiler. A man invested so much of himself in his son, and every year the commitment grew stronger, more demanding. Still, there was a limit to all things, particularly when he saw nothing of himself in the boy. Instead of gratitude, his efforts were met with defiance and youthful cynicism. A sort of jocular arrogance.

Pondering on it, Kruger recalled there was a time, not so long ago, when it might have worked out. If the boy had completed college and become a lawyer, their relationship

would be entirely different. Yet he'd simply quit, chucking three years of study, and returned home to announce that higher education was a crock of applesauce. It was then, openly confronted with rebellion, that Kruger realized the boy's mother had named him well. Young Hank was very much like his grandfather, rowdy and cocksure, squaring off against the world as though it were all an enormous prize ring constructed especially for his amusement. Then too, he was like his mother in many ways, thoughtless and undependable, with never a thought for tomorrow. It was an imperfect combination.

Curiously, though, Kruger found a spark of hope in the girl, Becky Hazlett. Today had been a revelation, opening up possibilities he hadn't even suspected. From the look on Hank's face, the gingerly manner with which he treated her, it was obvious she had him under some sort of spell. Whether it was mere infatuation, or something of a permanent nature, remained to be seen. But she clearly had him bemused, and with time she might very well clip his wings.

A wayward thought struck Kruger, forced a tight smile. Perhaps she was woman enough to keep him out of the compound at night, to stop his roaming the village like a drunken lord. That in itself would be a godsend for everyone on Santa Guerra.

And the daughters of *Los Lerdeños.*

CHAPTER 34

They were naked. The night was warm, the moon veiled by tall live oaks, modesty unnecessary. Stretched out on the grassy bank, a tangle of arms and legs, their breath grew shorter, coming faster, and along the creek the katydids went silent.

He clutched her buttocks and she moaned, exhaled a hoarse, whimpering cry. Then his strokes quickened and he thrust deeper. She bucked to meet him, hips moving in an urgent circle. He kissed her, their tongues met and dueled; she sucked his lips, licked his face, purring. Suddenly she drove at him in an agonized clash, legs spidered around his back, and he felt the heat building in her. The damp muff between her legs became an abundant swell of flesh, gathering and holding him within her until he rammed blindly, feverishly, to the molten core. She gasped, clamping him viselike, clinging wet with violent contractions, and then she screamed.

"Aaaaah Dios! Dios!"

She shuddered, fell back limply, and they lay panting for a long while. Then he withdrew, exhausted, and rolled away, one arm flung over her breasts. Slowly their breathing returned to normal, the night air cooled their moist bodies, and a sense of time and place came to them again. She shifted, levering herself up on one elbow, and nuzzled against him, lips pressed softly to his ear.

"Madre mío! You drive me crazy with that thing of yours."

"De nada, chiquita. It is nothing."

"Now you boast. Nothing indeed!"

"Yes, but it's all an illusion, done with mirrors and moonlight."

"Eh? Mirrors?"

"A small joke."

"Why do you jest, *caro mío?*"

"Because I'm a jester, *querida.* Why else?"

"Now you mock me."

"Would you have me gruff and long-faced instead?"

"Oh no, never! I love you the way you are. But this thing we have together is very precious . . . one should not make light of it. *Verdad?*"

"We agreed not to speak of sentiment."

Hank pulled away, rose quickly to his feet, and began dressing. The girl watched while he stepped into his pants, buttoned his shirt, and silently tugged on his boots. Then her bottom lip trembled and her eyes smoldered with green fire. Suddenly she jumped off the ground, breasts jiggling in the moonlight, and thrust herself in front of him.

"Where are you going?"

"I have work to do."

"Work! In the middle of the night?"

"*Sí, chica.* Very important work."

"You lie! You always lie. You use me and then you run off to that *gringa* bitch!"

"Hold your tongue, or I may indeed do that . . . and not return."

"Ha! And will she satisfy you the way I do? Will she?"

Hank laughed, and patted her rump. "Keep it warm. *Hasta la vista!*"

She stamped her foot, glowering at him, and he walked away. Several minutes later, hurrying through the village, he exchanged greetings with a group of *ancianitos* seated outside an adobe. The old men waited until he was past, then began chuckling among themselves, voices low and soft in the still night, vastly amused. The youngster looked like his grandfather, even had *El Patrón's* temperament, all that was true. But he had the hot blood and passion of his mother, as was apparent even to a blind man. Long ago she too once prowled the village and visited the creek at night. Of course she was more discreet, certainly more selective, but they recalled it well. Some of them, the quieter ones, recalled it vividly indeed, with great warmth and tenderness, and a yearning for things lost to time.

* * *

The dipper had rocked far down in the sky when they forded the river. Hank took the lead, alert and on edge, one hand gripping a Winchester carbine laid across the pommel of his saddle. Luis Morado and Julio Vega brought up the rear, their rifles out and ready, while the others herded the bull and almost a dozen oxen through the water. On shore, Hank waved the men forward, urging speed, then took a dead reckoning on the North Star and rode toward Santa Guerra.

Behind him, the vaqueros pushed the oxen along at a steady pace, whistling softly to keep the herd bunched together and on course. Yet every eye was on the bull, an enormous humpbacked beast that nearly dwarfed the oxen. So far, he seemed content to stay in the middle of the herd, away from the men and horses; the oxen had been brought along for that very purpose, to keep him calm and manageable during the drive. The vaqueros were nervous, however, and hadn't relaxed their guard since collecting the bull at a ranch some miles south of the border. Before tonight, none of them had ever seen such an animal, though they had heard tales about the breed, frightening stories of its ferocity and hair-trigger temper. Their apprehension had mounted with each mile, waiting for something to spook the bull, and no less than the young *patrón,* they wanted tonight's work completed. It was a job best done, and done quickly.

Hank left the vaqueros to worry about the bull. His task was to insure that they weren't discovered smuggling a Brahman into Texas. The quarantine had gone into effect only last year, and while most ranchers thought it was absolute nonsense, there were some who would delight in siccing the authorities on Santa Guerra. Once the bull was on home ground it was an altogether different matter. His father already had papers—acquired from a domestic breeder—and no one could prove the bull had been imported. But the first step was to get him there undetected.

For his part, barring the excitement, Hank cared very little one way or the other. There was a touch of irony about the whole affair. His father normally wouldn't trust him with the supervision of anything more important than calf branding. Yet here he was leading a $5000 bull and charged with the responsibility of pulling it off in total secrecy. All because the old man knew he could outride and outfight anything on

Santa Guerra. It was almost laughable, but in a queer sort of way it explained why the people called his father *El Alacrán*.

Hank shifted in the saddle, looking back at the vaqueros and the bull. He signaled with his carbine, indicating a change in direction, and reined his horse roughly northeast. The faint blush of false dawn lighted the horizon as his little column disappeared into a thicket of chaparral.

Early that morning Trudy and Ernest Kruger walked down to the stock corral. Hank was leaning against the fence, rolling a cigarette. He struck a match on his thumbnail and lit up as they stopped beside him. Then he took a deep drag, exhaling little spurts of smoke, and nodded toward the corral.

"There's your bull, safe and sound."

Kruger merely grunted and Trudy made no response at all. They peered through the fence, silent for a long while, inspecting the bull with a mixture of curiosity and awe. The Brahman stood in the center of the corral, pawing dirt, slowly swinging his head back and forth. The first rays of sunlight caught a pinprick of fire in his eyes, and he snorted. Then the pawing ceased and he raised his head, suddenly immobile, watching them with a look of suspicion and hostility.

The bull was a magnificent, dun-colored brute. Broad horns fanned out above his humped back; he was barrel-chested, thick through the withers. Almost five feet tall at the shoulder, long in conformation and heavily muscled, his weight easily topped a ton. A great fold of skin hung down from his neck, and in the sunlight his hide glistened like dusty pewter. His lines lacked grace, and viewed from any angle, it seemed that nature had fashioned a creature with mismatched parts. But he was a monster, supreme among all his kind, without fear of man or beast.

After a time Kruger cleared his throat and glanced around. "Have any trouble?"

"Nope." Hank smiled, flicked the ash on his cigarette. "Went off slick as a whistle. Nobody saw us, and we didn't see nobody."

"That's fine. You did a good job, son. I'm pleased, very pleased."

"All in a day's work. Or a night. Depending on how you look at it."

Kruger stared at him a moment, then turned to Trudy. "Well, what do you think, my dear? Quite an animal, isn't he?"

"You want the truth?"

"Of course."

"He's got to be the ugliest thing I've ever seen in my life. *Sangre de Cristo!* He looks deformed."

"His looks," Kruger told her, "aren't important. What counts is that he's full-blood Brahman, the only one in Texas."

"Maybe so," Trudy said, wrinkling her nose. "But for five thousand you should have at least got a handsome one."

Hank laughed. "Tell you something, Mom. What he lost in handsome, he sure made up for in mean. You're looking at *El Diablo* in the flesh."

"Excellent!" Kruger said firmly. "Just the quality we're looking for. If he's mean then he's got the instinct for survival, and that's what our cows need."

Trudy sighed, shook her head. "Ernest, no one could ever accuse you of being a pessimist. But it sure beats me . . . why you think you'll do any better than the others."

"I'll do better because I've talked to every Brahman breeder in Texas. I know how they've gone about it, and I have a pretty good idea of where they went wrong. And needless to say, I have no intention of making the same mistakes."

Brahman cattle were hardly new to Texas. The breed had been imported from India as early as 1885. In an attempt to develop a hardier strain of cow, one better suited to the climate and range conditions, several ranchers had introduced Brahman blood into their herds. The only notable result was that the offspring seemed less susceptible to tick fever; the experiments eventually ended, and with time the few remaining full-blood bulls simply died off. Then, early in 1906, efforts were made to revive the program. A rancher imported five bulls, all of which immediately died from an outbreak of surra, a virulent disease causing high fever and internal bleeding. The United States quickly placed an em-

bargo on all cattle from India, and the Brahman program appeared to be a thing of the past.

By the spring of 1907, however, Ernest Kruger was at a dead end himself. His experiments with Herefords had failed, and in casting about for an alternative, he became intrigued with the Brahman strain. While past results were not spectacular, there was faint promise of producing a sturdier breed, and he really had nowhere else to turn. The arrangements were made in secret, negotiated through a Mexican importer, and Santa Guerra now had a Brahman bull. Ernest Kruger was immensely pleased, confident he was at last on the right track.

Hank wasn't all that convinced, and like his mother, saw no reason to keep it to himself. He took a long pull on his cigarette, dropped it in the dirt, and ground it out with his boot. Then he smiled, watching his father out of the corner of his eye, and gestured toward the bull.

"Mom's got a point. What can you do that hasn't already been done?"

"It's a matter of how, not what. I'll start the usual way, crossbreeding Brahman with Hereford. After that, I intend to try some experiments with inbreeding."

"Inbreeding! I thought that was the big taboo."

"Talk to a dozen experts and you'll get a dozen different opinions. But it's all theory, none of them has accomplished anything worthwhile. So I believe I'll follow my own ideas for a change."

"Well, one thing's for sure," Hank noted dryly. "However you breed him, he'll produce some damn funny-looking cows."

"You and your mother seem to have a fixation with looks."

"Come on, Ernest," Trudy needled him. "That devil's ugly as a baboon and you know it." She cocked her head to one side, studying the bull a moment. "As a matter of fact, we ought to name him Baboon. He even looks like one!"

"Don't be ridiculous. That's no sort of name for a pure-bred bull."

"All right, then we'll call him Babs."

"I like it!" Hank crowed. "Great idea, Mom."

Kruger reddened. "No one in his right mind would call that bull Babs. Look at him . . . it's an insult!"

"For my money," Hank countered, "it's a stroke of genius."

"I think it's perfect," Trudy agreed. "Frankly, Ernest, anything that ugly needs all the help it can get."

"Perhaps, but you two certainly have a strange sense of humor. We'll be laughed out of the Cattlemen's Association."

"Not if he's everything you make him out to be."

Hank grinned. "That's right, Dad. If he's got it, he's got it! And if he don't . . . then what's in a name?"

"Very well," Kruger conceded wearily. "Babs it is."

The bull turned away, strolled to the opposite side of the corral, and stood gazing out across Santa Guerra. Then his tail twitched and, with imperial disdain, Babs broke wind.

CHAPTER 35

On a sweltering afternoon late in August, the people of Lairdsville gathered to celebrate Founders Day. It was the first community function to be held since the settlers arrived. The town's main street was draped with bunting and flags, and by high noon nearly a thousand people jammed the boardwalks along the business district.

The festivities were elaborate and well organized. There was to be a groundbreaking ceremony for the Henry Laird Memorial Hospital. A parade, sponsored by local merchants, would feature the volunteer fire department and a marching band imported for the occasion from Corpus Christi. The Southern Texas Railroad was offering excursion rides, free of charge, to Brownsville and back before dark. There were to be speeches and street dancing, and late that afternoon, a barbecue supper courtesy of the Kruger family. It promised to be a momentous day, honoring both the founders of Lairdsville and the settlers who had made it possible.

All that morning, arriving from every direction, wagons had trundled into town bearing farmers and their families. Nearly half the farm tracts had been sold by midsummer, and the daily train between Corpus and Brownsville invariably brought more settlers. Ernest Kruger's sales campaign, heavily financed and meticulously planned, had depicted the lower Rio Grande Valley as a modern-day Garden of Eden. Immigrants were lured straight off the boats in New York, and farmers who had failed elsewhere, principally on the high plains of the western states, were enticed by visions of a fresh start in a new land. A modest down payment, and an easily arranged mortgage with the Lairdsville Merchant's Bank, put them in business. Building materials were available from the Kruger Lumber Company; sturdy horses and

mules could be bought from Santa Guerra at reasonable prices; and the Kruger Cotton Gin was being erected to handle their first crop. Even the merchants found Ernest Kruger, who was president of the bank as well as the land company, to be an accommodating businessman. Some leased their stores, while others bought commercial property, and they all contracted with the lumber company to build their homes. Soon there was a hardware store and a mercantile emporium, then came a saloon and a grain dealer, followed by a café and a livery stable, and by early summer the town's main street was lined with businesses of every description. And now, only months after they'd begun, the townspeople and farmers paused to celebrate their good fortune.

Shortly after noonday there was a clattering roar, followed by several loud reports, on the wagon road west of town. People around the depot began shouting and pointing, hoisting children to their shoulders for a better view, and moments later a dazzling yellow Pierce-Arrow emerged out of a dust cloud. It was the only automobile in southern Texas, a massive lumbering affair tricked out with brass fittings, mahogany paneling, and a tonneau of lushly upholstered Morocco leather. As it crossed the railroad tracks, the engine backfired, rattling windows all along Main Street. Horses reared and spooked, wide-eyed with terror, and a pack of dogs, barking madly, chased after the car. Then the band struck up a march and the crowd roared, surging into the street.

At the wheel of the Pierce-Arrow, Kruger squeezed the horn, motioning people out of the way, while beside him Trudy waved and smiled. Packed together in the backseat were Hank and Becky Hazlett, along with her parents. John Hazlett was a wiry feist of a man, and his wife Josephine had all the mannerisms of an articulated kewpie doll. But Becky looked ravishing, and unlike her parents, her laugh was infectious and her eyes bright with excitement. As the car proceeded uptown, the band fell in behind, blaring a Sousa march, and throngs of people swarmed after them.

Kruger brought the car to a halt at the end of Main Street. Directly to the north was a large, roped-off area, with a sign identifying it as the future site of the Henry Laird Memorial

Hospital. A photographer from the newspaper, which Kruger also owned, already had his camera set up and was waiting expectantly. Several of the town's leading merchants were grouped before the sign, and as the guests of honor alighted from the Pierce-Arrow, there was a round of introductions and handshakes. Then someone produced a shovel, handing it to Trudy, and the Kruger family was hustled in front of the camera. Trudy planted the shovel in the ground, Kruger assumed a dignified pose, and Hank beamed like a trained bear. The flashpan exploded, freezing everyone in a blaze of light, and the spectators broke out in a thunderous ovation.

Walking to the car, Kruger hopped up on the running board and raised his arms for silence. One of the merchants gallantly assisted Trudy up beside him and a murmur ran through the crowd. Then the noise subsided and Kruger removed his hat, gazing out across the upturned faces.

"Good friends and neighbors! Allow me to welcome you to the first annual Lairdsville Founders Day. I have a few remarks of special interest, but if you will, allow me to introduce my wife, Mrs. Trudy Laird Kruger. She would like to express her thanks in person."

The onlookers applauded enthusiastically. Trudy appeared a bit uncomfortable, but she waited, smiling graciously, until they quieted down. Finally, drawing a deep breath, she raised her voice as the crowd pressed closer.

"Today we broke ground for a hospital to honor my father, Henry Laird. He would have been proud of that, just as I'm sure he would be proud of this town and all the people who worked so hard to make it happen. My husband assures me the hospital will be finished before winter, and he asked me to tell you that we've arranged for a doctor to set up practice here sometime within the month. Thank you."

Trudy stepped down from the running board, and quickly rejoined Hank and the Hazletts. The applause was even louder than before, and it took Kruger several minutes to quiet the crowd. At last, he jammed his hat on his head and stared them into silence, waiting until he had their undivided attention.

"I'll keep my remarks short. We have a full afternoon ahead of us and I know you came here to enjoy yourselves

. . . but I thought you'd want to know that the lawmakers in Austin have given us cause for real celebration."

He paused for effect, then resumed. "As you all know, our county seat is presently located in Brownsville. That's a long way off and it places many hardships on us. Not the least of which is the fact that we're a small community, and as a result, couldn't expect to have much of a voice in county politics."

From inside his coat a document emerged like a magician's dove. He snapped it open and held it aloft. "I have here a letter from the governor of Texas. He assures me that at the fall session of the legislature, the lower Rio Grande Valley will be divided into several new counties. And the county seat of one of those counties . . . will be Lairds-ville!"

There was a moment of stunned silence, then pandemonium broke loose. Farmers and townpeople slapped one another across the shoulders and hugged their wives, laughing and shouting and congratulating themselves on what was truly a stroke of fortune. Land values would rise, and they would have their own county government and, of still greater consequence, their own people would be representing them in the state legislature. It was indeed a day for celebration. A time to dance and get drunk and count their blessings. And a time to praise Ernest Kruger, the man who had made it all come true. The people surged forward, pressing around the Pierce-Arrow, but again he hushed them, motioning for silence.

"We've got a parade and a barbecue and a whole afternoon to talk good old country politics. But before we get started, there's one last bit of news, and because you're all my friends, I hope it will make you as proud as it does me."

He flapped the letter, grinning broadly. "They're going to call it *Kruger County!*"

The crowd erupted in a spontaneous, roaring cheer. Several men in the front row pulled Kruger off the car and hoisted him onto their shoulders. People jostled and shoved, straining to touch him, and the band burst out in a rousing march. Then they turned en masse, roaring ever louder, and carried Ernest Kruger down the main street of Lairdsville, their town.

* * *

Late that afternoon, as the sun dipped westward, farmers began loading their families into wagons. Their mood was boisterous, fueled by excitement and liquor, and they would have much preferred to spend the evening discussing the future of Kruger County. But prudence dictated; there was an exodus of wagons as everyone hurried to reach home before nightfall. Within a half-hour, the countryside was ribboned with trails of dust, and Lairdsville's main street appeared deserted.

Ernest Kruger and his guests departed with the last of the wagons. Though the Pierce-Arrow had acetylene headlamps, the roads leading to Santa Guerra were little more than rutted trails, and he too wanted to arrive home before dark. At Kruger's suggestion, John Hazlett sat up front, and the women crowded into the back with Hank. No one thought anything of it except Trudy; she was thoroughly infuriated with her husband, and alert to some underhanded design. His announcement about the county seat—Kruger County! —had shocked her as much as everyone else. Obviously he'd known about it for quite some time, but hadn't seen fit to confide in her. Nor were his plans for the future any too clear; everything seemed organized, highly calculated, yet shrouded in secrecy. She ignored Josephine Hazlett, who was prattling on about the day's events, and kept her ear tuned to the conversation up front.

Kruger was expounding on the necessity of creating new counties. There were clusters of population springing up throughout southern Texas; like Lairdsville, these communities were small and generally isolated; the larger towns, such as Brownsville, were able to control the political process and dictate to outlying areas. The change was inevitable, and fortunately the governor had agreed to expedite a division of the old counties. It was an equitable arrangement all the way round, and from a political standpoint, it made perfect sense.

"I'm not so sure," Hazlett observed. "We always came out pretty good under the old system. Leastways, we knew who our enemies were, and the way I see it, that's a darnsight better than dealing with strangers."

"By strangers, I take it you mean the farmers?"

"Yep, none other. They're not like us, Ernie, and I've got

an idea we're not gonna see eye to eye. Then it's farmers against ranchers, and I don't need to tell you . . . that could get a mite dicey."

"I don't agree, John. If we use our heads we can run this county pretty much to suit ourselves."

"How do you figure to do that?"

"Simplest thing on earth. I intend to vote my vaqueros."

"Mexicans!" Hazlett's mouth sagged open in amazement. "You intend to vote Mexicans?"

"I do indeed. And if we stick together—vote our vaqueros in a block—we can handpick a slate of candidates and carry the county by a landslide."

"That's risky business," Hazlett pointed out. "You give Mexicans the vote and you might find out you've got a tiger by the tail."

"Oh?" Kruger's eyebrows rose briefly. "Would you rather have farmers calling the shots?"

"Nope, didn't say that. But I sure get jittery thinkin' about greasers mixing in our politics."

Kruger fixed him with a stern look. "I can control my people, John. Are you saying your vaqueros won't vote the way you tell them?"

"Of course they will! Hell's bells, you ought to know better than that."

"Then there's no problem, is there?"

"Guess not," Hazlett said grudgingly. "But I'd feel a helluva lot easier if you hadn't played it so close to the vest. Least you could've done was told me you and the governor had it all rigged."

"That's politics." Kruger gave him a cryptic smile. "Wheels within wheels, John. But all's well that ends well, and don't forget . . . I always look after my friends."

From the backseat, Trudy studied her husband with an eloquent look, surprised and ruefully impressed. John Hazlett hadn't realized it yet, but what he'd just heard was a form of honesty, raw and simple, that she herself could appreciate. In a moment of candor, Ernest Kruger had once told her that men could never be trusted to know their own best interests. Now, reflecting on the conversation, she saw that he'd followed the precept to the letter. He had manipulated everyone, herself included, in order to bolster his polit-

ical influence. And in his strength, for all the days ahead, lay the promise of Santa Guerra.

Suddenly she hugged herself, suppressing a laugh. How clever he was, deliberate but crafty, utterly ruthless. Those were the very traits her father had admired, and it occurred to her that today had vindicated Hank Laird's judgment. He'd always said that cream and bastards rise to the top, and the very existence of Kruger County dispelled any lingering doubt.

Her husband was an unmitigated bastard.

CHAPTER 36

The engineer throttled down and set the brakes as the train approached the outskirts of Lairdsville. Up ahead, the stationmaster threw the switch, and the train eased into a siding along the stockyards. The engine rolled past the cattle pens, belching steam and smoke, and ground to a halt. A brakeman swung down from the caboose and walked forward. The engineer poked his head out of the cab window, watching the brakeman's hand signals, and slowly jockeyed one of the boxcars into position beside a loading chute.

At the north end of the stockyards, Hank left Becky seated in a buckboard, and motioned to several vaqueros who were standing near the pens. He moved along the siding as they lowered the loading chute and locked it into position. One of the vaqueros threw open the car door, then they all turned, waiting until he halted at the bottom of the chute. His expression was sober, and when he spoke his voice was crisp and businesslike.

"Tien cuidado, hombres! Go slow, and treat them gently."

His tone was that of *El Onza* rather than the young *patrón*, and the vaqueros quickly bobbed their heads. Then he nodded, and without a word they quietly entered the car. A horse whickered, and there was the faint sound of hooves stamping in manure and straw. Several minutes passed, and at last one of the vaqueros appeared in the door, leading a chestnut mare. One after another, ten mares were gingerly brought down the loading chute and led into a large holding pen. Hank scrambled to the top of the fence, calling out instructions in a low voice. While he watched, inspecting the mares for any sign of injury, the vaqueros paraded them around and around the pen. The mares were high-strung, skittish after the long train ride, but the vaqueros gentled

them with soft words and gradually walked off their nervous energy. Hank rolled a cigarette and lit it, seemingly in no rush. Yet his concern was evident, and he continued to scrutinize each animal as it was led past.

Every mare in the string was a Thoroughbred. Tall and graceful, with the sleek conformation and long legs of their breed, each of them approached sixteen hands in height. All were of champion bloodlines, and until last month any one of the mares would have commanded a price of $5000 or more. Hank had bought the entire string for twenty thousand.

Beleaguered by ministers and a coalition of churches, the state legislature, on the second day of the fall session, had abolished horse racing in Texas. Breeders throughout the state suddenly found themselves in an untenable position; the demand for Thoroughbreds simply vanished overnight. Hardset hit were the small breeders, who lacked the resources to play for time and locate an out-of-state buyer. An acquaintance of Ernest Kruger, who owned a string of ten brood mares, had written asking for a loan to tide him over during the interim. Kruger politely refused the loan, terming the mares poor collateral, and let the matter drop. Three days later, unbeknown to his father, Hank appeared at the breeder's ranch outside Austin. After inspecting the mares, and dickering nearly an hour on price, Hank laid down $20,000 cash—take it or leave it. The breeder damned Ernest Kruger, convinced the loan had been refused merely to force him to the wall. But his options were limited and the sight of hard cash was too tempting to resist. He took it.

Afterward, when Kruger learned of the transaction, he was infuriated that Hank had made him appear the villain. Still, he had to admire the youngster's audacity, and in the end, once he'd cooled off, he even admitted the mares might prove a sound investment. Santa Guerra dealt with several Eastern breeders, and it was entirely possible Hank could double his money come spring, when the mares foaled. Since it was Hank's money, honestly earned wagering on cockfights and horse races, he had seen no need to enlighten his father. Spring was a long way off.

Now, perched on the fence watching his mares, Hank felt quite proud of himself. A week ago he'd simply been another

hired hand, the heir to Santa Guerra, but nonetheless paid a
wage like everyone else. Today, he was a stockowner, and if
all went well and the foals looked promising . . .

Hank rose, straddling the fence, and ordered the vaqueros
to get mounted. They tied the mares in a line along the fence
and hurried off to their horses. Walking to the main gate,
Hank swung it open and waited until they returned. Then he
led the mares out of the pen, one at a time, and handed the
lead rope to a mounted vaquero. All the men were again
cautioned to go slow and take the utmost care with their
charges. Within a matter of minutes, the riders were strung
out single file, each leading a mare, moving at a sedate walk
toward Santa Guerra.

After closing the gate, Hank quickly circled the pens and
walked to the buckboard. Without a word, he climbed onto
the seat, gathered the reins, and gave the team a swat across
their rumps. Only when he'd closed the gap, trailing the last
mare by several yards, did he glance around at Becky. His
pale eyes glittered and a wide grin spread across his face.

"Aren't they something? Did you see 'em?"

"The horses? Of course I saw them."

"Godalmightybingo! Those aren't horses, they're Thor-
oughbreds. Pick of the litter!"

Becky gave him a bright, theatrical smile. "Well shut my
mouth! Never would've knowed unless you'd told me."

"Awww c'mon! So I've told you . . . one more time won't
hurt."

"Hank Kruger! One more time makes about fifty, and
that's on the conservative side. You haven't talked about
anything but those horses for the last week."

"Yeah, I know." He laughed, looking slightly shamefaced.
"But it's a big day, honey. The biggest day of my life."

"I still don't understand that. Lord only knows how many
thousands of horses you have on Santa Guerra, and you're
like a kid at Christmastime all because of ten mares. It's
almost comical."

"Nothing funny about it. Those mares are my ticket
to . . ."

His voice trailed off and Becky saw the carefree look dis-
solve into one of brooding. It was uncharacteristic of Hank
Kruger, yet a look she had seen more and more often over

the past few months. He seemed to be struggling within himself, and while he hadn't volunteered any information, she decided that today was the day to broach the subject.

She touched his arm. "Please don't shut me out, Hank. I'm sorry I made light of it . . . but you're . . . you never talk to me anymore, not about important things. I want to understand, really I do, but I can't if you won't tell me." She waited a moment, squeezed his arm. "Now, you started to say . . . ticket to what?"

"Well, it's hard to explain." He pondered for a time, shook his head. "I don't know exactly, it's got something to do with freedom . . . personal freedom."

"Are you talking about Santa Guerra . . . your father?"

"The whole ball of wax! It's him and Mom and the ranch; one thing seems tied to the other, except there's no place for me. I've never felt a part of it. Does that make any sense?"

"I'm not sure," Becky murmured. "When you say personal freedom, do you mean some sort of independence?"

"Yeah, that's part of it. All my life it's been a cat-and-dog fight between my folks. He's always had the upper hand and Mom's always trying to go him one better, and it's like I don't even exist. They're so wrapped up slugging it out with one another that I can't get a word in edgewise."

"Sweetheart, there's nothing unusual in that. Honestly, there isn't! You wouldn't suspect it, not the way my mother acts in public, but it's the same in my family. After people have been married a long time, it's almost like a game. They're constantly picking at each other, finding fault. It happens to everyone."

"Hell, I could handle that," Hank told her. "They could fight till they're blue in the face, and it wouldn't phase me a bit. I'm talking about something else."

"Now I'm lost again. Something else what?"

His gaze drifted out across the prairie, hung there awhile, then he blinked. "I guess it comes down to what separates the men from the boys. I've got no say-so at the ranch, and never will. I'm just an errand boy." His voice was suddenly edged. "A glorified errand boy! All I do is trot around delivering somebody else's orders."

"But you'll eventually take over, everyone knows that. Even the vaqueros already call you the young *patrón*."

"Eventually isn't soon enough." His face twisted in a grimace. "Damn it, Becky, I'm going on twenty-five years old! I want to be my own man."

She studied him a moment, finally nodded to herself. "That's why you bought the mares, isn't it?"

"You bet it is!" he declared hotly. "I am to have something all my own. Ten mares aren't much, but it's a start. In a couple of years I'll make enough off the colts to buy myself a blooded stallion, and after that . . . watch out! I won't be taking orders from anybody."

"Not anybody?" Her lips curved in a teasing smile. "What about me?"

"You? What about you?"

"Well, you're right, you know . . . eventually is a long time." She hesitated, watching him closely. "Sometimes too long."

"Could you break that down into simple English? Words of two syllables or less."

"Don't play the clown with me, Hank Laird. You know very well what I'm talking about."

"Awww hell, Rebecca Ann." There was mute eloquence in his shrug, somehow furtive and apologetic. "I told you we'd get married. And we will, you've got my word on it."

She pressed him. "When, Hank? How soon will we get married?"

"Just as soon as I'm not working for wages anymore. Hell, I can't even support myself on what the old man pays. If it weren't for room and board, I'd starve to death."

"Oh honestly! Can't you think of a new excuse?"

"It's the truth. Matter of fact, that's one reason I bought the mares. Thought it would give us a stake and sort of . . . you know . . . push things along."

"I've already waited a year! Are you telling me I'm supposed to sit around and twiddle my thumbs until your mares make you independent? Are you?"

"No, it'll be sooner than that, honey. Lots sooner."

"Oh, sure, the first snowfall this winter, right?"

"Snow?" Hank was impervious to any irony but his own. "It never snows here, you know that."

"Precisely."

Silence thickened between them. Becky had the sinking

feeling that she would never get him before an altar. Of all the men she'd known, he was the only one who gave her goosebumps. Sometimes her dreams were lustful and wicked, indescribably wanton. She wanted him in her bed, wanted him inside her, wanted his babies. There was a vitality and magnetism about him unlike anything she had ever imagined, and sometimes, when he kissed her and held her close, when she felt his hardness pressing against her thigh, it was all she could do not to tear off her clothes and experience in the flesh all those outrageous things she'd done in her dreams. She hadn't simply because she was too proud and too stubborn to let him have for free what was still negotiable for a wedding ring. Yet she knew he was equally stubborn, and for all his bullish charm, she had misgivings about his promises of marriage. His affection was genuine, and she believed he meant it when he said it, but she wasn't at all certain he'd ever given it a moment's serious thought. He was too busy chasing phantoms and daydreams, the image of a boy already become his own man.

After a long while he nudged her with his elbow. "Got an idea. Might not cure the rash, but it'd sure help the itch."

"Oh?" She eyed him warily. "What's that?"

"Maybe we could fool around a little, while we're waiting on the mares to do their stuff."

"You go to hell, Hank Kruger!"

"Yes, ma'am, just as soon as you gimme the key."

She laughed, unable to resist his devilish grin and his sly look of innocence. He put his arm around her and she snuggled up against his shoulder, ran her hand inside his coat. Then her fingers trickled across his belly, lingering above his beltline, and he groaned. She whispered something warm and suggestive in his ear.

CHAPTER 37

Early that evening Kruger drove into the ranch. Hank was seated on the veranda with his mother and Becky, still bragging volubly about his mares. Since arriving home, he'd talked about nothing else, and by now the women were barely listening. As the Pierce-Arrow came to a halt, Hank rose and hurried down the steps. His father represented a new audience, and though there was no lessening of strain between them, he circled the car with a broad grin. Kruger saw the look, greeted him with uncharacteristic warmth.

"Well now, it appears I've no need to ask. By your expression, I take it you're pleased with the mares."

"Wait'll you see 'em!" Hank grabbed his arm, tugging him in the direction of the stables. "C'mon, I'll show you some real bloodlines!"

"Hold on, there's no rush!" Kruger twisted around, waving at the women as he was pulled along. "Won't you ladies join us?"

"No thanks," Trudy called out. "He's just about talked our ears off."

"Well, it seems I have no choice. Pardon me if I don't stop to say hello."

"You're forgiven, but don't let him keep you too long. Becky's spending the night, and supper is almost ready."

"C'mon, Dad!" Hank tugged harder. "Plenty of time for them later. I want you to see the mares!"

"All right, I'm coming! Why do you think I drove all the way out here?"

"Yeah, I know. It's just that you're in for a real treat, that's all."

"Then why didn't you send for me this morning? I could have just as easily seen them at the loading pens."

"Because, I wanted to get 'em home. Stop dragging your feet, will you, Dad? C'mon!"

"All right, all right! Just quit manhandling me!"

Kruger attempted to retrieve his arm, but Hank kept hustling him along toward the stables. The mares were loose in the corral, munching on piles of fresh hay, and Kruger's protests diminished as they approached the fence. Watching them, Trudy laughed and shook her head.

"Have you ever seen it fail? There's something about fine horses that turns grown men into little boys. Sometimes I think if they had to choose between women and horses, we'd find ourselves running a poor second."

"Hallelujah!" Becky agreed wistfully. "Only I'm not even sure we're in the running. All the way out here I felt like a store dummy. Honestly, I did! Hank just went on and on and on about those mares."

"I know. His father's the same way! Once in a blue moon, he'll come to the ranch during the week. But mention Thoroughbreds and he comes roaring out here in that machine like a dragon with his tail on fire."

"You're right, Mrs. Kruger! At heart, they're nothing but little boys."

"Yes, and thank God for that. If they ever really grew up, we'd be in a fine pickle! Believe me, Becky, little boys are lots easier to handle."

Trudy fell silent, her gaze fixed on Kruger. She found herself pleased by his unexpected appearance. Which was indeed a change of heart for her, and curiously, one that gave her a measure of content. In the last year their relationship had altered gradually, quite subtly, in ways she sensed but hadn't yet defined. Somehow, though the precise reason escaped her, all her personal ghosts had been laid to rest. Perhaps it was the shock of his accusation, the fact he'd known her innermost secret all those years and restrained himself until goaded beyond control. Or perhaps it was the realization that her fantasies—the ghosts of Roberto and her father —were simply a childish invention. One conjured out of tattered dreams and faded memories, kept alive merely to avoid the reality of her husband and the demands of their marriage bed. She wasn't given to introspection, and felt no

compelling need to examine the change. She only knew it was true, unquestionably so. The ghosts were gone.

Kruger apparently sensed it as well. He sought her bed no more often than in the past, but these days there was a difference. They were now comfortable together, and with the lessening of tension she was able to give something of herself. It was a tentative passion, awkward though offered freely, and to her surprise, quite pleasurable. She discovered that her husband, encouraged by the change, was hardly as cold and insensitive as she'd always imagined. Outside their bed, he was still hard and ruthless, obsessed by his own ambition. Yet when he held her, slipped inside her, there was a tenderness and a concern for her needs unlike anything she recalled from the past. Perhaps it had been there all along, and in her bitterness she'd been blinded to the gentler side of his nature. She couldn't be sure of things past, but of one thing she sensed a growing certainty. She now felt something very akin to love for Ernest Kruger.

One thought led to another, and she glanced at the girl seated beside her. Becky and Hank were truly blessed, fortunate in a way she'd never even comprehended in the past. They were young and in love, caught up in the sort of wondrous enchantment that was fully shared. Their marriage would begin properly, not with reservation and misgiving, but with eagerness and anticipation and mutual need. Nor would they be forced to endure, as she had, thirty years of senseless antagonism before discovering the need to love. Indeed, they were the most fortunate of all people. Young lovers who were already companions and friends, content with each other, happy with themselves. She rejoiced for them, took heart from them for herself . . . and her husband.

Suddenly she felt a vast outpouring of affection. Her gaze swept back to her husband and her son, embracing them in a warm and very private moment. Then, deeply moved by her own fierce emotion, she turned to the girl.

"Becky, you'll probably think it's none of my business, but I want to ask you something . . . something personal."

"Of course, Mrs. Kruger. What is it?"

"When are you going to put your foot down . . . with Hank?"

"I beg your pardon?"

"Now, there's no need to play innocent with me. Maybe he's my son, but I'm on your side. So forgive the bluntness and just indulge an old woman with a straight answer."

Becky gave her an astounded look. "Mrs. Kruger, do you really mean that—do you—honestly?"

"You ought to know me better than that by now. I always say exactly what I mean."

"Oh god, what a relief! I've wanted to talk with someone, but I just didn't know where to turn. You see, my mother isn't . . . well, you know . . . she doesn't . . ."

"Let's forget your mother. You can talk to me, and I want you to be frank—woman to woman! You won't shock me."

"Yes, well, it's all a little sudden, Mrs. Kruger. I'm not really sure where to start."

"Then I'll do it for you," Trudy said, eyes narrowed in a firm stare. "He's giving you the runaround, isn't he?"

"I suppose so . . . in a way . . . but I'm not even sure he knows his own mind."

"Horseapples! He knows, all men know it when they've met the right woman. It just scares them. . . . That's their way of postponing the inevitable."

"If it were anyone else—" Becky paused, averted her eyes. "Hank's very confused right now, Mrs. Kruger. He feels he hasn't done anything with his life . . . and he's angry . . . hurt."

"You don't have to tell me. He's unhappy with his father and feels like he's forced to play second fiddle around the ranch, isn't that it?"

"Yes." Becky nodded, surprised. "That's it exactly."

"Hank's impatient—too much like me—but don't worry your head about that. One way or another, I'll get it straightened out. Your job is to get him in front of a preacher, and the quicker the better. You've let him run wild too long already."

"Oh, I agree, and I've tried, Mrs. Kruger, really tried!"

"Have you messed around?"

"Mrs. Kruger . . . I mean . . . really!"

"Come on now, don't act coy. Have you slept with him or haven't you?"

"No! No, I haven't, and to be perfectly honest about it
. . . I'm beginning to think that's the problem."

Trudy regarded her a moment. "The problem or the solu-
tion?"

"I've thought of that . . . and I'm tempted . . . but
it's . . ."

Becky looked away. Her features were immobile, and un-
der the dappled light of oncoming dusk, she betrayed not the
slightest emotion. Then her gaze went to the corral, fastened
on Hank. She stared at him a long while, her examination
deliberate, almost clinical, hard as diamonds. She seemed
abstracted, altogether lost in a maze of thought, but pres-
ently she blinked and her expression changed. She nodded,
her eyes suddenly vivid, and her look became one of brisk
determination. She turned, chin lifted defiantly, and smiled
at Trudy.

"I'm going to tell you something, Mrs. Kruger. It goes
against everything I believe to trick a man into making a
decision. But I love Hank and I want him, and I've just de-
cided I won't spend the rest of my life waiting for him to
settle down. If I have to trap him somehow, then that's ex-
actly what I intend to do."

"Wait a minute!" Trudy frowned, peering at her. "You're
not talking about a shotgun wedding . . . are you?"

"I don't know, not yet. But I certainly haven't ruled it out,
I'll tell you that much."

"Now, you listen to me, Becky! We'll think of something,
but don't go off the deep end. At least nothing that drastic,
all right?"

"I won't promise, Mrs. Kruger. We'll just have to wait and
see."

"You know something, young lady? I think Hank got more
than he bargained for in you."

Becky looked toward the corral, and her gaze once again
fastened on Hank. A slow catlike smile touched the corner
of her mouth, then she laughed.

"He hasn't yet, but he will, Mrs. Kruger. He will."

The hall clock struck twelve.

Becky eased her bedroom door open. She waited until the
last chime faded, then stuck her head out the door and

slowly inspected the hallway. The house was dark, wrapped in stillness, silent except for the measured beat of the clock. She stepped through the door, gently closed it behind her, stood listening a moment. Her hair was down, cascading across her shoulders, and she was barefooted, dressed only in her nightgown. At last, satisfied no one was awake, she padded quietly along the hall.

At the end of the corridor, she paused before a door, listening. All she heard was the thump of her heart and the hammering ring of her own pulsebeat. She took hold of the doorknob, turning slowly until the latch clicked, then swept the door open and quicly stepped inside. The bedroom had a pleasant man-smell odor, and a large brass bed gleamed in a spill of moonlight from the window. She stood with her back to the door for several seconds, listening to the rhythmic rise and fall of his breathing. Her heart was thudding now and she closed her eyes, took a deep breath, held it until she'd steadied her nerves. Then she turned and marched straight to the bedside.

She whipped her nightgown overhead and dropped it on the floor. In the moonlight the swell of her breasts and the curve of her tightly rounded buttocks were exquisite, at once voluptuous and statuesque. Without an instant's hesitation, she pulled the blanket aside and slipped into bed. He was sprawled out on his back, the hair on his chest matted in a tangle of gold and chestnut. She lay perfectly still a moment, watching him, then she wiggled inside the crook of his arm and pressed herself against him. Nothing happened; he snored lightly. She wiggled closer, snuggling her head into the hollow of his shoulder. She kissed his earlobe, let her fingers trickle through the curls on his chest, brought her leg over his hip, and rubbed gently with her thigh. The snoring stopped.

His arm moved, suddenly halted as his hand found the velvety flesh of her buttocks. He went still, lying motionless on an indrawn breath, then his arm tightened around her hips. She felt him growing firm against her thigh, swelling stiff and hard as his breathing turned rapid. His head moved, sleepy eyes focused on her in the moonlight, and his look was one of raw disbelief. He swallowed, managed a choked whisper.

"Becky?"

"Yes, Hank." Her voice was warm, husky. "It's me."

"I don't get it." He was awake now, all the more incredulous. "What made you change your mind?"

"Oh, something you said this afternoon." She ran her hand down his stomach, inserted her finger in his bellybutton, probed tenderly. "You know . . . about curing the rash."

"You mean it?"

"Silly." She snuggled closer, lifted his hardness erect and quivering with her knee. "I'm here, aren't I?"

"Ah Becky . . . god, honey, you'll never regret it . . . I promise you . . ."

He rolled over on top of her, fondling her breasts, kissing her neck and eyes and finally brought his mouth to her lips. His breath was labored, hot panting gasps, and his urgency too great once he touched the soft muff between her thighs. He levered his rump a bit higher, spreading her legs, and positioned himself. Suddenly her hand reached out, grasped his hardness, and he groaned, waiting for her to guide him into the warm dampness. She looked up at him, holding him in a firm caress, and saw his eyes glaze with pale fire. Her mouth curved in a sultry smile.

"Hank?"

"Ummm . . . what . . . what's the matter?"

"Hank, do you love me?"

"Oh—god—Becky—don't you know?"

"Say it, Hank . . . tell me . . . now."

"I love you, honey, love you, honest to god!"

"You're positive"—she squeezed gently—"it's not just this making you say it?"

"Holy God Almighty, no more talk. I love you, Becky, I love you!"

"And I love you too."

She wrenched his hardness aside and at the same time slammed him in the chest with her other hand. He toppled off her and fell away onto the bed with a strangled yelp.

"Jesssus Christ!"

Becky leaped out of bed, snatching her nightgown off the floor, and walked toward the door. Hank thrashed around, clutching himself, rolled onto his knees and stared after her

with an expression of oxlike bewilderment. She stood for a moment, allowing him to watch as the moonlight bathed her nakedness in a spectral glow. Then she shrugged into her nightgown and blew him a kiss.

"You can have it all, lover . . . on our wedding night."

She opened the door and stepped outside. As the latch clicked, she heard a muffled groan, followed by the squeak of bedsprings and a string of muttered curses. A vixen look touched her eyes, and deep inside, musical laughter flooded her heart.

She smiled and fled swiftly down the hall.

CHAPTER 38

Kruger spotted them through the plate glass window.

An instant later the door opened. The farmers entered the bank and marched straight past the tellers' cages. There were four of them, ranked two by two, and something about their stride reminded him of soldiers advancing on an enemy position. The head teller started toward them, then cast a hurried glance at Kruger, whose desk was guarded by a balustrade at the rear of the bank. Kruger warned him off with an almost imperceptible nod, and tilted back in his chair, watching the farmer. It was a visit he'd been expecting for the past week.

The men were led by Lon Hill, one of the first settlers, and according to rumor, self-appointed spokesman for the farm community. Their features were like whang leather, hardened in an expression of grim determination, and they looked tough as mules. Without breaking stride, they pushed through the swinging gate of the balustrade and halted before Kruger's desk.

A moment passed while Kruger studied them with a look of cool appraisal, then he smiled. "Gentlemen. Mr. Hill. How are you today?"

"Tolerable," Hill said shortly. "But this ain't no social visit, so you can forget the honors."

"Very well, Mr. Hill, down to business. What can I do for you?"

"Well, we've been holdin' meetings around the county . . ."

"Yes, I know."

"Yeah, I'll bet you do. Ain't much goes on you don't hear about, is there?"

Lon Hill was a gnarled, lynx-eyed man. He had a straight

mouth and a jutting chin, with a cleft so wide it looked as though it had been split with an ax. His life was a chronicle of failure—littered with a trail of barren homesteads—but he was undaunted by adversity. He'd come to the Rio Grande Valley, hopes revitalized, still clinging to a dream; there was no thought of failure, not this time, for he was fifty-three years old and desperate. The quarter-section outside Lairdsville represented his last chance.

When Kruger declined to answer, merely watching him, Hill dismissed it with a gesture. "Makes no nevermind anyhow. Everybody knows about your spies, but we've got nothing to hide. The fact is . . . we've formed a Grangers Association, and me and the boys here"—he jerked his thumb at the other farmers—"was asked to serve as a delegation on everybody's behalf."

"A commendable choice, Mr. Hill. But how does that concern me?"

Hill pulled a slip of paper from his coat pocket and slammed it on the desk. "There's my tax assessment—*two dollars an acre!*—and it's the same for every farm in the county."

"Yes, go on."

"Go on! Jesus Christ A'mighty, we're not gonna stand for it. We only paid five dollars an acre and now they're tryin' to tax us half of what it's worth."

"Not at all, Mr. Hill. I understand the assessments are based on current valuation, which is something over twenty dollars an acre."

"That's a load of horseshit, Kruger, and we both know it."

"On the contrary, your land has quadrupled in value since you bought it. I'd say you're very fortunate, very fortunate indeed."

Kruger's point was well taken. A resurgence of trade, generated now by rails instead of boats, had come to the Rio Grande Valley. The old Brownsville-Matamoros traffic was thriving and, along with the agricultural development, it had brought growth and prosperity to the entire area. By summer the first cotton crop was due to be harvested, and several farmers had already planted citrus groves, principally oranges and grapefruit. Land prices had risen at a dizzying pace, and today even unimproved land sold for nearly ten

dollars an acre. It was a boom-time atmosphere, with no end
in sight.

"It'll break us!" Hill protested angrily. "We're all strapped
for cash and you ought to know it better'n anybody else.
Hell, we're just livin' from hand to mouth till our first crop
comes in, and that's a fact. Valuation be damned!"

"Your worries are unfounded, Mr. Hill. The tax collector
is an understanding man; I'm sure he'll wait until your crops
are sold."

"Why, hell's bells, any fool knows that. Only trouble is
we're obliged to sell our crops to you! Ain't another cotton
gin within a hundred miles of here."

The farmers behind Hill muttered agreement, and there
was something ominous in the looks they exchanged. Appar-
ently they meant to force a showdown, and Kruger sensed
that the true purpose of their visit hadn't yet been revealed.
But if he was apprehensive, nothing in his manner betrayed
it. He spoke with authority, iron sureness.

"Gentlemen, let's clear the air on something. I have more
at stake than all of you put together, and if the farmers of
Kruger County fail, then I fail. In the past, my dealings with
you have been open and above-board"—he paused, staring
directly at Hill—"and if you think that's going to change in
the future, then you've been misled by a rabble-rouser who
hasn't the vaguest notion of business or economics."

"The hell you say!" Hill blurted. "You think we're a bunch
of dimdots? No, Kruger, we finally got your number, and it's
plain as a diamond in a goat's ass."

"Oh? Exactly what number is that, Mr. Hill?"

"You rigged the whole thing—start to finish—to keep the
bite off Santa Guerra."

"I presume you mean the elections?"

"Damn right! That and the tax assessments. Of course, I
haven't had any of your fancy book learnin', but lemme tell
you something, mister . . . I'm pure lightning when it
comes to figures."

"Is that a fact?" Kruger replied genially. "And what great
revelation have your figures unearthed?"

Hill gave him a bitter grin. "A little bird tells me that
Santa Guerra got stiffed for less'n sixty thousand in taxes.

The way I calculate, that breaks down to about five cents an acre."

"I take it you find that inequitable."

"No, Kruger, I find it plain old crooked. You and your goddamn greasers are gonna ruin us."

By now, the politics of Kruger County were the talk of Texas. In last fall's election Kruger and John Hazlett had voted their vaqueros in a block. The result was a landslide victory for their candidates, and a courthouse administration that governed Kruger County as though it were the private domain of one man. Since Kruger already controlled the economic lifeblood of Lairdsville, the elections gave him a virtual stranglehold on the county, absolute power to do as he pleased. He had handpicked his own legislators; he could deliver the county in statewide elections; and everyone in Austin considered him a political genius. It made him immune to outside interference.

The tax assessments, which had been distributed in early February, were the first overt demonstration of Kruger's power. Until then everyone had looked upon him as a benign patriarch, hopeful he would govern the county with the same indulgence that he ruled Santa Guerra. Those hopes were quickly shattered, however, both for the farmers and the townspeople. The ranchlands of Santa Guerra, combined with those of John Hazlett, comprised roughly eighty percent of Kruger County's total acreage. Yet it became apparent that the burden of taxation had been placed on small landowners, Lairdsville's merchants and the farmers. Ernest Kruger's intent was at last clear: the settlers were to be penalized for the benefit of the large ranchers.

The merchants, most of them politically astute, accepted the situation with a degree of fatalism. Since the gubernatorial election of 1908 was forthcoming—and Ernest Kruger could deliver the vote of an entire county—there was nothing to be gained in lodging an official protest. But the farmers were a stubborn lot, blind to the political realities, and not easily intimidated. The result was the Grangers Association, and a delegation headed by Lon Hill, waiting stolidly for Kruger's response.

"Gentlemen," Kruger finally observed, "my advice to you

is to heed perhaps the oldest adage in politics. There's no honey without stings."

"What the hell's that supposed to mean?"

"Why, it's really quite simple, Mr. Hill. You came here with little more than the shirt on your back, and now you own a prosperous farm. Moreover, at considerable personal expense, I provided your people with a church and a school, even a hospital." He hesitated, regarding the farmers with a flat stare. "The rest you'll have to pay for yourselves."

Hill squinted at him in baffled fury. "The rest of what?"

"Oh, town improvements, maintenance, that sort of thing."

"Spell it out, Kruger. What improvements?"

"Well, the courthouse has to be completed, and among other things we're planning a town waterworks. Lairdsville's growing, gentlemen. The people need services and facilities."

"Waterworks? Why in the name of Christ should we pay for a waterworks? We're farmers, we don't live in town."

"Civic pride, Mr. Hill. After all, it is your county seat."

"Come off it, Kruger. What you're really talking about is taxin' the little people to run *your* county. We never voted on no courthouse, and we sure as hell never approved no waterworks."

"Hmmm." Kruger considered that a moment. "Well, if you have a grievance, I suggest you take it up with the county commissioners."

"Don't make me laugh! They're all a bunch of stooges for you and your cronies, and everybody knows it. We'd just be wastin' our breath."

"Then I'm afraid I can't help you, gentlemen."

"Goddamnit!" Hill shouted. "We won't stand for it. You either call off your dogs or we'll hotfoot it up to Austin and have a talk with the attorney general. See, we're thickheaded, Kruger, but we ain't stupid. We know a little law ourselves."

"Yes, I can see you do. And what would the allegation be . . . the charges?"

"How about the way you and Hazlett rigged the elections? Just so you could work out a tax scheme where you wouldn't have to pay your fair share. That ought to do for openers."

"Very unlikely, Mr. Hill. The tax program of Kruger County is structured on land valuation. Obviously a farm is more productive per acre than a ranch, and therefore more valuable. As a result, it merits higher assessment. All that seems rather elementary."

"I got an idea the attorney general might see it different."

Kruger nodded to a crank telephone fixed on the wall. "Suppose I call the governor and arrange an appointment. He's a very good friend of mine, and I'm sure he'd be happy to speak to the attorney general on your behalf."

Lon Hill's chin came up, and his mouth set in a hard line. "Think you've got us euchred, don't you? Well you haven't heard the last of it, Kruger. Not by a damnsight!"

"Perhaps." A wintry smile lighted Kruger's eyes. "Let me give you another piece of advice, Mr. Hill. Never try to run a bluff when the other man holds your marker. You see, he'll call and tap you out because he's already playing on your money."

"That sounds awful close to a threat."

"Only to a man whose farm is heavily mortgaged."

His statement claimed their attention like a thunderclap. The farmers stood transfixed, glowering at him in tongue-tied rage. However subtly couched, the threat was very real, and none of them dared put it to the test. At last, with a murderous oath, Lon Hill wheeled away from the desk and led them out of the bank.

Kruger rose, watching through the window until they crossed the street. Then he lifted the receiver from the wall phone and twirled the crank.

"Central? This is Mr. Kruger. Connect me with the governor's office."

CHAPTER 39

Hank stood alone at the end of the bar. After a few drinks, he'd ordered the barkeep to leave the bottle. He was sipping steadily, like a man intent on drowning his troubles, and his expression darkened as the level of the bottle crept lower. His elbows were hooked over the bar, shoulders hunched, his gaze fixed on the glass. He hadn't spoken in the last hour.

Several regulars were clustered near the front of the bar, and two men were shooting a game of one-pocket on the pool table at the rear of the room. Though it was still early, the domino tables along the far wall were empty and the saloon was quieter than normal. The conversation was low key, curiously strained, and the men at the bar kept darting hidden glances at Hank. He seldom frequented the saloon, but they knew him to be a solitary drinker and a mean drunk. Once he went past a certain limit, something brutal appeared along the square line of his jawbone, and he became unpredictable, easily offended. By now, he'd consumed almost half the bottle and his glassy-eyed stare had them worried.

The Longhorn Saloon was Lairdsville's lone concession to the sporting crowd. Ernest Kruger, at the behest of the Merchants Association, had allowed the county commissioners to license one barroom in the whole of Kruger County. It was located on Main Street, but at the west end of town, only half a block from the railroad station. Travelers and salesmen were thus able to get a drink; townspeople and farmers had a meeting place where they could gather in a convivial atmosphere. But any similarity to a railhead saloon ended there. The owner of the Longhorn, as well as the general public, had been warned concerning barroom decorum. Any unseemly incidents, particularly fights or disorderly conduct,

and the license would be revoked. As a result, the saloon's clientele behaved themselves, and took a protective attitude toward the establishment. Troublemakers were hustled out the back door and unceremoniously dumped in the alley.

Yet tonight, the regular crowd was confronted with an altogether different problem. While Hank had never actually caused trouble in the Longhorn, he'd come close a couple of times. Watching him now, it seemed to them that tonight he might very well spoil the record. As the level dipped lower in his bottle, they grew quieter, their looks guarded. An altercation with the son of Ernest Kruger was a losing proposition all the way round. No one cared much for the prospect.

Hank was scarcely aware the men existed. Earlier, he'd ridden into town, intending to catch the train that evening and spend a few days in Matamoros. By the time he reached the depot, however, the idea had lost its appeal. His mood was bleak, and even the thought of cockfights and *señoritas* did little to raise his spirits. There was simply nothing to celebrate. Instead, he'd left his horse hitched outside the train station and walked over to the Longhorn.

For three hours now, he had been working on the bottle. His senses were dulled, and his tongue felt numb, but his mind still functioned perfectly. As he poured another drink, it occurred to him that it was a terrible waste of good whiskey. He lifted the glass, studying the amber liquid a moment, wondering why a man intent on getting drunk so very often developed a hollow leg. It was a paradox, and a damn shame. Normally, carrying such a load, he would have had the blind staggers. Tonight, with half a bottle gone, he had yet to outdistance reason or thought . . . or Becky.

His fist clenched around the glass, and he slowly lowered it to the bar. Perhaps there was no way to outrun her. Even if it were possible, he told himself, maybe he wasn't really all that determined anyway. Maybe that was the reason whiskey no longer worked and why he'd lost his appetite for other women. Instead of outrunning her, maybe he was really waiting to be caught, fooling himself into believing otherwise. It answered a lot of questions, but the thought was damned unsettling, even a little scary. He shook his head, pondering on it, thoroughly confused.

Some four months had passed since the night Becky

slipped into his bed. Yet it was as though it had all happened only hours ago. He could still feel the soft contours of her body, and in his mind's eye there was a vivid picture of her nakedness framed in a spill of moonlight. He ached for her, wanted her desperately, and time had done nothing to diminish his need. Whenever they were together the ache grew worse; merely to be near her was an exquisite form of torture. Even now, he could close his eyes and see her spread beneath him, feel again the touch of her hands and the warmth of her flesh. The image, that uncanny sensation of her hand gripping his hardness, was slowly driving him mad. Awake, he thought of it; and asleep, he relived it in his dreams. Try as he might, he couldn't forget. There was no escaping the promise of those moments, the vision of her loveliness.

All the worse, the memory intruded on every aspect of his life. He was surly with the vaqueros and rude to his mother, unable to converse normally with anyone. The few times he'd visited Matamoros, there was none of the old gaiety and laughter and bright moments of drunken revelry. It all seemed stale and flat, no joy in watching the cocks pitted or tumbling naked with some dark-eyed *puta*. Even the girls on the ranch now seemed a chore rather than a pleasant diversion; their lovemaking was somehow lackluster, almost tedious, and these days he rarely bothered. At first he'd resisted the truth, but gradually he was forced to accept the only possible explanation. Becky had ruined him for other women.

The thought terrified him. It conjured harsher images— lost freedom and an end to the sporting life—all the things he associated with marriage. But never once had he seriously considered breaking off with Becky. Secretly, he knew he couldn't, for he needed her now in a way he'd never before imagined possible. The idea of losing her was even more frightening than the thought of losing his freedom. Simply admitting it was perhaps the worst sign, one that triggered an inner conflict that left him vulnerable and defenseless. She had him hooked, and her assurance was monumental. Her whole attitude indicated it was merely a matter of time.

Still, despite all her wiles, he hadn't yet agreed to a formal engagement. She teased him with her body, used it as a form

of emotional blackmail, allowing him to squeeze and touch and keep fresh the memory of how she felt in bed. But it never went any further, and by now he had resigned himself to the rules, her rules. It was a mating dance, tease and tantalize, and until he'd slipped a wedding band on her finger, he would have to look elsewhere for relief. Mere physical relief, however, had proved not enough. Other girls were nothing more than a warm body, expending momentary lust but never once dulling the edge of his desire. He wanted Becky.

Thinking about her now made him groan inwardly. His loins ached, and between his legs a pair of cold stones, swollen and hard, throbbed like cannonballs struck with a hammer. His need had ripened into agony, and the pain reverberated downward from his groin in a steady, unremitting reminder that no other woman would do. The one he wanted he couldn't have—not at that price!—and those he could have he no longer wanted.

Damn her! Damn her for spoiling all the fun!

Hank knocked back the drink and slammed his glass down on the counter. The men at the front of the bar tensed, watching closely as he walked past. He ignored them, eyes fixed straight ahead in a dull stare, and marched out of the saloon. On the boardwalk he paused, wondering that his head was so clear when his legs felt wobbly and his mouth thick as paste. He took a couple of deep breaths, glanced toward the depot, where his horse stood hipshot at the hitchrack. The prospect of a long ride home suddenly lost its appeal. He puzzled on it a moment, then remembered the hotel.

His father had built a small hotel catty-corner from the bank. With the press of business matters, it had become his principal residence over the past year, and he now maintained a suite on the top floor. Hank had no wish to see his father, but the choice between a soft bed and a hard saddle was no choice at all. It occurred to him that a bribe would silence the desk clerk, at least for the night, and guarantee a room on the ground floor. Time enough to worry about the old man tomorrow.

He turned and walked unsteadily toward the main intersection uptown. The street was deserted, patches of shadow

broken by the dim glow of lampposts. His bootheels echoed
along the buildings, and as he passed the hardware store, his
reflection shimmered briefly on darkened glass. His glance
strayed across to the bank and he chuckled to himself, won-
dering who the old man had robbed lately. Of course, he had
to agree with his mother, though she'd said it only in so
many words: You have to give the Devil his due. The old
man was crafty as a chicken hawk; the way he'd rigged the
elections and the tax assessments, and set himself up as the
political kingfish of southern Texas, was a slick piece of work.
For Hank's tastes it was a little underhanded, too devious to
set comfortably. But he wouldn't argue about methods, not
where it concerned farmers. Anything that was good for
Santa Guerra was right by him; forcing the farmers to carry
the tax load of the county was, to his way of thinking, a
matter of poetic justice. Sodbusters deserved whatever they
got . . . and then some!

 Yet there was a side effect that seemed to Hank the para-
dox of all time. His mother was positively beguiled by the old
man's performance. Not that she would ever tell his father;
that wasn't her way. But he knew, from remarks she'd
dropped, that she thought the old man was a regular ball o'
fire. Once, in a moment of candor, she had even commented
that he'd done the family name proud. Which was no small
concession, since she was talking not of the Krugers but of
the Lairds, specifically her own father. Compared to years
past, when she and the old man were constantly at one an-
other's throats, it was a remarkable turnaround. He thought
it truly ironic that his mother would experience a change of
heart only after his father had proved himself a first-class
sonovabitch. It amused him, and he often wondered if the
old man even suspected. Probably not. Kingmakers and em-
pire builders had no time for the trivial.

 At the corner, Hank stepped off the boardwalk and
started across the main intersection. The glare of four lamp-
posts made it the brightest spot in town, and light spilled
over for half a block in every direction. As he approached
the opposite corner, a door at the side of the hotel opened.
He glanced around, saw a woman step outside, and thought
nothing of it. Then he halted, took another quick look as she
turned and hurried down the side street. Her features were

partially hidden by a hat, but he'd caught a glimpse of her face.

Lou Ann Newton.

He stood watching, struck by something peculiar in her manner. Only when she disappeared into the darkness, walking toward the residential section, did it occur to him. Why would his father's secretary have to sneak out of the hotel? There was definitely something furtive about the way she'd done it, ducking her head and—

What the hell was she doing in the hotel at this hour?

The question hung answered a moment, then he suddenly made the connection. But that was impossible, not the old man and Lou Ann Newton! Or was it? She was attractive enough, and at least twenty years younger, so maybe she had a thing for older men. Or maybe his father had a thing for younger women. Of course, she was married, but then the old man wasn't exactly unattached himself. Not by a damnsight!

Hank thought of his mother, and his perspective of things abruptly changed. He had a fleeting image of her at the ranch—alone all the time—faithful as a nun and damn near as celibate. Then he blinked, got an altogether different vision of the old man . . .

. . . and Lou Ann Newton!

A sudden fury swept over him, and the thought turned him cold sober. He walked to the hotel and barged through the door. As he crossed the lobby, the desk clerk looked up with surprise and rose from his chair behind the counter. Hank halted, nodding without expression, then jerked his chin at the side entrance.

"I just saw Lou Ann Newton go out that door."

"Lou Ann?" The clerk gave him a weak smile. "Oh no, Mr. Kruger, you must be mistaken. That was another girl, not Lou Ann."

Hank grabbed his coat lapels and pulled him halfway across the counter. The clerk let out a muffled grunt, then froze as Hank lifted him to eye level.

"You better get the wax out of your ears and pay attention. Now, I'll ask you once more, and I want a straight answer. Savvy?"

The clerk swallowed, bobbed his head rapidly.

"That was Lou Ann I saw, wasn't it?"

"Yessir, Mr. Kruger . . . Lou Ann . . . it surely was."

"And she was upstairs, in my father's room, wasn't she?"

"Mr. Kruger . . . *please* . . . don't ask me to—"

Hank shook him hard, knocked his glasses askew. "You're not listening. Now, let's try it again and keep it simple. How long was she up there?"

"Couple of hours"—the clerk grimaced, licked his lips—"maybe a little more."

"And it wasn't the first time, was it?"

"No . . . no, it wasn't."

"How often does she visit him?"

"Once or twice a week, sometimes more."

"How long has it been going on?"

The clerk rolled his eyes, and Hank pulled him closer. "How long?"

"Oh god, Mr. Kruger—"

"How long!"

"Several months . . . almost a year . . . but I've never told anyone, Mr. Kruger . . . honest to Christ! . . . Not a soul . . . no one!"

"Yeah, sure, you're a regular button-lip, aren't you?"

Hank dropped him on the counter and walked away. The clerk grabbed for a handhold, scattering the register book and inkwell, and slowly lowered himself to the floor. He adjusted his glasses, shirtfront splattered with ink, then stumbled to his chair and sat down. He watched wide-eyed as Hank crossed the lobby and hurried upstairs.

On the top floor, Hank turned left and walked to the end of the hall. He halted in front of Room 212, raised his arm, and pounded on the door. The force of his blows rattled the door, and when he stopped, there was a moment of acute silence. Then he heard a shuffling sound—footsteps—and the door was thrown open. His father stood in bathrobe and slippers, towel flung around his neck, dripping water.

"Hank!" Kruger looked surprised, then suddenly irritated. "What the devil's all that pounding about? You got me out of the tub."

"Trying to wash away your sins?"

"How's that again?"

"You know, Lou Ann . . . your little play pretty . . . I just saw her leave."

"Lou Ann Newton? I don't understand what you mean."

"C'mon, Dad, drop the act. The desk clerk and me just had ourselves a long chat. He told me all about it."

Kruger's expression changed. His features reddened and his eyes skittered away, then he cleared his throat. "Hank, believe me, it's not how it appears."

"Is that a fact? Well, appearances are sure deceiving then—"

"We're just friends, nothing more!"

"—because it appears you've been screwing your secretary pretty damn regular . . . like a couple of times a week!"

"Lower your voice." Kruger glanced down the hall, motioned him inside. "Let's sit down and discuss it, son. I can explain, if you'll give me a chance."

"Explain!" Hank jeered. "Jesus H. Christ! After all these years you've been preaching to me and you think you can explain away a married woman? Forget it!"

"It's not the same thing, not at all! And let me remind you . . . my personal life is none of your business."

"You! Hell, I don't give a shit about you. It's Mom! You're making a fool of her . . . everybody in town must know you're humping Lou Ann—"

"That's enough!"

"Oh, it's more than enough," Hank noted bitterly. "Matter of fact, I'm surprised Jack Newton hasn't come after you with a shotgun. Or have you got him by the balls too? Maybe Lou Ann's working off the mortgage by installment. Is that it?"

"Keep a civil tongue in your head! I'm your father, and you will talk to me with respect—*respect!*"

"Like hell! You're nothing but a phony . . . a goddamn hypocrite!"

Kruger's arm lashed out, struck at him in a vicious, open-palmed slap. Hank caught his wrist in midair and bore down with a crushing grip. Hauled forward, Kruger struggled to break loose, but his wrist slowly bent double and he winced with pain. Then he looked up, found his son watching him with a brutal smile.

"I want you to do something for me, old man."

"Hank . . . please . . . let go of my wrist."

"Shut up! I won't have Mom hurt by all this, you understand? I want you to break it off with Lou Ann Newton or I'll . . ."

"You'll what?"

"Don't make me show you." His grip tightened, brought tears to his father's eyes. "Just break it off with her—and damn quick!"

Hank released him and turned away. Kruger sagged against the doorjamb, clutching his wrist, blinked back the tears. His eyes followed Hank with a look of wounded rage, but inwardly he cursed himself. He'd been a fool—a careless fool!—and the boy was right. Trudy mustn't find out! That would never do, not now, not ever. There was simply too much at stake, a lifetime of work. Far too much to risk an open scandal or the enmity of his wife. As Hank disappeared around the corner of the stairwell, he nodded to himself, gingerly rubbing his wrist, and slowly closed the door.

He made a mental note to fire Lou Ann Newton. Quickly but with discretion.

CHAPTER 40

Early that spring, on one of his rare visits to the ranch, Kruger called a family meeting in the study. His time these days was devoted almost exclusively to politics and the myriad enterprises involving Lairdsville. The hotel in town, now more than ever, had become his place of residence. In part, his trips to Santa Guerra had dwindled in frequency due to the discord with Hank. Even though he'd ended the affair with Lou Ann Newton, his son avoided him whenever possible; their relationship was one of mutual bitterness, distant civility. But business and politics, rather than personal problems, accounted for his rare appearances. It was a matter of priorities, and to a great extent, he had allowed the ranch to run itself. Or so he thought.

Trudy was delighted by his long absences. His preoccupation with business and the upcoming gubernatorial election had brought a new element of harmony to their relationship. The *caporals* once again looked to her for direction, and while she generally followed the guidelines laid down by her husband, she had assumed increasing authority over the day-by-day operations. By now the three cattle divisions, along with the various breeding programs, were established and fairly autonomous. On-the-spot supervision, however, was still necessary; the *caporals* were of the old school, accustomed to a firm hand, and she gladly supplied it. Yet her most rewarding moments, almost the fulfillment of a dream, concerned young Hank. She had slowly made it known to *Los Lerdeños* that his orders were her orders, and with infinite patience she had rekindled his interest in the future of Santa Guerra.

There were problems, though. Hank had become terribly independent since purchasing the string of brood mares. He

was determined to establish himself as a Thoroughbred
breeder, and even more convinced that it would make his
fortune. On several occasions, when Trudy attempted to
point out the long-range nature of such a project, he had
laughed and politely informed her that he had all the time in
the world—a lifetime! She sensed he wasn't nearly as confi-
dent as he appeared, and she also knew he was counting the
days until his mares foaled. In her mind it had become a
dread event, and she worried constantly. If the foals looked
promising, he might be lost forever to Santa Guerra.

But tonight she had other worries. Her husband looked
exhausted, eyes bloodshot and rimmed with fatigue, his
shoulders stooped as though weakening under some enor-
mous burden. Clearly he had pushed himself too hard, and
she found herself concerned for his health. Within the last
year the depth of her feelings toward him had grown enor-
mously; though she kept it to herself, for he'd never been a
demonstrative man, what she felt was a blend of affection
and genuine admiration. All his accomplishments—the rail-
road and the town and the political coup—had prompted the
change. She saw him now as a man of ambition and power—
a visionary—and she liked what she saw. It reminded her of
her father.

Still, she recalled that it was obsessive ambition and an
unremitting workload that had killed Hank Laird. She also
recalled that no amount of argument had ever really dis-
suaded her father, and she suspected it would be equally
futile with her husband. Ambitious men rarely let go the
things they grasped, and as events had proved, Ernest Kru-
ger's sights were set very high indeed. Yet guile and flattery
might succeed where argument had failed, especially if he
were asked to relinquish only token authority. Not to her, of
course, but to the logical choice, his son. Which would very
nicely resolve her major worries with one swift stroke. And
lay the groundwork for young Hank to assume control of
Santa Guerra.

As they seated themselves in the study, grouped before
the fireplace, she decided that tonight was the night to try.
The purpose of the meeting was as yet unclear, but her hus-
band was worn and pale, and if ever he were to prove sus-
ceptible to guile, it would be in a moment of stress and

physical exhaustion. She sat very straight, alert and watchful, ready to act the instant an opportunity presented itself.

Kruger consulted his watch, almost as though he were late for an appointment, and snapped the lid closed with a decisive click. Then, without preamble, he trained his gaze on Hank.

"There's something I want to ask you. Now, you'll likely think it's none of my business, but I wouldn't ask if there weren't a good reason. So I'd appreciate a straight answer."

Hank gave him a dull stare. Since the night of their argument, they had spoken only on rare occasions. But his mother still had no inkling of the affair, and for her sake he attempted to keep up appearances. After a moment he offered his father a thin smile and shrugged.

"Guess a straight answer sort of depends on the question. But go ahead . . . fire away."

"How serious are you about Rebecca Hazlett?"

"I'll be dipped!" Hank glanced at his mother and saw that she was equally astonished. Then he shook his head, turned back to his father. "You were right the first time. It's none of your business."

"And I told you I have a reason for asking."

"Then I reckon I'll have to hear the reason."

Kruger hesitated, chose his words with care. "For the moment, let's just say I'd like some idea of how soon you intend to settle down."

"What you're really asking is whether I aim to marry Becky."

"That's correct."

"Well, Dad, you're a sackful of surprises, I'll give you that. But you still haven't told me the reason."

"All right, I'll try to be more direct. I believe Becky has two older sisters . . . no brothers?"

"Yeah."

"And as I recall, both sisters married well-to-do cattlemen, with spreads of their own."

"I'm beginning to see the light."

"Then explain it to me," Trudy demanded. "You two sound like you're talking riddles."

"No riddles, Mom, just a tricky mind at work. What he's saying is that Becky's sisters are all fixed, and whoever she

marries will likely wind up with the Hazlett ranch." Hank gave his father a sardonic look. "And if the lucky fellow turns out to be me, then that would automatically extend Santa Guerra's holdings to the county line."

"To be more precise," Kruger noted, "it would consolidate both properties into a single holding . . . and make Santa Guerra the only ranch in Kruger County."

"Why not say what you really mean? It'd just about make Santa Guerra and Kruger County one and the same, wouldn't it?"

"God in heaven!" Trudy blurted, staring at her husband. "Ernest, I think that's absolutely the most brilliant idea I've ever heard."

"Thank you, my dear. I'm rather proud of it myself."

"Hold your horses!" Hank said indignantly. "Don't you think you ought to consult me before you start congratulating yourselves?"

"Good point," Kruger agreed. "Which brings us back to the original question. How serious are you about Rebecca Hazlett?"

Hank stood and walked to the fireplace. He stared into the bed of ashes for a long while, mouth clenched tight and a steady tic pulsating in his jaw muscles. Finally, with a deep sigh, he turned to face his parents.

"You two sure make a pair. And I'm damn sorry you even told me what you had in mind. But to answer your question . . . Becky's promised to wait for me till I've got means of my own."

"Of course!" Kruger mused out loud. "That's why you bought those mares, isn't it? To build yourself a stake."

"Not the way you mean. I figured to sell off the colts and keep breeding the mares. Maybe buy myself a good stud."

"Son, I don't want to disillusion you, but that's a long road to prosperity. Very few Thoroughbred breeders ever strike it big."

"Some do, some don't. I'm willing to risk it."

"Perhaps. But a smart gambler always hedges his bet. The idea I had in mind would work out better all the way around . . . especially if you meant what you said about Becky."

"Yeah, what idea's that?"

"I want you to take over Santa Guerra."

The silence was tomblike. Trudy sat frozen, her mouth a perfect oval. Hank lifted his hand, lowered it when words failed, then stood rooted before the fireplace. Their reaction was one of stark disbelief, and it was obvious that neither of them could credit what they'd heard. Kruger had expected surprise, even shock, and he allowed them a moment to collect their wits. Then he smiled, glancing from mother to son.

"The explanation is really quite simple. There comes a time when a man has to delegate responsiblity. Things have progressed somewhat faster than I anticipated, and I suddenly find myself stretched too thin. Unless the other projects are to suffer, then I have no choice but to delegate, and Santa Guerra seems the place to start. That's all there is to it."

Trudy gave him a triumphant look. It was precisely what she'd planned, and had been accomplished without the need of guile. Somehow that made it all the sweeter, and she felt an enormous outpouring of affection toward her husband. Then she glanced at Hank and experienced a sudden stab of alarm. His face was fixed in a frown.

"Something wrong, son?" Kruger inquired. "You don't seem exactly bowled over by the news."

"Let me ask you something," Hank countered. "Would you have made the offer if I hadn't come up with the right answer about Becky?"

"One way or another I could always acquire John Hazlett's ranch. But you're my son, the only one I have. Does that answer your question?"

Hank searched his eyes for a time, finally shrugged. "Yeah, I guess so."

"Then it's settled," Kruger nodded. "You'll take over Santa Guerra."

"Thanks all the same, but I reckon I'll pass."

"What do you mean?"

"Just what I said . . . no deal . . . that's simple enough."

"Too simple, perhaps. Would you mind explaining your reason?"

"Oh, let's say it's a personal matter, and let it go at that."

Kruger stiffened, glanced at Trudy out of the corner of his eye. She was watching Hank intently, puzzled by the cryptic

remark. Kruger sensed there was no way to let it drop without further arousing her curiosity. He turned back to Hank, carefully stressing the words.

"I take it you don't approve of my methods?"

"Yeah, that's a fair statement."

"You think I'm using you—to further my own goals—and that makes you angry?"

Hank studied him a moment, slowly nodded. "Among other things."

"That's rather shortsighted, isn't it? You're allowing personal differences to affect your judgment."

"If you're saying I don't want any part of your scheme, then you hit it dead center. Hell, it wouldn't make any difference how I feel about Becky! I wouldn't marry her or anybody else just to give you a tighter grip on the county." Hank laughed a bitter laugh. "You don't need me, Dad. There's lots of ways to skin John Hazlett, and you know 'em all. I'll just sit this one out and tend to my mares."

"Son, you've been sitting it out all your life. Don't you think it's time you climbed down off your hobby-horse and got your feet wet?"

"Ahhh come off it! You're not talking about getting my feet wet. You're talking about getting my hands dirty! The way I see it, there's a helluva big difference."

"Stop it!" Trudy cried. "Both of you!"

She glared at them, looking back and forth with an expression of fierce dismay. In her heart, she knew they were both right. Ambition, the thirst for power, had corrupted her husband. The austere, highly principled man she'd married, the man of probity and Christian value, no longer existed. In his place sat a hard-bitten pragmatist, concerned not with rules but results. To some, he was devious and underhanded and never to be trusted. But to her, he was a man of vision and foresight, with the iron will and strong stomach to transform his dreams—her dreams!—into reality. She much preferred him to the callow young lawyer she'd taken to her wedding bed so long ago.

By the same token, she loved her son for his stubborn pride and rough assurance. In many ways, he was the very incarnation of her father, possessing all the traits that were perhaps the fondest memories of her childhood. All the

more important, it was natural to him, part of his nature. Unlike her husband, he hadn't learned it, he was born with it. Beneath the indifference and mockery, there was a man of determination and immense vitality, another Henry Laird. Yet he'd set himself against his father—for reasons that weren't entirely clear—and his stubbornness, his certainty of self, was now jeopardizing his own best interests. He had it all within his grasp, but he was on the verge of throwing it away, destroying everything she'd worked toward since the day he was born. Unless she turned him around tonight, the chance might be lost forever. She wouldn't risk that. She wouldn't allow him to. . . .

"Hank, I am not going to sit here and watch you make a damn fool of yourself. You've always had your way—done whatever you pleased, whenever it struck your fancy—but not tonight. You're full grown and it's high time you started acting like a man. So let's get it settled . . . right now!"

"Settled? Get what settled?"

"Whether or not you remain on Santa Guerra."

"Are you—"

Hank faltered, staring at her with a look of bewilderment. Her sudden outburst had stunned him. All his life, since he was old enough to remember, she had taken his side, defended him. But tonight her voice was cold and hard, the expression on her face implacable. He felt stricken, somehow unnerved by her threat, yet a part of him couldn't believe she'd said it. He shook his head.

"Mom, you're not serious . . . are you?"

"I've never been more serious in my life."

"You'd actually kick me out?"

"Yes . . . if I have to . . . yes, I would!"

"He's wrong!" Hank stabbed a finger at his father. "You know damn well he's wrong!"

"Oh for god's sake! Wake up, Hank. Wake up and grow up! Can't you get it through your head that you don't matter? Your father and I don't matter—nothing matters except Santa Guerra—the land, Hank!—the land!"

"I know that, Mom."

"You don't know anything. You just think you know!" Trudy's eyes burned with an intensity that left him transfixed. "Your grandfather killed himself building Santa

Guerra! He died before his time because that's what it took
to turn a wilderness into a ranch. He picked your father—
when he found out he was dying, Hank!—he picked your
father to carry on what he'd started." Her gaze swung to
Kruger, softened. "And your father kept his promise. Oh
god, how he kept it! He came to love Santa Guerra as much
as your grandfather did—as much as I do!—the way you
should." She turned back, frowning. "But you've never un-
derstood that, have you? You've always taken it for granted,
just assumed somebody waved a magic wand and—*magi-
presto*—there stood Santa Guerra. Now part of that is my
fault, and I take the blame. I taught you to believe Santa
Guerra was yours—all yours!—but I was wrong, dead wrong.
It's not yours until you understand what it means, Hank.
Until you understand why men died and burned themselves
out to build what you take for granted."

Trudy slumped back in her chair, breathing hard. She
stared at her son, a look of weighing and calculation, and
there was a moment of deadened silence. Then her fists
clenched and her chin jutted out proudly, defiantly.

"What you've never understood—what it means—is that
men don't count. Only the land counts! We're nothing, less
than nothing. When we're all dead and buried, the land . . .
Santa Guerra . . . will still be here. It's the only thing that
lasts—the only part of ourselves we can leave behind!—and
that's the reason it's the only thing that matters. Your grand-
father and your father understood that, and they always put
the land before themselves. Always!"

Her fist opened and closed, fell against the arm of the
chair. "Unless you understand it too, then you have no place
on Santa Guerra. The land takes everything a man has to
give . . . everything."

Hank regarded her with profound shock. He swallowed,
watching her as though mesmerized, struck dumb by the
force of her words. Several moments passed, the stillness
almost unbearable, while she waited for his reply. He tried to
speak, but there was no sound, and he found himself unable
to tear his eyes away. At last, his father cleared his throat,
broke the silence.

"Your mother's right, son. Whatever our personal differ-
ences, it's Santa Guerra that matters. You have an obligation

to the land, and perhaps an even larger obligation to yourself. You were born to the job, and you'll never be able to live with yourself if you run away from it. To put it quite simply, it's your birthright and your time's come. You are the *patrón!*"

Hank glanced at his mother. She held his gaze an instant, then her eyes misted over and she nodded. He paced to the end of the fireplace, turned and propped one hand on the mantel, stared into the ashes for a long time. Slowly, his features changed, the line along his jawbone tightened, and he seemed to come to grips with some inward part of himself. When he faced them, the old assurance was there, but somehow different. He was solemn, the look of mockery gone, his mouth thin and straight. His presence was commanding, vital.

"All right, I'll take over. But there's a couple of conditions attached to it, so we'd better get them ironed out now."

"Oh?" Kruger observed. "What sort of conditions?"

"Well, first off, I won't stand for any interference. Not from you"—Hank paused, looked directly at his mother—"not from anyone."

"By interference, do you mean—"

"I mean there'll only be one boss around here . . . and that's me!"

"You'll need help," Kruger insisted. "You haven't had the experience to take on the job overnight, not without some guidance."

"I'm not saying I won't take advice. But once we've thrashed it out among ourselves, that's it. I'll give the orders on Santa Guerra . . . *all the orders."*

Kruger and Trudy exchanged a glance. She nodded, and after a moment's deliberation he threw up his hands. "Very well, what's your next condition?"

"I'm through working for wages. We divvy up the profits once a year, and I take my third right off the top."

Kruger smiled. "If nothing else, I taught you how to drive a hard bargain."

"One more thing. And you'd better listen close, because it'll be the first order I give."

"Believe me, you have our undivided attention."

"I intend to post the ranch, every last acre."

"But that's unheard of!" Kruger declared. "Nobody posts their land."

"Nobody ever had reason until these sodbusters moved in."

"Good lord, they hunt for meat! There's no crime in that."

"Yeah, and they've already killed off half the deer and most of the wild turkey. Give them another year and they'll exterminate all the game on Santa Guerra."

"Perhaps it's good riddance. We need the graze for cows, anyway."

"C'mon, Dad, you know better than that. If we let 'em kill off the game, then the predators won't have any natural prey, and we'll really start losing cows."

"I suppose you're right," Kruger admitted. "But I already have trouble enough with the farmers. . . . This will certainly complicate matters."

"That's your problem. I intend to post the land, and once it's posted, I'll make it stick."

"Yes, I'm sure you will." Kruger deliberated a moment, then dismissed it with a quick gesture. "Very well, if there are no more conditions, can we move on to other matters?"

Hank pursed his lips. "If you're talking about Becky, forget it. I'll handle that in my own way, in my own good time, but she's not part of our deal."

"I'm referring to another matter entirely. In a way, it's what convinced me to put you in charge of the ranch. You see, assuming all goes well, I suspect it will occupy a major portion of my time in the future."

Kruger extracted a document from inside his coat and unfolded it. "I've formed another company. Unlike the railroad, however, this will be a family enterprise."

"God save us!" Trudy laughed. "Aren't you satisfied with what you've got, Ernest?"

"As your father often remarked"—Kruger handed her the typewritten sheet—"enough is never enough."

Trudy glanced at the document, suddenly caught her breath. "This says—I don't believe it!—the Santa Guerra Oil Company?"

"Indeed it does. We begin drilling next month."

CHAPTER 41

The year passed swiftly. Too swiftly for Hank Kruger, whose first year as *patrón* of Santa Guerra had been marked by ill fortune. On a warm summer day, accompanied by Luis Morado, he rode out to inspect the breeding pastures. It was an unexpected visit, almost a week ahead of his normal schedule, but it provided a respite from the worries awaiting him elsewhere. He needed a boost in spirits.

The sun was a polished ball lodged high in the sky, and a shimmering haze hung over the land. Luis Morado, long the *caporal* of the Coastal Division, found today's heat oddly oppressive. *El Patrón* had scarcely spoken since riding into division headquarters; his expression was somber and he appeared in a dark mood. Worse, he had offered no explanation for his visit, and that in itself seemed a bad sign. Morado was sweating profusely, eyes guarded and watchful.

The *patrón* had recently promoted him to *segundo,* a position left vacant following the death of his father, Ramon Morado. It was a signal honor, and indicated a return to the old ways. The promotion was to take effect in one month, allowing him time to train a replacement for the Coastal Division; thereafter he would be responsible for the whole of Santa Guerra, second only to the *patrón*. Morado was privately of the opinon that *La Madama* had influenced her son in the decision. She valued his friendship and discretion, and through the years they had remained *compañeros*. While nearly four decades had passed, she still loved to reminisce about their childhood and, perhaps the dearest of all her memories, Roberto. It was natural, then, that she would want her old friend elevated in rank, and brought to live at the main compound. Yet it was entirely possible the *patrón* was having second thoughts on the matter. Perhaps that was

the reason for his sudden appearance today, and his brood-
ing manner.

One leg hooked over the saddle horn, Hank rolled a ciga-
rette and lit it, puffing in silence. With Morado at his side,
they sat their horses overlooking a fenced pasture. A small
herd of two year olds grazed placidly in the noonday heat.
These were the initial offspring of Babs, the Brahman bull;
now approaching maturity, the cows had been bred earlier
that spring to a Hereford bull. Because of the long genera-
tion intervals with cattle, usually four years, the breeding
program constructed by Ernest Kruger was expected to span
a decade or longer. By culling and mating linebred cattle
with outcross offspring of the Brahman bull, Kruger hoped
to establish a fixed type of cow. The animal he envisioned
would be strong and heavily fleshed, larger than shorthorn
cattle, about five-eights Hereford and three-eights Brahman
ancestry.

Kruger's approach was iconoclastic and highly experi-
mental, in direct opposition to methods advocated by genetic
experts. At first, upon assuming command of the ranch,
Hank had argued for a return to orthodox breeding proce-
dures. But his father was intractable, and in the end he'd
agreed to stick with the original plan. Today, watching the
Brahman-Hereford crossbreds, he had to admit the first step
bore all the earmarks of success. The cows appeared hardy
and almost immune to the blazing Texas sun. Moreover, be-
cause of their tough hide, inherited from Babs, they had a
high tolerance to tick fever; the loose folds of skin also pro-
tected them from swarming insects which caused canker-eye
and screwworm in purebred Herefords. If nothing else, the
program had already produced an animal better suited to
the land and the climate.

Yet it was a long-range program, several generations away
from a proved concept. Hank still subscribed to all the tradi-
tional beliefs with regard to breeding; the modest success
he'd enjoyed with his mares had merely reinforced those
beliefs. Earlier that spring the colts had been auctioned off
at a handsome profit; with the proceeds he had imported a
Thoroughbred stud from Kentucky, and next year, when the
mares foaled, he would have a bloodline all his own. It gave
him impetus and hope for the future, and along with the

Brahman-Hereford crossbreds, it represented a ray of sunlight in a singularly gloomy year.

Last summer, shortly after he'd taken over Santa Guerra, the beef market had begun a steady decline. The slaughterhouses were still buying, but prices dropped daily, and by midsummer it became obvious that the Western cattle industry had simply outstripped the demand for beef. Toward the latter part of August, with ten thousand head still unsold, he'd been confronted with a crucial decision. Santa Guerra lacked adequate graze to support its natural increase and hold the unsold cows for another season; but to sell the cows would result in a loss of nearly a quarter-million dollars. His father advised him to take the loss, and chalk it off to the vagaries of the cattle business. Hank determined instead on a bold gamble. He leased grazeland in the old Cherokee Nation, located in northeastern Oklahoma; the cows were wintered there after being shipped north by rail in September. He'd staked everything on an upturn in the beef market, which as yet had shown no signs of recovery. Now, with another summer upon him, Santa Guerra was facing imminent disaster. If he was forced to sell the current crop, along with the wintered steers—roughly forty thousand head—the loss in revenues would total upward of $1 million. For a young cattle baron, it was baptism by fire, and often made him wonder why he'd so readily accepted the title of *El Patrón*.

The responsibility, compounded by the unrelenting pressure, had left its mark. Hank smiled less these days, and his happy-go-lucky manner had given way to an attitude of sober introspection. His tour of the Brahman-Herefords was meant to buoy his spirits and make him forget the thirty thousand cows, as yet unsold, awaiting him at the Northern Division. But he couldn't forget, and as he finished his cigarette, it occurred to him that he couldn't hide. He turned to the *caporal,* eyes grim, and nodded.

"*Bueno,* Luis. You've done well."

The comment came as a relief, but it left Luis Morado thoroughly bewildered. He still hadn't the vaguest notion of why the *patrón* had picked today to inspect his cows. Without another word, they reined around and rode back toward division headquarters.

* * *

The Coastal Division was almost a separate ranch, located closer to Lairdsville than to the main compound. A village had been built to house the vaqueros and their families, and a large adobe structure served as division headquarters. Here Luis Morado supervised the breeding program, maintained a commissary, and kept extensive records on the overall operation. As was the custom on inspection days, the *patrón* returned to headquarters for a monthly accounting by the *caporal*. Usually he spent the night, and with little excitement in their lives, *Los Lerdeños* always made it an occasion. There was a feast prepared by the village women, followed by music and dancing and a generous allotment of tequila, courtesy of *El Patrón*.

But today *Los Lerdeños* lost their excuse for a fiesta. Hank and Luis Morado had barely dismounted when the Pierce-Arrow roared into the village. Ernest Kruger braked to a halt, tooting his horn, scattering dogs and chickens in a cloud of dust. Beside him sat his wife, and in the back, waving gaily, was Becky Hazlett. Hank started toward the car, confounded by their sudden appearance, and his father motioned him to hurry.

"C'mon, slowpoke, climb aboard! We're running late."

"What's the rush? Where're we going?"

"Questions later . . . just get in!"

Hank jumped in beside Becky and Kruger gunned off in a thunderous backfire. As the car cleared the village, Kruger turned his head, shouting over the roar of the wind.

"Got a message from the driller. He's hit paysand! Said if we hurried, we could see the well come in."

"How'd you know where I was?"

"Didn't! Called the house and they told me you were here."

Hank glanced at his mother, then turned to Becky, thoroughly mystified. "Where'd you come from?"

"Your mother and I were in town together. When the news came, Mr. Kruger just grabbed us up and here we are."

"In town together?" He met her gaze, found something merry lurking there. "What gives? You look like you just ate the canary."

Trudy laughed. *"No, hijo mio . . . un vago!"*

"Yes!" Becky exclaimed. "The man who won't be caught."

Hank eyed them suspiciously. "What sort of plot have you two been hatching now?"

"Actually, darling, we were discussing your birthday present. A very special present."

"Yeah, what's that?"

"Me!"

"You?"

Becky nodded, gave him a catlike smile. "We've decided to hold the wedding on your birthday . . . that way you'll never forget our anniversary."

Though their engagement was official, Hank had been dragging his feet about setting a wedding date. In part, his reluctance stemmed from Santa Guerra's problems. He wanted to prove to himself—and his father—that he was equal to the job. Then, too, there had been no profits last year, and he was using that as an excuse to delay the wedding further. Now it seemed Becky had enlisted his mother in a conspiracy of sorts. . . .

Or perhaps it was the other way round!

Hank turned to his mother. "Whose brainstorm was this?"

"A joint effort." Trudy winked at the girl, mashed his hat down over his head. "Your roaming days are over, *vago*. So relax and enjoy it."

Becky grabbed him around the neck and hugged fiercely. Suddenly it all seemed too much, too quickly. An oil well and a firm wedding date—all on the same day—fairly boggled the imagination. He sank back in the seat, hat jammed down on his ears, glowering.

Oil had become a major industry in Texas. The spectacular growth, all occurring within the last eight years, could be traced to the Spindletop discovery outside the town of Beaumont. There, early in 1901, a gusher was brought in that electrified the world. The Spindletop well had a flow of 100,000 barrels a day, roughly half the daily production of the entire United States. By the end of the year, Beaumont had mushroomed into a boom town, with 138 producing wells, and an oil craze swept the land. Wildcatters and oil companies began drilling holes all across the state of Texas.

But Santa Guerra had thus far proved barren, and for Ernest Kruger, it had been a dismal experience. His com-

pany had drilled three dusters in the past year, and he'd
discovered that oil exploration involved staggering costs.
Still, despite the financial drain and the lack of results, he
wasn't discouraged. He was convinced there was oil on Santa
Guerra, and he had a hunch today was the day he would find
it.

The Pierce-Arrow was parked some distance from the der-
rick, and Kruger stood on the running board, watching the
drilling operation. Hank was still sulking, propped up against
one of the front fenders, trying to ignore his mother and
Becky. They chattered on endlessly, switching back and forth
between wedding plans and the thrill of witnessing Santa
Guerra's first well brought in. Becky's eyes gleamed with
excitement. Everything about the oil business was new and
fascinating, and she devoured it all with the greedy savor of a
small girl. She wore a dress of sheer cambric, and her hair
was arranged *à la Romaine,* the latest fashion, involving
twists and coils framed by wispy spit curls. She looked ravish-
ing, and the sunlight seemed to accentuate the swell of her
breasts through the fabric.

Feigning indifference, Hank couldn't keep his eyes off her.
He was experiencing subliminal flashes of what lay beneath
the gauzy dress, punctuated by distinct images of how she
would appear naked, wrapped in his arms, snuggled deep in
a featherbed. It was a tantalizing vision, and despite himself,
he began to think the wedding wasn't such a bad idea after
all. Then he glanced at his mother, and frowned. What he'd
merely suspected before had now been confirmed. She had
switched sides, joined forces with the old man—and Becky!
—in a conspiracy to marry him off. Suddenly he felt sur-
rounded, badly outnumbered, overwhelmed by a sense of
being trapped into something not of his own choosing. He
forced himself to look away from Becky, and focused his
attention instead on the drilling rig.

The derrick was an ancient contraption of wood and
squealing ropes, towering high above the prairie. A huge
wheel groaned, reeling a string of drilling tools from the
wellhead, and the crown block wailed in protest. On the der-
rick floor a man quickly engaged the band wheel and low-
ered his bailer into the well. Several minutes later, when he
brought the bucket out of the hole, it was full of pulverized

cuttings and water. He inspected the cuttings, rubbing sand between his fingers, smelling it, then stood and yelled something to another man in the enginehouse. He moved to the near side of the rig, went down a ladder to the ground, and walked toward the Pierce-Arrow.

Kruger went to meet him, and Spud Thompson, the driller, briefly explained the problem. Every load of cuttings he'd brought up in the bailer had shown streaks of color, but so far there was no flow of oil from the hole. Of course, as everyone knew, oil was embedded in sand at various depths in the earth. Below these beds, however, were formations of rock and clay, generally impregnated with water. The trick was to tap the oil sand without boring through to the water. All day he'd drilled down foot by foot, and bailed the hole after each drilling. By relieving pressure on the paysand, he'd hoped to coax the oil to the surface. Yet the oil hadn't budged, and at this point, he dared not drill another foot. One miscue and they might wind up with a very expensive water well.

"What we've got here," Thompson concluded, "is a bitchkitty of a teaser."

"Teaser? Are you telling me it's another duster?"

"Nope, never said that. There's likely oil down there, but it's just enough to tease you into drilling deeper. If you let her, she'll tease you into boring that last foot, and you'll strike water sure as hell."

"Then there's definitely oil down there?"

"Never said that neither. Leastways not the kinda well you're talkin' about."

"I don't understand," Kruger said wearily. "You just finished saying we've found oil."

"Yeah, after a fashion." Thompson jerked his thumb at the derrick. "This here well might produce fifty barrels a day. Then again, it might not cough up enough to fill a teacup. 'Course, I'd have to hire a nitro man and shoot it . . . explode the paysand. That way we free the oil—assumin' it's barrels instead of teacups—and force it to wellhead."

Kruger regarded him dourly for a minute. "Fifty barrels a day hardly seems worth the effort. In fact, I'm wondering why you brought me all the way out here for nothing."

"Well, you gotta admit, Mr. Kruger, it's better'n a duster.

'Course, I know it ain't exactly what you had in mind, but I thought you might like to go ahead and shoot it and make yourself a well.''

"I'm not interested in an expensive toy, Mr. Thompson. I want results! Now, does this hole indicate we're getting any closer to a strike . . . or doesn't it?"

"Yes and no," Thompson informed him. "Next hole we drill could bring in another Spindletop easy as not. On the other hand, we might keep drillin' dusters till Hell freezes over. See, irregardless of what some folks say, Texas ain't floatin' on a bed of oil, Mr. Kruger. There's a little bit everywhere and a whole lot in certain spots. But it takes a helluva lot of luck to tap the right spot, and you gotta be willin' to put your money where your mouth is . . . maybe for a long damn time."

"I'm not a great believer in luck, Mr. Thompson, but I have the money and I have the time. Come see me when you finish up here. We'll take stock and figure out where to spud in the next hole."

Kruger turned and walked back to the car. The others were waiting anxiously, their faces eager and expectant. His eyebrows drew together in a slight frown as he stopped, shoulders squared, thumbs hooked in his vest.

"It's not a gusher, but it's not a duster either. I'm informed it's a teaser."

Everyone began peppering him with questions and he warded them off with upraised palms. "All in due time. We have a long drive home, and I'll explain Mr. Thompson's definition of a teaser on the way." Then he paused, glancing around at the derrick and a strange light came into his eyes. "I'll tell you one thing right here and now, though. There's oil on Santa Guerra and one of these days the whole world will wake up and read about it in their newspapers."

His words had a ring of prophecy, and Trudy felt a shiver run down her spine. She regarded him with an odd steadfast look, and it occurred to her that she'd been very fortunate throughout her life. All her men had the gift of vision. Her father, her husband, and in his own way, even her son.

She suddenly envied Rebecca Hazlett the years ahead.

CHAPTER 42

The washed blue of the plains sky grew smoky along about dusk. Fall had come and gone, and with winter approaching, a dusty coolness settled over the land at sundown. High overhead a squadron of ducks, fleet silhouettes against the muslin twilight, winged their way southward.

Hank reined his horse to a halt and sat for a moment watching the ducks. Behind him Luis Romero and Umberto Mendez exchanged a glance, wondering that the *patrón* would stop for a thing of so little consequence. But ducks were not all that common a sight on Santa Guerra, and their appearance evoked a curious sense of restlessness in Hank. They were creatures of the wild, beholden to nothing, free to take flight when they heard the ancient call. Not at all like man, whose freedom was measured by the degree of his bondage. A bondage to people and the land, and now a girl.

Yet it was a velvet chain that held him. One most men would have gladly accepted, and counted themselves fortunate to be blessed by such restraint. In a week's time, on the tenth day of November, he would marry a girl of grace and charm who loved him perhaps more than he deserved. A girl, however much he'd resisted the notion, that he had always wanted and cherished, and knew in some secret corner of his mind that he would eventually marry anyway. And in an ironic twist, his last excuse for delay had vanished within days of the wedding announcement. The beef market began to rise and throughout the summer it had climbed steadily higher. By early fall, when prices peaked, his agents had contracted for Santa Guerra's entire production, including the herd in Oklahoma. The turnabout vindicated his judgment of a year earlier, and the gamble paid off beyond his wildest expectations. Today the last trainload of steers had been

shipped north, and by this time next week, when he left the church a married man, Santa Guerra would have cleared upward of $800,000 in profits.

Still, watching the ducks disappear in a dusky wedge, he felt some sense of loss. A deeper instinct, visceral in nature, to answer that call himself and vanish with them into the darkening sky. But the urge was quickly set aside. He was a fortunate man—damned lucky!—and only a fool dwelt on lost dreams. He turned in the saddle, pointing as the ducks faded southward, and smiled at the vaqueros.

"Qué bonito, eh, amigos?"

Luis Romero smiled, on the verge of replying, when a distant gunshot rolled across the plains. The three men froze, trying to fix the direction of the sound, and an instant later they heard the dull blast of a shotgun. Their heads swiveled in unison, eastward toward the railroad, and for a moment they stared at a ticket of woods almost a mile away. Then Hank jerked his horse round, spurring hard, and the vaqueros thundered after him.

Several minutes later Hank led them into the woods. At his signal, Mendez and Romero fanned out to the flanks, and they proceeded through the thicket on a line. There was no need of questions or instructions; by now the problem of poachers had become commonplace on Santa Guerra. Upon posting the land, Hank had issued orders that anyone caught hunting was to be restrained, by force if necessary, and held for the authorities. Since then, he had filed trespassing charges against dozens of farmers, and each of them had paid a stiff fine in county court. But the poachers continued to hunt Santa Guerra, scornful of the law, and all the more outraged that Hank Kruger allowed his "greasers" to apprehend and detain white men. Tempers flared, and on more than one occasion, when dusk settled over the woods, gunshots had been exchanged. The farmers grew bolder then, relying on darkness and gunfire to make good their escape.

Hank and the vaqueros came upon the deer in a patch of trampled undergrowth. It was a large buck, freshly gutted and still warm. The poachers were nowhere in sight, but their trail was visible through the tangled brush. Up ahead, the woods lay in deep shadow, and Hank listened intently,

disturbed by the silence. Clearly the poachers had fled only moments before, yet men crashing through underbrush made a racket that could be heard some distance away. And there was no sound whatever. He pulled a carbine from his saddle scabbard, motioning the vaqueros to proceed with caution, and they rode forward at a walk.

Some twenty yards farther the trail forked, indicating the poachers had split off in opposite directions. Still there was no sound, and after studying the sign a minute, Hank waved Romero to the left and Mendez to the right. The vaqueros nodded, rifles cradled in their arms, and as they moved out, Hank thumbed the hammer back on his carbine. Suddenly a farmer, dressed in tattered overalls and a straw hat, stepped from behind a tree, threw an old Winchester to his shoulder, and fired. Romero's horse went down, struck squarely between the eyes, and as he leaped clear of the saddle, Hank shot the farmer. A starburst of blood splattered the farmer's chest, then his knees buckled and he slumped to the ground.

Almost simultaneously there was a scream from the opposite direction and a figure rose from the brush, swinging a double-barrel shotgun to bear on Hank. Without hesitation, Mendez fired and only then did they see that it was a boy in his late teens. The slug sent him reeling in a limp, nerveless dance; as though his legs had been chopped from beneath him, the boy collapsed and fell spread-eagled in the undergrowth. Romero had scrambled to his feet, and for a long while the three men stared at the body in stunned silence. Then Umberto Mendez crossed himself and his lips moved in a distorted whisper.

"Madre de Dios. A boy, *patrón.* I've killed a boy."

The words jarred Hank out of his funk, and he quickly thrust the carbine back in the scabbard. He motioned Romero forward, but his eyes were fixed on Mendez, and when he spoke his voice was hard, commanding.

"Stay here! Touch nothing and allow no one near this place until I return. *Sabe?"*

The vaqueros bobbed their heads and Hank watched them with a steady gaze for a moment. Then he reined his horse around and rode off through the brush toward Lairdsville.

* * *

"That's it, exactly how it happened."

"You're certain? There's no chance Romero or Mendez could have fired first?"

"I told you, the farmer tried for Romero and missed, and I let him have it, then this kid popped up with a shotgun and Mendez fired out of pure reflex. Hell, we didn't even know he was a kid till he hit the ground. All we saw was that shotgun."

"And you haven't any idea who they were?"

"Never saw 'em before in my life. But they're sodbusters, one look'll tell you that."

"Yes, I'm sure it would."

Ernest Kruger tilted back in his chair, hands clasped across his chest. His gaze was abstracted, and as Hank paced back and forth in front of the desk, he seemed to fall asleep with his eyes open. But in his mind he carefully scrutinized everything he'd heard, examining it for some hidden danger. It occurred to him that it was fortunate he'd decided to work late tonight; that Hank had seen the light and stopped rather than riding straight to the courthouse. With the sheriff involved, his options would have been few and risky. Even now, with the incident still contained, it would be touch and go for a few days, perhaps longer. Yet it could be done, with no one the wiser, and done in such a way that it could never be traced to Santa Guerra. All of which presupposed he could convince his son to look at the matter in its proper perspective. That remained to be seen.

After long deliberation, Kruger leaned forward, elbows on the desk. His face was a mask and his tone was offhand, almost matter of fact.

"It appears there were no witnesses."

"Witnesses? What the hell's that got to do with anything?"

"A good deal. Without witnesses, our position improves enormously."

"Dad, maybe you weren't listening. We just killed a couple of people, one of 'em a kid! Christ, he couldn't have been more than seventeen, maybe not that."

"Yes, but they were poachers, caught red-handed."

"So what's the point? They're still dead."

"The point is quite simple," Kruger replied. "Without witnesses, who's to say the killings ever took place?"

Hank stopped pacing, suddenly whirled around. With a jolt he saw that his father was not in the least appalled by the killings. Instead he appeared thoughtful, curiously dispassionate, like a man contemplating some very involved gambit on a chessboard.

"I hope I heard you wrong. You're not talking about . . . keeping this under wraps . . . are you?"

"That's precisely what I'm talking about. Although I think 'underground' would be the better term."

"Goddamn! You're not serious. You mean, bury them?"

"The deeper, the better. In fact, I suggest that old bog southwest of the creek. I've seen it suck whole cows out of sight in three or four minutes."

Hank was struck dumb, momentarily unnerved by his father's quiet, cold-blooded manner. Several seconds passed as they stared at each other, then he shook his head, averted his gaze.

"I don't know whether you're trying to protect me . . . or save yourself some grief . . . but forget it. I've got nothing to hide. Hell, they're the ones that fired first, not us! It was self-defense, plain and simple."

"You might have a difficult time convincing a jury of that. Particularly if it's a jury comprised of farmers. Consider it a moment . . . do you think they'd believe you had to kill the boy—*a farm boy?*"

"I don't have to think about it." Hank rounded the desk, walked directly to the wall phone. "Before this goes any further, I'm going to call the sheriff. We'll let the law handle it."

"No!" Kruger's tone was harsh, roughly insistent. "You won't call the sheriff and you won't speak of this matter to anyone else, not even your mother. We have the family name to protect, and even if you weren't indicted, we'd still never live it down."

"Like hell!" Hank corrected him. "You're not worried about me or the family or anyone else. You're worried about yourself, aren't you?"

"It's a little more involved than that. We already have enough enemies, and right now we can't afford a scandal of this sort. Just take my word for it . . . leave well enough alone."

"It won't work, Dad. Either forget the slick talk and give

me a damn good reason, or I'm calling the sheriff. I mean it, so don't try horsing me around."

Their eyes locked, and after a long while Kruger nodded. "Very well, son, the truth. Next year I intend to run for governor. It's all arranged, and there's no way I can lose . . . unless you call the sheriff."

"Jesus Christ! You'd put me on the spot for that, your lousy politics?"

"Yes, you're right. It's selfish and conniving and you have every reason to be disgusted. But I've been aiming toward it for years, and I can do a great deal of good as governor. A great deal of good, both for the family and Texas." He paused, voice lowered, eyes downcast. "So I'm asking—father to son—don't spoil it for me."

Hank studied him for a time, finally looked away. "What about Romero and Mendez . . . want me to bury them too?"

"No need for sarcasm," Kruger observed quietly. "Romero and Mendez won't talk, not after they've killed white men and helped . . ."

"Go on, say it. Helped dispose of the bodies, isn't that what you meant?"

"I'm not proud of it, but I won't beg favors, not even from my own son. Just give me a straight answer . . . will you do it or not?"

"Yeah, I'll do it," Hank said in a resigned voice. "But after this we're quits, all accounts squared. You tend to your business and I'll tend to mine."

"I understand, and thank you, son. Thank you."

"Don't thank me, just keep your politics the hell away from Santa Guerra. Savvy?"

Kruger nodded but Hank had already turned away, walking rapidly toward the door. He slammed it on his way out.

Kruger left the hotel shortly before eight in the morning and walked toward the bank. He hadn't heard from his son in the past two days, which was hardly surprising under the circumstances. But he was satisfied Hank had kept their bargain. Talk of the missing farmers, now identified as Fred Jackson and his sixteen-year-old son, was all over town. There was a good deal of speculation about their disappearance, yet Kru-

ger was feeling rather sanguine about the whole affair. Talk
was cheap, and the Jacksons would never be found.

As he was crossing the street, someone called his name.
He turned, saw Lon Hill and another farmer approaching,
and immediately gathered himself to face a nasty situation.
They both appeared angry, and he recognized the second
man as Wendell Jackson, the missing farmer's brother. Hill
began talking in a loud, hectoring voice even before they
halted.

"Kruger, we'd like a word with you. We've just come from
the courthouse, and that mealymouthed sheriff of yours is
giving us the runaround."

"Oh, what's the problem now?"

"Don't play dumb, Kruger. You know damn well Fred
Jackson and his boy are missin'."

"Yes, of course." Kruger glanced at Wendell Jackson.
"Sorry to hear it, Mr. Jackson. Any word on them yet?"

"Save your sympathy!" Hill snapped. "We're after action,
and we mean to have it."

"I'm afraid I don't understand."

"The hell you don't! We asked that asshole sheriff to form
a search party and start combin' Santa Guerra, and the son-
ovabitch just flat refused."

"Why would you expect him to search Santa Guerra?"

"Best damn reason in the world. Go on, Wendell, tell
him."

Wendell Jackson wasn't a tall man, but his barrel-shaped
torso was thickly quilted with muscle. His features were
square and brutish, and there was a feral look in his eyes,
savagery and homicidal fury in his stance. He'd lost all rea-
son, all restraint, and his fists clenched in hard knots as he
strugged to choke out the words.

"My brother and his boy went huntin' on your place, night
before last. They been there lots of times, them signs of
yours don't mean nothin' to 'em. But this time they ain't
come back, and I'm done waitin'. I aim to find out what
happened."

"I see, and exactly what is it you think happned, Mr. Jack-
son?"

Hill grunted sharply. "Same goddamn thing that's been
happenin' ever since you posted that land. Only this time it

got out of hand. We think them greasers of yours killed 'em. Killed 'em and buried 'em, by the Holy Christ!"

Kruger regarded him with great calmness. "Mr. Hill, I can appreciate your concern, but to be quite blunt about it, I think you're going off half-cocked. My vaqueros don't kill people . . . not even poachers."

"Then you'll have no objection to us searchin' Santa Guerra, will you?"

"That's entirely up to the sheriff. If he feels there are sufficient grounds to warrant a search—"

"Bullshit! We're done askin' him, we're askin' you."

"I repeat, Mr. Hill, my vaqueros don't engage in violence. So there's really no reason to pursue the matter further."

Wendell Jackson's eyes hooded, and his jaws clenched so tight his lips barely moved. "If nothin' happened, then how come your boy rode in here hell-for-leather night before last and turned right around and rode back out again? Thought we didn't know about that, didn't you?"

"I assure you one has nothing to do with the other. You're jumping to conclusions, Mr. Jackson. All the wrong conclusions."

"Fuck you and your conclusions. You just got done tellin' us what we wanted to know."

Jackson wheeled away and walked off down the street. Lon Hill started after him, then stopped and turned back. "That was the biggest mistake of your life, Kruger. If you'd played it straight, we might've been able to cool him down. The way it sits now, I'd advise you to sleep damn light."

Hill hurried after his friend and Kruger stood watching them until they turned the corner. All things considered, he thought he'd handled it rather well, but that part about Hank bothered him. On impulse, he decided a trip to the ranch was in order. Probably nothing to worry about, and yet . . . it was best to keep Hank apprised of developments.

Hedge the bet, for the boy's sake. And his own.

CHAPTER 43

The stars were scattered like flecks of ice through a sky of purest indigo. Hank stood on the creek bank, lost beneath the shadow of the trees, staring intently at the heavens. His eyes roved back and forth, searching the patchwork sky, as though some immutable truth were to be found in the stars. He found instead the quandary of his own thoughts.

Hank had never before examined himself in terms of conventional morality. All his life he'd done pretty much as he pleased, following a loose code of personal conduct that had few limitations. He chased women and attended the cockfights and enjoyed *mano a mano* brawls in a way others considered a bit unnatural. He had little use for the church and even less for men of the cloth, and the decent, God-fearing people of the area were at once titillated and offended by his disreputable behavior. Yet he'd never welched on a bet or broken his word, and all along the border, even among the rougher element, he was known as a man of staunch integrity. By conventional standards it was a spotty reputation, but he had small regard for the opinion of others. He liked what he was and, by his own assessment, that had always been enough.

Now, forced to look within himself, he found there was less substance than he'd supposed. The last couple of days had been a brutalizing experience; two nights in a row he'd had nightmares about the bog. He saw the farmer rising from the slime, holding his son's body in his arms, marching step-by-step toward firm ground. In the dream Hank tried to drive him back into the marsh, but the farmer wouldn't be stopped, advancing with a ghastly smile and empty eye sockets that seemed to glow like dull embers. There the nightmare ended, with Hank jolted awake and bathed in sweat,

something vile and putrid lodged in his throat. Afterward there was no sleep, and he lay staring into the dark, filled with loathing for what he'd done.

In retrospect, he saw himself as a weakling. A man of so little character that he couldn't stand firm before his father's expediency and obsessive ambition. But if he was haunted by their confrontation in the bank, it was nothing compared to the specter he now envisioned for the future. Earlier tonight his father had arrived at the ranch; ostensibly it was one of his overnight family visits, all quite routine on the surface. Hank thought the timing rather too coincidental, and after his mother had gone to bed he discovered it was even worse than he'd suspected. His father briefly related the encounter that morning with Lon Hill and Wendell Jackson; while concerned, he expressed the opinion that there was no reason for alarm. Still, he'd thought it best to forewarn Hank, strictly as a precautionary measure. In the event the farmers came nosing around the ranch, they were to be shown the gate in no uncertain terms. A hard attitude, he declared, would soon convince them it was a waste of time, and discourage further efforts.

Hank thought otherwise, and he'd forcefully stressed the point. "All you've done is stall them. Suppose they bypass the sheriff and take that story to the Rangers . . . then what?"

"The Rangers," Kruger informed him, "wouldn't come near Santa Guerra unless they'd first cleared it with the governor. I can assure you that won't happen."

"Yeah, but what if the papers got hold of it? They could raise a big enough stink. The governor wouldn't have any choice."

"Even so, the law requires a *corpus delicti,* and we haven't any worries there, have we?"

"No." Hank paled, remembering. "No worries there."

"Then it's merely a matter of sticking to our story and waiting them out. We never saw Jackson or his boy, and that's that."

"Maybe, but there's another angle we ought to think about. The way you told it, Jackson's brother sounds like a hothead. What if he decides to take matters into his own hands?"

"An eye for an eye?" Kruger pursed his lips, shrugged. "I considered that, but it's rather unlikely. Those people respect Lon Hill, and he doesn't want trouble anymore than we do. By now, he's got Jackson calmed down and looking at the situation realistically."

"I don't know," Hank countered, "maybe it wouldn't hurt for you to start carrying a pistol. Just till things blow over. If Jackson jumps you some night, you might be damn glad you've got it along."

Kruger had joshed him for being a worrywart, and shortly afterward went upstairs to bed. The conversation left Hank in a dismal mood, even more disturbed than before, and the very idea of sleep filled him with dread. Once his eyes closed, the farmer would beckon him again to the bog, and he knew he couldn't handle the nightmare three nights running. He'd gone down to the creek for some heavy thinking.

Yet nothing had been resolved, and now, sickened by what he saw within himself, he realized there were no answers. He'd allowed himself to become enmeshed in a web of guile and treachery, and the time for pulling out was long since past. He was bound to his father in a conspiracy that had no end. In the days ahead there would be lies and more lies, one compounding the other until he was trapped forever in a tangled skein of deception. All his life he would live with those lies, for the terrible thing he'd done could never be undone. A man and a boy lay at the bottom of a muddy bog, and there was no way to raise them from the dead without destroying his father . . . and himself.

Hank turned from the creek and walked toward the house.

In the pale starlight Wendell Jackson emerged from the trees bordering the clamshell driveway. He paused for a moment, studying the house, then moved directly to the east end of the veranda. Hidden in the shadows, he stooped and set two five-gallon cans of kerosene on the ground. Uncapping one of the cans, he slowly circled the house, sloshing kerosene on the walls. He was methodical, seemingly in no rush, and when he'd finished, the rear and both sides of the house had been thoroughly drenched.

He returned for the second can and stepped onto the veranda. Walking the length of the house, he soaked the front

wall, swinging the can high in order to splash the eaves beneath the porch roof. Then he doused the veranda itself and backed down the steps, carefully spilling a trail of kerosene several yards into the driveway. He set the can down, dug a kitchen match from his shirt pocket, and dropped to one knee.

His thumbnail raked the head of the match.

Crossing the compound, Hank saw the flare of a match followed instantly by a thin streamer of fire running toward the house. For a moment it made no sense; his wits deserted him and he stood watching as the streamer leaped up the steps, crossed the veranda, and hit the door. Then the front of the house suddenly ignited and a second later the entire bottom floor exploded in a holocaust of flame.

Out of the corner of his eye, Hank saw a man standing in the driveway, calmly watching the house burn. A name flashed through his mind—Wendell Jackson—then his attention was diverted by vaqueros racing across the compound in their nightclothes. He started toward them, shouting orders to form a bucket brigade, but the vaqueros were screaming and pointing upward, their faces etched with horror. Hank whirled around, caught his breath in a sharp gasp, and froze.

The fire had spread rapidly, fueled by the dry tinderbox of the old foundation, and the upper floor was now in flames. Ernest Kruger had smashed a bedroom window, and was assisting his wife through the opening, on the verge of pushing her to safety. Suddenly the upper story caught with a roaring *whoosh* and a solid wall of fire forced them back from the window. Then tongues of flame leaped to the roof, and Kruger pulled Trudy into the hall, leading her toward the stairway. Smoke billowed through the window and they were lost from view.

By now the compound was jammed with *Los Lerdeños,* but the intensity of the fire kept them at a distance. Hank stood apart, shielding his face with his arms, edging ever closer to the house. The front door had disintegrated and his eyes were fixed on the stairwell in the ground-floor hallway. Screams suddenly pierced the night, swept back over the crowd in cries of terror, and in that instant Kruger appeared on the stairs, followed closely by Trudy. The inside of the

house was a raging inferno, with drapes and wallpaper and furniture quickly being consumed by the blaze. Kruger tried to reach the front door, but the flames again drove him back, and he retreated with Trudy into the hallway.

Hank shouted and waved, urging them to make another try, watching flames advance on them from all sides. Then he suddenly broke, crazed with fear, and ran toward the house. The veranda collapsed as he mounted the steps, peppering him with firebrands and sparks; he stumbled, reeling backward, spun around by a sheet of fire. Luis Morado and several vaqueros darted from the crowd, threw him to the ground, began pounding at his smoldering clothes. He levered himself upright and brushed them aside, started back toward the house. The men jumped him and he began punching and kicking, struggling to break loose. The scuffle lasted only a moment, and then, so abruptly they fell away, he stopped, went rigid. His mouth opened and a bestial moan rose shrill above the crackling flames.

Trudy and Kruger stood trapped in the hallway, locked in each other's arms. Her gown was ablaze and Kruger seemed to be talking to her, looking directly into her eyes. Her expression was composed, and even when his nightshirt burst into flames, neither of them lost control. Then her hair caught fire, and for an instant her head was framed in a luminous glow. Her features turned molten, began to melt, and as Kruger pulled her closer the heat fused them together, his own head wreathed in a florid incandescence. Mercifully, their ordeal ended in a volcanic roar.

The wall buckled and the house settled inward upon itself. Then the roof collapsed, demolishing the upper floor, and crashed downward in a thunderous firestorm. Cinders and sparks leaped skyward, and a searing blast of heat hurtled across the compound. Tongues of flame lapped at the rubble, and fiery timbers flashed a brilliant orange, consumed within the smoky pyre. There was one last flare, lighting the night, then the ruins leveled in a glowing bed of coals. A gentle wind fanned the embers, and with it came the faint stench of burnt flesh.

An eerie hush fell over the compound. *Los Lerdeños* stood like rows of bronzed sculpture, staring at the rubble, shocked beyond speech, their emotions blunted. Hank's eyes were

glazed, and his look was one of tragic disbelief. He seemed
rooted to the ground, and his gaze was riveted on the spot
where his parents had perished, almost as though he ex-
pected them to rise, miraculously unscathed, and walk from
the smoldering ruins. Yet nothing moved, and silence turned
to stillness, deathly quiet.

At the edge of the crowd, Luis Morado stood with head
bowed, tears streaming down his face. His thoughts were
confused and disoriented, vivid flashes of times past jarred
by the horror of flames. He saw Trudy as a young girl, splash-
ing joyfully in the old swimming hole, remembered her wild
recklessness and her beauty and her love for Roberto. Yet
the image was fleeting, turned quickly to fire and seared
flesh, that last glimpse of *La Madama* in flames, burned
alive. He shook his head, blinked and brushed away the
tears, unable to bear the thought of her, the memories. His
eyes went to the *patrón,* standing alone in the stillness, alone
and desolate. He suddenly realized his own grief was nothing
and he started forward. His features softened, arm stretched
out, reaching for the *patrón* and . . .

A crazed laugh splintered the night. It went on and on, the
gibberty laugh of a loon in darkened woods, bloodcurdling
and somehow maniacal. Hank whirled toward the driveway.
His eyes fastened on Wendell Jackson, forgotten during the
horror of the fire. He started forward, and an ominous mur-
mur swept back over *Los Lerdeños.* Several vaqueros, led by
Luis Morado, rushed to join him, but he waved them aside,
advancing on the farmer at a measured pace. Jackson's laugh
rose higher, oddly discordant, crested in an earsplitting
shriek of madness. He took no notice whatever of *Los Lerde-
ños,* nor did his expression change when Hank halted in
front of him. He seemed mesmerized by the glowing bed of
coals.

Hank hit him. A wild and devastating rage went into the
blow, and Hank swung again and still again, split the
farmer's eyebrow, heard the jawbone crack under his fist.
Jackson blinked, rocked by the blows, but he didn't fall. Nor
did he see Hank. He chuckled lightly and flashed a mouthful
of brownish teeth. His gaze was still fixed on the rubble.

Fist cocked, ready to strike again, Hank hesitated, slowly
lowered his arm. He took a step closer, looked straight into

Jackson's eyes. He found nothing there, only the blank emptiness of a man whose mind was gone, reason destroyed. Several moments passed while he debated killing Jackson anyway, then his rage began to fade, dulled by the hollow stare. He finally got a grip on himself and backed away, his mouth set in a grim line. As he turned toward *Los Lerdeños*, there was a silver flash in the glare of the fiery rubble. A swift whistling sound split the air, followed an instant later by the soft chunk of metal striking flesh and bone. Behind him, Hank heard a harsh grunt, and he whirled around.

Wendell Jackson looked surprised, the dull stare gone from his eyes. A broad-bladed *saca tripas,* the knife carried by all vaqueros, was buried to the hilt in his chest. He stood stockstill, alert now and fully aware, his gaze fixed on someone in the crowd. Then he smiled and a trickle of blood leaked out of his mouth. His grin became a wet chuckle, as though he were amused by a joke known only to himself, and he threw back his head, laughed louder. Suddenly he choked, the laugh broken by a strangled cough, and vomited a great gout of blood down across his chest. His eyeballs rolled back in his head, ghostly white sockets, and his knees collapsed. He dropped dead.

Hank stared down at the body for a long while. Then he seemed to collect himself, and turned to face *Los Lerdeños*. Gathered in a tight wedge, they regarded him without expression, their features hard and stoic. His gaze roved through the crowd, settled on Luis Morado, waited. The *segundo* met his look, held it for a time, then nodded once and lifted his chin with a faint smile of pride. Something unspoken passed between them, a private thing, resolved without words yet understood by all of *Los Lerdeños*. Hank nodded and walked away.

"Someone ride for the sheriff."

CHAPTER 44

Becky was waiting when he came out of the courthouse. His expression betrayed nothing, but she could tell he was surprised by the size of the crowd. There was a slight hesitation before he descended the steps; his eyes swept the throng of farmers and townspeople gathered on the courthouse lawn. Then she went to meet him, hands outstretched, and he hurried down the last few steps. She put on a brave smile.

"Are you all right?"

"I'm fine, just a little tired."

"What happened? Are they going to press charges?"

Hank winced, avoided her gaze. "How'd you find out?"

"Darling, the whole town knows."

"All of it . . . Jackson and the boy, too?"

Becky nodded. "Someone in the sheriff's office has a big mouth. People started gathering here before daylight."

"Wondered about that." Hank glanced past her at the crowd. "From the turnout, I guess most of them figure I ought to be lynched."

"Who cares what they think? The important thing is what the county prosecutor thinks."

"Let's save it till later." Hank took her arm. "It's a long story, and I've seen enough of this place for one night."

His eyes were sunken with fatigue, and he still wore the singed, soot-encrusted clothes he'd had on last night. Beside him, Becky looked like a subdued butterfly. Her dress was black, simple and stark, with an amethyst brooch at the throat and a brimmed black hat. She squeezed his arm, chin lifted proudly, and turned to face the crowd. As they started down the walkway, Lon Hill separated from a group of farmers and walked toward them. He halted, blocking their path, and a chilled silence fell over the courthouse lawn.

"Kruger." Hill bobbed his head. "Miss Hazlett."

"What can I do for you, Hill?"

"Well, first off, I'd like to offer my condolences about your folks. Your pa and me never got along too well, but I would've preferred it hadn't ended like this."

"Thank you." Hank's features softened. "Under the circumstances, I'm obliged you feel that way."

"Tell you the truth, I sorta feel like it's my fault. I should've kept a closer watch on Wendell, but it just never dawned on me he'd go that far."

"No, don't blame yourself. If I'd handled it right—you know, about Jackson and his boy—none of this would have happened. It's my fault for not reporting it the night we . . . jumped them."

"You started to, didn't you?" Hank gave him a startled look, and he went on. "That night, when you rode into town, you were gonna report it to the sheriff, weren't you?"

"Who told you that?"

"Nobody had to tell me. Guessed it for myself after we braced your pa yesterday mornin'." Hill paused, considering. "You've got a rough way about you, but I always took you to be an honest man. Figured if you was gonna try to hide it, you wouldn't've come into town at all, especially to see your pa."

Hank swallowed, glanced away. "Wish I hadn't now. There was a light in the bank and it seemed the natural thing . . ."

His voice trailed off in an uncomfortable silence. Becky hugged his arm, but he continued to stare into the distance, eyes filled with regret. After a time Hill cleared his throat, nodded toward the courthouse.

"Any idea what they aim to do about Wendell?"

"Nothing." Hank looked him straight in the eye. "It was ruled justifiable homicide."

"Pretty fancy term for a fellow that gets himself stabbed to death."

"Yeah, I suppose so. But then, I reckon you would've killed him too . . . under the same circumstances."

"You didn't kill him," Hill observed. "No need to tell me different either."

"Oh? What makes you so sure?"

"A knife ain't your sort of weapon. You might beat a man

to death—and I understand Wendell was busted up pretty bad—but a knife just ain't your style. No, I'd say it was one of your greasers. Like as not, one of 'em put that pigsticker in Wendell after you got through workin' him over."

"You'd have a hard time proving that, Hill."

"Think so?"

"I'd bet money on it."

"Now it's you that sounds awful sure of yourself."

"Well, there's better than five hundred vaqueros on Santa Guerra. Unless you've got a crystal ball, it'd be damn hard to prove your point."

"Tell you the truth, I never had no intention of tryin' to prove it."

Hank frowned, watching him. "I don't follow you."

"Nothin' to follow, not really. It's like you said a minute ago. I'd have killed him myself . . . under the same circumstances."

"I wish to God—" Hank faltered, looked down at the sidewalk. "I'm sorry it happened, Hill, sorry for the whole mess. Especially the boy . . . and his father . . . the way I handled it."

There was a moment of weighing, deliberation, before Hill spoke. "You figure they'll bring charges?"

Hank shrugged. "That's up to the grand jury. It was self-defense, but the county prosecutor says I'm still open to charges of conspiracy."

"Well, I wouldn't worry about that too much if I was you. We done talked it over, and everybody agreed—what with the fire and all—that it pretty much settles the account."

Hill pulled at his earlobe, thoughtful. "Way things worked out, I guess we've all suffered more'n we deserve. 'Course that's the trouble with life, ain't it? Hindsight don't change a thing, and most times it don't teach us nothin' either. Seems like the Good Lord in all his wisdom would've made it the other way round."

Hank stared at him a long time, finally drew a deep breath. "Mr. Hill, I can't change what's happened, and most likely I won't change the way I feel about farmers or posting my land or any of the rest of it. But there's one thing I can promise you. From now on, Kruger County will be run on the up and up. Come election time, your candidates are wel-

come on Santa Guerra, and if they can convince my people to vote your way, then I'll just have to learn to live with it." He hesitated, fixed the other man with a level gaze. "I won't help you, but you've got my word I'll stay the hell out of politics."

"I think that's what folks call friendly adversaries, Mr. Kruger. Not that it'll satisfy everybody, you understand, but it's good enough for me."

Lon Hill stuck out his hand and Hank shook it. Then the farmer stepped aside and he led Becky down the walkway. The crowd parted to let them through, watching in silence as they walked to the street and climbed into the Pierce-Arrow. Hank started the motor and drove west out of town, toward Santa Guerra.

The sun dipped lower, smothering in a bed of copper, as they drove into the compound. All that remained of the house was ashes and debris, with the chimney rising like a charred monolith against the plains sky. There was an acid tang of smoke in the air and a sense of desolation pervaded the compound. Work had come to a standstill, and the few vaqueros in sight quickly removed their sombreros, heads bowed in mourning.

Hank brought the car to a halt and killed the motor. On the ride out from town there had been little conversation, and not a word concerning the fire or his parents. He seemed to have withdrawn inside himself, nursing the pain and hurt like some wounded creature burrowed deep in its hiding place. But now, watching his face, Becky saw at last the enormity of his sorrow. Staring at the ruins, his eyes suddenly glistened and an expression of unbearable grief spread across his features. She touched his arm, but he turned away, quickly opening the door, and walked to the front of the car.

A long while passed as he stood gazing at the chimney. He felt a devastating loneliness, and all at once a frightful agony of despair mounted within him, became violently physical, left him chilled and his forehead beaded with sweat. Unbidden, those last moments materialized before him, and he saw again the blazing inferno, watched his father speaking

calmly, without fear or panic, as the flames engulfed them, and his mother. . . .

She had spoken!

In that final instant, with her hair ablaze and her features like clotted wax, she had spoken to his father. He forced himself to concentrate, looked deep within his mind's eye, trying desperately to see her lips. All the pain and anguish, the horror of watching them burn was suddenly transcended, somehow blocked out, and he saw her lips move. He stared hard, brushing aside images of flame and the smell of seared flesh, willing himself to grasp her words . . . to hear.

Then it was clear, the words formed on her lips, and he knew.

Slowly it drifted away, bright images faintly dimmed and lost, then it was gone. He shuddered, felt the touch of a hand on his arm, and turned away at last from death. Becky was watching him closely, her eyes troubled and bemused.

"Darling, what is it? What's wrong?"

"Nothing's wrong. Not now, anyway."

"But you're white as a sheet"—Becky wiped his forehead, gently smoothed his hair—"and you're soaked. Do you feel feverish?"

"No, it was something worse than that."

"Worse than what? I don't understand."

"Oh, I guess I was feeling sorry for myself. Got to wallowing around in all that self-pity and couldn't even see . . ."

He faltered, and Becky took his hand, brushed it with her lips. "Sweetheart, please, won't you tell me—see what?"

"I figured it out." His words were soft, almost inaudible, so quiet she had to strain to hear. "Just now, I figured out what they said to each other before it happened."

"Before they . . . in the fire . . . you saw them say something before they died?"

"Yeah, right at the very last. Probably never said it to each other in their whole lives, but they did then. I know they did."

Becky looked at him, gripped by the sudden awareness of change. In the midst of death he had found himself as a man, gained gentleness and compassion, the bedrock strength of all truly strong men. A tear spilled down her cheek, and she

hugged him fiercely. His arms went around her, pulled her into a circle of warmth and tenderness, and they held each other for a long time. Then he smiled, nuzzled her ear, his voice low and husky.

"Funny, the way things work out. One night Mom told me the land . . . Santa Guerra . . . was all that matters. I've got an idea she'd see it different now."

"Oh, in what way?"

"Well, she had the notion that the ranch . . . how you put your mark on the land . . . was the only part of yourself you leave behind. In a way, I suppose she was right, but there's more to it than that. The things you build, that's not all you leave behind . . . not of yourself anyway."

"No, not all," Becky murmured. "There's much more . . . the part of themselves . . . the thing they found there at the end . . . that part matters most of all."

"Yeah, I think they'd both agree on that. It'll last a long time, won't it?"

"Yes, darling, it will. All our lives."

Hank straightened, holding her close, and stared thoughtfully at the charred rubble. After a moment, he nodded to himself, laughing, and his arm tightened around her waist.

"You know something? We're going to rebuild on that same spot. Only bigger, lots bigger! By god, before we're through we'll knock their eyes out. A new house . . . and a new mistress—"

"And babies, Hank! Lots of babies!"

"Yes, ma'am! All you want, but especially one."

"Especially one or a special one?"

"Yeah, you're right, very special! The new *patrón.*"